I0779193

Worlds of Shadow

Other books by Lawrence Watt-Evans:

The Lords of Dûs

The Lure of the Basilisk
The Seven Altars of Dûsarra
The Sword of Bheleu
The Book of Silence

Legends of Ethshar

Night of Madness
The Misenchanted Sword
With A Single Spell
The Unwilling Warlord
Taking Flight
The Blood of A Dragon
The Spell of the Black Dagger
Ithanalin's Restoration

The Obsidian Chronicles

Dragon Weather
The Dragon Society
Dragon Venom (forthcoming)

Other Works

Touched by the Gods
Nightside City
The Rebirth of Wonder
Crosstime Traffic
Celestial Debris
Split Heirs (with Esther M. Friesner)
The Nightmare People

Worlds of Shadow

Lawrence Watt-Evans

BETANCOURT
& COMPANY
Doylestown, Pennsylvania

Worlds of Shadow
A publication of
Betancourt & Company, Publishers
P.O. Box 301
Holicong, PA 18928–0301

www.wildsidepress.com

For Julie

Part One:
Out of This World

Chapter One

*H*e was changing lanes, cutting in front of a silver-grey Toyota, when he suddenly felt as if he were being watched, as if someone were desperately trying to get his attention. He was alone in the car, though. He *knew* he was alone in the car.

He swerved back into line and checked his mirrors.

Everything looked normal.

He shook his head, puzzled, and began looking for another opening. His appointment was in five minutes, and he had three miles to go on the highway, another through the city streets. He wasn't going to make it on time, but all the same, he didn't want to be any later than necessary. He ignored the odd sensation, waiting for it to go away.

It refused. Instead of fading, it nagged at him like a sore tooth. Someone was *watching* him, somehow.

When he stopped at a light he looked in the back seat, just in case; of course, no one was there. For a moment he even thought about checking the trunk when he parked, but then he shook his head again. That was ridiculous.

The feeling was very definite. It was almost like one of those psychic things he'd read about — but he didn't believe in those.

The feeling was there, and it wouldn't go away.

He forced himself to ignore it.

*M*ommy?" Angela, seated cross-legged on the kitchen floor with her Raggedy Ann doll sprawled on her lap, looked up at her mother.

"Yes, honey?" Margaret Thompson went on scrubbing the saucepan, trying to get out every trace of the burnt-on cheese sauce.

"Mr. Nobody's talkin' to me again."

"Oh?" Margaret answered, not really listening. "What's he saying?" She peered critically at the pan, decided it would do, and put it in the drainer.

"He's in terrible trouble, Mommy," Angela told her, quite seriously.

"What kind of trouble?" Margaret asked, picking a skillet out of the soapy dishwater.

"There's this bad monster wants to get him, and eat him up, and make everybody do bad things."

Margaret looked down at her daughter. "Angie, there aren't any monsters. You know that. You tell Mr. Nobody that."

"I *told* him that, Mommy," Angela said very seriously, "but he just keeps talkin' about a monster in the shadows."

Margaret was a bit startled to hear a phrase like "a monster in the shadows" from her three-year-old, but she didn't worry about it. Kids pick up all kinds of things, and besides, Angie was almost four now. She was growing up fast. "Well, if he keeps talking about monsters," Margaret told Angie, "then just don't listen to him. Tell him to be quiet and stop bothering you with that stuff."

"Okay," Angela said, doubtfully. "I'll try."

PSYCHIC PREDICTS ARMAGEDDON

Ray Aldridge, noted West Coast psychic advisor, told reporters today that he has it on good authority that Armageddon, the final battle of good and evil, is almost upon us.

"It was the clearest message I've ever gotten from any psychic entity," Dr. Aldridge reported. "It was a warning sent by beneficent aliens far out in the galaxy, telling me that the powers of darkness are building up their forces for the final conquest of Earth. The aliens who contacted me say that the Galactic Empire they represent has tried to fight back Shadow, as they call it, but has been unsuccessful. It's up to us, here on Earth, to defeat it."

When asked how this evil force could be defeated, and what ordinary people could do that telepathic space aliens could not, Dr. Aldridge admitted, "I don't have any idea at all."

"Got a good one," the agent at the desk called, holding up an opened letter.

His partner looked up from the file drawer. "What's this one say?"

The man at the desk smiled. "Dear Mr. President," he read from the letter. "The angels from Venus who have been helping me with my garden called me up yesterday on the special telephone in my head to warn me that we're in big trouble. The Devil Himself . . ." He pointed and said, "That's underlined in red crayon." Then he continued reading. "The Devil Himself has found out about all the secret messages I've been relaying to you, to keep the Chinese from invading and to tell Americans how to grow better carrots, and he's really mad. I think my neighbor with the sick cat told him. I'm sure she's a witch or one of them Satan cults. The Venusians are going to fight the old bastard and chase him back to Hell . . ." The agent paused again and looked up, grinning. "'Hell' is in all capitals and underlined in red," he said, before turning his gaze back to the letter. He cleared his throat and continued, ". . . chase him back to Hell, but they need some help, so if you could send the 82nd Airborne to Goshen, Maryland, that's where they expect to meet him. Yours Truly, Oram

Blaisdell."

"Goshen?" the other man asked, bemused. "Why Goshen? Where the heck is it, anyway?"

"Just north of Gaithersburg, I think," the reader said. "One of those ritzy suburbs with three-acre estates."

"Does this guy live *there?*" The man by the files knew, intellectually, that the nuts whose letters came to this office sometimes lived in fancy suburbs, but it still didn't seem right. He expected them to come from either the inner city or the outermost sticks.

"No, no, of course not," the man at the desk replied. "He lives in Tennessee somewhere."

"Then why'd he pick Goshen? How'd he ever *hear* of Goshen, Maryland?"

The man holding the letter shrugged. "Who knows?" he asked. "Why the 82nd? Why Venus? Why carrots?" He tossed the letter aside. "At least that one didn't have Elvis in it."

*P*el Brown gave the screwdriver another turn and cursed when it slipped out of the slot and scraped across the metal. He dropped the screwdriver to one side, then brushed at the red-enamelled surface and leaned over to peer at it, wishing the light were better.

It looked okay.

Better light might be nice, Pel decided, but what he *really* wished was that wagons came ready-assembled. Had *his* father had to put together *his* old wagon? He'd never thought about that before; just one year there it was, under the Christmas tree, and he'd taken it entirely for granted.

Well, this one was going to be a birthday present, rather than for Christmas, but Rachel was probably going to take it for granted just as much as he had. And she probably wouldn't notice if he *did* scratch the paint. That wasn't something a six-year-old cared much about.

She was going to be six. Amazing. Almost ready for first grade.

Of course, the next school year was still almost four months off, but she would be six tomorrow.

She still wouldn't care about scratched paint, though. He sighed and reached for the screwdriver, then froze.

Standing next to the screwdriver was a . . . well, a person. Pel hesitated to call it a man, even in his thoughts; it stood just over a foot high, wrapped in a tattered cloak of coarse brown wool, black hair pulled back in a tight braid, revealing oversized pointed ears. It was looking about curiously and uncertainly, taking in the contents of the basement — the furnace, the water heater, the boxes of stored junk.

It was not a doll; no doll could look that lifelike and alert, no matter how many computer chips were stuffed into it. It wasn't a monkey, either.

And Pel sure hoped it wasn't a hallucination, as up until that moment he hadn't had any reservations at all about his mental health, and he hadn't taken anything more mind-altering than beer in weeks.

The creature had seen him, he was sure, but it wasn't saying anything, wasn't running or hiding or attacking. It was just looking around, a trifle uncertainly, taking in the scenery.

"What the hell are *you?*" Pel asked.

The thing looked up at him and grimaced. "I'm a bookkeeper," it replied. "Wouldn't know it from this outfit, would you?" Pel was relieved that it spoke, and spoke English; that probably simplified the situation, because it meant he could just talk to it and get some answers. Its voice was higher-pitched than a man's, but not squeaky or thin at all. Pel had heard grown women whose voices sounded far smaller and more childlike.

"No," Pel said, "I don't mean what do you do, I mean what *are* you?"

"I'm a human being, of course," the creature replied. "A small one. What do I *look* like?"

"You look like some kind of fairy," Pel replied, in honest bemusement.

The little person squinted up at Pel. "Are you looking for trouble, buddy?" he demanded. "I'm as much a lady's man as the next guy! If you weren't so damn big I'd punch your lights out!"

"Hey, I'm sorry," Pel said, holding up his hands in apology. "I didn't mean that. I meant an elf or something. I mean, you're a foot tall, with pointed ears — where'd you *come* from?"

Somewhat mollified, the little man said, "That's better. Yeah, I'm a little person. I came from a place called Hrumph — no jokes, I know it's a stupid name! That's what we called it, though, when it still existed. It was in . . . well, in another world."

"Oh, wow," said Pel, who had seen just as many episodes of 'Twilight Zone' and 'Lost in Space' as most of his generation. "You mean like another dimension?"

The creature looked puzzled. "Dimension? Um . . . I guess." He hesitated. "Not the word I'd have used," he said. "Another world, alternate reality, parallel universe, whatever." He waved vaguely, and his voice trailed off somewhat.

Pel blinked. After a moment of unthinking acceptance, a certain uncomfortable suspicion was growing in the back of his mind. Outside of movies and TV, things like this didn't happen, did they? Not for real.

"You're putting me on, right? This is a joke?" he asked.

"No, it's . . . it's not a joke." The person — he might not be human, in the usual sense, but after conversing with him Pel certainly thought of him as a person — looked uncomfortable. Not as if he were lying, but as if he were considering throwing up. "Hey . . ." he said, "I don't feel real good just now. Is it hot in here?"

"Hot?" Pel glanced around at the cool, moist basement. If this little person really did come from another world, maybe it was one colder than Earth — but that was silly. He shouldn't be taking it that seriously. "No, it isn't hot," he said.

"No?" The little man was swaying visibly.

"Are you all right?" Pel asked, concerned.

"No," the creature said. "I think . . . I think I better go." He swallowed hard. "Listen, we'll be back, okay? Or someone will. Don't go away!"

Before Pel could answer, the elf, or whatever it was, turned, stumbled away, and walked into the concrete wall.

Pel heard the smack clearly from where he sat. He winced in sympathy.

The little man got to his feet, let out a wail, and again stepped forward.

This time, when he hit the wall, he vanished into it.

Pel stared for a moment.

Then, moving slowly, he reached out and picked up the screwdriver.

He looked at the wall. In the movies, any character who had just seen such a thing would reach out and poke at the place the little guy had vanished, and maybe nothing would happen, and maybe not. He might get sucked into another world, or he might get killed by some sort of splashy special effects, or monsters might jump out at him.

Pel Brown was not going do that. He had no particular interest in watching the end melt off his screwdriver, or seeing his finger disappear into the fourth dimension, or even just poking the wall. It wouldn't prove anything. If he could hallucinate an elf, he could hallucinate anything.

He waited for a moment, but nothing happened, and he turned back to the wagon, shaking slightly.

Whatever he had just seen, real or not, seemed to be over. Maybe it had been just a weird sort of dream or something, or some kind of flashback to the one hit of mescaline he'd taken back in college, when he was young and stupid.

Or maybe he really had just talked to an elf from another dimension, and this sort of thing happened all the time, but most people didn't talk about it because they didn't want everyone thinking they were nuts. Maybe all those UFO aliens were real, Bigfoot was roaming the woods, and Elvis really *was* alive in outer space somewhere.

Maybe it happened all the time.

And maybe it didn't.

Whatever it was, it was not his problem; he still had to get the wheels on this stupid wagon in time for Rachel's party tomorrow. If the little man came back, Pel thought, he would worry about it then.

*A*my Jewell leaned back in her lawn chair, the book on her lap forgotten for the moment as she rested her eyes and listened to the pleasant hiss of the sprinkler. The sun was warm on her face, unseasonably warm for early May, and enjoying it seemed more important just now than reading whatever Danielle Steel had to say.

She wasn't sure she was going to bother finishing this one; she was beginning to lose her taste for Steel. And it was good to just lie here, eyes closed, enjoying the warmth, knowing that she had all day with nothing important to do. She liked that about Sundays.

Her eyes snapped open and she looked up, startled, at the crack of a sonic boom. It sounded as if it was almost directly overhead; she scanned the sky, but she couldn't see any plane.

Then suddenly she *did* see a plane, or something like one, but it wasn't flying, it was falling. It was brightly painted, like the old Braniff jets, mostly purple, and she didn't see any wings, just stubs. And it was *huge*, and it was almost directly overhead and it was falling almost directly toward *her.*

She rolled out of the lawn chair, scrambled to her feet, and ran for the house.

An instant later the thing hit with an immense, booming thud. The shock of its impact rattled windows and the dishes in her kitchen, and a planter at the corner of the patio toppled over, spilling scraggly geraniums across the flagstones. The sprinkler bounced, but did not overturn; its spray rattled against the thing's metal side.

The object had completely flattened the back hedge and had torn a major limb off the big sycamore. One of the stubby wings, or fins, or whatever they were had missed the lawn chair by just two or three inches.

It had stayed in one piece, though, it hadn't broken into sections like the crashed airliners she had seen on the TV news. The nose was no more than twenty yards from Amy's back door, while the tail was well across the property line, on Mr. Janssen's vegetable garden.

Amy had reached the back door just as it struck; she turned for a quick glance, paused long enough to lean over and turn off the sprinkler, then slipped inside. From the safety of her kitchen she stared out the window over the sink for a few seconds, then reached for the phone and dialed 9-1-1.

9-1-1 worked on Sundays, didn't it? Of course it did. Emergencies weren't limited to weekdays.

She didn't wait to hear what the person on the other end said; when she heard the phone picked up she said, "This is Amy Jewell, at 21550 Goshen Road, and an aircraft of some kind just crashed in my back yard."

"Do you need an ambulance?" a woman's voice asked calmly.

"I don't know," Amy said. "There hasn't been any explosion or anything, and the plane looks mostly intact; I don't see any bodies or flame."

"We'll send one. That was 21550 Goshen Road?"

"Yes." Amy heard other voices in the background.

"Even if there hasn't been an explosion *yet,* you might want to get well away from the wreckage. Was it a private plane? We have no reports of any commercial craft in trouble."

"I don't know *what* it is. It's purple."

The voice on the other end was silent for a moment, then asked. "Ma'am, where are you calling from?"

"I'm calling from my kitchen. I can see the plane, or whatever it is, out the window, about fifty feet away, and it's purple, and I never saw a plane like it before. Maybe it's some kind of experimental military thing."

"Fifty *feet?* Ma'am, I strongly suggest you leave the building and get well clear, quickly."

"Yeah," Amy said, staring out the window, "I think you're right." She hung up the phone.

The thing was lying across most of the width of her back yard, easily over a hundred feet long, with leaves and twigs from the sycamore scattered all over it. Amy's yard was three acres, what the real estate people called a "mini-estate," and the aircraft, or whatever it was, seemed to cover most of it, and a fair chunk of the Janssens', as well. Three fins, each shaped differently, projected from the near side, and a fourth jutted up from the top of the tail; the fins were pink and maroon, with yellow lettering she couldn't make out on them. The fuselage was mostly purple, with maroon detailing and more yellow lettering. It didn't look like any sort of airplane Amy had ever seen; it had a rather old-fashioned appearance, somehow.

And a hatchway over the central, largest, nearside fin was opening.

Amy knew she should turn and run, go out the front door and either wait for help or alert the neighbors, but she stared, fascinated.

The hatch swung wide, and a man stepped out. He was tall and blond, wearing a purple uniform with a black belt and high, shiny black boots — it wasn't any design she recognized, but it was clearly a uniform. He had a black holster on his hip — securely closed, to Amy's relief, with a flap that hid whatever weapon was in there; for all she could tell, it might be empty. He held a helmet in one hand, something like a motorcycle helmet; it was purple, too, with a yellow star on the side. He gazed around the yard. He said something.

Long ago, Amy Jewell had learned to read lips a little, just for fun. She couldn't hear him through the closed window, but she knew what the man had said.

He had said, "Shit."

He turned and called something back into the hatch, but Amy couldn't make it out, nor could she see his lips.

The man looked perfectly normal and ordinary, except for his rather outlandish attire. He was clean-shaven, his hair in a military crew cut that was beginning to grow out. He was tall and broad-shouldered and reminded her a little of Harrison Ford. She could see no sign of any injury; the thing's fall didn't even appear to have seriously mussed his uniform.

He was scanning her back yard, looking over the lawn chair, the still-dripping sprinkler, the spilled geraniums and the branch that had been torn off the sycamore. He did not look pleased.

Then he spotted her in the window. He waved and cupped his hands around his mouth and called, "Hello!"

Amy stared for a moment.

Then another head appeared in the hatch, looking out — another young man in uniform and crew cut.

Amy decided that she didn't want to talk to these people. They might be harmless — but they might not, and she was alone in the house, the neighbors were still off at their church, and there were at least two of the strangers and either one was bigger than she was. Those blond crew cuts brought Nazis to mind, which didn't help any.

She didn't think that the plane, or whatever it was, was going to explode. If there were any possibility of that the men would be running to get clear, not standing there looking around as if her back yard was some sort of disaster they had to clean up.

She locked the back door and then went upstairs to her bedroom. She got the little gun her father had given her from the bedside drawer, then crossed to the back windows and looked out again.

There were three men standing in her yard now, looking about. They looked nervous; one of them, the one she hadn't seen at all before, looked downright twitchy, his head jerking back and forth, scanning the shrubbery.

Naturally, he was the one with the gun.

It was quite a large gun, too, not one that would fit in a holster and not a kind Amy remembered ever seeing before. It looked oddly bulbous, but very complicated and ominous. He had it tucked under his right arm, he wasn't pointing it at anyone or anything, but Amy still had to suppress a nervous shudder. She was very glad she hadn't gone out to yell at the men for wrecking her yard; that man looked as if he might have shot her without even meaning to.

The second man righted the fallen lawn chair and sat down — making himself right at home, Amy thought with a stab of resentment. Then he put his head down in his hands and she felt a twinge of guilt for her resentment. She still didn't have the faintest idea what was going on, but obviously, whatever these people were doing had gone wrong. Let the poor man sit down if he had to.

The big blond who had been the first out cupped his hands around his mouth and called, "Hello, in the house!"

Amy didn't answer. She thought about it, but decided to wait.

"Hello!" he called again.

She put the gun down and opened the window-latch, then reconsidered.

"Where are we?" the man shouted. "Can you send for the authorities?"

Amy frowned. That seemed like a strange thing to ask. She opened the window a few inches.

"I already did!" she called.

The man blinked up at her, and the other man, the one with the big gun, turned to look. She ducked down and picked up her own gun.

This was crazy, she told herself. This was absolutely insane. These people were not acting like air-crash survivors at all. And that plane didn't really look that much like a plane.

So who the hell were they, then, and what *was* that thing? They didn't sound like foreigners, not really — though asking her to send for the authorities, rather than to call the cops, was odd phrasing.

That thing they came in — she had a better view of it from upstairs than she had had at ground level. It didn't look like an airplane.

It looked like a spaceship.

Not a real spaceship — not the space shuttle or a moon rocket. It looked like something out of an old Flash Gordon serial, only *real* — as if those comic-book spaceships had been based on this ship the way comic-book cars were based on real ones.

It bore the same relationship to those cheap models in "Flash Gordon," she thought, that a real 1947 Checker bore to Benny the Cab in "Who Framed Roger Rabbit?"

She blinked. Was someone shooting a movie, maybe? She'd never seen a ship like that in any movie, though. They wouldn't build it full scale and drop it in her back yard, in any case — not without asking her permission.

What the *hell* was going on?

Then she heard the sirens approaching and decided it wasn't her problem anymore.

Chapter Two

The nagging in the back of his head had been there for a few days, and he didn't really consciously notice it anymore — until it abruptly stopped. For a moment he was startled by the sudden mental silence; then he realized what had happened and smiled broadly.

It had stopped.

About time.

He had never figured out what caused that odd feeling, but whatever it had been, it was a relief to be rid of it.

Angela Thompson burst out crying, and when her mother finally got an explanation it took a real effort not to slap the girl for getting hysterical over nothing.

"Mr. Nobody stopped talking to me," indeed!

Ray Aldridge didn't like it when the messages stopped, but it was no big deal. They weren't providing all that much useful material, anyway — no bulletins from dead millionaires or miracle diet plans. He had gotten along without them for years, and he could get by without them again. He would just go back to making up his own.

Oram Blaisdell wasn't so complacent as the others. When the angels from Venus stopped talking to him, he concluded that Satan had somehow killed them all. He got his old twelve-gauge from the back room and went out to his pick-up and headed north.

He wasn't any too sure where Goshen, Maryland might be, but he reckoned he could find it.

He got as far as Radford, Virginia before the cops picked him up for speeding. Listening to his story, they decided the poor old guy shouldn't be running around loose. They called up his kids back in Paulette.

Between Henry Blaisdell's coaxing and the state troopers' story about a secret government campaign against the Satanists in Goshen, Oram finally decided to go home and mind his own business.

Satan wouldn't get him without a fight, when the time came, but why go looking for trouble where he wasn't wanted?

*P*el Brown was sitting in his favorite chair, re-reading C.S. Forester's *Ship of the Line,* when someone knocked.

He glanced up, annoyed. He had been in the middle of the scene where the *Sutherland,* Hornblower's ship, tears up an entire Italian army on the Spanish shore road, and he resented the interruption. He had been comfortably absorbed in ships' broadsides and Napoleonic politics.

Nancy and Rachel were out shopping, he remembered, partly to return the duplicate tape of 'Beauty and the Beast' Rachel had gotten at her party yesterday, but mostly after groceries. They weren't around to answer the knock — but maybe whoever it was would go away.

Whoever it was didn't go away, but knocked again instead.

Why would anyone knock, anyway? Was the doorbell broken?

Sighing heavily, Pel got up out of the recliner and put the book down on the end table, using the unpaid cable TV bill as a bookmark. He plodded to the front door and opened it.

No one was there. The porch and front steps were empty. No one was on the sidewalk or the lawn, either. More annoyed than ever, Pel turned and headed back for the recliner.

The knock sounded again, and he realized it wasn't coming from the front door. It was coming from the door to the basement.

Had Nancy come home without his even noticing it and somehow got herself locked in the basement?

No, because then where was Rachel? She was never this quiet. And besides, he hadn't been *that* involved with the book; he'd have heard them come in.

Maybe a meter reader had come in from outside and needed to talk to him about something?

On Sunday? Not likely.

There was one easy way to find out. He opened the basement door.

The man standing on the steps was a complete stranger. Pel blinked at him, startled. It was only when he saw this new apparition that he remembered seeing the little person while assembling Rachel's wagon two nights before.

"Good day, sir," the stranger said. He bowed, right arm across his chest, a hat in his right hand, a feather bobbing on the hat.

"Hi," Pel said. "Who the hell are you?"

"I am called Raven," the stranger replied, with another bow. "And whom do I have the honor of addressing?"

Pel stared for a moment.

He had, he felt, plenty of reason to stare. The man before him was of medium height, maybe five foot eight or so, with curly black hair and a tan. He was wearing a black tunic with silver embroidery and gold trim, black woolen hose on his legs, and a fine black velvet cloak thrown over one shoulder. The hat he held was a wide-brimmed, flat-crowned black felt, with a curling white ostrich plume in the band.

It didn't look like a stage costume, though — the materials were too heavy, the detailing too fine, without any of the glitzy look of theatrical attire. The clothes had a solid reality to them.

So did the man who wore them. He had a long nose, dark eyes, and lines at the corners of a thin-lipped mouth; Pel estimated him to be in his late thirties or early forties. He looked more like a Mafioso than an actor.

He was waiting for an answer.

"Pel Brown," Pel said at last.

The stranger straightened up a little more and said, "Your servant, sir. Are you the master here?"

"It's my house, if that's what you mean." Pel considered it odd that the man's speech was rather flowery, in accord with his garb, but his accent was faint and seemed somewhere between Australia and the Bronx, not at all in the traditional British upper-class manner.

"Indeed," Raven said. He moved his eyes.

Pel took the hint and stepped aside. "Come on up out of there," he said.

The man who had introduced himself as Raven obliged, and for the first time Pel realized that the stranger's tunic was belted with a wide band of black leather, and that a sword hung from that belt. Not a dueling foil, as his outfit might have led one to expect, but a sheathed broadsword.

"Come on over here," Pel said.

Raven's eyes darted about, taking in the passageway, the kitchen that was visible through the doorway, the family room, the bookcases, the etageres, the couch, the recliner, the video set-up, the Maxfield Parrish print on the wall.

Pel stepped back and closed the basement door, making sure that it latched and that the lock was set. Then he followed his guest into the family room.

Upon spotting the stranger the household cat, Silly Cat by name, leapt up from his place on the back of the couch and made a dash for the stairs. He was a timid beast, much given to hiding under the bed, and would hardly ever stay in the same room with an unfamiliar human being.

"Have a seat," Pel said, gesturing at the couch.

"Thank you," Raven said. He sank onto the sofa and seemed startled by how soft the cushions were. His sword got in the way; he swung it to the side, and had to unbuckle the belt to get comfortable. He pulled the leather band out, wrapped it around the scabbard, and then laid the whole package gently on the coffee table, carefully not disturbing the two issues of *TV Guide* or the beer-stained coaster. His velvet cloak he draped over the back of the couch, where, Pel was sure, the velvet would pick up cat hairs.

Pel settled back into his recliner, his hand reaching automatically for his book. He stopped himself, leaned forward, and asked, "So, Raven, you said?"

The stranger nodded.

"Okay," Pel said. "So what were you doing in my basement? You have anything to do with the elf who turned up down there night before last?"

"Elf?" Raven's face expressed polite puzzlement.

"Something like that — little guy, about this high." Pel held out his hands to show his tiny visitor's height. "Said he was from Hrumph."

"Oh." Raven nodded. "Aye, that would be Grummetty."

"Grummetty, huh?"

"Aye," Raven said. "A little person. He's no elf; the elven are another sort entirely. Of a time, we called Grummetty's people gnomes, but 'twould seem they find the term offensive now, so we .. well, most of us try to oblige them. Particularly now, in their days of exile."

"I asked him if he was a fairy," Pel said.

"Alack for that!" Raven exclaimed. A wry grin flickered quickly across his face, then vanished. "He made no mention on that. I'll hope he took not too great an offense at it."

"No, he accepted it as an honest misunderstanding, I think. So, he's a friend of yours?"

"An ally, more than a friend, I would say," Raven replied judiciously.

"Oh," Pel said, accepting the distinction without comprehension. "Well, so you got into my basement the same way he did?"

Raven nodded. "Exactly. It pleases me well to see that you're a man of such quick intelligence."

Pel gave a self-deprecating smile. "Sure. So now that we've got that straight — who the hell *are* you people, and how are you getting into my basement, and why?"

"Well . . ." Raven's eyes roamed the room again, the green wall-to-wall carpeting, the textured ceiling, the green drapes and the sliding glass door to the patio, the books and records and CDs and videotapes, the throw pillows that Rachel had stacked on the floor as a fort for her Barbie dolls.

Pel waited.

Raven sighed. "'Tis a long story," he said, "and I scarce know where to start."

"Begin at the beginning," Pel said, without thinking. "And go on till you come to the end; then stop." The quote from Lewis Carroll was an old favorite.

"Indeed, that's the wisest course for most tales," Raven agreed. "But I think I'd do best to start by asking you a question. What know you, sir, of other worlds than your own?"

"It depends how you mean that," Pel replied cautiously. He did not intend to set himself up for anything.

"What I mean, good sir," Raven replied, "is that I am not of your world. In truth, I know nothing of it save what Grummetty told me, and what I have seen for myself. Your pardon, but your world seems to me passing strange; your chamber here reminds of nothing so much as a wizard's secret chamber, yet the door — it is a door? — aye, the door yonder is sheerest glass, is it not? Not some mage's trickery?"

"It's glass," Pel agreed. "Go on."

"Doors of glass," Raven said, shaking his head in amazement.

"Get on with it!" Pel snapped. His patience was wearing thin. If this was all some elaborate stunt he was getting tired of it, he wanted the punch line. If it was real — well, that was another matter entirely. That was frightening.

It was downright terrifying, in fact.

"Your pardon, sir," Raven said, ducking his head. "As I was saying, your world is not my own, nor from what I see here does it much resemble my own, though men are yet men, and the trees and grass I see through the pane seem familiar, and we speak the same tongue."

That fact had already struck Pel. It seemed very unlikely that people from another world would speak English.

"It seems to me that you speak it as the little people do, rather than as my own, yet 'tis certainly the same tongue," Raven continued.

Pel began to wonder if he would ever get to the point. "All right, you're from another world," he said. "How'd you get in my basement?"

"'Tis the doing of our mage, Elani, with a spell stolen from the foe; she sent first Grummetty, and then myself, to see what manner of world it was that the Imperials had found in their quest for aid against Shadow."

"What?" asked Pel, thoroughly confused. Raven's accent seemed to be thickening, and his phrasing becoming more complex, as he settled into the conversation. The words didn't seem to make sense, but he tried a little free association. "You're in trouble with Lamont Cranston's Chrysler?"

"How's that?" Raven expressed polite puzzlement.

"Never mind," Pel said, waving it aside. "Go on."

Raven nodded. "As I said, 'tis a long tale. Know you aught of Shadow, or perchance of the Imperials?"

"No," Pel said flatly. He decided not to try any Little Anthony jokes.

"I feared as much." The stranger groped for words, then began. "Shadow," he said, "is an evil thing. 'Twas once a mortal wizard, the legends say, but I'd not swear to that. Whatever it is in truth, its magic is great, its slaves and servants many and mighty, and in its realm its power is absolute. For centuries, since before my family's first father began the archives, Shadow has been growing, spreading its power, fighting and defeating and devouring mages and wizards, learning their spells and consuming their power. In its wake come death and terror; castles are thrown down, their inhabitants horribly slain. Villages are burnt, the people devoured, crops and livestock vanished. For centuries, men of good will have struggled against Shadow, have resisted the offers it made of power in its foul realm — but weaker men have sold their souls for empty promises and brief pleasures."

Pel listened appreciatively. Raven told the story well, despite his curious accent. Pel had heard it before, of course, in any number of fantasy novels and movies. "And you've found some way this Shadow can be defeated?" he asked, anticipating the next step in the traditional plot. "Some talisman that can kill it, or something?"

"No," Raven said, startled. "Of course not. Such things are the stuff of children's tales. We know of no way Shadow can be fought save by slaying its creatures and combating its spells, as we have done since my grandfather was a babe."

"No?" It was Pel's turn to be startled.

"No! No, there can be no easy victory — can there?" An odd, hopeful note crept into Raven's voice. "Do you know of some way that Shadow can be defeated? Has something like this happened in your world, and was a way found?"

"No, of course not," Pel replied, confused. "Magic doesn't work in the real world."

For a moment Raven was silent, his face slowly reddening; then he stood up angrily. "You mock me, sir," he said, in a tone that was pure threat.

If this was a joke, Raven was a superb actor; he sounded utterly sincere. Pel blinked up at him, startled anew, and for a long silent moment the two men stared at each other.

"No, I don't," Pel said at last. "I'm sorry. I don't mean any mockery. Go on with your story."

Raven glared for a moment longer, then slowly settled back onto the couch. He stared at the far wall for a moment, where a blonde in white gauze rode a swing before a landscape of impossibly vivid colors.

Pel had always loved that print, but Raven seemed puzzled by it.

At last the stranger said, "Magic does not work in your world, you say?"

"No," Pel said. "At least, we generally don't think so, except for a few loonies. Real magic doesn't work. It never has."

Raven nodded.

"That," he said, "might well account for Grummetty's illness. 'Tis said by some that the little people are magical in origin, and yet need a trace of that magic to live. Perhaps in your world that magic is gone, and they cannot exist. Grummetty told us all that he felt as if his own flesh were burning him when he came here, and indeed he was sore ill when he returned to us. At first we feared he might not live, but when his fever broke and his strength began to return, I ventured through the portal. As yet, I've felt no ill here."

"Oh," Pel said. "He said he felt sick. I wondered about that."

Raven nodded. "We sent a little person at the first because he might more easily hide, should danger arise. He said he found no danger save the illness, only a metalsmith at work. Would that be you, sir?"

"I was putting together a wagon for my daughter," Pel explained, a little impatiently. "She just turned six, and we had a party for her yesterday. Now would you go on with your story about the Shadow, and what you're doing here?"

"Indeed," Raven said. "And gladly will I speak, an it be that my words can sway. That thing we call Shadow has conquered all my world, now; the darkness is everywhere. From one edge to the other it is supreme, and only in isolated pockets do a few of us still resist its dominion. In truth, we can do little 'gainst it. And having thus triumphed, 'twould seem that the evil seeks new challenge; our surviving free mages, working in secret, spied upon Shadow, and learned that it had sought new worlds to conquer — and had in fact found them."

"Earth, you mean?" Pel asked.

Raven stared blankly at him. "Earth?"

"This world, I mean," Pel explained.

"Oh," Raven said, with a glance out through the glass of the sliding door. "You call this Earth? How odd." He shook his head. "'Tis no matter, though. No, 'twas not this world Shadow found, but another, the realm of the Imperials."

"Oh. Okay, who are *they?*" The tale, Pel thought, was getting unnecessarily long and complicated, and he wished that Raven would get to the point.

"They are men, like us," Raven told him, "and they rule not one world, but many. Not worlds that are reached by magical portals, such as the one that brought me hither, but worlds that float separately in the sky, among the stars, and that can be sailed to in special flying ships — or so I am told. I do not pretend to understand it, not having been there. They call all the worlds gathered under their rule the Galactic Empire, though I know not whence the name derives."

"The Galactic Empire?" Pel objected. "Aren't you mixing genres?"

"What?" Raven asked. His confusion was beginning to have a constant visible admixture of anger, and Pel decided not to provoke him with explanations of the difference between science fiction and fantasy.

"Never mind," Pel replied. "Go on."

"As you will," Raven said, calming. He continued, "When 'twas learned that Shadow sought these other realms, certain mages among those who strove 'gainst the darkness took careful study and discovered the secrets of the spells Shadow had used in its researches — Elani was one such. Those mages then opened portals to the worlds of the Galactic Empire, that they might forewarn the Imperials, and thereby gain their aid in fighting Shadow. However, those who passed through these portals found that the Empire was strange beyond our understanding, and was perhaps itself no better than the lesser of two evils. Some, my group among them, therefore resolved not to trust the Imperials, but to proceed on our own."

"So you looked for another, better world, and you found us?" Pel asked.

"No," Raven answered. "The Imperials did that. Once they learned that one other reality existed, and that 'twas ruled by a hostile force, they set about finding another, in hopes of acquiring an ally in their coming battle against Shadow. They have no mages, but they have men and women who can hear the thoughts of others . . ."

"Telepaths?" Pel suggested.

"Aye, telepaths, the very word they use!" Raven agreed, startled.

Pel nodded. For once he'd guessed right about something in Raven's tale. "Go on," he said.

Raven continued, "'Twould seem that these telepaths had sometimes found traces of thought for which they could not account. Some, it seemed, had leaked through from my own native realm — but some, so it chanced, came from *your* world. Thus, they sought out your reality, and attempted to send messages to a few receptive individuals therein. When that yielded no useful results, they devised a means of transporting one of their sky-ships into whatsoever other realities they might find, and sent that ship hither, to your land. This morning it arrived, and if Elani's spell be sound, not far from here. My group learned about these plans, and our mages opened a portal, that we might communicate with your people — this, that you might have some contact with our realm other than through the Imperials, and that, perhaps, we, too, might benefit from whatever your people can teach us." He frowned. "We had hoped that our messenger might bespeak your rulers ere the ship of the Imperials came, but alas, Grummetty's illness cut short our first attempt, and 'twas not until some hours after the ship was sent that we made another."

Raven spread his hands.

"And here I am," he said, just as Pel heard the whir of the garage door opener.

*A*my Jewell watched as the last of the crewmen from the spaceship — if that's what it was — climbed reluctantly into the police van.

"What's going to happen to them?" she asked.

The plainclothes cop beside her looked up from his notepad. "Them?" he said, pointing his pen at the van.

Amy nodded.

The cop shrugged. "I don't know," he said. "I never heard of anything like this before. If it's a publicity stunt I expect the movie company will bail them out tomorrow morning — not today, because it's Sunday and the judge won't be in, but probably first thing tomorrow. *If* it's for a movie. And they didn't resist arrest or give us any trouble at all — hell, you probably heard them, they were *asking* to talk to the authorities — so even if they *don't* get bailed out we may not be able to hold them."

Amy nodded again. "I see," she said, though she wasn't sure she did.

"You worried about them?" the cop asked, giving her a shrewd glance.

Amy grimaced. "Not really," she said.

The cop didn't answer.

"What about the airpl . . . the shi . . . that thing?" Amy asked, pointing. "How are you going to get it off my lawn?"

The cop frowned. Then he sighed. "I don't know, lady," he said. "That's not my job. I'm sorry, but it's not police business. Either you can move it, because it's your yard, or they can move it, because it's their ship. Either way, they're liable, but you'll probably need to sue them to collect." He glanced at the huge purple object. "The FAA people are supposed to be on their way out here now, you know, Sunday or not — they want to look at the thing and figure out how it got here. You probably shouldn't touch anything until they get here."

A siren started up, then cut off abruptly; a white pumper truck with GAITHERSBURG-WASHINGTON GROVE FIRE DEPARTMENT lettered on the doors in gold pulled away, engine roaring and the tires spitting gravel from the roadside. Amy and the cop watched it go.

"I've gotta say," the plainclothesman remarked, "that this is the weirdest damn thing I ever heard of."

Amy nodded.

"If worse comes to worst," he suggested, "you could sell tickets and run tours."

"I suppose so," Amy said, unenthusiastically. She wasn't really very interested in the idea; she wanted her yard back, not a tourist trap. She didn't really need so dubious a source of additional income.

As she watched the pumper depart she spotted a blue sedan creeping up the road. She thought it looked as if it had writing on the door, but at that angle and distance she couldn't make it out.

"That's the FAA boys now," the cop said. "I'll be going along. If you could come to the station tomorrow and let us know whether you want to press charges or anything, we'd appreciate it."

"All right," Amy said distractedly.

"That's it, then," the cop said, closing his notepad. "Have a nice day."

He turned and ambled toward the remaining county police cruiser as the van pulled away and the blue sedan coasted to a stop.

Chapter Three

Nancy stared stupidly as Raven bowed deeply. Rachel giggled behind her hand, and dropped a small plastic shopping bag to the floor.

"Hi, honey," Pel said. He gestured at their unexpected guest. "This is Raven."

"Hi," Nancy said, looking questioningly at Pel as he came to take one of the bags of groceries from her arms.

"Your servant, madame," Raven said, bowing again.

"My wife, Nancy, and my daughter, Rachel," Pel explained as he carried the groceries into the kitchen.

"A pleasure to meet you, I assure you," Raven said.

Nancy murmured something vague, then followed Pel into the kitchen with the other bag.

"Who's *he?*" she demanded. "Why's he dressed like that?"

Pel put the sack on the counter and started putting cans of soup on the pantry cupboard shelves while he tried to think how to answer that.

"He says to call him Raven," he said. "I'm not sure if it's really his name or not. And he's apparently dressed like that because that's what he wears at home."

"Where's home? What's he doing here?"

A can of Campbell's cream of mushroom slipped, and Pel caught it in his other hand.

"I don't know, really," he said. "I mean, I sort of do, but it's . . . well, it's not that it's hard to explain as that nobody would believe the explanation." He paused, considering, and added, "I'm not sure *I* believe it."

Nancy stared at him. "Pel, what are you talking about?" she asked, worried.

Pel looked helplessly around the kitchen, as if hoping the cabinets would tell him what to say.

The cabinets remained blank.

He could hear voices from the family room, he realized — Raven and Rachel were talking. He crossed to the door and leaned through.

"You see?" Raven was saying. "It is indeed a real sword. And sharp — do you not touch it, lest you cut your pretty fingers." He had pulled about a foot of the blade from its sheath, and Rachel was admiring the dull gleam of the metal.

That wasn't cheap chrome, like some of the ceremonial swords Pel had seen, nor stainless steel, nor plain iron. Even from the kitchen door he could see the fine finish, the sort of finish one saw on very expensive carving knives.

Nancy came up behind him and looked over his shoulder.

"Pel," she whispered in his ear, "what's he *doing* here?"

Pel turned and pushed Nancy back into the kitchen.

"He's from some sort of fantasy world," he said. "Where magic works. He's a warrior of some kind, I guess."

"You mean he's crazy? An escaped lunatic?" In an instant, Nancy's expression went from mildly concerned to seriously worried.

"No," Pel told her. "Or at least I don't think so. I think he's for real. There's some kind of space warp that comes out in our basement."

The worried look now verged on panic. "Maybe *you're* crazy, too!" Nancy said. "Pel, what are you *talking* about?"

Pel groped unsuccessfully for words, and finally just said, "Come on." He took Nancy's hand and pulled her back into the family room, where Rachel was admiring the silver embroidery on Raven's tunic. Raven was watching the girl's little fingers indulgently as they explored the textures.

Raven looked up as the pair entered, and smiled. "A lovely child," he said. "And well-spoken."

"Thanks," Pel said.

"In her sixth year, you said? Or was it seventh?"

"She just turned six."

"Ah!"

For a moment the Browns just stood there, and Raven sat, and Rachel ran her fingertips down the silver piping. Then Raven carefully lifted Rachel off his knee, placed her on the couch, and stood up.

"My presence here troubles you, I see," he said, "and I've no wish to trouble anyone."

Pel chewed his lower lip, glancing back and forth between Raven and Nancy, while Raven awaited a reply. He was obviously hoping for a polite denial, but Nancy was obstinately silent as she stared at the stranger.

Raven sighed and picked up his sword. "I'll be going, then," he said.

"I'm sorry," Pel said, "but I can't think of any way to explain you that doesn't sound crazy."

"Ah," Raven said, comprehension dawning, "I see. I'd feared it was something else, that perhaps I'd given offense somehow. I know so little of your world, after all!" He looked hopefully at Nancy.

She remained silent; it was Pel who assured him, "No, you've been charming. But your clothes, and your name . . . well, it's strange."

Raven nodded.

"Madame," he said, "I beg your pardon for intruding, and for my garb, which I take it you find outlandish. In truth, I *am* outlandish — I've come here from another realm entirely."

Pel listened to this with interest; it was remarkable how much more believable that sounded coming from Raven than it did coming from him.

It still wasn't very believable, though, and in fact Nancy obviously still didn't believe it.

Rachel was also skeptical, judging by her expression. Nifty embroidery and shiny swords were all very well, but modern kindergarteners knew better than to believe stories about other worlds. Rachel had independently figured out just weeks before that Santa Claus wasn't real; she was still working on the Easter Bunny and the tooth fairy, but she wasn't about to accept Raven at face value.

Raven could see the disbelief as well as Pel could. He sighed. "You doubt me," he said, deliberately understating the case, "and I can scarce blame you, for who in her right mind would believe such an assertion without proof? But perhaps I can convince you. And if not, I'll go, and at least you'll be rid of me." He rose and reached for his sword and belt. "Pel Brown," he said as he fastened the buckle, "if you would be so kind as to lead us to the cellars?"

That was clearly the thing to do, though the idea had not occurred to Pel. "Come on," he said. "Everybody down in the basement, and you can see why I believed Raven about where he came from."

They trooped down the stairs, Raven in the lead, then Pel, then Rachel, and last Nancy. Raven did not hesitate; he walked directly across the basement and into the concrete wall.

Unlike Grummetty, who had whacked his head the first time he tried to return to his own reality, Raven vanished immediately.

Rachel's eyes widened, and her mouth opened.

Nancy turned to her husband and demanded, "Pel, what's going on here?"

"You saw," Pel said. "He vanished into the wall. See, night before last, when I was down here, this little tiny guy, like an elf or something, appeared out of nowhere, and talked to me for a minute, and then disappeared into the wall just the way Raven did." He didn't mention the bump. "Then this afternoon, when you were out, I heard knocking, and there Raven was, in our basement. And he gave me this whole story about another world, and I know it sounds stupid, but I bought it — it sounded real, and he looked real, and I couldn't figure out any other way it could happen."

"Well, he's gone now," Nancy said, and just then Rachel, who had wandered halfway across the basement staring at the spot where Raven had vanished, let out a shriek.

Raven was stepping back out of the blank concrete wall.

Rachel came running back across the basement floor to her parents and flung herself against her father, who bent down and picked her up, hugging her to him.

"It's okay, Rae," he told her, as Nancy laid a comforting hand on the back of the little girl's head. "It's just Raven. It's okay."

The dismay he saw on Raven's face over Rachel's shoulder could not be feigned, Pel was sure.

"My humble apologies, Mistress Rachel," Raven said, going down on one knee and lowering his head. "I'd not meant to startle you. Please, forgive me?"

Rachel lifted her head from her father's chest and peeked behind her. When she saw Raven's posture she pressed against Pel's shoulders, and he lowered her to the ground.

She turned to face Raven, but didn't say anything.

The man in black raised his head and looked at her. "Grant me your pardon, Mistress Rachel, please. Say you forgive me," he begged.

"It's okay," Rachel said. "I think. Isn't it, Daddy?"

"I think so," Pel agreed.

"Thank you," Raven said, rising to his feet and brushing the dust from the knee of his hose. He stood, waiting.

Nancy still didn't say anything.

"Shall we go back upstairs?" Pel suggested.

Nancy didn't say anything, but she turned and marched back up.

A moment later all four of them were back in the family room, and Nancy finally spoke.

"Pel," she said, "come in the kitchen for a moment."

Pel came.

When they were out of sight of Raven and Rachel, Nancy whispered loudly, "Do you really believe him?"

Pel shrugged. "I'm not sure," he said. "I don't have any better explanation."

"It could be some kind of trick," Nancy suggested. "Some kind of illusion."

"Sure, I guess it could be," Pel agreed. "But why?"

"*I* don't know," Nancy said, fretting, "but I don't like it."

Pel sighed again. "Nancy," he said, "the guy is not selling me anything. I'm just talking to him. He turned up in the basement, with this whole story about some kind of cosmic war, and I'm just listening to it. That's all. And frankly, I want to hear some more. If you want to go upstairs or something, go ahead."

"All right," she said. "You can talk." She turned and led the way back into the family room, then stopped suddenly.

"Can I get you a drink?" she asked Raven.

He glanced at Pel, then back at Nancy. "Thank you, aye," he said, "I judge I could put a drink to use."

"Um . . . beer?"

"Yes, that would suit me well, thank you."

Nancy spun on her heel and marched back toward the refrigerator while Pel resumed his seat on the recliner. Rachel was sitting on the couch, not touching Raven, Pel noticed, but staring at him intently. His performance in the basement had obviously impressed her.

"Now," Pel said, "you were telling me that you came here to talk to us about maybe joining forces with your people against something you call a Shadow?"

"Yes," Raven said, with a nod. "That's exactly right."

"Shadow is magical, right?"

"Aye," Raven said. "'Tis magical in nature. We know little enough of its true origins, but we know that much. It has gathered to itself all the magic that its evil allowed it, the greater part of all the world's magical might, leaving only crumbs for our wizards to pick at. Because the good magicians were not united against it, it has triumphed."

"But magic doesn't work here. No one in our world *has* any magic."

Nancy appeared from the kitchen, carrying two cans of Miller.

"You have nothing you call magic, perhaps, and nothing like our magicks, it would seem," Raven agreed, "but you have magicks of your own, I am sure, though perhaps you call them by another name. The Galactic Empire calls its magic 'science'; do you use that, perhaps?"

"Science isn't magic," Rachel said scornfully.

Raven turned to her, startled.

"She's right," Pel said. "Science isn't magic. It does some pretty amazing things, though."

Nancy put the two cans of beer on the table, then seated herself on the arm of the couch behind Rachel, at the far end from Raven. Pel leaned forward, picked one can up, and popped the top.

Raven blinked, then picked up the other.

"Cold!" he exclaimed, startled, as he quickly put it back down. He stared at it.

Rachel giggled. Pel and Nancy exchanged a glance.

"Maybe he's British," Nancy said, *sotto voce.*

"'Course it's cold!" Rachel said. "It just came out of the fridge!"

Raven glanced at her, then reached down and cautiously picked up the beer can. He held it up with one hand while the other explored it carefully, stroking beads of condensation from the side, feeling the smooth, thin metal. He studied it intently.

"I'd wondered," he said, "why you had no bottles or barrels in your cellar. It seems you have other ways of keeping things cool."

"The refrigerator," Pel agreed. "I guess that's some of the scientific magic you were asking about." He remembered his own beer and took a pull on the can.

Raven watched him, then looked at the top of the can he held. "How . . . there are letters here, stamped in the metal, or etched, perhaps. I cannot read them."

"Oh," Pel said. He put down his own beer and leaned over. "Let me show you," he said.

He took the can and popped the top, while Raven watched, fascinated. Beer foamed up, and Pel handed it back.

Raven tasted it.

"Good," he said, though his expression contradicted his words.

"It's American beer," Pel remarked. "I like the European stuff better."

"This is a trifle thin, perhaps," Raven agreed.

"So I guess we have technology you don't, like refrigerators," Pel said, leaning back with his beer in hand. "Is that what you came looking for?"

"I'd nothing specific in mind," Raven said, "but if you have this science, or . . . technology, did you call it? If you have this, and use it for weapons, perhaps we could use it against Shadow."

"I suppose you could," Pel agreed. "If it works in your world."

"Why shouldn't it?" Nancy demanded, addressing her husband rather than their guest.

"Magic doesn't work here," Pel pointed out.

Raven sipped beer. "There is that," he agreed. "So you do have technology weapons? Rayguns, perhaps, like the Galactic Empire's? Or mayhap you call them blasters? The Imperials use both terms."

"Not exactly," Pel said, amused. "The closest we have to rayguns would be lasers, I guess, and they only work as weapons in the movies."

"In the . . .?" Raven began.

"Never mind," Pel said, cutting him off. "In stories, I should have said."

"What works in reality, then?"

"Bombs," Pel said. "Guns. Tanks, airplanes, nuclear warheads. Poison gas."

"I know bombs," Raven said, a little hesitantly. "And I think I know what you mean by guns, but these others — what sort of tank is a weapon? What is a nuclear war head?"

"A nuclear warhead," Pel explained, "is a bomb that can destroy an entire city."

Raven sat silently for a moment, staring at Pel. Rachel got up her nerve to stroke the fine black velvet of his cloak, and Nancy got up to go to the kitchen again.

"How big be these warheads?" Raven asked at last. "Be they real, not just another fancy found in stories?"

"Oh, yes," Pel said. "They're real. But they're very big and heavy, and besides, only a few governments have access to them."

"You don't want them," Nancy said, startling both Pel and Raven. "Besides destroying cities they poison the air and soil, and kill or deform unborn children."

"In truth?" Raven asked, looking at Pel.

"Truly," Pel said, nodding. "They use atomic energy — the same thing that keeps the sun burning — and that produces radiation."

"Our sun burns with magic — I know nothing of yours. But your people fight with these bombs?"

"No," Pel said. "We keep from fighting because we're scared of them."

"Don't forget Hiroshima," Nancy interjected.

Raven looked a question.

"We used them once," Pel admitted.

"Twice," Nancy said.

"Right, twice. On Hiroshima and Nagasaki. Two cities in Japan. That was when the bombs were first invented, at the end of a long war, when we didn't know any better. Almost fifty years ago."

"Ah. So you know they work, then."

"Oh, yes, they work," Pel said bitterly.

"And are they strong enough to break through fortress walls?"

Pel stared at Raven for a moment, then said, "I don't think you understand. A nuclear bomb can totally obliterate an entire city — flatten it, leave nothing but a crater. When they tested them in the desert they fused the sand into glass. The Hiroshima bomb killed a hundred thousand people — and that was a small one, much less powerful than the ones we have now. If you dropped a nuclear bomb on a fortress, *any* fortress, the fortress would be gone. There wouldn't be any walls left."

"Even a magical fortress?"

"There's no such thing."

"There is in *my* world."

Pel had no immediate answer to that, but Nancy said, "It doesn't matter, anyway — you can't get a nuclear warhead, not even a Russian one. They're kept sealed away, heavily guarded. And you wouldn't know how to use one if you had it."

"I see. But guns and bombs and . . . and tanks?"

"You can get guns easily enough. And make bombs. I don't think you could get tanks, though."

Raven nodded. "I see. Thank you." He put down his can of beer and spoke slowly, as if making an effort to phrase clearly what he wanted to say. "I think perhaps I have imposed enough upon your hospitality," he told the Browns. "I'm very grateful for your kindness, but perhaps I had best return home now, to discuss what you have told me with my people."

"You haven't finished your beer," Nancy pointed out.

Raven looked at the can. "I fear my thirst is gone," he said, rising.

"All right," Pel said. "I'm sorry we couldn't be more help."

"I may return, sometime, if you have no objection," Raven said diffidently.

"We'd be glad to see you," Pel replied, getting to his own feet and not adding that he would be glad mostly because it would be further evidence that this wasn't all simply a dream or hallucination.

"I like your cape," Rachel said.

Raven smiled down at her. "I like it, too, child," he said kindly.

Pel led the way to the basement, and together, the Browns watched Raven vanish into the wall again.

As Pel had feared, there were cat hairs on the black velvet cloak.

"*A*re you people finished?" Amy asked.

"I don't know," the FAA man answered, not looking at her, "I really don't."

Amy stared at him without trying to hide her annoyance. "Why don't you know?" she demanded.

"Because I don't know what the hell is going on here," he told her.

She stared at him, and he explained, "That thing out there — it's not an aircraft. There's no way it could ever have flown under its own power. There's no engine, just this weird contraption of crystals and metal plates that doesn't do anything, attached to what looks like a pressure chamber. Some of the equipment aboard is ordinary electrical stuff, and works fine; other equipment is more of this crystal-and-metal nonsense that doesn't do anything. Those weapons those people were carrying — they have little batteries, but they don't *do* anything. All of them, the big one and the ones that look like pistols, they're harmless. They don't even light up or make noise like my kid's toy rayguns." He shook his head.

"It's some kind of hoax, I guess," he continued, "but why would anyone go to all this trouble? And all the *expense?* Some of the stuff in there looks like it's made out of gold and platinum, and if it's all a gag, wouldn't copper or tin do just as well? And how did the thing *get* here, anyway? Nobody tracked anything flying around here that shouldn't have been, and this thing would show up on radar like a Christmas tree, not to mention whatever must have carried it in and dropped it." He sighed. "Lady, you've got a really major mystery sitting in your back yard, and I'm glad I'm not the one who has to figure it out."

"You're not?"

"Nope." He smiled uneasily. "I passed the buck. This close to Washington it's all restricted airspace, you know — or just about. So I called the Air Force. They're sending someone out to take a look, and if he's as impressed as I am — which he will be — they'll be doing some serious investigating in the morning. And I think they called the FBI, too. I'm waiting around until their man gets here, and after that it's up to them. I'm hoping he'll just tell me to go home and forget any of this ever happened."

"But . . ." Amy turned and stared around the corner of her house at the huge purple object. "*I* can't go home and forget about it! It's on my land!"

The FAA man shrugged. "I know," he said, "and I'm sorry. You might want to start thinking about how much to ask if the national security folks decide to buy your property."

"*What?*" Amy whirled back.

"Well, they probably won't," he said, trying unsuccessfully to sound reassuring. "They may just haul the thing away." He paused, then added thoughtfully, "Though I'm not sure how they'd do that."

Amy stared around wildly, looking for a solution and seeing none.

"Listen," she said, "where'd they take the people who were aboard it?"

The FAA man shrugged. "County jail down in Rockville, I guess," he said.

"Thanks," Amy said.

She turned, leaving the FAA man leaning against the maple tree by the driveway, and went into the house. She wasn't sure just who to call to find out how she could get to talk to those people, the people who had been inside the thing, but she thought she could figure it out eventually.

And if she couldn't, her lawyer could.

She chewed her lower lip. It was probably time to call her lawyer in any case.

But then she remembered — it was Sunday. No one would be in the law offices on Sunday.

"Damn," she said, staring out the kitchen window at the ship. Then she shrugged. "So I'll have to wait 'til morning. It isn't going anywhere."

Chapter Four

"Any word yet?"

The lieutenant started, and looked around. The question had come from a woman in a major's uniform, a woman he did not recognize immediately.

"No, ma'am," he said, saluting.

She returned the salute briskly.

"Thorpe should have reported in *hours* ago, even if Cahn couldn't," the major said.

"Yes, ma'am," the lieutenant agreed.

"You haven't done anything about it?" she demanded sharply.

"No, ma'am," the lieutenant answered. "There's nothing in my orders that says I should, and after Major Copley took ill no one told me anything different."

The major's expression made clear what she thought of that argument. "You've dropped all the other contacts with that universe?" she asked.

"Yes, ma'am — at least, the telepaths were instructed to do so, as soon as the ship went through the warp. I was told that we wanted to be sure Captain Cahn didn't have any of our contacts interfering."

"That's right." The major chewed her lower lip for a few seconds, then ordered, "Get another telepath down here — one who's done those interdimensional contacts. I want to know what the hell Thorpe is doing."

"Yes, ma'am." The lieutenant started to reach for the telephone, then stopped.

Why bother? His post was supposed to be monitored at all times; the telepaths had already heard him.

Or if they hadn't, they were in trouble, which would suit him just fine.

"And this device of theirs, which they say will destroy an entire city and leave no stone upon another — believe you that it exists, and is not but some mad dream, or a tale to frighten strangers?"

Raven turned up his palms. "Who can say?" he replied. "They spoke of it as though 'twere but simple fact, they named names to me that meant nothing but had the ring of truth, yet how am I to know whether they speak lies? I'm but a man, not a wizard who can read men's souls."

The other snorted. "Would that I could!" he said. "I can see a lie betimes, when 'tis spoke, but beyond that I've no more insight into a man's secrets than you, my lord. I'm not one of these the Empire has, who claim to hear the innermost thoughts of others as if they were spoken aloud."

"Telepaths," Raven said.

"Aye," the other agreed. "That's the word."

For a moment the two were silent. Then Raven spoke.

"What of the Empire's expedition to this new world?" he asked. "Have we word of their success, or perchance their failure? Have they made contacts, perhaps obtained these terrible weapons?"

"Word is not yet received," the wizard replied.

"No?" Raven turned, startled, to look at the door of the chamber, as if he expected it to burst open on cue.

The door did not move.

"Did not Elani open the way for our messenger this hour past?" Raven asked.

The other nodded. "Aye," he said. "That she did, yet there's no word."

Raven stared at him.

"*Why?*" he demanded.

"Because the messenger tells us that the Empire has had no word of their sky-ship's fate, and our spies can hardly learn what is known to none," the wizard explained.

"No word?" Raven's brows drew together as he frowned. "Why would there be no word? They have their miracle-workers, their telepaths — why have they not heard?"

The wizard turned up his palms. "Who knows?" he asked.

"I may have to start believing in UFOs and Bigfoot," Nancy said, as she slumped on the couch and stared at the spot where Raven had sat.

"I wouldn't go that far," Pel said.

"Why not?" she asked, turning to face him. "I mean, if we can have swordsmen and elves walking through our basement wall, why are space aliens bringing Elvis back from the dead any less likely?"

Pel opened his mouth, then closed it again and considered the statement. He looked at Raven's unfinished beer, still sitting on the coffee table.

"I don't know," he said at last. "Maybe they aren't any less likely, but the evidence for them is pretty damn weak."

"Yeah, well, what evidence do we have?" Nancy retorted. "We didn't take any pictures or anything; all we've got is some memories and a can of beer. Is that any better than some of the saucer nuts?"

"No," Pel admitted.

"So maybe it didn't really happen at all," Nancy said; Pel noticed a hopeful tone to her voice. "Maybe we imagined it, got ourselves hypnotized somehow into believing it."

Pel took a deep breath, then let it out slowly.

That explanation was actually just about as believable as any other, he had to admit. He didn't like the idea that his mind could play such tricks on him, and he couldn't explain it, but really, a man from another universe wasn't a much better explanation.

He remembered Raven so clearly, though — the embroidery on his tunic, the greasy smudge on one temple, the cat hairs on his cloak, his odd accent. It didn't seem like something he and Nancy would have imagined, not with the weirdly confusing story about evil wizards and galactic empires.

That reminded him of something, and he sat up in the recliner.

"Hey," he said. "There was something he told me before you got home — he said the Galactic Empire sent a spaceship to Earth. Through a whatchamacallit, a gate or a space-warp or whatever, somewhere near here."

Nancy looked puzzled.

"So?" she said.

"*So,*" Pel said, "if it was all *real,* then don't you think a spaceship might make the evening news?"

Nancy blinked.

"I don't know," she said slowly. "Maybe."

Pel was annoyed at her lack of enthusiasm, but tried not to show it. "Well, if it's on the news, that would settle it, right? It would all be real, if it's on the news."

"And if it's not?" Nancy asked.

Pel shrugged. "Well, then we still don't know for sure," he said. "But we wouldn't be any worse off than we are."

"That's true," she admitted.

"And if it *is* on the news," Pel said with sudden enthusiasm, "this would really be big-time stuff! The first contact with another universe, my *God!*"

Nancy refused to share his excitement as he lifted the remote control and turned on CNN.

*A*my spoke quietly into the phone as she peered out her kitchen window. A man with what looked like a metal detector was walking across the back yard, swinging it slowly from side to side a few inches above the dewy grass. A team of men was taking photographs from every possible angle, with one of them holding a yellow measuring stick in various positions to provide a scale; about half of them wore Air Force uniforms, while the rest were in mufti.

They had started arriving right around dawn, and had apparently reached equilibrium now, with a few leaving whenever more arrived. And Amy's call had finally gotten an answer.

"This is Amy Jewell," she said. "I need to speak to Bob Hough right away."

"I'm sorry," replied the receptionist at Dutton, Powell, and Hough, "but Mr. Hough is on vacation in Cancun. I have the number of his hotel if this is an emergency, but Ms. Nguyen is handling everything for him while he's away."

Amy paused to think who Ms. Nguyen was. There was Susan, the Vietnamese woman who had helped out with the divorce — that must be her.

Susan had probably done most of the work anyway. The women with no titles or authority generally did everything except get the credit. "All right, then I'll talk to Ms . . . to her," Amy said.

"She's only just gotten in, but I'll see. Just a moment," There was a click, and insipid music began playing softly. Amy watched as the man with the metal detector thing wandered out of sight around the corner, and the photography crew paused to reload.

"Susan Nguyen," said a voice on the phone.

"Susan," Amy said, relieved; the voice was familiar. This was definitely the Susan she remembered. "This is Amy Jewell; I think you helped Bob Hough handle my divorce last year?"

"Oh, yes, Ms. Jewell; how are you?"

"I'm fine, but listen, something really weird happened yesterday. This . . . this thing landed in my back yard yesterday. It's like a . . . well, it's like a spaceship out of a comic book or something."

"A spaceship?" Susan replied dubiously.

"Not a *real* one," Amy said hastily, "I think it's some kind of gag — maybe a publicity stunt of some kind."

"Oh," Susan said. "It still seems strange. How big is . . no, never mind that. What is it you want us to do?"

"I want it out of my yard, that's what I want!" Amy's temper, carefully held in check until now, finally gave out. "I don't want anything to do with it! I want it *out* of here, and I want all these people who are out here looking at it off my land and away from here! And I want damages — it smashed my hedge and scared the hell out of me!"

"Have you called the police?"

Amy said, almost screaming, "They're the ones who started it!" Then she stopped herself, took a deep breath, and forced herself to calm down.

She could sense Susan waiting calmly on the other end of the line.

"I called 9-1-1," Amy said at last, "when the thing first fell here, because I thought it was a crashing airplane or something. So the police and the firemen came out and looked at it, and they took away the people who had been in it, and then the FAA came out and looked at it, and they said it wasn't a private plane, it was some kind of military thing. So now . . ."

"Wait a minute, Ms. Jewell," Susan said, interrupting. "There were *people* in it?"

"Yes! About a dozen of them, in silly purple uniforms. One woman and a bunch of men. All white, most of them blond, like a bunch of Nazis, with things like rayguns that didn't work. The police took them all away and charged them with trespassing. And I want you to find them and find out who's responsible and make them get this thing out of here!"

"I see," Susan said. "Was it the county police that took them?"

"I think so," Amy said. "Someone said something about taking them to Rockville, I think."

"Well, that would be the county, then," Susan agreed. "So you want to know who they are, and get the . . . the thing off your property. Anything else?"

"I want these people out of here. The FAA man called the Air Force, and one of them was here all night, sitting in his car, and a lot more got here this morning before I even woke up, and now there are a bunch of people out there taking pictures and measuring everything, and I want them off my land."

"Air Force?" There was a long pause before Susan said, "I'm not sure how much I can do about them, Ms. Jewell, but I'll try."

"I don't care who they are, I want them off my land!" Amy shouted. "Isn't there something in the Constitution about soldiers in people's houses?"

"Third Amendment," Susan replied automatically. "I doubt it applies in this case, but I'll see what I can do. I need to make a few calls, and then I'll probably want to come out there and see just what the situation is. I have your address and phone number in the files; are they still current?"

"I haven't moved," Amy said.

"Good. Just hold on, Ms. Jewell, and I'll see what I can do."

"Thank you," Amy said.

"Good-bye."

"'Bye." She hung up the phone and looked out the window at the photo team. Now they were pacing off the dimensions of her patio.

What business of theirs was that? She clamped her lips tight and turned away.

Maybe, she thought, if she didn't watch, it wouldn't be so annoying.

"*W*hat I can't figure out," the detective lieutenant said, "is that not one of them wanted to use the phone. You're *sure* of that?"

The booking sergeant nodded. "Absolutely," he said. "We read them their rights individually, just to be on the safe side, and we explained it all, and we told each of them he was entitled to one phone call, and all we got was blank looks. If I didn't know better, I'd *swear* that none of them had ever heard any of it before."

"What, they never saw cop shows on TV?"

"That's what it seemed like. I mean, when I read the line about if you can't afford an attorney one will be appointed for you, I got these looks you wouldn't believe — they were all of them astonished, like they'd never heard of such a thing. One of them, I mean, man, his jaw dropped open. And one said, 'Really? It's not a trick?' and Jesus, he sounded sincere."

The detective shook his head in wonder.

The sergeant slapped a hand on the desk. "It's *weird*," he said. "I mean, I know there are nuts out there, I've seen plenty of them. I've seen guys dragged in here trying to pick invisible bugs off their skin, and guys hopped up on PCP who needed a dozen men to hold them, and guys that looked like they'd been dead for a week and I was afraid they'd drop dead on the floor for real before we could get a doctor in, and I've had guys swear at me and curse me up one side and down the other, I've had rich guys screaming at me and street punks being Momma's little angel, but I have *never* seen anything like this bunch!"

"Gave you a lot of trouble?"

"Hell, no — that's what's so strange! They all of them looked around like this place was something out of a fairy tale, and did just exactly what they were told, and they gave us names and ranks and serial numbers, like they were prisoners of war instead of just busted for trespassing and littering, but they wouldn't tell us anything *else*. They didn't ask for lawyers, didn't make phone calls, nothing. It's like they really *believe* they're soldiers from another planet!"

"Maybe they do," the detective suggested.

The sergeant spread his hands wide. "*Ten* of them? Ten nuts with the same delusion?"

The detective shrugged. "So they were all ten like that?"

"Well, eight of 'em, anyway. The woman was a little different, I guess. She seemed real upset, where the others were calm as anything. And the captain, as he's supposed to be — he wanted to talk to someone official, and no, I wouldn't do, he wanted somebody from the military or the State Department. I told him I couldn't do that, especially on a weekend."

"Did he say why?"

"Well, yeah. He's an envoy, he says, from the Galactic Empire, and he wants to talk to someone about arranging a mutual defense treaty with Earth, or at least the United States. He can't make a treaty with local cops."

The detective considered that silently for a moment, then asked, "Think it's a movie stunt?"

"At first I did," the sergeant said, "but now . . . I dunno. Wouldn't they have called in the reporters by now? Wouldn't they have made some phone calls? And why would they pick this lady's back yard way the hell out in Goshen? Her lawyer just called, y'know — the lady's really pissed about it."

The detective nodded again. "So they all claim to come from the Galactic Empire?"

"As much as they claim anything, yeah."

"They're consistent?"

"Oh, yeah, absolutely. Not one of them has slipped out of character for as much as an instant, I swear."

The detective sighed. "All right," he said. "Where should I start?"

"Wherever you like," the sergeant said, pushing a clipboard over.

The detective picked it up and scanned the list of names. "Prosser-pine Thorpe?" he said. "Is that the woman?"

"Proserpin-*AH,*" the sergeant corrected him. "Yeah, that's her."

"Gave her rank as 'registered master telepath'?"

"That's what she said, yeah."

"She try to read your mind?"

The sergeant just shrugged.

"Not so you could tell, huh?"

"So how am I supposed to know? But she sure didn't talk about it, if she read anybody's mind."

"You said she was nervous?"

"Well, upset about something, anyway. Had a sort of trapped look — like a junkie who suddenly realizes she doesn't know where to get her next fix. You know what I mean."

"Sure," the detective said. "She a looker?"

The sergeant shrugged. "She's okay," he said. "Nothing I'd leave home for, but okay."

"What the hell," the detective said, dropping the clipboard back on the desk. "I'll start with her."

*P*roserpine Thorpe stared at the walls of her cell, baffled and frustrated.

Nothing. She had been straining her every nerve, focusing all her being on her telepathic sense, and there was simply nothing there.

This universe had some characteristics that nobody had mentioned or thought about in any of the briefings — presumably because nobody knew about them. The ship's main drive didn't work here. The crew's blasters didn't seem to work, either, though she wasn't sure they'd really been tested.

And, it seemed, telepathy didn't work here.

They should have expected this, or at least considered the possibility. After all, they had known that at least some of Shadow's magic didn't work in Imperial space. That demonstrated that there were differences. Why hadn't they considered what *other* differences there might be?

She felt as if her head were packed with wool, shutting out the constant background hum of other people's thoughts, and it was not a comfortable feeling at all. She had never experienced anything like it before.

What was even worse, though, was that no one had yet contacted her.

The plan had been that once they were through the warp she would send a quick verification that they had arrived safely, and that she then would devote her attention to the usual duties of a ship's telepath — accompanying Captain Cahn on his diplomatic mission, reading the minds of those around them, advising him when they were lying, and so on and so forth. All of that had obviously become impossible when the ship had crashed twenty miles from their objective and they had all been taken prisoner by the local constabulary, and when most of their equipment wouldn't work.

And she hadn't sent any verification because her telepathy didn't work, either.

Which meant that as far as she could tell, nobody back at Base One had any idea what had happened to them.

So why hadn't they gotten another telepath and contacted her? Surely, she could still receive as well as the natives here could, and her team had managed to make limited contact with half a dozen of the native psychics. Didn't they realize something had gone wrong? She had been here, isolated, all night, and there had been no contact.

Surely they knew something had gone wrong. Surely they had had plenty of time to try to get through.

Then, at last, something stirred in her mind, as if a mouse were moving inside that mass of wool. She tried to focus on it, and it became clearer, she could sense a sort of shape to the message.

And then it was through, it was Carrie back at Base One, calling her, calling desperately.

"Here!" she thought. "I'm here, Carrie!"

"Prossie!" Relief flooded through the contact, flowing both ways.

She didn't reply with words, but with reassuring thoughts roughly equivalent to, "It's okay, Carrie, I'm fine."

Carrie's thoughts caressed hers for a moment, and then a question came through, so clear that for a moment Prossie thought she had heard it spoken aloud.

"Prossie," it said, "what *happened?*"

Chapter Five

"No telepathy? No anti-gravity?" The Under-Secretary frowned at the papers on his desk.

"No, sir," the telepath standing stiffly before him reported. "Neither one. It appears that the laws of physics are totally different there — it's not just that the telepathic mutation never happened, or AG wasn't discovered. Not only do they have no telepaths or AG of their own, but ours don't work there; that's why the ship crashed, and why Prossie . . . why Telepath Thorpe didn't report in. It's a miracle that there are human beings so much like us in a place so alien, let alone that they speak the same language."

"But they have some sort of technology, don't they?" the official demanded. "I mean, they aren't just using sticks and stones?"

"Thorpe says that they have a *different* technology from ours, sir," the telepath explained, "but it's one that's very nearly as advanced as ours in some ways, sir, maybe even higher. She reports seeing a recording machine of some kind that's unlike anything we've ever imagined, and they appear to have a sophisticated mechanical communications system."

"But if our machines won't work there," the Under-Secretary asked, tapping the desk, "will their machines work here? Will their *weapons* work here? Or in the Shadow realm?"

"I don't know, sir," the telepath said. "Nobody knows."

"The reports say these people do have advanced weapons," he said. "Did Thorpe say anything about them?"

"Well, sir," the telepath said cautiously, "you have to remember, she was taken into custody before she'd ever had a chance to leave the landing site, and she can't read minds there, she has to rely on her eyes and ears, like anybody else. She spent the night in their jail, and there wasn't much to see there. And I didn't take time to go over every detail; I came directly to you to report."

The Under-Secretary's manner made his impatience clear as he said, "Yes?"

"So far as I know, she hasn't seen any weapons except the handguns the law enforcers carry," the telepath said. "And she hasn't heard anything about any others."

"Handguns?"

"Yes, sir. Projectile weapons, apparently, like the pistols of a century ago. She saw bullets on the law officers' belts."

"Bullets," the Under-Secretary said, frowning.

"Yes, sir," the telepath said.

"We're looking for help against the alien super-science of another universe," the Under-Secretary demanded, "science so advanced that they call it magic, and the best we can find is people who still shoot bullets at each other?"

The telepath shifted uneasily, struggling to stay at attention. "Well, sir, bullets can be very effective, really, and these were civilian law officers, after all, not military personnel. We've all read things in other minds there that hint at much better . . ."

"Which, even if it's true, doesn't mean any of these better weapons would work in our space, or in Shadow's space."

"True, sir," the telepath admitted.

The Under-Secretary shoved papers across the desk, letting the telepath continue standing at attention. After a moment he looked up.

"The natives think our people are crazy?" he asked. "I mean, certifiably insane?"

The telepath nodded. "Yes, sir," she said. "Either that, or perpetrating a hoax of some kind."

"Will they gas 'em?"

The telepath hesitated. "I don't think so, sir," she said. "When they were taken into custody, the arresting officers read each of the crewmen a statement of rights and privileges. It's Prossie's . . . it's Telepath Thorpe's impression that the culture is relatively non-violent and benevolent. Her cell is equipped with its own plumbing and electric light, and no one has struck her; she's still wearing her own uniform, in fact, though they did take her helmet and search her for weapons. She's seen no sign of a gallows or whipping post, nor any other means of torture or execution."

The Under-Secretary stared at her. "Bunch of wimps," he said. "Just like she said. And these are the people we thought might have super-weapons for us?"

The telepath didn't respond. She resisted the temptation to ask just who had said what about wimps, and the even stronger temptation to snatch the answer from the Under-Secretary's mind.

"All right," he said. "Go away. Dismissed." He turned back to his papers.

"Sir?" the telepath said.

The Under-Secretary looked up. "What is it?" he demanded.

Hesitantly, the telepath asked, "Will we be sending a rescue mission? What should I tell Prossie?"

"I'll be taking it under advisement, Telepath, but you can tell her, provisionally, that we plan no rescue mission," the Under-Secretary said. "It'd be a waste of time and money and manpower. How would we rescue anyone, anyway, when our warp comes out in mid-air and our anti-gravity doesn't work there? And blasters don't work; how would we get them out if our weapons won't fire? No, they're on their own. We can keep in touch, and reopen the warp if they can find a way to get to it, but beyond that I'm writing the whole thing off as a failure. We'll take care of Shadow ourselves."

"But, sir . . ." The telepath didn't finish her protest; even before the Under-Secretary spoke she had inadvertently, and against all her careful training and discipline, read his response.

"No buts. *Ruthless* was expendable, or we wouldn't have sent her, and she's lost. No point in wasting any more men trying to get her back. Copley probably shouldn't have sent her in the first place, not without more advance work. It sounds to me as if Cahn and his crew aren't badly off — hell, we've got plenty of men on active duty who live in worse than those cells, from what you've said. They may even be let go, and then they'll be free to look around and maybe find a way back. You'll be checking in with Thorpe every so often — say, every forty-eight hours, if your other duties allow. They'll be all right. So we'll get on to other things. Understood?"

"Yes, sir." The telepath offered no further argument. For one thing, she had seen at least part of the real reason underneath Under-Secretary Bascombe's thoughts.

There were the usual petty political concerns that flavored almost everyone's motivations, the personal jealousies and competitions that every telepath learned to ignore — in this case, the project was associated with Major Copley, who had been falling out of favor even before his appendicitis sent him to the hospital and knocked him out of the inner circle, so continuing it was a bad career move. Underneath that, though, Carrie found a good and logical reason.

If they sent in a rescue mission and shot up a jail in this other universe, they would be making an enemy of the people there, of the dominant nation, the United States of America, as it was called. If the super-weapons really *did* exist, they would then be more likely to be turned against the Empire than against Shadow.

She couldn't argue with that.

"Dismissed," the Under-Secretary said.

"Our messenger is bespoke," Valadrakul reported.

Raven sat up and thumped the chalice onto the table by his chair. "And?" he demanded.

"The sky-ship is fallen, and its crew prisoners in the land of Earth."

"Ah, evil tidings, 'twould seem," Raven muttered. "Fallen, you say?"

"Aye," the wizard said. "The magicks that hold it aloft failed, when the new realm was reached."

Raven considered that for a moment, then asked, "Wherefore was this word so tardy — was it said?"

The wizard nodded. "Aye," he said. "'Twould seem that the spells of telepaths have no virtue in Earth, as the flying spells have none, and as our own magicks do naught in the Empire."

Raven nodded. "I see," he said. He rubbed his temple, trying to think. "Prisoners, say you? Of whom, and wherefore?"

"Of — an' it be I have this right — of the constabulary of the County of Montgomery, in Mary's Land."

"And wherefore?"

"For trespass upon a lady's park, and the unlawful casting of debris upon the land, in that thereupon the ship was fallen."

Raven stared for a moment, then started to speak, then thought better of it.

Valadrakul waited.

"At first," said Raven, at last, "I thought to shout at you, good wizard, and denounce this tale as madness — knights held for letting fall their transport — but upon consideration, I fear you speak only simple truth, for the land of Earth is strange indeed. I saw as much with mine own eyes."

"Aye, marry," Valadrakul replied.

"What does the Empire intend, then? Have we word? Does mount an expedition to free the men, or offer ransom?"

"Nay," said the wizard. "That lordling John Bascombe, him that they call Under-Secretary for Interdimensional Affairs, has but moments ago said that such an effort would serve no good purpose, that the people of Earth do not harm prisoners. Among themselves, the mind-readers say he fears lest Earth be affronted thereby and fight on the side of Shadow 'gainst the Empire."

"Think you this is truth?" Raven asked.

Valadrakul shrugged. "Who can say?"

"Think you, perhaps, that this Under-Secretary Bascombe might himself be a creature of Shadow?"

Valadrakul considered that carefully before replying, "In truth, I know not, but methinks he be otherwise. His reasoning is not valorous, yet 'tis sound enough. Perchance he has such creatures among his counselors, but I think he be not one himself."

Raven nodded.

"What think you would befall," he said, "should we free these men from durance, and bring them hither?"

Valadrakul spread his hands. "Who can say?" he said.

"Perhaps," Raven said slowly, "Messire Pel Brown can say."

*T*here was nothing on the six o'clock news Sunday evening about a spaceship, nor on the ten o'clock on Channel 5, nor the eleven o'clock; in desperation, Pel even tried CNN and CNN Headline.

"They wouldn't have anything," Nancy told him. "Not if the networks don't."

Pel protested, "Sometimes they have stuff the networks don't. You remember the boys in Baghdad, don't you?"

"Of course I do," Nancy said. "And I know they break a lot of stories. But that's different, it's all international stuff. They wouldn't have something like this if the networks and locals don't."

"I know," Pel admitted. He put out the cat, and they went to bed.

It gnawed at them both through the night; at breakfast they were both surly, even after coffee.

Nancy spent most of the morning at job interviews, while Rachel was at her kindergarten. Pel made his Monday morning calls, but had no all-day projects or out-of-town appointments, so he was home again for lunch five minutes after Rachel's bus dropped her off.

Ordinarily, a family lunch together was a cheerful event, but the tension still lingered, poisoning the atmosphere; Rachel wolfed her sandwich and left the table, while Pel and Nancy ate in sullen silence.

"It was a joke," Nancy said, without preamble, as she carried her plate to the sink.

Pel didn't have to ask what she was referring to. He shook his head. "How could it be a joke?" he asked.

"What else could it be?"

"I don't know, but it wasn't any joke."

"Of course it was."

"No, it wasn't, damn it."

Nancy turned to face him, hands on hips. "It *had* to be, and don't you swear at me!"

"It was not a fucking *joke!*" Pel shouted.

"Well, then, what the hell *was* it?" she shouted back.

"Daddy?" Rachel said from the doorway.

"*I* don't know what it was, but no goddamn joker would be able to walk through our basement wall like that!"

"It was a *trick,* Pel! A hologram or something!"

"Daddy?"

"You think a *hologram* sat on our couch drinking beer? You think a hologram would wear a velvet cape that Rachel could *feel?*"

Nancy had no immediate rejoinder, and as she fumed, trying to think of one, Rachel was able to get Pel's attention by yanking at his sleeve.

"Daddy!" she yelled. "The man's back!"

For a moment, Pel didn't understand. Nancy was quicker; her mouth opened, then closed, and she demanded, "Where?"

"In the *basement,* of course." Rachel looked as disdainful as only a little girl can. "I heard him knocking and calling for Daddy."

That got through to Pel; he stood up so fast his chair started to topple over backward. He snatched at it and caught it before it fell, jostling the kitchen table. His coffee sloshed onto the place mat; he ignored it as he headed for the basement stairs.

"*T*hey may be back with a court order," Susan said. "They may even try to condemn your property and take it by eminent domain.

Amy sipped tea before replying. "Then what?" she said.

"Then I try for a restraining order, claiming their order violates your property rights and your right to due process."

Amy glanced out the window at the thing in her back yard; it was still damp from the morning dew and gleamed gold in the sun. "Then what?" she asked.

Susan shrugged. "I don't know," she said. "This isn't really my field. I've never done a national security case before."

Amy shuddered slightly and put down her teacup. "Do you think it's really a national security thing?" she said.

Susan considered carefully before answering, "I don't know." She took a deep breath and continued, "That's what the Air Force people claimed, but if that thing out there is a fake, the way they say it is, I don't see how they can make a national security claim stick." She picked up her own cup, which contained instant coffee rather than tea. "Of course, if it's a fake, there is the question of how it got here," she added just before she sipped.

"It fell out of the sky," Amy said.

Susan nodded and lowered her cup. "I know it did," she said. "So does the Air Force; they've measured the thing's mass and the effects of impact and can probably tell you exactly how far it fell and how fast it was going when it was hit. What they *can't* tell you, though, is how it got up in the air in the first place, because they don't know — and that's what has them so worried."

"So you think they'll be back?"

"Ms. Jewell . . . Amy, I really, honestly don't know."

Amy accepted that and delicately sipped more tea. Susan gulped coffee.

"At least you kept them from setting up those lights," Amy said a moment later.

Susan shrugged deprecatingly. "For now," she said.

"Thanks," Amy said. "I know I would never have gotten any sleep tonight with those things out there." She hesitated, then asked, "Did you talk to any of the people who were inside it?"

"No," Susan said. "I probably can, if you think it would help, but I haven't yet."

"Are they in jail?"

Susan looked at her watch. "So far, they probably still are," she said, "but the police won't be able to hold them for very long unless you press charges."

"Me?"

Susan nodded. "They were charged with trespassing, vandalism, and malicious mischief — they dumped that thing on your land, smashed your hedge, ruined your lawn — you could probably claim reckless endangerment, too, since you were out there at the time. But if you don't press charges, the cops will have to let them go. You don't hold people without a charge, not in the U.S."

"And if I press charges?"

Susan sighed. "None of them could give an address or show any means of support. None of them had any money or identification except for their 'Galactic Empire' stuff. None of them have asked for a lawyer, or used their phone privileges. They're all staying strictly in character. You can probably get them held for a couple of weeks, at the outside, since they can't make bond and the feds don't want them released, but more than that . . ." She shrugged.

Amy put down her cup and picked up the tea bag by the string, toying idly with it.

"Susan," she said, watching the tea bag, "what do you think is really going on here?"

Susan chewed her lower lip, then admitted, "I don't have any idea."

Amy looked up. "Do you think they could *really* be from some Galactic Empire?"

Susan hesitated, then said, "I don't believe in little green men."

"Neither do I — but how else do you explain those people, and that thing in my yard?"

Susan frowned. "If they're really from outer space, then why won't their ship fly?"

"But maybe it *did* fly — how else could it get there?"

"I don't know," Susan said. "I don't understand any of it." She rubbed her temple. "Maybe if I'd gotten more sleep over the weekend, but I didn't expect anything like this first thing on a Monday morning."

"Thank you for coming so early," Amy said gravely. "I appreciate it."

Susan waved away Amy's gratitude. "No problem," she said. "Shall we get down to Rockville and fill out the papers?"

*P*rossie lay curled up on the cot, staring at nothing.

She was betrayed.

She was trapped here, a prisoner, completely cut off from the minds of others, and most particularly from the minds of her fellow telepaths, the minds of her family and her community.

She was in jail, for reasons she did not understand — listening to words without being able to read the minds behind them was hard for her, and although she had heard the charges against her, she did not see why they had been leveled at her and the rest of the crew. Their ship had *crashed*; how could that be a crime?

And she knew that there would be no rescue. The brief moment of hope when Carrie had first reached her had died again when the news came through — her people had written her off. They had declared her expendable and expended. Carrie had told her — the mission had been abandoned as a failure, I.S.S. *Ruthless* given up as lost, and she and Captain Cahn and the other eight were considered prisoners of war. No efforts would be made to rescue them.

And since there were no other contacts between the Empire and this Montgomery County, there could be no negotiated freedom, no exchange.

She would rot here, in this bland little cell.

This was almost worse than a dungeon, really. If she were confined behind cold stone walls, in darkness and filth and hunger, she would be able to concentrate herself on resistance, on courage; she would have the romance of all those childhood stories to fall back on, all the tales of heroes who endured monumental suffering along the way to magnificent triumphs. The Earl of the White Mountain, the Man in the Sealed Helm, the people of Camp Eight — all the old stories of famous prisoners came back to her.

What romance was there in concrete block walls, a steel cot, and porcelain fixtures? What suffering did electric light and three meals a day provide?

She was no swashbuckling hero; she wasn't even a real soldier. She was just a telepath, sent along on this expedition because telepathy was the only good way to communicate over long distances.

Maybe, she thought, she should ask for an attorney — the officer had said that if she could not afford one, one would be provided for her.

But no; what good would that do? Why would a native attorney want to help her? How could an attorney get her out if the authorities wanted to hold her? If she got out, where would she go? What would she do?

She wished that Carrie hadn't told her Bascombe's decision. Captain Cahn and the others presumably didn't know about it, and they were probably stewing in their uncertainty, but that was better than despair.

She curled up more tightly, her head full of telepathic wool, and stared at nothing.

Chapter Six

"She's not taking it well." The telepath sat slumped in her chair, staring unhappily at the floor.

"Carrie, don't let it get to you," her supervisor said. "Prossie'll be okay, I'm sure of it."

Carrie looked up.

"I'm not," she said. "I read her mind, and I'm not sure at all."

There were four of them this time. Nancy hung back as they emerged from the basement, and despite their deferential manner, Pel found their numbers and armament somewhat intimidating himself.

Raven came first, and stood to one side, introducing the others as they stepped out into the hall and bowed.

"Stoddard, man-at-arms and a loyal friend to me since I was a lad," Raven said, describing a man who stood six feet tall and wore a dirty and somewhat faded red tabard over a stiff leather garment Pel had no name for. Stoddard bowed — more than a mere bob, but not a particularly deep bow. His hair was black and shaggy, his face brown and rugged; besides the tabard and leather, he wore baggy brown hose and brown leather boots. A scabbard hung from his belt, and from the look of it Pel judged his sword to be somewhat heavier than Raven's.

"Squire Donald a' Benton," Raven named the next. His bow was more perfunctory than Stoddard's, his green tunic considerably cleaner, his boots newer. He seemed about half Stoddard's size, and in fact was no taller than Nancy's five foot four, Pel realized. Like Raven and Stoddard, he bore a sword.

His green eyes darted about curiously.

"The mage Valadrakul of Warricken," Raven said, gesturing at the last member of his party. "Now sworn to Stormcrack Keep."

The wizard did not bow at all, but made an odd gesture with one hand instead. Most of his dull brown hair trailed loose, halfway down his back, while the rest hung in two narrow braids in front of either ear; he wore a long black vest, ornately embroidered in red and gold, that reached to mid-calf and mostly concealed a plain black tunic and breeches. The sheath on his belt was too small for a true sword, but held a good-sized knife.

"Mage?" Pel asked.

"A wizard," Raven said. "A magician. One who works spells and brings forth wonders."

Pel nodded, and tried not to stare. "This way," he said, motioning toward the family room, herding the visitors ahead of him.

Valadrakul did not fit Pel's image of a wizard. He was neither tall and imposing, nor small and wizened; his face was not long and hawk-nosed. He wore no robes, nor pointed hat, nor long white beard.

Instead, he was of medium height — five-nine, perhaps, or a bit over — and a little fat, with a pale, round face and a full brown beard, clipped short. His hairstyle reminded Pel of Val Kilmer playing the warrior in "Willow," though it wasn't exactly the same, and his outfit didn't seem like anything in particular. There were no moons and stars, no pentagrams; the embroidery was a graceful floral pattern.

Pel stepped down into the family room to find three of the four strangers standing in the center, staring in all directions. Raven stood with the others, but smiled politely at his host and did not stare; after all, he had been here before.

"Have a seat," Pel suggested.

Raven nodded and settled on the couch; the wizard, whose name Pel had not caught, took the other end. Squire Donald started toward the recliner, but threw first Pel and then Raven a questioning glance before sinking gingerly into it.

Stoddard ignored the invitation completely; he stepped back toward one wall, but continued to stand, arms crossed over his chest and feet braced apart.

Pel looked at his stolid pose and decided not to argue. Sitting down in that leather barrel the man was wearing might be difficult, and he looked as if he were accustomed to standing.

The man-at-arms looked incredibly out of place in that room, in his rough and archaic clothing. The other three weren't so bad, but Stoddard simply didn't fit in such a setting.

With a final glance at him, Pel decided against taking a seat himself; there were no good ones left. Sitting on an end table seemed undignified.

"So," Pel said, addressing Raven, "what brings you back?"

"Why, the same portal as erstwhile, of course," Raven answered smoothly.

"No," Pel said, "I mean, why have you come back?"

Raven smiled an acknowledgment of his slip. "As before," he began, "we seek your aid. Have you heard aught of the sky-ship the Imperials sent hither?"

"No," Pel replied. "And we should have, if it's really there."

"Oh, 'tis real, beyond question," Raven said calmly. Then he stopped abruptly and glanced at Valadrakul for confirmation.

"'Tis real," the wizard said. His voice, which Pel and Nancy had not heard before, was a pleasant tenor. "We've not been deceived, I assure you."

"It wasn't on the news," Pel said doubtfully.

"Nonetheless, the ship is real, and it reached your world," Valadrakul said. "However, its magic did not work here; it plummeted to the earth and has not moved since. Its crew has been taken prisoner by the Earl's men. This much we have learned."

"The Earl's men?" Pel asked, puzzled.

"The Earl of Montgomery," Raven explained. "'Twas the county constabulary apprehended the Imperials. Are we not in the County Montgomery here?"

"We're in Montgomery County, yes," Pel said, still puzzled, "but there's no earl. You mean it crashed, and the county police picked them up?"

"A county with no Earl? A Countess, then?"

"No, Montgomery County's democratic," Pel explained. "Or Republican, depending. We have a county executive, not an earl."

Raven and Valadrakul exchanged glances. Pel looked at the others; Stoddard was staring straight ahead, paying no attention to anything so far as Pel could determine, while Squire Donald was studying the shelves beside him, fascinated, and might or might not be listening.

For the first time Pel noticed that Nancy wasn't in the room; he turned, and saw Rachel watching from the door to the kitchen. Listening, he could hear Nancy moving about in the kitchen.

"Why call it a county, an there's no count?" Raven asked, annoyed. "Neither earl nor countess, then where's the county? Why not call it a shire?"

Pel shrugged. "I don't know," he said. "We do have a sheriff, I think, so yeah, shire would make more sense, but we call 'em counties anyway."

Raven waved it away. "It matters not a whit, then, who rules here, save that you understand your county police have taken prisoner the ten Imperials who came hither. And yes, their ship fell, and could not fly in your skies."

Nancy leaned through the kitchen doorway and called, "Would anyone like a beer? Or anything? I can put the kettle on if you'd like tea or coffee."

Stoddard turned a questioning look at Raven; Squire Donald glanced up from the bookshelves. Raven looked around quickly at all his companions, then up at Nancy.

"Beer would be most welcome, good lady, and our thanks."

Nancy nodded and disappeared.

"All right," Pel said, "so the cops picked up these Imperial stormtroopers. Why wasn't it on the news? It's not every day a bunch of people from outer space crash-land around here."

"I know not," Raven said, turning up an empty palm. "Perchance whoever retails your news has not yet learned of it."

Pel considered that. If a spaceship really had landed, the government might try to hush it up — but he would be surprised if they actually managed it. He had never bought the Hangar 19 — or 18, or whatever the number was — stories for a minute.

"Where'd it land?" he asked.

Raven looked at Valadrakul, who turned up his hands and said, "How are we to know the name of the place? It lies perhaps half a day's journey to the north, traveling on foot."

"But it's in Montgomery County?"

"That, or your shiremen crossed the border."

If the ship had come down somewhere out toward the Howard County line, that might explain how it had stayed off the TV news, so far; there was still a good bit of fairly empty countryside up that way, as Pel knew from driving the back roads to Baltimore on occasion.

"What are they charged with? I mean, why were they arrested?" he asked.

"The charges we were told are trespassing and vandalism," Valadrakul replied. "I fear we have no such word as 'vandalism' in our tongue, so we know not what it means."

"It means wrecking things just for fun," Pel explained.

The story didn't sound quite right to him; why would the county cops arrest a bunch of aliens on charges like that? Why weren't the feds all over the place?

Then an explanation occurred to him, one which made the whole thing make sense, including the fact that the news media had not reported anything.

"They don't think it's real, do they?" he asked.

"Your pardon, sir, but what do you say?" Raven replied.

"Nobody thinks the spaceship is real," Pel said. "Whoever found it thinks it's a hoax, right?"

"Indeed," Valadrakul answered, "you may have the truth of it; our reports cannot tell us everything, but 'tis hinted your constables think the crewmen mad. Certes, they do not accept them as envoys."

Raven turned to the wizard. "You'd said naught of that to me," he said, clearly irritated. "I had thought the captors mad, not the prisoners!"

"My apologies," Valadrakul said, bowing his head. "There was much to tell, and in my haste . . ." He turned up a palm.

"I'd like to see these guys," Pel said.

"Guys?" Donald said, looking up.

"A gnomish word," Valadrakul told him. "From a trickster of days agone, one Guiler by name, called Guy o' the Mews, who was famed for harassing the little folk."

This bizarre false etymology caught Pel's attention for a moment, distracting him.

Just then Nancy stepped in with a tray, carrying five foaming beer mugs. "I didn't think cans would go over well," she said to Pel.

The entire conversation seemed to be going in half a dozen directions at once, and Pel was becoming thoroughly confused. Reversing his earlier decision, he sat down on the edge of the stereo cabinet. "Fine," he told Nancy.

She smiled, not very confidently, and handed Raven a mug. He thanked her, as Pel wondered where she had found five beer mugs, since he only remembered owning four. Taking another look, he realized that the fifth was actually a small vase that they never used. It was about the right size and shape, though it lacked a handle.

She handed the vase to Stoddard, who nodded his head in polite acknowledgement.

Valadrakul and Donald accepted their mugs gratefully, and Pel himself took the last. He held it without drinking while the others sampled the brew.

He could tell they weren't impressed, but that wasn't anything he cared about just now.

"Let me see if I have this straight," he said. "The Galactic Empire sent a ship, with ten men aboard, to make contact with our government — in Washington, I guess?"

He glanced at Valadrakul, who made a sort of one-handed shrug while sipping beer with the other.

"They found out the hard way that some of the machinery doesn't work here, and the ship crashed, somewhere north of here, but still in Montgomery County. Right so far?"

Raven nodded.

"Then the county police came and arrested them all for trespassing," Pel continued, "and hauled them away somewhere — the county jail in Rockville, probably."

Valadrakul nodded this time.

"And they're still there, and the cops think they're crazy, they don't believe any of this stuff about spaceships and galactic empires."

No one objected to any of that.

"All right," Pel said, "I've got all that — so what are *you* people doing here?"

Raven put down his beer — what little was left of it. Pel noticed that Nancy was collecting an empty vase from Stoddard. "More?" she asked.

He nodded, and she slipped away to the kitchen.

"The Empire," Raven explained, "has given up their men as lost — aye, and the lady, as well, for the ship had a woman aboard. The man who has charge of the matter has decided against any attempt at rescue, or any further expedition hither. Thus, these ten are abandoned, at the mercy of their captors. 'Tis a coward's decision, say I, but 'tis made, nonetheless."

Pel nodded.

"The thought came to us," Raven continued, "that perhaps we might find a use for these abandoned men, ourselves. They might tell us much about the Galactic Empire. We might find a worthy ransom, should we offer to send them home. Failing all else, we could at the least find ourselves with nine more brave men in our fight against the creatures of Shadow."

"And a woman," Pel added.

Raven ignored the interruption; his speech rolled on as if Pel hadn't said a word. "We know naught of your world, however, and finding and freeing these Imperials could be a fearsome task. Our portal opens in your cellars and is not so very easily moved, nor can its point of arrival be precisely determined in advance; further, you seemed a good man and kindly disposed toward me. Thus, we came hither to seek your counsel."

Nancy reappeared with the vase refilled.

"You want me to tell you how to get these people out of jail?" Pel said. He saw smiles and nods starting, and asked, "How would I know?"

The smiles vanished and the nods never came. Raven and Valadrakul exchanged an unhappy glance. "We had thought," Raven said, "that you might perchance know something of this prison — its strengths and weaknesses, perhaps, whether a warder might be bribed, somewhat of that nature."

"You want me to help you get these guys out of jail?" Pel asked again.

Nancy looked up from the tray. "Have you talked to their lawyer?" she asked.

Raven and Valadrakul stared at her, startled.

"What's a lawyer?" Raven asked.

"Maybe I should talk to them," Amy said, uncertainly, as she toyed nervously with a ballpoint pen.

Susan looked up from the forms she was reading. "Why?" she asked.

"Well, I don't want to be vindictive or anything," Amy explained, "I just want everybody to get their stuff out of my yard and leave me alone."

"And pay for your hedge and your tree and all the other damage," Susan pointed out.

"Yeah," Amy admitted. "That, too."

The desk sergeant shook his head. "I don't think those guys are gonna pay for anything, lady," he said. "They didn't have a cent between them, they haven't called anyone about getting bailed out, nothing."

Amy stared. "They *still* haven't?" she asked.

"Nope. Not one of them. They're all sticking to their story about this Galactic Empire, and most of 'em won't give us anything but name, rank, and serial number."

Amy looked at Susan, who shrugged.

Amy frowned. "If they're real," she said, "then they *can't* pay for anything, can they?"

Susan answered, "Who knows? If they're for real, then it's all beyond me. If they're *not* real, though, and they're carrying it this far . . ."

"If they're *not* real, then screw 'em," Amy said, grabbing the pen. "They're carrying it much too far, and as far as I'm concerned they can rot here. Where do I sign?"

The desk sergeant pointed.

"Prossie heard someone calling her name, or at any rate something intended for her; she sat up and listened.

To her ears the cell was silent, save for the distant hissing of the highway that passed near the jail. It was her mind that had been touched.

"Carrie?" she said, whispering to make sure her thoughts were in words. "Is that you?"

Her ears still heard nothing, but the words reached her. "Yes, it's me, Prossie," the telepathic voice replied. "How are you doing?"

"Better," Prossie replied. "Much better. That woman filed formal charges against us this morning, so they sent an attorney for us, whether we wanted one or not, and he explained some things — oh, Carrie, I wish I'd asked for an attorney sooner!"

Carrie's response was a wordless questioning.

"They aren't going to keep us here," Prossie said. "They *can't* keep us. They have all these complicated rules they follow, and guarantees of rights — it's really incredible, if it's all true. We should be free in a few days, I think."

After a moment of mental silence, Carrie asked, "Then what?"

"I don't know," Prossie admitted. "But I'm sure we'll manage somehow. We can work, or live off the land, and find some way to get back to the warp eventually, I'm certain of it. It's just a hundred yards above where the ship crashed — that can't be all that inaccessible."

Prossie paused, and listened.

She sensed uneasiness on the other side of the conversation, as if Carrie doubted her, or as if she knew something Prossie did not. She certainly wasn't sharing Prossie's relief.

That troubled Prossie, but she thrust it aside as a new idea struck her.

"Listen, Carrie," she said, "once I'm free, what if I were to track down some of the people we contacted — Miletti, or Blaisdell, or Aldridge? Wouldn't they help us?"

"I don't know," Carrie answered, startled. "I hadn't thought of that. Are you *sure* they'll free you?"

"Well," Prossie admitted, "I have no way of being sure the attorney didn't lie to me — I don't have my telepathy here, so I couldn't check. I hadn't really thought about it — why would he lie? And if he told the truth, they definitely won't keep me here more than, I think he said thirty days, at most. They might try to send me to a madhouse, though — I think that was what he meant, anyway, though he didn't come right out and say so. But I'm not mad, and I ought to be able to avoid that."

"I see," Carrie said, and again Prossie sensed doubt. "There's something else, though; I don't know if any of the contactees are near where you came out. Some of them were thousands of miles apart. I'll have to see if we have any maps."

"Do it, Carrie, please — for me."

"Sure, Prossie. Hey, whatever happens, it's good to hear you sounding so much more cheerful!"

"It's good to be more cheerful, Carrie. Do check those maps for me, please. And thanks."

The contact broke.

Silent, Prossie sat on her bunk, puzzled.

She had been so pleased with her conversation with Jerry de Lillo, the attorney from the public defender's office, that she had not really considered the possibility that it was all a fraud, or that things might not work out as well as Mr. de Lillo said. Carrie, however, seemed to be taking it for granted that there was something wrong somewhere.

Why?

What could Carrie know that she, Prossie, did not? Had they been reading other minds here in Montgomery County, or whatever this place was called?

No, that couldn't be it; she knew perfectly well that contacting anyone in this universe was difficult, and only a handful of people had been sufficiently receptive to manage any sort of communication at all. Out of that handful, only three had been able to both send and receive.

Prossie hadn't been in on all the initial contacts, but she had done her share, and had carefully studied the files on those she hadn't personally attempted. None of them had been connected with law enforcement or government.

The chances of locating another new contact who just happened to know something about the fate of the crew of I.S.S. *Ruthless* had to be just about nil. Whatever Carrie had learned, she must have learned back at Base One, or through a contact somewhere else in the Empire.

Prossie tried to remember the conversation and spot just where it had begun to go sour.

When Prossie had first mentioned being freed, there had been a lack of certainty, but that was just an insufficiency of evidence — Carrie had been eager to be convinced, at that point. Then Prossie had gone on to describe her hopes for after her release . . .

That was it.

It was when she had mentioned going back through the warp that Carrie had started hiding something.

Any ordinary person would never have noticed it, but Prossie was a telepath; she knew how minds worked. Carrie would never have tried hiding anything from another telepath that way ordinarily, she would have known better, but where Prossie's talent was stifled she must have misjudged.

It must be that Carrie knew something about the warp that Prossie did not, and Prossie did not have to think very hard about the situation to guess what it might be.

The Under-Secretary had said that there would be no rescue, that the attempt to contact Earth was being abandoned; the next step was obvious and logical.

They must have shut down the warp.

Prossie slumped back against the wall. They had shut down the warp. The opening between universes was gone.

It would be possible to reopen it, she was sure. It had to be possible.

But would they do it?

Chapter Seven

"Ted, this is Raven," Pel said.

Ted held out a hand, but Raven was already bowing and did not see it. Discomfited, Ted pulled back his hand and stuck it in his pocket.

"Raven, this is our lawyer, Ted Deranian."

"'Tis an honor, good sir," Raven said, flourishing his hat as he rose from his bow.

"Uh, yeah," Ted said. He glanced at Pel, silently asking what the hell was going on.

"Raven's not from around here," Pel said hastily. "I mean, he's not just dressed up; that's his native costume."

Ted looked over the black velvet and elaborate embroidery, the sword and the bobbing ostrich plume. "I didn't know they still dressed like that anywhere anymore," he said.

Raven cast a questioning glance at Pel, who quickly said, "Don't worry about it. Come on into the living room and sit down, Ted, let Nancy get you a drink or something."

"Sure," Ted said. He turned toward the living room.

As he did, behind his back but in sight of Pel, Raven jerked his head toward the family room, down at the far end of the hall; Pel shook his head no. There was no need to bring Stoddard or Donald or the wizard into things at this point.

Ted accepted a scotch and water from Nancy, then settled into the fake-antique wing chair by the front window. Pel gestured for Raven to take the other armchair, while he seated himself on the couch and Nancy slipped out through the dining room, back to the kitchen.

"Look, Ted," Pel explained, when they were all seated, "Raven's got a problem. Some friends of his are in jail down in Rockville, charged with trespassing and vandalism. They're probably more or less guilty, but it was an accident, nobody meant any harm, and they're all foreigners, they don't understand the American courts and they haven't got any money for fines or bail or anything. We'd like you to go and look after them, get them out if you can — we need to talk to them, if you can arrange it."

"Foreigners?" Ted pursed his lips and put down his glass. "Do they speak English?"

Pel glanced at Raven, who nodded. "Aye," he said. "'Tis their native tongue."

Pel improvised, "They're from the backwoods of New Zealand someplace, I think."

Ted nodded. "Ordinarily, I'd say no problem," he said. "Do they all dress like, uh, Raven, here?"

Again, Pel glanced at Raven, who answered, "Nay, their garb is like neither mine nor your own."

Pel shrugged.

Ted hesitated, and then said, "I can't place your accent, Raven; where are you from?"

Raven glanced at Pel, then turned up a palm. "I come from Stormcrack Keep, in the Hither Corydians."

"Is that in New Zealand?"

Raven just smiled and didn't answer.

"Listen, would you do me a favor?" Ted asked.

Raven looked politely inquiring.

"Would you say, 'Yonder lies the castle of my father'?"

Puzzled, Raven looked at Pel, whose expression shifted quickly from thunderstricken to suppressed giggling.

"Yonder lies the castle of my father?" Raven said.

"No," Ted said. "Declaim it, announce it — you know."

"Ted," Pel interrupted, "Raven isn't Tony Curtis, and he doesn't know what you're talking about. The accent's real, he can't help it."

Baffled, Raven looked at Pel, who explained, "It's a line from an old movie . . . oh, never mind." He turned to Ted. "So can you get these people out of jail for us? As soon as possible? I'll stand bail, if it's not too much, or agree to be responsible for them."

"I'll see what I can do," Ted said, gulping the rest of his scotch. "If it's just trespassing and vandalism — they broke something?"

"Tore up someone's yard, I think," Pel said.

Ted nodded. "Simplest thing, then, would be to get the complainant to drop the charges; are you good for the damages, Pel, if that's what's wanted?"

Pel had to think for a moment before reluctantly agreeing. "I guess," he said. "If it's not too much."

Ted stood up. "Well, thanks for the drink, then, and I guess I better get down to Rockville and see what the story is. Ah . . do you have names for these people?"

Pel looked at Raven, who said, "Tarry a moment, please." He turned and hurried to the family room, leaving Ted and Pel standing where they were.

Pel looked apologetically at Ted. "Another drink?" he asked.

"No, no," Ted said. "I'm working, and I'm driving, and it's too early anyway."

"Coffee, maybe, or water?"

"No, thanks."

They stood, awkwardly waiting, for another few seconds; then Raven reappeared.

"Your pardon, sirs," he said. "The captain of the crew is one Joshua Cahn; his second is Alster Drummond. The lady with them is Mistress Proserpine Thorpe. Is that sufficient?"

"Should be," Ted said. "Joshua Cahn — how's that spelled, with a K?"

"I fear I know not, sir," Raven replied.

"Doesn't matter, I'll find him. Cahn, Drummond, and Thorpe. Got it."

"My thanks, sir, for your efforts in our behalf," Raven said, bowing again as Pel showed Ted to the door.

"*S*omebody named Ted Deranian wants to talk to you," Susan's voice said. "He's a lawyer, has an office in Germantown."

"A lawyer? What does he want to talk to me about?" Amy asked, puzzled.

"About the people from the thing in your back yard. He says he represents a friend of theirs who's willing to pay for the damages if you drop the charges."

Amy looked out her kitchen window at the ship, still lying where it had fallen. The Air Force people had not come back; she hoped they never would, though that did still leave the question of what she was going to do with the thing.

"I thought none of them knew any lawyers," she said.

"I don't think they do," Susan said. "They got Jerry de Lillo from the public defender's office appointed to represent them — he's okay. This isn't him. This Deranian person doesn't claim to be representing anyone directly involved in the case; his client is just a friend of one of them."

"If they're supposed to be from outer space, how can they have friends in Germantown?"

"That's a very good question," Susan said.

Amy considered for a long moment, then said, "I don't suppose it can hurt to talk to him."

"I wouldn't think so," Susan agreed.

"Maybe I'll finally find out what the heck is going on."

"Maybe. Should I send him out there?"

"Here?" Oh, no. Not here. I can come to your office, or his office — I don't want him here."

"All right. I'd like to sit in, so how about my office? When can you be here?"

I want to talk to them," Amy said. "The people who were in it."

"Fine by me," Ted replied, smiling.

"I mean, I'm making that a condition. If I drop the charges, I want to talk to these people. That's besides payment for the damages."

Ted leaned back in the chair. "Ms. Jewell," he said, "that's fine with me, but I don't know whether they'll say anything. I don't represent them; I'm acting on behalf of a third party."

"Who?"

"His name is Pellinore Brown. He's something of an old friend of mine."

"Pellinore?" Susan said, startled.

Ted swiveled in his chair and said, "His mother got it out of a book somewhere." He turned back to Amy. "Ms. Jewell," he said, "I can't make them talk to you, but how about this — you come to Mr. Brown's house, and I'll bring them there, and the lot of you can talk to each other all you want or not, whatever suits." He smiled. "It should be interesting; I've already met another of Mr. Brown's guests."

Amy considered for a moment, glancing from Ted to Susan and back. Susan shrugged.

"Okay," Amy said.

S omebody's put in for a writ to get those people out of jail," the lieutenant reported, holding the phone.

Major Johnston looked up, then back down at the reports spread on his desk.

Design analysis — nothing. The unidentified machines can't possibly do anything.

Field trials — nothing. The machines *don't* do anything.

Materials analysis — nothing. Steel, glass, simple plastics and ceramics, polished redwood, assorted metals — copper, brass, gold, platinum. Nothing untoward, unless you asked what the gold and platinum were doing there. No unidentified or unusual substances. No petroleum-based plastics, which was odd, and no aluminum, which was even odder. Who ever heard of any sort of flying craft made entirely without aluminum?

Electronics analysis — nothing. Not just nothing comprehensible, like the other reports, but nothing at all. No silicon chips anywhere, not so much as a single printed circuit. Everything electrical was hardwired, with simple copper wires and connectors. No transistors, not even any vacuum tubes — the most advanced equipment aboard that was recognizable at all was solenoids. *Good* solenoids, but solenoids.

This all assumed, of course, that the stuff that looked like random bits of wire, metal, and crystal wasn't some sort of circuitry, but whatever it was, it didn't *do* anything.

Aerodynamics analysis — nothing much. No airfoils. The guidance vanes were just that — guidance vanes. They would provide no lift to speak of. You could drive the thing up to Mach 1 and it still wouldn't fly, just fall. Air resistance would be very low, the streamlining was perfectly sound, there just wasn't any lift built into it anywhere.

Tracking analysis — nothing. The ship appeared out of nowhere about three hundred feet up, just barely high enough to show up as a blip at the county airport, and immediately plummeted to the ground. It didn't come in from above; if it had flown in below the radar, it had somehow done so without a single report being filed anywhere. No complaints from home owners, no sightings by UFO spotters, nothing.

Document analysis — still to come.

Somebody was supposed to analyze the food that had been stored aboard the ship, but that hadn't been done yet, either. At first glance it looked ordinary enough — canned goods, freeze-dried stuff, and so forth.

The thing didn't really look like a hoax, exactly; he would have expected hoaxers to rig up fancy displays and use lots of electronics, for effect. Hoaxers wouldn't use gold and platinum; they *would* use aluminum.

Unless, of course, they were very clever hoaxers indeed, trying to not look like a hoax.

The whole damn thing made no sense at all.

"The hell with it," he said, shoving back his chair. He looked up to see the lieutenant still holding the line. "Screw it," he said. "Tell 'em they can let 'em go. It looks like we aren't going to figure this one out until someone tells us something, and if those people haven't talked yet . . . just screw it."

"Yes, sir," the lieutenant replied. He uncovered the mouthpiece and spoke into it as Major Johnston angrily shoved the reports to one side and glared at them.

"Ms. Thorpe?"

Prossie looked up, startled. The jailer who brought her meals never called her that, never said "Ms.," and it was too early for dinner, anyway — she had only finished her lunch an hour or so ago. She wasn't expecting that wonderful Mr. de Lillo again until tomorrow.

And she hadn't sensed anyone coming, and she still wasn't used to that.

It was a uniformed officer speaking, and not the regular jailer. "What is it?" Prossie asked, concentrating on listening for spoken words.

The officer fumbled with the lock as he said, "Ms. Jewell's dropped the charges, and there's someone here with a writ, says he'll take responsibility for you people, so we're letting you all go." He swung open the door of the cell and stood to one side.

"Letting us go?" Prossie blinked.

"Yeah," the man said. "Letting you go. Get your things, if you have any, and come on."

"Really?" She did not understand this; why would that woman drop the charges? Who would take responsibility for her, and the rest of the crew?

What was really going on here?

"Come *on*, already," the officer said, annoyed. "Do you want to get out or not?"

Prossie didn't dawdle any further. Whatever the explanation might be, she wanted out.

Chapter Eight

Three cars would be needed — Pel's Ford Taurus, Nancy's little Chevy, and Ted's Lincoln — to transport the ten Imperials to the Brown home. Nancy was seriously unhappy about driving people who had just been in jail; Raven offered to ride along, or to send Stoddard to defend her, but that didn't really help much. While she had met them, they weren't exactly trusted friends.

Eventually she agreed to drive only on condition that Raven ride with her, that she transport only two of the ten prisoners, and that one of them be the woman, Proserpine Thorpe.

At first, Pel and Ted figured that that put four each in the other two cars, which was manageable. Unfortunately, it didn't really leave room for Rachel anywhere except in Ted's car, sitting beside a quondam prisoner, and Nancy objected to that. She wanted her daughter with a parent, not a lawyer — and certainly not home alone, or with the men from Raven's world. The Lincoln could hold six; the Taurus could not.

That called for another shuffle. A prisoner was shifted in the plans, so that the Chevy would carry Raven, Rachel, and Proserpine Thorpe, with Nancy driving. Four men would ride with Pel, and five, including Captain Cahn, with Ted.

That settled, the next problem was that Nancy didn't like the idea of leaving Stoddard, Donald, and Valadrakul unchaperoned in her house. Accordingly, the three men vanished through the basement wall, and the door at the top of the basement stairs was locked.

"That won't stop them, though," Nancy said, fretting. "They can step right back through, and that big one, Stoddard, I'm sure he can break the lock without half trying."

Pel sighed. "Nan," he said, "a random burglar could break a window and get in just as easily. Why would anyone want to bother? We'll be back in half an hour, probably. It'll be fine."

Reluctantly, Nancy agreed.

Up to this point the discussion of transportation had been theoretical, taking place entirely in the Brown home; now the party moved out, Ted to his car at the curb out front, the others to the garage.

Raven marveled at the vehicles, and ran a hand along the roofline of the Chevy while Pel raised the doors. "So smooth!" he said. "Is't lacquer?"

Nancy and Pel glanced at each other. "Um . . . yeah, I think they use lacquer," Pel replied. He opened the door for Raven and held it, while Nancy let Rachel climb into the back seat from the driver's side.

"Why do you build them so low to the ground?" Raven asked as he lowered himself in. "Would it not be better to sit higher, above the splashings of mud and whatnot?"

"Streamlining," Pel said. "Besides, our roads aren't muddy." He slammed the door as Nancy settled in on the other side, then turned away, headed for his own car.

Nancy pulled her seat belt and shoulder strap into place, and looked over to see Raven stroking the upholstery and staring at the various accoutrements, his own straps untouched.

"Fasten your belt," she said.

He started, looked up, and found the buckle. Awkwardly, he pulled it down and, after some fumbling, secured it.

"You, too, Rachel," Nancy said, turning her head.

Rachel displayed her fastened belt. "Already did, Mommy!"

The Ford's engine started up, and Raven jumped again; his hand fell to where the hilt of his sword would have been, had not the Browns convinced him to leave the weapon in the family room. His head snapped around, and he stared as Pel backed the Taurus out of the garage.

"'Struth!" he said. "They told me of such things in the Empire, but I'd not seen them for myself ere now. 'Tis true, you've no beast to pull it!"

Nancy and Rachel both giggled.

"And that noise!" Raven said. "What makes the noise?"

"The engine," Nancy explained. "The machine that makes it go." She turned her own key, and stepped on the gas.

Raven blanched at the roar — the car's muffler wasn't in the best of shape.

Nancy took pity on him and let up on the pedal before backing, slowly and carefully, out of the garage.

Raven watched in delighted wonder as they rolled down the street; he admired the houses, the mown lawns, the floral displays — he had apparently never seen azaleas before. He marveled at the cars everywhere, and at how fast they moved, and how smoothly — particularly the one he rode in.

"Why, 'tis as good as a wizard's wind!" he remarked.

Rachel giggled again from the back seat, and Nancy smiled a tight little smile. They were still on residential suburban streets.

A moment later, when they pulled onto Interstate 270, Raven stopped talking, admiring, and marveling; he was too busy holding on and fighting sheer terror as Nancy accelerated to about sixty miles per hour and wove in and out of traffic, all of it tearing along at what was, to Raven, an incredible pace.

When they finally pulled into the parking lot in Rockville and slowed to a stop Raven was shaking, odd bits of oaths bubbling incoherently from his lips. Nancy, after unbuckling her seat belt, turned a concerned look toward him.

Rachel, also unbuckled, was leaning over the seat and staring.

"What's the matter with him, Mommy?" she asked.

Nancy glanced at her. "I don't think he was ever in a car before, sweetie. He's not used to going so fast."

"By the impaled and bleeding Goddess!" Raven exclaimed.

Nancy frowned, and gestured toward Rachel with her head.

He saw the motion, and apologized. "Your pardon, lady; I'd bate my tongue, and mean no offense."

Inside the building a few moments later, while the cops and court officials stared curiously at a still-shaky Raven, Raven, Nancy, and Rachel hung back by the doorway while Pel and Ted greeted the freed Imperials and introduced themselves.

The purple-uniformed figures stood uneasily, purple-and-gold helmets tucked under their arms, newly-returned belts draped across shoulders or dangling from fists. Even their weapons had been given back to them; that had been the cause of some minor argument among members of the jail's staff, but since two of the "blasters" had been disassembled and proven to be absolutely harmless, not even as dangerous as a kid's spark-gun, the return had proceeded.

None of the Imperials spoke for a moment; then one stepped forward and announced, "I'm Captain Joshua Cahn, gentlemen; thank you for your efforts on our behalf." Pel could see no difference between Cahn's uniform and those of the others except a small black insignia on the collar.

"You're welcome, Captain," Ted said, shaking Cahn's hand vigorously.

"I don't know who you are, or why you're doing this," Cahn said.

"We'll explain," Ted told him. "Come on, let's get out of here."

"Will you be taking us back to our ship?"

Ted glanced at Pel, who gave his head a quick, negative jerk.

"Not at first, anyway," Ted said.

Cahn accepted that with a brisk nod. "Where, then?"

"My house," Pel volunteered. "To talk, maybe make some plans."

Cahn snapped another quick nod. "Good enough, then," he said. "Lead the way."

"We'll be traveling in three cars," Pel said.

"Groundcars?" Cahn asked. "Like the others we saw?"

"Groundcars are all we've got here, Captain," Ted said, grinning.

In the parking lot it took only a moment to divide the group up. Raven, with some trepidation, resumed his seat in the front of the Chevy, while Rachel and Proserpine Thorpe climbed in the back. Raven eyed Thorpe with passing interest, but then busied himself fastening his shoulder harness. What had originally struck him as a quaint custom he now saw as an absolute necessity, and he tugged at every point, making sure the straps were secure.

Prossie, in the back, studied Raven. He didn't seem to fit here; his clothing and manner were noticeably different from the others. One possibility occurred to her, but it seemed very unlikely. She debated asking him straight out, but then decided that would be rude, and she did not care to be rude with the people who had just bought her free.

"These groundcars of yours are interesting," she said, casually.

"Aye," Raven said. "That's a word for it."

Rachel giggled; Nancy concentrated on getting the car out of the parking slot and headed in the right direction.

"Not as smooth as they could be, though," Prossie added, as they bumped over the discontinuity between the parking lot and the road.

Raven, now secure in his seat, turned and stared. "Say you so?" he said. "We've none that ride a fifth part so well, whence I've come."

"Well," Prossie admitted, while absorbing Raven's implication that, as she had suspected, he came from somewhere else, "anything with wheels is going to be bumpy."

Rachel looked up at Prossie. "What kind of car hasn't got wheels?" she demanded.

Prossie looked down at the girl. "An aircar, of course." She paused, then added, "But I suppose you don't have them here, do you? If anti-gravity doesn't work, you couldn't."

"What's Annie Graffiti?" Rachel asked.

"Like Luke Skywalker's landspeeder," Nancy suggested from the front seat. "You remember, when we rented 'Star Wars'?"

"Oh," Rachel said. "But I thought that was just in the movies?"

Prossie struggled to follow this; she still had trouble with the accents and the lack of any thought behind the words, and she missed several of the references, but it was clear the little girl had thought aircars were fictional. Prossie smiled. "Not where I come from," she said.

"Then 'tis true," Raven said, "that the machines of this world, and the machines of the Galactic Empire, are different, one from the other?"

"Oh, yes," Prossie agreed, leaning forward between the backs of the front seats. "Very true." She paused, then added daringly, "And you, I take it, are from the realm of Shadow?"

"Aye," Raven said, "if you must call it that."

"What do *you* call it, then?" she asked. "The place you come from, I mean?"

"Simply the World," Raven answered. "We call it the World, for ere two years gone we knew no other — at the least, myself and my companions knew no other; I cannot speak for all the wizards and sages."

Prossie hesitated. She thought she was getting the hang of entirely-spoken conversations, but she was still wary of being rude; she had none of her accustomed feedback.

Still, she felt it should be said. She asked, "And you're not one of Shadow's creatures?"

"Nay," Raven barked, startling Nancy and almost causing her to swerve. "I've fought Shadow since I was a lad, and shall fight it ever whilst I live!" He shook a clenched fist to indicate his determination.

"I had to ask," Prossie said apologetically. "I mean, as far as I know, the only people from your world we've ever found in the Empire were constructs Shadow had created — things that are virtually indistinguishable from human beings, but . . well, they aren't really human."

"Fetches," Raven said. "And homunculi."

"Simulacra, we call them." She wasn't even sure just what words Raven had used.

"What are you two talking about?" Nancy asked, as she steered the car onto the entrance ramp for the interstate.

"Your pardon, lady," Raven said. "We speak of the foul creations of Shadow — things that mock humanity, that appear to the eye as men, that speak fair and feign good will, and that then turn on true humans when the time is ripe, all in the service of their evil master. They carry messages for Shadow, and work its will, all the while seeming no more than cheerful peasants or yeomen, or even gentry. Some even take the form of living men; such a one will slay the true man and usurp his place, live his life, even bed his woman, until the opportunity arises to wreak ill."

"They aren't really human," Prossie said. "Some of the details are wrong. They don't have appendixes, for example, and the structure of the brain is wrong, and none of them remember anything from their childhoods."

"They *had* no childhoods," Raven told her. "They are not born, nor do they grow as we do; they are made as adults, somehow, by Shadow's magic, brought forth full-grown and full of hate and treachery."

"Androids, you mean," Nancy said.

"Yes, only we call them simulacra," Prossie said, trying to avoid yet another unfamiliar word.

"Homunculi," Raven said.

"You're scaring me!" Rachel said, loudly and unhappily.

"Ah, mistress, I beg pardon," Raven said, turning and bowing his head.

"I'm sorry," Prossie said. "Uh . . . what was your name again?"

"Rachel," Rachel told her.

"Oh. I'm sorry, Rachel."

Rachel managed a small sniffle and turned away, obviously not accepting the apology.

A few seconds later she changed her mind and turned back. Prossie looked down expectantly.

"It's okay," Rachel said in a small voice. "But don't do it anymore, okay?"

Captain Cahn rode in the front seat of the Lincoln, with Spaceman First Elmer Soorn squeezed in between himself and the driver, and three more crewmen in back.

"So," Ted said, as he pulled out of the parking lot, "where are you guys from?"

Spaceman Soorn glanced uneasily at his captain.

Cahn considered the matter briefly before deciding that he might as well tell the truth. He didn't really know what was going on, but he had been sent as an envoy, not a spy. "We were sent here as representatives of the Galactic Empire," he said. "Our ship's home port is called Base One, in the Delta Scorpius system."

Ted threw him a quick grin.

"Sure," he said. "I figured, when I saw the uniforms, that it was something like that. Galactic Empire, huh? Knew it wasn't New Zealand."

Soorn, startled, turned to stare at the driver.

Cahn, moving more thoughtfully and showing no surprise, also focused his attention on Ted.

"I didn't get your name," he said.

"Ted Deranian," Ted said. "Call me Ted."

"Mr. Deranian," Cahn said. "You speak as if meeting emissaries from another universe is not particularly out of the ordinary for you."

"Oh, on the contrary, Captain," Ted said, as he accelerated to pass Nancy's little coupe. "I've never met anything remotely like you folks before. That's why I'm enjoying it so much."

Cahn blinked. "I see," he said. He turned his attention to the road ahead, marveling at the number of different vehicles that were using it.

It had been clear to him that none of the police agents or other, unidentified personnel he had spoken with since his ship's unfortunate arrival had believed a word he said. No one had come out and called him a liar; in fact, they had never denied anything, or disagreed with a single datum. They had also virtually never asked him to clarify anything, but had simply noted everything down, with assorted pens and typers, and with their mysterious recording gadgets.

It had become abundantly clear, within a few hours of his arrival, that they all thought him either insane or part of some elaborate conspiracy of deception.

Whether this was because the whole idea of other universes was held to be unacceptably fantastic in this culture, or because agents of Shadow had already infiltrated the society and somehow made sure the Imperial mission was not believed, he could not be certain. Or perhaps the explanation was something else entirely; this was, after all, an alien culture. They might speak good Imperial English, most of them might look white, but they were in truth more foreign than any of the wogs back home. He kept that always in mind; these people were alien.

Whatever the reason for their disbelief, he had resigned himself to a long imprisonment, and to the failure of his mission.

But now he and his crew were unexpectedly free, and in the hands of this person who seemed completely undisturbed by mention of the Galactic Empire. He didn't display the annoyance or resignation the law officers had shown.

Captain Cahn did not know what to make of it. Was this man, perhaps, one of Shadow's creatures?

If they had been back in normal space, where telepathy worked, Prossie Thorpe would have been able to tell if the man was truthful, if he meant them harm — but here, in this strange, warped reality, how was anyone to be sure of anything?

The wisest course of action, he decided, was to be noncommittal, to go along and see what developed.

He sat and silently watched the traffic; his men, taking their cue from him, did the same.

*F*irst Lieutenant Alster Drummond watched Pel Brown out of the corner of his eye, trying not to be seen doing it.

It was obvious that the Earthman was nervous, having the four spacemen in his vehicle; he had said nothing during the drive, and had refused to look at any of his passengers. Drummond had respected the man's emotions and had kept quiet, and the others had followed his example — though it was plain that they, too, were nervous, especially young Peabody, who was seated in the middle of the rear seat and who kept swiveling his head from side to side, like a scanner turret when an ambush is expected.

It might have been useful to say something to soothe the driver — Drummond had not heard his name — but the officer had no idea what to say. He knew nothing about this man, or about his society. Saying the wrong thing would be easy, and finding the right one might be impossible. It seemed better to just stay quiet and see what happened.

They had been in the vehicle for several minutes now, first on the streets, then on a great highway — these people, Drummond saw, having no anti-gravity, had performed miracles of highway engineering to compensate — and now they were on the streets again, cruising past shops and houses, all scattered among large expanses of grass and trees. Drummond wondered whether this was considered city or country, and whether these people *had* any true cities.

The groundcar was slowing; Drummond assumed they were nearing their destination, or at least a transfer point.

"That must be her," Pel said, suddenly.

"Who?" Drummond said, startled.

"There," Pel replied, pointing.

Drummond followed Pel's finger and saw two women, one tall and fair and the other small and dark and somehow exotic, standing on the sidewalk behind a blue vehicle that was slightly smaller than the one he was in.

A little farther along the curb a big brown groundcar had parked, and Drummond could see Captain Cahn climbing out of it on one side, the

Earthman who had driven it on the other.

Then his view was blocked by the garage wall, as Pel pulled the car into place and killed the engine.

Drummond discovered, when he turned to open his door, that the red car that had carried the ship's telepath, Thorpe, was already in the other bay of the garage. He fumbled with the latch and got it open before anyone could come to his assistance.

The men in the back seat did not manage any such feat, and Pel opened the door for them. They emerged, somewhat reluctantly.

People were getting out of the other car, as well — a woman in a peculiar costume of jacket, blouse, and skirt, a man in an even more peculiar and very archaic outfit of black velvet, a little girl in blue pants and a simple red shirt, and, finally, Prossie Thorpe.

"Thorpe," Drummond called. "Report!"

Startled, Thorpe turned and saw him and threw a quick salute. "Telepathic silence continuing, Lieutenant," she said. "Still totally dead, both reception and transmission. No other news; an interesting ride."

He nodded, and noticed that the others, the Earth people, were all staring, with various expressions.

Was that fellow in black an Earth person? His clothing did not seem consistent with the others.

But then, there was a great deal of variation in what the Earth people wore, as well as in their skin and hair — they were clearly a very mixed society, with no proper standards of racial discrimination. There had been black men in police uniforms and working at the jail who were apparently treated as equals.

This was an entirely new universe, Drummond reminded himself, with its own rules.

"I saw someone out front," Pel called to Nancy as he crossed to the overhead door. "I think it must be that Jewell woman."

Nancy nodded, while Drummond threw Pel a questioning glance.

"The woman who owns the land where your ship crashed," Pel explained, reaching for the handle. "Out front, there."

Drummond suddenly understood. "What about the other woman?" he asked.

"I don't know," Pel said, shouting over the rumble of the descending door. "Her lawyer, probably."

Drummond nodded. That would seem to make sense. This society obviously made extensive use of hired advocates and elaborate ritual confrontations.

"Shall we all go inside?" Nancy suggested from a small door at the back of the garage. The little girl was beside her, tugging at the handle and hauling the heavy door open.

"Come on," Pel said, making a herding gesture.

The crewmen obeyed.

Once inside, Nancy directed them all to the family room, while Raven slipped away and headed for the basement. Pel opened the front door to admit Ted, Captain Cahn, the remaining crewmen, and two women.

One was small and dark, younger than the other — no more than thirty, surely — with Oriental features. She wore a grey plaid blouse and black wool suit and carried a large black purse. "This is Susan Nguyen," Ted said, gesturing to make it plain that he was introducing her to everyone, rather than to a specific individual. Drummond noticed that he made no mention of her national origin, though she was the only Oriental he had yet seen here on "Earth."

The other woman was of medium height, with thick honey-blonde hair cut fairly short but elaborately curled. Pel judged her to be in her late thirties, or at most a well-preserved forty-five; her skin was pale, and she hadn't bothered to use make-up to disguise the fact. She wore a floral print dress, belted tightly. "This must be Amy Jewell, then," he said.

She nodded.

Rachel had recruited crewmen to fetch chairs from the kitchen and dining room to the family room, resulting in a temporary traffic jam as everyone bumped into each other. This was further complicated by Raven's return from the basement, accompanied by Stoddard, Squire Donald, and the wizard Valadrakul. As the chaos gradually subsided and everyone either found seats or places to stand, Nancy looked the entire array over with some dismay. She counted seventeen guests — and she hadn't had a chance to shop.

"Would anyone like coffee?" she asked, a little more loudly than she had intended.

Chapter Nine

*P*el looked over the gathering with an odd feeling of unreality. His house was full of characters out of fiction — spacemen and swordsmen and wizards.

Not actors, though; their clothes were all lived in, serious working clothes, not costumes made just for looks. He could smell sweat and perfume — the perfume, he thought, was coming from Squire Donald. He could see pimples and nose hairs.

These people were just as real as he was.

So if these people were all out of storybooks, did that make *him* a fictional character, too? Was he living out an adventure? If so, he hoped he was the hero, and that there would be a happy ending.

Up until yesterday he had thought he was all through with any chance at adventures, and that he had already gotten safely to the living-happily-ever-after part. He had a wife he loved, a delightful daughter, a pleasant home, and his own reasonably-successful business.

Maybe he was just background, then, just a spear-carrier, some bit player.

Or maybe it wasn't a story at all. After all, what sort of adventure story had both wizards and spacemen? And what were lawyers doing in it?

No, this was no story; this was the real world taking an entirely new and bizarre turn, such as his life hadn't done since college. And it had *never* before taken a turn *this* weird.

"We'll be sending out for pizza a little later," he announced as Nancy carried in the second tray of coffee. "For supper, I mean. I'm afraid we're not equipped to feed everybody anything more substantial than that."

"Will we be staying here, then?" one of the Imperials asked — Pel did not yet know them all by name, and this was not one he knew.

"What's pizza?" someone else asked, a little more quietly; Pel was not sure who had spoken.

That, at least, was a question he could answer.

"Pizza, for those of you who aren't familiar with it, is a sort of tomato and cheese pie you can eat with your fingers," Pel explained. "I think you'll like it, and it's something we can get delivered easily. As for whether any of you will be staying here for any length of time, I don't know; that's one of the things we need to discuss."

He looked around at the crowded room, and three dozen eyes looked back at him attentively. He was the host, the man in charge; it was his responsibility to get things moving.

"To start at the beginning," he said, "my name is Pellinore Brown, and this is my house; that's my wife Nancy bringing you all tea and coffee, and my daughter Rachel over there in the doorway." He pointed. "We have a cat somewhere, but he's probably hiding under the bed upstairs."

No one laughed; a few polite smiles appeared briefly.

Pel continued, pointing, "That's Ted Deranian, our attorney; some of you owe him a vote of thanks for getting you out of jail."

Ted, who had managed to snag the recliner and who now sat comfortably enthroned, his feet up, smiled and waved without rising. A polite murmur was heard; when it had subsided, Pel continued.

"Over there," Pel said, pointing to the step down from the hallway, "is Amy Jewell, who owns the land where the Imperial spaceship crashed, and beside her is *her* attorney, Susan Nguyen." The two women were seated side by side on the step; Amy did not react visibly, but Susan acknowledged the introduction with a nervous little nod.

"And," Pel said, looking around to make sure he hadn't missed anyone, "according to what I've been told, the six of us are the only people here from this planet. We have people here from three different worlds. I'll let Raven introduce the people from *his* world."

Raven rose from the white mesh patio chair he was using, one of three that had been brought in to augment the available seating. Pel noticed that at some point he had put his sword back on.

The man in black nodded an acknowledgment and said, "My thanks, friend Pel Brown. From my world there are at present but four of us come. I am called Raven of Stormcrack Keep; my companions," he pointed, "are the mage Valadrakul, Squire Donald a' Benton, and Stoddard, man-at-arms. We came hither by magic, seeking aid in the struggle against the Shadow that has darkened our homeland."

Ted, still ensconced in the recliner, snorted derisively.

"Thanks," Pel said, quickly speaking up before Raven could go any further. Raven essayed a quick bow to the gathered company, then sat again as Pel said, "And the rest of you are from the Galactic Empire; Captain Cahn, if you could introduce your crew?"

"I'm Captain Joshua Cahn, commanding *I.S.S. Ruthless,* detached service, Imperial Fleet," Cahn said, rising from his place on the couch. "My second in command is First Lieutenant Alster Drummond, my second officer is Second Lieutenant Geoffrey Godwin." With each name he pointed. "My men are Peabody, Smith, Lampert, Cartwright, Soorn, and Mervyn, and our Special is Registered Master Telepath Proserpine Thorpe."

"Thank you, Captain." Pel took a deep breath.

"Mr. Brown," Captain Cahn said, interrupting whatever Pel had been about to say, "why are we here? Are we your prisoners?"

"Oh, no, Captain!" Pel said, startled.

"No, you are *mine,*" Raven added, rising.

Astonished, Pel turned to see that Raven had his hand on the hilt of his sword, Squire Donald's hands were ready, and Stoddard was pulling his blade from its sheath. Valadrakul had made no move toward his knife, but had raised both hands in a very peculiar spread-fingered gesture that vaguely resembled a martial arts stance.

"What?" Pel said, baffled. "Raven, what d'you think you're *doing?*"

"Why, claiming my prisoners, friend Pel," Raven replied. "And my thanks to you and your comrade, and your lovely wife, for fetching them for me." He grinned, and Pel remembered that his very first impression of Raven had been of a Mafioso in Renaissance dress.

The Earth people all stared in confusion; the Imperials reacted with tension, anger, and befuddlement. Some stood, some started to and then froze, others never moved.

Ted smiled an uneasy smile. Amy muttered, "This is insane," and clutched her purse tightly. Susan watched, her face emotionless.

Captain Cahn did not bother to say anything; he hauled a blaster from the holster on his belt, pointed it at Stoddard, and pulled the trigger.

Nothing happened.

"Damn," he said. "I was afraid of that."

Ted giggled.

"Stoddard, put that thing away," Pel said. "And you, too, Captain; even if it doesn't work, I don't like people pointing guns in my house."

Stoddard glanced at Raven.

"Nobody is anybody's prisoner here," Pel insisted. "Raven, you three may have swords, but there are four of you and fifteen of us, and a drawerful of knives in the kitchen. If there's a fight someone's going to get hurt, and you might lose, and besides, it's just stupid. Put the swords away and let's talk about this, okay?"

"We have more than swords, Pel Brown," Raven said; he kept his right hand on the hilt of his own weapon and gestured at Valadrakul with his left.

"No, you don't," Pel said. "Magic doesn't work any better here than the captain's raygun."

Raven gave a Hollywood villain's laugh and called, "Valadrakul!"

The wizard's fingers moved in odd, twitching patterns.

For a moment, the room was silent; no one else moved. Then Rachel began crying.

"Rachel!" Nancy cried; she hurried to her daughter's side.

The momentary distraction did not break the tension; after a quick glance, everyone returned to the frozen tableau of a moment before.

Everyone, that is, except Pel, who was standing in the middle of the room grinning.

"Come on, Raven," he said. "Magic doesn't work here."

"Ah . . . my lord," Valadrakul said softly, lowering his hands, "I fear he speaks the truth."

Raven turned to glare at his wizard. "Canst do *nothing?*" he demanded.

"Naught, my lord," Valadrakul said. "Not the merest spell can I bring to fruit."

"As I was saying," Pel said, "three swords against a dozen steak knives isn't anything I'd care to see."

"I understood," Raven said, "that this realm was different, and that magic was not the same here — but to find that a mage can do *nothing* 'gainst armed men?"

"Raven, we have *no* magic here," Pel said. "It's not that magic is different here, it's that there isn't any. *None.* It isn't possible. People have been trying to work magic here for five thousand years, and it can't. Be. Done."

"Aaah!" Raven flung his hand from the grip of his sword in disgust. "Stoddard, sheathe your blade."

Stoddard obeyed. Squire Donald dropped his hands. Ted giggled inanely again.

"Now," Pel said, exasperated, "can we get on with it?"

No one objected.

"Good," Pel said. "Now, let me see if I have this straight. You people are not from other planets, in the usual sense of planets that orbit stars that you could fly to if you had a working spaceship. You're from alternate realities — places that are in entirely different universes that occupy the same space as ours. Right?" He looked at Raven.

"I cannot gainsay that," Raven said. "Though I'd not swear it be true."

Pel looked at Cahn.

"Sounds right to me, allowing for some minor variations in terminology," the captain said.

"Good," Pel said. "Raven, you and your people came here through an opening in the wall of our basement, right?"

Raven nodded.

"Now, how'd you make that opening?"

"'Twas conjured for us, by the sorceress Elani," Raven said.

"Fine. Now, Captain Cahn, how did you and your people get here?"

Cahn blinked, took a second to consider, and replied, "We flew our ship through a spatial continuum discontinuity — a space warp, we call it."

"And how'd that warp happen?"

Cahn tightened his lips for a moment, glanced at Prossie and then at Drummond, and answered, "It was deliberately created by a process developed by the Empire's Department of Science; I don't know the details."

"But it was done by science, and not magic?"

"Oh, yes; magic works no better in Imperial space than it appears to here," Cahn agreed.

"But it seems some of your science doesn't work here either, right?"

"That's right," Cahn admitted. "Though I'd be interested in knowing just how you learned that. It appears that certain physical laws are different here, including some that form the basis for much of our machinery."

"So your ship doesn't fly."

"At the moment, that's correct."

"But if it *did*," Pel asked, "could you fly it back through the warp and go back where you came from?"

Prossie coughed.

"In theory," Cahn said. "It hasn't been done, however."

"Ah. And in any case, your ship *doesn't* fly — so the ten of you are stranded here, right?"

Cahn did not answer that; instead he stared calmly back at Pel.

Pel waved the question aside. "It doesn't matter," he said. "I'm just trying to make sure everyone sees as much of the situation as possible."

"Keep it up, Mr. Brown," Amy called from the hallway step. "You're doing fine so far; it almost makes sense."

Several people, from all three worlds, smiled.

"Thank you," Pel replied. He paused, rubbed at a cheek with his forefinger, and considered, while everyone else waited expectantly.

"All right," he said. "Now let's consider *why* all you people are here. Raven tells me that something he calls Shadow has . . . um . . . conquered?" Raven nodded. "Conquered. Something called Shadow has conquered most of his home world — I guess he just means his own planet, and not whatever others there are in his universe . . ."

Valadrakul cleared his throat. Pel turned his gaze on the wizard. "Yes?"

"Your pardon," the wizard said, "but you misunderstand the nature of our reality. There is but one world; we have no planets in our cosmos, as you would use the term. I would take it that your own cosmos resembles that of the Empire, with a myriad of worldly globes circling many thousands of stars, but our realm is not like that; rather, we have but a single globe, and the sun and moons and stars, and the wanderers that *we* call by the name 'planet,' all travel about it."

"We used to think that, too . . ." Pel began.

Valadrakul cut him off with a shake of his head. "Still you do not understand," he said. "Wizards have *been* to the stars, long ago, and flown behind the sun. We have seen all our universe from afar, hanging alone in a black and empty cosmos. We know its nature."

"All right," Pel said, "I won't argue about it. At any rate, this Shadow thing has conquered most of the world, right?"

"Aye," said three of the four — Stoddard did not speak, but Raven, Donald, and Valadrakul all responded. "May Shadow be eternally damned," Donald added.

"It's conquered *all* the World," Raven said.

Pel nodded. "Right," he said. "And now it's looking for somewhere new, right?"

"Aye," said Raven.

"And that brings us to the Empire," Pel said, turning to Captain Cahn. "Captain?"

"Yes, Mr. Brown?" Cahn said, raising an eyebrow. The gesture was something Leonard Nimoy might have done playing Mr. Spock, but Cahn, with his close-cropped blond hair and square jaw, didn't look anything at all like Spock. He looked more like someone's idea of the all-American boy.

"This Shadow thing discovered your universe, right?"

"So it appears," Cahn said. "I believe that Telepath Thorpe can probably tell you more about that than I can."

All eyes turned to Prossie. She shrank back against the cushions of the couch.

"Report, Thorpe," Cahn told her.

"Yes, sir," Prossie said, standing quickly and snapping to attention. "About seven years ago," she began, "Imperial Intelligence started getting reports of oddities — strange creatures turning up in places they shouldn't, most often. The creatures in question either vanished or died before any Intelligence personnel or any telepath reached them, and the dead ones didn't explain much — the Department of Science couldn't figure out where they came from, or any conditions under which they could have survived naturally. Some of them seemed to lack vital organs, for example. A few were miniature humans, but most were monstrosities."

Cahn nodded; Pel blinked.

"Hellbeasts and homunculi, most likely," Raven said.

"The Empire investigated," Prossie continued, "and located certain people who were not what they pretended to be. Telepathic interrogation, carried out without the subject being aware of it, revealed that these people, and all of the anomalies, were the products of an extra-universal entity that they knew as 'Shadow.' This entity had sent its creatures to scout out Imperial space, explore it, and to send back reports. Shadow's reasons and long-term intentions were not known to any of its creations."

"Shadow is no fool," Raven remarked. Pel gestured for him to be silent, and he obeyed.

"Up until this point," Prossie went on, "the possibility of inter-universal travel was unknown to the Empire. However, the existence of this extra-universal threat was sufficient reason to begin a crash program at the Department of Science, to find and access other universes. Using knowledge gleaned from Shadow's creatures, telepaths assisted in this research, and in fact were central to it; it was discovered that under certain conditions telepaths could contact minds in other universes, that in fact such contacts had sometimes already occurred inadvertently, but that heretofore their nature had been misunderstood. It was determined that the foremost requirement for inter-universal contact, the one that appears to have been most limiting, is that the minds in question must all think in the same language as the telepath attempting to reach them."

"English?" Ted asked.

Prossie nodded. "It appears," she said, "that a similar limitation must exist on the magic that Shadow used in opening a way between its universe and Imperial space — or perhaps Shadow only discovered the Empire when a telepath accidentally contacted it. In any case, Shadow and its creatures, and most of the other inhabitants of its universe, speak a recognizable dialect of Imperial English. Accordingly, our telepaths were able to contact some of them. Shadow itself, however, was another matter; attempts to read its thoughts were unsuccessful, and sometimes damaging. One telepath died upon contacting Shadow; the autopsy found severe brain damage. After that we were all more careful."

Pel nodded. Amy shuddered.

"Although we could sometimes sense, around the fringes of our perception, beings that spoke other languages, we were unable to establish contact with anything other than English-speaking humans," Prossie continued. "Until very recently this meant that we could only communicate reliably within the Empire, or with Shadow's world. However, a few weeks back we achieved limited contacts with individuals in a third universe — the one we're all in right now."

"It's pretty goddamn unlikely, three different universes, *that* different, where the same species and the same language happened," Ted remarked. "That's the biggest flaw in the story so far — and there are plenty of flaws."

"Given an infinite number of realities," Prossie said, turning slightly to address the recumbent lawyer but staying at attention, "and we have no reason to think that the number is any *less* than infinite, the same species and language would *have* to recur somewhere, eventually."

Ted shifted and leaned the recliner further back. "I don't buy it," he said, "but go on with your story."

Prossie nodded. "There isn't much more. The Empire's been sure for a long time that Shadow is hostile and dangerous, and we wanted allies against it. Earth looked like a promising possibility. Telepathic contacts weren't clear and reliable enough, however, so the newly-developed space warp technology was used to send a diplomatic mission to your largest and most powerful nation." She shrugged. "And here we are."

"The United States isn't the largest nation on Earth," Susan protested.

Prossie slipped from her brace and stared. "It's not?" she asked.

"China is," Rachel piped up from the doorway. "They told us that in kindergarten."

"The United States is the largest country that speaks English," Nancy pointed out.

"That would explain it," Captain Cahn said.

"That's who *you* are," Ted said from his chair. "But who the heck are *they?*" He pointed at Raven and Valadrakul.

"We gave our names, sir," Raven said, a trifle stiffly.

Ted shook his head. "I mean, who the heck are you? Are you good guys, or bad guys, or what? You said you weren't on Shadow's side, so are you on the

Empire's side?"

"We are on our *own* side," Raven retorted.

"All right," Pel said. "But it's a good question — what side *is* that?"

Raven made a derisive noise. "Think you," he said, "that though all be conquered, even Shadow can control everything utterly? Think you that, though the fortresses fall, none will continue to bear arms 'gainst the tyrant? I and mine are those who have refused to give up, who have fought on beyond defeat."

"Could you be a bit more specific?" Ted asked.

Raven glared at him.

"Yes," Captain Cahn said. "I wasn't aware of any native resistance to Shadow's rule. Who are you, and how many? How are you organized?"

"Do you think me a fool?" Raven asked, annoyed. Then he stopped, and grinned. "Aye, perchance you do, after that exhibition I made but moments ago. And who could blame you? Yet I'm not such a fool as all that, and I'll not give away secrets before this many, when almost any of you could be a thing of Shadow."

Several of those present glanced uneasily at each other at this suggestion. Prossie realized she was still standing, and sank back onto the couch.

"This is all crazy," Amy muttered.

"Can't you tell us *anything* useful?" Lieutenant Drummond asked.

Raven turned to Valadrakul; the wizard said, "There are many of us, working 'gainst Shadow — but we are scattered, and needs must work in secret. We have organized ourselves in small councils, with no more than a dozen in each, and none but the leader of each council knows any save those within his own group — thus, should we be betrayed, no more than a dozen shall be found and slain."

"Cells," Pel said. "Revolutionary cells."

"And likewise, none save the innermost councils, of which those here have no part, can know our true numbers," Raven pointed out.

"So the four of you make up one cell in this underground?" Pel asked.

"Half a council, rather," Donald volunteered.

"Why didn't you all come?" Captain Cahn asked. "Seems to me that at least you'd be safe here."

Raven shook his head. "Nay," he said.

"Why not?" Cahn persisted.

"I should not say," Raven said, "for I know not whether any of you are tainted by Shadow, nor how far word might spread if spoken here. I'd not have any more known than I must."

"I think it's safe enough here," Pel said. "We're all of us opposed to Shadow, aren't we? Captain Cahn, you and your crew must have been checked over by telepaths before you were sent through the warp."

Cahn nodded. "We were, indeed," he said.

"And Shadow hasn't discovered Earth yet," Pel pointed out. "So none of *us* could be spies."

"We know not whether Earth has been found," Valadrakul corrected him.

Pel dismissed the matter. "Even if it *has,*" he pointed out, "there are five billion people on Earth; what are the chances that any of the seven of us here would be spies?"

"Fair enough," Raven said, after a moment's consideration. "Well, then, the truth is that we cannot all be safe here, for three of our council are wee folk — gnomes, as they were once known — who cannot abide this place. And another is the sorceress who maintains the portal; were she to step through, and her magicks thereby fail, we would all be trapped here."

Lieutenant Godwin growled. "We *are* trapped here, I'd think."

Cahn threw him a warning look, and he fell apologetically silent.

"Captain," Raven said, *"can* you return home, an we allow it?"

"I can't say," Cahn replied, shortly.

"He probably doesn't know himself," Nancy whispered in Pel's ear.

"If not," Raven said, "we have something to offer you, for your good services."

Cahn cocked an eyebrow at the black-clad foreigner. "And what might that be?" he asked.

"Our sorceress, Elani, has stolen Shadow's gateway spell, and has opened our portal to Earth — and likewise, she can open a portal to your Empire, and thereby send you home."

Prossie made a noise; Pel glanced at her, and she looked away.

Chapter Ten

"*A*n interesting proposition," Cahn said, in his most noncommittal tone. "And what sort of payment would you want for this service?"

"Why, 'tis obvious, is't not?" Raven asked, spreading his hands. "We wish your aid against Shadow."

"Our aid?" Cahn grimaced. "Mister, we're just ten men — ten people, rather." One hand made a vague gesture in Prossie's direction. "We've got a ship and weapons that don't work here, and that might not work in your universe, either — so what difference will ten men make against a force that has already conquered a world?"

"You are part of the Imperial Fleet, are you not?" Raven asked. "Yours but a single ship in a vast armada, with the power to lay waste whole kingdoms in mere days?"

"Oh, sure," Lieutenant Drummond said. "But the Imperial Fleet is *there*, and we're *here*. We're just the crew of one ship."

"Besides," Godwin added, "as the captain just said, the Fleet's weapons are based on the same principles as the captain's blaster that didn't go off a few minutes ago. They won't work here, and probably won't work on your world, either. We're disarmed — just like your wizard."

Raven ignored Godwin and addressed Drummond. "You are the crew of a *diplomatic* vessel," he pointed out, "sent as envoy, and empowered to make pact on behalf of your Emperor."

Pel considered Godwin's comments as Cahn said, "Our authority isn't as broad as all that. We're more a negotiating team than an embassy; anything we agreed to would have to be approved by higher authority, maybe by the Emperor Himself."

"Indeed?"

Cahn nodded. "In fact, the main thing we were sent to negotiate was an exchange of ambassadors. We sure don't have the power to declare war and send the entire Imperial Fleet through a warp to fight Shadow, if that's what you were hoping for."

"Raven," Pel said, "there's something here I don't understand. If magic doesn't work in the Empire, and the Imperial technology doesn't work in your world, how can they fight?"

Raven blinked in surprise. "Friend Pel," he said, "what mean you?"

"I *mean,*" Pel said, "how can Shadow do anything to the Galactic Empire if magic doesn't work there? And how can the Empire do anything to Shadow?"

Raven turned to Valadrakul, who said, "A good point, sir. Howsoever, there is some magic that can effect its purpose in other realms, even while it cannot be conjured there. Consider the gateway spell that manifests in your own cellars — the magic lies entirely in our own world, and yet it functions both ways. Likewise, consider the magic of the mind that these good people call telepathy." The wizard mispronounced the word, but as he gestured toward Prossie, Pel figured out what he meant. "It works not a whit here, and this maiden can no more hear your thoughts now than can any other.

Several people cast startled glances at Prossie or each other at this revelation. Valadrakul continued, unperturbed. "Yet from their own land, these mind-readers can know what others think in all our varied realms."

Pel nodded. "Still doesn't seem like Shadow's about to conquer the Empire," he said. "Or for that matter, that the Empire's about to conquer Shadow. I mean, if each side's major weapons don't work in the other one's worlds . . ."

"Ah, but Shadow's *greatest* strength is of value in either realm!" Raven said, interrupting.

"Its creatures, you mean," Prossie said.

"Exactly," Raven said. "Its homunculi can live in the Empire, and fight there, as can those true humans who are base enough to choose slavery to Shadow over death in resistance."

"The monsters died, though," Prossie pointed out. "At least most of them. And the miniatures, too."

"Gnomes," Donald muttered.

"And which would you rather face," Raven asked, "some misshapen thing brought from nightmare, or a well-drilled army? A beast, or a trained assassin?"

"Good point," Cahn conceded.

"And Shadow can be persuasive," Raven said. "Doubt me not, there are those among your own people who would yield willingly to its blandishments, and serve it of their own will. There were such among my own kin."

At that, Stoddard growled — the first sound most of those present had heard from him. Squire Donald spat in disgust, and Pel heard Nancy gasp at the sight of that.

"Don't worry," he whispered to her. "It'll come right out of the carpet."

Cahn nodded toward Raven. "I'm sure you're right," he said. "We've had trouble with spies and traitors before, and I doubt we've managed to breed the tendencies out of the human species in the last few years." He grimaced. "And as Thorpe told you, we've already had problems with Shadow's creatures infiltrating the Empire. Telepaths can spot them, or x-rays, but we only have four hundred telepaths out of thirteen billion citizens, and it's not practical to march everyone past a fluoroscope. Furthermore, Shadow seems to be able to send in duplicates and replace genuine people, so that the checks can't just be done once, they need to be repeated constantly. So we have spies among us, I'm certain."

"I think we all agree that Shadow has to be stopped," Drummond said. "The question is, how?"

"And your answer?" Donald demanded.

Drummond shrugged. "I don't have one," he said.

Cahn expanded upon that. "The Empire is preparing for war," he said. "We're stockpiling ships and weapons, and if ever Shadow attempts the open occupation of any part of Imperial space, it will find us ready to retaliate. We'll blast any colonies we find right out of space. And we're stepping up our security measures — of course, I couldn't give you details, even if I knew them, for fear of compromising them. We're doing everything we can to locate and stamp out any attempts at infiltration. When we find Shadow's creatures, we kill them, immediately."

"A noble effort, to be sure," Raven said, with a note of sarcasm creeping into his voice, "but knowing that Shadow's spies in your Emperor's kitchens will be found and slain gives me no great hope for the liberation of Stormcrack Keep."

"Nor Benton," Donald added.

"Nor anywhere else in our world," Valadrakul agreed.

"Hey," Godwin protested. "Who appointed us your rescuers, anyway? We have our *own* homes to worry about, first!"

"And would your homes not be best served," Raven demanded, "by encompassing the utter destruction of Shadow and all its creations, rather than nibbling away at its outer defenses?"

"Of course that would suit our long-term interests," Cahn said. "And it's just that, a *long-term* goal. As yet, we have no way to achieve it." He gestured at Pel. "We'd hoped that these people could give us a weapon to use against Shadow, but I doubt that these super-bombs of theirs would work in your space."

"You can't get any anyway," Pel pointed out.

Cahn drew his blaster, hefted it, pointed it at the ceiling, and pulled the trigger. Nothing happened, not even an audible click.

"Back home," he said, "that would have blown a two-foot hole through the roof. Here, nothing. Our weapons don't work here, and we don't think they work in Shadow's world, either."

"Nor do they," Raven acknowledged. "We've tested them."

For a moment nobody spoke; Pel took them all to be absorbing the implications. Among other things, it was an admission that Raven's people had visited the Empire, and had obtained weapons there.

But they hadn't done so openly.

"Well, then," Cahn said finally, "what do you want us to do, when our weapons won't work?"

"Some weapons work everywhere," Raven said, his hand dropping to the hilt of his sword. "Your Empire has great resources, thousands upon thousands of men and machines — you spoke of a populace numbered thirteen billions. Could you not make swords as easily as those . . . those things you carry? Could not your armies march 'gainst Shadow, as did those of Stormcrack Keep in my youth?"

"And where are those armies of your youth now?" Cahn demanded. "Why should we send our people to be slaughtered by that thing's magic?"

Raven frowned, and shifted his weight to his other foot before replying, "And what of your science? What of other weapons? We know that what you bear will not function, but have you no other armaments? We know little of what will or will not serve, in any of our three worlds; there may well be weapons known to you, and unknown to Shadow, that would serve as well in our world as your own. We know not whether this world's mighty bombs can destroy Shadow's fortress; mayhap they can, mayhap they cannot. Perhaps your magicians, your science-wielders, can discover ways to shield against Shadow's spells; perhaps the men of your world are not as susceptible to those spells as are mine. Dare we not venture the attempt?"

"I'll order the pizza," Nancy whispered in Pel's ear. "I figure five large pies."

He nodded, and she slipped away.

"I'm sure," Cahn said, "that when the Empire has had time to prepare, we *will* make an attempt. The Emperor doesn't want Shadow there any more than you do, but there's no point in throwing away resources in a premature attack."

"So you wait, and wait — seven years, now, since first Shadow showed its hand in your realm?"

"Seven years, yes," Cahn agreed. "But we haven't been waiting idly — if we had, I wouldn't be here talking to you."

"Not idle, perhaps, yet you wait," Raven insisted. "And I fear that when at last the Empire sees fit to strike, I'll be long in my grave, and our councils lost. Then even if Shadow falls, my people will be but yielding one tyrant for another."

"You're saying the Empire's no better than Shadow?" Cahn asked, his tone threatening.

Raven held up his hands. "Nay, I said it not," he said. "'Tis certain that your Emperor George cannot help but be preferable to the horrors of Shadow. But is there no other way? Are my people never to return to their own ways, their own rulers?"

"Watch how you talk about the Emperor," Godwin growled.

"His Imperial Majesty George the Eighth generally doesn't interfere much in the lives of his subjects," Cahn said, with enforced calm. "You people will probably have all your own little lords back, if that's what you want — it's just they'll be subject to the Empire."

Raven turned up his palms. "And you do not see why we are dissatisfied with that?"

"I see it," Cahn said, his voice hard. "I just don't see why it's any of my business."

"Ah, Captain," Raven said, suddenly changing manner from supplicant to salesman, "*that* brings us back whence we began. I can take you home to your own world; in exchange, I ask that you aid us against Shadow."

"It's a circle, all right," Cahn agreed, "because I don't see what we can do."

"Isn't there any way you can defeat Shadow, other than a full-scale war?" Pel asked.

Cahn turned to him. "For example?" he asked.

"Well, Shadow's a magician, right? I mean, underneath? Couldn't someone kill him somehow? Wouldn't that do it?"

"Shadow might have been human once," Raven said. "I doubt it still is."

"But could it be killed?"

Raven turned to Valadrakul, who turned up open palms. "Who knows?" he said.

"Well, maybe if someone tried, that would solve the whole problem," Pel suggested. "You know, like if someone had assassinated Hitler in 1938 maybe we wouldn't have had to fight World War II."

Fourteen pairs of eyes stared at him in utter incomprehension. Ted, in his recliner, giggled again; Amy was looking about the room, from face to face, while Susan was watching Raven. Nancy was in the kitchen, and Pel realized he didn't know where Rachel was; she had disappeared.

Probably got bored, he thought to himself. This must all be way over her head.

"Sir," Valadrakul said, "I know nothing of this Hitler, nor any World War, but yes, an we could slay Shadow, we would need no war."

"Well, *can* we slay Shadow?"

Valadrakul turned up a palm again. "Who knows?" he asked again.

"Well, where does Shadow get its power?" Pel asked. "Is there some magic ring we can throw into a volcano or something?"

Stoddard glanced at Raven, who glanced at Valadrakul, but most of those present simply stared at Pel.

"You know, like in *The Lord of the Rings* or something," Pel said.

"Friend Pel," Raven said, speaking gently, "what are you saying? Once before, you spoke of this; we know not what you mean."

"You aren't making sense, Mr. Brown," Cahn said.

"It's a book," Pel explained. "Three books, I mean, by J.R.R. Tolkien. There's this hobbit, see, who finds a magic ring that's the key to the Dark Lord's power, and he throws it into a volcano and melts it, and then the Dark Lord doesn't have any power."

"Nonsense," Valadrakul declared. "What fool of a sorcerer would put all his power in a single talisman? And Shadow uses no talismans at all; Shadow is at the heart of a great mystical matrix, a web of arcane potency built up over centuries. What would such as that need with wands and rings and baubles?"

"I certainly never heard of any such tale as you describe," Cahn added.

"I've heard of it," Susan interjected, "but I never read it."

"What's a hobbit?" one of the crewmen — Cartwright, Pel thought it was — asked.

"An imaginary little person," Pel explained.

"Like a spriggan?" Cartwright suggested.

"I don't know," Pel replied. "What's a spriggan?"

"Like in the stories," Cartwright said. "You know, like Plunkett's stuff."

"Who's Plunkett?" Ted asked.

"Edward Plunkett, the writer," Cartwright said, turning to look at Ted.

"Never heard of him," Ted said.

"Neither did I," Pel added.

"Of course not," Cahn said. "He's from *our* universe, not yours. He wrote picture books, died a couple of years ago."

"Well, I guess we all know things the others don't," Pel agreed.

"Like what that thing is," said Peabody, emboldened by Cartwright's comments. He pointed at the stereo.

"It's a stereo," Pel said. "It plays music."

"Like a melodeon?" Peabody asked.

"I don't think so," Pel said. "Wasn't that some Victorian thing?"

"Boy, has *this* conversation degenerated!" Ted called out to no one in particular. "From saving three different universes to sound equipment!"

"Indeed," Raven said, with a sour glance at Ted, "I must agree. We were discussing whether a way might be found to slay Shadow, without first defeating it in battle."

"I don't know of any," Cahn replied.

"I don't know anything *about* it," Pel said.

"Ah," Valadrakul said, "but you know much it does not."

Most eyes turned toward the wizard, Raven's among them.

"What mean you?" he asked.

"I mean that these gentlemen know many things that we cannot imagine, my lord — these tales of Messieurs Tolkien and Plunkett, an example. Who knows but that they *do* have a way to slay Shadow, but know it not?"

"But if we don't *know* we know it, what good does it do?" Pel asked.

"Perhaps," Valadrakul suggested, holding up a finger, "if men of all three worlds were to gather in ours, and together study the situation, a solution might be found."

Captain Cahn looked around thoughtfully.

"You may have a point, uh . . . wizard," he said. "If we all studied Shadow in your world."

"Yeah, and he may *not* have a point," Pel said. "Listen, I didn't ask for all you people to come here; I didn't ask anyone to put that thing in my basement. I've tried to be helpful, but I'm not going anywhere or studying anything. That's up to you guys."

"Well, I think I'd be willing to chance a visit to wherever these people are based," Cahn said. "I've already risked visiting one alien universe; I don't mind

passing through another on the way home, and seeing what we can do there."
He looked around at his crew. "This would be purely voluntary, men; if you'd
rather stay here and wait until rescue comes, that's fine. Or if you want to go
back to the ship and see about getting her airborne . . ."

"Oh, no," Amy said, interrupting.

Everyone turned to her, and Pel realized that she had hardly said a word
throughout the entire meeting.

"Nobody's going near that ship," she said. "It's on my land, and nobody's
messing with it."

"But, madam . . ." Cahn began.

"*No,* Captain!" she said, loudly. "I don't know what's going on, really I don't
— I've listened to all this, and I have no idea how much of it is for real, if *any*
of it is, and if it's not I don't know which of you are in on the gag and which
aren't, but whatever the truth is, *nobody* here, not *one* of you, is going to set
foot on my land or inside that ship until I *do* know exactly what's going on!
And maybe not then!"

"My lady," Valadrakul said, "everything said here today is purest truth, I
swear by the Goddess."

"I don't believe that," Amy replied.

"What part don't you believe?" Cahn asked.

Amy looked around uncertainly. "I don't know," she said. "I'm not sure I
believe *any* of it!"

"My lady," Valadrakul said, "we can easily prove to you the reality of our
native world; 'tis but a few steps to take you there, along the passage, down the
stairs, and across the cellars. A step through the wall, and you can see our world
with your own eyes."

"Oh, no," Amy said. "I didn't ask for any ship to fall in my back yard any
more than this person wanted a space warp in his basement." She waved at Pel.

Raven turned his attention to Ted, who held up his hands. "Oh, no," he
said. "I'm not like Ms. Jewell there; I *do* know what to believe, and I don't
believe a word of any of this. I'm enjoying the show, really I am — it's a pretty
good story — but I don't for a minute think any of it is real. I suspect I'm asleep
and dreaming the whole thing, I really do, but if that's not it then all of you
must be crazy. And I'm not letting any escaped lunatics take me anywhere,
thank you!"

Cahn turned to Nancy, who stood in the kitchen doorway.

"Don't look at *me,*" she said.

Valadrakul addressed Susan and said, with a slight bow, "That leaves you,
my lady."

"I'm not interested," Susan said, shaking her head. "Not at all. I saw enough
of war when I was a little girl."

"Well, then," Raven said, "'twould seem we have none of Earth who would
join us."

"What about those people you contacted telepathically?" Pel asked. "Would
any of them want to help?"

Cahn turned to Prossie, who leaned her head back and started counting
them off on her fingers.

"Well," she said, "there was Carleton Miletti. Every time we tried to contact him he was doing something dangerous, like driving a groundcar at very high speed, so we didn't force a contact for fear of distracting him and getting him killed, and he never responded to our presence."

"Doesn't sound promising," Pel commented.

"There was Angela Thompson — she's three years old. I don't think she'd be much help. A very sweet little girl, though; she called us Mr. Nobody."

Nancy smiled.

"There was a man named Ray Aldridge who claimed to be a . . a psychic," Prossie said. "He claimed to read minds and see the future, but we think he was lying. We never found any evidence of any real parapsychic abilities."

"Still," Pel said, "he might do."

Prossie looked up at Pel. "I suppose so," she said. "He lives in a place called California; is that anywhere near here?"

"No," Pel admitted.

"We could phone him, though, and ask him to fly out," Amy suggested.

"Phone?" Squire Donald looked about in polite puzzlement.

"Fly?" Raven turned toward Amy.

"You have aircraft?" Cahn asked, startled.

"Of course we do," Pel said. "Ms. Thorpe, did you get an address for him?"

Prossie shook her head. "No," she said, "but he lives in . . . in Oakville, maybe? Oakmont?"

"Oakland?" Ted suggested.

"That could be it," Prossie agreed.

"Big town," Ted remarked.

"Who else?" Pel asked.

"Well, Oram Blaisdell," Prossie said. "But he's an old man, and his neighbors think he's crazy."

"Where is he?"

"Tessenti? Something like that."

"Tessenti?"

"Tessenti, Tennessity, something — I don't remember."

"Tennessee?" Amy suggested.

"That's it, yes," Prossie said, thankfully.

"Any others?"

"One old woman who died," Prossie said. "She was in a place called Alice Springs — I'm pretty sure that wasn't anywhere near here."

"It's in Australia, I think," Pel said.

"And that's almost all that we even got names for," Prossie said. "There was one more, I think — a girl in another country, who sometimes spoke another language instead of English. Her name was Gwyneth something, I think."

"Sounds Welsh," Nancy remarked.

"That was the other language, yes," Prossie agreed. "She was about fifteen, I think."

"Not much help," Pel said.

"None of them are," Susan agreed.

"Where does this Carleton Miletti live?" Pel asked.

"I don't know," Prossie said. "We never got a strong enough contact to read any place names."

"Damn. Well, this Aldridge — you said he's out in Oakland, California? And he's a psychic advisor?" Pel began walking toward the kitchen as he spoke.

"Uh . . . something like that," Prossie agreed.

"Fine." Pel reached around the kitchen door and picked up the phone receiver; he said, "Just a minute." Then he stepped around the corner and pulled the phone book from the shelf.

"Nancy," he said, thumbing through the black-bordered pages at the front of the directory, "do you know the area code for Oakland?"

"No," she said, unhappily. "Area codes are page 29, though."

"Got it, I think." He dialed (415) 555-1212.

The motley collection in the other room waited silently while Pel spoke on the phone; a moment later he appeared in the kitchen doorway and announced, "Unlisted. Seems stupid for a psychic to have an unlisted number, but he does."

"Maybe he doesn't want you to phone him unless you're psychic yourself, and can *guess* the number," Ted remarked, grinning. Nobody laughed.

"What about the one in Tennessee?" Amy suggested.

"Oram Blaisdell," Prossie said.

"Yeah," Pel said. "What about him?"

Prossie shook her head. "He probably doesn't even *have* one of those telephone things," she said. "Besides, he's a crazy old man. He thought we were angels talking to him."

"Mr. Brown," Cahn said, "it was a good idea, but forget it. None of the original contactees are going to be any help. It'll be up to my crew and myself to lend whatever aid we can, in exchange for transport home; we won't drag you innocent civilians into it."

"Sir?" Soorn said, uneasily.

Cahn turned.

"Sir," Soorn said, "speaking purely for myself, I would prefer . . . well, you said that this was voluntary?"

"Yes, spaceman?"

"Sir, I'm afraid I must decline to volunteer. I'd prefer to wait here and hope for rescue. This world doesn't seem all that bad — I mean, dangerous. I'd rather stay here and wait than risk going into some fairyland where this Shadow thing is all-powerful."

Cahn stared at him, and Soorn, after a moment of awkward silence, added, "I saw some of what they found on Lambda Ceti IV, sir. I'm not going."

"All right," Cahn said, "I said it was voluntary, and it is. You can stay here, and fend for yourself."

"Thank you, sir."

"You can't stay *here*," Nancy protested. "I'm sorry, but not in *my* house you don't. I don't know anything about you!"

Soorn looked at her unhappily. "I can find someplace, then, can't I?"

"Maybe a hotel?" Susan said.

"Do you have any money?" Pel asked.

Soorn shook his head.

"Lad," Raven said, "Shadow is powerful, and nominal ruler of all the world, but it's not *all*-powerful. Come with us, and see for yourself! Lend your arm to a worthy battle!"

Soorn looked at him and said nothing.

"Come and take a look," Donald coaxed. "See for yourself! And should our land not please you, our wizards can see you safe home to your Empire, while those who would brave it may stay and fight."

Soorn glanced at Cahn, then at Nancy; neither of them gave any sign of yielding.

"You, too, mistress," Donald said, leaning forward and making a beckoning gesture to Amy. "And you," adding Susan, "come and see our realm! See what it is we wish to save! Then perhaps you'll think more kindly of us. All of you, come and take a look, and if you be not pleased, 'tis but a moment's work to step back through the gate to the cellars here — or should Elani wish it, to the Empire whence most of you came!"

"I could do that?" Amy said. "Just step through and take a look around, and step right back?"

"Why not?" Donald asked, with an expansive gesture.

"Then I'd *know* whether it was real," Amy said.

Donald nodded.

Pel glanced at Nancy. "Y'know, I think I'd like to take a quick look, too," he said. "I've always loved fantasy stories, and ever since that gnome first turned up — I mean, it's scary, but I'd like to take a look."

"You people are all crazy," Nancy said. "Especially you, Pel."

"Oh, don't be such a stick-in-the-mud, Nancy!" Ted said. "Let's *all* go see just what sort of dream-world I've come up with!"

"Nancy, think of it, seriously — a world where magic is *real*," Pel said.

"*Black* magic," Nancy retorted.

"Not all of it," Pel replied. "That gnome — you'd like seeing him."

"Ha."

"Well, *I'm* going to go look," Pel said, annoyed. "For one thing, as Amy said, how else will we ever be sure this is all real?"

"Are you going to take a camera?" Nancy asked. "And take pictures or something?"

"Sure, why not?" Pel said.

She glared at him, and then turned to Raven and demanded, "Are you *sure* we can step right back?"

"Oh, yes, my lady," he said. "Have we not done so, my comrades and I?"

"You're coming?" Pel asked.

"If you go, I'm going, too," she said. "To keep an eye on you."

"What about Rachel?"

Nancy hesitated. "She's upstairs playing," she said. "But we'll bring her, too. Maybe she'll like seeing those gnomes you talked about."

"She'll want to tell everyone at school about it," Pel said, smiling.

"They'll never believe a word," Nancy retorted. "Not even Jenny would buy a story like that, even if it's true. Which I'm still not entirely convinced of."

Pel shrugged. "You're probably right," he said.

"Then you'll come?" Raven said. "Perchance even a quick glance will tell you somewhat, and some thought may strike you that would serve our cause."

"Not likely," Pel said.

The doorbell rang, and Nancy's hand flew to her mouth.

"The pizza," she said.

Small feet pattered down the stairs as Rachel ran to answer the door.

Chapter Eleven

*A*my watched as the self-proclaimed spacemen sampled the pizza. If they were acting, they were doing a very convincing job of it; under other circumstances she wouldn't have doubted for a moment that they had never before seen pizza, or tasted Pepsi. If they had claimed to be foreigners, or from some isolated little place somewhere, that would have been fine.

But they claimed to be, not just from another planet, but from another *universe.*

Believing that would mean changing her entire way of dealing with the world. She had long ago decided that she was never going to be rich or famous, never going to have any wild romances, never going to climb Mount Everest or fly to the Moon or do anything else exciting and dangerous. It was safer and more comfortable to just stay at home and read about all that. She didn't need to do anything herself.

And if the books weren't enough, there were her decorating clients, with all their little stories about where this knickknack or that had come from, or why they had moved here, or what all the gadgets in the kitchen were for. She got customers who were in the foreign service, back stateside for a couple of years, and most of them were eager to tell stories about their time in places like Qatar or Tanzania. She got some buyers who were immigrants, who had *grown up* in places like Morocco or Taiwan or Syria. Listening to them was better than actually going to all those exotic, dangerous places.

Meeting people like that was fine; she could find Syria and Taiwan on the maps, hear about them on the evening news. But she didn't want to *be* one of them. She didn't want anything exciting to happen to her.

And she had her tidy little ideas of how the world worked, of how everyone was alike, really, the world over. All those people shared a single planet, and despite all the differences in language and culture, they were all part of the same reality, and that reality didn't include purple and gold spaceships falling out of the sky, didn't include swordsmen in black velvet or wizards wearing braids.

If she believed these people, it meant losing control of what was real and what wasn't. If magic could be real, if spaceships could appear out of nowhere, how could she ever be sure of *anything?*

It would change her entire perception of the world — and she'd already done that once, when Stan had come home drunk that night, and beaten her, and then left her for that bitch in Florida. She didn't want to do it again. Last time she'd had to learn that the world was not going to look after her, that she couldn't have everything she wanted, that bad things could happen even to her — what would she have to learn this time? That she couldn't trust anything at all, not even the sky overhead?

She wanted to find some nice, rational explanation, like movie publicity stunts or escaped lunatics.

She didn't think she would.

But at least, if she could really take a look at this other world of Raven's, she would *know,* just as she had *known* when Stan knocked her down with his fist, when he swore at her and kicked her.

Better to *know,* and have it over with.

*T*he matter of taking a look through the portal was discussed further. The pizza was eaten, and several liters of Pepsi were consumed. And finally, around seven, Pel and Nancy herded everyone down the stairs to the basement. Pel had his old Instamatic in one pocket.

Rachel was staring around wide-eyed at all the funny clothes the different people were wearing.

Raven went down first, to lead the way; he crossed quickly to the appropriate area of blank wall and stood there, waiting.

Stoddard followed immediately, and stood a little to one side.

The crew of the *Ruthless* came next, and at Raven's direction lined up against one wall, out of the way. Cahn and Prossie brought up the rear. As Pel watched them descend he heard Soorn's voice, carrying by some fluke of acoustics, as he told one of the others, "I guess it's just as well we're trying this; I don't know if I could ever get used to any world where people eat that 'Pete Sah' stuff."

"I kind of liked it," someone replied — Mervyn, perhaps? Pel was unsure.

"It tasted okay, but it's so *gooey* — and what *were* all those things on top?"

Pel laughed involuntarily, and the conversation stopped abruptly.

Susan descended next, with Amy close behind. Ted followed, and Squire Donald immediately after. That left Valadrakul and the Browns at the head of the stairs.

"Go on," Pel told the wizard.

Valadrakul bowed to Nancy. "After you, my lady."

"I need to check the locks," she replied.

"We're only going to be gone for a minute," Pel protested.

"I don't care," Nancy said. "If we're leaving the house I want it locked up."

Pel opened his mouth to argue, then shut it again.

"All right," he said. "Go ahead."

The others all waited patiently while she turned and made sure that yes, the deadbolt was thrown on the front door, and the bar was in place on the sliding door in the family room. The empty pizza boxes, stacked on the family room coffee table, caught her eye. "Maybe I should clean those up," she said uncertainly.

"They can wait," Pel said. "We'll be right back."

She looked around, hesitating. Pel started to speak, but she yielded before he could say a word.

"Oh, all right," she said. She took Rachel's hand and descended the steps.

Valadrakul followed, and Pel came last of all.

As he came down the steps he looked around at the crowd. It seemed somehow more surreal seeing all those people in the basement than it had in the family room; after all, the family room had been used for parties on occasion, and guests there weren't unusual, but the basement was strictly Pel's territory, where nobody else ever ventured.

Or at least, it had been until now.

Now, though, there were eight men in purple uniforms lined up in front of the water heater and related plumbing; there were two well-dressed women and Pel's lawyer over by the gas furnace; and there were four medieval weirdos and two more people in purple uniforms milling about near the boxes of Christmas lights and old baby clothes.

Stoddard stepped forward, slid a palm along the concrete wall; Pel watched as his fingers seemed to sink in at one point.

Then the man-at-arms thrust his entire arm into what still looked like solid concrete. He stepped forward, and vanished into the wall.

"Come on," Squire Donald cried, with a wave of his arm. Then he, too, stepped forward and disappeared.

"All right, men," Cahn said. "You saw how it works. Drummond, take the point."

"Yes, sir." Drummond marched across the dusty floor and, with only the briefest hesitation, strode into the wall.

Pel watched, marveling. It looked unreal, like something from a movie — but at the same time, it wasn't quite like any movie he'd ever seen. No special effects were that good.

Uneasily, Peabody followed Drummond; then went Cartwright, Lampert, and Smith. Smith had his arms curled around in front of himself, and Pel wasn't sure whether he was hiding something, or simply making a protective gesture.

Soorn was next; he stopped and turned to Cahn.

"Captain," he said, "I don't like this."

"Oh, get on with it," Mervyn said, shoving Soorn forward; Soorn lost his balance, put out a hand to catch himself, and toppled through the wall into invisibility.

Mervyn snorted derisively, and followed. Godwin went next.

"Now you, Thorpe," Cahn said.

Prossie obeyed.

Cahn himself went next.

"Ready, ladies?" Ted said. He bounded across the basement in mockery of a ballet dancer, and leapt through.

At the last instant, as he vanished, Pel thought he saw surprise on the attorney's face. He frowned; Ted had been acting very odd ever since he first met Raven, and Pel didn't like it at all.

Amy and Susan looked at each other nervously.

"You don't have to do this," Susan said. "You saw them vanish; they're gone now. You can go upstairs and go home and get the ship hauled away and forget any of it ever happened."

Raven started to answer, and Valadrakul held up a restraining hand.

"No," Amy said. She drew a deep breath and then let it out slowly. "Thanks, Susan, but I want to see. I want to get it over with. I want to know whether it's real or not. I think it'd drive me crazy if I didn't." She threw back her shoulders and marched across the basement, but then she stopped before the wall and reached out tentatively.

Her fingers vanished, and she snatched them back.

They reappeared.

"It's cold!" she said, startled, reaching out again. "And there's nothing there! I mean, nothing solid. It's just like putting your fingers in front of an air conditioner." Her hand vanished, sinking into the wall up to the wrist.

"Our land's but newly freed of winter," Raven remarked. "Spring comes late this year."

Amy threw him a glance, took a deep breath, and stepped forward.

She disappeared.

Susan's expression was plainly unhappy. She tugged at the strap of her purse, a big black leather bag that hung from her shoulder, and then looked around at the handful of people remaining.

"You could wait in the car," Nancy suggested.

Susan shook her head, and without another word stepped into the wall.

Nancy looked at Pel. Rachel pressed up against her mother's side.

"What if we can't get back?" she asked.

"Oh, mistress," Raven said, "fear not! Let me show you." He stepped forward and vanished into the wall.

And, seconds later, he stepped back out, reappearing as suddenly and inexplicably as he had gone.

"See you?" he said. "'Tis nothing!"

Abruptly Amy reappeared — or rather, her head and shoulders did, thrusting out of the wall, reminding Pel uncomfortably of a mounted hunting trophy.

"Hi," she said, relieved. "Just making sure it really worked both ways."

"Certes, it does," Raven said.

"What's it like?" Nancy called.

Amy had vanished again too quickly to answer.

Rachel giggled, her fear vanished as completely as Captain Cahn's crew. "They look silly," she said.

"All right," Nancy said. "Let's go see for ourselves, then."

"Carry me?" Rachel asked, arms raised.

Nancy bent down and picked her up, and carried her through the portal.

Pel gestured to Raven and Valadrakul. "After you," he said.

Valadrakul bowed and stepped through; Raven hesitated.

"You'll come?" he asked. "You'll come, and see my homeland? You'll lend your advice? I value your opinion, friend Pel."

Pel grimaced. "What opinion?" he said. "I'm just going to take a quick look and come right back."

Raven frowned, then quickly recovered his composure. "As you wish," he said.

He stepped through, leaving Pel alone in the basement.

Pel took a deep breath, gathered his nerve, and walked up to the wall. He put out his hand.

As Amy had said, he felt nothing but cool air as his fingers vanished into the wall. He closed his eyes, unable to bring himself to advance with them open, and then took another step.

Coldness swept over him; a shiver ran through his body, starting at the shoulder and sliding down through his spine and into his knees. His eyes snapped open.

For a moment he saw nothing but darkness, felt nothing but the chill, and terror began to grow, weedlike, somewhere in the base of his skull.

Then the door opened, and wan sunlight spilled in, illuminating the inside of the hut.

He was in a hut, a small one, with no light, no windows — only the door. It seemed quite solid, quite real — and it was definitely no part of his basement. It smelled of wood and earth.

Pel let his breath out, and it puffed into visibility in the cold air. Nancy was outside, she and Rachel were standing there, facing away, but Nancy was looking back nervously, watching for Pel.

Raven was in the hut, holding the door open.

The others were all there, scattered about outside; he could hear their voices, and he glimpsed them through the doorway. Pel stepped forward.

The movement felt oddly wrong; the air seemed preternaturally thick, as if he were wading through a foot of water. He looked down, but there was no water, only the hard-packed dirt floor beneath his feet.

The smell of black loam, sawn wood, and pine sap, carried on the sharp, cold air, reached him and swept images of long-ago winter mornings into his mind, mornings when he had gone walking in the woods, or watched his father cut a point on a Christmas tree before fitting it into the inverted cone of the green steel holder. He turned his head to see where the smell came from, and for the first time really noticed the shed around him, and its contents.

On either side, logs were stacked neatly, almost to the low, slanting rafters. Behind him stood a simple wall of rough-hewn planks, with no door nor other opening visible, and he realized he had stepped through it.

He thrust out a hand; it vanished into the wall, up to the wrist, as if the planks were not there.

Reassured that the portal was still there, that he could return home whenever he wanted, he turned his attention elsewhere.

He was one of three people in the woodshed; Raven was another, but the third he did not recognize. He could not see her clearly in the gloom, but she was just below medium height — no more than five foot four, he was sure —

with long, dark hair and wearing heavy robes. She was not thin, he was sure of that, but he thought part of her bulk came from her thick garments. One oversized sleeve caught the light from the door, where he could get a good, clear look at it; it was dull red, and appeared to be wool.

"Hi," he said, giving her a little wave with one hand, and smiling in her general direction. "I'm Pel Brown."

"I am Elani," she said, speaking with an odd, musical accent, completely unlike Raven's nasal twang.

"Shall we have a look at my world, friend Pel?" Raven asked, with a gesture at the door.

Pel nodded. He turned away from Elani, and together the two men stepped out of the woodshed into the world.

Behind them, Elani began mumbling something Pel could not make out.

*I*t hadn't been any forty-eight hours, but Carrie had no intention of sticking to silly limitation like that when it came to her own lost cousin. She settled on her bed and reached out with her mind, reached in that inexplicable direction that led around the corners of reality into the "Earth" universe. She shaped her thoughts to fit Prossie's familiar patterns, and searched down through the nameless irreality for Prossie's thoughts.

She couldn't find them.

Prossie wasn't in that jail anymore.

Carrie could sense a sort of after-image that she knew was the general vicinity of the jail, perceptible because she had seen it through Prossie's thoughts earlier — but it was dead and empty. No telepath was there, not even one of the pitiful "psychics" of Earth, like that Ray Aldridge or that little girl, Angela. There were guards, and prisoners, but they were all Earth people, all telepathically dead; she could barely sense that they existed, and certainly couldn't communicate with them, in either direction.

Prossie wasn't there.

Well, that was good, wasn't it? She'd been released, then.

Or killed. Maybe Prossie had been wrong about the Earth people and their soft-hearted rules. Carrie began searching, casting a telepathic net farther afield, wider and thinner, hoping for some touch.

For a moment she thought she felt Prossie's presence, but before she could home in on it, it was gone. She pushed on, minute after minute. Sweat began to sheen her forehead; her hands and jaw trembled.

Prossie wasn't there.

She found Carleton Miletti and passed him by; she found Oram Blaisdell, and Angela Thompson, and Ray Aldridge.

She didn't find Prossie.

Miletti and Blaisdell and Aldridge didn't notice the contact, but little Angela sat up in bed and shouted, "Mr. Nobody!"

"Hush," Carrie told her. "Hush!"

"What is it, Mr. Nobody? Is something wrong?"

"Not really, Angie. I'm sorry, I didn't mean to bother you."

"You didn't bother me. Whatcha doing?"

Carrie sighed. "I'm looking for a friend of mine."

"Who?"

"Her name is Proserpine Thorpe."

"I'll go ask my mommy!"

Before Carrie could protest, Angie was out of bed and scampering down the stairs, shouting, "Mommy! Mommy!"

Margaret met her at the bottom step, relieved to see that Angie was intact — no visible blood, nothing torn, no broken toys or furniture in sight. "What is it, Angie?" she asked, kneeling so that she could meet her daughter face to face.

"It's Mr. Nobody," Angie explained. "He's lookin' for someone."

Carrie winced slightly. Why was Angie always so certain the voice in her head was a man?

Margaret Thompson sighed. "Is that all?"

Somewhat cowed, Angie said, "That's all."

"I thought Mr. Nobody was gone," Margaret said.

"He was. He came back."

Angie's mother considered that.

She didn't really understand Mr. Nobody. She had never had an invisible playmate as a child; she'd heard about them, read about them in the parenting books, but the whole idea didn't really make much sense to her. And Angie was so utterly certain that Mr. Nobody was real. Her conversations with him didn't seem like anything a three-year-old should be able to invent.

Angie had never claimed to see Mr. Nobody, or to know where he was; she only heard him. That didn't fit what the books described for imaginary companions.

Was it possible that someone really *was* communicating with Angie somehow?

"All right, then, who's Mr. Nobody looking for?" she asked.

For the first time Angie hesitated. Then she said, "Basurpathork."

"Who?" Margaret blinked. She had been expecting a more recognizable name than that.

"Someone named Basurpathork."

Margaret sighed again. A name like that settled it; Angie was just making it up. "I don't know any Ba . . . Pa . . . anyone by that name. Now, you go back to bed and tell Mr. Nobody to let you sleep, and in the morning I'll ask around."

Chastened, Angie said, "All right, Mommy." She turned and made her way slowly back to bed.

And on her own bed, Carrie was fighting back tears. She had only been searching for a few minutes, really, perhaps twenty in all, but that was enough. She was certain. Prossie was not on Earth. And she wasn't back in the Empire, or she'd have made contact herself.

Carrie knew then that her cousin Proserpine, her childhood playmate, was dead. She had to be. What other explanation could there be?

And dying in that hostile other universe, where her mind could not speak, she had died in telepathic silence, in the sort of loneliness that ordinary people lived with every day, but which telepaths contemplated only with dread.

Cut off by that hideous silence, her family hadn't even heard the death-cry.

Chapter Twelve

"Hey," Pel said as he emerged, "it's daylight!"

"Aye," Raven said. "'Tis an hour or so past dawn, here."

"But it's after seven!"

"Not here, it isn't," Captain Cahn told him.

Pel turned, startled.

Cahn and Valadrakul were standing to one side; to the other side, he realized, were Stoddard, Donald, Susan, and Amy.

"The others went on ahead," Susan told him. "Your little girl was pretty excited."

"Oh," Pel said. "Thanks."

He looked around.

He was standing in a small clearing of bare black dirt. Behind him stood the woodshed. In the center of the clearing was a great flat-topped stump — the tree that had once grown there must have been huge.

Ahead and to the left was a cabin, built of rough-hewn logs and chinked with something greyish; there were no windows on the near side, but a fieldstone chimney bisected it, and to the left of the chimney a brown drape of soft leather hung from a gray wood bar. From the way the drape hung and what he could see below its lower edge, Pel guessed it covered a door.

Between the cabin and the shed, to the left, was a sunny little garden — though it didn't look particularly inviting just now. Most of it consisted of neat, fresh-tilled furrows in the black earth; a few had new green shoots springing up.

Beyond the garden was a steep embankment covered with a tangle of dead weeds, old vines, and fresh growth.

Atop the embankment, and ahead and to the right, was forest — old-growth forest, trees that seemed to soar up almost out of sight before ending in a maze of bud-speckled, crisscrossing branches, brown vines layered onto the black trunks like threadbare carpet, dark green moss spilling down from the crotches and smeared like jam on one side of each trunk — the north, was it? Pel seemed to remember that moss grew thickest on the north sides of trees, sheltered from sun and storm.

To the left the sky, visible through the greys and browns of the lower forest and the green and gold of budding leaves high above, was a rich blue streaked with high, thin clouds; to the right it washed out to uneasy off-white surrounding a pale, almost colorless sun, low in the sky, that seemed dimmer and smaller than natural.

The light of that sun was thin and watery and seemed to spill between trees as if running down sheets of glass, giving the entire landscape a cool, unfriendly appearance.

The air smelled of damp earth and wood smoke and something faint and unpleasant. It chilled his face and hands, and he could feel his nose preparing to drip. His breath rose in thin white swirls.

He shivered, and not entirely from the cold.

There was no one thing that Pel could point to as being out of place, but the scene seemed subtly wrong. The air in his lungs felt thick and heavy, the ground pulled at his feet, the colors and even the light itself jarred somehow.

Then he realized one thing that was wrong — it was the wrong time of year, as well as the wrong time of day. It was spring, yes, but back home the leaves were out and the azaleas in bloom; here, the trees were still just budding.

If the details had been right, he might have taken a place like this for a rustic retreat, or perhaps a historical re-creation intended to give tourists a glimpse of a bygone life; in that moist chill, the pale light, the heavy air, it didn't seem right.

"If you go around the cabin," someone said, in a high-pitched voice that reminded Pel of Bernadette Peters, "you can get a look at Stormcrack Keep."

Pel turned and saw no one; he looked down, following the voice, and found a tiny person, like the one who had appeared in his basement, the one Raven had called Grummetty.

This one was not Grummetty; it was a woman, even smaller than Grummetty. She came no higher than the middle of Pel's shin. She wore a simple white cotton dress with a thick blue sweater over it for warmth, and had a knitted woolen cap pulled down over her ears. A thick black braid trailed down her back. She was sitting on a rock the size of Pel's fist.

"Oh," Pel said. "Is that where Nancy and Rachel went?"

"The lady with the little girl?"

"Yeah."

"That's where they went. Also all those men in the silly purple outfits." She pointed.

"Thank you," Pel said. He followed the pointing finger around the right side of the cabin.

There was a well-worn path consisting of a strip of bare earth between mounds of rotting dead leaves, beaten down until it was too hard to show footprints. Pel followed it.

Every step seemed to take an inordinate amount of effort; he stopped and looked down at his shoes, trying to figure it out.

"Heavier gravity than you're used to," a voice said.

He looked up to find Lieutenant Godwin up ahead, leaning against a tree and grinning at him.

"Heavier gravity?" Pel asked.

Godwin nodded. "I'd judge your planet at, oh, maybe 1.2 gees, tops," he said. "This place has to be at least 1.3. Not a big difference, but if you aren't used to it, I guess it must be pretty disconcerting."

"Earth's one gee," Pel said.

"Well, of course it is, on *your* scale," Godwin agreed. *"Our* scale uses Terra as a standard. I'd say Earth's at least 1.1, probably closer to 1.2."

"But Terra and Earth are the same thing . . ." Pel began.

He stopped, confused.

"No, no," Godwin said. "Your planet's Earth, right? Back home, nobody's called Terra Earth for a century or so. It's Terra."

"But we call *Earth* Terra . . ."

"You do? I thought you called it Earth."

"Well, we do, mostly." Pel stopped again.

"Then why don't we just leave it at that? We probably both have a dozen names for the old home planet, right? But you people said Earth, when we asked, and we call ours Terra. Seems convenient."

"I guess," Pel agreed, reluctantly. Godwin smiled patronizingly.

Pel did not care to be patronized, and resolved to carry on the conversation as if he talked to people from other universes regularly. "So your home planet has lower gravity than this?" he asked.

"Mine? Hard to say — about the same, I'd guess."

"But you just said . . ." Pel began, feeling his resolve vanish.

"No, no, Mr. Brown — *I'm* not from Terra. I'm from Pennington, also known as Kappa Orionis Two. My *grandparents* came from Terra."

"Ah, I see," Pel said.

Lieutenant Godwin did not look like a Martian; with his blond crew cut and broad shoulders and round face he looked like a farm boy from Minnesota. His accent even sounded about right for a farm boy from Minnesota. Still, he was claiming to be from another planet.

"Pennington, huh?" Pel asked.

"Yeah. Grew up on the South Continent, near New Salisbury — and don't pretend you know what I'm talking about, okay?" The patronizing expression became an outright grin.

"Okay, Lieutenant." Pel tried to smile in response, but the result was only a weak grimace.

"I'm going back to the woodshed, see if they've got the gateway set to send us home yet. I'll see you, Mr. Brown." He pushed away from the tree, saluted, ducked past Pel, and marched on.

Pel watched him go.

So they were setting up a portal to send the Imperials back to their own universe? That was quick work.

He didn't blame Godwin for wanting to hurry, though. This place of Raven's was uncomfortable. It was cold and damp and the light was wrong, and if Godwin was to be believed, the gravity was wrong.

Just then the forest and path and cabin all darkened, and Pel looked up.

A cloud had hidden the sun. More clouds seemed to be gathering.

What a nasty, unpleasant place. How could people want to live here? He shivered and walked on.

*P*rossie was not really surprised to discover that her telepathic talent was just as dead in Shadow's realm as it had been on Earth; her head still felt as if it were stuffed with wool that blocked out all the thoughts she would normally have heard.

It was a good thing she would not be here long; she hadn't had a chance to warn Carrie. If the poor girl tried to make contact, she'd be unable to find anyone, and would probably worry.

As soon as she got back into Imperial space — assuming that the wizards could really open the portal they had promised — she would call Carrie, let her know what had happened.

For now, though, she was looking over Shadow's native world; her superiors in Imperial Intelligence would want to know as much as possible about it. Not that she was particularly fond of her superiors, but every telepath worked either in Intelligence or the Signal Corps, or both — that was the price the Empire demanded for letting a bunch of subhuman mutants live — and the better she did her job, the better she would be treated, and the more respect her entire clan would receive.

The gravity was higher than she had expected, maybe a gee and a third. The air was thick and damp, so while the primary's light appeared to be further toward the blue end of the spectrum than average, that might partly be due to the atmospheric conditions.

The trees looked Terran, as far as she could tell, but she was no botanist. Some certainly looked, even to her untrained eye, like oaks, but she supposed that might be a result of parallel evolution of some sort.

The soil seemed to be rich enough.

The only locals she had seen so far were the ones who had been on Earth, three little people, and the "wizard" Elani. The little people were definitely alive and intelligent, unlike the remains she had seen in Imperial space; and whatever mechanisms the wizard used to create her effects, Prossie had been unable to spot them.

And Stormcrack Keep was a rudimentary fortress, too far away for any serious look at its defenses.

She had gotten that far in her work as an agent of Imperial Intelligence when someone said, "It's like a storybook castle — only it's real, isn't it?"

Prossie turned and found Mrs. Brown standing there, holding her little girl.

"Of course it's real," she said. "Why wouldn't it be?"

*A*my watched the others traipse off for their look at Stormcrack, but for her own part, she couldn't yet bring herself to move that far away from the gateway home.

And she couldn't leave Susan, who was even more frightened than she was herself.

And why shouldn't they be frightened? It was all real.

Even though Amy didn't want it to be, even though she had desperately hoped it would all turn out to be some incredibly complex fraud, it was all real.

She did want to look at the castle, to see it all — but it would take her a few moments to work up the nerve. She had to adjust.

Her safe little world had come apart at the seams.

Again.

*P*el could hear voices ahead; he turned a corner, around a huge oak, and found the rest of the party gathered in an open, grassy area, looking out across a wooded valley.

Nancy was holding Rachel in her arms as she spoke to Prossie; Ted was standing nearby, talking to Mervyn. Drummond was arguing with Soorn and Cartwright. Smith, Lampert, and Peabody were sitting on the grass, not talking to anyone, facing away from the path where Pel stood.

Pel stepped forward; Peabody turned and looked at him, and Pel realized he had missed someone.

Grummetty, or someone very much like him, was standing just in front of Peabody. So was somebody even smaller — another gnome, a young one.

"Hi," Pel said.

Several voices returned his greeting.

"See the castle, Daddy?" Rachel asked.

Pel looked out across the valley.

The land dropped away steeply from the clearing, in a slope that was almost a cliff, too steep for large trees to grow on; that provided the first real view of a broad area that Pel had seen since stepping through his basement wall. Up until now, everything had been bounded by trees and walls.

Here, though, he could see.

Below, at the foot of the steep slope, the forest continued, deep green and extending to either side, as endless as a river.

On the other side of the valley — or perhaps canyon — rose another cliff, symmetrical to the one on which they stood, perhaps a half-mile distant.

And atop that cliff stood Stormcrack Keep — such as it was.

The main body of the structure was of windowless stone, at least on the visible side; it was simply a solid, flat-faced mass of masonry. Pel had trouble judging the scale at such a distance, particularly since there were no other referents handy except the outsize trees, but he judged it to be perhaps a hundred feet across and forty feet high.

At one side rose the remains of a round tower, built of the same featureless grey stone. About ten or fifteen feet above the top of the keep wall it was pierced by several tall, narrow windows.

And about ten feet above that, it ended in jagged ruin, roof gone, walls shattered, a few blackened beam ends projecting from the rubble.

The whole thing was in the shadow of a cloud, as was the clearing where the new arrivals were; patches of light and shadow were gliding across the surrounding forests.

Most of the world seemed to be in shadow; the clouds were spreading.

All in all, Pel thought, the castle didn't look like much. He had seen far more interesting and elaborate ones when he toured Europe as a young man.

But Europe wasn't in his basement.

And, obviously, neither was this place, whatever it really was.

Up until now, he thought, he might eventually have been able to convince himself that the whole thing was an underground soundstage, or some sort of illusion done with mirrors and tapes, but that valley, and the castle on the far side — that was no illusion.

A hawk was gliding above the valley; a smaller bird, too far away for identification, vanished behind the ruined tower before the predator could spot it.

It was almost as if they had fallen into a fantasy novel — except that when he read fantasy novels he never had so many of the details, the leaves on the trees, the chill in the air, the slippery spot of mud under one foot, the fibers frayed from that tree root catching the pale sunlight. Fiction never had this solid reality.

"Can we go home now, Daddy?" Rachel asked.

"We figured you'd want to see the castle," Nancy explained, "so we waited . . ."

"It's cold," Rachel interrupted.

Nancy smiled. "But it's cold, and Rachel's tired — it must be about her bedtime, back home."

Pel nodded. "Sure," he said. "I just wanted to see." He put out a hand to the trunk of a nearby oak, and felt the cold, rough bark. "I guess it's all real."

Ted snorted; startled, Pel turned to face him.

"It's all a dream," Ted said. "And this place proves it."

Pel blinked. "What?"

"I'm dreaming, all of this and all of you — I mean, come on, you think this is real? Castles on cliffs? Fairies, or whatever those little guys are?"

Grummetty and the other one turned to glare angrily at Ted.

"Ted," Pel said, "if you're dreaming, what am *I* doing here? We can't be having the same dream!"

"Of course not," Ted agreed. "You aren't here at all; I'm just arguing with my subconscious. It doesn't like it when I know I'm dreaming."

"Come on," Nancy said, taking Pel's arm. "Let him think it's a dream if he likes."

With Nancy carrying Rachel on one arm and pressing Pel along with the other, they started back around the cabin. Ted's words nagged at Pel as he walked, and he turned for one more final look at the castle.

A beam of sunlight, breaking through the thickening clouds for a moment, sprayed color across the gray stone, and then vanished.

If they had fallen into a story, now they were about to climb back out. They had just been bit players, spear-carriers, part of the background.

"We should take a souvenir," Pel said. "Something to prove we were really here."

"Did you bring the camera?" Nancy asked, just as Pel remembered it.

He pulled it out of his pocket. "Hang on," he said. "Let me get a picture of the castle."

"Hurry up, Daddy," Rachel said, as Nancy stopped and turned.

Pel hurried; after all, he didn't *want* to be inside a story. He was quite sure that they always looked like a lot more fun from the outside, curled up reading somewhere, rather than living them. He took a quick snapshot of Stormcrack Keep and the surrounding greenery, then turned back toward the woodshed. "Let's go," he said.

He kept the camera ready in his hand, though.

Half a dozen paces down the path he paused and took a picture of the front of the cabin, with its two shuttered windows and leather-hung doorway and the huge trees to either side.

Then he snapped a quick shot of Nancy and Rachel on the path, the woodshed just barely visible through the trees.

Amy appeared as he did.

"I hope I didn't ruin your picture," she said. "I wanted to see the castle."

"Don't worry, it's no problem," Pel assured her. He stepped aside, as did Nancy, to let Amy squeeze by on the narrow path.

"Where's Susan?" Nancy asked.

"She wouldn't come," Amy said. "This whole thing has her really scared; she said she didn't want to get out of sight of that shed we came out of."

Nancy just nodded.

Before she and Pel could continue they heard another set of approaching footsteps; they glanced at each other and stayed where they were.

Lieutenant Godwin was returning. He said nothing, but threw them a quick salute as he strode past.

Pel and Nancy waited for a second or two, but no one else appeared; they turned and walked on, Pel snapping a picture every few steps.

Raven was standing at the end of the path, at the edge of the clearing, when they arrived. He smiled at them and stepped back.

"Saw you the Keep?" he asked.

"We saw it," Pel said.

Rachel, curled in her mother's arms, made a noise, but didn't say anything intelligible; Pel realized she was sucking her thumb. It was obviously time to get her home to bed.

"My home, once," Raven said. "'Tis in the hands of the foe now, and I dare not show my face there."

"Yeah," Pel said. He hesitated, then added, "I'm sorry, Raven. I can't think of any way to help."

"Ah, but you've seen naught as yet but this forester's holdings!"

"That's all we're *going* to see," Nancy announced. "Rachel's worn out, I'm tired, and we've seen enough. We're going home now."

"Ah? Oh, but . . ." Raven glanced at the shed, then uneasily at Pel.

"What's wrong?" Pel asked, suddenly nervous. He felt the muscles in his back tightening.

"Oh, 'tis naught," Raven said. "Save that . . that man Godwin, and the Captain Cahn."

"What about them?" Nancy asked.

"They were here, and you were not, and they spoke fair — I fear Elani is conjuring the portal to *their* realm."

"So?" Pel demanded.

Raven spread his hands. "Friend Pel," he said, "Elani is a sorceress of the first rank, but she can maintain only a single portal at any one time. To open a way to the Empire, she needs must allow the way to Earth to close."

"Damn it, Raven," Pel said angrily, "I *told* you we were only taking a quick look! Has she already begun? Maybe the portal's still open." He started toward the woodshed; he wanted to get *home,* back to normal reality, out of this fantastic setting he had stumbled into.

Raven reached out a restraining hand, and on the far side of the clearing Stoddard stepped over to block the door to the shed with his body.

"No, no, friend Pel," Raven said. "Know you no better? 'Tis folly to interrupt a mage at his work — or hers, as it be in this case."

Pel glared angrily at Raven, but could think of nothing worth saying; he fumed silently.

Rachel took her thumb out of her mouth and announced, "I wanna go home."

"So do I," Nancy said, hugging her closer.

"My lady," Raven said, "I assure you, at that instant that the last of these Imperials is vanished, that would not stay to our aid, then shall I command Elani to restore the way to your home."

"How long will *that* be?" Pel demanded.

Raven turned up his palms. "What know I of such magicks?" he asked. "Perhaps the fifth part of an hour, perhaps twice that — certainly no more than the half of an hour."

"Well," Pel said, reluctantly, "I guess we can stand to wait that long."

Rachel obviously didn't think so; she didn't quite cry, but her expression made it plain that she was holding back tears only by superhuman self-control. "I want Harvey!" she wailed. "I want to go to bed!"

"Harvey?" Raven asked, with an inquiring glance at Pel.

"Her stuffed alligator," Pel explained. "It's her favorite toy; she takes it to bed with her."

"Ah, poor weary poppet," Raven said, giving Rachel a sad, funny little smile. "It shan't be long, I promise you."

Leaves rustled, and Pel turned to find the crew of the *Ruthless* marching single-file down the trail toward him, Lieutenant Godwin at their head.

As he looked at the forest, Pel noticed that the daylight had dimmed; the path was now shadowy and dim. The clouds obscuring the sun were thicker and darker.

That was all they needed — to get caught in a thundershower in this already-uncomfortable world.

He stepped aside, and let the Imperials march on past him into the clearing.

Captain Cahn stepped out to confront them, and the march stopped; the crew stood at ease, facing their commander.

"All right, men," he said, "and you, Thorpe — you all know the situation.

We're on Shadow's home planet here, and we've been asked to aid the resistance to its rule. Our first duty is to the Empire, of course, and for that reason I've asked these people to open a warp to our own reality, to Base One if possible. Right now the woman Elani is working on it." Pel heard leaves rustle again, and he turned to see Amy and Ted strolling along the path toward the little clearing, side by side, not speaking.

He glanced around, and saw Susan standing by the corner of the woodshed, watching silently. They were all back from the cliff top.

"I'll be going through that warp," Cahn announced. "However, if any of you wish to volunteer to remain here and join the resistance, I'm willing to accept that and give orders allowing it. Now, the warp isn't ready yet. You have until it *is* ready to make your own personal decisions." He looked over the nine uniformed people before him, and nodded.

"That's it," he said. "I'll call you when we're ready. Until then, stay in this immediate area."

Leaves rustled yet again; startled, Pel turned to see Grummetty and the other gnome — no, little person — approaching. The other was a young man with a sparse blond beard, wearing a dark green hooded robe. Grummetty was attired just as he had been in Pel's basement, three days before.

Pel was about to say something, to point the little people out to Rachel, who didn't seem to have noticed them yet, when the ground shifted slightly beneath him.

Startled, he glanced down at his feet, then looked at Rachel and Nancy.

They had felt it, too — Nancy was staring at him, and Rachel had raised her head from her mother's shoulder and was looking about, puzzled.

Thunder roared overhead.

"What was . . ." Nancy began.

Then the ground burst open beneath them.

Chapter Thirteen

*P*el's first thought, as he began to fall backward, was that Ted was right after all. None of this was real; it was all a dream, and now he was waking up. The dream's superficial appearance of sanity and logic was disintegrating, and it was going to turn into the more usual irrational dream nonsense, or maybe a falling dream, maybe he was going to fall through the ground and fall for what would seem like hours, and then he would wake up, and he would be back in bed at home, where nobody had ever walked out of his basement wall with stories about spaceships in people's backyards or evil world-conquering wizards.

Or maybe he was falling out of bed, for the first time in years, and he would wake up on the bedroom floor.

Instead he landed on very solid, very cold, hard-packed ground, landed on his backside and one elbow. Nothing vanished or changed shape or behaved like anything in a dream — except for the head that had thrust up through the earth and knocked him off his feet.

It was black and smooth and hard, with great blazing red eyes and pushed-back pointed ears. More than anything else, it reminded Pel of the terror dogs in the first Ghostbusters movie — but it was larger. Much larger.

Much, much larger.

The head, which was all he could see, looked about the size of a Volkswagen Beetle.

It stank, like fresh sewage.

And no matter how much Pel wanted to think otherwise, it really didn't look like a special effect. It looked real.

Rachel was shrieking, one piercing wordless yell after another, as she watched the thing thrust itself upward. Black dirt seethed around it, and even over the shrieks Pel could hear the grinding noises it made.

Nancy started screaming as well, as she backed away with her daughter clutched tightly to her, but she used words: "Pel, no! Pel!"

Pel scrambled to his feet and backed up a step, watching the thing.

It was in a pit now; its movements had broken in a circle of dirt about twenty feet across, and the dirt had fallen inward, away — to *somewhere.* Pel wondered where. Did the thing have a *burrow* down there?

One of the huge trees beside the clearing swayed, and wood cracked some-where.

The head was not shaped like a dog's head, not now that he could see it all; the snout was much shorter, proportionately, than any dog's. Pel tried to find a comparison — the demon atop Bald Mountain, in Disney's "Fantasia," perhaps? There was a resemblance, but that was only an approximation.

The thing didn't look like anything he had ever seen, not really — not in real life, not in movies, not even just in his imagination. The muzzle wasn't human; the rest of the face wasn't really anything else.

A demon ape, perhaps? But no ape ever had floppy ears like that.

The head tilted back, the lower jaw pulling free of the crumbling dirt, and then the mouth opened. Pel braced for a roar or a bellow or a shriek.

None came. Instead of sound, new horrors spilled out, little black things that crawled and flapped and fluttered, things the size of a cat or a bat or an insect. They scampered and scuttled, knocking clods of dirt aside, rustling and thumping, but none squealed or grunted. The only voices Pel heard were human.

Thunder rumbled again; the daylight dimmed further.

People were shouting, Pel realized. He looked past the horrors in the pit and saw people on the far side, the crew of the *Ruthless,* and Raven and his comrades. They were crowding back against the woodshed, calling to each other.

Something hit the back of Pel's head, hard and sharp; he heard wings flapping, felt them beating against him, felt the rush of air, and he smelled rotting meat. He started forward, then turned.

The thing struck again, its claws tangling in his hair — it was glossy black, with wings and talons, and it was flapping and struggling, moving so fast that he couldn't get a good look at it.

It was obviously kin to the things in the pit, the things that had come from the monster's mouth, but it couldn't have come from there, there hadn't been time for any of those to have reached him.

He slapped at it, knocked it away, and it lunged at him again. He knocked it away again, knocked it to the ground, and this time he stamped on it.

He heard bone snap. He stamped again.

The thing was like a lizard with bat's wings, a *big* lizard, with fangs and talons and a four-foot wingspan. He had broken one wing, near the base, and it scurried for cover, limping slightly and dragging the broken wing behind it.

He turned for a glance back at the pit; dozens of creatures had poured from the big one's mouth, and now other things, things like snakes or great worms, things like a cross between a snake and a squid, were burrowing up out of the surrounding soil that the big one had loosened up in surfacing.

Pel started to turn, to head for the woods, but now he saw where the bat-lizard had come from — there were more of them, in the trees, and in the underbrush, and there were other creatures, things like furry dog-sized spiders, like fanged black stumps walking on pulled-up roots, like gigantic black rats. Oily fur glistened darkly, white teeth gleamed, eyes of red and gold and cat-green shone.

There were scores of them, all coming silently closer.

"Oh, shit," Pel said, his muscles tensing as he backed away slowly.

The shouting and screaming had faded somewhat, had blended with the grinding of the immense creature in the pit and the rustling of the creatures into a dull cacophony, and Pel heard the sudden loud crack clearly.

At first he thought it was a tree-limb snapping; he looked up, startled.

The shouts had suddenly ceased. He turned and looked across the pit, past the huge glaring head, at the people clustered around the woodshed.

Susan Nguyen was braced against the wall of the shed, her big black purse hanging open from one shoulder. She had a short-barreled revolver clutched in both hands, held out in front of her, pointed straight ahead. Something like a large black monkey lay face-down on the ground in front of her, oozing thin purple fluid.

Even from this distance, Pel could see she was trembling.

And most of the others were staring at her.

Still trembling, she heaved the gun a few inches to one side and took careful aim at the head in the pit; it was turning slowly toward her.

She fired, and her hands jerked with the recoil. Pel didn't see where the shot went; he heard the gunshot and saw the flash, but that was all.

"Come on!" someone shouted, tugging at Susan's arm.

Pel suddenly realized that there were fewer people over there than there should have been. Squire Donald was gone, and Prossie Thorpe, and maybe others.

"Nancy," he shouted, "run for the shed! Around the pit! They have the portal open!"

Nancy was already moving, carrying Rachel. Pel started after her.

One of the creatures landed black and writhing on a crewman's back —

Cartwright's, Pel thought it was — and the man screamed. Susan turned the gun, aimed at the monster, and then stopped as she realized she would have to shoot Cartwright, too.

Godwin was pulling at her arm, and she finally yielded; he yanked her around and thrust her through the door into the shed.

Something flashed red, and one of the monsters near the shed door exploded silently into bits of meat and bone.

"Valadrakul!" someone called.

Another creature exploded, this time with an audible bang.

Something was chewing on Pel's ankle, and he kicked it away and ran.

Godwin was by the door of the shed, herding people in; he grabbed Nancy's shoulder as she came within reach and shoved her through into the darkness.

Pel stopped, ready to turn and join Godwin in guarding the door, but Godwin's hand closed on his upper arm, closed *tight,* and Godwin's voice barked, "No civilians!"

He stumbled into the dark, into the shed that had now added the stink of urine to the smells of pine and earth; someone unseen, someone large who smelled of sweat, took him and thrust him at the back wall.

Pel's hand flew up to fend off a collision with the wall, and the wall wasn't there, he tumbled through the darkness into light, and fell forward rolling on sand, thinking for an instant, once again, that it was all a dream and now he would fall forever, or maybe wake up on the bedroom floor.

Then he landed, grit scraping his arm and cheek.

He blinked, and saw sunlight on fine white sand, sand that was cool against his cheek and hand, while the air was warm.

Sand?

Shouldn't he be back in his own basement?

Someone else tripped over his legs and fell, and Pel gathered his wits sufficiently to roll out of the way as others continued to appear.

He rolled over twice, ending on his back, and then sat up and looked around.

He was definitely not in his basement.

He was sitting on drifted sand, sand that stretched off in all directions, pierced here and there by outcroppings of weathered white stone. A few feet away was the largest outcropping in sight, a diagonally-upthrust slab of stone at least ten feet high.

The sand reached the horizon, but the horizon was too low, as if they were all sitting atop a gigantic dune.

As he watched, Amy stepped out of the slab of rock — that was clearly where the portal was. She was bleeding from scratches on her forehead, and something had torn up one side of her skirt.

Pel realized that his own ankle was bleeding; he dabbed at it ineffectually, getting blood on his fingers. The sand seemed to be helping it clot.

He hoped that that thing hadn't been venomous. The wound didn't look bad. It certainly didn't look as worrisome as the surrounding landscape.

This was not his basement. He had a horrible suspicion that it wasn't anywhere on Earth. It would appear that Elani had opened her portal to the Galactic Empire.

The plot thickens, he thought, fighting back an insane urge to giggle.

W hen Prossie fell through the back of the woodshed it was as if a door had been flung open, as if a faucet had been turned on; the wool was gone from her mind, and she could hear again!

For a long moment she gloried in the sensation, letting the shapeless thoughts of the entire galaxy pour through her. She didn't look for meaning, didn't try to find any individual thoughts; it was enough to have the raw "sound" of all those minds reaching her again.

But after a moment the realization came — that sound was weak and distant. Compared to Earth or Shadow's world, it was a thunderous, constant roar, of course, but still . . .

This was not Base One, obviously. There were no telepaths close by. There weren't even any *people* close by — not really — except for the ones who were coming through the warp.

It was only after she had come to this realization that she bothered to use her eyes, and noticed the barren wasteland around her.

P el hadn't expected the Empire to be an uninhabited wasteland; that didn't fit very well with any story he had read. He had been thinking more in terms of huge buildings and broad avenues.

Of course, Luke Skywalker's home planet had been a desert, hadn't it? Was that part of the Galactic Empire?

He knew he should stop thinking in terms of falling into a story; this was *real.* The idea, however, wouldn't go away — particularly not when the whole bizarre episode didn't end, but kept on happening. He left the wound on his ankle alone for a moment and looked around.

Nancy was sitting cross-legged on the sand a few feet away, holding Rachel tightly, rocking back and forth, trying to comfort the child. Rachel was crying, and her thin sobs were the only sound Pel could hear.

Susan was standing, watching the portal, her revolver in one hand, her purse hanging from her shoulder, the flap closed now, but the clasp still unfastened.

Squire Donald, too, stood a few feet away, his hands swinging uneasily at his sides, as if looking for something to hold onto.

Prossie Thorpe was walking slowly away, in the direction Pel tentatively identified as east, assuming that it was morning wherever he was. It felt like morning, somehow. She seemed to be paying no attention to anyone else.

C arrie sat up abruptly.
"Prossie?" she asked, inadvertently speaking aloud.
The contact was weak; wherever Prossie was, it was still a long way off.

"Hi, Carrie — I just wanted to let you know that I'm all right. We're back in Imperial space, I think, but I don't know just where. I'm going to track down someone local and find out. I'll get back to you when I know more."

"Prossie," Carrie said, "I was so . . . I thought you were dead!"

"For awhile," Prossie told her, "I thought so, too."

*T*he sun, Pel noticed, was the wrong color — it was very small and intensely white, not the washed-out pale yellow of the sun in Raven's world, but *white.* The sunlight was, for lack of a better term, *richer* than in the forest they had just left, but it was still not right. The air was thin and he felt lightheaded.

The person who had tripped over Pel's legs was Soorn; like Pel, he was now sitting on the sand.

Ted had followed Amy out of the stone; he was apparently uninjured.

Two of the little people, Grummetty and the woman, were standing beside Squire Donald — Pel had missed them at first. The woman had her hand to her stomach, as if she were ill, and Grummetty's expression was worried.

A fluttering black thing burst out of the rock, soaring upward into the thin air; Susan started to raise her pistol, but Squire Donald had his sword out before she could take aim. He shouted, "Leave it to me!"

The shout was startling — until he heard it, Pel hadn't realized how quiet this place was. It was as if everything was muffled somehow. Even Donald's shout seemed thin and weak.

The Squire slashed, and the thing tumbled to the sand, one wing hacked halfway off. Once it was down, Donald stepped up and proceeded to methodically chop it to pieces. His movements seemed oddly sharp, almost jerky; experimentally, Pel lifted his own hand, and found it seemed to almost fly up. It was buoyant, as if he were in water.

Even without Godwin telling him, he guessed that wherever he was now, the gravity was weaker than in Raven's world, weaker than on Earth.

Mervyn backed out of the stone, followed closely by Lampert.

"Where the hell are we?" Mervyn asked, as he looked around. As with Squire Donald's shout, his voice was muffled.

Before anyone could answer, Smith appeared, holding up what looked like a plastic club of some kind, and then Peabody. Peabody was holding his right arm in his left, trying to staunch the bleeding of a long gash in his forearm. His uniform sleeve hung in bloodstained tatters, and there were several scratches on his face; blood trickled down one cheek. Pel realized that Mervyn and Lampert and Smith had all been scratched up, as well.

And the club was a two-liter soda bottle, held by the neck — Pel could make out the Pepsi logo on the crumpled label. Smith must have brought it along from the Browns' basement.

Lieutenant Drummond appeared, limping, with a black creature clinging to his scalp; he snatched it off and flung it away. The creature flapped, tried to fly, but seemed unable to do so. Drummond hauled his blaster from his belt-holster, pointed it at the thing, and squeezed the trigger.

A sharp crack and an electric sizzle sounded, something flashed, and the black thing exploded. The scattered fragments were aflame, and shriveled quickly to black ash.

Half a dozen creatures came spilling through the portal then; Drummond blasted two of them out of the air, rather spectacularly, while Squire Donald skewered a third one with his sword.

Raven was next to emerge, sword drawn and dripping with ichor. Close behind came Captain Cahn, Valadrakul on his heels. More creatures accompanied them, and Drummond, Donald, and Raven disposed of several with blaster and blade.

They didn't get them all, Pel noticed, but on the other hand, the survivors weren't attacking; most of them appeared to be wandering aimlessly off across the landscape. A couple of the most gruesome specimens had collapsed, for no apparent reason, to lie twitching on the sands.

Lieutenant Godwin emerged, panting.

"Who's left?" Smith asked.

Peabody looked up from the improvised bandage Mervyn was binding around his gashed arm. "Where's Cartwright?" he asked.

"Down," Godwin said. "We couldn't get him."

"Who's left?" Smith repeated.

"All present but Cartwright, it looks like," Lampert announced.

"What about the Earth people?" Soorn asked.

"We're all here," Amy told him. "Mr. and Mrs. Brown, their little girl, their lawyer, me, Susan — that's everybody."

"What about the locals?" Mervyn asked, looking up from the bandage.

A larger creature, roughly the size and shape of a German Shepherd but slick and black and saber-toothed, burst through the portal; Raven impaled it on his sword, where it writhed briefly, and died.

Stoddard appeared close behind it, Elani cradled in his arms; his scabbard flopped about at his side, obviously empty. He staggered out onto the sand and fell to his knees.

A black tentacle reached out, and then abruptly fell to the ground, chopped off where it had emerged from the portal. Pel rose to his feet and moved slowly closer, staring in horrified fascination at the severed limb.

It twitched once, then lay still.

"No more," Raven announced. "The way is closed."

"Well, everybody made it, right?" Amy asked.

"Except Pete Cartwright," Godwin corrected her.

"Where's Dundry?" Grummetty called. "Has anyone seen him?"

"Who?" someone asked.

"Isn't he here?" someone else asked at the same moment.

"Be he not here?" Raven asked, frowning.

Grummetty shook his head.

Elani, trying to get to her feet, said, "I'm sorry, Grummetty. I could hold no longer."

"Perhaps he'll find refuge somewhere," Valadrakul suggested. Pel noticed for the first time that Valadrakul had lost the braid in front of his left ear, along with a patch of skin, leaving a red, oozing spot. Something black, like ash, was smeared across his face and his left hand, while his right was still clean.

Grummetty blinked, and drew his lips tight, but said nothing more.

"What about Cartwright?" Soorn asked.

For a moment no one spoke; then Raven cleared his throat. "You have my deepest sympathies, sir," Raven said, bowing to Captain Cahn, "on the death of your man Cartwright. He fought bravely and well, 'gainst a foe not his own."

Susan made a choking noise.

Nancy stood up, still holding Rachel, but said nothing. Rachel buried her face in her mother's shoulder.

"Captain," Mervyn said, *"where the hell are we?"*

Cahn looked about; so did most of the others, and an uneasy silence fell.

"It sure ain't my basement," Pel remarked, trying unsuccessfully to lighten the mood.

"I want to go home!" Rachel shrieked suddenly.

"'Twas Elani's spell that brought us hither," Raven said. "Speak, then, lady, and tell us — where are we?"

Elani, finally standing upright, hesitated, and then turned up her palms.

"I don't know," she said.

Chapter Fourteen

After a moment of general consternation, Susan demanded, "What do you mean, you don't know?"

"'Tis plain enough," Elani said, somewhat offended. "I know not where this place might be. I had not the time required to complete my incantation. I had called forth a portal to Messire Godwin's..." She hesitated, groping for a word. "World?"

"Universe," Godwin suggested.

"As you will, then — universe," Elani agreed. "But I'd no time to steer it small, and in this ... this universe there are many ... worlds? Planets?"

"Aye," Valadrakul said, as he dabbed lightly at the blood that seeped from his cheek. "They do call them by both names."

Elani nodded. "I had no time, as I said, to find the right one, in so many. So I found one where men dwell — that much, I could do — and cast forth the way, and opened it, and here we are."

"There are people here?" Amy said, scanning the empty horizon.

"Aye," Elani said. "Somewhere."

"It's not as bad as it might be, then," Cahn said. "If there really are people somewhere, and it's in our space, then the odds are that it's a part of the Galactic Empire — there aren't more than a dozen rebel worlds in all the galaxy, so far as I know."

"And how many worlds does your empire hold?" Squire Donald asked.

Cahn shrugged. "Not sure of the exact count just now," he said. "Something around thirty-one hundred."

"And how big are these worlds?" Donald asked. "How far must we travel to find whatever people there might be?"

"They come in all sizes," Cahn answered. "From the gravity, assuming a typical planetary density, I'd guess this one at, oh, six or seven thousand miles in diameter. A little smaller than Terra."

Donald nodded. "And your mile is, pray, how many feet?"

"Five thousand," Cahn replied.

Donald accepted that and withdrew to do some calculation.

Pel had listened with mounting discomfort.

This episode — this story, this series of events, whatever it was — was taking an unpleasant direction. He wanted to get out of it now. "That's all very interesting," he said, "but it's time for us to go home, now. Rachel's exhausted and terrified." He grimaced. "So am I, for that matter."

Raven turned to stare at him. "Friend Pel," he said, "perhaps you do not understand our situation."

"I understand it well enough," Pel said defensively. "I know what's going on. Shadow sent those things, right? The big monster and all the little ones? It found us somehow . . ."

"The portals," Elani said, interrupting. "It sensed the portals. I should have known that it would."

"Yeah, well," Pel said, "so it was the portals. Anyway, it found us, and it chased us all away from that place, whatever it was, and we wound up here, which is too bad for you guys, Raven and you others, I guess, because you can't go home. And it's not great for you others, Captain Cahn and the rest of you, because it looks like you're out in the middle of nowhere and it may take awhile to get home, but it's not bad, really, because at least you're in the right universe." He paused for breath, and saw Drummond nod.

"Well, for us Earthpeople," Pel continued, "I don't see that it makes any difference. Elani, here, can just open a portal to my basement, and we can go home and Rachel can go to bed and we can just forget any of this ever happened, right?"

Raven and Elani looked at each other unhappily.

"Friend Pel," Raven began.

"Stop calling me that!" Pel shouted, his anger sounding weak and futile in the thin air. "Elani, *right?* You can send us home?"

Silently, Elani shook her head.

"Messire Brown," Valadrakul said, "we are in another realm now, an alternate reality. In this place, our magic cannot work."

"I wanna go home!" Rachel cried.

Pel glared angrily.

"We're *stuck* here?" he said.

Amy, Nancy, and Susan had inched closer during the conversation; now all the Earth people but Ted were facing Raven, Donald, Stoddard, and the two wizards across a few feet of sand.

Raven nodded.

"Yes," he said, "I fear you are."

Pel looked about desperately, and saw the crew of the *Ruthless,* gathering to one side.

"They got to Earth, didn't they?" he said. "There's *some* way to get back!"

Raven looked at Cahn, who nodded. "If we can get back to Base One," he agreed, "there's the equipment there necessary to open a space warp back to your Earth."

"So how do we get there?" Pel asked. "Where's this Base One? Is it in this area?" A dreadful thought struck him. "Is it . . . is it even on this *planet?*"

"No," Cahn answered. "I don't know where the hell we are, but I know that much."

"We're on Psi Cassiopeia Two, Captain," Prossie Thorpe called from atop a distant outcropping.

Startled, everyone turned.

"I've made contact," she said happily. "Locally, I mean." She pointed eastward. "There's a small colony town about four hundred miles that way — Imperial, of course. If I can convince the governor there that I'm real, and not just a figment of his imagination, he can send a car or a hopper for us."

"Psi Cassiopeia Two?" Smith asked quietly.

Drummond shrugged. "I never heard of it," he muttered. "Must be way out in the middle of nowhere."

"Oh, it is!" Prossie called.

"Thorpe," Cahn called back, "watch it!"

"Sorry, Captain," she said, not sounding sorry at all. "It's so wonderful to have my talent back, though — I can't help it!"

Peabody saw Pel's puzzled look, and explained, "She can't possibly hear us talking, when she's all the way over there — not in this thin air, she can't. So she must be listening telepathically, and that's seriously against regulations, spying on your own people without orders."

Pel nodded, and asked, "What was that about convincing someone she's real?"

Peabody shrugged, then winced at what the motion did to his slashed arm. "I guess she's been calling someone," he said, "and the local brass never heard a telepath before and isn't sure he's hearing one now."

"Why wouldn't he have ever heard one before?" Nancy asked. "I thought you people used them all the time."

"Hey, there are three thousand inhabited planets in the Empire, and only four hundred telepaths," Peabody explained, "and more than half of those four hundred are serving communications duty in the Imperial Fleet. Hardly *anybody* outside the fleet's ever heard a telepath."

"Why are there so few?" Pel asked. "I mean, can't you train more?"

Peabody blinked in surprise, and threw Prossie a quick glance. Her attention was focused entirely on the eastern horizon; her crewmate leaned forward and raised his uninjured hand to shield his mouth as he whispered, "'Course you can't train more! It's something they're *born* with — you either have it or you don't." He threw Prossie another glance. "I mean, they're all mutants, really."

"Oh," Pel said.

Peabody nodded, and continued, "In fact, they're all one family — all descended from one woman. Prossie's great-great grandmother."

"Oh," Pel said. He considered, and then pointed out, "Well, then, they aren't really mutants — I mean, *she* was, but her kids weren't. The trait bred true, that's all."

Peabody pulled away slightly. "You making excuses for mutants, Mr. Brown?"

"No," Pel said, confused, "I don't think so."

"Good," Peabody said.

*A*my looked about her, then settled down and sat cross-legged on the sands.

That five-minute look at another world had gone wrong, just as she had feared it would. Now they needed to find this space warp thing.

Something would probably go wrong there, too.

Still, if everybody else could handle this, so could she. Her world had been snatched away from her, in an incredibly literal way, but she would just have to deal with it. She was still alive; that poor man Cartwright wasn't, she'd seen him fall with that *thing* ripping at his back, tearing away skin and cloth, but she herself was unhurt except for the little scratches that other horrid flying creature had given her — she hoped the scratches wouldn't get infected. Her skirt was torn up, but the scrapes on her leg hadn't even broken the skin.

All that blood, those monsters, that was gruesome, traumatic stuff, but she could handle it. She was a healthy, intelligent woman, and she was not going to let all this mess her up.

She'd been through all that. She could take anything the universe — or universes — cared to throw at her.

She glanced at Susan, who was sitting curled up, almost in foetal position.

Susan was Vietnamese, and hadn't she said something about already having seen enough war? Amy guessed that she must have been through hell as a girl, seen things that made those black monsters look like nothing.

She'd survived, though.

Well, maybe there were *some* things Amy wouldn't be able to handle, but she intended to try. She intended to be, like Susan, a survivor.

No matter what path her life was dragged down.

*S*ee you, friend Pel," Raven said, interrupting Pel's talk with Spaceman Peabody, "think you not, 'tis just as well that we found ourselves here, and not in your world?"

Pel glared at him. "How do you figure that?" he said.

"Because hence we can go, by means of the 'space-warp,' and all of us be sent safely home again. Had we reached your world, then I and mine would be trapped there."

"Would that be so bad?" Pel asked. "I mean, how can you go back? Those monsters were all over everything!" He kicked at a dead one that lay near his feet.

"Oh, I think they'll not stay," Raven said with an airy wave. "Shadow saw us fled, and will surely summon home its creatures, so that they might be dispatched elsewhere as needed."

"Maybe," Pel said, unconvinced.

"Where was that, anyway?" Nancy asked. "I mean, that place where we came out. It wasn't your castle, because we saw that across the valley."

"Certes, madam," Raven agreed. "We made our lodgings in the forester's cot of my ancestral lands, for my brother holds Stormcrack as vassal to Shadow, and in disgrace of our family's honor."

"Your *brother?*" Nancy threw Pel a worried glance.

"Aye," Raven said.

Pel decided that a change of subject was called for. "Those monsters that got through, before the portal closed," he said. "What's going to happen to them? Should we hunt them down and kill them?"

Peabody shook his head. "Don't need to," he said. "They'll die on their own."

"Will they?"

"Oh, sure — just ask Soorn. He was on the clean-up crew on Lambda Ceti Four. Those things can't live for long in normal space."

Pel glanced around, not at Soorn, but at Grummetty and the little woman. They were sitting side by side on the sand, arms around each other's shoulders. They looked pale; Pel wasn't certain whether that might be partly due to the abnormally-white light.

"What about them?" he asked, surreptitiously pointing a thumb.

Peabody and Raven followed his gesture.

Raven looked grim, and Peabody shrugged his good shoulder.

"I wouldn't make any long-term plans for them," Peabody said.

"Perchance poor Dundry was the fortunate one," Raven said. "An he found shelter, he might outlive us all; an he died, at the least it was quick."

"Dundry was the other one, the one in green?"

"Aye," Raven said, "Alella's son, by her first husband."

"I met Grummetty, but not the others," Pel said. "That's Alella, there?"

"Aye," Raven said. "Grummetty's wife."

"So Dundry was — I mean, is Grummetty's stepson?"

Raven nodded, making no comment on Pel's initial use of the past tense.

Pel took a surreptitious look at Grummetty.

"You know," he said, "Grummetty was in my basement for maybe ten minutes before he started getting sick. *Really* sick. He's been here longer than that, hasn't he? And he looks all right so far."

"Raise no hopes, friend Pel," Raven said. "Mayhap the death is slower here, for 'tis plain truth that this realm is not your own, but death is certain, all the same."

"Unless you can get them back through the . . . the warp in time, anyway,"

Nancy suggested.

Pel looked at her, and realized that Rachel had fallen asleep in her mother's arms.

"Do you want me to take her for awhile?" he offered.

"No, that's all right," Nancy said. "We're fine." She hesitated, then asked, "*Can* you get them back through the warp in time?"

Raven looked at Captain Cahn; he wasn't listening. He was discussing something else entirely with some of the others.

Pel looked at Peabody.

"Doubt it," he said, frowning. "I don't know just where the hell we are, even with the name, but if I never heard of it, it's got to be at least a week, probably a lot more, from Base One. If those gnomes could last a week here, we'd probably have caught a few of them alive sometime."

Pel's jaw dropped.

"A *week?*" he shouted.

"Yeah," Peabody said.

Pel turned and grabbed Raven by the front of his embroidered jacket. "A *week?* I can't spend a *week* here! I didn't even want to spend an *hour!* I have a business to run! I left the lights on, and the cat — what's going to happen to our cat?"

"I'm sorry, Pel Brown," Raven said, pulling Pel's hands away from his garments with surprising ease; he was even stronger than he looked.

"Pel," Nancy said worriedly, watching Grummetty and Alella, "this isn't our space any more than it's theirs. Are *we* going to be all right here?"

Pel glared at Raven.

"I know not, my lady," the nobleman said. "But I see no reason to fear. My people and Messire Peabody's have lived in each other's lands for months, even years, and suffered no ill; likewise, the neither took harm from our stay in your own realm. 'Tis only the creatures of Hrumph and Shadow and Elfindom, the creatures of magic, that cannot abide here."

"Sure, lady, don't worry about that," Peabody said. "You'll be fine." He hesitated, then added, "I'm sorry about your cat, though. Maybe the neighbors'll do something?"

"Yeah," Nancy agreed, stroking Rachel's hair. "Maybe. He'll have water, at least, if nobody closed the bathroom door."

For a few seconds they were silent, sunk in gloom; then a joyful shout, audible even in the thin air, roused them.

"Aircar on the way!" Prossie called. "No Imperial ships are available, so they're sending a car. Be here in a few hours!"

A ragged cheer went up, and quickly faded.

"We need to put up a marker, so it can spot us," Prossie added. "I'll tell them what it is."

That brought on a puzzled silence, followed by disjointed muttering, until finally somebody thought to start collecting the dead monsters, and fragments of monsters, into a heap.

"Should really show up, against all this white," Peabody remarked, wincing, as he used his injured arm to help steady a mashed spider-thing before heaving it onto the growing mound.

Pel, dragging something resembling a saber-toothed wolf, nodded. He hesitated, and then said, "I'm sorry about that man Cartwright," he said. "Was he . . . Did you know him well?"

Peabody turned away from the pile and shrugged. "Well enough," he said. He sighed. "It'll probably be me has to tell his wife back on Terra."

"Wife?" Nancy, still seated holding Rachel, looked up, startled.

Peabody nodded. "Cute little thing. Her name's Maureen; last I saw she was about seven months pregnant, probably had the kid by now. She and Pete have a place in New Dorset, in North Columbia."

Pel looked uneasily at Nancy; she stared at Peabody in horror.

"They sent him out there with his wife pregnant?" she demanded.

Peabody shrugged again. "Sure. It didn't look all that dangerous. It was supposed to be a diplomatic mission, after all — we didn't know we'd wind up fighting monsters in the middle of nowhere." He gestured at the surrounding landscape. "And we didn't expect to wind up *here*, either, but this doesn't look too bad."

Pel glanced around, at the cold white sand, the various people with torn clothing, bloodstains, and improvised bandages, the pale sun and too-close horizon. He stared for a moment at the heap of fanged, clawed, and tentacled horrors, all of them dead. He took a deep breath of the warm, thin, oddly flavorless air.

"Well, no one's attacking us, anyway," he said.

Peabody grimaced.

"At the moment," Pel added.

"Hours," Nancy said, looking at the corpses. "She said a few hours?"

Pel frowned and nodded.

"I'm going to get some sleep, then," Nancy said. "It must be after ten back home, and I'm tired."

Pel looked at his watch, and saw nothing; the display was blank. The light came on when he pushed the appropriate button, but had nothing to illuminate.

He shrugged. "I don't think it's really that late," he said, "but sure, if you like."

Nancy lowered Rachel gently to the sand, arranged her comfortably, then curled up beside her. Pel watched them silently.

He sat up himself for awhile, but eventually, for lack of anything better to do, he joined her.

He was awakened by Peabody jostling him. He blinked, sat up, and looked where the crewman pointed.

At first he didn't see anything. The sun had crossed the sky and was descending toward the western horizon; the air had progressed from warm to hot, while the sand on which he lay had also warmed, though far less. He peered out over the sand and rock, and finally spotted it.

A glittering object had appeared over the horizon and was coming quickly nearer.

"Oh, my God," he said, tensing. "Now what?"

"It's okay!" someone shouted. "That's our ride!"

Pel relaxed slightly, but remained wary as the thing neared. Someone — in the dimming light it took Pel a moment to recognize Mervyn — had improvised a small torch, somehow, and was waving it enthusiastically over his head, signalling to the approaching craft.

The vehicle was roughly the size and shape of a car, but had no wheels; instead it cruised along at roughly the height of Pel's head, with no visible means of support.

"It *is* just like Luke Skywalker's landspeeder," Nancy said, sitting up.

Pel looked at her questioningly. "Prossie said they had cars with anti-gravity — aircars, she called them," Nancy explained. "And I told Rachel they were like the one in 'Star Wars.' And they *are*, see?"

Pel nodded. The thing certainly traveled like the one in the movie.

It didn't much resemble it otherwise, though. It wasn't pink and battered. The cockpit wasn't open, and the lines were more bulbous than sleek. It was glossy black, with elaborate brass trim and numerous running lights in various colors, and it reminded Pel more of a 1953 Buick Roadmaster his father had once had than it did of anything else — though of course, the Buick had been festooned with chrome, rather than brass.

By this time the entire assorted party was awake, and everyone had noticed the approaching vehicle. They were all watching it, with varying intensity. Susan was frankly staring, her mouth open; Amy was a bit more restrained, while Ted was grinning like an idiot, as if the thing's appearance were something he had contrived himself that had turned out better than expected. Stoddard was watching other people as much as the aircar itself, judging their reactions to it; Squire Donald's expression was unreadable; Valadrakul's gaze seemed coolly appraising.

Most of the crew of the *Ruthless* seemed mildly relieved and completely unsurprised.

The aircar glided to a standstill and hovered over a slab of white rock, a few yards away. A window whirred open and a white-haired head thrust out.

"Proserpine Thorpe?" the man in the aircar called.

"Here!" Prossie replied, waving cheerfully.

The head swiveled around to peer at the telepath, then turned back to the main party and called, "Captain Cahn?"

"Yes," Cahn answered.

The man nodded, and pulled his head back inside the vehicle. An instant later, with a high-pitched whine, the aircar settled slowly to the ground.

Pel glanced at Nancy, making sure she and Rachel were all right, and then jogged toward it.

As he drew nearer, he saw that the resemblance to an old Buick was less than he had initially thought. The thing was bigger and far more complex, with exposed tubing in several places, running lights in yellow and green and red, and protuberances that Pel couldn't identify at all.

It also bore an elaborate gold seal on its side, showing a lion and unicorn rampant against a sunburst. That was not something Pel had expected — a ringed planet or a spaceship would have struck him as more appropriate. The gold-leaf beasts looked positively medieval, and made a curious contrast with the multicolored lights and all the other signs of a fairly high technology.

By the time Pel reached the aircar's side Captain Cahn had strode the three paces necessary to reach the vehicle and was already bent down, talking quietly with the driver through the open window.

Pel frowned; the vehicle had a pair of bucket seats in front, and two rows of three behind, rather than the two bench seats his father's car had had, but even so, there was no way the entire party could fit into it at once.

"It'll take three trips," the driver said, looking past Cahn, seeing Pel's expression and guessing the reason.

"Couldn't you have sent something larger?" Pel asked, struggling not to shout.

The driver grimaced. "Nope," he said. "This is it. Psi Cass the Deuce isn't exactly London; this bucket's about it for official transport. They were trying to scrounge up more, but for the first run, I'm all you get."

"We'll take the wounded first," Captain Cahn said, in a tone that implied argument was flatly impossible.

The driver nodded. "And I take the telepath, of course, right?"

"Of course," Captain Cahn agreed.

"What about my wife?" Pel asked. "And our daughter?"

"Second trip, probably," the driver replied, reaching for a lever.

Captain Cahn stepped back and turned, looking the group over and choosing who would go.

"Peabody, you go and get that arm looked at," he called. "Drummond, you're in charge, and get the leg taken care of. Wizard . . ." Elani and Valadrakul both looked up. Valadrakul's face was bloody, but he was basically intact; Elani was unmarked, but clearly suffering from exhaustion.

Pel was distracted by the driver clearing his throat. He turned, startled.

The driver's hand was on the polished wood knob atop a black lever, and he was glaring at Pel. Pel blinked.

"Step away, please," the driver said.

"Oh," Pel replied. He took a step back.

The driver pulled the lever, and the aircar made a noise like a vacuum cleaner warming up. It stirred, and then hovered, a few inches off the ground.

As the machine rose Pel felt suddenly off-balance, as if he were about to fall toward the aircar; he backed away another step, and the feeling vanished.

Peabody stepped up, apparently untroubled by any falling sensation; he opened a door and climbed in, then turned and held it open. Valadrakul handed in first Grummetty, and then Alella — they were far too small to board without assistance.

The two little people both rode in a single seat, the center one of the back row, with Peabody to one side. Elani went in next, taking the other side.

"Nobody else's hurt that bad, sir," Peabody said, leaning forward. "Why not take Mrs. Brown and the girl?"

Cahn frowned. "All right," he said. "If they want, but there isn't room for all three of them. If the mother and daughter go, the father waits here. You want to do that, Mr. Brown, or would you rather wait and all go together?"

Pel turned to Nancy.

Nancy looked down at Rachel, who was huddled, sound asleep, in her arms. She looked around at the empty sand, the descending sun, and the gleaming aircar.

"We'll wait," she said.

Cahn looked around.

"You two, then," he said, pointing to Susan and Amy. "I want *somebody* from your world in this group."

The two women glanced at each other, then stepped forward together and boarded.

A moment later the aircar was loaded — Prossie Thorpe rode shotgun in the front, Susan, Amy, and Lieutenant Drummond were in the second row, and Peabody, Elani, and the little people rode in back. Doors slammed, the engine sound rose to an ear-piercing shriek and then upward in pitch, into inaudibility, and the vehicle lifted from the ground, swung around, and began to pick up speed, back the direction it had come.

Pel had been standing too close; the backwash of the anti-gravity drive left him dizzy.

"Next load," Cahn said, "Lieutenant Godwin, you'll be in charge. You'll take the Browns, the other wizard, that Squire Donald, and Ben Lampert. The rest of us should all fit in the third."

There were answering nods, but Pel paid no attention. He was too busy watching the aircar as it disappeared over the horizon.

Despite the hot, dry air, he shivered.

A thought struck him, and he snatched out his camera; it appeared to have survived undamaged, thus far. He pointed it after the aircar, but it was too late; the vehicle was out of sight.

He sighed, and contented himself with snapping a quick shot of the remaining group, scattered on the sands.

Chapter Fifteen

Amy found herself seated in the exact center of the aircar, between Susan Nguyen and Lieutenant Drummond. The sound of the engines was not the same as any car or plane she had ridden before; it was a steady whine, and it took a few moments before she could adjust to it and block it out.

Drummond was obviously back on familiar ground — so to speak, since they were cruising about eight feet up. He was leaning back, relaxed and smiling. His injured leg was stretched out, the foot under the seat in front of him, while the other leg was bent, knee out to the side. His blond hair was matted with blood, and Amy wondered what had happened to his helmet. He had had a helmet before, she was certain.

Then she realized where she had seen him with his helmet on — stepping out of the *Ruthless* in her back yard. He had been the first to emerge from the ship.

Despite his wounds, he looked a lot happier now than he had then — and why not? He was on his way home.

Amy wasn't so lucky. She didn't know where she was headed.

She *hoped* it was home.

*T*he richness of telepathic contact was so wonderful, after the long drought on Earth and in Shadow's realm, that Prossie was tempted to just lean back in her seat and let the whine of the aircar's engine shut out distractions while she soaked in impressions — but she knew she couldn't do that. She had duties to attend to.

She sent a wordless status report to Carrie, back at Base One — Carrie and the family were always her first concern, of course, whatever her official orders might be. And Carrie would keep the higher-ups in the military hierarchy informed and happy, anyway, so that was all right.

Then there were plans to be made here on Psi Cass Two. They would need a ship, to get everybody back to Base One as soon as possible. That barbarian who called himself Raven, and his bodyguard Stoddard, and the rest of them, she supposed they would all be unspeakably valuable to Imperial Intelligence; Shadow was a top concern, and this was the first time a group of friendly natives from that universe had ever been found.

At least, as far as Prossie knew, it was, and as far as she was concerned that was definitive — if any telepath knew it, now that she was back in normal space and in contact with the family, she would know it, on some deep unconscious level. And if anyone who ever came anywhere near a telepath knew it, or if anyone a telepath contacted from a distance knew it, then the suspicion would leak through.

The telepaths all knew things they didn't know they knew, things that had registered deep in the back of the mind, far below consciousness — it was one of the more useful side-effects of their talent, really.

It was also one that they tried not to let normals know about. Prossie wasn't going to tell anyone that she knew how important these people were; she would let her superiors tell *her* how important they were.

And not just Shadow's people; the Earth people were potentially valuable, too. An entire new universe, with its own science — even if much of it didn't work here in the real world, that still had to be valuable.

Not that Under-Secretary Bascombe thought so. He thought the Earth people were barbarians.

Prossie knew better; she hadn't snooped deeply, but even a light brush showed her that their minds were rich, sophisticated, crammed with a wealth of stories and information. She couldn't even understand much of what she found in there — especially when she tried this Susan Nguyen, whose back-

ground was so different from the others, and who had spent her early childhood
speaking an utterly alien language.

Raven and company, on the other hand, *were* barbarians. Oh, they had their
own culture, with plenty of elaboration and ritual, and their wizards had a
great deal of esoteric knowledge about their "magic," but they had the single-
mindedness and ethnocentricity typical of primitives.

She conveyed all that to Carrie, in mental shorthand.

But then she turned her attention to the governor in Town — Psi Cass Two
had only one settlement, and nobody had bothered to think up a fancy name
for it yet.

A ship. They needed a ship. And Captain Cahn held a special commission
as emissary to Earth that, despite what he had told Raven, gave him plenipo-
tentiary powers.

And there were all those people still stuck out in the desert.

She had some arguing to do, to speed things along.

*R*aven watched the vehicle depart. No single part of it touched the sand
beneath, and yet these people denied the reality of magic?

What else was their science but another magic?

Yet deny it they did, always and vehemently. It was a curious thing indeed.

Would that the more ordinary, commonplace magic functioned in this
hellish realm wherein he had found refuge! Alas, he knew from the reports of
his compatriots and their spies that it did not and could not; the currents of
power that wizards tapped did not flow here, those lines of the web Shadow
had strung did not reach here, in this so-called Milky Empire.

What power was it, then, that these machines used? A pretty puzzle, that;
perhaps, were it solved, wizards of Elani and Valadrakul's ilk could draw upon
that same source. That was a thought for another day.

For the nonce, the need was to reach the heart of the Empire from this
barren outpost, and there to find the portal back to Stormcrack.

And of course, to bring through the Empire's men and machines, to do
battle with that infernal Shadow that had fallen upon all the true lands.

Thus, to ride the machines, this aircar, and then some other — would it be
as that other vehicle, in the realm named Earth?

Raven did not quail to face man or monster, with blade or less; he feared
not death, as must needs come to all in the end. Still, at the memory of that
ride his lips tightened.

He did not *trust* these machines, nor the men that built them!

*P*el's digital watch was still not working. He had no way of telling, therefore,
how long the aircar was gone.

It seemed like days. The sun — or rather, the star Psi Cassiopeia — vanished
below the horizon not long after the vehicle departed, and the air cooled

quickly. Darkness fell suddenly and more completely than the suburbanite Browns were accustomed to; there was no glow of street lamps and headlights, but only the light of a few million stars.

The stars were brighter and more numerous than Pel ever remembered seeing before, even on trips to the country, but that still hardly made up for the lack of a moon.

The air temperature dropped with astonishing speed once full dark had arrived; where the sands had seemed cool in the heat of the day, they were quickly the warmest thing around.

That, Pel thought, explained why they had been cool in the first place — the sand held the heat far better than the air, which had turned downright chilly. Captain Cahn used his blaster to heat the rock face where the portal had been, just like Lieutenant Sulu in an old Star Trek episode, and the party huddled around it, but in fact the night air was not actually as cold as all that — at its worst, it didn't approach freezing.

There was no food to be had, no supplies of any kind except the half-bottle of Pepsi that Smith had somehow hung onto throughout their adventures; there was nothing to do here, nowhere to go, no place worth exploring, just miles upon miles of empty sand and rock. The remaining travelers, whether from Earth, Terra, or Shadow's realm, had little choice but sleep.

Pel was very glad they had eaten the pizza *before* venturing through the basement wall; that ensured that hunger, while real, was not a serious problem. Rachel did complain, when she was awake, about being thirsty, but she accepted the fact that there was nothing to drink. Captain Cahn was holding the Pepsi in reserve, doling it out in capfuls as he deemed appropriate. He was very cautious about it, and nobody came away satisfied.

The captain did allow Rachel more than her share, Pel had to admit.

At least there were no live monsters, nor even shadows that monsters might hide in. Their situation was not pleasant, but neither was it particularly frightening. Mostly, it was simply dark, dull, and boring, and just chilly enough to make sleep difficult.

Pel had the feeling, sometimes during the long wait, that he ought to be *doing* something. A storybook hero would be doing something — Captain Kirk, or Arnold Schwartzenegger, or Horatio Hornblower wouldn't just sit and wait, would he?

But what could he do?

Besides, he wasn't a hero. If this whole mess was someone's great adventure, it probably wasn't his. He didn't feel like the star, but just a bit player. His role was to go along until he could get back home, out of the story entirely and back to real life.

Some time before dawn, when heating the rock didn't seem to be doing much good anymore, and maybe in part just because he was bored, Cahn set fire to the heap of dead monstrosities — that not only provided some warmth, but served as a beacon for any approaching rescue vehicles to home in on.

Unfortunately, it also stank horribly, making further sleep almost impossible.

The night seemed to drag on forever, but Pel suspected that it was really only five or six hours before Psi Cassiopeia again appeared on the eastern horizon. The star in question seemed to move considerably faster than Earth's sun.

Or rather, he corrected himself, the planet he was on rotated more swiftly than Earth.

The *planet* he was on — somehow, the concept of being on *another planet* was more mind-boggling than being in an entirely different universe.

Were those stars up there really more numerous than what he'd seen from Earth? He had no way of being sure. He was quite certain, though, that he saw no familiar constellations. The familiar planets, Venus and Jupiter and Saturn, were nowhere to be seen; if the Psi Cassiopeia system had other planets, he didn't see them, or at any rate he didn't recognize them as planets.

(There had to be at least one other, he told himself, or this place couldn't be Psi Cassiopeia *Two,* could it?)

The sun had only just cleared the horizon when its light glittered from something moving; Pel happened to be looking in the right direction, and let out a shriek at the sight.

Half a dozen drowsing people started, and a sudden babble arose.

Rachel screamed in terror, and Pel and Nancy rushed to comfort her.

"She was asleep before," Nancy pointed out. "She didn't see it."

"It's okay, Rae," Pel told her. "That's the magic car that's going to get us out of here and take us back . . ." He stopped. He didn't want to lie about that, to get her hopes up too high. " . . And take us somewhere we can maybe get a ship that will take us home."

"I wanna go home," Rachel agreed. "I want Harvey."

"Well, then, behave yourself, and we'll do everything we can to get you home. It's a long ride, I'm afraid . . ."

"Anything's better than sitting out here freezing," Nancy interrupted.

"Oh, for sure," Pel agreed. "But three or four hours, or whatever it is, sitting in a car isn't going to be much fun, either."

A moment later, as the aircar slowed to a stop, he added, "And it isn't that cold out here, anyway."

"You're wearing heavier clothes than I am," Nancy retorted — accurately, Pel had to admit. His shirt was definitely warmer than the flimsy blouse Nancy had on.

He had also been willing to sit closer to the smoldering signal-fire than Nancy had — she had always been more sensitive to smells than he, and close in the stench was unbearable.

"Daddy," Rachel asked, "are there *more* magic cars?" She pointed.

Pel turned, and saw that two more aircars were approaching, a blue one and another black one. His attention had been so focused on the first that he hadn't noticed them before.

"I guess so, Rae," he said.

Nancy frowned. "If they have more than one," she said, "then why didn't they send them all out here the *first* time? Why did we all have to spend the whole damn night out here freezing?"

Pel shrugged. "Ask him," he said, pointing to the driver — who was not, Pel noticed, the same man who had picked up the first group.

Nancy did just that.

"Didn't think of it, ma'am," he replied. "Or, well, actually, you see, the first time we weren't all that sure that the call was genuine, so we didn't want to send everything we had out on a rabbit hunt. We didn't have anything to go on but that telepath's say-so, and we don't have much truck with mutants out here, so we wanted to see she was on the level first. And then we needed Lennie to give us directions, so we had to wait until he got back . . ."

"There must have been *something,*" Nancy insisted.

The driver just shrugged. "I guess Lennie couldn't think of anything, ma'am."

The blue aircar was pulling up — it was smaller and sleeker, with a sort of central nose cone that made it resemble a Studebaker or an Edsel, rather than a Buick. Its color was a sort of robin's-egg blue that really didn't seem appropriate at all.

The other black one didn't look like anything Pel had ever seen before. Unlike the first two, it had no brasswork; its trim was painted matte black. Its lines were simpler than the others, and its running lights were few and simple and all yellow. It had a rather nasty air about it that Pel didn't care for; he hurried to load Nancy and Rachel into the back seat of the big one.

Lieutenant Godwin herded Valadrakul, Lampert, and Squire Donald into the middle seat, then took the front passenger seat himself.

Captain Cahn, Ted, and Raven boarded the little black aircar; the blue one took the others.

Pel saw the captain swig down the last trace of Pepsi, hardly more than a few drops, and then toss the empty onto the floor of the aircar before he climbed in.

"No luggage?" the driver of the Browns' car called back. "You folks got everything?"

His answer was a muttered chorus of assent.

"All right, then," the driver said. Engines whined, and one by one the three aircars lifted off, turned, and sped away. Pel took a final glance back at the faint column of smoke rising from the burning pile of dead Shadow-creatures, the odd bits of litter they had dropped here and there, and the endless rocks and sand.

That was one campsite he would remember, but would never miss.

Once they were airborne, the driver announced, "I heard the other bunch came in real hungry, so I figured you didn't have any food out here, and I brought shrewsburies."

Godwin and Lampert brightened visibly; the others looked at each other, puzzled.

It must be food of some sort, obviously, but Pel had no idea what a shrewsbury might be.

Not that he and the others cared very much. They were ravenous, having had nothing to eat for at least half a day.

"They're in the map box," the driver said, pointing to what Pel would have called a glove compartment.

Godwin opened the indicated container and pulled out a stack of objects wrapped in foil — not, Pel noted, in plastic, the way most foods were back home. From the size and shape, Pel guessed that they were sandwiches of some kind.

Godwin took the top one off the pile, then turned around, stretching, and passed the rest to Lampert. Lampert gave one each to Valadrakul and Donald, kept one himself, and passed the remaining four to Pel.

"Last one's mine," the driver called.

Pel took a moment to peel back a corner of the foil on each packet and look the contents over. They were, indeed, sandwiches; he guessed that for some reason the Imperials called sandwiches "shrewsburies" instead. Maybe there hadn't been an Earl of Sandwich in the Galactic Empire.

Or maybe this particular sort of sandwich was called a shrewsbury. The sandwiches, or shrewsburies, all appeared to be the same — white bread, yellow cheese, and a slab of pink lunchmeat, the exact nature of which was not clear.

The exact nature of the foil wasn't clear, either, Pel realized; at first glance he had assumed it was aluminum, but it didn't feel quite right.

Could it be tinfoil, perhaps? Some other details of the Galactic Empire seemed oddly old-fashioned; perhaps they still used tin, rather than aluminum, here. Or was their aluminum just processed differently, somehow? *Could* aluminum be different? Metallurgy wasn't something Pel knew about.

Well, it didn't matter. This was another universe, so why should the aluminum foil be the same?

Why should the sandwiches be the same, for that matter?

He didn't know, and right now he didn't much care. He handed one foil-wrapped sandwich to Nancy and one to Rachel, then handed one back to Lampert and unwrapped his own.

It was edible, but unexciting — there was no mayonnaise or other condiment, just bread, meat, and cheese, and the meat was bland — some sort of ham loaf, Pel decided.

A jug of lukewarm water was passed around, as well, and at the driver's request the used foil was collected and passed back to the front.

"The stuff isn't cheap, out here," the driver explained. "We re-use the metal."

Food and water improved Pel's condition considerably. However, once the last crumb was gone, the ride was, as Pel had expected, very dull indeed.

Rachel was fascinated for perhaps six or seven minutes by the fact that they were flying, and stared intently out the window as she chewed on her sandwich. She climbed on Nancy's lap for a better view, watching the sand and stone rush by below.

Around the eighth minute, the sandwich gone, she climbed back into her own seat and asked, for the first of what seemed like several hundred times, "When will we get there, Mommy?"

Pel sighed, and tried to ignore her.

He wished he had made a last visit to the impromptu latrine that had been established behind a rock. That particular discomfort at least served to distract him from Rachel's restlessness.

She shifted, squirmed, leaned this way and that, climbed from her seat onto first her mother's lap, and then her father's, before being forcibly placed back where she belonged, with her seat belt fastened securely.

(The seat belts, Pel noticed with something approaching astonishment, had actual *buckles* — metal rings with a hinged central prong that went through a hole in the strap, just like the belt he happened to be wearing. He wondered why a civilization that had interstellar travel made do with anything so primitive.)

Perhaps an hour after they were picked up, Rachel announced, "I have to go to the bathroom."

Pel, secretly relieved, passed this information forward to Lampert, who passed it on to the driver.

A moment later the vehicle settled to the ground — a stretch of empty sand indistinguishable from where they had started, save that the outcroppings were more scattered, and veined with something grayish, instead of being entirely pure white.

"Five minutes," the driver announced. "Stretch, do your business, whatever, but just five minutes and then we get airborne again."

Five minutes was plenty. The bleak surroundings were hardly an invitation to do anything beyond the necessary. That out of the way, when they were moving once again Rachel curled up quietly and went to sleep.

Pel found himself with no distractions at all, now. He stared out the windows.

The other two aircars were out of sight, presumably gone on ahead, and Pel wondered how the things navigated. The desert below all looked the same, to him.

Just as he thought that, of course, they sailed over a canyon, by far the most distinctive feature he had seen yet. That didn't explain how the driver — or was he a pilot? — knew where to go, though. Pel regretted sitting in back, where he could see nothing of the controls.

This whole new world — whole new *universe* — was all so strange . . .

Pel paused, blinked, and looked down at the upholstery.

There wasn't anything strange about that at all, he corrected himself. The brass-plated door handle and window crank were completely, utterly ordinary, if old-fashioned. Rachel was curled up asleep, fingers tangled in her hair, looking just as sweet as ever; Nancy, on the other side, was leaning against the glass, lost in her own thoughts, and she, too, was familiar.

But outside the car the sun was white, the horizon too near, the ground seven feet away, and instead of rolling over asphalt they were flying over an endless wilderness of lifeless sand.

It was the contrast of the strange and the familiar that was most troublesome, somehow.

For one thing, it made it all seem real. It wasn't a dream, where everything was odd, nor a theme park, where everything was clean and plastic, nor any other sort of fantasy. It was like a visit to a foreign country, in a way — like his trip to Mexico a few years back, where the strange and the familiar had been mixed, where he had bought Coca-Cola with thousand-peso notes, where Mayan ruins had been built of stones no different from those in his own back yard, where the tropic light had been clear and golden, shining on Volkswagens and concrete-block walls as well as palm trees and sandy beaches.

Here the light was wrong, the air was wrong, the gravity itself was wrong; cars flew, and monsters emerged from the earth, but still the door-handles were cheap brass, probably plate, and there were little flip-top ashtrays in the armrests.

He didn't like it at all. It was too real. In all his dreams, he had never once imagined cars with flip-top ashtrays in the armrests. In the science fiction books and stories he read no one ever mentioned flip-top ashtrays. If they mentioned ashtrays at all they were exotic devices of some sort, sucking away smoke and ash or evaporating cigarette butts in atomic disintegrators, not just dirty little metal dishes with chintzy lids that clicked open at the flick of a thumbnail.

Ashtrays — did that mean that the Galactic Empire had tobacco? There were no butts or ashes, so Pel could not be sure they actually *were* ashtrays at all, but that was certainly what they looked like.

How closely parallel to Earth *was* the Empire's homeworld, anyway?

And did he really want to know?

No, he decided, he just wanted to get *home*. Silly Cat (originally Sylvester, but long since shortened) would be seriously upset by now, his food supply probably exhausted, though he could still get water from the toilet — if no one had put the seat down or closed the bathroom door tight.

That mundane little worry somehow made the whole thing worse.

Pel wished he could just dismiss this entire adventure as a dream, as his imagination running amok, even as outright insanity accompanied by hallucinations, but it all felt too real, too solid and detailed. He never worried about toilet seats in his dreams.

He stared out at the sand and rocks sliding by.

*I*t might be, Raven bethought himself, that he was become accustomed to the uncanny. Else, it might likewise be that this aircar, as it was, rode higher and more smoothly than the groundcar at Earth, and thus removed from him the worst of the sensations.

He watched the bare sands that flashed beneath, and listened warily to the mutterings of Captain Cahn, in the forward right-hand seat, as he spoke, seemingly to some familiar spirit. The driver of the vehicle said naught, but paid all his heed to his craft — and that as it should be, minding the speed at which they flew.

Beside him, the man called Ted Deranian, the advocate for hire, dozed fitfully, twitching occasionally. Raven glanced at him.

That poor fool still thought the waking world to be a dream; did he then take his dreams for truth? Was he now, perhaps, back in his home, his strange and frightening life untroubled by the common affairs of empires?

Raven smiled to himself at the thought.

*P*el only realized he had dozed off when he woke up; the whine of the aircar's engine had changed.

They were descending, sinking down into a sort of open-topped box, comprised of four concrete walls painted battleship gray. Pel could see two doors in the wall directly ahead. They were already below the tops of the walls by the time he was awake enough to understand what was happening, so he saw nothing of the surrounding structures except a quick glimpse of black and gray rooftops.

"Welcome to town, folks!" the driver called back over his shoulder.

"What do you call this place?" Pel called back.

"Town," the driver replied, a bit embarrassed. "It's the only one on the planet, so we haven't bothered to give it a real name."

"The only one on the *planet?*" Nancy asked, as she roused Rachel.

"'Fraid so." With a bump, the aircar was down, and the engine's whine died away suddenly.

Hesitantly, Pel pulled at the door-handle.

The door opened and he stepped out, then turned to take Rachel from her mother. When the three of them were out, he took a look around.

They were in a bare, featureless enclosure perhaps fifty feet by eighty, standing on coarse gravel near one corner, surrounded by blank gray walls. The two doors at one end were the only way in or out; the only colors anywhere were the blue aircar, resting in the opposite corner, and the various running lights. The dark hues were in sharp contrast to the bright, pale sky overhead.

The third aircar was in a third corner, but even as Pel first spotted it its engines came on, and it rose upward, into the brightness above.

A car door slammed; Pel started, and turned to see that Lampert was standing nearby, one hand on the door as he looked around.

"Doesn't look like much, does it?" he said.

"No," Pel agreed.

The driver slammed his own door, on the other side of the aircar, and called, "Okay, folks, right on in, through the door on the left, please!"

The passengers obeyed, shuffling across the gravel and through the door; a man in a purple uniform, not quite the same as those worn by the crew of the *Ruthless,* held it open for them. He said nothing as they trudged past.

Inside they found themselves in a large, windowless and mostly-bare room, concrete walls painted a dull peach color, the floor grey tile, the ceiling off-white. The only furnishings were two rows of white stone benches, and some red-print-on-white posters on the walls. There were four doors, counting the one they had just entered through, one centered in each wall. Light came from white glass globes that hung from the ceiling, looking very much like ordinary electric lights.

Pel would have expected fluorescent fixtures instead, but there were none, only the globes.

People were sitting on the benches — Stoddard, Ted, Smith, Soorn, and Mervyn. They had obviously not yet had a chance to clean themselves up; scabbed-over scratches were still in evidence, sand in their hair, uniforms wrinkled and frayed. Ted's suit would probably never recover.

Stoddard looked up and smiled as the others trailed in; Soorn waved, and Smith called, "Hello! What kept you?"

Ted grinned foolishly and said nothing.

Mervyn ignored them all; he was leaning back against a wall with his eyes closed, and did not stir. Pel was unsure whether he was asleep or awake.

"Slow old bus," Lampert replied. "How long have you guys been here?"

Smith shrugged. "Maybe ten minutes. They called in the captain and the nut in the velvet just before you people came in. The two of them, and that one —" He pointed to Ted, who waved in reply. "— were here before we were. Don't know how long."

"The nut in the velvet" was obviously Raven. Pel hadn't thought of him in those terms.

If that was how they saw Raven, Pel wondered how the crewmen saw him — the nut with the kid? It was probably something just that impersonal and unflattering.

The man in the purple uniform closed the door and stood silently against the wall. Nancy and Rachel settled cautiously onto an empty bench.

"Oh, I guess I got here about ten minutes before you," Ted said to Smith. "I must say, this is the longest and most complicated dream I can ever remember having. I wonder if I have a lot of dreams like this, and I just don't remember them when I'm awake?"

Smith grimaced, and turned slightly away from Ted. Pel felt his own stomach shift uneasily.

That sandwich had been some time ago, and he never had gotten enough to drink, but still, Pel knew that his discomfort wasn't merely physical. It was Ted making him nervous. Ted was acting crazy — literally insane.

Well, Pel told himself, if they could just get him safely back home to Germantown, Maryland, it wouldn't matter if he thought he had dreamed the whole thing.

Pel wished he could think of it as *when* instead of *if.*

Chapter Sixteen

Raven listened with approval as Captain Cahn conversed with the local lordling, the so-called Governor. This Cahn had the makings of a good commander, and such was recognized even in so dismal a place as this. Put him in armor and a sword in his hand, and he'd be fit for the service of Stormcrack, fit even to lead a hundred men.

Ah, but to get him there . . .

Best to say nothing and leave it all to Cahn. These misbegotten fools doubtless thought Raven mad; were he to speak it would serve no good. Leave it, then, in terms of the Empire's good, the Empire's authority, and say nothing of the need to fight Shadow.

*P*rossie watched in admiration as Captain Cahn told the Governor what to do. It was really quite educational; he didn't shout, didn't argue, didn't ask anything. He used a sort of tight, determined anger to drive his thoughts and words, but Prossie doubted a non-telepath would sense any of that — the Captain was calm and efficient, simply taking his authority as a given.

And of course, it was quite real. The Empire had given its emissary pretty much a free hand, and the legal power to go with it.

The Governor couldn't really know that, though. He had no telepath to verify anything — Prossie worked for Cahn, and the Governor didn't know enough about telepaths to realize that that meant Cahn had the Empire's full blessing. His orders had always come by ship, prior to this.

For all he could prove, Cahn could be a rebel, a mutineer, a lunatic — but when Cahn spoke the Governor never doubted for a moment that he was just what he claimed to be.

Prossie could see the theory of how to do it, of course, but she couldn't possibly have done it herself; quite aside from the near-universal antipathy to telepaths, and aside from her sex, she just didn't have the knack. Watching Cahn was like listening to a first-rate musician. Prossie might read the same notes, might pick them out, but she didn't have the talent to make the same music.

Cahn was magnificent. Prossie had been relaying messages to the Governor, had been telling him much the same thing that Cahn was now saying, and had been virtually ignored, because she simply didn't have Cahn's presence and aura of authority; the Governor had made a few tentative gestures, but no more than that. Now that the Captain was here in person, though, he was getting instant compliance.

It took less than fifteen minutes to establish martial law, with Cahn himself in charge, and to commandeer much of what they needed.

*T*he stay in the waiting room hadn't been long — twelve minutes, according to Godwin, whose analog watch seemed to have survived better than Pel's digital one. Half a dozen of the purple-uniformed men had then appeared and escorted the party out.

The next stop was a crowded men's room — at least, for everyone except Nancy and Rachel, who had a ladies' room to themselves. Soap, towels, and various brushes were provided, and Pel emerged feeling much better than he had entered. Clothes were still torn and wrinkled, faces unshaven, but at least the worst of the dirt had been cleared away.

The facilities were indistinguishable from what Pel would have expected in a men's room back on Earth, in, say, a bus station or a rest station on an interstate — white tile, bare bulbs in wire cages overhead, green-painted steel partitions, white porcelain fixtures.

It was only when he ran water in the sink, and found himself bothered by something about how it flowed, that Pel was reminded that this was *not* Earth.

The difference wasn't really very great at all, he decided, watching the water, but *any* change in how water flowed was enough to make him uneasy.

It was slower, he realized. In the lighter gravity of Psi Cassiopeia Two, objects — including water — fell more slowly.

He had more or less adjusted to how the air and gravity *felt,* but he had had few opportunities to see anything fall. He stared.

Then he shrugged, and went on washing.

After clean-up came food — cafeteria food, served in a more or less standard-issue cafeteria, but that was quite good enough for the Browns at this point. Rachel gobbled two hot dogs — which were labeled "hot reds" — along with several dozen sugared french fries and large quantities of canned milk; Nancy tried the macaroni salad, frowned, and then settled on ham slices, green salad, and cold tea.

Pel took a "Homburg shrewsbury," which looked like a cheeseburger, and discovered that there was cornmeal and chopped onion in the meat, which appeared to be a blend of pork and beef, rather than pure beef.

Another quirk in the local cuisine, obviously, like the confectioner's sugar on Rachel's fries, or for that matter, the word "shrewsbury" replacing "sandwich."

It was edible, though, and he ate it, washing it down with watery root beer.

"Everything tastes funny," Rachel said, staring at her empty plate.

"Well, we're on another planet," Nancy said, throwing an uneasy glance at the smear of potato salad on the edge of her plate.

Pel said nothing; he had sampled a french fry and decided against eating any more. Rachel was quite right; everything *did* taste funny.

Well, why shouldn't it? This wasn't their own land. Foreign food was *always* strange at first.

He hoped that the stuff would nourish them. This was not only another planet, as Nancy had pointed out, but another *universe.* The molecules in the food could well be arranged differently — he vaguely recalled reading something about right-handed and left-handed proteins.

Well, the crew of the *Ruthless* hadn't had any visible problems with the pizza.

He wondered about the people from Shadow's universe — was this food strange to them, too?

What about the little people? Were they all right?

The later arrivals had not seen anyone from the first carload since arriving in Town, nor had Cahn and Raven rejoined them. The purple uniforms had denied knowing anything at all except where the group was to go next.

Pel stared down at the table, which was topped with black glass.

The cafeteria wasn't quite standard issue, really. The tables were steel and glass, the chair seats made of something like fiberglass on steel frames. It struck Pel suddenly that except for some trim in the aircar, he hadn't seen any wood in this entire place — none of the rooms had any woodwork, the chairs and benches and tables were all stone or steel or glass. Plastics and paper products were present, but scarce — the men's room had been equipped with fluffy white terry cloth towels, rather than paper towels. The cafeteria plates were ceramic, the napkins cloth, the flatware steel.

He hadn't seen any trees, anywhere, on this planet. There was nothing to make paper or wood out of. And most plastics were made from petroleum, weren't they? Petroleum came from dead dinosaurs — well, maybe not dinosaurs, but dead things from millions of years ago. A planet as lifeless as this probably had no oil deposits. For all Pel knew, there was no native life here at all.

"Okay, folks," someone called, "let's clean up and move on."

"Hell," Pel muttered. "Let them clean it up themselves." He did not find himself exactly brimming over with gratitude for the treatment he and his family had received here; while it was true they had been cleaned up and fed, they had hardly been pampered. After waiting around without any explanation, or any contact except the silent guards, Pel was hardly in a mood to show his hosts much consideration. He stood up and headed for the door, leaving his tray where it was.

Nancy and Rachel followed.

In a moment, the full dozen — the Browns, Valadrakul, Stoddard, Donald, Ted, Godwin, Smith, Soorn, Mervyn, and Lampert — were marching down another bare concrete corridor, with purple-clad guards ahead and behind.

Double doors swung open, and while two guards held them, others indicated that the visitors were to turn right into another corridor — but this one was not entirely empty. Captain Cahn and Raven of Stormcrack Keep were waiting there.

Smiles broke out, but after a few quick words of greeting there was no conversation.

Fourteen strong, the party continued down this new corridor, and through another set of doors — glass doors, this time — into a large glassed-in vestibule.

Pel scarcely had time to look out through the glass at the vast expanse of flat gray before he was swept on through another set of doors, out onto the gravel pavement.

Gravel — the tar in asphalt is another petroleum by-product, Pel realized.

For the first time he saw the exterior of the building he and the others had been in — a blank white concrete façade, only two stories, few windows. (Well, who needed windows? What was worth seeing on this bleak little world?) It extended several hundred yards in a gentle concave arc; the glass vestibule was the rightmost one of three, spaced well apart along the curve.

Red letters were painted above each of the vestibules, reading, "Welcome to Psi Cassiopeia II." The lettering had clearly been done by hand, and the letters were shaped a bit oddly.

That was to his left; to his right the gravel pavement ran for perhaps a hundred feet, and then gave way to white concrete.

The broad strip of gravel ran the full length of the building, however, and in fact continued on past each end of the arc; it appeared to Pel that it formed a full circle, around the circular concrete.

And on the concrete —

There were three of them.

The smallest and farthest away, almost directly across the circle from them, was about the size of a tractor-trailer combination, back on Pel's Earth; it had once been painted white, with red trim, but the paint had worn away in several places, exposing dull grey metal. A small bubble cockpit protruded from the top; two huge, swept-back fins adorned the sides. It rested on three legs; a hatch in its belly was open, and a ladder descended from the hatch to the pavement. Its lines were graceful, but it had obviously seen better days.

Flash Gordon, twenty years after, Pel thought.

He had never seen the *Ruthless*; had it looked something like that?

The largest, its bullet-shaped nose near the middle of the circle, was gigantic — the size of an ocean liner, perhaps, its tail assembly projecting well out over the gravel ring on the far side. It was also squat and ugly, its gray paint obviously several layers thick, its surface dented here and there. Three glass-and-steel observation blisters, reminding Pel of the gun turrets of a B-17, protruded near the nose. There were no fins or foils or trim, simply the immense cylinder, rounded at one end, flaring slightly at the other. Two support struts kept the thing from rolling over on its side in one direction; Pel assumed there were similar struts on the opposite side. He could see the outlines of three hatches in the behemoth's side, any one of them large enough for the smallest ship to fit through sideways, but all three were closed.

A freighter, probably, Pel guessed.

They were headed toward the third and closest spaceship — the three craft had to be spaceships. This one was midway between the others in size, and apparently newer, with green and gold paint that had not yet begun to flake or peel. The stern was adorned with a profusion of gracefully-swept-back fins. A door in the side was open, and a boarding stair in place.

"The others are already aboard," someone said.

It suddenly struck Pel that they were being herded aboard a spaceship — they were going to leave Psi Cassiopeia Two.

"Hey," he said, "we're leaving?"

Captain Cahn heard him, and turned to reply, "Yes, Mr. Brown — they're giving us a ride back to Base One, just as we wanted. Nine days, I'm told, and we should be back there, ready to send you and your family home to, uh . . . to Earth."

"But I thought . . . didn't your telepath Thorpe say there weren't any ships available, when we were out on the desert?"

Cahn nodded. "They *weren't* available — that freighter just got in this morning, they couldn't find the owner of that little one back there, and the liner here was just down, hadn't cleared quarantine yet. And none of these are Imperial property, you know; we've had to invoke martial law to get the use of the liner. Don't worry, Mr. Brown, we're doing the best we can to get you home just as fast as possible."

"But we haven't *seen* anything here yet!"

Someone snorted; someone else chuckled.

"Believe me, Mr. Brown," Cahn answered, amused, "you've seen everything worth seeing on *this* planet!"

Pel didn't argue; for one thing, Nancy was glaring at him. It was quite obvious that she wanted him to shut up and not do anything that might delay their return home, and he belatedly realized that *he* didn't want himself to do anything that might delay their return home, either.

Still, it seemed wrong, somehow, to visit another planet, an outpost of the vast Galactic Empire, and see nothing but a few hundred miles of desert and the spaceport waiting rooms.

This was another *planet*, after all, thousands of miles across, big enough for whole oceans and continents, entire new civilizations — and all he'd seen was a little of one town.

Maybe rushing home as quickly as possible wasn't all that necessary . . .

He cut his chain of thought right there.

Getting home as fast as possible *was* necessary. He had responsibilities there, Silly Cat not the least of them. He had a home and a business and friends and family, all of whom would be wondering what had become of him.

And while he might be in the Galactic Empire, he didn't have so much as a toothbrush with him.

The possibility of coming back here later, properly prepared, occurred to him. It was an idea, certainly.

If Earth had anything the Galactic Empire wanted, then they could probably open a healthy tourist trade; who wouldn't want to visit an entire new universe, with strange new worlds, different air and light and gravity — and where everybody spoke English?

The business prospects in that began to percolate through his mind. That was certainly full of marketing possibilities, and marketing was what he did, after all.

But on the other hand, the Empire didn't seem to be a particularly friendly place, and seemed to be unhappy about the very existence of other universes. It might well be that they wouldn't want tourists.

And Earth might not, in fact, have anything they wanted — would a culture with interstellar travel and the resources of a galaxy be interested in a single planet's output?

Looking around, Pel thought that they just might, at that. Psi Cassiopeia Two was a backwater, admittedly, but it seemed to him that what he'd seen of the Empire and its works wasn't all that impressive, in many ways. They did have anti-gravity, which was amazing and wonderful and useful and all that, and they had blasters, which were effective enough, but they seemed to be rather backward in their use of metals, and he hadn't seen anything using any sort of electronics anywhere — no digital clocks, no LED read-outs anywhere, certainly no computers. No one had even mentioned television.

There were innumerable possibilities, not just in tourism, but in trade of all sorts.

Where Shadow's universe fit into this he wasn't sure. And of course, he had no idea what the difficulties of inter-universal travel might be; so far, it had seemed simple enough, stepping through portals, but those had been magical portals, opened from Shadow's realm — the technologically-created space-warps the Empire used might not be so easy.

Scientifically-created space-warps, he corrected himself — the Empire didn't seem to like the word "technology" much, and preferred to call it "science."

Had the Empire considered the possibility of trade?

Oh, they must have, he told himself. How could they not? Just because nobody had mentioned it to him, because everything anyone had said so far was about diplomatic or military interactions, that didn't mean that no one had thought about trade.

Somebody must have thought of it. Surely, once the preliminaries of opening relations and dealing with Shadow were done, the Empire didn't intend to just shut itself off from Earth again!

He stumbled slightly, the toe of his shoe catching in an uneven patch of gravel, and brought himself back to the present reality. Right now, nobody was talking about doing business between universes, because right now they all needed to get back to Base One and pick up where they had left off, in coping with Shadow and its creatures.

Raven probably wasn't concerned with trade possibilities at all — he just wanted Stormcrack Keep back. Captain Cahn was just doing what he was told to do by his superiors, and not worrying about long-term consequences.

And there wasn't really much point in his worrying about them, either, he decided. He squeezed Rachel's hand, and on a sudden whim, leaned over and kissed Nancy on the cheek.

They stepped up from the gravel to the concrete pad, and marched on toward the ship. Pel could see her name now, painted on the side near the nose, in gleaming gold letters — *Emerald Princess.*

Captain Cahn stepped to one side at the foot of the steps, and started counting noses; Raven's boots clanged loudly on the metal steps as he led the way up, into the waiting vessel.

The narrow steps created a slight bottleneck, and the Browns had to wait their turns for a few seconds while Stoddard and Valadrakul and the rest sorted themselves out.

"Nine days," Nancy whispered, leaning over close so Rachel wouldn't hear. "The cat will be frantic!"

"*Everyone* will be frantic," Pel whispered back. "And unless these guys prove they're real, somehow, no one's going to believe our explanations."

"Well, we'll just say we were kidnapped by a UFO," Nancy said. "It's almost the truth, isn't it?"

Pel started to protest; this was real life, not the absurd fantasies of little men with big heads who went around mutilating cattle. Then he stopped, before a word had escaped him.

After all, if one other universe was trying to contact Earth and botching it, why couldn't there have been dozens, over the years? What if all those flying saucer stories were true?

Now *that* was a terrifying thought. Pel had grown up with science fiction and fantasy, in books and in movies and on TV, and while he enjoyed the stuff immensely, he'd always been very clear on where the line was between fantasy and reality.

Flying saucers and UFO abductions and psychics and all the rest of the material found in tabloid headlines he had always put on the "fantasy" side — and he'd considered them bad fantasy, at that.

But here he was, boarding a spaceship, and that woman, Prossie Thorpe, was a telepath — a psychic, in other words. He'd been abducted from Earth, after a fashion, and had found himself in a world of little men — though Grummetty's appearance in his basement had hardly been the stereotypical close encounter of the third kind. Grummetty had seemed thoroughly down to earth, despite his impossible size.

The stairway was clear, and Captain Cahn was waving them forward; Nancy went first, leading Rachel by the hand. Pel brought up the rear, with a steadying hand on Rachel's back.

As they climbed toward the warmly-lit doorway into the ship, Pel considered UFOs and the Galactic Empire.

This ship made *sense,* though. The people had an *explanation* for what was happening — the whole thing about Shadow and space-warps and telepaths all fit together. The space creatures in the UFO stories never made sense, flying around conducting mysterious experiments with no rhyme or reason to them, kidnapping people at random.

But on the other hand, would the *Emerald Princess* and all the rest make any sense to, say, an Australian aborigine?

Pel didn't know anything about Australian aborigines, but he suspected that it wouldn't.

Then he was at the door, being helped in by Susan Nguyen, of all people; she was wearing an unfamiliar outfit, a white blouse and maroon wool skirt combination cut oddly.

The door, or hatch, or whatever it was opened into a small chamber, presumably an air lock, painted in a friendly mustard color; a wine-colored drapery on one side incompletely hid a bank of gadgetry of some sort, probably the pressure controls.

The inner door was open; he stepped through into a room, or cabin, or compartment, whatever the correct term was, about the size and shape of a one-car garage. Amy Jewell, in white and maroon like her attorney, was standing there, welcoming people aboard; behind her was Spaceman Peabody, his arm in a cast and sling, the rest of him in one of the purple uniforms the guards had worn, rather than his own ruined outfit. Grummetty and Alella were perched atop a cabinet bolted to one wall — their clothes were the same, but somewhat cleaner.

A loud clang interrupted Pel before he could say more than a quick general hello; the last arrival, Captain Cahn, was aboard, and had just slammed the outer air lock door shut.

Now he was in the lounge, closing and locking the inner door as well.

Pel had looked first at the people, but now he considered the chamber in which he found himself.

The walls were covered in rich yellow wallpaper, flocked in a stylized floral design; the floor was covered in lush plum-colored carpet. The several doors leading elsewhere were dark polished wood, set with round, brass-rimmed windows. Plum-upholstered seating was bolted to the floor — two round things, like circular sofas, that reminded Pel of an old-fashioned hotel lobby. Light came from lanternlike brass fixtures on every wall. The overall impression, he decided, was of a turn-of-the-century ocean liner.

The *Titanic,* for example.

As Pel greeted the others he wished he hadn't thought of that particular comparison.

Chapter Seventeen

As had been obvious from the first glance at its interior, *Emerald Princess* was a luxury vessel; that it had stopped at Psi Cassiopeia Two was, Amy later learned, merely a lucky chance. Psi Cass the Deuce, as it was known, happened to lie along the route between Omicron Cygnus Three, better known as Avalon, and Alpha Ophiuchus Three, better known as Ishmael. Noticing that fact on the charts, the party of Avalonian tourists who had chartered *Emerald Princess,* bored by the long flight, had decided to stop in at Psi Cass, unaware that the planet was home to nothing more interesting than a small and rather dismal mining colony.

Amy hadn't noticed any mines, but she was assured that Psi Cass the Deuce was a mining colony.

From the point of view of the Avalonians their timing had been absolutely abominable. Pleas of injustice, threats of punitive action, and attempted bribery were all insufficient to prevent Captain Cahn and the local governor from using their authority, as agents of the Empire, to seize the ship temporarily, in order to transport the crew of *Ruthless,* along with people from two other universes, to Base One with all possible haste.

A suggestion that the freighter, or the battered little scout, be used instead was rejected; the freighter had no room for passengers and was too slow, and the scout was simply too small for the entire group.

The *Princess* was perfect.

Getting the entire group safely from Psi Cass the Deuce to Base One was obviously a matter of importance. If there had been any doubt of that, orders authorizing the seizure had come through, by way of Registered Telepath Thorpe, even before Captain Cahn had added his voice to the Governor's in suggesting it.

That the Governor had hesitated when Prossie relayed orders, and had only paid heed when Cahn showed up and started talking, was not mentioned in Amy's hearing.

Nor did anyone mention that the more desperate charter passengers had tried to throw doubt on Thorpe's reliability and trustworthiness. Once convinced, however, the Governor had been unyielding, and when word reached the Captain he was seriously offended. While it might be true that Thorpe, being a telepath, was a damnable mutant bitch, as one man had called her, she was *his* damnable mutant bitch, and no mere civilians were going to impugn her honesty and get away with it.

Cahn had made no explicit threats, but he did calmly point out that interfering with a ranking Imperial military officer in the performance of assigned duties could draw the death penalty. This remark was passed aboard by the same Town guards who had first informed Captain Gifford that his ship was being claimed by the Empire.

That ended the debate, and the frustrated passengers and crew of *Emerald Princess* had mostly huddled in the control room or the aft salon, complaining bitterly to each other, while the first batch of refugees, as they were now called, came aboard and sorted themselves out in the forward lounge.

This was the party that had been put aboard the first aircar, under the command of the limping but still mobile Lieutenant Alster Drummond; his second in command was Spaceman James Peabody, with his chewed-up arm. Prossie Thorpe was undamaged, and they had in tow Susan, Elani, Grummetty, and Alella, in addition to Amy.

This group, led by an armed and wary Lieutenant Drummond, came aboard while the later groups were still eating. They were greeted in the forward lounge by Captain Gifford and his chief steward.

Both sides seemed nervous, as if expecting a nasty confrontation; the sight of Drummond's hand on the butt of his blaster didn't help any. Blasters were not subtle little things, either; nobody would fail to notice the hardware.

Peabody, with his injured arm, made no move toward his own weapon. Prossie Thorpe, as a Special, carried no sidearm. Elani was carrying the two little people, who were both now seriously ill, and none of that threesome was very clear on just what was going on; they were also unarmed.

Still, that blaster was there, ready to draw.

And Amy noticed not just Drummond's weapon, but also that Susan's hand had strayed into her big black purse, as if fiddling with something; they were both stepping out of the air lock into the lounge before Amy realized what Susan was doing.

Susan had a gun of her own in that handbag, the pistol she'd fired at the monsters back in Raven's place — Raven's world, though Amy really didn't like thinking in terms of multiple worlds.

Did that mean Susan was ready to get into a firefight with these people? Amy couldn't really imagine that; she was glad that she had left her own gun safely at home. Using it to defend her house against Captain Cahn's men would have been one thing, and she thought she might have done that, but getting into a battle here, with all these people who presumably knew far more than she did about what was going on — no. No way.

But Susan was Susan; if she wanted to have her gun ready, Amy wasn't going to try to stop her.

And maybe she was right.

The spaceship's captain was eyeing his unwanted guests cautiously, very much aware of Lieutenant Drummond's blaster, but probably with no idea at all that Susan was armed.

For a moment they all stood there, not speaking.

Oddly, what finally broke the silence and settled the situation peacefully was Amy — to be precise, her appearance. When the chief steward finally looked past the tall threatening blond man in the rumpled, worn, and bloodstained Imperial uniform and saw the deep, half-cleaned scratches on Amy's forehead, the tattered condition of her flowered dress, his protective instincts took over. Here was a female in distress, and one who was to be a passenger aboard his ship, at that.

"Come in, my dear," he said, beckoning, "and we'll get you fixed up and find you something to wear!"

Susan made a small, wordless noise, and tugged at the jacket of her suit. Her hand was no longer in her purse, and Amy felt a definite relief upon seeing that.

"You, too," the steward said.

"If that's all right," the captain said, glaring at Drummond.

"Absolutely," Drummond said, smiling. "Excellent idea. We're going to be stuck with each other for awhile; I don't suppose anyone's going to like it, but there's no reason we can't make it as comfortable as possible."

The captain thawed slightly.

"I'm not going to interfere with the way you run your ship, Captain," Drummond continued, "and I'm sure Captain Cahn won't, either, just so long as you get us all to Base One as quickly as possible."

Captain Gifford nodded. "Yes, sir," he said.

*P*el and most of the others were blithely unaware of any prior conflict as they trickled in through the air lock. It didn't even occur to Pel to wonder whose ship he was on, or where the crew was, until someone else brought the subject up.

The earlier arrivals, once aboard and with Drummond's authority accepted, had sorted out the accommodations. Despite the complaints, the refugees posed no serious hardship to anyone. In fact, the ship wasn't even crowded; all the original complement had to do was double up, so that the unmarried passengers were two to a stateroom instead of one, and that provided enough space to fit the twenty-two refugees in at three or four to a room. Crew quarters, far less luxurious to begin with, were not disturbed at all.

The Browns were given a cabin for the three of them, with a double bed for Pel and Nancy a folding cot for Rachel.

Susan, Amy, Elani, and Prossie, the four unmarried women in the group, took the largest cabin aboard — a suite, actually, with a tiny sitting room and minuscule bedroom, one of two suites aboard the vessel.

Raven, Stoddard, and Drummond were grouped together, as were Godwin, Ted, and Valadrakul. Peabody, Lampert, and Squire Donald were assigned to a single room. The more observant noticed that this put at least one Imperial in each group of men — either one lieutenant or two spacemen — but nobody bothered to comment on the fact.

The other suite, opposite the one the unmarried women shared, went to Captain Cahn, who claimed the bedroom for himself, and left Smith, Soorn, and Mervyn occupying the sitting room.

The little people, Grummetty and Alella, were given an unused storage locker; since the ship's furnishings weren't suited to them, nobody saw any point in giving them a stateroom. They made no objection; the locker suited them just fine.

Besides, they were really too sick by then to care very much.

While these assignments were being made up forward, the twenty original passengers divided themselves into pairs for the ten remaining staterooms. Since that happened to work out to a nice even two to a room, there were no serious accusations of added unfairness or injustice.

By the time these arrangements were settled and explained Pel was thoroughly bored with the whole affair. He had begun to tune out the chatter and wonder how much time this group would waste before getting under way.

Nine days to Base One, they said, and there were bound to be delays there, as well — the Galactic Empire seemed to be full of delays. They did some things quickly and well — Prossie had made the original telepathic contact with Town within minutes — but others they seemed to dawdle on. It had taken forever, it seemed, to actually pick everyone up.

He probably wouldn't be home for another two weeks, at this rate. He worried about Silly Cat. He was pretty sure he had left the lid up on the upstairs toilet, so even if someone had closed the downstairs bathroom the animal could reach water, but the food in his bowl wouldn't last more than a day or two. The poor beast might well starve before Pel and Nancy and Rachel got home to feed him.

And God only knew what would become of Pel's business after more than a week of missed appointments. He had a report to write up for that computer dealer in Rockville, explaining why their radio ads weren't working — that wasn't getting done while he was here, instead of home.

"Mr. Brown," a steward said, startling him out of his gloomy thoughts.

"Yes?" Pel turned and found himself facing a young man in a white jacket and dark pants, with his crew cut and bristling mustache looking oddly mismatched.

"This way." The steward gestured toward a brightly-lit passageway.

"To where?"

"Your cabin, sir."

"Oh," Pel replied, feeling foolish. He brushed Nancy's arm to make sure she was paying attention, then followed the young crewman. Nancy and Rachel came close on his heels.

Their cabin was the fourth door on the left; it was moderate in size, perhaps ten feet square, with its own miniature bathroom and a more generous closet, all of it decorated in shades of blue. A square of royal blue velvet drapery hung above the bed.

The steward bowed and left, closing the door gently.

While Nancy and Rachel were examining the closet, Pel kneeled on the bed and pulled the curtain aside, revealing, as he had expected, a porthole.

At least, it looked like a porthole, but then he reconsidered. Perhaps it was a backlit painting on glass.

He shifted his angle of view slightly, and decided no, it was definitely a real window.

Beyond the porthole the sky was black and full of stars; the ship had taken off.

Pel had felt no jarring, no acceleration, but with anti-gravity that didn't seem to mean much. He stopped to listen, and could hear a faint, steady, high-pitched hum, but nothing like the roar of jet engines or rockets.

But then, with anti-gravity drive, why would you need rockets?

And there wasn't any weightlessness, but presumably, if the Empire had anti-gravity, they could also provide artificial gravity.

That took some of the fun out of a trip among the stars.

Then he paused in his chain of thought. *Were* those stars? Something looked wrong. They looked fake, somehow.

Was this a video screen, rather than a real porthole, perhaps? Or was it a glass painting after all, done with some unfamiliar technique?

If it was video, it was some kind he'd never seen before, something that made the best HDTV stuff he'd seen look primitive. It was *not* video. And he couldn't imagine any technique that would give a painting such a flawless illusion of depth. Was it a hologram, perhaps?

No, it had to be a real porthole. But then, what was it that looked wrong? He stared out at the star-spattered darkness for a moment, and finally figured it out.

The stars weren't twinkling. They burned as sharp and clear as tiny headlights, out there in the emptiness.

No air, he realized. There was no atmosphere blocking his view.

He had never really thought of stars on a clear night as "twinkling," despite the popular descriptions — not the way Christmas lights twinkled, or those spinning mirror balls. Stars didn't blink on and off, or anything even remotely similar to blinking.

He had to admit, however, that in comparison with the steady, sharp brilliance he saw now, stars back on Earth were dim, fidgety things. The intense points of light beyond the port looked quite unstarlike in their stability, their unchanging blaze.

Tearing his gaze away, he turned his attention back to the others. Nancy was bent over, bouncing her hands, stiff-armed, on the cot's mattress to show Rachel that the cot was sturdy enough to hold her.

"We're moving," Pel said.

Nancy looked up, startled; first she looked at Pel's face, and then past him at the porthole.

"Oh," she said.

"You stay here," Pel said. "I'm going back to the lounge."

Nancy nodded.

*T*he stars of the Galactic Empire, Raven noted, did not shine as the stars of home, but instead with a clear, hard light that was not particularly pleasant to look upon. He closed the little drapery.

A ship that sailed above the sky, and yet they disdained all talk of magic. Incomprehensible, these Imperials. The reports he had received had never fully conveyed their strangeness.

Consider, he thought to himself, that their lord Governor's palace, just departed, was built of bare stone, ugly and harsh — not even a fine stone like marble, nor any polished thing, but that unpleasant substance they called "concrete." Consider that it was, insofar as he had seen, furnished in the rudest fashion, almost unadorned, and lit everywhere in harsh and discomforting manner.

And then compare this vessel upon which they now rode, this mere transport, that by rights might be cramped and malodorous, bare of all luxuries, as had been every ship Raven had heretofore sailed upon.

Instead, though the chambers were small, it was rich in comforts, with the finest of fabrics and woods, with polished brasses and the warm glow of artificial fires. There was no rocking or sway, no stench; the ceilings rose well clear of even Stoddard's head. The beds were fine and soft.

What sort of people were these, who made their vehicles finer than the homes of their lords?

It was wisely said that men devote their most thoughts to that which is to them most important, and lavish the most care upon that they value most highly. Did then the Imperials place the transport of goods more highly than the administration of their colonies? An it were so, it spoke ill of them.

Or might it be perhaps that attention was paid to such craft as this because the distances in this realm were so great that more time was spent upon the journey than at the end thereof? This passage was to be nine days, which was no great time — but was this place just departed the most far-flung of the Imperial possessions?

It was all a mystery; indeed, the minds of all those around him, save his own handful of faithful allies, were as inscrutable as cats. Further, worrying at such a knot did nothing to aid him in all that mattered, to wit, the defeat of Shadow and the liberation of Stormcrack Keep.

He would, he swore, worry it no more. He flung himself upon the bed and closed his eyes, resolved to rest whilst the opportunity availed itself.

*P*el made his way back up the passageway, moving carefully — somehow, the knowledge that the ship was under way made the floor seem less steady than it had a few moments earlier.

He reached the lounge without incident. Amy and Susan were there, on one of the sofas, and Smith was leaning against a wall nearby, chatting with them — and trying to pick Amy up, Pel decided. A white-jacketed, brown-haired man Pel didn't recognize was standing quietly in one corner, observing.

Maybe he had designs on Susan, Pel mused, and was waiting for Smith and Amy to leave. He was presumably a crewman — another steward, perhaps.

Pel wandered in his direction, and the steward, or whatever he was, spotted his approach and quirked his eyebrows upward questioningly.

"Hi," Pel said.

"Hello," the other replied. "Was there something you wanted, sir?"

"I was wondering about our departure." He deliberately phrased this question with a certain ambiguity.

"It went quite smoothly, sir — all things considered. Captain Gifford piloted the ship himself."

Pel nodded.

"Are there any, um . . . viewports?"

"Yes, sir, of course — isn't there a port in your stateroom?"

Pel admitted there was. "But what I wanted," he explained, "was to get a look back at the planet."

The steward pursed his lips thoughtfully, then pulled a gold pocket-watch from his jacket and glanced at it.

"Come with me, sir," he said, as he put the watch away.

Pel followed as the steward led the way aft, explaining, "You won't be able to see much, sir; that military officer, Captain Cahn, has insisted on maximum acceleration, so we've already come a long way."

Pel nodded. He wasn't all that interested in seeing the close-up details, but he did want a look at the planet. He had never seen a planet from space.

He had never *been* in space before.

He was now, though. He supposed he should be impressed, or awed, or something, but he wasn't. Somehow, the mere fact that he was on a real starship, flying through outer space, didn't seem all that mind-boggling anymore.

Maybe, he thought wryly, he was all boggled out. The shock at Grummetty's appearance, at Raven, at the crew of the *Ruthless,* at stepping through into Raven's world, at the attack of the monsters, at finding himself on some strange planet he'd never heard of — he was having real trouble being boggled anymore.

The steward opened a door, and the two of them stepped into the aft salon.

Though still compact, it was a good deal more elaborate than the forward lounge; the crystal chandelier was the most obvious exemplar. The room was decorated in several shades of green, with gold and silver trim, and was inhabited by perhaps a dozen people, most of whom Pel did not recognize.

Before Pel had had a chance to look at any of the details, however, a familiar voice cried, "Ah, two more figments of my imagination!"

"Ted?" Pel turned, and saw his lawyer grinning maniacally at him.

"This one," Ted announced to everyone present, "is a simulacrum of a client of mine, one Pellinore Brown, freelance marketing consultant. It was he who supposedly got me involved in all this."

Pel glanced at the steward, who discreetly shrugged.

"He's been trying to tell us," an elegant redhead in a green evening gown explained, "that we're all just part of a dream he's having. I haven't decided if he's serious or not, and if he *is* serious, I haven't decided if he's crazy or just confused."

"Ted," Pel said, "what are you talking about?"

Ted leaned forward, still grinning. "I'm *talking*," he said, "about this interminable, boring, complicated dream I'm having. I've never had one quite like this before — at least, not that I can remember. This one just seems to go on and on."

"Have you been drinking?" Pel asked, uneasily.

"I don't know," Ted replied. "Have I? I really don't remember just *when* I went to sleep. Maybe I *was* drinking. That might have something to do with it."

"No," Pel said, "I meant here, now."

"In the dream? No, I haven't been dreaming about booze, oh figment of mine. Odd thing to ask — are you a subconscious worry that I might wind up an alcoholic, maybe? I've heard that alcoholics dream about booze, but as far as I recall, I've never done that. Maybe I've been suppressing it, eh? Maybe you're some little bit of my mind trying to break through a wall of denial and suppression, to warn me off the sauce before it's too late. But hell, figment, it's nowhere near that late, is it?"

"Ted, I'm not a figment. You're not dreaming. This is real." Pel hesitated, then added, "At least, I think it is."

"Well, if you're not a figment, what are you doing in my dream?" He smiled a humorless, challenging smile. "Are you a telepath, Brown? Sending psychic messages to me while I sleep? Is that why there are telepaths in this dream? I never thought about telepathy much before, that I can recall. So are you sending this to me?"

Pel glanced uneasily about; everyone else in the room, save the steward and the bartender at the far end, was staring at the two of them. The steward was carefully not looking anywhere; the bartender was polishing glasses.

"No, Ted," Pel said. "This is *real.* You are *not* dreaming. I swear you aren't. You're making a fool of yourself."

Ted shook his head vigorously and held up his hands as if pushing the very thought away.

"No, no, Pel," he said, "or figment, or alter ego, or whatever the hell you really are. This *is* a dream. It has to be."

Desperately, Pel said, *"No,* Ted! I know it's all strange, but it's *real!"*

"Nope," Ted replied. "Can't be. You think I don't know a dream when I see it? A bunch of bad swipes from Tolkien and Buck Rogers, all twisted around? Gotta be a dream."

"It *isn't,* Ted . . ."

"Pel, look," Ted interrupted, "I'm open-minded and all that, and if a spaceship landed on the White House lawn tomorrow I'd accept that — though I'd be amazed as hell, believe me. But this stuff is all too much. I mean, you hire me to bail a bunch of spacemen out on behalf of some guy out of Shakespeare by way of Brooklyn, and then we all eat pizza together and walk through your basement wall into somebody's back yard in Appalachia, except there's a castle on the next ridge, and then a bunch of El Greco monsters jump out at us and chase us through the wall into a bleached-out desert where the horizon's too close so it looks like a cheap Hollywood set, and we sit around for a few minutes except that dream time can stretch all out of shape so it seems like hours, and we get picked up by a flying Oldsmobile . . ."

"Buick," Pel corrected him. "I thought it looked more like a Buick."

"No," Ted said, shaking his head. "*You* went in the Buick. I was in the other one, the little one. But you're right, it wasn't much like an Oldsmobile. Reminded me a little of this primer-black Camaro my nephew has, actually."

"Ted . . ."

"*Anyway.* So I fly off in this car with the Shakespearean guy and the spaceship captain and a driver who thinks he's CIA, and halfway there the captain starts getting psychic flashes or something and talking to the air and telling us stuff, and none of it makes any sense, so then we land at what looks like the Pittsburgh Greyhound station and eat a dinner that all tastes like tofu, and then we get aboard a spaceship that looks like the Emerald City turned sideways on the outside, and like a French whorehouse inside, and here we are."

"That's right, here we . . ." Pel began, soothingly.

Ted paid no attention to Pel's interruption; he demanded, "And you're trying to tell me all this crap is *real?*"

"*Yes,* damn it!" Pel glared at Ted. "Yes, it's real, and I'm telling you that!"

Ted stared back, his expression merely mild surprise — no anger, no doubt at all.

"But, figment," he said, "it's *silly.*"

"*Life* is silly, Ted," Pel told him. "I mean, think about it — isn't it all a bit ridiculous? But it's real. And all this is real, too."

Ted simply grinned foolishly at him.

"Sir," the steward suggested quietly, "if you want to see Psi Cassiopeia Two . . ."

"Right," Pel said, turning away from the silent Ted. "Lead the way."

The steward led the way to the curved rear wall, where a window, perhaps two feet high and six feet wide, was centered.

This gave a view looking back over the tail assembly; Pel stretched up, peering out the topmost part of the glass, trying to see the planet. The tail of the ship was apparently hiding it.

All he could see was stars.

And the stars were mostly various shades of orange; they covered a range from pale yellow to deep red. Pel supposed the glass was tinted, though the green paint on the ship's tail looked its natural color.

"Where is it?" he asked.

The steward pointed. "Right there," he said. "That big faint one."

"Big one?" Pel followed the pointing finger, and found a pale orange dot of light, virtually indistinguishable from all the others, save that it seemed marginally larger and not very bright.

It did have one odd feature, he realized after staring for a few seconds. It was shrinking, while all the other stars remained constant.

"I didn't realize we'd come so far," he said at last.

"Oh, yes, sir," the steward said, beaming modestly. "*Emerald Princess* is a very fast ship."

"How fast?" Pel asked, looking away from the window. "Nine days to Base

One — how fast is that?"

"Oh, our top speed is around point three."

"Of C?"

"No, sir — I don't know that term. I mean, point three light-years per hour."

Pel turned to stare at him. "Light-years per hour? It's faster than light?"

The steward smiled at him, almost smirking. "Well, of *course* it is, sir," he said. "How else is interstellar travel possible?"

"You don't use space warps or something like that?" Pel asked.

The steward looked puzzled. "No, sir," he said.

Pel turned back to the glass. "Is that . . . the color out there . . ."

The steward glanced at the window. "Yes, sir, the red shift is quite visible now, isn't it? You'll see a bit more of that, but then in a little while, when we pass the speed of light, you won't be able to see anything at all looking out in this direction."

"So what happens then, do we pop into hyperspace or something?"

"Hyperspace?"

Pel turned, exasperated. "Look, *I* don't know your terminology! I mean, you can't go faster than light in normal space, right?"

"You can't?" The steward looked baffled. "Why not? What other kind of space is there?"

"*I* don't know," Pel snarled. His grasp of the theory of relativity was sufficiently weak that he had no intention of trying to explain it to someone — and most particularly, someone who worked on a spaceship and ought to *know* all that stuff. He glanced out the window again, and an unpleasant thought struck him.

Maybe this wasn't normal space, as he understood the term. It certainly wasn't *his* space.

Maybe this universe had entirely different rules.

Maybe here, everything he knew was wrong. Everything he had learned in a lifetime of dealing with his own world was open to question.

He had been thinking of his situation in terms of having stumbled into a science fiction story of some sort — something with spaceships and rayguns and monsters, but still grounded in logic and common sense. But if the laws of physics were different, then *anything* might be possible.

It wasn't science fiction at all, it was fantasy. He might as well be in the twilight zone.

Or in a dream.

He backed away, then turned, all his confusion and frustration boiling up in him at once.

He found the elegant redhead standing there waiting for him. "Mr. Brown, is it?" she asked.

"Excuse me," he said, pushing past her. Right now he did not want to talk to some stranger from another universe, no matter what she looked like.

She turned to stare, and the other strangers made way for him as he stamped across the room to Ted.

Ted, bemused, watched him come.

Pel grabbed the lawyer by his lapels.

"Listen," he said, "what would it take to convince you that this is real, and not a dream? Would a punch in the nose do it? I mean, if it hurt, just like real life?"

Ted considered this quite seriously. He looked around the room, at the oddly but splendidly dressed passengers, at the dimming orange stars beyond the window, at the crystal chandelier and the brass railings.

"I don't think so," he said. "It'd probably just mean I fell out of bed. It might wake me up, though."

Pel nodded.

"Let's see," he said, as he swung.

The steward was almost in time to stop him, and his restraining arm, flung up in front of Pel's, slowed the impact; Ted staggered, nose red and starting to bleed, but he didn't fall, and nothing broke. He made no protest, no defense, and no counter-attack. After the blow had landed he simply stood, staring blankly at Pel.

"*Sir,*" the steward began, shocked.

"Oh, shut up," Pel replied, as he stalked off toward his cabin.

Chapter Eighteen

By the time they were two days out from Psi Cassiopeia Two, Pel understood why the original complement aboard the *Princess* had wanted to land there in the first place.

Space travel was *boring*.

It was very nearly as boring as, though far more comfortable than, sitting out in the desert waiting for the aircar to come back.

Obviously, anything that broke the monotony would be welcome, even if it was just a stopover somewhere like Town — which Pel, angrily remembering Ted's words, had to admit probably did resemble the Pittsburgh bus station more than it did anything else.

So much for the romance and adventure of being in another universe.

The fact that none of them had so much as a toothbrush in the way of supplies didn't help any. Having to either wear the same clothes constantly or borrow ill-fitting substitutes from condescending strangers was a constant irritation for them all; Amy and Susan had wound up with spare stewardess uniforms, but there hadn't been enough of those to go around even for the women, so the crew and the original passengers had made donations to the poor, pitiful refugees.

"Condescending" was the politest word Pel could apply to their attitude. He would have paid his entire fortune for a well-packed suitcase — preferably one with a couple of paperbacks in it. A nice trashy novel would have been just right for passing the time.

Pel had initially assumed that the ship would have some sort of library, or a theater of some sort — just a VCR hooked to a TV would have been wonderful. This assumption had not panned out; some of the paying passengers had brought their own books, but there was no library, and none of the people native to this universe seemed to understand what he was talking about when he mentioned "TV," or "video," or "VCR."

Movies they understood, films, motion pictures — though Pel had the impression that they only knew silents, that the Empire hadn't yet developed talkies. In any case, there weren't any films on board.

And books were too bulky. Keeping a good selection would have been, a steward told him, completely impractical; far better to let the passengers bring their own and swap.

None of the passengers seemed interested in simply *loaning* books to the refugees, and of course, the refugees had nothing to offer in trade.

This was not to say that there was nothing at all on board for entertainment; on the contrary, the *Princess* was, the stewards assured him, fully equipped in that regard. They carried a plentiful supply of playing cards, poker chips, backgammon boards, dice, and other gaming devices.

Pel was not quite ready to resort to such mundane pastimes — for one thing, he had no money with him, which really made poker and other gambling games rather pointless. He had never much liked backgammon, never even learned craps.

There were other card games, and he knew he would probably resort to them shortly, but for now he was still hoping to find something more exotic. He didn't want to be like those people who go to Europe and eat at McDonald's; he wanted to sample the local culture.

Unfortunately, the local culture was not cooperating. The native passengers, after the incident in the aft salon, avoided him even more than they avoided the other refugees. The crew spoke to him, but kept relations strictly business-like and formal.

Nancy and Rachel had found something to occupy *their* time — caring for the two little people, who were growing weaker and weaker with no visible cause for their illness. The two of them were in constant pain now, and unable to move, and Nancy had taken it upon herself to stay with them and tend them as best she could, feeding them thin soup and aspirin, sponging off the heavy perspiration that bathed them, and talking to them soothingly. Rachel was acting as her mother's messenger, running whatever errands needed to be run.

That was all very well, and in fact Pel was proud to see it, but there wasn't room or need for another person in the storage compartment the little people occupied. That left him unable to help out, and without the company of his wife and daughter.

The others all seemed to have found ways to stay busy, as well — except for Ted, and Pel was avoiding him.

There wasn't even anything to see out the ports; to the stern the stars had red-shifted into invisibility, while ahead they had blue-shifted into areas of the spectrum hazardous enough that the ports were kept closed.

This left him sufficiently desperate for entertainment to stand around asking stupid questions of the crew.

"How does anti-gravity work, anyway?" he said casually.

The navigator looked up from the periscope, annoyed. "What?" he asked.

Pel repeated his question.

"How the hell should I know?" the navigator snarled.

"Well, I just thought . . ." Pel began. "I mean, I don't know *anything* about it, not even schoolboy stuff, we don't have it where I come from."

The navigator returned to the eyepiece, but said, "It's simple enough. Matter absorbs gravitons, so that particles are drawn toward each other by the streams of gravitons flowing into them — that's gravity, right?"

Pel made a noise of agreement, but was in fact bewildered; that was not at *all* the explanation he remembered from high school physics.

But then, why should it be? This was another universe, with its own laws.

"Well, anti-gravity makes solid matter spit the gravitons back out again, that's all," the navigator explained patiently, never moving his eyes from the periscope. "So it counteracts gravity. And if we make it spit the gravitons out all in one direction, we can use it like a rocket, only of course it's far more powerful."

"Oh," Pel said.

It would appear, he thought, that gravity did not work here in anything like the way it did back home. No wonder *Ruthless* had dropped like a rock.

"How do you get matter to emit gravitons?" he asked.

The navigator let out an exasperated sigh and looked up from the lens. "You compress it until the space it occupies collapses, of course," he said. "You take a lump of uranium, or something else really massive, and run a vibratory current through it to destabilize it, and then you apply pressure."

Pel started to ask another question, then saw the navigator's expression and thought better of it. "Thanks," he said.

He started to turn away, and then something else occurred to him. "If we're traveling faster than light," he asked, "how can you see to navigate?"

"I'm not *seeing* anything," the navigator said. "I'm reading the gravity fields."

"Oh," Pel said.

The whole thing sounded crazy. That bit about making the space an object occupied collapse sounded a little like black hole theory, but the rest of the explanation didn't, and how would creating a miniature black hole result in anti-gravity? That didn't make any sense.

It was clear that he had come upon this other universe's version of quantum physics, and that he wasn't going to make sense of it anytime soon. He wandered off, baffled.

The navigator had at least answered him with more than monosyllables, however, so he drifted back an hour or two later and hovered nearby, trying to think of something intelligent to ask.

He was still working on the phrasing of a question about telling one star from another when the spectra had shifted when the navigator said, "Shit."

This was almost the first time Pel had heard any citizen of the Galactic Empire use foul language. He blinked in surprise.

The navigator adjusted something and stared into the eyepiece, then repeated, somewhat louder, "Shit!"

"What is it?" Pel asked.

The navigator didn't answer; instead he turned and pushed Pel aside as he reached for a button and pushed it hard. A bell chimed somewhere.

That done, the crewman looked at Pel as if only now discovering his presence.

"You'd better get to your cabin," he said. "And lock the door. And if you have any weapons, get them."

"Why?" Pel asked. "What is it?"

"I don't know," the navigator said, "not for sure, but we're slowing down. It looks like something's got a gravity beam on us."

"A gravity beam?" Pel was getting tired of feeling stupid and lost and asking dumb questions, but he couldn't help himself. "What's that mean?"

"It means someone's slowing us down and pulling us in."

Pel blinked. "It does?"

The navigator made a disgusted noise and pushed the button again. "Yes, it does," he said.

"How does that work, though?"

"Where the hell are they?" the navigator asked, not speaking to Pel.

"Who?"

"The captain. It works . . . well, I told you we spit out a stream of gravitons from our main drive, right?"

Pel nodded.

"Well, you can spot that beam pretty easily, and track where it came from, and then if you fire a faster, more powerful beam back along the same line, it cancels out our main drive — and in fact . . ."

A buzzer sounded, and a distant, dull thump reverberated through the flooring beneath Pel's feet. He felt suddenly lighter; his gorge rose in his throat, and his ears hurt.

"Damn!" the crewman said. "In fact, it can blow out the drive completely, which it just did, and then we're just coasting until we can get it running again, and that gravity beam can reel us in like a fish on a line."

Pel started to say something, and almost choked; the crewman glanced up and asked, "Feeling lightheaded?"

Pel nodded.

"With the drive blown we don't even have the full on-board gravity," the man explained. "We're on emergency power. Most ships don't even have this sort of back-up, but the *Princess* is top of the line — on an ordinary ship you'd be drifting a foot off the floor right about now. And those bastards would probably like that just fine; we'd be even more helpless."

"But why?" Pel asked, with his composure back but still utterly baffled, more confused than worried. "Who would want to do that?"

"Pirates," the navigator said.

And then the alarms went off, and an officer chased Pel out of the room.

*P*rossie had been asleep, afloat in the pleasant current of dreams, both her own and others she soaked up from her surroundings. She had picked up some wonderful imagery from somewhere nearby, from one of the non-telepaths aboard *Emerald Princess,* and had tangled it into the warm, comforting network of her own family. A faint touch of the pain and hurt and heat and worry from the forward storage locker had wormed its way into her sleeping thoughts, but so far it was just a little background noise, and had not turned the dreams into nightmares.

Then the alarm bell sounded, and she snapped awake, as much from the psychic shock of a score of other minds being startled as from the actual physical sound.

She felt the disciplined worry of the crew, the confusion of passengers, but the rule was "Don't snoop," so she didn't snoop. She called Captain Cahn for orders.

He didn't know what was going on, and latched onto her light contact.

"Find out," he told her.

She thought a question.

"Just find out," he replied. "No rules to get in the way until we know."

She dropped the contact and reached out elsewhere. She found Captain Gifford, found the navigator —

And woke up Carrie, back at Base One, with her mental shout. Captain Cahn heard it, too.

Then she stopped worrying about anybody else for the next few minutes, as she found her uniform and began carefully searching for anything else that would mark her for what she was, an Imperial telepath. She had to hide it all, or better still, destroy it; had to remove all the evidence.

Because everybody knew what rebels and pirates and anyone else who feared the Empire did to telepaths. No outlaw could risk, even for a moment, having someone around who could relay their very thoughts to the Imperial military.

If the pirates reached *Emerald Princess* and spotted her for a telepath, killing her would be the first thing they did.

They wouldn't even take the time to rape her first.

*P*el stood in the passageway, dazed, for several minutes, watching crewmen hurrying back and forth, most of them looking worried and determined and purposeful. A few looked angry, or frightened, or as dazed as Pel, instead. He kept himself pressed flat against one wall, out of the way.

After a time it occurred to him that there were probably better places to be. The navigator had told him to go to his cabin; that sounded like a good idea.

Pirates — had the man been serious?

Something was obviously wrong, and the navigator certainly hadn't *sounded* as if he were joking, but pirates?

Space pirates?

That sounded so *silly,* like something out of a low-budget, straight-to-video movie, that Pel found it hard to believe it could be serious. *Pirates?*

Pirates were a childhood game, something out of kids' adventure stories or old films. They were an absurd anachronism, a word that brought an image of peg legs and parrots and that ridiculous accent. Captain Hook and Errol Flynn and "Arr, me buckoes" — those were pirates.

Pel smiled uneasily as he began inching toward his cabin, still keeping his back to the wall and staying out of the way of oncoming traffic in either direction. Pirates?

Ted wouldn't believe in any pirates — but then, he didn't believe in *any* of this. Raven and the rest from that world probably wouldn't have any trouble with the concept, though, and Rachel might think it was exciting — or scary.

And he didn't know about the other Earth people, Nancy and Amy and Susan . . .

Susan.

Susan Nguyen.

Pel grimaced. She probably wouldn't think there was anything funny or unbelievable about pirates at all. Pel had no idea how she had gotten to the U.S. — she might even be native-born, really — but she was obviously Vietnamese by ancestry, and plenty of Vietnamese refugees knew first-hand that pirates weren't just something out of old adventure stories.

And Pel and his family were refugees now, like those boat people . . .

Suddenly Pel didn't see anything particularly amusing about the idea of space pirates anymore. He picked up his pace.

The cabin was empty, and he remembered belatedly that Nancy would still be tending to Grummetty and Alella. He turned back and headed that way.

At the door of the storage locker he found Rachel sitting against the bulkhead to one side, arms wrapped around her knees and her head down. She didn't stir when he approached.

That wasn't how she would react to the alarms, or to talk about pirates; Pel knew his daughter better than that.

"What's the matter?" he asked her.

She shook her head and didn't answer, didn't look up.

"Rachel?"

She refused to speak, refused to move.

The locker door opened and Nancy peered out. "Oh, Pel," she said. "It's you."

"Yeah," Pel said. "What's wrong?" He belatedly remembered why Nancy was there in the first place. "Are they worse?" he asked.

Nancy nodded. "Grummetty's dead," she said. "About ten minutes ago." Her voice was unsteady.

Pel felt his own throat drying and tightening at the news.

"Oh," he said helplessly. "I'm sorry." He paused for a second or two, out of respect for the little man, and then said, "Listen, the ship's in trouble." He couldn't bring himself to mention pirates, not yet; it still sounded stupid.

"I heard the bells," Nancy said. "What's wrong?"

"I don't know exactly," Pel said, "but the navigator said we're under some kind of attack — something that shuts down the anti-gravity."

"Is it Shadow?" Nancy asked. "Is it sending more of those creatures?"

Pel had not even thought of that; what if it *was* Shadow that was responsible, and not pirates?

"I don't know," he admitted. "I don't think it could be the creatures, because they can't live in this universe any more than Grummetty could, but it could be people working for Shadow, I guess."

"Are they shooting at us? At the ship, I mean?"

"I don't know," Pel repeated. "Listen, I really don't know much of anything, but we *are* under some kind of attack, and the navigator said we should get to our cabins and lock the doors and wait there."

Nancy shook her head. "I can't leave Alella," she said. "You take Rachel, and I'll stay here."

Pel chewed on his lower lip, considering, and then nodded. "Come on, Rae," he said. "Let's get back to our room."

Rachel looked up unhappily. "I want Harvey," she said.

"I know you do," Pel said, "but he's not here. Now, come on, and we can cuddle up together, if you like."

"Is Grummetty *really* dead?"

"If your mother says so," Pel said, "then I'm afraid he is. Your mom's pretty reliable about these things."

"I don't want him to be dead."

An officer trotted past, almost running. Something was buzzing loudly somewhere forward.

A storybook hero would find some way to make himself useful, some way to save the ship, but Pel was no storybook hero, he knew that more certainly than ever. Right now, dealing with Rachel seemed much more important than saving the ship. He knelt down and spoke softly to his daughter.

"I don't either, Rae, but we have to go. Right now. Come on!" He reached over and took her hand, and then stood up again. She allowed herself to be pulled upright, and followed him, unresisting, as he led her by the hand back to their cabin.

There, they sat on the bed and waited.

*A*my had decided to make one more attempt to convince Ted that he was awake, and that everything that had happened was real.

For one thing, she wanted to be sure that she was convinced herself; for another, she thought Ted might be useful somehow if he once started taking things seriously.

She had been leading the conversation gently in that direction, listening to Ted ramble on about how everyone misunderstood what lawyers really did, when the alarm bells sounded. She looked up, startled.

"I wonder what that is?" she asked.

Ted shrugged, looked around, and saw nothing different about the aft salon. "I guess I haven't decided yet," he said.

Amy frowned.

A crewman ran through, without so much as glancing at them. The two Earthpeople watched him go.

"Or maybe we should go see," Ted said, getting to his feet, "just what I've come up with this time."

*T*he tocsin roused Raven from a doze. He frowned; he had slept far too much and too easily, of late. Perhaps the strain of these strange adventures in fantastic lands was telling upon him, and were it so it would be sorry news indeed; he would need all his powers when he led attacks against Shadow.

"A bell?" he asked no one in specific. "Wherefore does it ring?"

"I know not," Stoddard replied. "Perchance the lieutenant can say?"

"An he be here," Raven agreed.

"It's an alarm," Drummond said, hurriedly pulling on a boot. "I don't know why."

"An alarm?" Raven said, swinging his feet to the floor and sitting upright. "Be the ship endangered?"

"I said I don't *know*," Drummond snarled. "I'll go find out." He stood, boots on.

"Shall we accompany?"

Drummond hesitated, thinking.

"No," he said at last. "No, you two stay here. And don't cause any trouble. You're valuable; if there's some kind of fight we don't want you getting yourselves killed."

"I've no fear to give my life in a good cause," Raven said. "Better to die waging war 'gainst evil than to live in an evil world."

"This isn't any war against evil," Drummond said. "It's probably some stupid mix-up. You just stay out of trouble."

"I reserve, sir, the right to judge my best role myself," Raven retorted. "I am no child."

"Fine," Drummond said. "Fine. Just stay out of it this time, though, okay?"

Then he was gone, the door closing behind him.

"'Tis not our fight," Stoddard said. "'Tis not our world, so how could be?"

Raven looked at his sword, leaning against the nightstand, but did not reach for it. "Shadow has its agents in this realm, as in ours," he said, settling back. "But 'til we know more, best to bide."

*S*omehow Pel had assumed, from what the navigator had said, that the pirates, whoever they were, would be arriving, however they would arrive, within a few minutes, but instead he and Rachel sat on the bed, hugging each other and whispering quietly, for what seemed like hours. Nothing happened; no one burst in, or even knocked; there were no loud noises, no screams, no explosions, no sign that anything out of the ordinary was going on. A few times they heard footsteps passing the door, sometimes running, sometimes not.

Rachel fell asleep after perhaps a quarter of an hour, and Pel tucked her into bed. Then he sat, alone, waiting.

And still nothing happened.

He wished fervently for a book to read, or a TV to watch, or *something* to pass the time. A deck of cards to play solitaire would have been a taste of heaven, and he wished he had taken one when he had the chance.

His watch still wasn't working; after some thought he had concluded that as near as he could figure, liquid crystals didn't exist in Imperial space, and probably *couldn't* exist. He wasn't sure about chip technology in general, whether it was impossible or just hadn't yet been developed.

Whatever the exact reasons, he had no way to tell how long he sat there, watching Rachel sleep and waiting for the pirates. It was very inconsiderate, he decided, to not provide every cabin with a working clock.

He lay back on the bed, trying to think of what he should be doing and reaching no conclusions at all. Nothing that he came up with seemed very important, and they all involved leaving the room, and that meant leaving Rachel alone, which seemed like a very bad idea.

*A*my had reluctantly followed Ted to the forward lounge, where they watched the confusion and worry. Three times, crewmen ordered them to leave, to go back to their cabins, but Ted simply ignored them — he didn't need to obey orders from figments of his imagination. Amy followed his lead; she wanted to see what was happening, not be cooped up in the suite with Susan and Elani and Prossie.

Nobody had time to argue with them, or force them, and they stayed in the lounge.

They stayed there right up until the pirates boarded the *Princess* and burst in through the air lock.

Ted looked at the grey-uniformed men, at the heavy blasters they held, and shook his head. "No, no," he said. "I don't like this part. It's nasty, and I don't want any more of that. The monsters were bad enough."

"On the floor," a man in a grey coverall ordered.

Ted ignored the order; instead he stepped up and reached out for the man's blaster. "Give me that," he said.

"He's crazy," someone called.

Ted's hand started to close on the barrel of the blaster, and the man holding it said, "I'll give it to you, all right."

A dream it's all a dream it's a fucking *dream* it can't be real.

The pain blazed through the side of his head, screaming agony that ripped at his consciousness.

It's a dream.

It *has* to be a dream.

But a dream can't hurt like this.

I must have fallen out of bed, that's what happened, I fell out of bed and hit my head on the floor, and it hurts like hell, why can't I wake up? God, is it a concussion or something?

Why can't I wake up?

As he fell, as he struggled to remain conscious, Ted remembered an old story called "The Knight's Tale," from a book of puzzles, a book called *Mazes and Labyrinths,* a story about a mysterious death. The man in the story had dreamed his own death, and had died in his sleep as a result.

Could that happen? Could he really die from this stupid interminable dream?

No, the knight had lied. And he couldn't possibly sleep through pain like this. He would wake up any second now, he knew he would wake up, and the dream would be over.

Please, God, it would be over!

"Get away from there," someone ordered.

Nancy looked up, startled.

"What is that, anyway?" the man in the grey coverall demanded. He was standing in the doorway of the storage area with a blaster in his hand.

"Alella," Nancy said. "She's dead, too."

The man looked at the little corpse.

"What is that, some kind of freak? Or just a doll?"

"She's . . . she was a little person," Nancy said.

"You sure it's dead?"

Nancy just stared at him; the inside of her chest seemed hollow and aching.

"Whatever, just leave it and come out of there."

Nancy didn't move.

"Damn it, bitch! Get out here!"

In some part of her mind Nancy knew that she should do what the man in grey wanted; he had that gun, and he was getting angry, and it wouldn't do Alella or Grummetty any good to linger here.

That logical, sensible part of her was overwhelmed, though, by the grief and emptiness she felt, and she still didn't move.

With a wordless growl, the man reached in and grabbed her by the hair, one-handed, the other hand keeping the blaster at ready. He tightened his grip until, even through her grief, she felt the pain; a small gasp escaped her.

Then he dragged her out into the corridor.

Exhausted from her long hours tending the little people and from all the cumulative strain of being swept out of her own world, awash in despair, she never did find the strength to scream.

*W*hen the door opened, Raven expected to see Lieutenant Drummond enter. By the time he saw the stranger's face it was too late.

"Touch that sword and I'll blow your fucking head off," the man in gray told him.

Stoddard glanced at Raven, who gave a quick negative jerk of the head. The weapon in the stranger's hand would not have worked back in the real world, nor in Pel Brown's Earth, but this ship sailed in the Empire's skies, where such devices were effective indeed.

"Surely, sir," Raven answered. "Whatever please you."

Stoddard accepted this hint, and made no move for his weapons.

"Get out here." The man gestured with his blaster.

"Certes. Might I ask, though, whether Lieutenant Drummond . . ."

"No questions."

Raven shrugged and obeyed.

He had no fear of any fight, but unarmed men against one of the Empire's fire-weapons was a senseless waste. He would heed, for the present, Lieutenant Drummond's advice. Perhaps this was some jurisdictional squabble between Imperial factions, or a disagreement over the succession to the throne, but in any case, this gray-clad fellow with the rude speech gave no impression of being one of Shadow's monsters. Surely, in time, all would be made clear, and when matters were settled Raven and his companions would be free.

And perhaps whatever faction this person represented would be more eager to fight Shadow than had been Captain Cahn and his crew.

*P*el was awakened by a pounding on the door; it was only when he started up that he realized he had dozed off.

He turned the knob, struck once again by the incongruity of ordinary wooden doors, with knobs and hinges, aboard a spaceship.

The door was shoved open, the knob yanking out of his hand before he could react, and he found himself facing three unfamiliar men in grey uniforms. Two of them held drawn blasters; one needed a shave.

"Out," one of them ordered.

"What . . ." Pel began.

"*Out,*" the man repeated, gesturing with his weapon.

Pel reluctantly stepped out into the passageway, then turned and said, "My daughter . . ."

"That her?" One of the men pointed at Rachel, still asleep.

"Yes," Pel said.

"Get her."

Pel obeyed. He crossed quickly to the cot and stooped over her, then stood again, lifting the girl to his shoulder. She protested sleepily, then flopped against him, her arms around his neck.

"Out," came the order.

Nervously, Pel returned to the corridor.

"That way," he was told, and one of the men herded him forward, toward the lounge, while the others vanished into the cabin.

Farther aft, down the passage, Pel could see armed men at other cabin doors, and ahead he could see a knot of people.

In the lounge he found the ship's doctor bent over Ted Deranian, who lay on the floor, arms flung out to either side. One side of Ted's head was . . .

Pel couldn't see it clearly. He couldn't bring himself to look at it, but he couldn't look away, either. There was black, and red, wet and shining, and the hair was gone. He was glad Rachel was asleep, and not able to see it.

"What happened?" he asked.

"I don't know," someone said.

"He tried to play hero," Amy answered. "When they came charging in here Ted tried to take away one of their guns, and the man with the gun shot him. He didn't have time to aim, though, so he's still alive." She made a choked little noise, apparently suppressing a hysterical giggle, and said, "I mean, the man didn't have time to aim, so Ted's still alive."

Pel realized that the doctor was feeling Ted's chest, rather than his head, but before he could ask anything, Amy added, "They kicked him after he fell; we think a couple of ribs are broken."

"Was anyone else hurt?" Pel looked around, checking who was present.

There was Susan, standing quietly, and Prossie Thorpe, and Soorn, and Valadrakul. There were three, four, five of the *Princess*'s original passengers, and three of her crew, in addition to the doctor.

"Where's Nancy?" Pel asked.

Amy turned and glanced about, worried. "I don't know," she said. "Wasn't she with you?"

"No," Pel said. "She stayed with Alella."

Raven and Stoddard emerged from the corridor behind Pel, their swords gone, a blaster leveled at their backs. Beyond them Pel could see more of the original passengers, and farther back Captain Cahn and two of his crewmen.

"All right," one of the grey-clad men ordered, "through there. Let's go." He pointed toward the air lock.

"What about my wife?" Pel called.

"Don't worry about it," another man ordered him. "Just move."

Pel started to say something, and the man shoved a blaster under his nose with one hand, pointing to the air lock with the other. "Move," he said.

Pel moved.

Chapter Nineteen

*T*he corridors of the pirate ship — if that's what it actually was — were gray-painted metal and resembled the inside of a submarine Pel had once toured. This vessel was far more what he had always expected a spaceship to look like than *Emerald Princess* had been.

He had little time to study it, though; he was hurried to a large, bare chamber, where he and some of the others were locked in, without any further explanation.

For a moment after the heavy steel door slammed shut Pel stared at it, expecting something more to happen. When nothing did, he turned to consider his surroundings.

A row of stained, bare mattresses lay along one of the long walls; at the far end were two small bathrooms, the doors standing open. There were no other furnishings, no windows, no other doors. In the room with him were Amy and Susan; the navigator of *Emerald Princess*; two passengers, one a young man, one a middle-aged woman; and of course, Rachel.

"What happened?" Amy asked. "Who are those people? Where are we?"

"Pirates, right?" Pel asked, looking at the navigator.

He nodded. "Pirates," he said. "From one of the rebel worlds out on the fringe, I suppose. Though I don't know why they picked on the *Princess*; I'd think there were juicier targets out there."

"And those juicier targets are probably better-guarded," the young man said knowingly. "The *Princess* was small enough that we weren't worried about pirates, and we didn't have any defenses. Made us a sitting duck."

The navigator's expression made it plain that he wasn't impressed with this logic. "There's a good reason we weren't worried," he said. "A gravity gun's an expensive thing to operate, and bringing in a ship in mid-flight isn't any picnic; the *Princess* shouldn't have been worth the trouble."

"Well, how much trouble was it, really?" the young man argued. "The ship itself — she's a nice little boat, and they've got her for next to nothing, really. And the passengers — we had money and jewels along, some of us, and they can probably collect ransoms on most of us . . ."

"No, they can't," the navigator interrupted. "How the hell could they collect any ransoms? If they tell anyone where they are, so someone can make the payment, the Empire'll hunt them down and wipe them out."

"Well, there's still the ship . . ."

"I suppose," the navigator admitted. "But it still seems strange. The ship isn't anything all that special."

Amy, Pel, and Susan exchanged glances.

"Do you think it might have had anything to do with us?" Amy asked.

"I don't know," Pel said. "Could Shadow have tracked us somehow?"

"Why would it bother?" Amy asked.

"Does it need reasons?" Susan said. "It tried to kill us once, back in that forest; it could just be trying to finish what it started."

"In that case," Pel argued, "why didn't it already kill us? I mean, why didn't these pirates just shoot everybody?" A thought struck him, and he added, "And even if they aren't working for Shadow, if it was the ship they wanted, why didn't they shoot us?"

That question made everyone uneasy; Amy cast a glance at the mattresses.

"Those stains don't all look like blood," she said uncertainly.

Pel followed her gaze. "No," he agreed. "They don't. I think if they were just going to kill us, they'd already have done it."

"They killed some," the navigator said.

The others all turned to face him.

"They did?" Amy asked.

"Yeah," the navigator said. "There was some fighting. One of the spacemen, that man Jim Peabody, he pulled a gun and picked off two pirates, and they blew his head off, in the starboard crew compartment. And when they found someone hiding in one of the storage lockers they dragged her out and beat her, and . . ." He glanced at Rachel, who was drowsing but not fully asleep, and then finished, "And worse, and I'm pretty sure they killed her when they were done."

"Her?" Pel asked, suddenly nauseated, his ears starting to ring. He had seen Prossie alive and unhurt, and some of the original female passengers, and Amy and Susan were here with him. Nancy was missing, though. "Her?"

It didn't have to be Nancy, he told himself. There were some missing females among the ship's original passengers, too, weren't there?

"A woman," the navigator said. "One of your group. I saw part of it and got a look at her, when they were done, but I don't know her name."

Elani was still unaccounted for — but hiding in a storage locker?

"Nancy," Pel said, gasping. "My wife."

There was a long moment of silence as Pel's strangled words sank in.

"Oh, God, Pel," Amy said, "I'm sorry."

"Mommy?" Rachel asked, waking. "Where's Mommy?"

Raven considered his surroundings with interested distaste.

It would seem that the luxury of the other ship was not a universal trait of sky-ships in the Empire's world. This sorry vessel — assuming that this was indeed the interior of another ship — was just as drab as the Governor's installation in Town, perhaps even more so.

Well, he had endured hardship before, and would undoubtedly do so again, in his battle against Shadow.

All that troubled him was that he still had no notion of who had captured him, or why. Pirates, the others taken with him said — but pirates in whose pay? Freebooters or privateers?

Amy watched miserably as Pel tried to comfort his sobbing daughter. She wished she could help, but she hadn't been able to do any more than provide a used tissue out of her purse. No one had actually told the child directly that her mother was dead, but none of them had denied it, either.

This was perhaps the worst moment yet in the long string of dislocations and horrors that she had been living through ever since that damned spaceship fell out of the sky on her back yard. Monsters bursting up out of the ground, being stranded in an alien desert, all the other things had been frightening and uncomfortable, but nothing that equaled the feeling of sick helplessness she felt right now.

"Why *didn't* they just shoot us?" she muttered.

The young male passenger heard her, and cast a sideways glance at Pel before muttering in reply, "I've heard some rumors."

Startled, Amy turned to look at him. "What rumors?" she asked.

"Well, they *are* just rumors," he said, "but you heard the crewman there mention the rebel planets. There are some nasty rumors about them."

"What rumors?"

"Supposedly — and I don't know, it's just what I've heard, but supposedly they've revived the slave trade."

Amy stared at him. For a long moment his words failed to connect with anything. Slave trade? What was that? What did it have to do with anything? What did it have to do with *her?*

Then it clicked into place.

She had been captured by pirates. Spaceships and drab grey uniforms notwithstanding, she had been captured by pirates.

And they were going to sell her into slavery.

The image of the "wenches" being auctioned off in Disney World's "Pirates of the Caribbean" came unbidden to her mind. She had ridden through with her ex-husband years ago, and had found that bit of scenery slightly offensive and oddly uncomfortable, though she knew it was intended to be harmless fun. Now, in retrospect, it seemed downright horrible — there was nothing at all amusing about auctioning people off.

But this wasn't the eighteenth-century Caribbean; she was in a spaceship. The Galactic Empire had anti-gravity and rayguns; didn't that mean it was more advanced than Earth? Didn't that mean they would have no use for slaves, would have no tolerance for slavery?

Didn't they have robots, or something?

"What sort of slaves?" she asked.

The passenger shrugged. "Labor for the mines and farms, I suppose," he said. "And . . . well, other things." He blushed faintly.

He actually blushed. It wasn't a bright red, but it was unmistakably a blush. Amy hadn't seen a man blush in years. She didn't inquire any further.

"I still don't understand," the female passenger announced, "why they picked on the *Princess.* There must be dozens of ships out there that would have been worth more — the big liners, or freighters. Why pick on *us?*"

"Maybe it was random," the navigator suggested. "Maybe they just saw the gravity field and attacked because it was close, without even knowing what ship it was."

"That seems stupid," the young man said. "What if they hit a warship that way?"

"I hadn't thought of that," the navigator admitted.

"They must have known what ship it was," the woman said.

"I guess they must have," the navigator agreed.

"How could they?" Amy asked. "I mean, aren't we sort of in the middle of nowhere? And they couldn't have gotten close enough to *see* it until after they'd decided to attack, could they?"

"Shadow," Susan suggested, gripping her big black purse tightly. Noticing the bag, Amy wondered whether it had been searched; no one had bothered to check her own. "It was Shadow," Susan said.

"What's Shadow?" the female passenger asked.

Susan looked helplessly at Amy, then glanced at Pel and Rachel, still huddled together in the corner.

"It's this thing from . . . from another universe," Amy explained. "It's why we're here."

"Why who is where?" the young man asked. "Do you mean why all of us are *here*, in this room?"

Amy shook her head. "No," she said, "I mean it's why Susan and Pel and the rest of us are in your universe." She sighed. "It's a long story."

The passengers and the navigator glanced at one another, puzzled.

"Are you claiming you're from another universe?" the young man asked.

Amy nodded.

"We are," she said. "That's why we were important enough to need your ship to get us to . . . to wherever they were taking us. Some military base, I think."

The navigator nodded. "Base One," he said. "It's the headquarters for the entire Imperial military."

Amy nodded again.

"So this Shadow thing," the navigator asked, "it's from your universe? It followed you, you think?"

"No," Amy said. "It's from a third one. There are three. Some of those other people are from Shadow's world, but we aren't."

"But it followed you?"

"Maybe," Amy said. "We don't know."

"This Shadow," the young man asked, "just what is it, exactly?"

Amy looked at Susan, who shrugged.

"We don't know that, either," Amy said. "I don't think anybody does, really."

"How could it have known anything about us, anyway?" the middle-aged woman asked. "Does it have a telepath working for it, or something?"

"I don't know," Amy said. "Maybe Shadow didn't have anything to do with it; maybe the pirates just have a telepath of their own."

The navigator shook his head. "All the telepaths work for the Empire," he said. "They always have."

"Maybe one went rogue," the young man suggested.

"If that ever happened," the navigator said, "the Empire would hunt it down and kill it."

"I wonder what happened to Prossie?" Amy said, more to herself than anyone else.

"Prossie?"

"Is that the bitch telepath that came aboard with you people?" the woman asked.

Startled by the harsh term, Amy didn't answer immediately.

"She was in the lounge," the navigator said. "I saw her there right before they brought us across."

"If the pirates know she's a telepath . . ." the young man began.

"She's probably *working* for them," the woman snarled. "She probably called them down on us!"

"She's an Imperial officer," the navigator objected. "And her entire family works for the Empire. Why would she work for pirates?"

"Because she's a stinking mutant, and she hates everybody normal!" the woman replied angrily.

"I don't think that's true," Amy objected. "I've talked with Prossie — I don't think she hates anybody."

"Well, of course you wouldn't think so," the woman retorted. "She can read your mind and act however you want her to act, do whatever it takes to fool you, and you'd never know the difference."

Startled by the woman's anger, Amy didn't reply.

"If she's not working for the pirates," the young man said, "she's the best hope we've got."

Amy and Susan looked at him inquiringly.

"Well, it's obvious — she can call for help. Maybe she already has. If she's not working for them, they've made a big mistake, not killing her the minute they got aboard."

"Maybe they don't know she's a telepath," Susan suggested quietly.

"She was in uniform," the female passenger said scornfully. "Of *course* they know."

"But she wasn't," Susan said. "In the lounge she was wearing a dress."

"Her uniform was aboard the *Princess,* though," the young man pointed out. "When they find it, they'll know."

"Well, let's hope they don't find it, then," the navigator said.

"Of course they'll find it eventually," the woman said. "I mean, won't they strip everything out of the ship?"

Amy glanced at Susan's purse again.

"They might not look at it closely enough," the navigator suggested. "And even if they do, she's probably already called for help."

"But when they find it, they'll kill her," the young man pointed out. "That would make it harder for any pursuit to track us."

"Serve the bitch right," the woman muttered. "Snooping in people's heads. Mutants."

"They may have killed her already," the navigator said, "but let's hope not."

"Can she really call for help from way out in space?" Amy asked. "I didn't know telepaths could do that. I thought they had to be close to someone." She remembered the distance from Town to where the portal had first delivered them all to Psi Cass the Deuce, and corrected herself. "I mean, on the same planet, anyway."

"Oh, sure," the young man said. "She could call the other telepaths from clear across the galaxy. I don't know about reading minds, or anything to do with normal people, but telepaths can reach *each other,* no matter *how* far apart they are. That's why the Empire uses them, they're the fastest form of interstellar communication we've got."

"Then the pirates couldn't have a telepath working for them, could they?" Susan asked. "Wouldn't he or she be spotted by the Empire's telepaths?"

"What if he were?" the woman asked. "Those mutants all stick together against us. They wouldn't squeal on one of their own."

Nobody bothered to argue with that — not because they agreed, since in fact none of the others believed it, but because there was no way to prove anything.

A moment later, the young man said, "Suppose they had their own *family* of telepaths? I mean, suppose the telepathic mutation happened *again,* and this time working for the rebel worlds instead of the Empire?"

"The Empire's telepaths would have spotted them," the navigator said.

"Are you sure?" the young man asked. "Suppose they communicated on a slightly different level, as it were; suppose that there was some sort of mutual interference, in fact, so that the two families blanked each other out, couldn't detect each other."

"You're just guessing," the navigator said. "I never heard about anything like that."

The young man shrugged. "Sure, I'm guessing," he said. "But it *could* be true."

"I still think it was Shadow," Susan said.

*T*he discussion, and sometimes argument, continued off and on for hours, perhaps days; no one was quite sure how long they were confined to that room and ignored. Long enough to grow very hungry, certainly, and no one brought any food. They were left entirely to their own devices.

They took turns sleeping; there were enough mattresses for everybody, but it seemed like a good idea to always have someone awake.

Rachel gradually calmed down; sleeping helped. She and Pel listened to some of the conversations, but neither of them had much to add. Topics included the nature of their captors, their destination, the fate of the other people who had been aboard *Emerald Princess,* and other such matters.

The navigator confirmed, out of Rachel's hearing, that the woman he had seen raped and murdered fit Nancy's description, and not Elani's.

More generally, the four Earthpeople learned that the Galactic Empire did not actually rule the entire galaxy, or even the majority of it; most of it was still uninhabited, at least by humans — and so far, no intelligent aliens had been encountered, though that didn't mean there weren't any. The female passenger, whose name turned out to be Arietta Benton, took any suggestion that a non-human could be sentient as a personal affront, apparently on theological grounds; the navigator and the other passenger were more open-minded, but neither one had ever heard anything more than tall tales about aliens.

Even among human-inhabited worlds, the Empire was not as all-powerful as it might have liked. The galaxy was vast, and space travel fairly cheap and easy; anyone who could get a ship could reasonably hope to find himself an uninhabited planet of his own. It might take a few years of looking, and if the Empire found the planet later it would promptly be conquered, but people were willing to try it. A good many of them succeeded, and set up their own little fiefdoms.

Nobody was sure just how many of these independent worlds were out there — that was inherent in their nature, since if they were sufficiently well-known to be counted, they would already have been conquered.

The male passenger, Alex Gorney, was of the opinion there were a hundred or more rebel worlds; the navigator, Lieutenant Martin, put the number much lower, at maybe half a dozen. "Ships aren't *that* easy to come by!" he insisted.

Gorney argued that one ship could colonize a dozen worlds, and Martin agreed it *could,* but maintained it wouldn't. One habitable planet, after all, was big enough for a few dozen miniature empires.

All three of them, Gorney, Benton, and Martin, agreed that the sort of people who wound up on the rebel worlds tended toward the fringes of sanity. The colonies the Empire had found so far had ranged from eccentric to downright bizarre; some had destroyed themselves before the Empire ever got there, and atrocity stories were common.

Naturally, some had turned to piracy. And some had turned to slavery. Not to mention those that had taken up communalism, theocracy, torture, murder, cannibalism, and any number of other barbaric practices.

The Earthpeople listened to these explanations — Amy with visibly-growing worry, Susan with a veneer of calm acceptance, Pel far too concerned with Nancy's fate and Rachel's reaction to care much at first.

As time wore on, though, the subject percolated in Pel's mind, and finally he found himself sitting on his mattress grinning wryly at the thought.

The clean, hard frontier, where men were strong and brave; the fine new worlds beloved of science fiction writers, away from the decadence and bureaucracy of old, worn-out, overpopulated Earth — all that was a cliché, of course.

And here was the reality, it appeared — pirates and slavers and lunatics.

That he and his daughter were about to be delivered into the hands of these pirates, slavers, and lunatics did not fully register until the hour — day or night he could not tell — when Lieutenant Martin shook him awake and said, "The drive's shut down. We've landed."

Chapter Twenty

*T*hey were all awake when the door finally opened, all of them dressed and waiting. Martin and Gorney were standing straight and tall, waiting to face whatever might come; the others were sitting in a group on two of the mattresses, waiting with more resignation than defiance.

"Come on," one of the grey-clad pirates ordered. "Out of there."

"Where are you taking us?" Benton demanded. "To see the captain?"

"Just get out here," the pirate said, gesturing with a blaster.

Pel, Susan, and Amy got to their feet, Pel giving Rachel a reassuring hug. Benton crossed her arms over her chest and looked defiant.

"I want to know where you're taking us," she announced.

The pirate in the doorway cast a disgusted glance over his shoulder, then stepped aside. Two men entered, stepping past him; they carried no guns, but in Pel's opinion they didn't need them. Both of them were huge, built like linebackers or pro wrestlers.

Pel glanced doubtfully at Amy, who returned the look uncertainly. Susan stepped out of the way immediately, her back against one wall. She didn't meet anyone else's eyes. She held her black purse tight to her side and didn't move.

Gorney and Martin stood firm, unyielding and motionless, between the door and Benton.

The first of the oversized pirates reached out and grabbed Martin around the throat, one-handed. Pel immediately remembered the scene in "Star Wars" where Darth Vader picked up a rebel one-handed and broke his neck; the pirate was not doing anything quite so dramatic as that, but the gesture was still extremely effective.

Martin's hands flew up, trying to pry the death-grip loose; Gorley, horrified, flung his own weight on the outstretched arm.

The other large pirate marched past, undaunted, to where Benton sat on the mattress, glaring up at him. He pushed past Pel and Amy as if they weren't there, and neither of them dared resist; instead they backed away, one on each side. Pel almost stepped on Rachel in his retreat.

"You coming?" the pirate asked, as he looked down at the disobedient captive.

"No," Benton began, a bit less steadily than before. "Not until . . ."

That was as far as she got; the pirate kicked her in the belly, hard. The air burst out of her lungs, and she curled forward, gasping. Rachel let out a little wail and buried her face in her father's shirt, clutching the fabric with both hands; Pel put a soothing hand on her head.

The pirate reached down with one hand and roughly yanked Benton upright. She didn't resist; the fight had gone out of her with her breath. She was unable to walk at first, and the pirate dragged her by one arm until, halfway to the door, she got her feet under her.

Martin and Gorney had been unable to release Martin from the other pirate's stranglehold; now, though, the grip was suddenly released, and Martin almost fell.

"Come on," the pirate said.

There was no further resistance; the entire party allowed itself to be herded out of the room, and on out of the ship.

*T*he holding facility had rough concrete walls and rows of steel benches, but not everybody used them. Some stood along the walls, some crouched on the floor. The room was cavernous, big enough that even without crowding everyone together the entire party of dozens occupied less than a fourth of it. Light came from a row of clerestory windows, far overhead. A narrow corridor at one end led to toilet facilities. The place was dusty and cool and had a faint unpleasant odor to it, compounded of mildew, sweat, urine, and other, less definable traces.

Pel looked over the crowd.

In addition to the handful he had been with aboard the pirate ship, he spotted Lieutenant Drummond and Captain Cahn, Raven, Valadrakul, Elani, Squire Donald and Stoddard, Prossie Thorpe, Smith, Lampert, Soorn, and Mervyn. Ted Deranian, his head a mass of bandages, sat dazed in one corner, and Pel was relieved to see him alive. Most of the passengers and crew of *Emerald Princess* were present, but Pel had never become familiar enough with them to put names to them all or say if any were missing.

He looked back to Prossie Thorpe. She was alive — that was promising. She was out of uniform, now wearing a ragged bathrobe rather than the borrowed dress she had been in before; maybe their captors didn't know she was a telepath. Maybe, even now, she was relaying messages to the Galactic Empire.

He didn't want to draw attention to her. He returned to scanning the crowd, looking for familiar faces.

Nancy was not there. Neither was Peabody, nor Lieutenant Godwin, nor Alella.

There were three doorways, with pirates guarding each of them; each pirate held a blaster. Susan, Pel noticed, was standing with her back to the wall once again, stiff and tense, trying to watch all three guards at once.

"Now what?" someone whispered.

"Shut up," one of the pirates called — not angrily, just giving a necessary order. The hand holding the blaster lifted somewhat.

Silence descended, broken by shuffling feet and rustling clothes. Someone coughed.

One of the doors opened, and three more of the grey-clad pirates entered, accompanied by a tall man in blue coveralls. The four of them strode into the room with an air of calm and certain purpose, then stopped.

"All right, everyone hold still," one of the pirates bellowed. "Sit down, and hold still."

With varying degrees of reluctance, those who were standing obeyed. Susan's descent was so quick Pel thought at first she had fallen.

When everyone was seated, the man in blue stretched out a finger and began counting heads. Pel could see his lips moving; he wasn't sure if he could hear muttered numbers or not.

"Forty-three," the man announced.

"You missed one," the smallest of the accompanying pirates said. "I counted myself. Did you see the little girl, there?"

Rachel raised her head from Pel's lap and blinked.

"You're right," the man in blue said. "Missed her. Forty-four, then, and the dead midget. Forty-two healthy adults at fifty crowns each, and half each for the kid and the one with his head shot up. That's twenty-one fifty, plus twenty for the freak, makes twenty-one seventy."

"What, half for the kid and the dummy?" the small pirate protested. "Come on! He's just got his hair burnt off, he's not hurt bad! And she's older than she looks!"

The man in blue shook his head. "She's not twelve," he said. "She's not even eight. Just take a look at her. Hell, *ask* her!"

"I'm six," Rachel volunteered.

"There, see?"

"All right," the pirate conceded, "but the one with the bandage . . ."

The man in blue sighed. "Oh, hell, it's not worth the argument. Twenty-one ninety."

"Ninety-*five.*"

"Right, ninety-five."

One of the other pirates handed him a clipboard and a pen — Pel noticed they looked much like the same implements back on Earth. The man in blue filled out a few lines, then signed at the bottom, tore off the sheet, and handed it to the small pirate. He smiled, folded it, and tucked it away in an inside pocket.

All the pirates were smiling, in fact — not just the four in the central party, but the three at the doors as well.

Then the party of five turned and marched back out, leaving the captives where they were.

"What the hell was that about?" Pel asked, half to himself, before he remembered that the guards preferred silence.

"Prize money," the nearest guard replied, smiling. "That chit's sixty crowns for every man on the ship — double shares for the officers, and a bonus for the captain."

"Sixty-five, I make it," one of the other guards called.

"Whatever," the first replied, grinning. "Enough to get good and drunk. And that's just on these — prize court hasn't even looked at the ship yet!"

"Shut up, both of you," the third guard snapped.

They shut up, and Pel sat, thinking. This was the first time any of the pirates had deigned to answer any questions at all, and he rather hoped it was the beginning of a trend.

Prize money — he knew about prize money, more or less, from the novels he had read. It was a method of rewarding ships' crews for capturing enemy vessels in wartime, by buying their captures from them. It had been dropped over a century ago back on Earth, and with good reason. The whole system struck Pel as a really barbaric idea. It made the crews greedy, made them more interested in catching enemy merchant shipping off-guard than in winning battles.

And even at its worst, back on Earth, he thought it had only been applied to ships and cargo, not to *people.*

Why would anyone pay prize money for people?

He could think of a few possibilities, and he didn't like any of them very much. The only good one was also the least likely — that it was just a humanitarian gesture, a way of convincing the pirates to deliver prisoners alive, rather than dead.

Somehow, Pel couldn't imagine any government making such a gesture.

Of course, that assumed that they were dealing with a government here. If they were, then perhaps "pirates" wasn't the right term for their captors at all; "privateers" might be more accurate, or perhaps they were actually part of the navy — or space force, or whatever the correct term was — of this particular world. Or country, if the government in question didn't run the entire planet.

One of the doors opened, and half a dozen men in dark blue uniforms ambled in. Most of the prisoners watched intently.

"Okay, boys," one of them called. "You can go."

Mervyn got to his feet, and the man in blue called, "Not you, stupid."

Mervyn sat down again, as the three grey-clad guards, grinning and slapping one another on the back, jogged out of the room. The newcomers split into pairs, and took up posts at the three doors.

"You people might as well settle in," one of them called. "You're staying here tonight, and you'll go out in the morning, around nine, I think." He pulled a watch from his pocket and glanced at it. "That's fourteen hours. We'll get you in some breakfast before that, I guess, but for now, you might as well sleep."

"May we talk?" someone asked; Pel didn't see who it was.

"Nope," the guard said, smiling. "Sorry. No escape plans. And if any of you gets within five yards of a door, we'll shoot you dead, no warnings." He drew a blaster, then leaned back against the wall beside the door. "Good night!"

*D*azed, Ted looked out at the gathered prisoners.

This dream went on and on and it was so boring! Why hadn't the pain in his head woken him up? He must be lying on the floor, he might have a concussion, and he had always thought he had a better imagination than this.

Why wouldn't it stop?

Maybe he was dead, not dreaming, maybe he was dead and this was some antechamber of Hell.

But no, he didn't believe in any of that, he hadn't believed in it since he was eight, not really, maybe he *never* had.

He was dreaming.

He had slept and woken, he had eaten, he had been hit and burned and abused, and the dream still went on and on and didn't end, and he really wished he would wake up.

He would need to talk to someone about this, he really would. He'd never seen a psychiatrist, never wanted to, but a dream like this might change his mind.

Maybe if he attacked one of the guards, he'd be shot, and that would wake him up . . .

Or maybe he'd die. Maybe he was really hurt from falling out of bed, maybe he'd had a heart attack, or a stroke.

He wouldn't risk it.

But he wished he would wake up.

Raven pursed his lips angrily.

How utterly foolish, to have fallen prisoner in some petty little raid like this!

It was clear to him now that this was no grand factional dispute, nor any great crusade against the Empire; instead this was some minor warlord's action, an attempt to gather a little loot without drawing the Empire's wrath. *Emerald Princess* would be reported lost, doubtless, but the loss ascribed to wind or weather, monsoon or monster. Even were pirates suspected, how could they know which or where?

And so here he was, Raven of Stormcrack Keep, about to be held for ransom, or sold to slavery, and there was naught he could do to prevent it.

Thus was his struggle to end, then?

Or might he yet win free? Might he draw the aid of whatever warlord was responsible, by promises of booty from Shadow's conquered lands?

That was a thought to consider, most certainly.

First, though, to survive that long. Would that someone would spare him somewhat to eat!

They hadn't eaten, Pel realized, for at least a day and a half; poor Rachel was starving, her stomach hurting. "Breakfast soon," he whispered in her ear, as she shifted on the bench beside him, trying unsuccessfully to get to sleep.

She whimpered.

They had dozed fitfully for hours, surrounded by others doing the same. Some of them snored, or at least breathed loudly and sometimes irregularly; some tossed and turned. At least once, someone had fallen off a bench with much commotion and noise.

The guards at the doors were replaced every four hours, as nearly as Pel could judge; after the first change they all wore the dark blue uniforms, rather than the drab grey of the pirates.

He wondered just where they all were, and who these people were, and what was really going on.

And he wondered what he was doing here, and what had really happened to Nancy. Was she truly dead?

She couldn't be. He looked down at Rachel.

Nancy couldn't be dead. Martin the navigator must have been wrong, somehow. The whole thing had to be a mistake.

Nancy couldn't be dead.

He looked up, swallowing hard, his eyes wet.

The line of windows had been visible as a slightly lighter strip of darkness, sprinkled with stars; now, though, the stars seemed to be fading, the darkness lightening.

Dawn?

He hoped so, if only because of the promise of breakfast.

Amy felt as if she had just gotten to sleep when the banging woke her. Someone was beating on a metal tray, making a great clanging racket.

"All right, you people," a man shouted. "Up and at 'em! Breakfast in five minutes!"

The struggle between hunger and fatigue raged for a long moment, but amid the general stirring and muttering, bringing home the realization that they weren't going to let her sleep anyway, hunger won out. She got to her feet, stretched, and yawned.

The inside of her mouth felt gummy, and she was sure her breath stank, but that wasn't anybody's business but her own anymore. Stan had been given to rude remarks about it, back when she was married.

He had also been given to rude remarks whenever she put on weight, and she'd noticed that her breath always smelled worse when she was dieting, which had created a no-win situation — one of many in her relationship with him, even before the whole thing went down the tubes once and for all.

Stan wasn't here, though. He wasn't even in this *universe,* if all this was really happening.

If it was really happening, she repeated to herself. Ted's dream theory did have a certain undeniable appeal to it.

But she couldn't imagine herself dreaming about bad breath, and there was Ted with his head bandaged up, and the echoes from the blank walls, the rattle of the metal benches, all the solid little details made the dream theory seem pretty untenable. She couldn't manage to believe it, though she rather wished she could.

Who was it that could believe six impossible things before breakfast?

Well, it wasn't her; she seemed to be stuck with a choice of believing one or the other of two, either this was all real or it was all a dream, and she was having trouble accepting either of the available options.

But there just wasn't any third choice.

"Breakfast! This way to breakfast!" shouted a man at one of the doors. People were beginning to line up there, Amy saw; she tugged her maroon stewardess skirt into place, hung her battered purse on her shoulder, looked around and saw she had nothing else to pick up, and then ambled in that general direction.

The door opened into a short, gloomy, gray-walled passageway. At the far end of the passage the prisoners found themselves in a cafeteria that closely resembled the holding room they had slept in, save that there were tables between the rows of benches, and a serving counter across one end. The line that had formed in the holding room and moved down the little corridor now swerved directly to the serving area without breaking formation; grey metal trays were stacked at the near end, waiting.

Back in Town, on Psi Cass the Deuce, they'd all had to sit and wait, and then had gotten fed — but it had gone much more quickly, and they'd been treated more considerately, and the place, drab as it was, hadn't smelled or looked anywhere near as unpleasant.

Amy's stomach pinched at her as she waited her turn; she could smell coffee, could smell food. The contrast with the odor of the waiting room was drastic indeed.

It had been much too long since she had eaten. It had been much too long since *any* of them had eaten; she could hear stomachs growling.

The one good thing about that was that it meant the line moved quickly; each person was eager to fill his or her tray and get it to a table. No one was kept waiting a moment longer than necessary.

Breakfast was biscuits and sausage and corn flakes and coffee — no eggs, no orange juice, no fruit. The biscuits were fluffy, but almost tasteless; the sausage plainly contained as much filler as meat; and the coffee was thin, watery, and cool.

The corn flakes were fine, except that there was no milk or sugar or fruit to put on them.

It had been long enough since her last meal that Amy ate everything on her plate anyway, and went back for seconds on the biscuit and sausage.

As she worked her way through the narrow gap between benches, back toward her seat, she saw Rachel Brown twisting about in her place, her face set in a scowl. "I don't like this stuff!" she said. "Don't they have any milk, or soda, or anything?"

"No," her father told her, "they don't. Just coffee."

"They have water," someone — Lampert, Amy remembered his name now, Ben Lampert — said from across the table. "Would you like me to get you some?"

Pel looked down at his frowning daughter.

"Well, it's better than *this* stuff," Rachel said, pushing her cup away and spilling coffee onto her tray.

Pel caught the cup and righted it while it still held half its contents; Amy stopped watching and proceeded back to her own seat.

The food ran out before everyone had eaten his or her fill, but Amy no longer heard stomachs complaining; everyone had at least eaten *something*. Now they sat, looking about, talking quietly with their neighbors.

Amy had Susan on one side, and an unfamiliar middle-aged man on the other; across the table were strangers, save for Bill Mervyn, one seat to her right.

"Any idea what's going on?" she asked Susan.

Susan, lips tight, shook her head no. She clutched at her purse.

Mervyn looked up from his empty coffee cup, at Amy. "I don't know if . . ." he began, then stopped.

Amy looked back at him. "You don't know what?"

"Well," Mervyn said, reluctantly, "I think I can *guess* what's going on, but you won't like it. You'd probably be better off not knowing."

"No," Susan said. "We would not."

"Especially not now, now that you've said anything," Amy added.

Mervyn sighed and looked back at his cup; the coffee had run out, as well as the food.

"Well," he said, "when I was on *Devastation* — that's I.S.S. *Devastation*, Captain Morley, that was my ship before *Ruthless*. . ."

Amy nodded. "Go on."

"When I was on *Devastation*, we did a run on one of the rebel worlds out on the fringes of the Empire. They'd been supporting pirates, same as these people here, and they used the people the pirates brought back as slave labor. Auctioned them off. And about half a dozen ships got away — these might even be the same people."

"So you think . . ."

"I think they're feeding us because hungry slaves don't look as good to the buyers, and hungry people are more likely to do stupid, desperate things, like trying to escape."

"Only at first," Susan said. "Go without food long enough and you don't have the strength anymore. You need to choose your time carefully." She adjusted her purse on the bench beside her.

"Well, that's true," Mervyn acknowledged, "but they want us healthy."

Amy and Susan nodded reluctant agreement. "At least we have that much," Susan said. "I've known worse."

Amy glanced at her attorney, startled, but Susan was not looking in her direction.

She had known worse?

Amy decided not to pursue that. For a moment, the two of them sat, contemplating their situation. Amy was, once again, finding it all hard to believe; slavery? She, Amy Jewell, was going to be sold into slavery by pirates?

That was something out of stories, something out of the past . . .

Then she stopped and glanced at Susan again.

"I've known worse," Susan had said.

Susan was Vietnamese, and her family had escaped to Thailand by boat when she was a child. Amy didn't know any of the details; she had never asked, and Susan had never volunteered anything.

Still, Amy had heard stories about the boat people. Robbed, raped, murdered by pirates; stuck in camps and abandoned by civilized governments on all sides — to Susan, this might well seem all *too* real and familiar.

To *most* people outside the United States, Amy supposed, this wouldn't seem so outrageous. The world was full of cruelty and injustice, it always had been; why should this other world be any different?

She told herself that, and she knew enough history to know it was true, but still, she didn't really *believe* it, in her heart and her gut. All her life she had been safe, had been protected, had known what the rules were. She didn't walk through certain neighborhoods at night, she generally kept her doors locked, she stayed out of bars, and that was enough; her world was safe and serene.

It wasn't perfect; she'd had her bad moments when her marriage fell apart, when her dorm room was broken into her long-ago junior year of college, when she wrecked her car on that trip to Phoenix, but those seeming disasters looked pretty trivial in retrospect. She had worried that Stan would walk out, would leave her broke, would take the house away from her, might even slap her; she had feared that she might lose all her things, all her money and mementos, that she would never be able to sleep again without worrying; she had wondered how long it would take to get home without a car, where she would stay, how she would pay for everything, what would happen to her insurance rates.

Stan had done worse than slap her, but she had survived it, and it hadn't been so very bad, she hadn't wound up broke at all, or anywhere near it. And when it was over she was rid of him and that was all right.

She hadn't been robbed again, she had burglar alarms, all her things were safe at home waiting for her.

She had flown home, bought a new car, paid her bills off eventually.

So she had worried about all those things, and they had all turned out all right in the end — but she had never, in all her life prior to the crash of *Ruthless,* had to worry about where her next meal was coming from, or whether she would be alive to eat it; never worried about whether she would ever again see her house, her family, her friends, her entire *world.*

She had sometimes feared rape, robbery, and murder — but piracy? Slavery?

And in *another universe?*

It was absurd, it was crazy.

And it was true, wasn't it?

Or would she be rescued at the last minute? Would the cops come, the neighbors, the lawyers, the way they had after the robbery, the way they had after Stan had beat her? Prossie Thorpe was still alive, Amy had seen her; had *she* called the cops, the Imperial soldiers, this time?

And would they come?

"Your attention!" someone shouted above the room's babble. "Your attention, please!"

The hum of conversation and general hubbub faded. A man in a blue uniform was standing on a chair against one wall, his arms spread wide.

"Next step is hygienic," he announced. "I'm sure most of you haven't had a good bath in days, and you may have . . . well, you could probably use one."

Amy threw Susan a glance; the lawyer shrugged. Other people were also trading looks, worried or questioning.

"We don't have facilities for individual baths," the announcer continued. "Instead we have showers, one for the men, one for the ladies. If the men would please leave the cafeteria through *that* door . . ." He pointed. " . . . And the ladies through *that* one . . ."

"Now?" someone asked.

"Whenever you're ready," the announcer replied.

Showers.

They were prisoners being herded into mass showers.

Amy tried very hard not to think of what that immediately brought to mind.

Did any of these other people, the ones not from Earth, have anything like that in their histories? Had this monstrous, inhuman Shadow that they talked about ever sunk to the level of the Nazis? Had the Galactic Empire ever faced an evil to equal the one the Allies had conquered?

Very probably, she thought; after all, Stalin had killed as many as Hitler, and Pol Pot and a dozen others had tried. There had been murderous dictators all through history. The people of the Empire, and the people of Shadow's world, all looked human enough; they probably had plenty of murderous dictators in their own histories.

But had those dictators used poisoned showers? Was anyone else here making the same connection she was?

Probably not. She was probably just being paranoid. And Prossie Thorpe must have called for help. Even the people at Auschwitz had been saved eventually, when the Allied troops came marching in.

A few of them had been saved, anyway.

A few of them.

She turned to Susan. "What do you think?" she asked. "Should we go?"

The lawyer shrugged.

"Do we really have a choice?" she asked.

Chapter Twenty-One

P el Brown was arguing with the announcer as Amy left the cafeteria. She couldn't make out the words, and decided against snooping; instead she just followed the little crowd through the indicated door.

Once inside, she looked around the bare little room and noticed that there were no lockers in the changing room, just cardboard boxes — stacks of them, grey inside, blue outside, with loose-fitting lids. There were no markers, no pens, no labels, no serial numbers, and Amy found herself very suspicious indeed.

How would they ever get the right stuff back?

Did anyone ever expect to return anything?

"Just put your clothes in there, dearie," the blue-uniformed woman with the billy club told her. "They'll be safe."

"How'll I find the right box?" Amy asked. "I mean, afterward?"

The guard, or matron, or whatever she was looked annoyed. "Write your name on it if you like," she said.

"There aren't any pens," Amy pointed out.

"We ran out; don't you have anything in that purse you're carrying?"

Amy was not satisfied, but she began fishing in her purse, looking for a pen. If nothing else, it let her stay dressed a moment longer. The room was not particularly warm — and there were those other fears, not entirely suppressed.

Around her the other women were slowly, reluctantly removing their clothes. The first shower was turned on in the tiled room beyond and for a moment Amy froze, listening for the hiss of gas.

There was no gas; just water, splashing on the tiles. Someone squealed. "It's cold!"

"It'll warm up," the guard called.

Amy felt an altogether unreasonable rush of relief, and was annoyed at herself. Had she really thought they were about to be gassed?

Did she really know they weren't going to be killed by some other method?

She shook her head. She was being paranoid again, and it wasn't going to do anybody any good. Her hand brushed through the contents of her purse, and for a moment she could see an old Bic, and then something slid over and it was lost again.

Someone knocked on the door from the cafeteria, interrupting her thoughts, and a male voice called, "Is there an Amy Jewell or a Susan . . . Susan Goyen in there?"

Amy looked up, then quickly scanned the room. Susan was already naked and about to step into the shower room, but incongruously, she still had her purse, held so the matron could not see it.

"I'm Amy Jewell," Amy called back.

"We have a . . . could you come to the door, please?"

Cautiously, Amy approached the door. It swung open a few inches, then stopped.

"Excuse me, miss," the voice said, and Amy recognized it as the man who had made the announcement about showers. "I don't want to intrude on anybody's privacy."

"It's okay," Amy said, leaning around the edge of the door, "I'm still decent. What is it?" She looked out.

The cafeteria was almost empty now, and a man in a dirty apron was collecting trays and debris. The announcer was standing with his back to the door, holding it open with one hand.

His other hand was on Rachel Brown's shoulder.

"We have a bit of a problem here," he said. "It seems this little girl doesn't have her mother here. She wants to stay with her father, but I'm afraid we have very strict rules about that; we just *can't* let her through the men's side. So could you please take charge of her for now? Her father says she knows you."

Amy looked down at the child; Rachel looked back, her eyes wide. She had been crying, and Amy had the distinct impression that the wrong word would start more tears flowing.

Amy had never been very good with children, and had always been relieved that she and Stan had never had any. Still, this poor thing needed *somebody* to look after her, and her mother, Amy remembered . . well, her mother wasn't here.

And it was only for a few minutes.

"Would that be okay, Rachel?" she said. "It'll just be until we're washed up, and then you'll be back with your father, I'm sure."

The announcer's face was carefully expressionless, and Amy suddenly knew, beyond any question, that it would not just be a few minutes before Rachel was returned to her father. She knew that these people had no intention of ever returning the child to her father, and she knew that this time she wasn't just being paranoid. Still, she could hardly back out now.

And they weren't planning to return those personal belongings, either. She threw a glance at Susan and her purse; Susan was being smart, if she could get away with it.

Just what they *did* plan, Amy didn't know. She pushed that thought aside, though, at least for the moment, and forced herself to smile at the girl.

Rachel stared at her for a moment, then pulled away from the announcer's hand and slipped through the door.

*P*el watched Rachel go, then reluctantly allowed himself to be pushed through the door into the men's changing room.

He took his clothes off with dull mechanical efficiency, trying not to think. Nancy was dead, and now Rachel had been taken away; he was lost two universes away from home — he didn't *dare* think. He knew that Rachel was supposed to rejoin him after they had showered, but on some level he didn't dare believe that, *couldn't* believe it, because the possibility of disappointment was too horrible to contemplate. Better to give her up as lost now, while he knew she was still alive and in the hands of someone who, if not exactly a trusted friend, was at least familiar and not obviously hostile or alien.

If he let himself think, he knew he would start anticipating Rachel's return, would start wondering if Nancy was *really* dead, would start planning a return to Earth — and Rachel was gone, Nancy was dead, and he would never get home, he knew that and dared not let himself hope.

So he dared not let himself think. He peeled off his worn clothes quickly and dropped them in the box provided, focusing his eyes and mind on the texture of the concrete floor, the scuff marks on the steel bench, the grain in the box's cardboard — all of it simple visual data that occupied his attention and filled his mind.

Some part of him probably wondered how he would reclaim the right box, but right now he really couldn't worry about it.

Mechanically, he walked naked into the shower room, where the other men were already bathing themselves, Cahn and his surviving men, passengers and crew of *Emerald Princess,* Raven and his companions. Ted Deranian was not merely bathing, he was singing quietly.

Pel plodded into the room, but made no move toward the showerheads.

And behind him, between the shower room and the changing room, a heavy steel door dropped into place.

The others started, turned, shouted. Pel didn't bother; he stood, spray from the showers splashing his legs, water running down across his ankles and onto the tile floor.

He had known. Something like that had to be coming. He had known. And it didn't matter anymore.

Nancy was dead. Rachel was surely gone now, closed off by that metal barrier, as he had known she would be. He was trapped. He was doomed.

They were going to kill him. They were going to kill everybody. He was going to die. Maybe he was already dead. Maybe this was Hell, this Galactic Empire, not part of any living reality at all.

Maybe he was mad.

Maybe he was dreaming — but no. That was Ted's theory, and he had seen what happened to Ted. Besides, that was the way to false hope, because every dreamer must wake eventually.

Pel knew he was not going to wake up.

*T*his mass ablution was distasteful, but Raven had acquiesced, had taken off his garments and placed them neatly in one of the odd little boxes provided. He had stepped into the water chamber, and had allowed the water to wash over him. He was not yet ready to draw attention to himself, beyond the comments already made upon his attire.

When the portcullis fell, though, he cursed his own foolishness in playing along this far.

Now, with his clothes gone, what was to mark him apart from the common mass of humanity? How was he to assert his identity?

True, the clothes would not have been proof, for the veriest madman might contrive himself the appropriate garb to support his tales, but they were all he had, save his own words.

Now, he had only his tongue and his wits.

Further, this locking away seemed a sign that the lordling that had captured them was done with them, and was now consigning them to whatever fate awaited them.

Slavery, most likely — a sorry life tilling the soil somewhere, back bent to the hoe and burnt by the sun.

Cold anger grew in his chest as warm water spilled down his side. Raven of Stormcrack Keep, a mere tender of vegetables?

Not so long as breath remained in him!

*A*my stared at the steel door. After an initial yip of surprise she hadn't bothered to shout or scream or protest; some of the other women, though, were not so resigned. Three of the passengers from *Emerald Princess* were pounding on the metal with their bare wet hands, calling out until the shower room echoed deafeningly.

Slaves, Amy thought, they were going to be slaves. Bill Mervyn was right. That was why the door had dropped, she was certain — buyers would want to see what they were getting. No fancy packaging, no clothes. The showers were genuine enough, because the slavers wanted their merchandise clean, but they also wanted them naked, and how else could that be accomplished without argument?

She looked down at Rachel, who was looking up at her in silent puzzlement.

"It's okay, honey," she said. "They don't want us going back that way, that's all. They aren't going to hurt us."

At least, she thought, not yet. Slavers wouldn't be eager to damage the merchandise.

But the new owners . . .

The new owners could be anybody and anything. Sadists, perverts — or just people looking for cheap labor.

If she were lucky, whoever bought her would just want cheap labor.

"All right, ladies," the matron called. "Out this way, when you're done washing."

Amy turned and found that the drab grey door at the far end of the shower room, the door that had looked so much like access to a broom closet or furnace room that nobody had consciously noticed it at all, was now open. The matron was standing there, her billy club in her hand, her blue uniform starting to sag and darken with the moisture in the air.

Amy managed a smile as she told Rachel, "Come on; we might as well get on with it."

"What about our clothes?" someone shouted; other voices chimed in.

Amy, Rachel, and Susan didn't bother shouting, but they heard the matron's explanation. "We'll have them waiting when you're dried off. This way, please."

The women from Earth exchanged glances. They knew better. They would not be getting their clothes back — at least, not for some time yet. Amy wondered if Rachel knew, too.

Susan's purse was not in sight, and Amy had no idea what her attorney had done with it.

*P*el toweled himself off quickly, though he had never gotten all that wet; then he stood and waited.

This was no dream, no fairy tale. He wasn't going to wake up back home. This shower room wasn't going to melt away like morning mist. He wasn't going to get out of here by wishing. He couldn't get back to his own world that easily.

This was real life, and real life was never that simple, there were never any ruby slippers.

In the stories everything came out right in the end. In the stories someone would rescue them, Nancy would still be alive, it would all be a mistake.

This was no story.

Someone might rescue them. It did happen. There were possibilities. There was Prossie Thorpe — or at least, there had been Prossie Thorpe, he had seen her in the waiting room, maybe even in the dining hall, but she might be dead by now. Death only took an instant.

And there might be some way to save himself. The hero of a story would do that, he wouldn't wait to be rescued. In stories there was always a way out.

But in real life, sometimes there was and sometimes there wasn't. Sometimes the hostages were rescued; sometimes they died. Sometimes the innocent were saved; sometimes they were slaughtered.

Real life was never as tidy as the stories.

"You done?" one of the guards asked.

He nodded.

"Toss me the towel, then, and I'll see if we're ready for you."

Pel obeyed, and stood naked and waiting while the other men, seeing their protests did no good, finished drying themselves and stood chatting uneasily among themselves.

There were three guards, each with a baton — no blasters, no blades. It occurred to Pel that the thirty or so prisoners could easily overpower them. In the stories, the hero would organize them and they'd do it, they'd overpower the guards — but then what?

Thirty men, naked and unarmed, on a hostile planet, with no idea where they were — what could they do?

In the stories they'd find a way, but this was no story.

Three guards were plenty.

A loud click was audible over the general background noise; Pel turned to see that the door opposite the shower room, a door that had been locked, was now open. One of the three blue-clad men stood beside it, baton at ready.

"Okay, one at a time," he called. "You!" He pointed at Pel. "You ready? You first."

Slowly and deliberately, Pel crossed the room.

This was it; he was about to die.

This was the last minute, when the rescuers would burst in with blasters ready — in the stories.

In real life, it was when the victims died like sheep.

Would it be a bullet? A shot from a blaster? Would they cut his throat, butcher him like an animal?

He didn't know, and wasn't really sure he cared. He stepped through the door.

Two men were waiting for him in the corridor.

"Hands behind your back," one of them ordered, as the other grasped his upper left arm. Pel obeyed, and cuffs were slapped on.

He didn't get a good look at them, and couldn't turn his head far enough to see them once they were in place, but he could tell from the feel that these were not the slim steel bands used by modern police; they were wider and heavier than that, like old-fashioned manacles.

He considered that dispassionately. Would he be blindfolded, next? Posed against a wall for a firing squad, perhaps? Led up the steps of a gallows?

The guard who had cuffed him took his right arm, the other still held his left. He was led down the corridor and through another door.

As the door opened Pel blinked, and tried to stop, but the pressure on his arms forced him onward. Suddenly horribly aware of his nakedness, he struggled, but to no avail. He felt his scrotum contracting, as if he had just plunged into cold water.

He was being dragged out onto a stage, in front of a crowd of at least a hundred people, men and women; those he could see were dressed in strange but elegant clothing.

This was *worse* than death, worse than the gallows or firing squad. He trembled, and might have screamed if one of his guards hadn't jerked him back and shoved a gag in his mouth.

The stage was lit, but so was the audience; he was on display, but this was no play, no mere performance.

An announcer stood behind a lectern at the far side of the stage. "Lot Number One," he called, "a healthy adult male, age and history uncertain. What am I bid?"

Raven stood straight and proud as the auctioneer called out the bids. He thrust out his chest, threw back his shoulders, and set his jaw.

If he were sold as a mere farmhand or miner he would stand no chance of gaining authority's ear. Were he to be bought as a conscript for the guard, as a bodyguard perhaps, or as someone's personal attendant, his chances were that much better.

He had heard the bidding on other men, and he allowed himself a smile when he heard the auctioneer call out, "Four hundred! Four hundred and ten! Do I hear . . . I have four hundred and ten!"

The smile broadened when he heard a woman's voice from the audience and the bid jumped to four twenty-five.

None of the others ahead of him had gone for so much. He had guessed that four hundred was the ceiling for simple labor. If he went for more than that . . .

Amy could hear the remarks as she was led out.

"No yearling this time, hey?"

"Drooping a little."

"Is this somebody's grandmother?"

She started to react, to glare at the audience, then stopped herself. This wasn't some stupid movie; acting up wouldn't impress anyone with her spunk. It would probably just get her a whack from one of those damned billy clubs.

Just as arguing with Stan hadn't impressed him, hadn't cowed him, hadn't won him over, hadn't gotten an apology. It just got her hit and finished off the ruins of their marriage.

The lights were on the audience as well as the stage, so that bids could be spotted, and Amy looked out at the bidders, but she didn't glare, didn't make any stupid defiant gestures. This was no movie.

If it *were* a movie, of course, rescue would probably arrive right about now. And there were so many things about this that seemed unreal — castles and monsters and spaceships — that why *shouldn't* there be a last-minute rescue? All those Imperial troopers in their spiffy purple uniforms ought to be good for *something,* and surely Prossie Thorpe had had plenty of time to send a telepathic cry for help.

In fact, why hadn't help already come?

She had glimpsed Prossie Thorpe briefly in the showers and in the drying room; she should have asked. She had been busy with Rachel, though, and when she had looked elsewhere it had been at Susan and her mysterious vanishing handbag, or the passengers off the *Princess* banging on the door.

Mostly she had paid attention to Rachel. Now she and Rachel had been separated by the guards anyway, to be auctioned off individually.

The thought of that poor little girl being sold like an animal was ghastly. It couldn't be allowed. Something would have to happen to prevent it.

Prossie Thorpe was the only hope, though. *Did* the pirates and slavers know that Prossie was a telepath? They were treating her like anyone else. Did they have some way of blocking her telepathy?

How would they know what she was? How could they block something that could work between universes?

Help had to be coming. It had to be on the way.

But there was no sign of it. She was standing naked on a bare stage, about to be auctioned off, and she could see the cracks in the plaster walls, could smell the cologne someone in the front row was wearing, could hear someone whispering, but she couldn't see or hear or smell any sign that anyone was coming to save her. No ships rumbling overhead, no soldiers shouting, just rustling clothes and muttered asides, and somewhere behind her the clink of manacles.

"What am I bid?" the auctioneer called, and the moment of silence before the reply was the most embarrassing few seconds in Amy's entire life.

*P*el wondered how much two hundred and eighty crowns actually was. It didn't sound like very much.

But then, why should he be worth much? Somehow he didn't think a place like this would have much use for a marketing consultant, and without that he was just another warm body, another set of not-very-developed muscles.

He didn't put up any fight when his new owner came and collected him; he was so relieved to be off that stage, away from all those staring eyes, that he was almost glad to see the man who had paid two hundred and eighty crowns for him. The whole experience had been exhausting, terrifying, unbearable; he was more certain than ever that he had somehow found himself captive in Hell.

Rachel — would they auction *Rachel* off that way?

Who would buy a six-year-old girl, and why?

He was so involved with his own thoughts, with trying to keep them away from certain subjects, that he barely noticed when he was loaded into an airbus, barely noticed when he was turned over to someone else, when he was led into the mine shaft, when the manacles were removed.

The overseer had to slap him to get his attention.

"All right, new boy," he said. "You listening now?"

Pel nodded, gently touching his stinging cheek.

"You're new, you don't seem too bright, we'll keep it simple for you. Those guys over there are breaking rock; your job is getting that rock off the floor and into the carts, so we can get it out of here. You can use your hands, or if you ask nice we'll give you a shovel." The overseer glowered at him, hands on hips, the overhead light emphasizing his downturned features with streaks of shadow.

Pel took the hint. "Please, sir," he said, "may I have a shovel?"

One of the workers at the rock face grinned and kicked a shovel over toward Pel; it clattered loudly in the enclosed space. Watching the overseer's face, ready to duck or drop the shovel, Pel cautiously picked it up.

The overseer gave a snort and turned away.

Pel, holding the shovel but not moving, watched him go. He made no move to smash in the overseer's skull with the edge of the shovel; the urge was there, at least slightly, but he knew it would do no good. It couldn't be that easy.

Then the overseer was out of sight and the opportunity had passed.

"Hey, new boy," one of the workers called. "You got a name?"

"Pel," Pel admitted, turning.

"I'm Jack. You really stupid, or just confused?"

"Disoriented, mostly," Pel answered.

"Yeah. I figured. Well, it's not really all that bad here; we get food and shelter and as long as we get the ore out they don't bother us. You'll get clothes, too."

Pel registered for the first time that the other men — there were half a dozen in sight — wore pants and boots. No shirts — but then, the mine shaft was hot. Sweat gleamed on every side in the light of the four electric work-lights that hung from the shaft's ceiling.

"They'll give you your duds at supper tonight," Jack told him. "After we change shifts. You do the first day naked to remind you that you ain't worth shit, but after that they'd just as soon you didn't get scratched up."

"We change shifts?" Pel asked.

Jack nodded. "We got two shifts, twelve hours each, work here; meals before and after, and they send down food and water around mid-shift."

"Are we . . ." Pel swallowed; his throat was suddenly dry. "Are we the day shift or the night shift?"

Jack smiled. "Neither one; guess you *are* new. Local day is something like seventeen hours, so everybody just ignores it; all the clocks are on Terran time."

"Oh."

"We're the Blue Shift; the other one's red. Somebody's idea of a joke, I guess. You'll get a cot, share it with someone on Red Shift."

Pel nodded. He stood, the shovel in his hands, trying to absorb all this.

"Hey, buddy," another man called, "enough with the lessons. Get to work."

Pel looked at Jack, who nodded and pointed to the pile of ore and slag. "There you are," he said.

The rock was on one side, the empty cart on the other, and Pel between, with his shovel. The rock was fist-sized lumps; the cart was a battered black metal box on steel wheels; the shovel was a shovel.

He started shoveling.

*A*my looked over the interior of the aircar apprehensively. She didn't like the situation at all.

She had seen most of the others, male and female, sold to men in various uniforms, and formed into gangs — obviously destined for manual labor somewhere. A few who had had specific skills announced had drawn higher-than-average bids and had presumably been bound for jobs that could use their talents.

But the auctioneer had announced Susan with an audible leer in his voice. "A really *nice* young woman," he had said, grinning. "History unknown, looks a bit exotic." And the bidding had been enthusiastic — she had gone for eleven hundred and something, higher than anyone else Amy saw sold. Susan was small and slender, with no known skills, so nobody was buying her as a laborer. It was obvious what her value was.

And one of the bidders for Susan — one of the losing bidders — had been the one who bought Amy for five hundred and ten. He hadn't bid on anyone else after that; he had just stood in his spot along the right-hand wall, watching her, waiting until he could claim her. He wore no uniform, no fancy clothes, just a dull white shirt and black slacks; he had no clipboard, no notes, none of the totems and devices the other buyers flourished.

And when the paperwork was done, and he could collect her, he hadn't said a word; he had just grabbed her by one manacled wrist and had dragged her out to the parking lot where his aircar waited.

That had given her her first glimpse of the outside world on whatever planet this was, save for the quick dash across bare concrete from the pirate ship to the holding facility, and she had been interested by the look around, despite her worries. They were clearly in a city — she really hadn't been sure of that from the glimpse between the ship and the entrance tunnel. None of the buildings in sight from the parking lot were over three stories high, but the streets were lined solidly with masonry, showing no gaps in the stone and concrete façades. The architecture ran to colonnades and pilasters, with little ornamentation — it reminded her of old pictures of the Soviet Union under Stalin.

Then she had been shoved into the rear seat of the aircar, and a moment later they were airborne, just the two of them. She wondered if she should say something, anything, but she had no idea what would be appropriate. After all, she had never been auctioned off before.

She studied the interior of the aircar.

The dark red upholstery was worn; a tear in the back of the rear seat had been darned with heavy thread, but the off-white stuffing still showed through. The nap of the rough fabric scratched her bare bottom, her manacled hands made it difficult to sit back, and she shifted repeatedly in an unsuccessful attempt to find a comfortable position.

If she had been wearing anything, she thought, she would have been much more comfortable.

The windows were clean; the cranks to open them had been removed, she noticed, leaving bare threaded metal. The metal was dull, not shiny — the removal wasn't recent.

The rear shelf, behind the seat, was dusty and empty. The front seat was more of the same, dark red fabric, worn but clean and serviceable.

The driver — well, the driver was medium height, heavy, with a round, sweaty face. His expression seemed to vary from hostile and blank to an unpleasant smile, and his gaze had never yet met her own. All she could see of him now was the back of his head, thick black hair that could have used a shampoo and trim.

He hadn't said a word to her.

And he had just *bought* her, for five hundred and ten crowns, however much that was.

However much it actually came to, it was less than half what Susan had been valued at; Amy wondered if she should be offended by the difference. Of course, Susan was at least ten years younger, and ten pounds thinner — or maybe twenty. She wasn't sagging anywhere yet, the way Amy was.

She was just as sold, though. Amy had seen her standing motionless on the stage, her face calm and resigned; almost everyone else who had stood there had been visibly nervous, trembling or sweating, glancing in all directions as if expecting sudden rescue.

It was about time for that rescue, Amy thought. It was *past* time. Prossie Thorpe must have called for help days ago; wasn't it due to arrive by now?

After all, in the movies help always arrived before anything really terrible could happen, didn't it? And this whole thing, spaceships falling out of the sky into her yard, Raven and Shadow and the Galactic Empire — wasn't it all something out of the movies?

If help didn't come soon . . .

She didn't want to think about it.

Not just for herself, but all the others. What was going to happen to Susan? What had become of Rachel? Amy hadn't seen her out on that stage; the girl had been pulled away by the female guards and put at the rear of the female line. Maybe they had the decency not to make slaves of little girls, Amy thought; maybe they would find a good home for her.

And maybe not.

Chapter Twenty-Two

*T*he aircar set down on a gravel square in the front yard of a rambling one-story house; the little patch of pavement was surrounded on all sides by grass, and that, in turn, was surrounded on every side by cornfields. The crops stood from knee- to waist-high, and stretched off as far as Amy could see in every direction. In the distance she could see the wind drawing patterned ripples in the fields, but where she stood the air was still.

A few scraggly oak trees had been planted near the house, but as yet none were much taller than Amy, and while she wasn't short, she was hardly

Amazonian.

The driver got out, slammed the front door, then turned and opened the rear.

"Get out," he said.

Amy got out, not hurriedly, but not hanging back, either. The manacles made it a bit awkward.

Once she was out the gravel hurt her bare feet, and she danced a painful two steps to the grass. "Ow," she said.

"Come on," the man ordered, turning away from her and toward the house.

Amy looked around.

She stood beside a gravel square, connected by a gravel path to a concrete stoop; the house behind that stoop was half-timbered, with something like orange clay forming most of the walls, while the frame and trim were dark unpainted wood. The roof was thatch. The windows were large, with only a few large panes, which seemed at variance with the rest of the architecture.

A front lawn of neatly-trimmed grass extended out from the house and around the gravel landing area. On all sides of the lawn green corn plants marched in neat rows across the reddish earth.

The idea of escape struck her. Her feet were free; the man had made no move to stop her when she hopped off the gravel, and now she was a good five feet away, out of his reach. He didn't look like much of an athlete. If she were to turn and start running, she thought she could probably outrace him and outlast him.

But where would she go?

She couldn't see any human-made structure except the house and aircar, anywhere. She was naked, her hands chained, on an unknown and hostile planet. There weren't any lawyers or cops to help her this time, no friends or family she could hope to contact.

Where *could* she go?

Reluctantly, she turned and followed her captor toward the house.

*W*hen Raven was first informed of his duties he balked. The rightful lord of Stormcrack Keep, kept to play the stud for some fat old mare?

"Why else would someone pay five hundred crowns for you?" asked his new mistress' majordomo, who had bid for and bought him on the woman's behalf.

Raven had no quick reply.

In truth, he had no reply at all; he knew too little of his new home to make any guesses.

And upon further consideration, he decided that perhaps this was for the best. A woman who could afford such luxuries must needs be powerful indeed, in the local hierarchy, and what better way to ingratiate himself than by such services as she was demanding?

Nor was there any great hurry; she had ordered that he be fed and pampered for a day or two, that he might be up to the task.

He had not as yet seen her; her agents had collected him after the auction.

As he ate and drank he found himself imagining what she might look like. A wealthy woman, they told him, and as his purchase demonstrated; she was presumably not of noble birth, for these people, degenerate barbarians that they were, put no store by ancestry, but he would make allowances for that. And no great beauty, surely, else she would have no need to buy a man's services. Still, doubtless she would have her virtues.

Doubtless.

*T*he food was boring, with a peculiar off taste to it, but it was nourishing. Pel found the work boring, as well, and tiring, but not particularly difficult — it called for endurance, but no great strength or skill. No one abused him; the overseer checked in maybe once an hour, billy club in hand, and then went on to inspect the other work gangs. There were no whips, no groaning wheels, no one dying of exhaustion, none of the clichés of slave-worked mines that Hollywood had taught him. The men worked hard, but were a long way from killing themselves, and as long as the broken rock came out of the shaft on schedule nobody bothered them.

In fact, the workers exchanged bitter jokes about their situation, and laughed at them.

Pel didn't laugh with them. He was gradually coming out of his funk, but was not yet ready to laugh at anything.

There was a sort of dull comfort in the steady work, in pushing the shovel under the rock, lifting it, and dumping it into the cart. It kept his body busy, kept him moving, so that he couldn't sink completely into apathy and despair, but it still left him free to think if he wanted to.

And it tired him, so that when he was off-shift he slept soundly.

That twelve hours on, twelve hours off was deceptive, he discovered. His gang, along with the rest of Blue Shift, was only permitted to leave their shaft when their replacements from Red Shift had arrived and actually begun working. Walking back out to the refectory and dormitory, being checked out by the clerk at the shaft mouth, finding a seat in the refectory — that took half an hour or more. The refectory crew wasn't in any great hurry, either. And the meals were fairly leisurely; no one rushed.

On top of that, if he wanted his sweat-soaked pants laundered, he had to wash them himself, in the lavatory sinks — and most of the men did just that, because odors lingered in the unventilated shafts. Each slave had been issued one pair of pants, and one pair of wool-lined boots — no socks. Not much could be done about the smell from the boots, but washing the pants out each night was a social necessity. Lines for drying ran the length of the dormitory halls, and every night a pair of damp trousers hung over each bed; if a man was too exhausted to wash them, at the very least he hung them to air out. Aside from the smell, moisture seethed constantly in the cool night air; anything left damp with sweat and *not* hung out was an invitation to mildew and rot.

With the walk to and from his work area, the leisurely meals, the washing up, and the lines everywhere, Pel found he only had about nine hours to sleep, and no time left at all for any sort of diversion. Nine hours was not excessive at all, given the unaccustomed heavy labor.

He could speak to the other slaves, of course — on the job, at the table, in the lavatories and dorms. At first, though, he didn't. They were strangers, not even from his world, and he was still too caught up in his losses.

The men around him accepted that; nobody bothered him. Occasionally someone would try to include him in a discussion, but nobody forced it, nobody pressured him.

But he gradually came out of his funk, and by the third day he was thinking again, thinking about just one thing, the one thing that any storybook hero, or any sane man, would think about.

Escape.

*A*s Amy and the black-haired man approached the house the front door opened, and a woman appeared. She was short and dumpy, in her forties, her dull brown hair tied back. A shapeless brown floral-print dress covered her from throat to ankle.

She looked critically at Amy.

Amy was reminded anew that she, herself, wasn't wearing anything at all. Even an ugly brown dress would have been an improvement.

She hadn't exactly had a choice, though, and at least the weather was reasonably warm. Walking around naked in snow would have been much worse.

"I see you got one," the woman said.

The man didn't bother to reply.

"What'd she cost?"

"Five hundred," the man growled, pushing past the woman into the house.

Amy was mincing across the gravel to the stoop by then, trying to keep her feet intact. The woman watched with interest. "That's not too bad, five hundred," she said. "And she's got nice hair, it looks like — hard to be sure, the mess it's in."

The man growled something Amy couldn't make out as she gratefully stepped up onto the smooth concrete and found herself face to face with the woman in brown. She hesitated, looking down slightly at this person, apparently the mistress of the house.

"Go on," the woman said, gesturing. "Get inside."

Amy got inside.

The door opened into a large, open room; the floor was gray concrete spread with bright rag rugs, the walls papered in a wine-red pattern of stripes and blossoms on primrose. Most of the furniture used black iron frames to support upholstered seats and backs, the iron seemingly in rough imitation of early American woodwork.

The man who had bought her stood by an open door; beyond, Amy could see a cheerful bedroom. "Come here," he ordered.

Amy glanced at the woman.

"Guess I'll go take a walk," the woman in brown said. She stepped out the door, closing it behind her.

"Come here, bitch, if you want those cuffs off," the man called.

Amy hesitated.

Wasn't it about time for the space cavalry to come charging over the hill? Hadn't Prossie done *anything*? Couldn't the Empire find her?

The memory of Stan was far clearer than she wanted, just now. This man didn't look anything like him, but something in his voice had the same ugly edge Stan had developed.

"Get the fuck over here, bitch!"

Reluctantly, Amy crossed the room, stumbling over the upturned edge of one of the rugs. The man stepped back into the bedroom as she approached, and to one side.

"On the bed," he ordered. "On your knees."

"Why?" Amy demanded, her throat dry.

"Why do you *think?*" he retorted. "If I just wanted someone to do housework, I could've gotten someone cheaper than you — a kid or somebody's grandmother. I couldn't afford that black-haired one, but you'll do."

"You're planning . . ." She swallowed, moistening her throat, and tried again. "Planning to rape me?"

"What the hell else did I buy you for?"

The woman was outside somewhere; as far as Amy knew, if she could overpower this one man, she would be safe, at least for the moment. Amy considered kicking him in the crotch, but he was off to the side, the angle was wrong — he could dodge. And she was still manacled, her hands behind her back, which would throw her balance off.

She didn't have any weapons, but neither did her captor, so far as she could see.

She was still trying to think of something when his patience ran out and he grabbed for her arm, saying, "Get *over* there!"

She dodged, turned, and ran, with no plan at all except to get away.

With a growl, he ran after her.

She was turning, trying to get her hand on the door handle, when he caught up with her and punched her in the belly.

The air rushed out of her lungs, and she felt a sudden constriction, a cramping of her diaphragm, as if she were about to vomit. She doubled over, and his other hand came down on the back of her head, knocking her off-balance. She fell to her knees, slamming her right knee hard against the concrete floor; before she could regain her balance he drove both hands, clenched together, against the back of her head, knocking her forward. She caught herself on one shoulder just before her face hit one of the rugs, but then the man's booted foot came down on the back of her neck and pressed her cheek down against the coiled fabric.

"Stupid bitch," he growled. "Where the hell would you have gone, bare-ass naked and with your hands chained?" Holding her down with his foot, he unfastened his belt. "Get it through your head, I *own* you. You do what I tell you, or I'll beat the shit out of you. Give me too much trouble and I'll kill you

— and don't think it'll do me any harm, either; on this planet, nobody thinks twice about killing a slave. I've done it once already." He fumbled at the buttons on his fly; from the corner of her eye Amy could see his fingers working.

This was the time for a rescue, all right. This was it, the last minute, when help was supposed to come.

It didn't.

He bent over her and grabbed her manacled hands, pushed them up behind her back with one hand while the other stroked slowly down her side and across her buttocks. She squirmed, trying to pull away, and he shoved the cuffs viciously.

She had her breath back now, but if she struggled she knew it wouldn't help any.

She screamed.

That didn't help, either. He laughed, a harsh, nervous laugh, as he knelt behind her.

And rescue didn't come.

*R*aven's first impression was of an infinite field of lace and fine fabric beneath a mountain of flesh. As the door closed behind him he thought that this was surely some mistake, that the bed already held two or three people; was he expected to service them all?

Then she lifted her head from the pillows and beckoned to him, and even in the dim orange light, even among the myriad pillows and cushions and hangings, her shape became clear, the huge masses of her belly and breasts and thighs.

The partial erection beneath his robe, prompted by anticipation and imagination, vanished.

"Come here," she said, in a thin soprano. "Come and sit beside me." She patted the bed, her fingers like thick pale sausages.

Reluctantly, he obeyed.

The odor of perfume and her own scent, horribly sweet and cloying, reached him even before he sat down beside her. He did not look at her.

"Take off that silly robe," she told him.

He stood and slowly removed the robe, letting it fall to the floor.

He had not considered what would happen if he were unable to perform. It was simply not a question that had ever arisen for him before. Refusal, yes, he had thought about that — and he had decided against it. Inability had never occurred to him. He turned to face her, trying to think of other women, beautiful women.

A little plumpness was a good thing in a woman, certainly, a little flesh on the bones, and he wouldn't have wanted one of those gaunt, bony scarecrows he had seen betimes, with hipbones that would grind against you and ribs that would dig into your own, but this great pile of powdered flesh scarcely looked human at all, the skin was coarse and pasty, with none of the smooth resilience of a woman's . . .

Yet she *was* a woman, and he could smell her musk. She was waiting for him, she held the power of life and death over him. However repulsive she might be, she wanted him to make love to her.

And however repulsive she might be, he would have to try.

Chapter Twenty-Three

There was only one way out of the mine, so far as Pel could determine. That was through the building complex that included the dormitory and refectory, as well as a great deal of industrial equipment he couldn't identify — machines that sorted and processed the rocks that were sent up in the carts. Pel never got a clear look at most of that area; he had no business there. He saw glimpses when he came up out of the shaft; he heard the distant rumblings as he ate or slept.

He had come in that way, but the airbus had landed in an enclosed courtyard, at the bottom of an air shaft somewhere — he would not go out by that route.

There were no side-shafts, no back way out of the mine itself, so far as he could determine.

Where he emerged from the shaft each day the cart tracks ran straight ahead, through a large black pair of swinging doors; he and the other workers always turned right into a gray-painted corridor that ran between the refectory and kitchen on the left, the dormitory and lavatory on the right.

He figured that the ore must eventually leave the complex somehow, and probably not by air, but trying to follow it seemed far too risky; judging by the sound, he was as likely to find himself in a crusher or a furnace as outside.

So any escape route would have to be from the living areas, rather than the work areas.

That didn't look very promising, either. The dormitory's light and air came from a handful of small clerestory windows — this planet's architectural preferences, and in fact those of the entire Galactic Empire, from what Pel had seen, seemed to run to clerestories. Getting up to them would not be easy, and since he could not look out, he had no idea what lay beyond.

He tried watching for shadows when the sun shone — or rather, whatever star served as the sun here; the light was a little more orange than seemed natural. He determined that a chimney or similar structure stood near one window, but beyond that he could learn nothing that way.

The adjoining lavatory was arranged similarly, and the single clerestory there was frosted and barred. A filthy skylight added a little more light, but no more hope for his escape.

The refectory had a row of tall, narrow, heavily-barred windows looking out on a small, paved courtyard — little more than an overgrown air shaft, really. It did have a gate into a passageway at one end, but Pel was unable to see where that gate led.

That left the kitchen, and ordinary workers were not allowed in there. The slaves were not heavily guarded, in general, but at meals the two doors to the kitchen *were* watched, a billy-club-wielding overseer standing by each.

Food had to come in somewhere, Pel decided, and where it came in, he could go out.

Through the kitchens, then — that was the way to go. That was where he would find a way out of the mine complex.

Even though he was still somewhat dazed with grief and the confusion of his situation, he was rather proud of working this out. This was the sort of thing that a storybook hero would do, Horatio Hornblower or Captain Kirk or whoever — work out the best way to escape, plan it all out logically and then carry it through.

In a movie or a novel, of course, this whole episode, being captured by pirates and sold into slavery and all the rest of it, this would all just be a minor episode on the way to the big final confrontation with Shadow, the climactic battle that would save the world — but screw all that, Pel told himself, he would settle for just getting home safely. Let someone else worry about Shadow, or about the Galactic Empire, or about Earth itself; he had his own problems.

A World War II POW wouldn't have worried about assassinating Hitler (though he might dream of it); he'd worry about getting home alive.

And that was what Pel was doing. Take it one step at a time, he told himself, and the first step would be to get out of the mine complex by way of the kitchens.

Of course, he would still be stranded on a hostile planet, with nothing but his pants and the boots on his feet and whatever he could grab on the way out. He would still need to find Rachel somehow — but he might be able to bring back help to rescue her if he could just get off the planet. Besides, if he was ever to get home to Earth, he would need to find some way to get back to Base One.

Stowing away, perhaps, or stealing a ship — though he realized he had no idea how to navigate a spaceship.

Stowing away, then. He would make his break through the kitchen, hide wherever he could, and find his way to the nearest spaceport. That was the only possible route. If he found any friendly faces along the way, he would see about finding and freeing Rachel.

No storybook hero could do any better, he was sure.

He arrived at these conclusions without ever mentioning a word about escape to any of his fellow slaves; it was only after he had reached this point in his plans that he decided to risk a few whispered questions while working.

Jack, the unofficial leader of his work gang, picked up on his hints immediately. He put down the pick he had been swinging.

"Thinking about making a run for it?" he said, sympathetically. "We all think about it, sometimes. I suppose you were figuring on the kitchen route? You don't look like the sort who plans on going out the dorm windows. Or hadn't you got that far?"

"I was thinking about the kitchen," Pel admitted, dismayed that this didn't seem to be news.

"Doesn't hurt to think, I guess," Jack said, nodding. "We've had a few people try it, but nobody's ever made it. A couple have gotten themselves killed. Farthest anybody ever got without dying . . ."

"How do you know they died?" Pel interrupted.

"Because they hauled the bodies back to show us, of course," Jack replied, unruffled. "Wouldn't do anyone any good to let any rumors about successful escapes get started. They don't want to kill us, after all; we cost good money."

Pel grimaced.

"Anyway," Jack went on, "the farthest anyone's gotten is the back courtyard. See, when you go through the kitchen, there's just one door outside, and that goes into a walled courtyard where they keep the trash cans and so forth, with this big sliding iron door at the back — and the door's been closed every time anyone's gotten that far. Apparently it's always closed when anybody from inside is on that side of the passageway."

"It can't always be shut," Pel protested.

"Of course not," Jack agreed. "But it is during meals, and the rest of the time the kitchen's locked."

"So nobody's gotten past that door?"

"That's right. And nobody's going to. There are only two ways to get even that far, and neither of them is going to be real popular."

"What two?" Pel asked.

"First, you can rush it — ten or fifteen guys charge in there, and the guards can't stop them all. Everybody knows that; the guards don't even try if they see it's a whole mob. What they do do is sound an alarm, and when everybody goes charging out into the courtyard to try to haul that door open, they find a bunch of thugs with blasters looking down at them from the walls."

Pel nodded.

"And the second way," Jack said, "is to create a diversion, so that one or two people can slip through. That's tough — those guards aren't stupid, or at least, whoever gave them their orders isn't. And there are cooks and people in the kitchens; you can't sneak past them, you have to make a dash for it. The cooks won't bother you — that's not their job — but you can't hide, either, because they'll see you. So you'll get out to the courtyard, and you can't move that door, it takes more than one man to get it open, and before you can come up with anything else the guards will catch on and come out after you and beat the shit out of you."

Pel thought for a moment, pushing his shovel as he did. He had been disappointed to hear that all his plans were old hat, but surely, there was some overlooked possibility here, one that he could spot.

He had a rule of thumb from his marketing work that came to mind, a question he always asked himself: When you have two possibilities, can you combine them?

"Well," he suggested, "what if you did that, got one or two guys through to the courtyard, and *then* ten or twelve guys stormed through, and caught the guards from behind?"

Jack blinked. "I don't know," he admitted. "I don't think that one's been tried while I've been here."

"I think we should try it," Pel said.

Jack didn't answer for a long moment. He lifted his pick and hefted it thoughtfully, eyeing Pel.

"Maybe we should," he said.

W hen he was done he fished a key from somewhere, unfastened the manacles, and stood aside, dangling the cuffs from one hand. Amy didn't move.

"All right, bitch," he said. "Get up and clean yourself off, and then let's get some clothes on you."

Amy didn't move; she crouched, trembling with fury and shame, on the floor.

Even Stan had never done that to her.

"Oh, come on," he said, kicking her in the side. "You weren't any goddamn virgin."

She still refused to move.

"Goddamn stupid bitch," he muttered. He pushed her aside with his foot, the rug where her face and arms rested slipping easily, and opened the front door.

Amy considered a lunge for his leg, now that her hands were free. She shifted her weight, judging the distance.

He glanced down and saw the movement; cautiously, he stepped further away.

"Beth," he called, "get in here, will you?"

Amy bit her lower lip. The woman would be coming back, and in a minute it would be two against one. This was probably the best chance she would ever get; he probably thought she was cowed and helpless. She lifted herself up on one arm, then threw herself sideways, grabbing at the man's leg, trying to throw him off-balance. If he fell, she saw, he would hit his head against the wall or the door frame.

She hit him, but not as hard as she had hoped; the distance was too great. He stumbled back and dropped the manacles, but caught himself, and kicked her in the face.

The cuffs clattered on the hard floor just as his boot hit her jaw, and for a moment Amy confused the sound with what she saw and felt and thought she was hearing her bones rattle. She staggered, but did not fall.

"Shit," he said. He disentangled himself, stepping back a few feet.

Amy tried to bring herself upright and get out the front door, all at once, but she was still stooped and still inside when one hand closed on the back of her neck. Awkward and off-balance, she was unable to resist as he rammed her head forward, driving her forehead against the door frame.

Dazed, she slid back to the floor.

He reached down, grabbed her arm just below the shoulder, and hauled her up to her knees.

"Listen, stupid," he said, "I *told* you, there's nowhere to go. So just settle down and live with it, all right? You might even get to like it, if you give it a chance."

Dazed, her vision blurred, aching a dozen places, Amy reluctantly nodded. She would wait.

She would not yield, but she would wait.

*S*he allowed him a second attempt, and a third.

It made no difference; the sight of her unmanned him.

At the second trial Raven had managed to drive himself from shame to rage, in hopes that his anger would bring his blood to move, would allow him to function, but it did no good. The blood suffused his face and chest, his hands trembled with it — but not his loins.

At the third trial he forced himself not to see her, conjured up in his mind's eye all the women he had loved before, from sweet little Elenor to the fiery Alison, and still, at her touch, all his lust had faded, he had withered, and again he had failed.

She had him whipped, of course; he had expected that.

And then she sold him.

*T*alk about large-scale diversions and massed rushes was all very well, but Pel didn't expect it to work. He had his own ideas, ideas he didn't intend to share.

Jack might well be an informer, after all. He seemed to know almost *too* much.

The information about the courtyard door was probably accurate, though, and could be useful.

Pel didn't really expect his first attempt to work; it was more in the nature of a scouting expedition. It was extremely difficult to manage the first step, he found; it wasn't until the third attempt that he was able to stay awake long enough during his off shift without anyone realizing he was still awake. The heavy lifting and hauling was responsible, he knew.

Eventually, though, he did manage it, and found himself the only person conscious in the entire dormitory.

It was daylight, as it happened, and light slanted in through the windows overhead, so he was able to see clearly. Darkness could have made things more difficult — or given him additional cover, and he wasn't sure which would be more significant. Carefully, he arose from his cot and stole as silently as he could across the floor to the door.

It was locked.

He had expected that, really. He turned and crept to the lavatory. That door was never locked; after all, someone might well need the facilities at any time.

And the lavatory had another door, opening onto the central passage. That should be locked, too — but he had noticed that the latch was rusty. In the damp air of the building practically anything ferrous was likely to rust.

He had not only noticed that, he had done something about it, hammering at it surreptitiously whenever he could, trying to knock it out of shape.

His efforts had had the desired result; the door hadn't latched properly. By giving the knob a good hard tug to the left he was able to spring the door open.

Then he was out in the passageway, where he tiptoed quickly to the refectory. The doors between the dining hall and the corridor were open — Pel had noticed that they never seemed to move, from one shift to the next, and had concluded that nobody ever bothered closing them.

The doors to the kitchen were locked, of course, just as they were supposed to be.

He crossed to the tall, narrow windows, and measured the gaps between the bars. They weren't as wide as he had hoped; he would not be able to slip out that way.

He was improvising, scouting out the situation; he had no coherent plan yet. He stood for a long moment, looking around, trying to think of some way to get through the windows, or through the kitchen.

When did they post those guards at the kitchen doors?

He would come back to that.

He slipped back into the corridor and crept down toward the mine.

And that was where the guard spotted him.

He was beaten methodically, without any particular animus, and then thrown back in his cot.

He lay there, planning the next step.

*T*he man's name was Walter, but Amy was not permitted to call him anything but "master." Beth was just Beth; Amy wasn't sure of the reason for this difference.

Amy's duties were simple enough; she was to keep the house and its contents clean. Later on, if they trusted her enough, she could help tend the corn, and Beth would take over part of the cleaning, but for the present Amy was not permitted outside the house. Amy was also to be available to Walter whenever he felt the urge — which was fairly often.

She was given a simple white shift, undergarments, slippers, and an apron. She slept on the floor, with a rug underneath and a blanket on top. When she refused an order or resisted in any way, Walter would beat her into submission. If a beating didn't convince her, she would not be fed until she relented. The manacles were kept handy, and on occasion, when she had disobeyed, they were used to secure her to furniture, where she could watch Walter and Beth eat.

She did not resist very often — enough to maintain her self-respect, but not enough to seriously endanger her health. She knew that she wasn't going to do herself any good by starving, or letting Walter break bones. If she was ever to get out of this unbearable situation she would have to keep herself reasonably fit.

She thought about escape, but knew she had nowhere to go. She could not get far on foot in any case, and had no idea how to fly the aircar — even if she could start it without the key, which was doubtful. She had heard of hot-wiring a car's ignition but didn't know it was done, and in any case aircars were not necessarily the same as the cars back on Earth in such details as ignition switches.

Walter was not interested in speaking with her, and besides, he spent most of his time out of the house. Beth was out much of the time as well, but less, and she was willing to talk, and even answer questions — at least, sometimes.

She explained about the inconveniently short day, and the arrangements they had made to deal with it. She explained the basics of corn-farming, and showed Amy how to handle unfamiliar household equipment.

She answered more personal questions, too.

Yes, Amy was the only slave they had at present; they had had two others at one point, both women, both subject to Walter's whims, but last year's crop had been very bad and first Walter had sold the little one, Maggie, and then the other one, Sheila, had died.

At first, Beth insisted that Sheila had gotten sick and died before they could get a doctor for her, but eventually she admitted that Walter had gotten drunk and angry one night and had strangled her. She was buried out back. Beth pointed out the grave, visible from the back windows.

Amy had thought that the bare ground there was a small garden patch; now she stared at it and felt ill.

"He's not going to really hurt you, though," Beth said. "He couldn't afford to buy *another* slave."

Somehow, Amy did not find that very comforting.

*W*hen Raven learned the identity of his new owner, and what the man wanted of him, he realized that this was Arabella's final insult, her final comment on his own sexual prowess, or lack thereof.

It was, he supposed, to be expected.

He put it to his buyer directly, in blunt terms — how much fun could there be if Raven had to be beaten into submission every time? Raven was stronger than this new owner, so that other slaves would have to do the beating, would be required to hold him down. Was that what this Roland wanted?

What point in owning him, then?

Roland did make one test of Raven's resolve; thus convinced, and nursing a black eye as a result, he put Raven up for sale.

That was after the flogging, of course.

There were no buyers at first; nobody cared to risk any money until they knew whether or not the slave would live.

*R*eaching the clerestory windows wasn't as difficult as Pel had feared; standing a cot on end and climbing the ladderlike frame lifted him high enough to reach the sill.

The other slaves simply watched with amused interest; they made no effort to help him, but didn't hinder him, either. Nobody called for the guards. They all just watched as he chinned himself on the sill, threw up first one arm and then the other, his feet waving wildly all the time.

He hung there for a moment, looking out through the window at gray asphalt roofing and, some distance away, the tumbled gray stone of a mountainside. There were no obvious hazards or obstacles.

Encouraged, he struggled to inch upward, to swing one leg up.

It was harder than it had looked in all those old movies, all those times Indiana Jones had hung from a cliff by his fingers or whatever, but eventually he got himself out the window onto the roof.

He got cautiously to his feet and looked around.

He stood on a long, narrow rectangle of slate-gray roofing, extending the full length of the dormitory and lavatory, but only about six feet wide. The "chimney" he had located by its shadow was close by, and he now discovered it to be a vent-pipe from the lavatory's plumbing.

Behind him, the windows were set in a sheer wall extending much higher than he had expected — it had to be at least twenty feet high, and was topped with an overhang. The edge of the overhang was wrapped in dull grey metal that glinted oddly in the orange sunlight. It looked very sharp.

The height of the wall seemed to imply that there was another story to the building, but there were no more windows above the set he had climbed through, nothing above them but blank concrete. It might simply be intended as an obstacle.

That wall was too high and bare for him to climb. He turned to look at the other sides. Before him was the edge of the roof; he crouched down and peered over.

The wall dropped sheer for a ridiculous distance, given that he was only one story up — at least thirty or forty feet, it looked like.

And about thirty feet away another wall rose, a wall that appeared to be hewn out of the mountainside itself, the space between the walls forming a sort of dry moat.

He worked his way around all three sides, and the moat went all the way around. Nowhere was it narrow enough to make an attempt to jump it reasonable; nowhere was it shallow enough to make a leap down into it reasonable; nowhere did it look possible to climb back out if he once did get in.

Frustrated, he climbed back down into the dormitory — and found four guards waiting for him.

They beat him soundly and removed his bedding, to prevent any attempts at making climbing gear from the fabric.

Major Johnston swore quietly under his breath, wishing he could think of some new obscenity. The old ones had all lost their flavor by this time.

"All of them," he said. "*All* of them."

"Yes, sir." The lieutenant stood beside the desk, trying to look suitably unhappy and hide the relief he felt that this wasn't his problem.

Johnston tapped his pen on the desktop and stared up at the lieutenant. He knew the man was glad to not have the responsibility on this one, and he didn't blame him. Johnston wished *he* didn't have the responsibility, either.

And to think he had *asked* for it, and had been pleased when the FBI decided to leave it all to the military.

"The cars are really theirs? The vehicle numbers match, not just the plates?"

"Yes, sir."

"And that damned phony spaceship hasn't moved? Nobody's been inside?"

"No, sir."

The Major stopped tapping, and for a moment he sat silently. Then, abruptly, he hurled the pen across the room and roared, "*Where the hell did they go?*"

"I don't know, sir."

"You talked to the neighbors?"

"Someone did, sir, not me, personally."

"And searched the house?"

"Yes, sir."

"Legally?"

"Yes, sir; we got a warrant."

"Nobody saw anything?"

"No, sir."

"And there wasn't *anything* to say where they'd gone? Notes? Maybe something on a computer disk? *Anything?*"

"Nothing, sir. Some empty pizza boxes, a very hungry cat — nothing else out of the ordinary."

Johnston growled. "This is ridiculous. The spaceship appears out of nowhere, but does *that* disappear? No, it just *sits* there, and instead this . . this marketing consultant bails the crew out of jail, and invites the Jewell woman and her lawyer over, and they all vanish. All the cars still there. Like the goddamn *Marie Celeste.* Lieutenant, does *any* of this make sense?"

"No, sir."

"Damn right it doesn't. Almost makes me believe in the fucking Bermuda Triangle and Charles Fort and all that crap." He slumped back in his chair.

For a moment he sat silently, and the lieutenant stood, equally silent, and waited.

"The cat," Johnston said at last. "What happened to the cat?"

The lieutenant cleared his throat. "Well, sir," he said, "I've got the cat at home. He's a cute little fellow."

Johnston chewed on his lip for a moment, then snarled, "Good. Keep it. And I want that place bugged. Both places. And watched. If anyone goes in or out of Jewell's house, or Brown's, I want to not just know it happened, I want to know who it was and every goddamn word they said. Bug that ship, too. Bug the lawyers' homes and offices. *Everything.*"

"Yes, sir." The lieutenant started to turn away, but the major's voice stopped him.

"Lieutenant. Do it legally. Get court orders.

"Yes, sir."

"Lieutenant."

"Yes, sir?"

"You think we'll ever find them?"

The lieutenant considered that carefully, then shrugged.

"No, sir," he said, "I don't think we will."

Chapter Twenty-Four

By the end of the first month after the capture of *Emerald Princess* Amy had given up any hope of rescue. She had also given up resisting Walter's advances. She still neglected the housework as much as she dared, but when she received a direct order she obeyed it without argument.

She had also made the rather startling discovery that Beth was a slave, like herself, rather than Walter's wife. Walter had never bothered trying to deal with free women; he had bought Beth about twenty years ago, when they were both young, and had kept her.

This revelation left Amy feeling betrayed — right from the first, and at every point since, Beth had consistently sided with Walter against her. Bad enough that Beth had sided with a man against one of her fellow women, that she had helped Walter to rape and starve and torment Amy — but when she was herself a slave, and at least theoretically in the same situation that Amy was?

When she learned the truth Amy refused to speak to Beth for a day and a half.

She had just decided that this was a mistake, that she was only making everybody's life more difficult and making Beth less likely than ever to sympathize with her, when the whine of an aircar made her look up from the sink.

Walter hadn't said anything about expecting company. He and Beth were out in the fields somewhere.

Then another whine sounded, and another. Amy put the dishrag aside and reached for a towel to dry her hands.

Voices were calling back and forth out there; Amy tossed the towel on the counter and crossed to the window. She hesitated, then lifted the curtain and peered out.

There were a dozen men in purple uniforms out there, and three matching purple-and-gold aircars — or vehicles, anyway; they didn't look much like ordinary aircars. One of the vehicles had landed beside Walter's aircar, half on the gravel and half on the grass; the other two had set down on the corn, flattening it. The men had blasters drawn.

One of them saw her and pointed. She let the curtain drop, and her fingers trembled as she did. Her heart was racing, and her chest felt tight with excitement — was this *rescue?* Finally? Weren't those Imperial uniforms?

What should she do?

"All right, in there," an amplified voice called, "come out with your hands up!"

That answered her question. For the last few weeks she had had lesson after lesson in not resisting — and Walter hadn't even had a blaster.

She opened the door and edged out, her hands raised, fingers spread, empty palms forward.

Half a dozen blasters were leveled at her by men crouching behind aircars — armored aircars, she realized. Each had a swivel-mounted weapon on top, something vaguely resembling a machine gun; all three of those were pointed at her, as well.

One of the men motioned for her to come forward; nervously, she did.

When she was well clear of the house, a man dashed forward, grabbed her by the arm, and pulled her away, across the little front lawn.

"Who else is in there?" another man — an officer, she supposed — barked at her.

"Nobody," she said. "They're out working the fields." She pointed with her thumb in the direction Walter and Beth had gone that morning.

The men exchanged glances.

"They must've seen us coming in, or heard us," someone remarked.

The officer nodded.

"Get her aboard," he said. "Jonas, Medfield, search the house."

After that, Amy didn't get to see much; she was dragged into the back of one of the vehicles and strapped onto a steel bench, sitting up with a purple-clad soldier on either side. A third man was perched in a raised seat nearby, his head and shoulders sticking up through an open hatch — manning the swivel gun, Amy realized. A fourth man sat up front, in the driver's seat.

A moment later the driver called, "Right," out a window and threw a lever into position; the car lifted off and began moving, but with the usual almost-undetectable acceleration of anti-gravity vehicles, which made it impossible to judge speed or distance by feel.

From where she sat, Amy's only view of the outside was through a narrow strip of windshield that was visible between the two high-backed front seats; most of what she could make out through that was either sky or rapidly-passing cornfield, and not enough of either one to mean anything to her.

She heard the whine of anti-gravity engines, the rush of wind, distant shouts, and once the electric hiss of a blaster, but she really had no idea what was going on outside the steel walls of the vehicle.

"What's happening?" she asked.

"You're a slave here, right?" the soldier on her right asked.

She nodded.

"Then we're rescuing you. The Empire's clearing out this whole planet, bringing it back under civilized control."

Amy felt a flood of relief; she had hoped, but hadn't dared believe, that that was what was happening. "Thank you," she said. She groped for more words, for some way of expressing what she felt, and could only repeat, "Thank you."

"Hey," the driver called back, "ask her who else is around here. Whose farm is it? Any other slaves?"

"A man named Walter," she said. "It's his farm. And a woman named Beth. She . . ." She hesitated.

Beth was a slave — but she hadn't acted the part, had she? She had sided with her master, every time. *Beth* wasn't beaten when she talked back. *Beth* wasn't raped almost every night. And she hadn't lifted a finger to stop it when *Amy* was.

Together, the two of them might have done something against Walter, but Beth had chosen to side with her master.

"She's his wife," Amy said.

*S*omeone kicked Pel awake; startled, he raised his head.

Pain shot through his neck, which was stiff and bruised from his latest beating.

"It isn't really time, is it?" someone asked.

"Doesn't *feel* like it," someone else replied.

That was the truth; after three weeks, Pel was fairly well settled into the rhythms of his life in the mines, and it simply didn't feel like time to get up for breakfast.

Maybe it was just his bruises saying that, though. Reluctantly, he sat up.

"All right, boys," one of the overseers called. "Line 'em up and march 'em out."

Grumbling, the slaves got themselves up, pulling their stiff, dry pants from the lines, fishing malodorous boots from under cots.

One man refused to stir.

"Hey," an overseer said, prodding him, "rise and shine, boyo."

"The hell with breakfast," the slave said without moving. "I'll starve today, if it means I can have another ten minutes' sleep."

The overseer glanced at his boss, who was standing in the doorway. The head overseer shrugged.

"Listen, Sunshine," the guard said, "this isn't breakfast. Wouldn't be your shift for another two hours. This is special. Everybody out."

Pel blinked, and hesitated, with one leg in his pants and the other out.

Two hours early? No wonder everyone was sleepy.

What sort of special?

He pulled his pants on.

*R*aven's third owner had bought him as a personal plaything. He had no duties to carry out; he was simply to be there when Wilf was in the mood to inflict pain.

Wilf was astonished by just how stubborn his new acquisition was. Roland had told him the man was tough, but for someone not yet fully recovered from a serious whipping to take broken bones without even a whimper — that was impressive.

It drove him to greater efforts.

Raven had given up any idea of ingratiating himself with his owners; right now he was far more interested in surviving with his honor intact — honor that was far more important than his bones. To cry out in pain might not be unmanly, and the Goddess knew that any man would cry out if pressed hard enough, yet he was reluctant to give this filthy barbarian the satisfaction.

He knew that he could survive without breaking; it was just a matter of refusing to yield until eventually, his captors would give up.

Eventually, either they would give up, or he would die. He refused to admit any third possibility.

He was watching his new owner's face, studying the greedy look in his eyes, trying not to think about the pain, when the soldiers burst in.

*F*or the long flight away from the farm the soldier on Amy's left traded places with the driver. The others stayed where they were. Walter and Beth, captured as they fled, were in one of the other vehicles, and Amy was relieved not to see them.

"Hi," the off-duty driver said, as he belted in.

"Hi," Amy replied.

"Listen, are you sure there were just the three of you?" he asked. "And that that woman is this Walter Fletcher's wife?"

"Of course I'm sure," Amy said. "Why?"

"Oh, well . . . because she swears she's a slave, too."

"She's lying," Amy snapped.

The soldier nodded. "I figured she probably was — trying to get off, I suppose." He shook his head.

"I guess she tried to tell you *I* was . . . was that man's wife?"

"No," the soldier said. "She wasn't that stupid; nobody would buy that for a minute, not with that thing you're wearing, and that shiner, and all those bruises."

Amy felt an odd mixture of emotions in reaction to the man's words. He meant to be sympathetic, she was sure, but she was struck by anger, shame, embarrassment, and an uncomfortable sort of righteous self-pity, rather than taking any comfort from his words and presence.

After a moment of awkward silence, she asked, "Where are you taking us?"

The soldier glanced at her, then at the opposite bulkhead and the tangle of equipment that hung there. "Well," he said, "old Walter's going to a prison camp — and his wife along with him, I suppose. Keeping slaves is a felony. Beating them is assault — we'll want to have a doctor check you out, take some photos. You'll need to give a statement. We aren't going to bother with full-blown trials here — too many people for 'em. Besides, the whole planet's under martial law right now. We'll hold tribunals, a panel of judges'll check the evidence and figure out what to do with him." He shrugged. "He'll probably be in the camp for a good long time."

"Beth told me he killed a girl," Amy said. She wasn't sure why she was telling him this, but the words spilled out. "Her name was Sheila. They buried her out back, Beth said — I saw the grave."

The soldier frowned, and stared at Amy for a moment. She returned his stare, unflinching.

She wasn't sure why she had told him, but she had, and it was true. If it meant Walter would be imprisoned longer, that was fine, it was what the son of a bitch deserved.

"That's murder," the soldier said at last. "If that's true, old Walter's going to hang. Or maybe they'll just shoot him, to save time. And his wife's an accomplice, I suppose, so she'll get the same."

"How'll they know?" Amy asked. "I mean, I don't think he and Beth are going to tell the judges about that."

"You'll put it in your statement. The grave will be there, if it's true."

It was not a question, saying she would put it in her statement. It was definitely not a question, and even after fighting Walter, Amy knew she did not dare to refuse. She bit her lower lip.

Hang Walter? And Beth?

She hadn't meant that to happen, not really. She hated Walter, but . . .

Well, why the hell not, if they'd really killed Sheila? Why shouldn't the bastard hang?

But Beth hadn't killed anyone.

She would have to think very carefully about what she would put in her statement.

"What about me?" she asked.

"You," the soldier said, leaning back with his hands behind his head, "are on your way to what they call a repatriation center, where they'll sort you out and send you home — or if they can't do that, at least send you *somewhere.*"

"Uh . . . where?"

He glanced at her. "You have any family? Anyone who'd be looking for you? Friends who might take you in?"

"Not in the Galactic Empire," Amy said bitterly.

"Well, where the heck are you *from,* then?" the soldier demanded. "You second-generation or something?"

"I'm from a planet called Earth," Amy said. "In another universe." She shrugged. "Not that I expect anyone to believe that."

The soldier froze and stared at her. On her other side, the other soldier, who had been lounging and listening halfheartedly, sat up and stared as well.

"What did you say your name was?" the soldier on the right asked, fishing a clipboard out from under the bench.

"I didn't," Amy said. "It's Amethyst Beryl Jewell. Amy Jewell."

The man stared at the paper on the clipboard, then made a fizzing noise and said feelingly, "Son of a *bitch*. She's on here. Amy Jewell." He looked up at Amy. "Why didn't you tell us sooner?"

"I didn't know it mattered," she said timidly.

"Shit," he said. He looked down at the clipboard, then flipped a few pages. "Okay, if you're Amy Jewell," he said, "what was the last thing you ate before leaving Earth?"

Amy blinked.

Before leaving Earth?

Before her three weeks with Beth and Walter?

Before she was marched naked across a stage and auctioned off?

Before she was locked aboard a pirate spaceship for days on end?

Before those boring, pointless days wasted on *Emerald Princess*?

Before sitting out on that white sand desert for hours, freezing?

Before fleeing from black, monstrous creatures that had appeared practically from nowhere?

Before she had stepped through a concrete wall and found herself in a rather cold, damp corner of Fairyland?

Before taking five minutes to see another reality, five minutes that had turned into more than a month of Hell?

How the hell was she supposed to remember that far back, remember that other life, when everything had been safe and sane and she had been free and in control of her own life? That was another universe entirely.

But of course, she *did* remember, which was, she supposed, the whole point.

"Pizza," she said.

"That's it," the soldier agreed. He flipped the pages back and tossed the clipboard aside, then leaned forward, between the two front seats. "Hey, Bill," he called to the driver, "we got a hot one here! Straight to the port!"

The new driver glanced back. "You serious?"

"Absolutely," the other replied.

"You got it," Bill said. He turned the wheel and began tapping at switches. The others sat back and stared at Amy.

"You, my dear," the one on the left said, "are on your way to Base One."

*T*hey marched into the refectory in single file, but instead of taking seats they marched straight on, through the kitchen doors, through the courtyard, through the great black sliding door into a much larger yard, where a line of airbuses stood, surrounded by various smaller but equally wheelless vehicles, all of them at least partially purple, and crewed by men in purple uniforms. Blasters were much in evidence.

Another line of men was there, as well, coming along the central passageway from the mine shaft, through the other door of the refectory, the other door to the kitchen; at the door to the first courtyard the two lines merged into one.

They were being loaded onto the 'buses, Pel realized, all the slaves — the other line was the men of Red Shift.

One of them was Elmer Soorn, the crewman from *Ruthless,* Pel realized with a shock. He had never known that anyone else from the party captured on *Emerald Princess* was at this mine; the only part of Red Shift he ever saw was the gang that his own gang shared their shaft with.

And at the sight of the purple uniforms, Soorn began cheering.

The others stared at him at first, not comprehending; then someone else joined in, and a moment later all the slaves were whooping and shouting.

Dazed, battered, still sleepy, Pel was slow to understand, but at last it sank in.

Those were Imperial uniforms. Those were the soldiers of the Galactic Empire, and the Galactic Empire had outlawed slavery.

He didn't need to worry about escaping. He didn't need to be the hero. He could just be a minor character, somewhere in the background, while other people dealt with Shadow and Earth and the Empire.

They were rescued. The Galactic Empire had come for them at last.

Finally, they were rescued.

Chapter Twenty-Five

They had offered him a set of fatigues, but Pel had kept his gray miner's pants. He had accepted a military-issue T-shirt, though — purple, of course, but comfortable and practical. Thus outfitted, he had settled in aboard one of the spaceships to wait while the other survivors from other universes were gathered.

Several ships were collecting freed slaves; two of them, however, were special. The passengers and crew from the *Emerald Princess* were being taken aboard one particular ship, where they would be treated, questioned, and taken home; the people from Earth, from Shadow's universe, or from I.S.S. *Ruthless* were all sent to another.

It was a big ship, a military ship, and when the soldiers took him aboard they led him to a large room apparently intended for meetings or briefings of some sort. A long metal table stood at one end, with a row of chairs behind it, and a dozen uneven rows of folding chairs faced it from elsewhere.

Prossie Thorpe was there, behind the table, back in uniform, checking each person as he or she was brought aboard. She smiled at Pel.

Captain Cahn was there, also in uniform, but he was not behind the table. He was obviously not in command. Not only was he not in command of the rescue force, he did not seem to even be in command of himself. One side of his face was a huge purple bruise, the cheekbone obviously broken, lips swollen, drool seeping from the corner of his mouth; he sat motionless near the back, saying nothing, barely moving at all.

Arthur Smith and Bill Mervyn sat beside their captain, exchanging silent glances.

Stoddard stood against one wall, arms folded across his chest. He wore only a sort of fur loincloth and open black felt vest — Pel wondered how he had come by such a costume It seemed to suit him. His sword and armor were gone, but even half-naked he still looked dangerous enough; he had no bruises or welts, and his hair had been cut short, where the others, including Pel himself, had gotten rather shaggy. Pel wondered what could have happened to Stoddard while he was a slave to leave him thus. His expression gave no clue.

Elmer Soorn arrived just a few moments after Pel, back in uniform, and he seemed cheerful and healthy — but then, as Pel knew, life in the mines had not been all that harsh, really. Soorn greeted the others, grinning broadly, then got a look at Cahn.

The grin vanished.

"What the hell happened to the captain?" he asked.

Cahn closed his eyes.

Smith explained. "He tried to lead a revolt. Two days ago. Thorpe had told him help was coming, and he wanted to hurry things along a little. Didn't work. In the fighting someone threw him off a building."

Soorn dropped into a seat. "Shit," he said. "He couldn't have just laid low and waited?"

Smith shrugged; Cahn turned his head away.

Embarrassed, Soorn scanned the room. "Hey, Pel Brown," he called. "Saw you at the mine — I'd hoped we'd be on the same bus, so we could talk."

Pel just shrugged.

"Looks like we'll get you home this time," Soorn said. "We must have half the Imperial Fleet here!"

"I hope so," Pel muttered.

"Don't everybody cheer at once, or I'll go deaf," Soorn said. "Hey, we've all just been rescued; why are you people so miserable?"

"Well," Mervyn said sourly, "we don't know how bad the captain's hurt, for starters. Pete Cartwright is dead. Jim Peabody is dead. Lieutenant Godwin is dead. Ben Lampert and Lieutenant Drummond are still missing. Nancy Brown's dead. Rachel Brown and Susan Nguyen are missing. That twit who called himself Squire Donald is dead — hanged, I heard. What's-her-name, Elani, is missing, and the lady gnome. Will that do?"

"You're sure Nancy's dead?" Pel asked.

Mervyn glanced at Prossie Thorpe, who nodded. "She's dead," Prossie said. "I'm sorry, Mr. Brown. They'll try to recover the body, so you can arrange a decent . . . burial, is it? Yes, you bury your dead." She winced at the pain her clumsy phrasing caused, and wished she could read the future, as well as minds — just a few seconds of precognition would let her avoid such awkward moments.

After a moment of uncomfortable silence, Soorn tried to change the subject. "What happened to *him?*" he said, pointing a thumb at Stoddard.

"I don't know," Prossie said. "I try not to snoop, you know. Sometimes I can't help it, but I do try."

"'Twill bother me none that you read my thoughts," Stoddard said, startling everyone. He had looked so motionless that it was hard to remember he was alive and able to talk. "Doubtless you'd speak better than I on what befell."

Prossie smiled wryly. "I'd be none too sure of that," she said. She blinked, as if startled by her own words, then continued. "He was a wrestler," she said. "The woman who bought him challenged all comers to beat him, best two falls of three, in fair fight. She made that costume for him, called him the Space Barbarian, said he came from a lost colony somewhere. He was undefeated in twenty-three matches."

Stoddard nodded an acknowledgment.

Prossie started to say something else, then stopped, hesitated, and announced, "Latest reports are in. They've found Lieutenant Drummond and Susan Nguyen, both alive and well, but Alella is definitely dead — they've found her body, pickled in alcohol."

The men exchanged uneasy glances.

"What about the others?" Pel asked. "What about Rachel?"

Prossie shook her head. "Still no word on Rachel or Elani or Spaceman Lampert."

"What about the others?" Soorn asked. "That guy Raven, and the wizard, Valdakrul, or whatever it is. And the other Earth people?"

"Amy Jewell, Lord Raven, and the wizard Valadrakul are all alive and on their way here," Prossie said. "Miss Jewell will be coming aboard in just a few minutes — she may already be aboard, in fact. And Ted Deranian definitely is on board now, but he's in the ship's infirmary."

"They found Amy? Rachel isn't with her?" Pel demanded angrily.

"No," Prossie said, uncomfortably. "They were separated at the auction. I saw it happen, but there wasn't anything we could do."

"Damn it!" Pel growled. Then something else struck him. "You said Ted was in the infirmary," he said. "Why?"

Prossie sighed.

"Two reasons," she said. "First off, he got the crap beaten out of him several times when he just stopped what he was doing and refused to move, so they're setting broken bones, checking him over for internal damage, and so forth. Second, he did that because he's convinced himself that this entire universe isn't real, that he's still at home in bed, dreaming all this — either that, or that he's gone mad and is imagining it all. The alienists are trying to find some way to cure him of this delusion."

That led to another uncomfortable silence.

"What about the people from the *Princess?*" Mervyn asked at last.

"Well, they aren't really my department," Prossie said, "but last I heard there were three dead, a fourth probably dead, and eight still unaccounted for. But they aren't our problem anymore, the Empire's taking care of them."

"So," Soorn asked, "what happens when we're all present and accounted for here?"

"This group, you mean? We go to Base One," Prossie replied. "At full boost. About four days. In fact, we'll be leaving in a few hours even if the others aren't found. The Earth people, and Shadow people, are a top priority right now."

As she spoke, Amy Jewell stepped into the room. Pel looked up.

She looked older; her hair was partly grown out straight and a shade darker. One eye was spectacularly blackened. She wore a military-issue white blouse and purple slacks, but instead of the shiny black boots that went with the uniform she had ragged bedroom slippers on her feet. She stood by the doorway, looking the room over and listening.

She wasn't his problem, though. "What if they haven't found Rachel?" Pel asked.

"Then we'll leave anyway," Prossie said. "And when someone finds her they'll send her on another ship, as quickly as possible. We don't have the time to wait around; the search might take awhile. It's a big . . well, no, it isn't really that big a planet, but *any* planet is a big place."

"Who's going to take care of her?" Pel demanded. "Listen, if she isn't found, I'm not going — she's my daughter. I need to stay here until she's found."

Prossie shook her head. "I don't think they'll allow that," she said. "You people are absolutely a top priority; they want you at Base One as fast as possible."

Amy made an unpleasant noise, and all eyes turned toward her.

"We're a top priority?" she asked, her voice a trifle unsteady. "They want us there fast?"

Prossie nodded. "That's right."

Pel could see that Amy was angry — in fact, furious, and trying hard to restrain herself, to calm herself down. He thought at first it was because of Rachel, but then caught himself. Rachel wasn't that important to Amy.

She wasn't that important to anyone, it seemed, anyone but him.

"If we're so damned important," Amy said through her teeth, "then why didn't they rescue us *sooner?* I've been through three weeks of hell out there — I'd given up! I could have killed myself before these idiots bothered to come save us!" She lost control, and began shouting wildly, "I could have *died* out there! I was beaten and raped and abused, and they could have stopped it!"

"Miss Jewell," Prossie called. "Please, Miss Jewell . . ."

Amy continued to shout.

The others looked helplessly at each other, impotent and embarrassed, while Prossie tried to make herself heard without screaming.

All except Stoddard, who straightened up from where he had leaned against the wall. Without a word, he crossed the room and put a hand on Amy's shoulder.

Startled, she broke off and looked up at him.

"Sit," he said, pointing to a chair. "Listen. An you be not satisfied, I'll side you, and we'll have what you will of them."

Slowly, Amy sat, watching Stoddard as if hypnotized.

When she was sitting, Stoddard turned to Prossie.

"And now, Mistress Thorpe," he said, "what is it you would say?"

Amy, too, turned to look at the telepath.

Prossie paused to catch her breath and clear her throat, then began, "Miss Jewell, I'm very sorry for whatever indignities you may have suffered. You aren't alone, you know; I was raped, too, and if you'll look around, I think you'll see bruises on several faces. And the preliminary report I got on your barrister seems to indicate she had it worse than any of us."

"Susan?" Amy asked.

Prossie nodded. "She's on her way. She's all right, more or less — just as you are. No permanent physical damage. Not everyone was as lucky — Mr. Brown's wife was killed, as were at least two of my crewmates, and some of the people from *Emerald Princess.* And there are some we still don't know about."

"So why didn't somebody *do* something . . ." Amy began. Stoddard silenced her with a hand on her shoulder.

"We did," Prossie said wearily. "I sent an alarm as soon as I knew *Emerald Princess* was under attack, and the Imperial High Command responded immediately — but space travel isn't instantaneous, and there were no warships nearby. So *Emerald Princess* was captured, and all of us were taken prisoner aboard the raider. I was able to disguise myself as a civilian passenger, and the pirates never found out I was a telepath; if they had, they'd have killed me instantly. Since they didn't, I was able to stay in communication with the High Command — but because telepathy is non-directional, they couldn't use that to locate us. They knew where *Emerald Princess* was, but not the course the pirate ship took after capturing it."

Amy started to interrupt again, then glanced up at Stoddard and thought better of it.

"I tried to ask where we were going, but nobody bothered to tell me — I was locked in a room, just the way you were, with nobody who knew anything. I read a few minds, very carefully, trying to find out something useful, but I never managed it. So the pirates were able to reach their home base unmolested — and that made the job harder, because you can't defeat an entire planet with a single warship, no matter how much firepower it carries. You can't even free a bunch of slaves, not once they've been scattered all over two continents the way we were — you'll just wind up with a hostage situation, a stand-off where you have to deal with criminals. In case you didn't notice, that isn't what happened; nobody sent just one ship. The Empire put together a task force — Task Force Umber, it's called, and you're currently aboard its flagship, I.S.S. *Emperor Edward VII.* They put together a force that could do the job, could conquer the entire planet so fast that nobody would have time to fight back, to take hostages. They got eighty-two ships and eleven thousand troops organized and supplied in about two weeks, and then got them all here at top speed once my reports of the nighttime constellations had been analyzed and the planet located. It worked — you've seen that. It was a huge operation, but it worked, and it went as smooth as ice. They took the entire planet without losing a ship, without more than a dozen casualties, and you're complaining because they couldn't do the impossible any faster than they did."

"I didn't see any fighting," Amy muttered.

"You were way the hell out on the southern plains," Prossie reminded her. "Besides, they didn't put up much of a fight." She took a deep breath, and smiled crookedly. "I haven't done this much talking out loud since I was a girl," she said. "I think my voice is worn out!"

Raven had three broken fingers on his left hand. He walked stiffly, slightly bent, like an old man, and flinched when anyone came near his back. Ridges of fresh scar tissue broke the line of the borrowed shirt he wore.

Valadrakul's remaining braid had been cut off, but he was otherwise unharmed.

Susan Nguyen had burns on her back and arms, and scars on her back, but insisted she was fine. "I've had practice with this sort of thing," she said bitterly.

Elani was found, finally, hiding in a cave — she had been the only one to successfully escape from slavery, using tricks learned in years of avoiding Shadow's agents. She had, of course, avoided all contact with other people thereafter, so that she had been slow to learn of the planet's liberation by Imperial forces.

Ben Lampert seemed to have disappeared without a trace. The auction records listed him as sold for three hundred and ninety crowns, paid in cash, no name or address given — a dead end. No one who had been at the auction and was still alive was willing to admit knowing anything about him. Prossie could not locate him telepathically — but because he had no trace of psychic talent, no particularly distinctive thought-patterns, that didn't mean much. She couldn't pick out one ordinary person on an entire planet without a little more to go on.

Several boxes of personal belongings were recovered from the auction house, to everyone's surprise — apparently the people in charge of sorting and pricing such things for resale had not been in any hurry. Susan's purse was found, apparently unopened, where she had hidden it — she would not tell the others where that had been — and it was returned to her intact shortly before *Emperor Edward VII* lifted off.

Prossie noticed Susan radiating a certain morbid pleasure upon the return of her purse, even while her face remained absolutely blank, and couldn't resist snooping a little. She found that Susan was pleased because her gun was still there, untouched, apparently undiscovered.

Prossie also inadvertently shared Susan's wish that she'd had the gun with her on a few occasions during the past three weeks.

Emperor Edward VII launched on schedule, despite Pel Brown's protests. Rachel's probable location had been traced through the auction records and eyewitness reports, but she had not yet been found; Pel had to be sedated and confined to his assigned quarters to keep him from interfering with the flagship's departure.

Prossie tried to tell him that she would stay in touch with the search teams on the newly-liberated Zeta Leo III, and would let him know the minute Rachel was found, but that failed to comfort him.

And in fact, it was a lie.

Telepaths can lie quite effectively when they choose to. After all, they can tell when they're believed and when they aren't.

It was only partly a lie, though. She had every intention of telling him immediately when Rachel was found, on one condition — that she was found alive.

And Prossie didn't think she would be.

Nothing would interfere with an Imperial fleet at full strength, and nothing did. *Emperor Edward VII* reached Base One on schedule and without incident.

The body now called Base One had once been an asteroid of no special distinction. It was mostly nickel-iron, but so were a million other asteroids The only things that marked out Base One were that it was about the right size, and it was about where the Empire wanted to put their military headquarters. By hollowing it out and using the material they thus removed to build on additional sections the Empire had transformed it into a vast deep-space complex, the heart of the Imperial military, and home to the High Command.

Pel never did see what it looked like from the outside during the approach; *Edward VII* didn't bother with unnecessary viewports. His primary impression of the inside was of endless corridors — not spotless, gleaming white corridors, as he had seen in any number of science fiction movies, but steel corridors, painted in battleship gray or olive drab or maroon, most of them floored with worn linoleum tile in various colors — sometimes mismatched. He found black grit in the cracks between floor tiles, black streaks on the wall here and there where a cart had rubbed, and other signs of long and heavy use on every side.

He had to be dragged off the ship; he was demanding to be taken back to Zeta Leo III, to find his daughter. He was dragged off and given a small room, with a cot and a bureau and a chair, and he was locked in.

By the time he had been there a full day he had calmed down enough to be interviewed — they didn't call it interrogation, but that term would probably have been more accurate. He answered as honestly and completely as he could — and there was no reason not to, as a telepath always sat in on the sessions. It wasn't Prossie Thorpe; instead, it was a young man named Theobald Carver who appeared, from comments various people made, to be Prossie's second cousin.

There were many sessions.

He was questioned about Zeta Leo III, about Psi Cassiopeia II, about Shadow's realm, about Earth, and he answered as well as he could.

Between interviews Pel was given a brief tour of parts of Base One, including an observation chamber where thick windows looked out onto the surface of the asteroid and gave a view of a gigantic complex of equipment — copper busbars at least ten feet in diameter supported a ring of intricate crystal and metal gadgetry.

"That's the warp generator," his guide explained. "The gateway to your home universe."

Pel took more of an interest once he had heard that; he looked out at the huge tangle of machinery.

Soon, when they found Rachel and brought her safely back here, he would be going through that thing, back to the safety and sanity of his own world, his own home, his suburban quarter-acre twenty miles from Washington.

As soon as they found Rachel.

It was three days later when he was brought into the interview room again. This time, though, instead of his usual questioner in the standard purple uniform, he found himself facing an older officer in more ornate garb, with gold braid and a row of medals.

"Mr. Brown," the man said, folding his hands on the table in front of him, "this time, instead of asking you to tell us things, *we'll* be telling *you* what we've found out."

Pel took his usual seat and said nothing.

"You were captured by pirates and sold into slavery on Zeta Leo III," the officer said. "While it's true that pirates and slavers are a recurring problem on the fringes of the Galactic Empire, they are a *minor* problem, and the odds of the particular ship that Captain Cahn had commandeered being attacked — well, let's just say that it was unlikely enough that we were very suspicious indeed."

Pel listened without much interest. The attack had happened; he didn't really care why.

"With that in mind, once we had taken control of Zeta Leo III, we began a thorough investigation of pirate activities based there, and of the attack on *Emerald Princess* in particular. We took a dozen telepaths with us to aid in the investigation — an unheard-of measure. I don't suppose you realize just how extreme a measure that is, unfamiliar as you are with our society, but let me assure, it's extreme. Never before have we allowed more than eight telepaths to gather in a single place, other than at military transfer points or this base." He raised a hand to make a gesture at the ceiling.

Pel sat, listening. He blinked occasionally.

"We found what we'd expected," the officer said. "Several people died inexplicably under interrogation, *not* from anything we did, but eventually we found what we were after. Agents of the extra-universal thing known as Shadow had secretly controlled the government of not just Zeta Leo III, but an entire network of rebel worlds — the others are being reduced even as I tell you this. It was already expanding its sphere of influence from its own universe into ours, and it was this thing, this Shadow, that ordered the attack on *Emerald Princess.*"

That was scarcely a surprise, really, Pel thought. They had guessed at it, without any evidence at all, aboard the pirate ship.

"That means that it was Shadow that was responsible for the death of your wife."

Pel blinked. He really hadn't thought of it that way, but it was true — Nancy hadn't just died. Someone had killed her. Some person had deliberately killed her.

He sat up a little straighter.

"And I'm afraid that I have some very bad news."

Pel knew, with a cold, crawling certainty, what was coming. His lips formed the word, "No."

"I'm afraid we found your daughter, Rachel. And . . well, we'll be bringing the remains here to Base One, so you can make your good-byes."

"No," Pel said, quietly.

"That's another death that this Shadow is responsible for, indirectly," the officer said. "More directly, of course, someone else was, and while I can understand it if you find this a disappointment, if you'd have preferred a more personal vengeance, I'm afraid that the procedures of military justice have already taken care of him. A man named Lemuel Burgess has been hanged for your daughter's murder. If you wish, transcripts of the tribunal and other evidence can be provided to satisfy you that we found the right man." He cleared his throat. "Your wife's killers were never specifically identified, but the entire crew of the ship *Reaper* has been apprehended and executed for piracy, slave-trading, and other high crimes, so she, too, is avenged — in part."

Pel stared at him.

The Empire did things with dispatch, certainly, if this man was telling the truth — and why would he lie?

They were all dead — Nancy and Rachel and the men who had killed them, all dead.

"Thank you," Pel whispered, unsure why he said it.

The officer hesitated. "There's a little more," he said.

Pel sat motionless, watching him.

"As I said," the man continued, "this Shadow is responsible for the deaths of your wife and daughter. And it's waging a sort of secret war against the Empire, as well. We can't just march in and bring Shadow, whatever it is, to trial; we can't hang it or shoot it, much as we'd like to. In plain truth, we don't know much about it. We do know, though, that it's evil, that it's criminal, that it's responsible for the deaths, not just of your family, but of hundreds of innocents." He paused dramatically.

Pel watched.

"We want it stopped," the officer continued. "It's a murderous, monstrous thing, intruding where it has no business, and we want it stopped as quickly as possible. What's more, we think that you can help us stop it. We want to send you into Shadow's world, as part of a team effort to track down and destroy it. This is the thing that gave the orders for your wife and daughter to die that we're asking you to fight; it's a chance for revenge. Will you take it?" He looked down at Pel, awaiting a reply.

Pel looked back. He stared up into the bright, brown eyes of this man from another universe, this officer in the military of a Galactic Empire, this figure from some pulp space opera, offering him a chance at lurid vengeance against the killer of his wife and child.

It was all like a scene from a novel or a movie, more than ever — he was James Bond being offered his assignment, Mr. Phelps listening to the tape, he was a man being offered a chance to be a hero. He was supposed to say yes, whereupon the officer would shake his hand, and the camera would cut away, and the next scene would be the determined little war party preparing for the assault upon the enemy's fortress.

It was all laid out in the books. This was where the hero differentiated himself from the lesser characters.

James Bond wouldn't hesitate in taking his assignment, no matter how risky. Horatio Hornblower would never turn down a command, no matter how outgunned he would be. Indiana Jones would go after the artifact, no matter how many booby traps there might be, no matter how many enemies might try to stop him. Any real hero would answer instantly.

But in the books the officer's breath didn't smell of the onions he'd eaten at lunch, and there wasn't an incipient pimple on the side of his neck; the table didn't have someone's initials scratched in it; the hero's stomach wasn't wrenched out of shape by the thought of his daughter's death, there weren't tears itching at the corners of his eyes, he didn't feel as if he was about to faint or vomit or, worst of all, burst out in hysterical laughter. In the books the world was all smooth and simple, not hard and solid and arbitrary; there were good guys and bad guys, right and wrong, and right always won out in the end.

Was the Galactic Empire right? Maybe it was better than the alternative, but it was no bastion of purity. Since leaving Earth he had not seen a single black person, or any Oriental except Susan Nguyen — where were they all? What had the Empire done with them? He had heard the Imperials openly voice hatred for "mutants," he had seen a society that to every appearance was racist and sexist and imperialist and saw nothing wrong with any of it. They had hanged every man aboard the pirate ship, had hanged or imprisoned most of the population of Zeta Leo III — mercy was not one of the Empire's strong suits. Were these the good guys?

And in truth, all he knew about Shadow he had heard from its enemies. True, it had attacked him, but it might be acting in its own defense.

Was *he* one of the good guys, really?

The bad guys offered their people these choices, too — the agents Bond sent to gruesome deaths, the assassins assigned to kill the hero, they had these offers and they accepted them. Was the Empire in the right?

And if it was, so what?

This was no story. This was real life. There was no author making sure justice was done. Right hadn't won against Shadow before; why should it now? And how did he even know whether anything this man had said was true?

Rachel might still be alive; he had only the officer's word that she was not.

He didn't know what was true. He didn't know what was right.

The officer was still waiting for his answer.

This was his chance to be the hero, he knew that. All he had to do was say yes. Be brave and strong and true, and despite tragedy, the hero would win out, the evil would be destroyed, the survivors would live happily ever after.

All the stories said so.

Raven would say yes in an instant, he was certain. Raven had all the makings of a traditional hero. He believed in honor and courage and duty, in right and wrong, good and evil.

And look what it had gotten him; the doctors were still working on his back, and his traitor brother was still lord of Stormcrack Keep.

All Pel had to do was say yes.

James Bond would say yes, Indiana Jones, Horatio Hornblower, they'd say yes in an instant.

But Bond was a spy, Hornblower a sea captain, Jones an archaeologist — those were their *jobs*. Pel Brown was a marketing consultant; his job was telling small businesses why their ads didn't work.

All he had to do was say yes to be a hero, instead of just a marketing consultant.

All he had to do was say yes.

All he had to do was say yes.

. . .

"I don't know," Pel said.

— end part 1 —

Part Two:
In the Empire of Shadow

Chapter One

*T*he spaceship shone vivid purple in the unfiltered light, brighter than any jewel, bright as a skateboarder's gear. Its nose and tail fins were golden; the forward fins were patterned in gold, white, and purple. At first glance, it should have been as gaudy and absurd as a cartoon.

But out there in space, with the glow of Base One's sun cutting sharp-edged divisions between light and shadow, with the utter black of deep space and the hard, unblinking blaze of a myriad stars behind it, it didn't look silly at all. It looked impressive, more real than reality itself.

Pel Brown supposed that this was what all those comic-book artists and movie special-effects crews had been trying for, and, limited by the media they used, had been unable to achieve. It took the reality of airlessness, free-fall, and starlight to create such an intense image.

The bright colors were what did it; the bland greys and whites of NASA's shuttle or most of the movie spaceships just didn't have the same power.

Pel had never expected to see a real spaceship — not like *this*, anyway. After all, he was just a freelance marketing consultant from Germantown, Maryland, and until recently the only spaceships he'd ever known existed were the ones built by NASA or the old Soviet space program.

Three months ago he had had no idea that parallel universes were real, and not just science fiction. Three months ago he hadn't met the velvet-clad thug who called himself Raven, or any of Raven's motley companions. He hadn't asked his lawyer to bail a bunch of stranded spacemen out of jail. He hadn't stepped through a portal in his basement wall into Raven's world, a universe where magic worked, and something called Shadow was the absolute ruler of the world. He hadn't escaped from Shadow's monsters only to wind up in a third universe, the one the spacemen came from, where the Galactic Empire ruled three thousand inhabited planets. He hadn't spent weeks as a slave working in a mine on a planet called Zeta Leo III.

And three months ago he had had a wife and daughter, and now they were gone, and he had been told that they were both dead, murdered by space pirates.

Space pirates! God, that sounded like something out of the old pulp magazines, or a low-budget movie — only they'd been all too real, and altogether serious. They'd captured Pel, along with Raven and the others, and sold them into slavery.

And they hadn't gone in for gaudy colors. The ship out there was not their style at all. The colors marked it as part of the Imperial fleet.

This particular combination of colors wasn't quite the standard set; gold and white were unusual. The purple meant the ship was the property of the Galactic Empire, of course; Pel wondered what the gold represented. He guessed that it probably meant the ship carried some high official.

There were plenty of high officials at Base One already, in Pel's opinion; he had been harassed by a few of them. A good many of the Galactic Empire's big shots had been interested in seeing the people from another universe.

Pel watched, vaguely annoyed, as the ship slid smoothly into the huge air lock a quarter-mile farther down Base One's surface.

That surface was an uneasy blend of raw meteoritic stone and riveted metal — the Imperial military had hollowed out the orbiting rock, and then built outward, as well. Pel's window looked out from a bulge of asteroidal stone onto a broad vista of sheet steel, pocked and patched as a result of collisions with celestial debris, but untainted by any trace of rust.

Then the infinite depths of space and the long metal walls of the station dimmed to near-invisibility and his own face leapt out at him from the glass; someone had turned on the light in the room behind him.

He blinked, and continued to stare at the glass, at his own features super-imposed on the universe, almost blocking it all from sight. His nose, recently broken by the overseers at the mine where he'd worked as slave labor, did not look quite right, and the bruises elsewhere had left dark traces that looked like shadows, but it was still the same face he had always had.

He was in the wrong universe, but he was still in his own body. Reality hadn't gotten *that* strange.

"Mr. Brown?" an unfamiliar voice inquired.

*T*he clerk looked at the clipboard, then at Amy. "Miss Jewell?" he asked.

Amy dropped the magazine on the table, losing her place. The tentacular monster in the cover picture grinned lewdly up at her, ignoring the screaming girl in its coils.

Losing her place was no great inconvenience; the stories were all pretty bad anyway. Men's adventure stories weren't any better written here than back home on Earth, and in general were even more offensively sexist. Not to mention that the line between adventure and science fiction had been hopelessly blurred by the existence of interstellar travel and huge areas of unexplored galaxy — odd, to realize that stories of heroes fighting monsters from other planets didn't qualify as science fiction here.

The stories still sucked, though. She was very tired of evil mutant master-minds and big blond heroes.

Reading this tripe was better than nothing, but not by much. It generally took her mind off feeling lousy, but nothing more than that. When her bruises healed completely and she got back home to her three acres in Goshen, Maryland, that would probably help a lot more.

Of course, there was presumably still a stranded spaceship in her back yard. The Empire's first attempt to contact Earth, to arrange an alliance against Shadow, had ended when I.S.S. *Ruthless* plummeted out of the sky and crash-landed there.

They'd planned on appearing twenty miles from the White House, one the crewmen told Amy later — they didn't want to just drop right into the middle of the capital.

Twenty miles or so northwest of the White House had put them right over Amy's yard, and the moment the ship popped out of the space-warp that let it into Earth's universe the crew had made the unexpected discovery that anti-gravity, the basis for much of the Empire's machinery, didn't *work* in Earth's universe, and there was therefore nothing holding the ship up.

It had crashed, and it was probably still there, and it was never going to fly again. The laws of physics were apparently very different in each of the three known realities.

They were different enough that something called "magic" worked in the world Shadow and Raven came from, something that had let Amy and the crew of *Ruthless* step through a basement wall into that world.

And when they'd fled into the Galactic Empire, the monsters that followed them had died for lack of that "magic," just as *Ruthless* had fallen for lack of anti-gravity. The three universes were *different,* all right.

Some things didn't change, though — people could still be rotten, in any universe. Like her ex-husband Stan. Like that son of a bitch Walter, who had bought her from the pirates and kept her as a slave until the Empire rescued her and brought her to Base One.

At least the Empire made an *attempt* at being civilized.

Even if, she thought with a final glance at that god-awful collection of violent, sexist, racist, imperialist adventure stories, they weren't all that good at it.

She forgot the magazine and looked up at the clerk.

"Ah . . . Miss Jewell? Or is it Mrs.?"

"It's Ms.," Amy said, perversely. Her stomach was slightly upset, as it often was lately — the food here was at least as bad as the fiction — and she was in no mood to cooperate with the Empire in its petty oppressions.

"Mrs.?" the clerk asked again.

"Ms. It's a word we use back on Earth."

"Oh. Yes, of course." The clerk noted something, then looked up again and said, "Could you come with me, Miss Jewell?"

"Why? And where?"

The clerk did not answer; instead he said, in a surprisingly definite voice, "I was told to bring you *at once.*"

Amy sighed, and decided not to argue any more.

"Mr. Deranian?"

Ted ignored them, and the two men cast knowing glances at one another.

"You take the right arm," one of them said. "Be careful, though — the doctor said that besides the head wound, his ribs aren't completely healed yet."

The other nodded.

Side by side they advanced, and grabbed Ted by the arms.

"Come on, Mr. Deranian," one of them said. "Dream's not over yet."

"Miss N'goyen?"

"Nguyen," Susan said, without moving from her cot. She was lying face-down; the burns on her back no longer hurt all the time, but lying on them was still not a good idea. Her time as a slave on Zeta Leo III had been very rough on her.

But then, having been a refugee as a child, she'd survived rough times before. She'd thought that she was finally through with all that when she'd made it through law school, passed the bar, and joined the firm of Dutton, Powell, Hough.

Obviously, she'd been wrong.

When Amy Jewell had called on her to provide legal assistance in dealing with the spaceship that had crashed in her back yard, Susan had not expected it to lead her to this.

The messenger tried again, and almost managed to pronounce the name.

"What is it?" Susan asked.

"Could you come with me, please?"

Susan raised her head and looked at the messenger. "Do I have a choice?"

"Not really."

She sighed, sat up, swung her feet to the floor, and stood.

"Lead the way," she said.

*P*el took the seat on the far left, and Amy settled beside him. Pel noticed that she was no longer wearing heavy make-up to hide the bruise on her face; the discolorations had faded to a faint, sickly yellow tinge. Pel knew that his own injuries, too, were no longer obvious.

Ted was led in, unresisting, and seated on the far right; the fresh bandage on his head was smaller than the one Pel had last seen there, and the visible cuts and bruises had healed. There were scars, of course.

Susan, arriving last, took her place between Amy and Ted. A long-sleeved tunic hid the bandages that still covered much of her back and her forearms.

That was all of them, Pel thought, all four of them — the only living Earthpeople in the entire universe, according to the Galactic Empire.

At least, in *this* entire universe. So far as Pel knew, there were five billion others back on Earth, all blithely unaware that any universe but their own existed. And he secretly harbored hopes, despite his own better judgment, that his wife and daughter might still be alive somewhere. Their deaths had been reported to him, had been confirmed repeatedly, but he hadn't seen either of them die, hadn't seen their bodies.

He knew, intellectually, that they were both dead, but accepting it emotionally was another matter.

Nancy and Rachel weren't here, though, even if by some miracle they weren't both dead. The four of them, Pel and Amy and Ted and Susan, were the only Earthpeople here at Base One. Pel found something peculiarly amusing in the thought that half of them were lawyers, here because they had been representing the other half.

The Galactic Empire didn't seem to care about lawyers, though. Ted wasn't representing him here, and Susan wasn't representing Amy; they were all here on their own. Pel looked around, wondering why they had been gathered.

This was a new room to them all. It was small and bare, with walls of whitewashed stone — that meant it was within the asteroid itself, rather than in the later additions, where everything was steel. The tiled floor might once have been white, too, but was now a dull gray. The four steel chairs were not particularly comfortable. The purple-painted lectern bore the lion-and-unicorn seal of the Imperial Military — but then, so did any number of objects scattered about Base One.

It looked like a small briefing room. That was, at least, an improvement on the debriefing and interrogation chambers where Pel seemed to have spent most of his waking hours for the past ten days.

The door opened, and a man in the familiar purple uniform of an Imperial officer marched past them, papers in hand, and took his place at the lectern. Pel was beginning to learn the insignia; he placed this character as a major in the political service.

That was mildly unusual; up until now they had mostly been bothered by people in Imperial Intelligence.

"Welcome to Base One," the major announced, in jovial, booming tones that were almost painful in so small a room. "I'm Major Southern."

Pel winced, not just at the tone, but at the words. He and the others had been here at Base One for over a week — Pel, without a regular cycle of sunrise and sunset, had lost track of exactly how long it had been, but he knew it was over a week. They didn't need any more welcoming speeches.

Ted grinned foolishly. "Major Southern," he said. "I like that. Glad I thought of it. Southern, warm, friendly — a summery sort of name."

At that, *Amy* winced.

"Now, you're all intelligent people," the major proclaimed, in somewhat more moderate tones. "You all know what the situation is."

Pel glanced at Ted, who grinned back and winked broadly at him.

"We're fighting a powerful, mysterious enemy," Major Southern continued. "A force that has conquered an entire universe, and that now threatens two others."

Ted nodded, smiling happily. Susan sat in polite and motionless silence. Amy's lips tightened. Pel could almost hear her thoughts — he could imagine her muttering, "I haven't seen it threatening Earth."

"This force called Shadow uses methods we don't understand, methods that are impossible in our own universe; the people of Shadow's world call it magic, and that's as good a name as any. It's used that magic to send its agents, its spies, and its monsters into our universe. It has attempted to subvert the Galactic Empire, which has brought peace and security to all mankind — at least, in this reality."

Amy's lips twitched, and Pel could easily guess the cynical thoughts running through her mind.

All mankind, except where it hadn't gotten yet, which was far more than the Empire cared to admit — all of the little group had seen more than they wanted of the odd corners where the Empire had no dominion. And the Empire might bring security to *man*kind, perhaps, but not necessarily women. It also helped if the men were white.

Just how different was the Empire from Shadow, really? Both were imperialist; Shadow just seemed to be a little farther along in its conquests.

Of course, as one point in its favor, the Galactic Empire was run by humans; nobody knew just what Shadow was.

"You know that we have representatives of Shadow's universe here at Base One," the major said. "Lord Raven of Stormcrack Keep has taken temporary refuge here, and he and his party have fought against Shadow all their lives."

"So they say," Amy muttered, and this time it was not just Pel's imagination.

He thought this might be carrying cynicism a little far; Raven and his man Stoddard and the two wizards had certainly seemed sincere enough.

The major either didn't hear her, or chose to ignore her. "They've sworn to continue that fight," he said, "and to join their efforts to ours, rather than to continue operating independently. In just a few days, we'll be sending Lord Raven and the others through a space-warp, back into their home universe — and with them we'll be sending a squadron of our best men, and a trained telepath. This combined force will be the first step in taking the battle onto Shadow's home ground, the first step in overthrowing this unnatural tyranny and freeing the oppressed people of Shadow's realm."

And probably bringing them under Imperial domination instead, Pel thought.

"I'm here today to invite the four of you to join that combined force," Major Southern said. "As natives of a universe different from both ours and Shadow's, you have a different viewpoint, you have knowledge and techniques that might be just what's needed to defeat this . . . this inter-universal horror."

"Fuck off," Pel said, unable to resist any longer. Did this beribboned idiot think they didn't know what the Empire wanted? They knew, and they weren't interested. They had all made that clear enough. "Just send us home," he said.

"It's not our fight," Amy added.

Ted giggled.

Susan's lips were a tight line; she said nothing.

"I'd been told that some of you felt that way," Major Southern said, frowning. "You're civilians, and subjects of another nation — one we don't recognize, of course, but still, we realize you aren't soldiers we can order into battle. Further, you probably wouldn't be of much use if we sent you out there involuntarily. We don't seem to be getting anywhere by appealing to your patriotism and common decency — you've all turned us down. Revenge doesn't seem to have been enough, either."

"We don't know it was Shadow that sold us into slavery," Amy said. "We only have your word for that."

"Why would we lie?" The major spread his hands in a gesture of bewilderment.

"You might have staged the whole thing to get us on your side," Amy suggested. "If it was Shadow that captured us, why would it sell us? If it's after us, why weren't we killed?"

"We don't know," Southern admitted, "and that's something we'd like to find out, but we can't." He hesitated, but Amy had said her piece; no one interrupted further, and he returned to his speech.

"You won't go voluntarily, as I said," he told them, "so we're offering you a choice. Lord Raven and the rest will be sent into Shadow's universe three days from now, whether any of you four are with them or not. Those of you who don't go — well, we can't keep you here forever, living on the largesse of the Empire. You're free to join the Imperial military; we can always use bright people like yourselves. If you're not interested, though, I'm afraid you can't stay at Base One, which is, after all, a military installation. Instead, we'll send you to any nearby planet you choose; we'll land you where you ask, and from then on, of course, you're on your own."

"Send us *home*, damn it!" Pel shouted.

The major pretended to ignore him and continued, "Of course, we can't create an inter-universal space-warp just for the convenience of a handful of uncooperative civilians, but I suppose we can arrange grants of citizenship and provide the necessary papers to keep you out of jail. For brave volunteers, once the crisis is past and Shadow defeated, no reasonable reward would be refused, and opening a space-warp would be considered; but for civilians who've turned down a chance to serve the Empire? Not likely."

The four Earthpeople stared at him — or at any rate, three of them did.

Ted Deranian shrugged and said, "I'll go with Raven if you like; it's all the same to me. Might make a better story that way, if I don't wake up before I get that far."

Amy let out a low moan of disgust at Ted's insistence on his delusion. Pel glanced at her, but said nothing; he understood her reaction.

Ever since the party had stepped through the magical portal from Earth to Shadow's world, Ted had been convinced the entire thing was a dream. Beatings, torture, wounds, and the passage of days and even weeks had failed to dislodge this conviction. Almost two months had now passed since the May evening when they had passed through Pel's basement wall, but Ted persisted.

The man's exact mood varied; sometimes he seemed to be struggling to maintain his belief, sometimes he sank into near-catatonia. Right now he was treating it all as a joke that had gone on a little too long, a story that was slow in reaching the point.

It got on everyone's nerves, and Pel and Amy both feared that Ted had slipped irretrievably into insanity weeks ago. Pel suspected the head wound he had acquired resisting the pirates aboard *Emerald Princess*, or the beatings he had received on Zeta Leo III, might have caused brain damage, as well.

"What about the rest of you, then?" Major Southern asked, smiling.

"You're a sadistic bastard, you know that?" Pel answered calmly.

"Now, now, Mr. Brown," the major said, feigning shock. "That's no way to talk!"

No one replied. He looked them over, then stepped out from behind the lectern.

"I've said my piece," he told them. "From here on, it's all up to you."

"Sure it is," Amy said. "We get our choice of two universes — but neither one of them's ours."

The major smiled and patted Amy on the shoulder. "That's right," he said. "I'll let you think about it." He looked around the room, gave everyone a cheerful grin that was only slightly patronizing, and strolled out.

Amy glared after him, and muttered, "Where'd they find *that* stupid prick?"

Pel shrugged. "Same place as all the others, I suppose," he said. "Wherever *that* is."

Susan suddenly spoke, for the first time since entering the room.

"I'm going with Raven," she said. "And I'd advise you both to consider joining us. I don't have any power over you, Mr. Brown, but as your attorney, Amy, I strongly recommend you take my advice."

The other three all turned to stare at her.

"Susan, are you . . . what are you *talking* about?" Amy demanded.

"Amy, just think it over."

She turned and marched out.

Baffled, Pel and Amy and Ted watched her go.

Chapter Two

"W"e've no need of them," Raven repeated.

"We don't need them here, either," General Hart replied, "and they might be useful to you. Our telepaths tell us they have the most amazing assortment of odd information tucked away in their heads; this Earth of theirs seems to make a fetish of spreading information every which way, whether it's needed or not."

"And what know they of *my* world?" Raven protested. "Not so much as a newborn babe at the nurse's breast!"

Hart shrugged. "So? My men aren't much better."

"Soldiers?" Raven waved that away, the natural gesture stiff because of the bandaged fingers of his left hand. "A soldier's a soldier, man — an they know their jobs, we'll find use for them in Stormcrack and in Shadow's lands. But the Earth-folk . . ."

"Are you bothered because two of them are women?"

Raven, pacing by the wall-map, glanced at the general. "Aye," he said, "there's that, and I admit it freely. 'Tis no place for a woman, in the midst of battle."

"One of your own party's a woman," Hart pointed out.

"Elani? Nay, she's a *wizard*; 'tis another matter entire."

"Looks like a woman to me," Hart said.

Two rooms away a telepath listened in on the conversation, and on the thoughts of the participants. Proserpine Thorpe had been reading the minds of those around her, sometimes whether she wanted to or not, since her earliest childhood; she was rarely surprised by the lies and deceptions of non-telepaths dealing with one another. Even so, the cynicism underlying this particular discussion was more than she would have expected.

General Hart really didn't care about any plans to destroy Shadow, had no interest at all in the people the mysterious evil had harmed or killed; he just wanted to get rid of all the extra-universal troublemakers before some idiot politician or ambitious underling found some way to exploit them and make him look stupid or ineffective. He didn't really completely believe in other universes, or that this Shadow thing posed a serious threat; this whole business had happened because nobody kept a close enough eye on that overzealous geek Copley, who should never have made Major, and that pompous civilian fraud Bascombe, the so-called Under-Secretary for Interdimensional Affairs — a post in the Department of Science that existed only because Bascombe had invented it and pulled sufficient strings to get it for himself.

But Copley was out of the way now, thanks to a burst appendix, and Bascombe would be harmless enough by himself once these foreigners were disposed of. If Hart had a chance to send along a couple of his own unwanted subordinates as well, that would be just fine, even if it meant losing a couple of dozen men from his command. The Empire had plenty of soldiers, after all; sending a few on a ridiculous mission was no great loss.

And he seemed quite certain that whoever was sent would be lost.

For his part, Raven cared about almost nothing *except* destroying Shadow — not so much because of what it had done to thousands of innocents, though to give him credit he did feel a certain regret and anger at such needless cruelty, but because Shadow had harmed him, his family, and his honor. Had Shadow never touched Stormcrack Keep, Raven would still have opposed it, but only from a safe distance.

That was hardly a shock; after all, Raven was, as Prossie had known for weeks, a barbarian.

As it was, though, with his younger brother ruling Stormcrack Keep as Shadow's puppet, Raven was willing to sacrifice anyone and anything, including Stormcrack itself, to defeat Shadow and avenge himself. He did not care in the least that Amy and Susan might be in danger if they ventured back into his native reality; he cared, rather, that they would be useless, and that their presence might be an inconvenience him, and increase the risks of the party as a whole.

However, he would, in the end, agree to anything General Hart proposed, because it was General Hart who controlled access to the gate between universes — at least for the moment. Once back in his own land Raven would be free to ignore any plans and promises made at Base One — and he intended to do just that. He thought General Hart's plan for a small, fast-moving strike force that would penetrate Shadow's fortress and assassinate Shadow to be utter nonsense. Shadow, he knew, was a magical being, and if confronted directly must be fought with magic — though its creatures could be slain with sword or spear, certainly, he doubted that Shadow itself would be bothered by anything so mundane.

Raven's own plan was to gather whatever magic he could and fling it against Shadow until something got through.

To Raven, as the telepath had seen before, "magic" included not just the magic of his own universe, but any force that he did not comprehend, including Imperial science and Earthly technology.

If he took this proposed Imperial raiding party in, and brought back a few survivors who would attest to the need for other weapons against Shadow, then perhaps the Empire would provide those other weapons. Perhaps, if their "science" could do nothing, they would at least provide the men and swords to dispose of Shadow's creatures.

So he was agreeing to Hart's plan, even while he knew it was absurd, in order to draw the Empire into more direct conflict with Shadow.

Prossie knew that according to the rules the Empire set for telepaths, which required the immediate reporting of any sort of treason, or deception of government officials, or other anti-Imperial thought that a telepath might accidentally uncover, she should tell General Hart — but the general already assumed that the whole thing was a suicide mission. He misjudged Raven's motives for agreeing, thought the man was acting out of some silly romantic notions of courage, honor, and chivalry, but Hart knew that the proposed attack was insane and impossible.

He was deliberately trying to get Raven and the others killed, to get them out of the way. He *liked* the idea of keeping Shadow there as the Empire's enemy; it made the military more important if there was a serious foe out there somewhere, rather than just occasional rebels and outlaws to be suppressed.

So he intended to send Raven and his companions, and the Earthpeople, and a few of his own less-desirable underlings off to get killed.

And he intended to send Prossie along. Like most Imperials, he didn't mind at all if telepaths got killed. Almost everyone hated telepaths; that was a fact that Prossie had lived with all her life. Hart was no exception.

It was only reasonable to want to send a telepath, for communication and espionage reasons, and Hart thought that Prossie, after her previous visit to Earth, might be tainted with dangerous notions.

General Hart wanted her dead.

And as far as Prossie was concerned, that meant that he didn't deserve to be warned of Raven's plans.

Besides, even if Hart knew the lordling's true motives, his own plans wouldn't change.

Likewise, even if Raven knew Hart's own intentions, he wouldn't change his own mind; cooperation was the only way to get home to his own world.

Maybe some of the others should be warned, Prossie thought, but not these two. Aside from the uselessness of such a warning, nobody really wanted to have telepaths telling them what to do, telling them what they had misread or misunderstood or forgotten.

And for that matter, Prossie was not supposed to be listening in in the first place. She had heard her own name mentioned earlier, and had, almost inadvertently, begun eavesdropping. That was a violation of the rules; the Empire had strict penalties for telepaths who spied on innocent citizens, and even worse for those who spied on government officials. If she warned General Hart, or if she warned Raven and he let it slip to an Imperial officer, she could wind up at the whipping post, or on the operating table for a lobotomy, or even hanged.

General Hart was far more likely to order a flogging than to thank her.

Let them go on with it, then.

As for the others — well, that remained to be seen.

Prossie liked the Earthpeople, or at least three of them — Pel and Amy and Susan had such interesting, complicated minds, and so little real hatred or hostility in them. Ted's poor tangled thoughts she avoided now, but the others she enjoyed, even when Amy was feeling sick and sorry for herself. Raven's liegeman Stoddard was a good person, the wizards Elani and Valadrakul were no worse than average — Elani had a noble streak under her motherly warmth that was intriguing. Prossie didn't want to see any of them killed, and she certainly didn't want to get killed herself.

But although Prossie wished the Earthpeople no ill, getting off Base One and into Shadow's realm was probably the best thing that could happen to them.

She would not say a word to General Hart.

Roughly an hour after the briefing, if that was the name for it, had broken up, while he rambled along one of the endless metal-lined corridors that laced Base One, Pel encountered Susan Nguyen and fell in beside her.

He would not admit, even to himself, that he had been deliberately tracking her down. It was just good luck, he told himself, that he had happened upon her.

Just good luck — but he did have a question or two he very much wanted her to answer.

After mumbled greetings and a few paces of polite silence, he cleared his throat. She glanced up.

"Susan, are you really going to go with Raven's party into Shadow's universe?" he asked. "You saw what sort of monsters Shadow controls — you really think this stupid attack squad is going to get anywhere? It seems to me that it's practically suicide!"

He waited for an answer and was on the verge of concluding that he wasn't going to get one when Susan suddenly said, "You've noticed that the Empire's technology is different from ours, haven't you, Mr. Brown? They've got anti-gravity and telepathy, but we haven't seen any sign of computers or electronics, or even radios or telephones. All the same, do you think they might know how to make bugs of some kind, Mr. Brown?"

"Bugs?" Pel blinked.

He hadn't thought about that. He chewed his lower lip for a moment, glancing along the drab gray walls.

"I suppose they might," he admitted, "but it doesn't . . ."

"Just keep walking," Susan suggested.

Pel obeyed; together, the two of them strode down the corridor.

"A telepath could hear us, anyway," Pel muttered.

"But a telepath would have to be listening," Susan pointed out, "and they really have very few telepaths."

"For all we know, they have spy-rays or something," Pel pointed out.

Susan just nodded.

A moment later, as they turned a corner, she said, "You know, all of them are going back to their own universe, not just Raven. Elani's going."

Pel glanced at Susan, then turned his gaze resolutely ahead. "I know that," he said.

He was puzzled by the reference. He was sure Susan had some good reason for mentioning Elani, and not any of Raven's other companions. Susan and Elani weren't particularly close; in fact, Pel couldn't remember ever seeing the two of them together for more than a few seconds at a stretch, or speaking to each other at all beyond common courtesies.

Elani was one of the two wizards in Raven's band, and the only surviving female; did either of those facts signify anything important?

"You know, I'd rather go back home to Earth, instead of Shadow," Susan remarked. "It's a shame we can't go back the way we came."

Pel started to reply, but just then Susan turned, adding, "And here's my door. It's been a pleasure seeing you, Mr. Brown."

She stepped into her room, and left Pel standing in the passageway, staring stupidly at the blank closed door.

Back the way they came?

They had arrived at Base One by spaceship. They could hardly use an ordinary spaceship to get back to Earth; spaceships couldn't travel between universes. In all the Galactic Empire, so far as they knew, there was only one space-warp generator, and it was a huge thing here at Base One, not something that could be mounted on a spaceship.

Before that spaceship they had been on another one, Pel remembered, and another before that — but before *that*, they had arrived on a worthless desert planet called Psi Cassiopeia II through a magical portal from Shadow's realm.

Pel blinked.

They had come through a magical portal.

A magical portal that Elani had created.

And they had gotten to Shadow's realm by stepping through another, similar portal from Pel's own basement.

Pel suddenly felt very stupid.

They didn't need the Empire's gigantic space-warp machine to send them to Earth. All they needed was Elani.

Of course, the laws of nature differed drastically from one universe to the next, so none of Elani's magic worked here in the Galactic Empire, any more than his long-lost digital watch had, any more than anti-gravity worked on Earth. Elani couldn't send them back home from Base One.

But if they went with her into Shadow's realm, she could certainly send them home from *there*.

Now why, Pel wondered, hadn't he thought of that himself, and much sooner?

He shook his head. He'd been too busy with other thoughts to look at the situation logically, he decided. He twisted his mouth into a wry smile as he started back toward his own assigned room.

It appeared he'd be volunteering to join Raven's strike team after all.

In the next corridor, Prossie Thorpe smiled to herself. The telepath hadn't had to so much as drop a hint; Susan Nguyen had figured it out for herself, and she would let the others know. The mission would go on as planned — but not necessarily as General Hart expected.

Chapter Three

*P*el eyed the gathered group with some dismay.

All four of the Earthpeople had eventually gotten the idea and realized that the road home led through Shadow's world; now they all stood in a little bunch to one side of the staging area. They wore hand-me-downs and cast-offs; their own clothes were lost or ruined, leaving them in borrowed slacks and surplus T-shirts and old boots. Susan Nguyen had managed to hang onto her big black handbag through all their adventures, but everything else they wore came from the charity of the Galactic Empire, and in consequence they looked mismatched and scruffy.

In the center of the assembly room stood Raven of Stormcrack Keep, dramatically clad in his customary black velvet, calling and waving for order. Three fingers of his left hand were bandaged together, and his movements still had a certain stiffness to them; his arms were raised, but did not move as smoothly and freely as they ought.

It was a mystery to Pel just where Raven had gotten his clothes; when he had been taken aboard *Emperor Edward VII* for the flight to Base One he had worn only a tattered green silk bathrobe. Perhaps the Empire had been generous with him in return for his enthusiastic opposition to Shadow — or perhaps his own garments had somehow been recovered and repaired.

Beside Raven on his right stood Stoddard — none of the Earthpeople knew any other name for him, or even whether Stoddard was a family name or his given name — in a borrowed purple uniform with the insignia removed, since his own leathers had been lost or ruined somewhere along the way.

On Raven's left stood the wizard Valadrakul of Warricken, and a step behind him was Elani, also a wizard. Some of their original garments, like Susan's purse, had been recovered, somewhat the worse for wear, so that Elani wore her dark red wool robe, now heavily stained and with a few tears in the fabric hastily sewn shut. Valadrakul's calf-length embroidered vest incongruously covered most of a borrowed Imperial uniform. He had worn braids and long hair before his arrival in the Galactic Empire, and had lost one braid and some skin on Zeta Leo III; now his hair was cut short and trimmed in the bristly Imperial military style. Where Imperial soldiers were always clean-shaven, however, Valadrakul wore a full beard, which made for an odd combination.

These four, Pel knew, were all that remained of Raven's cell of the organized resistance against Shadow's rule in Stormcrack Keep's demesne; all the other members of Raven's little group were dead or lost, their remains scattered across two universes.

Of course, Raven claimed that there were other resistance groups, dozens of them, and that they formed a network that had even placed spies in the Galactic Empire and sent envoys to the Imperial Court. Pel had no way of knowing how much of that was true, but in any case, Raven's party had been cut off, and no longer knew how to contact the others.

At least, so they said.

Facing Raven was a stocky, balding man in a purple uniform, his insignia proclaiming him a full colonel. He had given his name as Carson. Behind him was arrayed his squad, some fifteen men — all of them white, of course, and most of them blond. The Galactic Empire did not believe in mixing races; Pel had learned that much during his time here. The Delta Scorpius system, where Base One orbited, was entirely reserved for whites. Pel had been told that planets and bases existed where there were blacks and Orientals and other non-whites, either alone or in combination, but he had never seen any. The only non-white at Base One was Susan; even Raven, with his Mediterranean complexion, was dark enough to sometimes draw curious and uneasy looks.

So here were fifteen of the Empire's finest, which meant Aryans, in full uniform, hair cut short, tall polished boots gleaming, helmets hung on their Sam Browne belts. The fancy belts apparently indicated that they were a special elite force of some sort; the crew of I.S.S. *Ruthless* hadn't been so equipped.

If the uniforms had been black or gray, instead of purple, Pel thought they'd have looked like fine little Nazis.

And why a group that small was under the command of a colonel, rather than a lieutenant or even just a non-com, Pel didn't know. Maybe Carson's rank was intended to impress someone. It did not, however, impress Pel.

Standing off to the side was one more person in an Imperial uniform, this one with an ordinary belt, dull-finished half-boots, and the black and gold patch of a Special on her shoulder, a rather plain young woman Pel knew from his previous adventures. She had no helmet in sight, and no sidearm. Pel knew her as Registered Master Telepath Proserpine Thorpe — Prossie, to her friends.

Hers was the only familiar face in the Imperial contingent. Pel had hoped that the surviving members of the former crew of *Ruthless* would all be included

— he had gotten to know them somewhat, and to respect them. Especially, Pel thought, in comparison with most of the Imperial military personnel he had encountered at Base One, many of whom seemed virtual parodies of dim-witted pomposity.

The military didn't have to be like that, Pel knew; back on Earth, in the U.S., even the Marines generally weren't as absurd as the bunch at Base One.

He looked for a familiar face in Carson's squad, and didn't find it. Captain Cahn was not there, nor Smith, Mervyn, Soorn, or Lieutenant Drummond.

Lampert was not there because he was still missing, last seen on Zeta Leo III. Cahn himself was probably still in a hospital somewhere, getting his bones reassembled — he had been thrown off a rooftop on Zeta Leo III.

And Cartwright, Peabody, and Lieutenant Godwin were dead, of course. Like Squire Donald a' Benton, and little Grummetty, and Alella, all of them dead, somewhere in the Galactic Empire.

And like Pel's wife Nancy, and their daughter Rachel.

So there were eight survivors from the other two universes here, and even counting Prossie as an ally, that left them a minority of the group. Carson's fifteen men — fifteen strangers — were the majority.

Pel was of the opinion that that was likely to cause trouble. Raven was certain to consider himself the leader of the entire enterprise, and from the look of it, Colonel Carson did not care to yield the point.

Colonel Carson might also have some pretty serious reservations about allowing the Earthpeople to go home. Pel thought that he and Amy could probably have convinced Captain Cahn to let them go — after all, the Earthpeople had gotten Cahn and his crew out of the Rockville jail; shouldn't he return the favor?

But Carson was a complete stranger, and his presence could be a real problem.

Still, once they were in Shadow's universe, the Imperials would no longer have their whole empire backing them up, and their blasters would not work.

Did they know that? Had they picked that up from Cahn's reports?

Pel remembered the battle that had sent the earlier group fleeing through the magical opening from Shadow's universe into the Empire's reality. Shadow had sent hordes of monsters against them, and the Imperials' blasters might as well have been harmless toys for all the good they did. Valadrakul's spells had worked, and Susan's pistol . . .

Susan's pistol.

Pel blinked, and looked at Susan.

Yes, she had her purse. The big black handbag hung from one shoulder. Despite everything, she still had it.

Carson and Raven were arguing about something, and everyone else was watching the dispute, or else busy with their own affairs. Pel leaned over and whispered to Susan, "You armed?"

She threw him a quick warning glance, then answered, not looking at him, "Yes."

He took his cue from her, and did not look at her as he asked, "Loaded?"

She lowered her head slightly, in a barely-perceptible nod.

A moment later, as some minor official was herding the entire party of twenty-five into the ship that would carry them through the space-warp, Susan managed to step away from Ted and closer to Pel.

".38 Police Special," she whispered. "Six-shot revolver, but I only have four rounds left. Why?"

"Just wanted to know what's available, in case we have any disagreements on the other side." He threw a meaningful glance in Colonel Carson's direction. She nodded.

Just behind them, Amy asked, "What are you two talking about?"

Pel glanced at Ted, and at the Imperials, and said, "Tell you later."

Amy, annoyed, decided not to press the issue on the spot.

"You'd better," she said.

Pel smiled. He glanced about.

His gaze fell on Prossie Thorpe, and his smile vanished. If she read what he was thinking, the whole game might be up right there.

Or it might not; he wasn't sure just what side Prossie would take.

To be safe, though, he decided it would be best not to think about any of that stuff. Not about the pistol, or using Elani's magic to get back to Earth, or anything the Empire might not like. But of course, trying not to think about it was almost impossible.

If he thought about something else instead, maybe he could distract himself.

Well, here was something — just how were they going to go through the space-warp? He had seen the machinery the Imperials used to generate their opening between universes, and it was absolutely gigantic — Hoover Dam would make one of the support brackets, and the Washington Monument an insulator. The resulting field was a couple of hundred yards across — and a few hundred yards away from the machinery, out in the vacuum of open space. They would need some sort of transport to reach it.

Captain Cahn's expedition to Earth had flown through the warp aboard I.S.S. *Ruthless,* and had immediately discovered, on the other side, that anti-gravity didn't work in Earth's universe.

Their blasters hadn't worked on Earth, either.

And their blasters hadn't worked in Shadow's realm.

Pel suspected that meant that anti-gravity wouldn't work in Shadow's realm, either.

So how would the whole group get there?

Was the Empire going to throw away another ship, and count on Raven's wizards to send everyone back? Had they come up with some other approach?

A glider might work. The space-warp generator operated in the hard vacuum of space, but an anti-gravity craft with wings could use its engines on the Imperial side and its wings on the Shadow side.

"All right, folks — everybody, your attention, please!"

Pel realized he was staring at the dull gray asteroidal stone of the floor; he looked up, startled. Colonel Carson was speaking.

"We're all here, and I think we're all ready. We've got our team equipment loaded already, and if you'll all bring your personal belongings, I think it's time to board the ship and get this show on the road!" He smiled — Pel supposed the smile was intended to be encouraging and friendly, but it came out rather stiff and stupid.

Pel had very little in the way of personal belongings; unlike Susan, he had been unable to retrieve anything after his stint working the mines of Zeta Leo III.

Not that he'd had much of anything, in any case. He hadn't carried a purse; when he'd stepped through the magical portal in his basement, planning a five-minute visit to Stormcrack Keep and a quick return home, all he'd had was the clothes he wore and the contents of his pockets. A shirt, a belt, pants, socks, and shoes; his wallet, with credit cards and a few dollars in currency that wouldn't pass anywhere in this universe; the key to his car; and that was about it.

And even those items were all lost.

Nancy had had her purse, but she was dead and her purse was gone.

Rachel was dead, too.

So all Pel had to carry were the pair of pants he had been given at the mine, and somebody's cast-off Imperial uniforms.

With a sigh, he picked up the little bundle and marched in the direction Carson had indicated.

*T*he Empire, it seemed, had decided to throw away another ship.

This one, I.S.S. *Christopher,* was a small short-range personnel transport, smaller than *Ruthless,* perhaps seventy feet from nose to tail — certainly no more than that. It was purple and pink, but not particularly elaborate in its design or decoration — at least, not by Imperial standards. To Amy, with its fins and curves and two-tone paint job, it still looked like something out of a comic book or a campy movie.

She shivered slightly; the air of the flight deck felt thin and chilly. She knew that had to be an illusion, though; the door they had entered through had been wide open to the rest of Base One, so the air would have equalized. It was just the knowledge that the flight deck itself was an air lock that was bothering her, she was sure — that, and the general stress and uneasiness she had been living with since arriving at Base One. She glanced up at the immense outer door; that mass of steel girders and panels was all that stood between them and outer space, and in a few minutes it would be opened.

She quickly looked away, back at *Christopher.*

The entire party trooped inside and found seats in the main cabin, which was starkly utilitarian — gray steel ribs overhead, gray steel plates underfoot, and eight rows of four seats apiece, gray steel seats upholstered in worn maroon leatherette, arranged in pairs on either side of a central aisle, like some military imitation of an airliner. Three bare lightbulbs, in a line down the center of the curving ceiling, provided light.

Amy thought that *Ruthless,* from what little she had seen of it, had been far more luxurious. But then, *Ruthless* was a long-range craft, Captain Cahn had told her, and had been on a diplomatic mission.

Furthermore, they hadn't known they were throwing it away. This time they presumably did, so naturally they'd picked a less valuable ship.

There were no seat belts — Amy had noticed long ago that the Galactic Empire wasn't much on safety equipment. Personal belongings were stowed under the seats; anything large or awkward was taken to the back of the cabin, where one of Colonel Carson's men heaved it through a door and onto a shelf in the storage area astern, where the soldiers' packs and various other supplies were already stowed. The soldiers retained their helmets and sidearms, but not much else; the Earthpeople generally kept whatever they had.

Two more of Colonel Carson's men split off from the main group and trooped forward, into the cockpit; Carson himself stayed until everyone else was sorted out and seated, and then he, too, vanished through the forward door.

There were half a dozen portholes, small ones with opaque covers dogged down over them; Amy found herself seated beside one, and immediately set about uncovering it.

Susan, seated beside her, watched with interest.

As Amy had suspected, the ship was already off the deck and moving slowly toward the air lock door. Anti-gravity was quick and silent, and the Empire, once it finally started something, didn't waste time.

The space-warp machine was out on the surface of Base One, halfway around the asteroid. They would be out in empty space for a few minutes. Amy had traveled through space before, on *Emerald Princess* and *Emperor Edward VII*, but those were big, comfortable ships, and appeared far safer than *Christopher*. She felt a twinge of uneasiness.

They stopped moving; there was no change in sensation, any more than there had been when they lifted off, but Amy could see that the flight deck wall was no longer sliding past. For a long moment they hung suspended as air was pumped out of the chamber, the ship no longer moving forward, but swaying gently in the air currents. The process began with a distant boom that was audible even through the thick steel of the ship, and then a dull roaring that gradually faded as the air thinned.

At last silence fell; the ship was floating in vacuum, with nothing to carry vibration. Then, finally, the outer door swung open before them — Amy had to press her face against the after edge of the porthole to see it clearly, but she managed it. There was no sound, of course; the immense steel barrier moved in utter silence, swinging slowly aside and revealing the white blaze of stars beyond.

The ship began moving forward again — as always with anti-gravity, there was no sensation of motion, but Amy could see the air lock walls sliding by again.

Then they turned about. Amy's inner ear still registered nothing, but she saw the universe wheel vertiginously past the porthole. The open door of the air lock was replaced by an infinity of stars and blackness; then the gray steel of Base One's artificial walls appeared along one side, followed by a rough, dark stretch of the original asteroid, then by more steel.

She had hoped to have a good look at the space-warp generator, but she realized quickly she was on the wrong side of the ship to see it clearly. Still, by repeating her edge-of-the-port maneuver, she was able to see it ahead.

It was ablaze with light. The gargantuan ring of equipment was glowing violet-white, so bright Amy found she couldn't look at it directly even when she found the right angle. Everything else vanished into the blackness of space in contrast.

The airless void gave the whole scene an impossible sharpness, a clarity that perversely made it seem dreamlike and unreal. The waking world as Amy knew it was never so stark and clean-edged.

Then the ship surged forward — still with no sensation of acceleration — and that intense light surrounded the vessel, spilling in through the port so intensely that Amy turned away, momentarily blinded. Others exclaimed in pain and surprise at the unexpected brilliance as she groped for the porthole cover and slammed it shut.

Her eyesight was almost back to normal when, abruptly, there *was* a feeling of motion.

The ship was falling. Amy could feel it. Her stomach surged uncomfortably; she clutched at her seat, wondering why the hell the Empire didn't use seat belts and shoulder harnesses.

Everyone else felt it, as well; Elani screamed, Prossie Thorpe shrieked something that might have been, "Here we go again!," and several of Carson's men swore.

To add to the confusion, the cabin lights went out, plunging them into utter darkness.

They struck something, hard; the ship rocked wildly, and Amy heard crunching and snapping. They fell again, and then, again, struck something and broke through it.

Then, with a sudden hard bump, they were down. Amy's head rocked back and forth, but she kept her seat and was undamaged. Judging by the sounds she heard in the stygian gloom not everyone was equally fortunate.

She waited for a few seconds, to be sure the ship was not going to move again; she realized that it lay at a slight angle, the artificial gravity that made it always seem level gone. It wasn't much of an angle; she didn't hear anything rolling or sliding down the slope after the first second or two.

At first it felt as if they had bounced, as if the ship were now rising, but then Amy realized that was just higher gravity. Base One had artificial gravity set at one Imperial gee — which was less than Earth's gravity. Earth, she had been told, had a gravitational field approximating 1.15 gees, by Imperial measurements.

And Shadow's conquered world was 1.3, which, she was sure, was what they were now experiencing. That heavy feeling, as if they were in an ascending elevator, was not going to go away.

Once she was convinced they weren't going anywhere, she groped her way up the wall and found the porthole. Carefully, she lifted the porthole cover slightly; light spilled in. This was not the incredible eye-scorching glare of the space-warp, however; the light that now shone around the rim seemed quite manageable. In fact, it looked like ordinary daylight — perhaps a bit thin and watery, but daylight.

Amy swung the cover aside and looked out at Shadow's world.

She couldn't see much. The trunk of a huge tree, standing no more than two yards away, blocked most of her view. Turning slightly, she could see that broken branches and foliage were scattered across the ship's fin, a few feet aft of the port. The fin itself was bent and battered, its pink paint scratched and scraped, revealing black primer and shining steel. Yellow sunlight slanted down, glittering coolly on the pink paint and green spring leaves — the sun here in Shadow's realm, in what she and some of the others had taken to calling Faerie, was paler than Earth's, its light not the warmer hue Amy would have expected back home.

Although she had no reason to think she could tell the difference, the light seemed to her like morning light, rather than afternoon.

"What the hell happened?" an unfamiliar male voice demanded of no one in particular.

Amy turned away from the port and peered into the gray gloom of the main cabin.

"We landed," she said. "Hit a few trees on the way down."

"Trees?" a timid voice asked.

"Big plants," a more confident voice replied. "Some of them get to be a hundred feet tall, or more. They're what wood comes from."

"We know what trees are, idiot!" a new voice snapped.

"Not all of us, we don't," another retorted. "Or at any rate I've never seen any!"

"Well, you'll see plenty of them here," Amy called, while wondering how anyone could have grown to adulthood without seeing a tree.

Then she remembered what she had seen of the Galactic Empire — the backwater world Psi Cassiopeia II, which was mostly lifeless desert and entirely treeless; the rebel colony on Zeta Leo III, where she had been held captive on an immense corn farm where the only trees were a handful of six-foot shrubs near the house, obviously just recently planted; and the hollowed-out asteroid called Base One. She might have seen a tree or two somewhere besides that farm, but there certainly hadn't been very many. She had to remember that these people weren't from Earth; most of them weren't even from the equivalent homeworld of the Empire, Terra.

Maybe trees had never evolved anywhere in the Galactic Empire's universe except Terra. Even so, she would have expected the Imperials to have exported them to all their colonies.

Well, she had expected a lot of things that didn't seem to have happened.

"Your pardon, milady," Raven said from very near behind her, startling Amy. "Might I trouble you to allow me a look?"

"Of course," Amy said, getting out of her seat and allowing Raven to lean over and peer out the port. "I'm afraid you won't be able to see much."

"Indeed," Raven agreed wryly, as he took in the sight of the immense tree-trunk. "'Tis scarcely the broad panorama that one might have hoped for."

"Any idea where we are?"

Raven shook his head. "Marry, milady, though 'tis a grand oak, 'tis hardly one I recognize — for that, how to tell one from the next, an you see but the bole, with no mark upon it save those put there by our craft's descent? The Empire's telepaths were consulted in the devising of yon opening 'tween worlds, and our goal was to arrive far enow from Shadow's demesne for safety, yet close enough to approach it in time, and perchance that's done, but that scarce names a single spot. Grand oaks such as this might be found in any number of suitable places."

Emboldened by Raven's presence, several of the others were now gathering around the port, trying to see out; poor Susan, in the seat beside Amy's, was being crowded quite rudely, and was twisted almost into fetal position trying to avoid pressure on her burns.

A rush of anger swept through Amy at the sight of that. It was bad enough that the lot of them had been sent off on this stupid journey before their injuries were fully healed, but all those big, strong, healthy men crowding around poor wounded Susan . . .

"There are other ports you people could open," Amy pointed out sharply.

Before anyone could reply, the door to the cockpit swung open and Colonel Carson appeared.

"Lord Raven," he called, "we could use you up front."

"Your pardon, milady," Raven said, managing an approximation of a bow despite having his head and shoulders wedged into the narrow space between the back of Amy's seat and a curving steel rib. He withdrew, made his way past the press of bodies, and strode up the aisle to the cockpit.

Without waiting for an invitation, Stoddard rose and followed his master.

*P*el took his time unclogging the porthole. After all, the ship wasn't going anywhere — not unless the Empire had some utterly uncharacteristic surprise up its collective sleeve, some way to get the thing moving in a universe where anti-gravity didn't work.

And he didn't really care all that much about Shadow's universe, except as a step back to Earth.

Ted Deranian was sitting beside him, watching as Pel uncovered the port. Ted was smiling foolishly. Looking at him, it was hard for Pel to believe the man had ever gotten through law school; he looked more like a village idiot than like an attorney.

Still, there was something he had said that tickled at the back of Pel's mind. It didn't really make sense unless you accepted Ted's theory that both Shadow's universe and the Empire's universe were all an elaborate dream, but Pel *wanted* to believe it.

It had been said back at Base One, when Ted had found Pel sitting alone, on the verge of tears as he thought about Nancy and Rachel.

"Don't worry, Pel," Ted had told him. "They woke up, that's all — they're back on Earth. When you get back there they'll be waiting for you."

Then he had caught himself and asked, "But why am I talking to you? You're not really here."

He had wandered off, leaving Pel furious at his insensitivity, but the idea that Nancy and Rachel were alive back on Earth had stayed, no matter how hard Pel tried to suppress it.

Maybe they were.

He knew that this wasn't all just a dream, all these strange things they had been through; he knew that Ted had it wrong, and the Empire and Shadow were real. They weren't a dream in the usual sense.

But on the other hand, this was an alien universe; Nancy and Rachel did not belong here. The Empire's universe was equally alien. Had they really, fully crossed over into these alternate realities?

What if they were all really doing some sort of astral travel? Wouldn't Nancy and Rachel snap back into their own world when their astral selves were destroyed?

Or even if the physical bodies made the transition, was time the same here?

Pel had read plenty of science fiction and fantasy as a kid; he had seen hundreds of movies over the years. Wasn't there always something somehow unstable about someone who had been removed from his or her proper place? What if that wasn't just a literary convention, but a deep subconscious understanding of some fundamental fact about reality?

Mightn't there be some way to change the past, to make Nancy and Rachel have never left Earth?

He and the others were in another dimension, a parallel world, an alternate reality; they were, as Amy put it, in Faerie. The very existence of such a place went against all common sense and previous experience; it threw Pel and Amy and Susan and Ted into the realm of legend, of myth, of fantasy. How could they know any more what the rules were? Back home, dead was dead, and nobody came back — but here? Who knew? Death might be different.

Hadn't someone written a story about a land like that? "Death Is Different," that was it — by Lisa Goldstein, perhaps? About a small country somewhere where death wasn't permanent, where the dead could be seen strolling about.

What if that author had somehow known a truth about this place where Shadow ruled? After all, the worlds of Empire and Shadow so resembled the settings for any number of stories that Pel found it hard to believe it a coincidence; it made more sense to credit it to some sort of psychic leakage between universes, images from one realm finding their way into the subconscious minds of writers in another.

And if that were so, what about all those stories where people rose from the dead, where the protagonist awoke at the end home safe in his own bed, everything restored to what it was before? Were those based on truth?

What if death *was* different?

On one level he knew that was nonsense. He knew this was all hard fact; Nancy and Rachel were dead. Cartwright and Godwin and Peabody, Grummetty and Alella and Squire Donald, they were all equally real, and all equally dead, and all really dead. He had seen Grummetty's corpse himself. He had seen Cartwright bleeding as the monsters overwhelmed him. They were all dead, and would stay dead until Judgment Day.

But somewhere, in the back of his mind, where he wanted so much to believe

Nancy and Rachel were alive that he could believe anything at all, he still hoped.

He swung open the porthole cover and stared out at the green and gold and deep gray of the forests of Faerie.

Chapter Four

Raven of Stormcrack Keep had seen many strange things in the hard, sad days since his brother had betrayed the clan and yielded the Keep and its lands to Shadow. He had fled through haunted forests by night, and had seen creatures there whose nature he still did not know, things he dared not contemplate too closely. He had lived for a time among the little people of Hrumph, the people his grandfather had called gnomes, before they were driven into exile; he had dwelt like a giant among them, and had been amazed by their ways and customs. He had fallen in with a handful of the few remaining wizards, had seen them in their own strongholds, where they lived unhampered by the dictates of the nobility and used whatsoever magic they might please. One of those wizards, Elani, had opened for him portals into the Galactic Empire, and into the world of Earth, where he had seen wonders that even the mightiest magic could not equal. He had been slave and supplicant in those other worlds; he had been beaten and abused, and still bore scars and wounds not yet healed from those encounters. He had thought that nothing could faze him any more. But now, as he stared at the men who had piloted the Imperial vessel, he discovered that he had not lost his capacity for surprise.

It was not any new marvel of science or magic that astounded him, but the depths of idiocy to which allegedly intelligent men could sink.

"Colonel," he said, "what might those two be about?" He pointed at the two men crouched beside an open panel, poking at the tangle of wires and baubles inside.

"They're trying to fix the engines, of course," Carson replied edgily.

"Be your engines broken?"

"Well, of course they are!" Carson snapped. "Why else would we have crashed?"

Raven considered this question for a moment, admiring its magnificent ineptitude. "Prithee," he asked eventually, "has none told you the nature of this realm?"

Carson glared at him. "What do you mean?"

Raven hesitated, then waved the matter away. Perhaps it would be best if he were to leave the man's ignorance intact for the moment; an opportunity might arise to exploit it at some other time. "Mayhap later," he said. "Erst, you sought my favor in some matter?"

"Yeah," Carson said, looking distastefully at the broad forward viewport. "I want to know where the heck we are. I'd figured on reconnoitering from the air, taking a look around — but then the drive quit on us. In fact, nothing seems to be working; must be a break in the power system somewhere."

"I fear, sir, that I know not where we be," Raven said. "Did they not tell you where the great portal would be?"

"They told me we'd come out around two hundred miles from this Shadow thing," Carson said. "I didn't listen to all the damn details; I figured we could straighten that out from the air once we came through."

Raven nodded. "And I've no more than that."

"You know this country, don't you?"

"Aye, for the main, an I've landmarks . . ."

"Well, then, take a look, damn it!" Carson waved at the viewport.

Raven looked.

The view here was a good deal more extensive than that from the porthole by Amy Jewell's seat, but it still revealed little more than that they were in a mature forest somewhere. Broken branches and scattered leaves were every-where, signs of the ship's fall strewn in a web of sunlight and shadow; oaks towered overhead, while moss and fungus flourished below. The light was the clean sweet white of home, not the hot glare of Earth's sun, or the harsh blaze of the lights of Base One. He judged from its angle that the day was just short of mid-morning.

"'Tis a forest," Raven said, "and I and mine drew best we could a map for you ere we left, and thereon we indicated those forests we knew — and some would put us your two hundred miles from Shadow's stronghold. How to tell one forest from another, who can say? Saw you aught before we fell — a keep, a mount, any such as that?"

Carson turned and glared at one of the pilots.

"No, sir," the man replied. "We didn't have time to see much of anything. Just trees."

"There might have been mountains off that way," the co-pilot offered, pointing to the left.

Raven considered that, studying the angle of the sun and the patterns of the moss on the trees. "Then, an those were the Further Corydians, we might be in the West Sunderland," he said at last, "but I've no certainty."

"All right," Carson said. "If we're in Sunderland, where do we go, and how will we know if we've got it wrong?"

Raven bit back a retort; he took a second to calm his voice, then replied, "An we're in the Low Forest of West Sunderland, we need but make way to the west, and in due time we should either strike the Palanquin Road, or reach the edge of the forest and the Starlinshire Downs. If it be the road, turning south will bring us in time to the River Vert; if it be the Downs, we should find landmarks enow."

Carson nodded. "And then what?" he demanded.

"And then? Why, then we strike out westward for Shadow's keep, should our plans be made and the omens favorable, and if they be otherwise, then seek we shelter with those who yet serve the cause of the Light." Raven's own plans were already made, and consisted mostly of the latter choice, locating a surviving part of the resistance to Shadow's rule; he had no intention of flinging himself against Shadow's keep in some pointless, suicidal raid.

However, throwing Carson and his men into such a raid might be the best way to rid himself of a nuisance, and to provide the evidence needed to convince the Empire to devise a *serious* attack. And who could say that they might not learn something from such an assault? To Raven's best knowledge, no one had been foolish enough to attempt anything of the sort in centuries.

"You can contact these others?" Carson snapped.

"Certes, I can," Raven replied, meeting his eye. He had developed the knack of lying straight-faced as a child, and had never lost it, but in this case he spoke very nearly the truth. Contact could be made, though it would best be done by a wizard, rather than by himself.

"And they can contact the Empire?"

Raven hesitated. "Aye," he said, "that's within their powers." That was beyond question; the hesitation was due to uncertainty as to the wisdom of letting Carson know it.

He didn't mention that in plain truth, either Elani or Valadrakul could doubtless make contact with others in the anti-Shadow network at any time, now that they were once again in their native realm, where good magic worked as it should. In truth, Elani could most likely make contact with agents in the Galactic Empire at any time, and they could, in their turn, carry messages to the Imperial authorities.

Of course, that would most probably put an end to their usefulness as spies. Furthermore, Raven did not trust the Empire. He would communicate with it only on his own terms, not at the urging of this arrogant oaf of a commoner.

He had not yet fully settled upon his own preferred course of action to be followed once he had found a new place in the resistance. That the Empire had some fool notion of using him as native guide in their assault on Shadow's keep he knew; that he had assented to the Empire's instructions, however, did not mean he would actually obey them. He had agreed because such an agreement was his only way to leave Base One and return to his own world.

Here, though, he was in command. Colonel Carson might not have realized that yet, but Raven knew who was master here, in the natural world, away from the topsy-turvy Empire. He was the heir to Stormcrack Keep, and as such he need take no heed of such as Carson.

*C*arson glared at the damned foppish barbarian who called himself Raven, trying to decide whether or not he could be trusted.

He didn't *really* trust any foreigner — none of them could think straight, they all had minds as twisty as their infernal streets in those little outworld colonies or the Azean backwaters on Terra. He had been told to cooperate with this Raven, though; the savage was supposed to be sworn to fight Shadow, and it was Shadow that really scared those pissant politicians back home, especially that twit Bascombe in the Department of Science, with his fancy title that he'd made up and got his father-in-law to make official.

And, Carson admitted to himself, the people who gave him his orders might actually know what they were doing this time — though he wouldn't bet his pension on it.

They'd told him that the space warp would put him in a whole new universe, where space itself was different; he'd had his doubts, and for that matter he still wasn't *entirely* convinced that this planet wasn't just someplace off in an odd corner of the galaxy, that the space warp wasn't just a shortcut from here to there, but it did seem to operate as advertised.

They'd told him to expect equipment failures, that some of the machinery wouldn't operate in the space here, maybe most of it, and sure enough, the damn ship had fallen like a rock, the AG drive working about as well as a popped rubber. He still suspected a break in the power feed somewhere, but he couldn't prove it.

So maybe they knew what they were doing when they told him to trust this fancy-talking twit.

"We can breathe the air here?" he demanded.

"Most assuredly," Raven replied gravely.

"All right," Carson growled. "Let's get out and take a look around, then, and maybe find these friends of yours."

*A*my scuffed one half-booted foot through the dead leaves, enjoying the rustle that made.

It wasn't quite the same sound she'd have gotten doing the same thing back on Earth, in, say, Vermont; the air was slightly thicker here, and the higher gravity made the leaves pack down more tightly. That made it an effort to just stand and breathe, really; the tired irritability that had hounded her ever since her rescue from Walter and Beth, back on Zeta Leo III, was still with her as well.

Still, it was good to be outdoors again after all the weeks at Base One. They had been lucky enough to arrive on a beautiful day — warm in the sun, cool in the shade — and the contrasts were delightful after the stuffy boredom of the hollowed-out asteroid. And it was good to see trees and leaves; she hadn't realized it, but she had missed them, not seeing a proper forest, or even a decent grove, since she had first arrived in the Galactic Empire.

The rich smells of black earth, rotting leaves, and growing things were absolutely wonderful after weeks of steel walls and stale air.

The forest seemed awfully quiet, though. She heard no birds, no squirrels or other animals; perhaps the spaceship's crash had frightened them away. The heavy, still air wasn't stirring anything overhead, either; the only sounds came from the stranded humans.

She looked up as the Imperial soldiers, in response to a brisk order from Colonel Carson, formed up in a line alongside the ruined spaceship, facing into a small clearing. At the sight of them, all together in their neat uniforms and silly purple helmets, it occurred to Amy that they had all been lucky that the ship had not smashed directly into one of the huge trees.

But then, the trees weren't all that close together, for the most part; a few giants had crowded out most of the lesser competition.

Even so, it appeared to Amy that they had been fortunate in falling into one of the larger gaps. Trees crowded close around the ship's nose and one side, but farther back the vessel lay in a relatively open space — open enough, at any rate, for Carson to stand there and order his men about, while the rest of the party stayed in sight but out of the way.

She saw Raven and Valadrakul exchange a derisive glance at seeing the soldiers standing in their tidy row, chests out and shoulders back.

"Popinjays," Elani muttered. "Gaudy purple popinjays, ready to have the stuffing knocked from them."

Stoddard didn't say anything; he crossed his arms on his chest and watched. Pel and Susan were still helping Ted down from the ship, and not paying any attention to the rest.

Amy turned and whispered to Elani, "You don't think much of them?"

"Pah!" Elani said. "Soldiers such as these perished in their thousands in the wars against Shadow. The others, Captain Cahn and his men, at least showed small signs of wit; this lot, ha!"

"You haven't had a chance to get to know them," Amy protested.

Elani made a noise of disgust. "I need not," she said.

Amy remarked, "Raven seemed eager to have them along."

Elani muttered, "My lord Raven is a wise man at times, but he can be a fool, as well. Look you now, and see what he thinks of these."

Amy looked at Raven, who was making no attempt to hide his disdain for Carson and company.

Well, that was fine. It might serve as a distraction.

"Elani," she said, "now that we're here, is your magic working again?"

The wizard turned to look at her. She waved a hand, and something flickered briefly in the air, and then vanished.

"Aye," she said. "The craft's with me again."

Amy smiled. "Then we have a favor to ask — Pel and Susan and I."

Elani quirked one side of her mouth upward in a crooked smile of her own. "It seems to me that I might guess whereof you speak," she said. "In truth, I'd wondered when you might speak of it."

"Then you'll do it?"

The wizard shook her head. "In time, aye," she said, "for we'd have none with us who'd not be there freely, and indeed, what would we with such as your man Deranian? And yourself, a dealer in knickknacks and drapery, what have you to do with deeds of high courage and state? So aye, I'll see you home — in time, in good time. But this is no place suitable, nor have we time enow, and 'twould be impolitic to attempt this ere I have spoken to Raven."

Amy pursed her lips and reluctantly nodded. "I can see that," she said.

"And it might have risks, as well," Elani added. "There's reason to believe that the opening of the gates between worlds is what drew Shadow's eye before, when erst you came to our land. An that be so . . . well, you'll be safe in your own realm, but those of us who remain behind . . ." She shook her head.

"I hadn't thought of that," Amy admitted.

"I had," Elani replied. "But naught of it, i'truth, for I'll have the risk, an you're quick. We'd the gate to Earth a time or two ere ever Shadow caught us at it, and all I ask is that we have at the ready a way to make good our flight when the portal again closes. For that, 'twould seem wise to know better where we stand."

Amy hesitated. "You mean you want to wait until we know where we are?"

"Certes, you have it."

Amy would greatly have preferred it if Elani had opened the portal immediately, but that evidently wasn't going to happen. She frowned, but in the heavy gravity and thick air, with her stomach uneasy, she found that she didn't have the energy to argue.

"All right," she said. "We'll wait."

*P*el watched with interest as the black-garbed nobleman and the purple-uniformed colonel stood almost nose-to-nose, glaring at each other.

"Colonel," Raven said patiently, "imprimis, you know naught of this land. Would not it be wise, then, to heed the counsel of those who do? Secundus, is't not but common sense to dissemble, when in the enemy's lands?"

Carson glowered at Raven.

"I don't like it," he said. "I want my men in uniform. We aren't a bunch of spies."

"Are we not?" Raven demanded sarcastically. "What are we, then?"

"We are a fighting squad sent to destroy this Shadow of yours, Mr. Raven, or whatever your name is."

"And you think, then, that such a motley party as this can best a power that has laid waste twice a dozen kingdoms, and brought all this world 'neath its sway?"

"I think, sir, that one properly-disciplined squad of Imperial soldiers can do a better job of damn near anything than any bunch of foreign barbarians!"

Raven threw up his hands in anger and disgust. He turned away, and spotted Prossie Thorpe.

"Mistress Thorpe," he called, "come hither, lend me your counsel!"

Several sets of eyes swiveled toward the telepath, who had been leaning against an immense oak and picking idly at the bark.

Prossie started and looked up, dropping flakes of bark. "Me?" she asked.

"Aye," Raven said, beckoning. "You."

Prossie had not expected anyone to notice her presence; she had no idea that she would be dragged into an argument between Raven and Colonel Carson, and had hardly even been listening. She sometimes had trouble paying attention to people whose minds were closed to her, and telepathy did not work in this universe — in what Amy called "Faerie." Prossie had picked the name up in passing, and rather liked it.

She still found it somewhat odd, being so out of touch with the thoughts of those around her. In fact, after the crowding at Base One, and the constant buzzing of thoughts on all sides, it was rather restful.

And it wasn't the same horrible cut-off loneliness she had felt in her cell on Earth, because here she was in constant contact with her cousin Carrie. That was the communications line between this party and the people back at Base One; it was also a natural and comfortable link between the two women. The two of them could chatter away while Prossie took in the physical sensations of this strange new world.

She had been in Shadow's world once before, but weeks ago, and in a different place. The trees here were taller, older, more imposing, the atmosphere more restful — if warmer, perhaps uncomfortably so.

It was rather intriguing to look at things, to touch things, to smell them, without having any preconceptions impinging from other minds about what the things *should* look like, *should* feel like. Prossie had really been too concerned with other, more urgent matters to take an interest in that before.

So instead of listening to the others she was picking at the bark of a gigantic oak when Raven called to her, picking at it and enjoying the feel of it.

She started and looked back at the others.

"Thorpe," Carson said, "get over here."

Reluctantly, Prossie left the oak and obeyed. Her stride was brisk and military; her expression was not.

"Mistress Thorpe," Raven said, "you can look into the minds of others, is't not so?"

"Well, ordinarily, I can," Prossie admitted hesitantly, "but not here, or on Earth. Only in normal . . . I mean, Imperial space."

"Then you cannot see what I am thinking, nor what Colonel Carson believes?"

"No, sir."

"Is that right?" Carson demanded angrily.

"Yes, sir," Prossie said.

"Well, then, what the hell did they send you for," Carson shouted, "if you can't read minds here?"

"I can maintain telepathic contact with my cousin Carrie, sir — Registered Master Telepath Carolyn Hall, that is, back at Base One," Prossie explained. "I can still handle communications with General Hart and the High Command." She did not add that he had been told all this previously; she knew perfectly well that Colonel Carson had ignored most of his briefing, assuming, as he always did, that he knew better than all the pantywaist experts and fat-bottomed generals.

Carson glared at her, and Raven took the opportunity to ask, "But ere we left Base One, you could see into the minds about you?"

"Yes, sir," Prossie admitted warily. Although it was an interesting novelty, she was never *entirely* comfortable when her telepathic ability was blocked off, and any sort of talking to other people without it was unpleasant. This questioning, about matters she preferred not to discuss, was much worse than ordinary conversation. She had no way of knowing whether Raven suspected that she had illicitly eavesdropped on him earlier. He hadn't suspected anything at the time, but the idea could easily have come to him after the ship passed through the warp.

"And your cousin Carolyn Hall," Raven continued, "she can still see into the minds of others about her?"

"Yes, sir," Prossie admitted, "but there are strict rules to protect privacy."

Carson rumbled, muttering something that might have been a remark about it being a damn good thing. One good thing about having her head blocked off, Prossie thought, was that she could ignore the distrust and hatred everyone felt toward telepaths.

Raven nodded. "Assuredly," he said. "But then, perhaps you could answer a question of mine, as it regards the thoughts of General Hart and the others above you."

Prossie hesitated. "Maybe," she said.

"Perhaps you can tell me, Mistress Thorpe," Raven said, "why these men should have chosen to saddle me with a blockhead such as Colonel Carson."

Prossie's mouth opened, and then closed again. Someone snickered.

Had the time come to admit what she had done, and tell them all the truth?

"I didn't snoop . . ." Prossie began uncertainly. Then she stopped. Her expression wavered for a moment; Raven, who had started to turn away from her to argue further with Carson, saw the colonel's expression and turned back.

She had been nervous as Raven and Carson questioned her, but Carrie, who was listening in, had thought the whole affair was thoroughly amusing. Prossie could sense her mental giggling. Carrie could afford to giggle; she was safe at home, not out here in an alien forest.

But then Raven asked why he had been saddled with Colonel Carson, and Carrie, at first amused by the question, had read what Prossie knew.

And suddenly she wasn't giggling, mentally or otherwise. Her amusement had vanished. She sent a feeler out to General Hart, and then to others . . .

By now everyone, from all three universes, was staring at the telepath, though several of them were not sure why. Pel, watching, felt a growing tension; for his own part, he had a sense of impending doom.

But then, he had felt a sense of impending doom for much of the time since Nancy's death.

Prossie's face went oddly blank as Carrie, panicking, pulled her briefly into a full linkage; then her expression returned more or less to normal.

"What troubles you, lady?" Raven asked.

Prossie hesitated, trying to think over what she had read herself, and what Carrie had relayed. Trying to decide what to say, when she couldn't read her listeners' reactions, was very difficult.

"It's a mistake," she said at last. "General Hart . . . there's been a lot of factional fighting about Shadow . . there were several plans, and they got confused, what with Major Copley being ill. It should have been Captain Haggerty in command, not Colonel Carson . . ."

It was actually worse than that, but Prossie had had a lifetime of not telling everything she knew. She didn't relay what Carrie had just told her.

General Hart's choice of personnel, and entire attitude toward the mission, had been subtly affected by undeservingly trusted subordinates. Prossie had known that Hart had intended to send an officer he wanted to get rid of, but it had actually gone beyond that.

Colonel Carson had been selected by agents of Shadow as absolutely the worst possible officer for the job.

"Bull!" Carson shouted.

For a moment, Prossie thought Carson was replying to her unspoken thought, but then she realized he was simply denying that his appointment was a mistake.

Prossie felt lost without her mind reading. She knew what everyone wanted; the Earthpeople wanted Elani to send them home, Elani wanted to send them. Raven wanted to take command of the rest and take them to join the underground. Elani and Valadrakul and Stoddard trusted Raven and would support him in whatever he had planned against Shadow.

Most of the fifteen troopers just wanted to finish whatever the job was and go home; they had no idea of what they had gotten into.

And Carson wanted to prove that he was a great leader and a true man among men, but since he was not, in fact, either one, he had no idea at all how to accomplish that.

She knew what they all had wanted, up to the moment they hit the space-warp — but what they intended to do about it, she had no idea. Why hadn't the Earthpeople taken Elani aside? Amy had been talking to her, but nothing had come of it, so far as Prossie could see.

Why wasn't Raven playing along with Carson, as he had with Hart? Didn't he see that the man was an arrogant fool who could be coaxed into doing anything, so long as he thought it was his own idea? If Raven didn't see it, what about Valadrakul or Elani?

Prossie wished she could take Raven aside for a few moments, or Elani, or almost any of them, but instead here she was, trapped between Raven and Carson in the most public manner possible. She regretted, now, that she had taken time to look around and admire the trees.

"It's bull, I said," Carson repeated, and Prossie realized that everyone was looking at her. She stared back at Carson. Even without her telepathy, Prossie could almost feel the hate Carson felt for her.

"Maybe I misunderstood something," she said.

"Nay, lady," Raven protested, "'twould explain much, if this man was sent in error. 'Tis plain he's no master of subtlety, and ill-fitted for our task here. What, then, shall I, as a rightful lord, take the charge? What say you all?"

"I say it's bloody treason, you barbaric fop!" Carson bellowed. He reached for his sidearm.

Raven stepped back and reached for his sword-hilt — but he had no sword. The weapon was lost long since, somewhere back in the Galactic Empire. "Valadrakul!" he called.

Carson's blaster was out and pointed, and Prossie stared at it in horror.

Didn't they know it wouldn't work here?

Carson pulled the trigger as Valadrakul raised his hands; the wizard's fingers twisted strangely as he spoke a word.

For a moment, Prossie thought the blaster had worked after all, as something flashed, pale and quick as heat lightning, between Carson and Valadrakul. Then she realized that the weapon was pointed at Raven, that the shimmering flare had traveled from the wizard's upraised hands to Carson's body.

For an instant the colonel stood motionless, an expression of astonishment spreading slowly across his features; then it turned to a rictus of pain, and he crumpled to the ground, still holding tight to the useless blaster.

The sound of his fall into the dead leaves seemed impossibly loud and prolonged. Accustomed to a constant telepathic echo behind every voice, the eternal hum of other minds drowning out the ordinary noises of the inanimate universe, Prossie rarely heard mere sound so clearly, but here, in this telepathically dead environment, there were no distractions. She thought she could almost hear each individual leaf crumbling, each separate impact as first one knee, then the other, then a hand and the blaster and the other hand struck, his belly and finally his face landing in the rustling detritus.

And when the sound of the impact had faded, she heard a strange arrhythmic chorus of faint clickings. At first she took it for leaves settling, but then she realized it came from the wrong direction.

She turned, and saw a dozen blasters, drawn and aimed, triggers clicking uselessly against copper contacts. Carson's men were avenging their fallen commander — or trying to.

"Men of the Empire!" Raven called, his hands upraised in an orator's gesture. "Yon usurping fool is dead; drop your arms, an you'd not taste the same!"

"The hell you say," someone called.

"Raven," a quiet voice said — a woman's voice, speaking from the side, not from the line of men by the ship.

Startled, Raven turned, and found Susan Nguyen standing straight, legs braced, her pistol held out before her, gripped firmly in both hands. Her black handbag, whence the revolver had come, lay open at her feet.

The barrel of the little gun was pointed directly at Valadrakul's head, from a distance of perhaps four feet away. The wizard was utterly motionless, his hands hanging stiffly at his sides.

"*This* gun works here," Susan said, speaking calmly but emphatically. "You've seen it."

"Aye, mistress, I do so recall," Raven replied warily.

"You are not going to hurt anyone else. Neither is Valadrakul. If anyone else is harmed, your wizard dies. Clear enough?"

Raven flicked his gaze to Elani; Prossie's own eyes turned to follow, and she found that Pel and Amy stood one on each side of the female wizard, each gently restraining one of Elani's arms.

"Now," Susan said, "we are all going to sit down quietly, and talk this out, and settle what we're going to do, and we're going to do it without any sort of violence, because the first person to use violence is going to get a bullet in his gut. Is that clear?"

"Aye, mistress," Raven said, "'tis plain as the day. And it pleases me well — I'd no wish for strife. Yon fool drew 'gainst me, and I've no blade; am I to perish undefended by the hands of such as he?"

"You know perfectly well that blasters don't work here."

"Ah, but mistress," Raven protested, "in the heat of the moment I misremembered."

Susan did not reply to that.

She didn't lower the gun, either.

For a moment, no one spoke; then Ted Deranian burst out giggling.

"What an anti-climax!" he shouted. "No gunfight, no wizard war! My subconscious is wimping out on me."

"Shut up, Ted," Pel said.

Ted ignored him, and turned to Susan.

"Lady, if you're a real person and I didn't just dream you up," he said, "I sure hope you don't try this sort of thing in the courtroom!"

Chapter Five

"*B*ut I tell you, I *am* your rightful lord!" Raven shouted.

The Imperial soldiers shuffled their feet and cast uneasy, mocking glances at one another.

"The hell you say," one man muttered.

"Mr. Raven," the lieutenant explained patiently, "leaving aside that you killed the colonel, or at least your man did, and while it may have been self-defense, I'm not saying it wasn't, still, that ain't the approved procedure for promotion, and as I was saying, even leaving that aside, you aren't in the chain of command."

"And I have the word of General Hart that I *am*," Raven insisted.

"You got the paperwork, the signed orders, you let us see 'em," the lieutenant answered. "Otherwise — you don't have the uniform, you don't have the rank, you don't have anything. You're a civilian."

"I am a nobleman born!"

"That don't mean shit to us, sir. Our oath is to the emperor, nobody else. You could be the bloody King of the Franks himself, and we'd still have to tell you to call your Dad and get the papers."

Pel, watching and listening from a few yards away, could see that a couple of the soldiers were not happy with that particular claim; he wondered who the King of the Franks was. He supposed it might be a title given to the heir to the throne, like the rank of "Prince of Wales" in Britain. It seemed a very odd thing to him that there would be such archaic titles in an interstellar empire.

"Listen, man," Raven argued, "your master is dead, and you are in the enemy's lands, lands that you know naught of, and where I am all that you have to guide you. Your lord, the General Hart, sent you hither to aid me — me, and none other. Then is't not madness and folly to deny that command is fallen to me, that Colonel Carson is no more?"

"Mr. Raven," the lieutenant explained wearily, "you are not in the chain of command. *I* am. I was the colonel's second-in-command, and with him gone, *I* am in command. *You* are a civilian, and as long as you are, you can't possibly assume command. That doesn't mean we can't cooperate."

"Permission to speak, Lieutenant?" one of the men called.

Startled, Raven and the lieutenant turned.

The man who had spoken — Pel didn't know any of the soldiers' names yet — was leaning comfortably against a tree; now he straightened, and pointed to Prossie. "We've got a mu . . I mean, a telepath with us, Lieutenant," he said. "Why not ask *her*? Check with Base?"

"Aw, come on," someone called. "She's the one who started this and got the colonel killed!"

"No, that was the guy over there in the funny clothes," another voice protested.

"I don't mean she killed him," the first replied, "but she was the one who said things were screwed up!"

"So maybe they *were* screwed up!"

The lieutenant looked over his men, chewing his lip as he did so, then turned to look consideringly at Prossie.

"All right, Thorpe," he said. "You call home and tell us what we're supposed to do."

"'Tis a waste . . ." Raven began.

The lieutenant thrust out a warning hand.

Susan Nguyen cleared her throat warningly.

Raven fell silent, and two score eyes focused on the telepath.

*W*hen Colonel Carson fell, Prossie had not waited for orders; she had immediately relayed the news to Carrie and told her to tell someone in authority.

Carrie had done so — she had left her cubicle and gone running for the Office of Interdimensional Affairs. Her orders were to report anything received from other universes to the Under-Secretary, and that included messages from Prossie, as well as contacts with the handful of psychics on Earth, or with Shadow's creatures.

The Under-Secretary was not in.

"It's urgent," Carrie told the receptionist.

"I'm sure it is," the receptionist replied. "Have a seat, and the Under-Secretary will be back momentarily."

Carrie hesitated, and glanced toward the door — she made it look as if she were seeing if there were any sign of the Under-Secretary's approach, but in fact she was turning away so as not to stare while she read the receptionist's mind in hopes of finding out just where the Under-Secretary was.

The receptionist was not thinking about Under-Secretary John Bascombe; she was thinking about an idealized, muscular, blond and handsome male figure. This was the man she felt she deserved to have married, and she was convinced that she had not found him because telepaths, with their sneaking and spying, had stolen him away. There were hundreds of the dirty mutants out there, far more than anyone knew, but they kept themselves secret, only a few admitted what they were in order to get into the government where they could spy on everything better, and steal all the good men away from deserving ordinary women.

It took Carrie several seconds to dig down past this depressingly familiar paranoid fantasy and locate recent memories.

"Why don't you sit down?" the receptionist asked, mentally adding, "Mutant bitch."

Carrie realized she had been staring foolishly out the door of the office. The receptionist, despite her belief in a conspiracy of evil, lawless telepaths, didn't yet realize that her thoughts had been illicitly spied on, but the idea might occur to her at any second.

"No, that's all right," Carrie said. "I'll try again later." She turned and headed back out into the corridor.

The Under-Secretary had been taking a long lunch, and was lingering over his final cup of tea; Carrie hurried to the cafeteria, to catch him before he left.

He looked up in surprise as she entered.

"Telepath," he said, "what are you doing here? This room's off-limits for you!"

"Yes, sir," Carrie said, "but I think this is an emergency."

He put down his cup.

"Colonel Carson has been killed, sir," Carrie told him, coming to attention.

"By Shadow?"

"No, sir. By one of the wizards in his own party."

Bascombe let out a long, deep sigh. "Are you sure?"

"Yes, sir."

"Well, get out of here, anyway — no telepaths are allowed in here. I'll be out in a moment."

"Yes, sir." Carrie turned and trotted out to the hall.

She waited, and a moment later the Under-Secretary emerged, walking quickly. "Come along," he ordered.

She followed, but to her surprise he did not return to his own office; instead he led her down to Level Six, to General Hart's office.

Five minutes later the three of them, Hart and Bascombe and Carrie, were seated in Hart's office with the door closed.

"Now," Hart said, "tell us all about it."

"*T*hey're still arguing," Prossie told the others.

"Who is?" Lieutenant Dibbs demanded.

"General Hart and the Under-Secretary for Interdimensional Affairs," Prossie replied.

"Just what are they arguing *about?*" Amy asked.

That was not easy for Prossie to answer. Carrie was relaying not just the two men's words, but some of their thoughts, as well. While the spoken debate purported to be a discussion of the best way to ensure the survival of the rest of the expeditionary force, the actual subject, as both men knew, was the fact that General Hart had deliberately tried to screw up the Under-Secretary's project and had been caught at it. Both Hart and Bascombe knew, however, that Bascombe could not come out and say that openly — if the mission failed he would take at least part of the blame, and trying to shift it to Hart would just make him look worse.

He could, however, take Hart down with him, in a variety of ways, since Hart's sabotage had shown up so quickly. If the party had been wiped out by Shadow's forces, both men would have been able to get out cleanly — underestimating the enemy was a mistake, but an understandable and forgivable one, relatively minor, nothing at all like deliberately sending people to be killed.

So each man was now looking for a way out that would leave him blameless. Branding Raven as a dangerous lunatic or treacherous foreign outlaw was one possibility — in that case, Lieutenant Dibbs should be put in command and Raven arrested or killed. Denouncing Carson posthumously as a renegade was also a possibility, but if he had surviving family or friends that might be risky. And in either case, what should the survivors do next? Should they continue their mission and attempt to penetrate Shadow's stronghold, or should they abandon the enterprise, take shelter, and wait for rescue?

That latter possibility assumed that rescue was possible. General Hart was not at all clear on how travel between universes worked; the Under-Secretary had a better grasp of the subject, but did not care to enlighten a man who was, when all was said and done, his political adversary. And even knowing what he did, the Under-Secretary was thinking in terms of reopening the space warp and lowering a line; the possibility of using wizards' magic had not yet occurred to him.

"Whether to continue the mission," Prossie said.

*A*my was seated cross-legged on dry, dead leaves, forearms resting on her knees, watching as Raven and the Imperials argued, and feeling sweat moisten the back of her T-shirt; it wasn't really very hot, and she hadn't been doing anything very active, but the thicker air seemed to make perspiration come more easily. She felt a vague discomfort in the general vicinity of her stomach, as well, and wasn't sure whether or not that could be attributed to the climate and atmosphere.

Beside her stood Elani; Amy was staying close to the wizard, who was, after all, her ticket home to Earth, to peace and sanity and her own home.

As far as Amy was concerned, it made no difference at all who was in charge of the group, so long as Raven agreed to let Elani send the Earthpeople home.

Still, she could see that it mattered very much indeed to some people — with a shudder, she stole a glance at Colonel Carson's body, lying undisturbed on its bed of fallen leaves.

More death. That was not anything she wanted to see. She had managed to live forty years on Earth without seeing more than half a dozen corpses, and those were mostly at funerals; she had never seen anyone die until she had stupidly agreed to step through Pel's basement wall and take a quick look at Raven's world.

But then there had been Cartwright, killed by Shadow's monsters — though he might have still been alive, Amy told herself, when she escaped through the portal into the Empire. There had been Peabody, killed by the pirates aboard *Emerald Princess.* And others. She hadn't seen them all die, but Pel's wife Nancy was dead, and their daughter Rachel, and Raven's friend Squire Donald, and Lieutenant Godwin, and the two little people, Grummetty and Alella. People aboard the *Princess* — she didn't know all the names. People killed in the fighting when the Empire's Task Force Umber came to the rescue.

And the two on Zeta Leo III who had held her prisoner, Walter and Beth — they had both been hanged by the Empire. She hadn't seen that, it had happened after she was aboard *Emperor Edward VII* on her way to Base One, but it had happened, and the two of them were dead, and it was partly her fault.

It was partly their *own* damn fault, of course, for keeping slaves, and abusing her, and killing that other woman, whatsername, Sheila. Walter was a murderer, and Beth was his accomplice — but if Amy had kept her mouth shut, probably no one would have known that, and the two of them would still be alive in an Imperial prison camp somewhere.

If anyone asked her now, she wouldn't testify — she was over the need for vengeance, and had had her fill of death. She looked at Carson's body and swallowed hard, feeling suddenly queasy.

Elani looked down at her, eyes bright.

"Is aught amiss, lady?" the wizard asked.

"I don't know," Amy replied. She felt no need to explain her misgivings. "I just don't feel very good."

"Ah, certes, you'd be home, I'll wager. Well, methinks this parley is near its end, and we'll soon be sending you hence." Elani's motherly smile suddenly dimmed. "Or be it more? Have you the Sight, lady? Is danger at hand?" She raised her head and lifted a hand.

Amy started to protest, then stopped.

If Elani wanted to check for danger, it might not be necessary, but it couldn't hurt.

"*A*n they summon you home," Raven said, "'twould be simple courtesy that I call for volunteers 'mongst your men."

"My men are under *my* orders," Lieutenant Dibbs insisted loudly.

"Ah, but you'll see that *you* might soon be under *my* orders, an your superiors so state — true?"

"Yes, sir," Dibbs agreed, "but until I get orders to that effect, I'll just do as I think best. And if we're ordered home, we go home. Thorpe, any word yet?"

Prossie shook her head. "They're still talking," she said. "I think they're planning to go on, but they haven't settled the details."

"They've said naught of who's to command?" Raven asked.

"No."

"Have you inquired?"

Prossie hesitated.

"Lord Raven," she said, "I've told Carrie that we need to know who's in charge, but she can't just interrupt a general and an undersecretary, she can't make them listen to her. They've got what they consider more important matters to settle first. If it's any help, the Under-Secretary wants to put you in charge, but General Hart says you should be in an advisory capacity, since you're not only not in the military, you aren't even an Imperial subject."

"Ah . . ." Raven turned away angrily, spat on the ground, then turned back. "You've no doubt of that, lady? That lying scoundrel Hart would have me play the native guide, and no more, and his promises that I'd command are no more than devil's smoke?"

"I'm afraid so," Prossie said.

"In my own land, he'd have me a mere servant to this ill-born stripling?" Raven gestured toward Dibbs with the three bandaged fingers of his left hand.

Prossie nodded.

"I'll not have it," Raven shouted. "I will not and I shall not!"

"So what are you going to do about it, then?" Dibbs demanded.

The rightful lord of Stormcrack Keep turned his attention from raging at the treetops to defending his right. "Silence, fool," Raven commanded. "Hast forgotten that thy Under-Secretary would place me above thee? Durst address thus one who shall perhaps shortly hold thee in thrall?"

"I'm a freeborn Imperial citizen, sir, and I'll speak as I please," Dibbs retorted.

Raven grabbed at his swordless belt in frustration, and cast a glance at Susan. The revolver was no longer aimed directly at Valadrakul's head, but it was still held securely in the lawyer's hands.

"'Tis all . . ." he began.

"Raven!" Elani cried, interrupting him. "Shadow!"

Pel, who had been sitting nearby and listening to the debate, started; he looked about wildly, but saw only the downed spaceship, the cluster of people, the surrounding trees and underbrush.

"Damn!" Raven said. He, for one, clearly did not doubt Elani for a moment. "Valadrakul, wards!" he called. "Elani, where away?"

Elani pointed upward and to one side, past the spaceship's nose.

"We're under attack?" Susan asked, turning the gun away from Valadrakul.

"It's a trick, lady," one of the soldiers called. "He's just trying to get the gun!"

Susan started, and her grip on the pistol tightened, but none of the natives of "Faerie" were paying any attention. Raven was looking about for cover, glancing every so often at the sky; Stoddard was shading his eyes and looking up at the treetops; Elani and Valadrakul were both muttering and gesturing, preparing spells.

Pel got slowly to his feet, not sure just why, or what he hoped to do; he was unarmed, and had no way to fight if Shadow's creatures really were approaching.

"Aye," Elani called, in a pause between mumbles, "Shadow's creatures draw nigh. Hellbeasts, carried by another, one that flies — they approach, yonder — a score, perhaps, aboard the flyer!"

The Earthpeople and the Imperials stood, baffled, or milled about in confusion; the natives were more alert. "Shelter in the ship?" Stoddard asked, nodding toward *Christopher.*

"Nay," Raven replied, "an we might be trapped within and besieged, or the vessel crushed and us thereby."

Stoddard nodded an acknowledgment; Pel, who had been heading for the door of the ship without realizing it, stopped dead in his tracks.

A better means of escape occurred to him. "Elani," he called, "can you get us out of here? Open a portal?"

Amy had gotten to her feet, as well, and was standing close beside the little wizard; she added her own voice, saying, "Please, Elani?"

The sorceress shook her head. "We've not the time," she said.

"Look!" one of the soldiers called, pointing upward.

Something big and black was moving, up above the trees, blocking the sunlight and plunging them into shadow. Pel, watching it, thought it resembled a blimp passing overhead. Did Shadow use airships?

"All right, men," Lieutenant Dibbs called, "form up, two lines, helmets on, weapons ready."

"No," Raven shouted, "flee! Take shelter, wherever you may!"

"These are *my men* . . ." Dibbs began.

"Sir," a soldier said, cutting him off, "our blasters don't work here."

Dibbs froze for a second, then said, "Damn. All right, then, we'll take cover — but in proper order. We aren't running away. Shelby, you take that end, and the rest of you form up, we'll move over there, under the starboard vane."

"Lieutenant . . ." another man began.

"Move!"

For a moment, no one spoke; leaves rustled, boots stamped, as everyone did what he or she thought best to prepare for an assault. A faint humming that reminded Pel of distant insects came from somewhere overhead, and he realized it came from that dark shape.

Pel remembered his previous visit to Shadow's realm, and the horrific fight near the forester's hut on Stormcrack lands, the fight where Spaceman First Class Cartwright had died; there, Shadow's creatures had burst up through the ground and come showering out of the trees from every direction. There was no safe place. The only chance to survive was flight.

He considered turning to run now, dashing off into the forest at random, but that, he realized, might just take him into the jaws of some slimy black monstrosity.

Besides, if he died, perhaps he would be reunited with Nancy and Rachel. If he died bravely, went down fighting, didn't he *deserve* to join them, wherever they were? Maybe if he died here he would wake up safely back home on Earth, in his own bed, alive and well.

But there was no point in being stupid, in making it easy for Shadow. He headed for Valadrakul and Susan; Valadrakul had his spells, Susan her revolver.

"'Tisn't seeking us," Elani said abruptly, breaking the silence.

"Is't not?" Raven asked, startled. Pel saw that the nobleman had found a broken limb among the debris that the ship had brought down, and was holding it in his right hand like a club. His bandaged left hand was empty.

"Nay. 'Tis come to study the portal that brought us hither."

Pel started to relax, then realized what that could mean. "It'll find us soon enough, then," he said.

"An it flies not on through, into Empire, aye," Elani agreed.

"Mistress Thorpe," Raven called, "can you send word, warn those who remain at Base One?"

"Of course, sir," Prossie replied. "But I can't promise they'll pay any attention."

Raven muttered a word Pel didn't catch. It sounded like an archaic obscenity.

"The flying creature is at yon portal," Elani announced, pointing upward.

"Goes it through?" Raven called.

Pel looked about, and saw that the party had collected into three groups — and one individual.

One group consisted of Elani, Amy, and Ted, clustered at the base of a large tree of undistinguished species; another was composed of himself, Susan, Valadrakul, Stoddard, and Prossie Thorpe, standing by the side of the downed ship; and the third was made up of Lieutenant Dibbs and his fourteen men, gathered under the ship's stubby wing, farther astern. Raven stood alone, on an upthrust root of a gigantic oak, swinging his makeshift club stiffly and watching the leaves overhead.

And Colonel Carson's body lay in the open part of the little clearing between the ship and the trees, near the center of the uneven quadrilateral formed by the survivors. Pel turned away, and found himself looking at the dead officer's troops.

Dibbs had his men arranged in two rows of seven, one line facing forward, the other aft, with himself at the outer end; all of them were crouching, as the fin provided slightly less than six feet of headroom. Some, Pel saw, were clutching their blasters by the barrels; others were searching the ground for sticks or rocks.

"Are there any other weapons aboard the ship?" Pel called to the lieutenant, shifting back to the rear of his own cluster.

Dibbs shook his head.

"Nay," Elani cried. "It turns away! It senses us!"

A dozen faces turned upward.

And a moment later, a dozen assorted black-winged horrors plunged down through the green leaves, claws outstretched, fanged mouths agape.

Chapter Six

Valadrakul gestured, and the foremost hellbeast exploded in golden fire. Pel ducked instinctively as football-sized gobbets of black slime spattered across the ground and the side of the ship. Another flash he guessed to be Elani's doing.

The other hellbeasts came on without slowing, and before Pel could raise his head one of them struck him on the shoulders and spun him around, slamming him against the hull. Dazed, he could see nothing but purple paint on smooth metal as sharp claws or teeth — he couldn't tell which — chewed at the back of his head.

Then there came a brilliant yellow flash, and Pel could feel things sliding down his back, across his buttocks and down the back of his legs.

People were screaming, he could hear them, and there were other noises, gnashings and scratchings and gurglings. He heard a loud popping, and realized that it was the sound of a gunshot — Susan had fired her pistol. Another flash sent spots dancing before his eyes.

He remembered the other fight against Shadow's creatures. That had been different; they had come up from beneath the ground, rather than down from the sky, and then hundreds more had come in from all sides, from the surrounding forest. There had been no warning at all, and the group there had been somewhat different — Cahn and his crew were there instead of Dibbs and his squad, the little people had still been alive, Nancy and Rachel were there. There had been no ship, but a woodshed with a magical portal in it, and the party, hopelessly outnumbered and outmatched, had fled through the portal.

This time, there was no portal — unless one of the wizards could open one, and that seemed unlikely, in the midst of battle, without any previous preparation. Pel knew nothing about how the portals worked, but he remembered that Elani had needed several minutes to open one.

If they faced those limitless hordes again, the hundreds of horrible things that had come leaping out of the forest, they were surely all as good as dead. A few might escape into the surrounding forest, but what would become of them then? They would be lost, to starve or be picked off one by one by Shadow's creatures.

Maybe, Pel thought, it was almost over. Maybe, in a few minutes, he would be joining Nancy and Rachel — either in death, or waking up again safely back home on Earth.

Unsteadily, shielding his face with one arm and bracing himself against the ship with the other, Pel turned.

Twisted fragments of monster were strewn everywhere, horribly out of place in the bright midday sun — some like the remains of a gigantic burst black balloon, some like black jelly, some like charred driftwood or burned roasts, all dark and harsh against the gentler colors of the forest. Valadrakul stood amid the debris, systematically targeting the survivors — a fifth exploded as it gnawed on someone, one of the group that had stood to the side, Amy and Ted and Elani. All three of them were down, lying on the ground with hellbeasts atop them. As Pel watched, something in that heap flashed white, but the monsters continued their assault. Whatever magic Elani had attempted had not worked.

Pel's own group, by the ship, was also under attack — there were creatures assaulting Prossie Thorpe and Stoddard, and one lay dead at Susan's feet, the back of its head blown apart. Pel judged that Susan had thrust the .38 into its mouth before pulling the trigger.

A single monster had gone after Raven, who had warded it off with his club; the antagonists were now facing off, a few feet apart. It seemed to Pel that there was something unnatural about Raven's position, and for a second that puzzled him. Then he realized what it was; the natural pose for a man with a club would be to hold the weapon in both hands, or to keep his free hand up, ready to grab. Instead, Raven's bandaged left hand hung uselessly at his side.

None of the beasts had attacked the Imperial soldiers; hiding under the ship's wing had apparently been a successful ploy. Pel found himself irrationally resenting that.

And there was no second wave, no throng of monsters spilling out of the trees and underbrush. In fact, this time the humans seemed to be getting the better of the fight.

Stoddard had his attacker, a thing like a greyhound with bat-wings and elongated, tentacular forelegs, by the throat, and was squeezing; the monster was trying to wrap its own snakelike limbs around the big man's neck in return, but its head was twisted back so that it could not see its foe, and Stoddard jerked it from side to side, so that it was having trouble finding its target.

Prossie's opponent was smaller, and resembled a flying spider, or perhaps a winged monkey; at first glance it didn't look big enough to be seriously dangerous, but Pel could see blood on Prossie's hair and uniform as she rolled on the ground struggling with it.

"Lieutenant!" Pel shouted. "Do something!"

Valadrakul flung out a hand, and the thing attacking Prossie exploded.

One hellbeast had landed atop Colonel Carson's corpse; realizing at last that its prey was already dead, it turned toward the ship and slithered forward, wings dragging behind. Pel was not sure who it was aiming for, Valadrakul or Prossie or himself.

Stoddard began slamming his antagonist against the side of *Christopher,* a steady dull thudding.

"Come on, men!" Dibbs called; he came charging out of his shelter brandishing a thick chunk of tree-limb. Several soldiers followed; Pel, startled, saw that three or four did not, but remained where they were, huddled under the guidance vane.

Half a dozen men landed atop the slithering creature, arms rising and falling as they pounded at it with rocks and clubs; other men flung themselves at the two monsters that were still atop Elani's group.

A sharp crack sounded, and Stoddard's creature went limp. Thin liquid oozed down the side of the ship.

Valadrakul worked his magic once more, and Raven's opponent burst into ruin without ever striking a blow.

In seconds, the remaining creatures were dead, and the humans were brushing themselves off, gingerly testing wounds, assessing the damage.

Pel had superficial scratches on his head and back, and the T-shirt he wore had been shredded, but he was not seriously injured. None of the soldiers had received anything worse than a few scratches on their hands and arms. Valadrakul and Raven were untouched; Stoddard had bruises on one forearm and a red abrasion on the side of his neck.

Prossie had received dozens of shallow slashes from the razor-edged feet of the thing she had fought, and had lost enough blood to make her dizzy. She sat against the base of a tree, resting, while the others gathered.

Elani, Amy, and Ted were in a pile, under several dead monsters; it took the others a few moments to dig them out.

Ted was on the bottom, and had had the wind knocked out of him, but was otherwise not visibly damaged any further than he had been before. The bandage on his head had been torn off, but the wound beneath appeared no worse.

Amy had three long gashes on one forearm, but had fended off all other attacks; she was pulled upright, dazed and panting.

Elani was dead; she had thrown herself atop the other two, and one of the monsters had torn open the back of her neck, as well as slashing at her head and elsewhere. Her hair and clothing appeared singed, though none of the creatures had used fire in their attacks. Pel wondered if some sort of acid or venom might have been responsible.

"I thought she was supposed to be a wizard," one of the Imperials muttered.

"She was," Prossie said.

"Then why didn't she defend herself, the way whatsisname did?"

"She defended Ted, instead," Amy explained dully, staring down at the dead sorceress. "She saw he wasn't moving, so she destroyed the one that went for him, instead of the one that was after her."

"I saw a flash," Pel said, "but it didn't seem to do any good."

"That was the last time," Amy said. "I'm not sure . . ."

"'Twas her death," Valadrakul said, interrupting. "At a wizard's death the web of energies that's been woven about her through all her life comes unraveled all in an instant, and betimes there's a flash, or a display of one sort or another." He stared at Elani's remains with an expression Pel couldn't interpret — it might have been grief, or anger, or almost anything.

"Well, we . . ." Dibbs began. He cut off short and looked up, startled, as a deep shadow suddenly fell over the party, blotting out the patchy sunlight.

"What's that?" a soldier asked.

"The big one," Valadrakul said, looking up, his face suddenly intent. "'Tis the hellbeast that carried the others hither." He raised his arms and began a spell.

"Is it attacking, too?"

No one answered, but from overhead came a sudden snapping and crunching — tree-branches were being smashed aside as the thing tried to fight its way to the ground. Leaves and twigs showered down.

Pel looked up, puzzled, trying to locate the descending creature. The trees and shadows made it difficult to see just what was happening.

"Why doesn't it just come through the hole the ship left?" he asked no one in particular.

Valadrakul was too busy with his magic to answer, and no one else had a ready reply, but then Pel managed to figure out what he was looking at, and realized why. The thing *was* coming through the hole the ship had left. It still had to break off limbs.

Otherwise, it couldn't fit.

*P*rossie stared up at the hellbeast in weak and horrified fascination. Behind her, someone screamed, but she didn't bother to turn and look.

She had heard stories about animals of incredible size that were found on various obscure planets on the outskirts of the Empire — or even worlds that were closer in, but off the main routes. She had generally assumed that such tales were exaggerated; she knew that non-telepaths had a tendency to distort things. Telepaths had something of a self-correcting mechanism, since their memories would automatically be compared with those of the other telepaths, and even so, some events grew in the retelling, so it was no wonder that non-telepaths might blow things all out of proportion.

On the other hand, it was a big universe, and the Empire was full of marvels, so she had never completely dismissed stories of beasts the size of spaceships.

But now that she was actually looking straight up at one, she found it impossible to believe. That thing up there could *not* be real, she told herself.

A heavy tree-limb plummeted down and smashed ringingly against the grounded spaceship's metal hull, leaving the opening in the treetops a little larger, giving her a better look at the thing. She stared up, ignoring the leaves, bark, and branches that fell around her.

The hellbeast was roughly bat-shaped, but with a huge, bloated body, a body the length of *Christopher* but easily twice as thick. The head was raw nightmare, with saw-edged ears the size of sails, man-sized compound eyes where each facet was a slit-pupiled green disk, a mouth that could swallow an aircar; the clustered fangs were like swords, and the dangling purple tongue, thick as a man's thigh, writhed like a wounded squid's tentacle.

The wings were still tangled in the surrounding trees, tearing their way through; Prossie glimpsed at least four sets of claws, rather than the two that an ordinary bat would have. And the monster's shadow covered *Christopher,* the narrow clearing where the ship had fallen, and a broad stretch of forest to either side.

There was simply no way such a creature could exist in any sane universe.

But then Prossie reminded herself that she was not *in* a sane universe — she was in Shadow's realm, in Faerie, where magic ruled and science was powerless.

Regardless of what universe it was, there was still only one sensible reaction to such a monster, and that was to run. The thing might be able to smash its way through the forest, but judging by how slowly it was making its way down to the ship it would not be able to do it with any speed; she ought, she thought, to be able to escape it easily, even in her weak, wounded condition.

She forced herself up onto her feet, bracing herself against the tree she had sat beneath, and was about to flee when Carrie's mental voice called to her.

"Prossie, they want you to continue the mission, to go on to Shadow's fortress."

Prossie stumbled, and looked up at the monster overhead.

She hadn't been transmitting, there was no way that Carrie could have known what was going on here, but still, the message seemed so irrelevant as to be ridiculous. A dozen dead monstrosities were scattered across the landscape, she was bleeding from a dozen cuts, Elani had been killed, and a nightmare with a quarter-mile wingspan was fighting its way down through the forest, trying to get at them — who *cared* what a couple of pompous idiots back at Base One wanted? She turned to run.

As she turned, she glimpsed Valadrakul as he flung his spell at the gigantic creature; eldritch energy flashed upward from his raised hands, and sparks flickered across the monster's belly — but that was all. Nothing exploded; no tattered bits of black monster-flesh fell.

A faint whiff of something unpleasant reached her nose as she ran, but Prossie could not tell whether that meant Valadrakul's attack had singed the thing slightly, or whether it was the monster's natural aroma.

Prossie glanced back over her shoulder, and saw Susan point her pistol at the thing. The lawyer looked at the weapon in her hand, then up at the descending horror; she let out a quick bark of laughter, then dropped the gun in her handbag, turned, and ran, following Prossie.

Most of the others were scattering now, as well, and Prossie could only see a few of them; the rest had vanished behind the trees. Valadrakul was standing his ground, chanting; Ted Deranian was lying where he had fallen, watching everything, not moving; but all the others were departing or already gone, at paces ranging from a slow, backward-facing, step-by-step retreat to a full-tilt heedless run.

Prossie's own pace was somewhere in between; she was moving at a brisk trot, but watching where she was going and glancing back every so often. She didn't need any more scrapes or scratches, and she didn't want to leave a trail of her own blood for any of Shadow's creatures to follow. Right now, she really didn't want to think about the fight against Shadow itself, or what was happening back at Base One, or long-term plans of any kind; she just wanted to get away, to stay alive and in one piece.

*A*my had panicked. When she had seen that thing coming down through the trees, had seen its shadow block out the sun, had been showered with twigs and leaves as it broke past the treetops, she had frozen for an instant, and then she had screamed, and she had turned and run.

It was all too much, Colonel Carson's death, and the hellbeasts, and Elani falling on top of her and dying there, and then that gigantic horror appearing overhead. She had gotten used to the relatively sane and normal life at Base One, and this succession of shocks had broken her nerve temporarily.

But only temporarily; as she stumbled across the uneven floor of the forest she was slowed by the irregular footing, by mounting nausea, and by a wave of guilt.

She knew better. Running away didn't solve anything, that's what the counselors and therapists all said. A person must face her fears. The others were still back there, fighting that thing.

She forced herself to stop and turn around.

For a moment, as she stood sweaty and panting, her gashed arm throbbing, she couldn't see the monster or the ship, only trees — she had covered more ground than she had thought. In her unthinking panic it had seemed as if the creature was right behind her, just inches away; that it was not seemed somehow miraculous.

And then an entirely new sort of panic set in — she was alone, lost in the forest, wounded, with no one to help her and no chance at all of finding her way home. For an instant, from sheer terror, she stopped breathing.

And when the sound of her own breath stopped, she could hear the sounds from the ship — wood breaking, people shouting. She followed them with her gaze, and spotted first the hellbeast's shadow, then the spaceship, and finally the creature itself.

It was at that moment that Valadrakul flung his new spell; Amy could see it spilling upward from a tiny figure she had not realized was there until the orange plume of fiery magic burst forth.

The scene was so distant that it didn't seem entirely real; framed between two tree-trunks, it was like a tableau, like some sort of outdoor drama staged for her amusement. The spell was a special effect, something midway between smoke and flame, vividly painted across the image but not entirely convincing It wove upward through the air, into the monster's open mouth, moving not with the speed of fire, nor the slow grace of smoke, but like the ascending trail of a skyrocket on the Fourth of July.

And then it entered the creature's mouth, and something exploded, and for a moment light and smoke seemed to obscure everything; Amy had a glimpse of what looked like glowing green crystals where the creature's eyes should be.

The sound of the explosion reached her, a dull thud that echoed and re-echoed through the forest; she blinked, and when her eyes were open again the monster was falling down through the air, covering the spaceship and the wizard in a lumpy black shroud.

Amy blinked again.

The wizard — that was Valadrakul.

The other wizard, Elani, was dead; with a shock, Amy realized that she still had Elani's blood on her, in her hair and on her borrowed T-shirt, smeared down her right arm and across the back of her hand.

Elani, the wizard who had agreed to send them home to Earth, was dead.

And Valadrakul, buried under the dying monster, was the only other wizard in the group.

"No!" Amy shrieked. "No, no, no!" Her feet seemed to move of their own accord, and she found herself running back toward the clearing, the ship, and the monster just as desperately as she had fled a moment before.

Upon first spotting the hellbeast above, Raven had known instantly that this gigantic manifestation of Shadow's malice could only be fought with magic; his makeshift club could be of no effect against a beast the size of a castle.

This was Valadrakul's fight, then. Elani was fallen, and her skills had never lain in the area of combat, in any case.

"An I can serve," Raven called, "you need but speak!"

Valadrakul ignored him — and quite rightly.

A woman screamed, and Raven heard running feet. For his own part, he bethought him that a cautious retreat might be advised, lest he be struck down by the monster's struggles, all unintended. He began pacing slowly back, away from the wizard and the arena.

The first spell was launched, to no effect, but that troubled Raven not a whit; Valadrakul was but trying out his foe, using against it the spell that had sufficed to destroy the lesser beasts. Raven had seen wizards do the same upon many a previous occasion.

Debris was falling freely now, leaves and branches; Raven retreated farther. He judged that the monster was free of obstructions, and stared upward, trying to determine why it did not fall, in all its fury, upon those below.

Men were shouting — undoubtedly the odious Dibbs and his underlings, but Raven spared no glance for such as they.

The beast, he could see, was gripping the great trees with its claws, holding itself aloft as it studied what lay below. It could see the sky-ship, but surely knew not what it might be. Likewise could it see Valadrakul; did it know him for what he was? If so, it might strike him down before another spell could be cast.

Raven hesitated. Valadrakul was too intrigued in his magicks to move of his own choice; should one then try to pull him thence, out from beneath his foe, ere disaster might arrive? An it might disrupt a casting, yet would it save the wizard to fight again.

Ere he could decide, another spell went up — no mere bolt like the last, but a torrent of glowing force, orange and gray, smoke and fire bound into one. It leapt up from the wizard's hands and into the beast's gaping maw.

The thing, in anticipation of the attack, had released its hold upon the trees, had drawn in its claws and begun to fold its great wings.

And then all happened with such speed that Raven could not follow. Valadrakul's fire caught at the inside of the monster's throat, and its head seemed to be burnt out from within, the glow of the flames visible for an instant through its crystalline eyes; smoke and fire billowed forth, obscuring all; and the creature fell.

Sound and wind forced Raven back; he flung up his arms to protect his face, and thus did not see the actual impact. The rush of air knocked him back against a tree; his head struck hard against the wood, and for a moment his thoughts were scattered.

When he could see again, and understand what he saw, the spaceship was gone from his sight. The clearing, too, was gone. Valadrakul was gone, and Colonel Carson's remains, and poor Elani's. The demented Earthman, Ted Deranian, had vanished as well.

And in the place of all of them was only a great black heap.

It needed a moment ere Raven understood that that heap was the remains of the fallen bat creature.

And that Ted Deranian and Valadrakul lay somewhere beneath it.

Chapter Seven

*P*el approached the dead monstrosity carefully. The thing was obviously dead or dying; Valadrakul's fireball, or whatever it was, appeared to have burned out the entire interior of its skull, and surely even one of Shadow's magical creations couldn't survive that.

But on the other hand, with a thing that size, even a final spastic twitch of a wing could probably break a person's neck.

He saw no twitching, though. He couldn't hear if the thing was making any sounds; Amy was screaming as she ran toward him, drowning out almost everything else.

Her screaming was not particularly piercing, just loud; Pel judged that she was not so much frightened or hurt as working off accumulated tension. He ignored the screams and looked the situation over.

The body had fallen directly atop I.S.S. *Christopher* and then slid partway down the far side, but the outstretched wings seemed to cover the entire area; the bony claws had gouged huge raw yellow chunks from the surrounding trees on the way down. Pel kicked aside a curl of bark the size of his head from one such wound; he stepped over a fallen branch and stopped a few feet from the black membrane of the wing.

It looked like thick rubber or polished leather. At first Pel thought he could see the shapes of tree-branches showing through from beneath, but then he realized that those were veins within the wing itself.

He started to reach out, then stopped. He didn't really want to touch the thing.

Ted and Valadrakul were underneath it, though. They might even still be alive. Forcing himself, Pel reached out, grabbed for the edge of the wing, and tried to lift.

It was still warm, and it felt horribly like human skin with a thin coating of fine fuzz. It was thicker than he had realized; when he slid his fingers underneath he couldn't get his hand all the way around the edge to close his thumbs over the top. Prying upward with just his hands did nothing at all; the wing did not budge, and his fingers slid out from beneath.

That black fuzz was as smooth and soft as cat fur; it didn't give him any easy purchase.

"Someone give me a hand!" he called.

He tried again, thrusting his arms under the wing as far as his elbows and heaving upward. His muscles strained; his breath stopped. The veins in his face distended, and he felt as if something would burst at any moment.

The monster's wing did not move.

"You think they're still alive under there?"

Startled, Pel recognized Susan's voice. He also realized that Amy had finally stopped shrieking. He relaxed and turned to Susan, who had come up behind him.

"They might be, anyway," he said. "But they may not have much air left, if they are."

"You think it's airtight?"

Pel waved at the huge black covering. "What do you think?" he asked.

"I think you need better leverage; there are plenty of branches you could use." She, in turn, waved at the scattered debris left by the creature's descent, and the ship's fall before that.

"More men," another, deeper voice said. Pel realized that Stoddard was standing at Susan's shoulder. "Sticks are well enow, but this needs more men than one."

"You're right," Pel said.

"We're two, then," Stoddard said.

"Three," Susan corrected him.

Stoddard looked down at her from his six feet or so of height; she smiled crookedly up at him from an inch or two over five feet, her still-bandaged arms folded across her chest, and corrected herself, "Two and a half."

Pel called, "Lieutenant Dibbs!"

*D*ibbs had wanted to find all his men before attempting any rescue efforts; four of them had not returned yet. Only when Prossie Thorpe had reported a decision from Base One would the lieutenant agree that uncovering Valadrakul and Deranian was more urgent.

And only Prossie knew that she had lied — there had been no decision to report. The people back at Base One had completely lost touch with the situation; they were still talking about whether Colonel Carson might not be completely dead, and what medical assistance might be appropriate. Bascombe and Hart were concerned with an attack on Shadow's stronghold, with setting up a proper chain of command that they could duck out of to avoid accountability if they had to. Even Carrie had not really followed the sequence of events after the arrival of the first group of hellbeasts; she was far more concerned with assurance that her cousin was safe, that there weren't any more monsters lurking somewhere nearby, about to leap out and eat everybody. No one at Base One understood about the black wing, about how big it was. No one there appreciated that Valadrakul was the only wizard left, and that magic was their only hope, both in any fight against Shadow, and as a way home.

Valadrakul *had* to be saved, or they were all trapped here, all as good as dead. And no one was listening, no one at Base One, none of the Imperials in Faerie. Pel had tried to explain, but Dibbs had almost ignored him — Brown was a civilian, a passenger, with no authority. Raven argued that the two should be freed, but he said nothing about a need for magic; he spoke only of how Valadrakul was a faithful servant and owed loyalty. Amy and Susan babbled of a common humanity that meant nothing to an Imperial soldier.

And Prossie could not speak on her own account; she was a telepath, and a woman — a mutant bitch. She had been called that all her life; she knew that that was how Dibbs saw her. No one would listen to her as herself.

But they would listen to her as a relay.

So Prossie had lied. *She* knew that Valadrakul and Ted needed help immediately, that saving Valadrakul was vital, and she had said they should be saved.

And by doing so, she had committed a capital crime. The technical term in the Imperial Articles of Service was "usurpation of representational authority by specially-empowered communications personnel," and it was an offense invented as a direct result of the widespread fear and mistrust of telepaths. No non-telepath had any way to verify what a telepath reported, but telepathic communication was too valuable to leave unused; the Empire had responded to this dilemma by setting up draconian rules for all telepaths. From birth, they were trained to tell the truth, to obey non-telepaths, never to venture their own opinions — they were communication equipment, not people; spies, not soldiers.

And one reason that the Empire had only four hundred and sixteen telepaths, out of thirteen billion citizens, was that in the years since telepathy first appeared, forty-three telepaths had died for violating those rules.

If the Empire ever learned what Prossie had done, she would be the forty-fourth.

And since one of the other rules required that any telepath who learned of a violation and failed to report it was subject to the same penalty as the person who committed the original violation, she had dared not let Carrie know what she was doing.

Pel Brown had started it, asking for a decision from Base One, and Dibbs had objected; he didn't need to have headquarters overseeing his every move.

"What do they say?" Pel Brown had demanded, as Dibbs continued to protest.

Carrie was not listening in; she was still asking if there might be more monsters, and ignoring Prossie's own questions.

"Carrie, calm down," Prossie had sent, trying to hide what she intended to do, "I'm fine. We're busy here right now; I'm going to break contact for now.

Find me again in about twenty minutes, all right?"

"Prossie, are you sure?" Carrie's concern was touching — and also annoying.

"*Yes,* I'm sure. Now get out of my head!"

No telepath ever refused that order; it was a family rule. Carrie broke conscious contact.

"We might as well settle this," Dibbs had said. "Thorpe, report!"

"Yes, sir," Prossie had said, snapping to attention, long habit overcoming her weaknesses.

And then she had lied. "General Hart says that the survival of extrauniversal personnel is absolutely essential and must take first priority, sir! Please use all efforts to uncover Raven's man Valadrakul and the solicitor Deranian."

"Damn," Dibbs said. "I think they're making a mistake, but an order's an order. All right, Singer, Wilkins, the wizard was right by the ship, he could be under the curve of the hull — see if you can crawl in there and find him. Maybe take a couple of those branches to shore things up. Hollingsworth, Moore, you others, we've got half a dozen lumps under the wing — some of them are wood or rocks, but that one by the rib must be the Colonel, and those two close together are probably the dead woman and the one we're after. See if you can pry up the edge and get a look at them."

Prossie watched with an odd mix of emotions. She admired the way Dibbs and the soldiers set out efficiently to get the job done, once they accepted an order — she'd seen it before, of course, hundreds of times, but it still amazed her that non-telepaths could work together so well without direct communication.

And tired as she was, she felt a peculiar sensation of pride and pleasure because the men were obeying *her* orders — they didn't know it, they would never have obeyed if they had known, they would kill her for it if they ever found out, but they were obeying *her* orders.

This, she realized, was the feeling of power, real power; she had never felt it before.

And tied to it was a feeling of terror. She had broken the law, the law that was all that kept non-telepaths from murdering every telepath in the galaxy. She was a criminal, an outlaw.

If Carrie ever found out . . .

Would Carrie tell, or would Carrie risk her own death sentence?

Prossie didn't want to find out. She had fifteen minutes before Carrie would call to her again; in that fifteen minutes she had to forget what she had done. She could never dare think of it again.

Not that the Empire could put her to death here in Faerie, of course. Not that Dibbs and the others could ever find out what she had done — she was their only link to the Empire. But if she ever wanted to return home, if she wanted Carrie to be able to live a normal life, she had to never again allow herself to consciously remember her crime.

*A*t the age of eighteen, Albert Singer had signed up to be a soldier. He had enlisted because he was thoroughly bored with farming, because he liked the way the fancy purple uniforms looked, and most importantly, because he saw how much the girls liked the way the fancy purple uniforms looked. He had signed up for space service because it looked a lot more interesting than hanging around the little garrison at Cochran's Landing, and he figured it would impress the girls even more.

It had never once occurred to him that this would one day lead to crawling through the stifling, malodorous darkness underneath a wrecked spaceship and the corpse of a gigantic monster bat, shoving his way through damp earth and brittle dead leaves, trying to rescue a fat little foreigner who was probably already dead.

He couldn't see a thing, not really; a little of the afternoon light filtered in around his own boots, but the dust from the leaves was a thin haze everywhere around him, grit had gotten in his eyes, and there wasn't anything to see, in any case. He sneezed, spraying warm goo on his upper lip and the back of one hand, and could hardly wipe it off. The entire front of his uniform, chest to toe, was becoming coated with dirt — he could feel it, could feel the cool moisture and the grainy texture.

He belatedly decided that he should have taken off his boots; the shiny finish was going to be ruined, and he thought he'd have been able to crawl better without them.

He pushed with his toes and elbows, forcing himself deeper into the narrow passage. One shoulder brushed against the steel of the ship's hull; the opposite knee rubbed against the furry, rubbery flesh of the dead monster.

Why the hell did the lieutenant have to pick *him* for this? And why had he not argued when Wilkins had said to go in first? Good old Ronnie Wilkins was squatting back there watching, not doing a damn thing except staring into the dark, where he probably couldn't even see the bottoms of Singer's boots any more.

The first part had been easy, crawling under the ship's starboard guidance vane, but this part . . .

Singer coughed, without meaning to, and hoped very much that he wasn't going to cough up anything that would wind up smeared on his chin or his uniform. The dust from the leaves was ghastly.

As much to clear his throat as anything else, he called, "Anyone in here?"

To his utter astonishment, a voice called back weakly, "Aye, lad."

Not only was the bearded foreigner still alive, Singer realized, but he was conscious, and only a few feet away.

"Hold on, sir, we'll get you out," Singer said, trying unsuccessfully to sound reassuring. Then he coughed again. The powdered leaves felt like ground glass scraping the back of his throat.

He saw something flutter indistinctly in the dimness ahead, and suddenly his throat cleared. He swallowed experimentally, and everything worked.

Singer remembered that the man ahead was supposed to be a magic-worker of some kind. "Did you do that?" he asked.

"Aye," the voice replied. "An it please you."

"Thanks." Singer shoved himself forward again, then stretched out one arm and found he could touch Valadrakul's embroidered vest.

Then the roof fell in, or seemed to; the blackness that was the dead monster's wing suddenly sank in, pressing down on him, and Singer found his face pressed into the dirt beneath. "Hey," he managed to shout, his voice muffled.

Wilkins heard him, and called in, "They're lifting it off the other one, the loony with the head wound. They were picking it up, and everything shifted."

"Well, tell them to hurry up, for God's sake," Singer called back.

"Right." Wilkins turned away and shouted something, but Singer was no longer listening; he was trying to see through the gloom ahead of him.

"Are you okay?" he asked.

"Aye, lad," the wizard answered.

"Can you move?"

"After a fashion, aye," Valadrakul replied. "My head is free, 'neath the ship's hull, like your own. And I can move hands, arms, and all, despite the weight of the flesh atop. But alas, one of the beast's bones lies across the back of my legs, and holds me fast. An that be moved, I'd be free."

"You can't lift it?"

"Nay."

"I saw you doing those fire tricks before; you can't burn your way out?"

"Nay, I'd but set myself afire, as well. A blade might serve, but I've none, mine was lost long since."

"A blade . . ." Singer mentally cursed himself for not bringing a knife. He had one, of course, a standard military-issue combat knife, but it was in his pack, inside the ship, and the ship was underneath the dead monster.

Then, abruptly, the thick layer of flesh above him shifted again, this time pulling up and away. Twisting around so that his helmet was out of the way he looked up at it, and realized that the rest of the squad must have heaved the wing out a little.

He still couldn't see much, though. His flashlight was in his pack, aboard the ship, as well. Another stupid mistake. At least he wasn't the only one who had made this particular mistake; as far as he knew, everybody, even Lieutenant Dibbs, had left his pack aboard ship.

He peered into the darkness. The dust had settled, and his eyes had adapted; he could see the wizard's face as a pale, colorless blur.

He had room now to get up on his knees, his back pressing up into the creature's wing; he did, and leaned forward, groped ahead until he was able to grasp Valadrakul's hand.

"Maybe I can pull you free," he suggested.

"Mayhap you can," Valadrakul agreed. "An you haul, I'll push."

Singer grabbed the wizard's arm in both hands, braced himself, and said, "Ready? Heave!"

They heaved.

Nothing happened. There wasn't enough room for Singer to really dig in his heels, and his grip was on Valadrakul's sleeve more than on the arm within.

Someone shouted, back out there in the world of light and air; Singer glanced toward the opening, then decided to ignore it. It couldn't have anything to do with him or the trapped foreigner.

"'Tis the ankles that hold me," Valadrakul said. "And the thing's wing-bone."

"Maybe if I dig down underneath?"

"'Tis a sound idea, methinks," Valadrakul agreed.

Singer took a deep breath, cupped his hands, and started burrowing.

*P*el watched as Ted got unsteadily to his feet.

"Are you all right?" he asked.

"Guess I got the blanket over my face," Ted said, looking back at the huge black wing. "Or maybe a pillow. Maybe I pulled it down off the bed — I think I must've fallen out long ago."

Lieutenant Dibbs snorted with disgust; Pel didn't blame him. Ted's persistence in his delusion had long since passed the point of evoking sympathy, concern, or even amusement.

Pel had long ago run out of ideas for dissuading Ted, though; nothing worked.

Dibbs and the civilians watched as the soldiers heaved at the wing, trying to pull it out, away from the ship, as much as possible. The soldier who was helping in the attempt to free Valadrakul — Wilkins, was it? — had said that his companion was having problems, being squeezed in there.

That would not do. They *needed* Valadrakul, needed him badly.

So the soldiers were trying to give Valadrakul and his rescuer a little more room. They were too far under to have the wing lifted off them completely, the way it had been lifted off Ted, but it should be possible to stretch it a little tighter, so it didn't hang down so heavily upon them.

Pel thought it was a very good idea. "Can I help?" he asked.

Dibbs looked at him, at the tattered remnants of his shirt and the blood and dirt smeared on his face and body, then turned back to his men. "No, sir," he said flatly. "We're doing fine."

Pel didn't argue, but he wondered just how fine Dibbs was actually doing. His commanding officer had been killed — and, Pel realized, Dibbs was now, under orders, trying to rescue the man who had killed Carson. Four of his men had vanished during the panic as the bat-thing approached, and still had not returned. His supplies, other than the useless sidearms, were all aboard the ship, which was inaccessible — and for that matter, the ship had crashed, stranding them all in an alien universe.

Pel reminded himself that this universe was just as alien to the Imperials as it was to the Earthpeople.

It would be perfectly reasonable for Lieutenant Dibbs to be feeling some pretty serious strain. Pel decided not to push the man about the rescue efforts, or anything else, just yet.

As Pel decided this, one of the soldiers happened to look to one side. Startled, he pointed and shouted. Equally startled, Pel turned.

A rather shamefaced Imperial soldier was stumbling out of the forest, toward the dead monster and the buried ship. His helmet was gone, and his face smeared with something.

Well, that was one of the four, anyway; Pel glanced surreptitiously at Dibbs' face, and caught an expression of intense relief.

Then it vanished.

"All right, Sawyer," the lieutenant shouted, "about time you got back! Get over there and give the others a hand!"

*D*irt sprayed into Singer's face; his eyes had closed immediately, but not fast enough, and now they stung horribly. Dirt was blocking his nose; he huffed most of it out. He could taste the earth in his mouth, on his tongue and lips; he spat out as much as he could.

"Your pardon, good sir, a thousand times, I beg your pardon!" the wizard said hastily. "I am shamed and dishonored to have discomfited you, who sought to rescue me — and who did so! Look you!" He wiggled his newly freed, booted foot.

"No problem," Singer muttered, wiping away dirt. "Let's get out of here."

"Aye," Valadrakul agreed fervently, "with a good will!"

Chapter Eight

*Y*ou cannot see it," Valadrakul remarked, gently probing his jaw, "but 'neath this beard, all my chin's but a single bruise, by the feel."

He stood a few feet from the corner of the tail assembly that was the only exposed portion of I.S.S. *Christopher*; his long black vest and borrowed uniform were smeared with grime. Still, he was smiling.

Lieutenant Dibbs, a few feet away, was not. "All right, they're out," he said. "And Sawyer's back, so that's one out of four. Now, can I find the rest of my missing men, Thorpe, or has Base got some other stupid order?"

"I'm sorry, Lieutenant, I've been out of contact," Prossie replied, not mentioning that this was deliberate and entirely her own idea. "Should I ask?"

"Don't bother," Dibbs answered. "If they aren't calling us, then there can't be anything very urgent, and maybe we'll do better if we don't have a bunch of bigwigs watching over our shoulders."

"I don't see how we could do much worse either way," someone muttered.

Dibbs whirled to spot the speaker.

Before he could say anything, someone else interrupted.

"Whoe'er spoke has the right of it," Stoddard said, startling everyone. "Scarce in this land a second hour, and we'd seen Elani die, seen your Colonel Carson die, lost three men to the forests, and been found by Shadow. All this, and we've yet to say who's to lead and who's to follow, yet to say whither we go, yet to step a dozen paces from this sky-ship, save we flee in panic. I've my fill of it."

Prossie turned, startled; she had never heard Stoddard make so long a speech.

"Not to mention," Singer pointed out, "that all our supplies are in the ship, and we can't get at them with that dead whatever-it-is draped across everything."

"Stoddard, hold tongue," Raven snapped. "We've had misfortune, aye, but 'tis no fault of any of us gathered here. That Carson was a fool was none's fault save his own, and he's paid the price that folly must bring. All else follows upon Shadow's magic, that told it of yon sky-portal ere we were well through it, and how to counter that, how to prevent?"

"I'll *not* hold tongue," Stoddard said, "for I've words to say. Ask me not of how to counter Shadow, for I'm but an honest warrior, but ask rather yon corpse that was a wizard, and wise in the ways of magic." He gestured at Valadrakul. "Ask likewise this, that stands before us, brushing dust from his garb with no thought that Shadow must still seek us."

Prossie's mouth opened in astonishment; she had never before heard Stoddard defy Raven in even the slightest degree.

Valadrakul, too, looked at Stoddard, startled. "I am ever aware of Shadow's threat, man; what wouldst have me do?"

Stoddard turned. "Hast no wards, no warnings, naught that might guard us?"

"Nay, I've none," Valadrakul replied angrily. "Magicks are not all as one, and I've no spell that would stand 'gainst Shadow."

"Then of what use art thou?" Stoddard demanded.

"'Gainst Shadow itself, little more than any man," Valadrakul retorted, "yet I've spells that serve us well enow in other regards!" He waved at the gigantic remains that covered the ship.

Stoddard looked at the dead monstrosity, and seemed to soften and shrink. "Aye," he said. "Aye, wizard, I've wronged thee. Your pardon."

"Freely given, Stoddard," Valadrakul answered.

"Fine, so that's settled," Dibbs said.

"Nay," Stoddard said, "'tis not settled; yet do I say, I've had my fill. An we do no better, I'll depart. This is mine own world, not Earth nor Empire, and should I go, who's to say me nay? Now, you who would lead us, my lord Raven and Messire Dibbs, Mistress Thorpe who speaks for the Empire, what do you propose to do?"

Prossie decided that this would be a very good time for Carrie to reestablish contact; weren't the twenty minutes up yet? Surely, they must be! She tried to listen, despite the mental wool that this universe stuffed in her head; she strained, threw her senses open . . .

And jumped when Carrie's greeting came through.

"Prossie," she asked, "what's happening?"

Prossie quickly ran through the basics: Attack survived, monsters slain, three men deserted, ship at least temporarily inaccessible, Elani dead. Carrie already knew Carson was dead.

"I'll take my orders from Base One," Dibbs was saying, "but personally, I think the whole thing's a disaster from the start, and once I find my other three men we should just go home. They can try again later, with a better-equipped force — I mean, our guns don't work, our ship can't fly, we've got a dozen of us out here fighting with rocks and sticks."

"And what if there be no home that one may flee to?" Raven asked angrily. "I've no welcome at Stormcrack, much as I might wish it otherwise."

"Not my problem," Dibbs said, shrugging.

"Flee, then," Raven said. "Flee, and be damned. I and mine will struggle on."

Dibbs glanced meaningfully at Stoddard.

"In time," Raven said warningly, "your Emperor and all his empire will come to see the need to destroy Shadow. I pray to the Goddess that that time will not come too late."

Prossie listened approvingly.

She agreed with Raven that Shadow must be destroyed; she had seen enough of Shadow's horrors, both firsthand and in dozens of memories, to have no doubts of that.

But she agreed with Dibbs, too; this expedition had been a farce, doomed from the outset, and the best thing to do now would be to call it off before anyone else died, to send the Earth-people home, let Raven and his people rejoin their underground, and then go back to Base One and start over.

The only question was whether the Empire would agree that there was a need to start over, rather than to abandon the entire thing. Without Raven there at Base One, prodding them, the generals and politicians might decide to wait and see what happened.

"Listen, Raven," Dibbs said, "you're back in your own land, and you can go on with your resistance movement. And if I'm told to, I'll help out. But do you really think that a dozen strangers are going to make a big difference against something that plays with monsters like that?" He gestured at the gigantic wreckage of the bat-thing.

"Methinks you've changed your position," Raven remarked, his head cocked as he eyed the lieutenant.

"I sure have," Dibbs said. "That thing convinced me. My men are tops, but we're out of our league with stuff like this."

"Then perhaps we're agreed," Raven replied.

"I know *we* are," Amy interjected, seizing the opportunity. "We want to go home, Raven — Pel and Susan and I. We're no use here. Send us back to Earth."

Raven turned, startled.

"So hasty, mistress . . . Are you certain, then?"

"We all are," Pel said, stepping up beside Amy. Susan was a few feet behind; Ted had wandered off to inspect one of the trees.

"I've no wish to keep you 'gainst your will," Raven said. "I promised you could return to your homes, and I meant that promise — but are you certain that you're of no use here? Mistress Susan, that device you carry — methinks that's of good service."

"The gun?" Susan tugged at the strap of her purse. "Raven, I only have . . . well, it's very limited. If you send us home, though, we can give you lots of guns, lots of ammunition — better stuff than this."

"Aye? Truthfully?" Raven eyed her thoughtfully.

"Absolutely," Pel said.

"Then indeed, 'twould be folly to keep you," the nobleman said emphatically, "and I'll be sending you to your Earth at the first hour I may."

"Why not *now?*" Amy demanded. "Tell Valadrakul to send us!"

Raven turned to the wizard, who held up his hands. "Messires, mesdames, methinks you mistake the situation," Valadrakul protested. "I've no power to send you home."

The three Earthpeople present stared at him in outraged silence. Somewhere a bird whistled, the first that Prossie had heard since her previous visit to Faerie.

"Why *not?*" Amy demanded. "You're a wizard, aren't you?"

"Oh, aye, I'm that," Valadrakul agreed, "but I know naught of the portal spell."

"*Elani* knew it!" Pel shouted.

"Indeed she did," Valadrakul affirmed. "And she mastered it well, caught it in the structure of her magicks. But I know it not; the webs of my work are otherwise. I'm learned in the spells of fire and destruction, magicks that send forth the raw energy of magic in fiery outbursts; likewise, I know the spells that send forth and draw in in other ways, and have caught the strands of those in me. But the spells that shape worlds, that link the several realities, those I ken not a whit."

"But Elani did!"

"Aye; in that, she was far my better. The worse for us, that she's no more."

Prossie heard all this with growing unhappiness. She had not consciously known that only Elani knew the portal spell, but somehow she felt none of the shock the Earthpeople felt; perhaps she had telepathically sensed the truth, on some subconscious level, back at Base One.

Still, it was very bad news.

And while Valadrakul was admitting his impotence, Carrie had received Prossie's report and was relaying parts of it to General Hart and Under-Secretary Bascombe. Prossie suspected, from the flavor of Carrie's thoughts, that it was not going over well.

That was no surprise. Hart and Bascombe did not want anyone coming home bearing tales of disaster and incompetence.

Well, it looked as if they might not have anything to worry about; without magic, it appeared that no one was going to leave this universe. The Empire's own space-warp was up above treetop level, where they couldn't get at it. Dibbs and his men were not going home any time very soon — and neither, that meant, was Prossie.

"Raven," Amy demanded, "where can we find another wizard who knows the portal spell?"

"I've not the slightest notion," Raven replied. "Wizardry is none of mine."

"Valadrakul?" Pel asked.

The wizard frowned deeply, then winced as the movement affected his injured jaw.

"The brotherhood of magicians is scattered and broken in these sad times," he said. "A handful survives here, another there, but we've no central councils, no trustworthy messengers, canny or otherwise. For the most part, we dare not use the greater lines of power, for those are Shadow's. The portal spells are likewise Shadow's; they were stolen from Shadow, and taught quickly to those few who could learn them well, who could draw down those strands from the web of powers; there was Elani, and likewise Taillefer, who served us betimes, but of others, I know not. 'Twas thought unwise that any should know too much of others' skills, lest we be captured and questioned by Shadow."

Prossie nodded slightly to herself; she had known that. While the wizards didn't follow the system of revolutionary cells as carefully as the other members of the resistance did, they did keep plenty of secrets.

"This Taillefer," Pel asked, "where can we find him?"

Valadrakul considered that carefully.

"You don't know," Amy said. "Do you?"

"Nay," Valadrakul admitted, "I do not."

The Earthpeople accepted that, but Prossie, watching Valadrakul carefully, wondered if the wizard might be concealing something. She was no expert at reading facial nuances, really, because she had never had to resort to such crude methods in her own universe, but still, something seemed wrong about Valadrakul's answer.

Could she be remembering something she had learned from Valadrakul's mind earlier, without realizing it?

"Well, damn it, if you can't find him, we better start looking for him!" Amy shouted.

"You go right ahead," Dibbs said. "Meanwhile, I'll be rounding up my men and calling for pick-up. Wilkins, Moore, Dawber, I want you three to take a look around, see if you can spot any sign of where our missing men went. Stay in sight, we don't know what's out there; you see anything moving, you call it in, don't play hero."

"Right, Lieutenant," Wilkins said. He picked a direction and started walking; the other two Dibbs had chosen followed him.

"Uh . . . permission to speak, sir?" Prossie said uneasily, glancing after the three.

"What is it, Thorpe?" Dibbs stepped away from the rest of the group, and Prossie followed.

"I'm not sure there's going to be a pick-up, sir."

"You aren't," Dibbs said. "Why not?"

Prossie hesitated, wishing she felt better and stronger; what she really wanted to do was curl up somewhere and rest, not argue.

But she had to warn Dibbs if she could.

The real reason she was fairly sure there would be no pick-up was that Bascombe had shown her once before that he felt no compunction about abandoning a failed mission, rather than risking further complications; the Under-Secretary had left Prossie and the rest of Joshua Cahn's crew in jail on Earth without a second thought, and in that case there hadn't even been evidence of incompetence or mismanagement, where the current expedition had been a disaster right from its inception.

Telling Lieutenant Dibbs this did not seem like a good idea, though. He didn't like cynics — and for that matter, he didn't like telepaths. A telepath accusing a superior of callous political gamesmanship was asking for trouble.

"Technical reasons, sir," Prossie said.

Lying really wasn't very hard at all, she was finding, despite all her years of training.

"Go on."

"The Department of Science has confirmed earlier theories, sir — anti-gravity cannot operate outside normal space. This world we're on is not in normal space; that's why *Christopher* went down. And any rescue ship would lose all lift, too. We'd need a vehicle that can fly in the distorted space here, and Base One hasn't got any. So they *can't* pick us up."

"You sure of that, Thorpe?"

Prossie hesitated. She had sinned once; she would resist the temptation this time. "It's not relayed, sir, it's my own conclusion," she said.

Dibbs nodded slowly. "Got a reason they can't just drop a *rope* through that space-warp up there, Telepath?" he asked sarcastically.

"No, sir," Prossie answered truthfully. She had no idea whether a rope was possible or not. She could see no reason that it would not work, but then, she didn't understand space-warp science. If the warp was as open as that, wouldn't air from Faerie be boiling off into Imperial space right now?

She didn't know. Maybe a rope would work.

But she was quite sure nobody would be sending one.

"*A*s you wish," Raven said, with a tight little smile. "We'll away, then, in pursuit of Taillefer. For that, we must make our way westward, as there lies the fastest route from these woods, to clear air where Valadrakul's spells might best work, to summon his compatriot, that a portal to your Earth might be opened. An you be safely home, we'll arrange a thousand of these 'guns' be sent. Then see we will whether the things of Shadow can withstand them!"

"You'll not be marching hence to beard Shadow in its lair, then?" Stoddard asked. "If this be Sunderland, Shadow's hold lies to the west."

"Nay," Raven answered. "What good of that, with a band such as this — fools and fainthearts and women, with only you and I and the wizard that would stand fast? We fare west only to be free of the forests."

Stung by Raven's words, Pel said, "It's not my fight, you know — there's nothing wrong with my running away. And I'll do you a lot more good buying guns back home than getting myself eaten by monsters here."

Raven turned to face the Earthman, caught sight of his battered and bloody appearance, and hesitated. Then he smiled ruefully. "True enow, friend Pel," Raven admitted, "and you've my apology that I spoke ill of you."

"Where are you going to get a thousand guns, Pel?" Amy asked. "And where are you going to get a thousand men to use them?"

"I'll buy them," Pel replied. "A few at a time."

"I'll help," Susan said.

"And for men," Raven said, "perhaps the Empire has better than our friends to offer." He waved his bandaged hand at Dibbs and his men. Dibbs was talking quietly with Prossie; the others were chatting amongst themselves, leaving the Earthpeople and the natives alone.

Amy looked at Pel, at Susan, and at Dibbs, then shrugged. "I guess you're right," she said, "and what do I care, anyway? As long as I get home."

Pel frowned.

Getting home was what he cared about, too. He intended to keep his promise to buy guns, but then, why shouldn't he? If he didn't, Raven and a couple of oversized swordsmen like Stoddard might walk out of his basement wall at any time and drag him away on more idiotic, dangerous, deadly adventures.

And when he got home . . .

The house would be empty, just him and Silly Cat — wouldn't it? Nancy and Rachel wouldn't be coming home with him.

Unless Ted was right, in which case they already *were* home, waiting for him

He knew they weren't, he knew they were dead, he really did know that.

But he had to *see.* He had to see for himself. He had to get home and see.

"*A*ll right, Thorpe," Dibbs said. "Unless we get orders telling us otherwise, we're going to sit right here and wait for a pick-up. That clear?"

"Yes, sir." Prossie knew better than to argue. If she were to suddenly manifest an order from Bascombe or Hart at this point in the argument, Dibbs probably would reject it outright. Maybe later, when the men started to get bored, she could "receive" an order to move on.

Or maybe she could leave without Dibbs and the rest, go with Raven and his group instead; certainly, they would be more interesting companions.

That thought was treasonous, she told herself; she didn't dare think it.

Dibbs turned away, and shouted, "Raven, all the rest of you! We're staying right here until Base One sends someone to get us. Anyone who wants to stay, that's fine with us. If the rest of you want to go, we won't stop you — it's your world, you're not Imperial citizens."

"It's not *my* world," Susan said quietly; Dibbs ignored her.

"Messire Lieutenant," Raven said, "methinks you might best reconsider. I'll not ask you to join us if you've no wish to, but in all true compassion that the Goddess bids us, I'd warn you that this place be perchance more dangerous than you realize."

"*This place,*" Dibbs replied, "is where the space warp comes out."

"Aye, so 'tis, and therefore of interest to Shadow; would you face more such as this?" The nobleman gestured at the dead monster.

"You think more are coming?"

"Aye, so I do."

"Well, I don't," Dibbs said flatly. "And if they do, we'll take shelter."

"And what can shelter you from such as that?" Raven was clearly trying hard to be reasonable and persuasive; Prossie wondered why, since she was fairly sure he didn't particularly want Dibbs and his men along any more. Could it be honest concern?

That was a frightening thought, that there was something so fearsome approaching that Raven would worry about what it might do to other people.

More likely Raven was afraid that if Dibbs and company stayed here at the ship they would somehow interfere with his own schemes against Shadow.

"We'll be safe enough in the trees," Dibbs said. "We can take care of ourselves."

Raven considered for a moment; Stoddard and the Earthpeople all watched him. Valadrakul was studying the dead monster; the soldiers were looking in various directions.

"An it please you," Raven said at last, "I'd ask a favor. Could call for volunteers, that would come with us?"

"Lieutenant," Prossie said, before Dibbs could reply, "Base One agrees with Raven that there's a risk here."

No one at Base One had said any such thing. Prossie had once again yielded to the temptation to play God, to alter the facts to suit herself — or at least to exceed her authority and lie.

Prossie could sense that Carrie, who had not been paying much attention, was suddenly much more interested. Prossie tried to ignore her questions. Did someone here say that? Did I relay that? I don't remember anything like that, Prossie . . .

Dibbs did not like what he heard, either. He frowned at Prossie.

"I'm not going anywhere," he said.

"But volunteers?" Raven asked, his tone almost wheedling.

Dibbs glanced at his men, then yielded. "All right," he said, "you can take volunteers. I doubt you'll get any."

"I'll go," Prossie said immediately. "Base One will want to stay in touch with the advance party." It would get her away from Lieutenant Dibbs and, she hoped, eliminate any further temptation to lie about relayed messages. More importantly, it would get her away from the space-warp; she was now convinced that Raven was sincere in his warning, and that this place was a death trap.

"Wait a minute, Thorpe," Dibbs protested. "What am *I* supposed to do for communications, then?"

"With all respect, sir, you won't need any, if you're just waiting right here. And Base One can send messages through the warp if they have to."

Besides, Prossie thought, she wasn't reliable anyway. She had lied about messages more than once already. The farther she got from Lieutenant Dibbs, the less likely she would be to do it again — and the less likely she would be to think about it, and perhaps let Carrie know what had happened.

She tried not to let those thoughts come clear; she didn't want Carrie to hear them.

Carrie wasn't receiving, though, she was sending, objecting to Prossie's decision. Prossie hadn't cleared it, she hadn't even asked anyone at Base One, how could she volunteer for anything that way? Telepaths didn't do that! Telepaths don't choose for themselves! And who had told her that there was any danger?

Then Spaceman Singer said, "I'd like to go, too, sir," and suddenly everyone was distracted; Prossie felt a surge of relief that she was no longer the center of attention.

But she dared not think about it, dared not enjoy the relief; Carrie would notice. Instead, she forced her mind into a receptive blank, and passed the scene in the forest on to Carrie without comment, as mindlessly as she could, struggling to be only a camera.

"*D*o we wait until morning?" Pel asked, as he carefully felt the scratches on the back of his head; they were scabbing over. He tugged a lock of hair out of the congealing blood and winced at the sharp pain that resulted.

"Nay," Raven said. "And spend the night here, with that?" He gestured at the dead bat-thing. "More, 'tis by night and the dark that Shadow's strongest. We'll depart as soon we may."

"It's already well after noon."

"And I know it well, friend Pel; think you I'd not? It may be we'll not get far, but every pace we put betwixt ourselves and this place will be a pace away from wasting our lives."

Pel nodded. "Right," he said.

"Who all is coming?" Amy asked.

"Well, we are," Pel said, indicating himself, Amy, Susan, and Raven. "And Valadrakul, and I think Stoddard . . ."

"Aye," Stoddard said. "I've no wish to linger in this foul spot."

"And three of the soldiers . . ." Pel said.

"Three?" Amy asked. She turned, and saw only one Imperial trooper standing near. Dirt was smeared down the front of his uniform; he had obviously hit the ground at some point, but nothing appeared torn or bloody. He had his helmet tucked under one arm.

"That's right," the soldier said. "Me, and Ronnie Wilkins, and Bill Marks. Four, if you count Miss Thorpe."

"So where are the others?" Amy asked.

"Ronnie and Bill are arguing with the lieutenant," the soldier explained. "I'm not sure where Thorpe went."

"'Twill do no good," Raven said. "'Tis plain Messire Dibbs' mind is set firmly in its course."

"That's why I'm over here with you folks," the Imperial agreed.

"What about Ted?" Amy asked.

Pel frowned, and glanced at the lawyer, who was standing to one side, alone, gazing idly at the dead bat-monster. "I don't know," he admitted.

"We better take him," Amy said. "He'll get killed if he stays here. The lieutenant isn't going to want to look after him."

"I don't know," Pel said reluctantly. "He's pretty far gone. He could really slow us down . . ."

"Pel Brown, how can you say that?" Amy shouted. "If he doesn't come with us, he'll *never* get home to Earth! And getting home is probably the only chance he's ever got to recover, and you know it!"

"It's not a hell of a great chance," Pel shouted back. "If we drag him along, maybe *none* of us will get back!"

Amy prepared to shout a reply, but Pel raised a hand to forestall her. "You're right, you're right," he said. "I know that. We have to bring him. Stoddard, could you go bring him along, please?"

"I'll go," Susan said quietly.

"Together, then, lady," Stoddard said.

As if echoing the Earthpeople's shouts, a loud argument broke out just then among the Imperials; startled, Pel and Amy turned to see two soldiers marching angrily away from their companions and toward Raven's group.

A third hesitated, and then followed. This one had no helmet, Pel noticed.

The pair marched up; the shorter of the two addressed the soldier who was already there.

"You better be right about this, Al," he said. "The lieutenant says that he'll let us go and won't try to stop us, but if Base One calls it desertion, he won't argue with them, either."

"Lord Raven," the first soldier said, "this is Ronnie Wilkins. And beside him there is Bill Marks."

"And your own name, good sir?" Raven asked.

The soldier smiled. "Guess I forgot to say; I'm Albert Singer."

The fourth soldier, the one who had followed Wilkins and Marks, cleared his throat. He stood behind and between his companions, speaking over their shoulders. Pel recognized him as the man who had been missing for an hour or so after the hellbeasts had attacked.

"Excuse me," the soldier said, "but are you people serious about it being dangerous here? That this dead monster's going to attract more?"

"Aye, and indeed we are," Raven answered. "'Tis a thing of Shadow, and where one falls, a dozen follow."

"In that case . . ." He glanced back over his own shoulder, then turned toward Raven again and said, "In that case, I'd say I'm coming with you." He held out a hand. "My name's Tom Sawyer."

Pel started.

Raven made no move to take the soldier's hand, so Pel stepped forward and shook it warmly. "Tom Sawyer? Really?" he asked.

Puzzled, the soldier nodded. "Spaceman Second Class Thomas James Sawyer," he said.

"Tom Sawyer," Pel repeated, grinning foolishly. "I'll be damned."

The soldiers and the Faerie folk were all staring curiously at Pel; Amy shoved him.

"It's not so strange as all that," she said. "Now, come on, let's get out of here. We have a wizard to find."

"Right," Pel said, dropping Sawyer's hand and turning to Raven. "Which way?"

Chapter Nine

Something rustled in the dark leaves overhead; Pel started and looked up.

"Probably just a squirrel," Wilkins said somewhere behind Pel; he looked upward, as well.

Pel turned at the comment, and realized that Sawyer had his blaster drawn — for all the good that would do him, here in Faerie.

Sawyer was next to Wilkins; Marks and Singer were a step ahead. The four Imperial soldiers had stayed close together, talking mostly with each other, as the group proceeded; Pel didn't suppose he could blame them for that, for wanting to stay with their friends and compatriots while trapped in this alien reality. He had noticed, though, that they seemed to avoid Prossie Thorpe — wasn't she an Imperial, too? Her uniform had been somewhat slashed up by Shadow's hellbeasts, but she still had the proper purple blouse and slacks, and the insignia on her shoulder.

Of course, for himself, he avoided Ted, who was a fellow Earthman, but that was different. Ted was . . . well . . . damaged. Prossie wasn't. And she was a woman, too; why would soldiers avoid a woman, especially one with those peek-a-boo tears in her blouse? It seemed out of character.

This stupid Imperial prejudice against telepathic "mutants" was probably responsible.

Pel glanced at Prossie; she seemed content to walk with Stoddard and Amy and Susan. Raven and Valadrakul had moved on a few paces ahead of the others; then came Ted, herded forward by Stoddard and the women. Pel, not inclined to talk just now, was close behind; he had taken off the remains of his borrowed T-shirt, since he hardly needed it in the warm, damp evening air of the forest, and wore only purple pants and black boots. The sweat was starting to dry on his back, though; what he would do when the air cooled further he didn't know. And he thought he might be developing a blister on his right foot; the boots were a fairly good fit, but unfamiliar, and he wasn't used to walking so much.

Behind him, the Imperial soldiers brought up the rear, still fully dressed, and wearing boots and helmets — except Sawyer, of course, who had lost his helmet. Pel wondered why they weren't stinking of sweat.

Maybe they were, and he just didn't smell it over the rich, heavy odors of the forest.

"What're you planning to do with *that*?" Wilkins said, pointing to Sawyer's blaster.

"Nothing," Sawyer replied defensively, holstering the weapon. "Just habit."

"You really think it was just a squirrel?" Marks said uneasily.

Wilkins shrugged. "Or a bird, or something."

"It's getting hard to see what's up there," Marks pointed out. "How do you know it wasn't one of those black things?"

"Because if it was, it would have attacked us already," Wilkins said.

No one had an answer to that; Pel turned away, and they all marched on.

A moment later, Wilkins stubbed his toe on a tree root hidden in fallen leaves, and swore quietly — though Pel doubted it had actually hurt, through the heavy boot the soldier wore.

"Hey, Raven," Singer called.

Ahead, Pel saw Raven and Valadrakul stop and turn.

"It's getting dark," Singer called. "The sun's been down a good half an hour, at least. When are we going to make camp for the night?"

"Yeah," Amy said, loudly. "I'm tired. It's been a long day."

That, Pel thought, was an understatement. They had gotten out of bed that morning in Base One; now they were in the forests of Faerie, Elani and Colonel Carson and a score of Shadow's monsters were dead — and it had been a very long day literally, as well as figuratively, since they had departed Base One in late afternoon by the artificial local time, and arrived in Faerie around midday, going by the sun.

Amy added, "And we've been walking forever. My feet are killing me."

Pel could sympathize with that. The Imperials were all soldiers, and presumably accustomed to marching, while the Faerie folk came from a world where human feet were still the primary form of transportation, but Pel and Amy, at least, weren't in the habit of walking when they could drive. Pel wasn't sure about Susan or Ted; they didn't seem inclined to complain.

Susan never seemed inclined to complain about anything, of course, and if Ted had had anything to say about pain in his feet, or tired legs, he'd probably have attributed it all to twisted bedsheets or something else suited to his insistence that he was dreaming.

Raven looked at Valadrakul, who made a gesture with his hands that Pel couldn't interpret.

"As you will, then," Raven said. "'Tis true we've put a league and more behind us, but I'd thought to fare on until the night grew too deep. The darkness draws fast o'er us; perhaps 'tis best we stop."

"Nay," Valadrakul said. "Not yet. Shall we not find water ere we rest? There's no sign of stream or brook here."

"Oh," Amy said.

"No water?" Ted asked, startling everyone. "More nightmare, I guess. Haven't done thirst in awhile."

Pel clenched a fist and wished he could reach Ted with a good punch on the nose.

"Oh, shut up," Amy muttered wearily.

"Can't the wizard get us water, somehow?" Sawyer called.

"Would that I could," Valadrakul called back. "I can, perhaps, take game, that we might have our supper, but water is beyond my powers."

"Maybe we better keep walking, then," Susan said quietly.

"I *can't*," Amy protested. She dropped abruptly, to sit cross-legged on the ground. "I can't go any farther."

"As you will, then," Raven said. "We'll camp here."

"What about the water?" Wilkins asked. "We crossed a stream a ways back."

"We'll not retrace our steps so far!" Raven said, shocked. "Surely, we'll find water nearby, and can fetch it hither, if the women can go no more."

Pel looked around as the others spoke, and found himself agreeing. There had to be water around here somewhere, didn't there? Where did rainfall here go?

He looked at the slope of the land. "That way?" he said, pointing to the left, where the ground dropped off somewhat.

"Aye, of course," Raven answered. "Wouldst join me, friend Pel?"

Pel just wanted to get off his feet, but he couldn't let himself be seen as a whiner or shirker. "I don't have anything to carry water in," he replied.

"Then these others? An they've naught else, surely those helms they bear will hold water."

Pel turned, and saw Wilkins shrug and remove his helmet. "If you want," the Imperial said. "I'm in no hurry to wear the thing again, anyway, and it should be dry by morning."

"I'll get firewood," Pel offered, feeling a bit guilty.

"A fine thought, friend Pel. And if the ladies would clear a space that the fire might be set . . .?"

"We will," Susan said.

A thought struck Pel. "Valadrakul," he said, "we saw something up in that tree a little while ago." He pointed upward.

"Ah," the wizard said, smiling. "And you think it might serve to feed us?"

Pel smiled back. "It might."

Twenty minutes later, when Raven, Wilkins, Marks, and Singer returned with three helmetfuls of water, Stoddard was midway through skinning a fair-sized opossum, and Pel was tending the campfire Valadrakul had, by means of his magic, lit. Amy, Ted, and Susan had brushed away branches, leaves, and underbrush, and were sitting around the fire; Sawyer, bearing a good-sized tree limb, was standing guard, after helping gather wood.

"A fine sight to return to," Raven remarked.

Pel eyed the half-skinned, slightly scorched opossum.

"Well," he said, "it could certainly be worse."

Amy awoke shortly before sunrise, her back stiff from sleeping on the hard, dewy ground and her feet still sore from the long day's hike; she felt chilled, and her stomach was churning. The overripe scent of decay was in her nostrils. She sat up slowly, then suddenly sprang to her feet — or tried to. She got as far as her knees before the remains of her share of the roast opossum came up.

She retched several more times after her stomach was emptied.

When at last she was able to stop heaving and straighten up, she found the rest of the party awake and staring at her in the dim predawn light.

"I never ate 'possum before, okay?" she said, glaring around at them.

No one answered; embarrassed, most of them turned away and set about getting themselves up, since there was obviously no point in going back to sleep.

Susan, however, took the three steps necessary to reach Amy's side and knelt beside her.

"Are you all right, Amy?" she asked.

Amy nodded. "I'm okay. Really."

"It's just the food, you think?"

"What else could it be?" Amy asked, hopelessly. "I mean, it's not like I've had anything decent to eat in months, now." She laughed unhappily. "It's hard to believe I'm looking back on that cheap pizza we ate at Pel's house as the last good meal I had."

"Some of the food hasn't been bad, just different," Susan said. "You'd get used to it."

"I don't *want* to get used to it," Amy said. "I want to go *home.*"

"I know," Susan said quietly. "Me, too."

"Everything's tasted *weird.* Even when I know what it is, and it's something normal, like chicken, it'll taste funny. The whole time we were in the Empire, everything tasted funny. And here in Faerie, what do I get to eat, after an entire day of running around being chased by monsters? Dirty water and one-twelfth of a possum. What kind of a meal is that?"

"An improvised one," Susan said. "It'll get better. When we get to civilization, or whatever passes for it here, we'll have real food again."

"If it doesn't poison us," Amy muttered.

"It won't poison us," Susan said. "We're all human beings, even if we do come from three different worlds. Anything they can eat here, we can eat." She smiled. "Did I ever tell you about when I first came to the U.S., and they gave me a cheeseburger? I'd never eaten cheese before, my mother called it rotten milk. I couldn't imagine how anyone could eat that stuff. But I had to, if I wanted the beef it was on, so I peeled off what I could, and ate the rest, and then I waited to get sick from eating spoiled food. And nothing happened to me, of course."

Amy gestured unhappily at the mess on the dead leaves. "I wasn't so lucky," she said.

"It's probably just strain," Susan said. "It's rough on everybody, getting stranded here all over again, and worrying about Shadow sending more monsters after us. And you'd hardly even recovered from what happened on Zeta Leo III when they sent us here."

At the mention of her enslavement Amy lost control again, and bent over, retching. She brought up a thin stream of clear fluid, nothing else.

Susan put a reassuring hand on her back, and with the other scrabbled in her purse and came up with a somewhat used tissue, which she offered.

Amy accepted the crumpled paper and wiped her mouth, then stared at the result distastefully.

"I've ruined your Kleenex," she said. "And you probably don't have any more."

"I still have a couple of others," Susan said. "It doesn't matter."

"I'm sorry, anyway," Amy said. "And I've got to find the little girls' bush." She got to her feet. "Thanks, Susan," she said.

"All part of the service," Susan said, smiling. She, too, stood.

*A*s Amy ducked behind a tree in search of privacy, Susan noticed Prossie, standing quietly a few feet away, watching. The men were going about their own affairs — many of them undoubtedly doing the same thing Amy was, while others were fetching water or clearing away the campsite.

"Is there anything I can do to help?" Prossie asked uncertainly.

Susan glanced after Amy, then shrugged. "I don't know," she said.

"I didn't want to intrude," Prossie explained, a little ashamed that she hadn't done anything for their stricken companion.

"Oh, go ahead and intrude," Susan said. "After all, there's just the three of us with all these men."

Prossie hesitated.

She wasn't from the same universe as Susan and Amy. Besides, she was a telepath, a mutant, unfit for the company of normal humans. But right now Carrie wasn't communicating, and this world of Faerie was so silent and strange with her telepathy cut off.

"Thanks," she said.

*N*o breakfast," Pel remarked, as he splashed his face at the stream and wished the water was cleaner and warmer.

"Not unless you can spot us another 'possum or something," Wilkins replied.

"I was hoping to see a fish or two, maybe, now that there's better light," Pel said.

Wilkins considered the stream, then shook his head. "Doesn't look too likely," he said.

"No," Pel agreed. He shivered, and wished he still had a shirt.

"The sooner we get moving, the better," Wilkins said, seeing Pel's actions. "Let's fill these helmets and get up there." He was holding his own helmet as he spoke, and gestured toward the other with it.

Pel picked it up. "Whose is this?" he asked.

"Bill Marks'," Wilkins answered. "Al keeps hold of his, and Sawyer's is missing."

"Right." Pel scooped water from the stream, and together the two men headed back up the slope.

*T*he entire party was regrouped and moving by the time the sun was a hand's breadth above the horizon.

"I'm hungry," Ted said. "I wish I could wake up and get myself a snack."

No one bothered to hush him this time; Sawyer remarked, "I'm hungry, too."

"I don't think I could keep anything down if we had it," Amy said. Susan eyed her uneasily, but said nothing.

They walked on; Amy could hear someone's stomach growling, while her own seemed to be tying itself in painful knots. She felt tired and ill.

Of course, she hadn't felt *good* since *Emerald Princess* was captured by pirates. They'd starved their captives on the journey to Zeta Leo III, and then after the one meal there everyone had been hurried through the showers and put on the stage for auction, all nervous, even terrified. She'd been tired and scared, and Walter had bought her and taken her back to his farm, and then he'd raped her, and beaten her, and for all the weeks she lived with Walter and Beth she had been abused, over and over.

And then she'd been rescued, and flown to Base One aboard *Emperor Edward VII*, and she'd mostly recovered there, the bruises were healing, she was sleeping better, but she still felt tired all the time, still felt sour and irritable — and then, before she could get over it, they'd sent her off to Faerie.

She hoped it was just strain and fatigue.

But as she walked through the forests of Faerie she remembered poor little Alella, and Grummetty, the little people from Hrumph who didn't like to be called gnomes, the little people who had died because their bodies didn't work right in Imperial space.

What if *her* body didn't work right in Faerie? What if she had been uncomfortable in the Empire as much because the nature of space itself was wrong, as anything else?

Susan had said, that morning, that they were all human beings, regardless of which universe they came from — but what if she was wrong, and they weren't the same at all?

That was a terrifying idea. She hadn't watched Grummetty and Alella fade away, she hadn't had the nerve to face it, and had left all the nursing to Nancy Brown and little Rachel — she felt guilty about that now, especially since Nancy and Rachel were dead, and she also selfishly regretted that she didn't know more about how it had worked. How could she tell if the same thing was happening to her?

None of the other Earthpeople seemed to be troubled by any such effect, though.

At least, not yet.

"*I* wonder what Lieutenant Dibbs and his men have to eat," Susan said, stepping neatly over a tree root that, a moment before, Ted had stubbed his toe on.

"There are supplies in the ship," Prossie said. "Maybe we should have taken our share before we left."

"We couldn't get at them," Singer pointed out. "That monster's wing covered the door."

"By now Dibbs probably has that thing propped up like a front porch,"

Wilkins said. "They'll be fine."

"They've no water within a hundred yards or more," Stoddard pointed out.

"There's some water in the ship, too," Sawyer said. "At least, I think there is."

"They'll be fine," Wilkins repeated.

"Then why the hell are we here, instead of there?" Marks demanded.

Wilkins glared at him. "Oh, shut up," he said.

Chapter Ten

*T*hey struck the road around mid-morning, and emerged from the forest shortly after noon.

Not that it was much of a road, by the standards of either the Earthpeople or the Imperials. Pel had noticed the four soldiers exchanging derisory glances when Raven called the narrow path a highway. He had sympathized, but had kept his mouth shut; Raven knew this world, and the Imperials didn't.

"Do you know where we are?" Pel asked Raven, as they all paused, blinking in the bright pale sunlight, atop the gentle slope that led down to cultivated fields and half a dozen crude huts. Rolling farmland stretched out before them almost as far as they could see, broken by streams and occasional small groves and ending in a grassy ridge topped by a massive structure Pel could not make out clearly.

The air had warmed again, and a trickle of sweat was running down his back and into the waistband of his pants.

"Not as exactly as I would choose, friend Pel," Raven replied, scanning the landscape. "This must surely be the Starlinshire Downs, and behind us the Low Forest, but this road we follow is not the Palanquin Road — 'tis not of the size to be that. Thus we must be well to the north, but I'd know no more than that until we find landmarks or ask the dwellers here."

"My lord?" Valadrakul said quietly.

"But ah, look you, friend Pel," Raven said, turning suddenly, his hand on the wizard's shoulder. "Look you all, we've no need to limit ourselves to means natural, for we've a practitioner of the arcane arts with us! Speak, then, Valadrakul — where are we now, and where may we find he that we seek, your compatriot Taillefer?"

"I know not, my lord, but a spell can tell me, an you allow me a moment."

"'Tis safe, my friend, e'en in this realm of Shadow?"

Valadrakul spread empty hands. "Who can say, when we know not the extent of Shadow's power? At this moment, we might yet be pursued by creatures keen to avenge those we slew beside the sky-ship, and perchance even the merest trace of an incantation will draw disaster upon us. But 'tis only the very simplest of magicks, and I've practiced its like many times before, without mischance."

"Thus, wilt know our whereabouts?"

"Aye, and more," Valadrakul answered. "Though I know not where we be, yet I sense that this place is a goodly one for magicks, and that hence can I send word to Taillefer through the currents of the air and ether. It might chance that such a message Shadow will feel likewise, but 'tis only a small risk; ne'er has Shadow troubled itself with the signals that we lesser magicians send each other betimes."

Raven hesitated, then nodded — Pel noticed that he didn't bother to look around at any of the others, let alone to consult them.

"Go, then," Raven told the wizard. "Work thy wonders — methinks 'twill give the ladies a needed rest. And if thou canst discover us whence our next meal may come, as well, surely shalt thou have the gratitude of us all!"

It seemed to Pel that Raven and Valadrakul were getting carried away, their phrasing becoming more flowery than ever for no good reason, even while their peculiar Australo-Brooklyn accent grew stronger. Pel didn't like that. Any time Raven began to talk too much, it meant trouble.

But the man in black did have a point; a glance at Amy convinced Pel that she did, indeed, need a rest. She looked terrible. She hadn't thrown up again since that morning, but her face was pale, and she appeared to be on the verge of collapse. Susan was keeping a solicitous eye on her; Pel was relieved that someone was.

The four Earthpeople and Prossie settled to the grass in a group; the other four Imperials settled a few feet away. Raven and Stoddard remained upright, roaming along the slope, studying the countryside.

And Valadrakul crouched on the slope, muttering, working his magic.

*A*my was ravenously hungry, but at the same time she doubted she could keep anything down if she ate it. She felt achy and exhausted; her feet throbbed. The stop for Valadrakul's magic had been very welcome indeed.

She wondered what was wrong with her. There were so many things it could be.

Stress, hunger, weeks of bad food — that could be it. The others weren't visibly suffering, but stress didn't affect everyone the same way. Ted Deranian wasn't exactly suffering, but he'd snapped completely. And Pel Brown had become sort of detached since his wife and daughter were killed; that might be his way of dealing with the strain.

Susan, of course, could cope with anything; Amy was convinced of that. She'd been through it all before, as a child in southeast Asia.

And the others — well, they were different. The Faerie folk were in their own world, they were *used* to dealing with Shadow's monsters and all the rest of it. The Imperials were all soldiers, even Prossie; they'd been trained for hardships. And they'd only been out of their own reality for a day and a half, not a couple of months.

So maybe it was just stress affecting her. Stress, and the thin air, and the heavy gravity, and the heat, and the humidity, and the weird washed-out sunlight.

She liked that idea, the idea that it was just stress, much better than the other possibilities. If this space wasn't quite right for Earthpeople to live in, then finding a way home wasn't just a way to get back to normal, it was a matter of life and death.

But none of the other Earthpeople were showing any symptoms that she could see, so she hoped that that wasn't it.

If it were, then she was the most sensitive. If the others *did* start showing symptoms, then she would be the first to die.

Right now, she felt as if she might die if she didn't get a few days' rest and some good food.

There were other possibilities, of course, and in a way those were even more frightening. What if she'd contracted some alien disease somewhere? What if she'd caught something from her rapist, Walter, back on Zeta Leo III? She'd been free of him for weeks — heavens, he'd been *dead* for weeks, hanged on her testimony — but how could she be sure she hadn't picked up something from him? Who knows what loathsome alien diseases he might have had?

Oh, hell, who needed anything alien? If he had syphilis or herpes or something, that would be bad enough, though she didn't think her symptoms fit either of those.

What if Walter had AIDS? Did AIDS exist in the Galactic Empire? In the space movies on the late show they never talked about things like that.

And what were the symptoms of the early stages of AIDS? Despite all the scare stories on TV she didn't have any idea. Feeling tired and sick and nauseous didn't seem very distinctive. And didn't AIDS usually take years to appear?

That brought a terrible thought — could she have gotten AIDS from her ex-husband and have had it all along, for the past year and a half? Despite all their arguments and accusations, she had no idea whether Stan had ever really been unfaithful, whether he might have picked up the virus somewhere.

This was all silly, though, she told herself; it wasn't AIDS. It was more likely to be mononucleosis, or that "yuppie flu," or something. She could have caught *anything* on Zeta Leo III. Or on Base One.

And that was all the more reason to get home to Earth. Somehow, she doubted that modern medicine was easily come by here in Faerie.

Valadrakul was crouched a few yards down the slope from her. "How's it going?" she called.

"Don't bother him," Prossie said, from where she sat just behind and to Amy's left. "He's working magic, or whatever you want to call it."

Amy glanced at her, startled.

"He needs to concentrate," the telepath explained.

"Are you reading his mind?"

Prossie grimaced. "No," she said. "I can't, here. Telepathy doesn't work any better here than it does on Earth."

"But I thought . . . weren't you relaying instructions from Base One?"

Prossie nodded. "That's right," she said, "but only as a receiver; it's my cousin Carrie who does the sending."

"Oh, that's right, you said that." Amy waved a hand at herself and said, "I forgot."

Prossie shrugged.

"So, is Carrie sending anything right now? Does she have any news about Lieutenant Dibbs?"

Startled, Prossie stared at Amy. "How could she have any news about him?"

"Well, if they sent a rescue party, or something."

Prossie shook her head. "They're not sending any rescue party," she said. "If there were any chance they'd do that I'd probably have stayed there myself."

Amy frowned. "Then what's going to happen to those men?" she asked.

"I don't know," Prossie said. "I hope that eventually they'll have the sense to leave. Or maybe we can send Taillefer to help them, after he's sent you Earthpeople home."

"That sounds good," Amy agreed.

"What I'm afraid of, though," Prossie said, "is that Shadow's going to send more monsters, and more, and more, until Dibbs and his men are all dead. That's what Raven's expecting, you know; that's why he fled, but didn't argue more about everybody coming."

"I don't understand," Amy said uneasily.

Prossie picked up a pebble and tossed it down the slope. "It's simple enough," she said. "Shadow knows something's happened back there at the clearing where we crashed, right? It sensed the space-warp, and it sent those creatures to investigate, and we killed them all. So it'll be expecting a report, and it isn't going to get one; what'll it do then?"

Amy stared at her.

"It's pretty obvious, isn't it?" the telepath said. "It'll send another force, a larger one. And if that doesn't work, it'll send a third, and a fourth. It'll send trackers, too, in case whatever it's after has left."

"Then they'll be coming after us," Amy whispered, suddenly terrified.

Prossie shook her head. "No, they won't," she said. "Or at least Raven doesn't think so. He thinks that they'll find the ship and Lieutenant Dibbs and the rest there, and they'll kill them all, and it'll never occur to Shadow that there were more, that the rest of us got away."

"Is that . . ." Amy began. Then the implication sank in. "But that's . . . that's horrible . . ."

Prossie grimaced. "Raven set them up," she said. "A decoy, so we could get away."

Amy glanced at Raven, standing further down the slope, showing no sign at all of a troubled conscience.

"He did ask for volunteers," Prossie said unhappily. "He gave them a chance."

"Do you know for sure that that was what he was doing?" Amy asked. "Did you read his mind?"

Prossie shook her head. "I told you," she answered, "I can't read minds here."

"You're just guessing?"

"You can call it that if you like."

That was exactly what Amy liked; she didn't want to think of Raven as being as callous and calculating as Prossie claimed. She swallowed, then changed the subject. "So what *is* your cousin Carrie saying? What's happening back on Base One?"

"Not much," Prossie said, a trifle uneasily.

"Oh," Amy said.

Her stomach cramped.

"I wish Valadrakul would hurry up," she said. "And I wish . . . oh, the hell with it. I wish I were safe at home and this was all *over,* that's what I wish!"

"Me, too," Prossie.

*P*rossie watched as Amy lay back on the grass and closed her eyes. The Earthwoman had a hand on her belly, and winced occasionally at some internal discomfort.

There were advantages to being cut off, Prossie thought; she couldn't feel Amy's discomfort, whatever it was, at all.

And of course, being in this other universe made it possible to keep her contacts with Carrie to a minimum, as well; Carrie had not yet been forced to realize that Prossie was deliberately disobeying orders, that Prossie had lied, had given false reports.

And she didn't know that Prossie had willingly let Raven set Dibbs and the others up to be sacrificed, in order to preserve the group he led, the group Prossie was in.

Of course, the brass back at Base One had sent the entire expedition out as a sacrifice to save face for themselves, but Carrie would expect better of a fellow telepath, wouldn't she?

Prossie knew that Carrie suspected something was very wrong, beyond what had been reported; Prossie suspected that Carrie knew Prossie had gone rogue.

That's what it was, of course; that's what she had done. And that was one more reason, aside from her increased chances for survival, that she was very glad that she had gone with Raven's group. If she had stayed with Dibbs people would have asked her questions, demanded she relay orders, and her treachery would have been revealed. With *this* group, no one bothered her — even the four soldiers seemed to have forgotten that she was a telepath, that she could talk to Base One at any time. She could keep her secrets.

She could never go back to Base One, though. She could probably never again risk reentering the Galactic Empire anywhere.

She would never again be able to live in her own reality, and that meant that she would never again have her full telepathic ability. She would always be able to touch the minds of her family, back in the Empire, but no one else.

That was a frightening and lonely thought, in a way, but it wasn't all bad. She would never again have to feel the fear and hatred of others, would never be forced to share in someone else's pain or sick terror. She had been mulling it over for hours now, as they traveled, and she was beginning to reconcile herself to the idea.

She didn't think much of Faerie as a place to live, though; she thought Earth would be much more enjoyable. When the others got their space-warp, their magical portal, open, she would go through it with them.

Prossie?

Carrie. Prossie looked up; no one was watching her.

"What is it?" she sent.

"You've been ignoring me. All today and last night, and even before that. I don't think you even heard some of what I sent."

"I probably didn't," she admitted. "I was thinking."

"Prossie, you're in trouble. I can't get answers out of you. General Hart and Under-Secretary Bascombe are both . . well, they say they're furious, but they're relieved. They can write off the whole mission if they lose contact with you. They've already written off that poor lieutenant and all those men. They can't admit that, of course, but it's true — and Prossie, they'll blame it on you. They'll say that the crazy mutant bitch screwed up communications and got everyone killed. And if they need a scapegoat on this end, they'll get *me*. Prossie, I'm really scared about this."

Prossie hesitated, then said, "Carrie, it's okay. Don't worry about me. Save yourself, Carrie — tell them I really have screwed things up. Tell them anything you like — anything *they* like. Let them blame me. I really *did* disobey orders."

"Prossie, you didn't, did you? Have you gone *crazy?*"

"Maybe I have. You tell them whatever you need to tell them to get yourself out of trouble, Carrie, and don't worry about me — I won't be coming back."

For a long moment, Prossie heard only with her ears, only the gentle near-silence of the Faerie hillside — a gentle wind rustling leaves, Wilkins muttering something, a distant bird's call. She hadn't heard many birds in the forest, but now one was singing somewhere.

Then Carrie asked, "Are you really sure?"

"I'm sure."

Before either of them could transmit more, Valadrakul made an unexpected noise, a sort of great wheezing sigh, as he let his breath out all at once.

All eyes but Amy's turned toward the wizard, but no one spoke as the man got slowly to his feet and turned to address the rest of the party.

Amy, Prossie noticed, stirred, but did not sit up.

For a few seconds, no one spoke.

"He is bespoke," Valadrakul announced. "Taillefer is called, and he comes. We're to meet him at yon ruin, at nightfall." He pointed to the misshapen edifice on the ridge ahead.

"Prossie, what's happening?" Carrie asked.

"Nothing," Prossie said. "It's not important any more. Don't worry about it."

The contact wavered as Carrie floundered for something to say, for the right way to respond.

"You're really leaving the family?" she asked at last.

Prossie frowned. She hadn't thought of it that way, but of course, that's just what she was doing.

"Yes," she said, "I really am."

"Then good-bye, Prossie."

"Good-bye, Carrie — but hey, I'd still like to hear from you sometimes, you or any of the others. If you can't find me here, check on Earth, too."

"Earth? But, Prossie . . ."

"Good-bye, Carrie."

"Well, come on, folks," Pel said, marching down the slope. "We've got to get there by nightfall."

Chapter Eleven

"We've no need to rush headlong 'cross the vale," Raven said, as the party splashed through the small stream at the foot of the slope. "A meal would do us all good."

"Where are we going to get a meal?" Pel asked, looking about. "I don't see any shops or restaurants or anything."

Stoddard stared at the Earthman; Raven let out a bark of laughter.

"Hardly, friend Pel," Raven said. "These slopes are the Starlinshire Downs, deep in the heart of Shadow's domain, and to the best of what I know, there's neither village nor keep nearby. Yet are there people, and the customs of hospitality surely have not been forgot entirely, even here."

Amy shuddered. "This is Shadow's territory, then?"

"Aye," Stoddard said sourly. "All the world is Shadow's."

"And this part fell to Shadow centuries past," Raven added, "yet surely some semblance of decency must remain."

Pel looked about, startled. "This land's been under Shadow for hundreds of years?" he asked.

"Aye," Raven said, looking at the Earthman with sudden interest. "What of it? Think you of aught that might aid us, then?"

"No," Pel said, "it's nothing important." He blinked, rubbed his nose, and gazed about.

The surrounding landscape was not at all what he would have expected after centuries of rule by an evil wizard. In the movies and stories, when evil fell over the land everything died, everything was dead and black and gray. Clouds were supposed to blot out the sun, if the sun still rose at all. The countryside was supposed to reflect the gloom and despair of its people.

This place didn't. The sun still shone — a bit pale and watery, but bright enough The grass was green, the trees bore leaves, the crops were growing in the fields and most of the huts they had seen from the slope, while primitive, had looked reasonably clean and well-kept; Pel remembered noticing that the thatch on one was obviously fresh and new.

Of course, he had only seen the outsides of the houses, and only from a distance.

Still, Pel didn't think that Mordor had looked like this. There was no stink of evil in the air here — neither brimstone nor blood nor burning oil — but the smell of raw earth and things growing. No suspicious smoke rose anywhere, nor did ominous fires glow in the distance. The air was a little chilly just now, but there was no soul-deadening cold or exhausting heat, and he was comfortable enough without his shirt; in fact, the occasional breezes felt pleasantly stimulating on his bare back. Shadow obviously wasn't up there with Sauron or Lord Foul or Skynet as a despoiler of countrysides.

On the other hand, Shadow did just fine at creating and sending monsters, he remembered.

At least, if it was really Shadow that sent those creatures. What if they were just ordinary beasts that had happened along, and Raven and his crew blamed Shadow unfairly?

Well, no, Pel admitted to himself, they were scarcely *ordinary* beasts. They were clearly unnatural in their appearance, and they had attacked without reason and fought to the death where ordinary animals would have turned and fled. They probably *were* Shadow's doing — whatever Shadow was.

Raven and his people always spoke of Shadow as if it were an individual, but was it really? Was it a person, a force, an organization?

Pel didn't know, and was not at all happy that he didn't.

As he had been thinking this, the party had continued on, up the west bank of the stream and further along the little road. Now, suddenly, they halted.

"Here," Raven said, pointing with his bandaged hand. "Here's the house that will give us to eat, an any human hearts remain in these lands."

*A*my winced as Stoddard pounded on the door of the cottage — if "cottage" wasn't too generous a term for the place. "Hovel" perhaps went too far the other way, but it certainly wasn't anywhere Amy would have wanted to live.

Even so, it seemed rude to hammer like that when they had come seeking the occupant's charity.

The door opened, and a frightened face peered out at them — a woman's face, thirtyish, Amy thought, and not attractive, with unkempt hair and coarse skin.

"Open, in the name of the Goddess," Raven said. "We are famished, and claim hospitality by the ancient laws."

The woman glanced up at Stoddard's raised fist, resting on her door, and seemed much more impressed by that, and by Stoddard in general, than by Raven's words. She opened the door, staying behind it.

Stoddard and Raven and Valadrakul marched boldly in; the others hesitated at first, but then Wilkins shrugged and followed, with Sawyer and Marks and Singer close behind.

Ted went next, then Pel, and the three woman brought up the rear, Amy last of all.

She found the cottage's main room jammed; it had never been meant to hold so many. The Imperials and Earthpeople were standing near the center, milling about in a crowd that practically filled the available floor space, while the Faerie folk had found their way to an alcove that, Amy realized, must be the kitchen.

At the other end of the little house was an earthen hearth before a crude stone chimney and mantle. A rough trestle table and benches stood beside the hearth; Sawyer and Singer were crowded against the near end of the table, leaning up against it.

Pel was standing a few feet from the table, staring at it — or under it, Amy realized. As she watched, he closed his eyes tight, and stood, swaying slightly, with them shut. Puzzled, Amy glanced under the table.

Hiding beneath it was a child — Amy couldn't be sure whether it was a boy or a girl — who stared out at the strangers with frightened eyes. The poor thing wore a dull brown sacklike garment and nothing else, had mousy brown hair hacked off unevenly at shoulder length.

The child didn't really look anything like Rachel Brown, but Amy knew that that was who Pel was thinking of. Uncomfortable, Amy looked up, away from the child, away from any memories of Pel's dead daughter.

Above the table was a loft. The central portion of the cottage was open from dirt floor to thatched roof, but the kitchen alcove and the hearth area both had plank ceilings. Another child sat in the loft, this one, dressed in faded blue, almost certainly a girl; she clutched a baby in her arms. For a moment Amy thought the baby might just be a doll, but then it waved an arm.

No one who lived in a place like this would have a doll that could wave its arms, Amy was sure. She swallowed.

The space above the kitchen alcove was smaller and lower, and appeared to be used for storage; at any rate, there were no children to be seen there.

The woman closed the heavy door, the bang and the sudden dimness startling Amy.

"Ah, goodwife," Raven called. "We claim but a single meal. What would you give us?"

"We have nothing to give you," the woman said, her voice high and unsteady, her tone flat.

"Oh, come," Raven replied. "I see much here before me — fruits and grain and vegetables, and surely that keg holds ale."

"'Tis not for you," the woman insisted. "We've children to feed, and our taxes are not yet paid." Amy noticed that she didn't seem to have quite the same accent to her speech that Raven and Valadrakul and the others did.

"And what of the Goddess' decree that all Her children owe hospitality to one another, whenever they might be wanderers upon the land?" Raven demanded.

"We pay no heed to the old faiths," the woman replied. "We heed only Shadow's orders."

"And what does Shadow say, then, in how one is to treat travelers?"

"Know you not, then?" The woman stood, hands on her hips, eyeing the intruders.

"I'd hear it from you," Raven answered.

"Shadow commands that we feed and shelter those who come on Shadow's business, and to deny all others," the woman told them, "but not when that would risk our own lives, for they are not our own to sacrifice, but are Shadow's, and valued more highly than whatever else might be stolen from us. Better to lose a year's crops, and Shadow's tax thereupon, than a lifetime's, and there are many of you, while I am alone here, save for my children."

Amy glanced up at the loft again, at the children there. Pel, standing near, still had his eyes tightly closed.

She wondered if Shadow could use its magic to spy on this somehow, here in its own territory. Would Shadow, whatever it was, feel the instinctive desire to protect those children that she felt? Did their mother have any way of informing Shadow of the presence of intruders?

"And you admitted us, then, in fear of your life?" Raven asked the peasant woman.

The woman gestured in the direction of Stoddard and Valadrakul. "That," she agreed, "and in hopes that you might prove yourselves to be servants of Shadow."

"You do disgrace to your ancestors and your spirit, in this sad acquiescence to that evil power and the renunciation of the true faith and its customs," Raven said.

"And you prove yourselves fools, to oppose the Shadow that shades the world!"

Amy, already uneasy, had listened to this exchange with mounting discomfort. Now, as the woman and the three intruding natives of Faerie glared at one another through the little crowd, she called, "Raven, let's get out of here, if we're not welcome." She didn't mention anything about the possibility of drawing Shadow's attention, but she thought that Raven would see it.

If Prossie was right about why Raven had left Lieutenant Dibbs back at the ship, then Raven certainly ought to have that in mind.

"Nay," Raven said angrily. "By the bleeding Goddess, I say you nay! We've a right under the ancient law, and we'll take a meal here before we go!"

"She's got a right to her own home," Amy protested. "It'd be stealing!"

"I don't care about that," Sawyer said, before Raven could say anything more, "but I might worry about her men getting back. She's got a husband, at least, or there wouldn't be that baby up there."

Amy bit back a comment about the naïveté implied by that comment; there wasn't necessarily a husband anywhere — but there certainly *might* be one.

"We can handle a husband," Wilkins said, "if it's only one."

"Aye," Stoddard agreed, "an it's but one; what, then, if that one brings friends?"

"Then we'll take what we can carry," Raven said. "I'll not leave here without our due."

Amy watched unhappily as the men of Faerie and the Galactic Empire picked through the contents of the kitchen alcove, but she did not protest further. It was stealing, no matter what ancient rights and privileges Raven might claim, stealing from a woman and her children — but Amy was hungry, very hungry, and the woman wasn't arguing any more, and there were seven men doing the stealing, compared with two men, four women, and a few children who were not — and Amy was fairly sure that if it came down to open conflict, Susan and Prossie and perhaps even Pel would side with the thieves, while Ted would be useless to either faction.

Pel might be useless, as well, lost in his grief; he was still standing with eyes closed.

She stood and watched, and wished she could think of something to say to comfort the woman they were robbing, but nothing came.

She was sure that the woman would report their presence to Shadow, if she could — but then, she probably would have reported the presence of strangers even if they hadn't robbed her.

And ten minutes later, when the entire party was moving again, across the valley toward the ruin where they were to meet Taillefer, Amy ate the raisins and dried apples and sticks of hard-baked bread that were her share of the booty without complaint.

She did not so much as glance back at the cottage, where the woman still stood in the open doorway, watching the thieves depart.

*T*hey had finished their meal as they had started it, while walking. The intermediate stage, when they had settled briefly by the roadside to sort out their loot and prepare anything that required preparation, had lasted no more than fifteen minutes, at most, Pel was sure.

Of course, he had no way to check; digital watches didn't work in either Faerie or Imperial space, and his was long gone, anyway. He relied on his own time sense, which he knew was not particularly good.

Still, he was sure that they were moving again less than half an hour after the robbery — despite Raven's claims, Pel could not help thinking of the way they had acquired their meal as a strong-arm robbery.

He almost wished he had joined in, though, and taken a shirt. He hadn't seen any, but there had probably been some, somewhere.

He hadn't seen any, because he hadn't wanted to look.

He tried very hard not to think of the girl under the table, not to associate her and her mother with Rachel and Nancy.

Maybe they would realize, when they thought about it, that Pel and the others hadn't taken very much; maybe they wouldn't hold the robbery against him. Maybe they would accept that it had been a necessity.

Robbery or not, it was done, and the party was well along the dirt track that Raven insisted on calling a highway, passing farms and fields on their way to the ridgetop ruin. This time the Earthman had not hung back; instead he walked in the front, with the three natives of Faerie.

"We don't have any hereditary nobility with special privileges back home," Pel remarked to Raven as they walked. "Not any more, anyway."

The nobleman glanced at the Earthman, but did not break stride or comment.

"I'm not complaining, I was as hungry as anyone," Pel continued, "but back home, taking that woman's food would have been outright theft."

"'Twas hospitality, not theft," Raven snapped. "The custom is required by the Goddess who brought forth all life, and has naught to do with the patents of nobility."

"Well, but it was because you're a member of the nobility that you thought you were entitled, wasn't it?"

"Nay, of course not; these lands are not mine, nor am I brought here to guest, nor are you my retinue, that I'd have the right to feed you." Raven paused, then remarked, "'Tis clear that your homeland's customs are not as our own, friend Pel — hospitality to travelers is a religious duty put upon us by the Goddess, and any who walk Her green earth are entitled, merely by virtue of being Her children, to the boon of a single meal from any who dwell upon the land and share in Her bounty. 'Tis this right and duty that I sought to claim, not some privilege due my gentle birth."

"Oh," Pel said, comprehension dawning. "It's a sort of tithe, you mean?"

"Aye, a tithe indeed," Raven agreed, nodding. "I'd not thought you had the word. A tithe and a duty, yet one that that woman sought to deny us, so debased has this realm become under Shadow's rule! Yon wife placed her duties to Shadow above all common duties to the Goddess — a greater disgrace to Shadow I cannot imagine."

Pel suspected this was hyperbole; he could think of a great many things worse than abandoning the customs of traditional religion. He decided against saying so, however.

He squinted at the sun as it descended steadily toward the ridgetop before them. The sky was reddening about it, the wisps of cloud were edged in golden fire — it promised to be a spectacular sunset.

There was nothing abnormal or threatening about it at all, nothing reflecting Shadow's alleged presence.

The lands to either side were green with the lush growth of spring, save where fresh-tilled fields showed rich and black, clean-edged and tidy squares set in the landscape, as if to break the monotony of green. Pel could see men and women and even children working in the fields, here and there; although none were near enough for a good hard look at their faces, they all seemed to be going about their business cheerfully enough. He saw no whips, no tears; backs were bent with labor, but not, so far as he could see, with undue hardship. The people didn't appear to be suffering any more than peasants anywhere might suffer, be it medieval Europe or some Third World country in Africa or South America.

Yet this land was under Shadow's rule, had been under Shadow's rule for centuries, and the Faerie folk spoke of Shadow as this hideous monster, this unspeakable evil. When Pel had first heard Raven's story he had immediately associated Shadow with Tolkien's Dark Lord, Sauron; with Donaldson's Lord Foul; with Bakshi's Blackwolf; with all the evil powers of fantasy films and novels.

By those standards, this land should have been a blasted wilderness, all ash and stone; the people should be crippled by floggings and torture; the skies should be black with unnatural clouds.

None of that fit.

Not for the first time, but far less idly than ever before, Pel wondered whether Shadow might be less a villain than it was a victim of bad press.

Despite the meal, despite the prospect of rescue and a return to Earth that lay ahead, Amy found herself wearing out quickly. She struggled to continue, to keep up with the others, but she felt weak and sick.

At least, she thought, she was able to keep down the stolen food. She pushed on, placing one foot ahead of the others, but the mound of brush and vine-wrapped stone atop the ridge seemed to be taking forever to draw any nearer.

The sun was reddening in the west and the sky darkening, they were finally at the foot of the ridge itself, and Amy was on the verge of collapse when Pel dropped back from the main group, coming even with Amy and Prossie, who had fallen behind.

"Hi," the Earthman said. "You two doing okay, back here?"

Prossie glanced at Amy, who was in no hurry to answer. She shrugged and said, "I'm fine, I guess; I've been thinking, and keeping Amy here company."

"I'm okay," Amy said. "At least, I think I am. Tired, but otherwise I'm okay."

"Not throwing up any more?" Pel asked.

Amy grimaced at this grotesque lack of tact. "Not throwing up," she said. "Not feeling real good, maybe, but not throwing up."

"I've been thinking about this Shadow thing," Pel said. "I think maybe I had a wrong idea about it."

Amy had been staring at her own feet, willing them to keep moving; now she looked up at Pel. "What sort of wrong idea?" she asked.

"Well, I'd been thinking of it as really being this all-encompassing evil that Raven claims it is — a big supernatural force, like in a horror movie or something. Like Sauron in *The Lord of the Rings.*"

"Yeah, so? Maybe it is. Raven seems to think so." She jerked her head in Valadrakul's direction. "And we know there's real magic here."

"But if it *were,*" Pel said, "then would everything here look so *normal,* here in Shadow's own territory?" He gestured at the evening sky, the darkening fields, the looming ruin atop the ridge.

"Normal," Amy said, glaring at him. "The sun's the wrong color and everyone talks funny and we all weigh about half a ton and I'm getting sick for no reason, and we're going to meet a wizard, and you're saying everything's too *normal* for you?"

"No, I mean . . . I mean if this is Shadow's country, shouldn't the skies be dark?"

"They *are* getting dark," Prossie pointed out.

"No, I mean all the time," Pel persisted. "Shouldn't it be a wasteland, all smoke and ash?"

Amy stared at him, then shook her head. "You're being silly, Pel," she said. "This isn't some stupid movie, like that one, 'Wizards' . . . did you ever see that? It was an animated film . . ."

"I saw it," Pel said. "That's the sort of thing I was thinking of. I mean, we've fallen into a story like that, haven't we? Wizards and Galactic Empires and all the rest of it, it's all a story — so why isn't the bad guy acting the part?"

"How do you know he isn't?" Amy said. "How do you know who the bad guy *is*? This isn't a story, Pel; this is real life."

"Then you don't think Shadow's really evil?"

"I didn't say that," Amy protested. "I don't know anything about Shadow. It could be just as bad as Raven says."

"But then why doesn't the countryside show it?" Pel asked, waving an arm at the farms behind them.

Amy sighed. "Pel," she said, "suppose someone popped you through a magical portal into some nice, quiet rural area in Germany in 1943 — would the skies be dark? Would the landscape be all twisted and evil?"

Pel frowned. "I guess not," he said. "Not necessarily, anyway, if it was someplace that wasn't getting bombed, and away from the camps. But Hitler wasn't a wizard, there wasn't anything supernatural about him."

"So maybe Shadow isn't supernatural evil incarnate," Amy said. "So it's not Sauron. It could still be Hitler."

"Or it could be nothing much. Maybe it's *Raven* who's Hitler — or Napoleon returning from Elba."

"And it could be that we don't have any idea what's going on, and we shouldn't worry about it, we should just all go home," Amy replied, exasperated.

Pel looked uncomfortable and didn't answer. Instead he turned away, and the party continued silently up the ridge in the gathering twilight.

Chapter Twelve

"And where is he, then?" Stoddard demanded, directing his question equally to Raven and Valadrakul.

Valadrakul shrugged. "I know not," he replied. "He gave the sign for nightfall, I am certain; thus, I understood he would be here by nightfall."

"He will come, I am certain," Raven said.

"Night has fallen," Stoddard pointed out, gesturing at the darkening sky overhead. Stars were beginning to appear.

Pel, standing a step or two away from the Faerie folk, looked up at the sky and shuddered.

The stars were wrong. The constellations were strange, and the patterns and groupings just didn't seem natural. He remembered what Valadrakul had said once, that the stars here were not unimaginably-distant spheres of gas, burning by atomic fusion, as they were at home; instead, they were mere thousands of miles away, and burned by magic.

That shouldn't really make any difference, he told himself. After all, that was what people had believed back on Earth, for thousands of years. They had learned better, eventually.

But Valadrakul said that the wizards here had gone up and *looked*, that they *knew* the stars were small and near.

Something dark moved across the sky, and Pel blinked. He stared.

Then, as he watched, the dark object suddenly flared into light, and Pel saw that it was a man, a man holding a staff, and the end of the staff was ablaze with something that wasn't quite flame and wasn't quite sparks.

"We must give him time," Valadrakul was saying. "Perchance some delay has befallen . . ."

"'Scuse me," Pel said loudly, "but is that him?" He pointed.

Raven and most of the others whirled, or at any rate snapped their heads around quickly; Stoddard turned more deliberately.

"Aye," Valadrakul said, "'tis him; Taillefer a' Norleigh." He raised a hand, and a yellow glow shone from his palm, casting a weak and uneasy light over the entire party as they huddled in the ruined castle.

The flying figure was approaching rapidly; now, seeing the light, the man waved, and adjusted his course to head more directly for Raven's party.

"Can *you* fly?" Pel asked Valadrakul.

Startled, the wizard glanced at him, then turned his attention back to his incoming compatriot.

"Aye," he said, "an some, though none so well as yonder."

"I haven't seen you do it," Pel said.

"I've had no need," Valadrakul answered.

Pel's mouth opened, then closed.

No need, perhaps, but wouldn't flight have been useful against Shadow's hellbeasts? Wouldn't it have been useful in scouting ahead, in finding food and water, in ensuring that at least one member of the party would be at the ruin by nightfall? Pel could see a dozen ways in which flying might have been convenient, yet Valadrakul's feet had always remained firmly on the ground.

If nothing else, wouldn't it be a way to avoid blisters and aching feet? Pel's own feet were certainly suffering, and he assumed that Valadrakul's hurt, too.

Still, he reminded himself that he shouldn't pry. It wasn't any of his business. If Valadrakul didn't care to fly, he presumably had a reason; there might be a cost he didn't want to pay, or some danger inherent in it.

Or maybe, despite his claim, he just couldn't fly, any more than he could open the interdimensional portals; wizardry was obviously not all a single skill. There was nothing wrong in that, either, and Pel could hardly question Valadrakul's power or value, since the wizard's magic had saved Pel's life when the hellbeasts had attacked.

And then Taillefer was coming in for a landing, not in a slow upright descent like a movie superhero, but in a headlong tumbling plunge; at Raven's direction Stoddard and the four Imperial troopers were preparing to catch him, Stoddard at the point of a V, the soldiers two on either side of the big Faerie native, obviously a bit unsure of what they were doing.

"I'd aid, as well, an I could," Raven said, holding up his bandaged hand, and calling to the others. "Friend Pel, here, stand you ready by the side. Ted Deranian, would take this side with me, and be my other hand? And the women, though you be frailer, stand to the rear and watch, lest any fall."

Pel stepped up, taking a position behind Wilkins and Sawyer, not at all sure what he was doing; then, before anyone else could react, before anyone could ask any questions, Taillefer came plummeting into the wide end of the V, headed straight toward Stoddard.

"Catch you him!" Raven and Valadrakul called in near-perfect unison, as Stoddard stepped forward, arms out and knees bent, and the four soldiers thrust out their hands.

The flying wizard hit Stoddard hard; Pel could see that he had curled up as best he could, and Stoddard had positioned himself to have an arm under each shoulder, but still, Taillefer's head drove into Stoddard's belly hard enough to knock the wind out of the big man. The wizard's legs flew up, and the Imperials grabbed at them.

And then Stoddard and Taillefer and Singer were all in a heap on the broken flagstone floor of the ruin, and the others were all crowding around at once, trying to help them up.

All except Amy, that is, who was leaning against a broken wall, looking sick.

*T*he ruins had been a castle. That had not been obvious at all until they actually reached the outer wall and fought their way through the entangling vines, but once they were inside, even Amy could see that the structure had once had a central mass, an encircling wall, and guardian towers at the corners.

It had obviously never been a graceful fairy castle like the one at Disney World, or the one that crazy Bavarian king had built on a mountaintop; from the look of it, this had been a practical and very ugly fortress, with thick walls of heavy gray stone, few windows, and little in the way of comforts or ornamentation.

Whatever it had been, however, not much remained. The curtain wall, as Raven called it, was broken down into rubble in several places; the courtyard was overgrown with weeds and thornbushes; the roof was gone entirely, the supporting arches and columns broken off short. The great hall had one side missing, the other three jagged remnants.

Oddly, the tower at one end still stood, apparently almost intact, though it was hard to be sure through the thick layer of ivy that covered it. That tower, and the adjoining mass of stonework, had been what they had seen from afar, what they had steered for.

When they had reached it, though, no one had shown any inclination to enter the tower or most of the rest of the structure; they had simply gathered in the ruined hall, where the remains of a stone floor had kept the undergrowth from getting out of hand.

When the men had begun arguing about why Taillefer wasn't there yet, Amy had almost suggested that perhaps he was, maybe he was in the tower somewhere

— but then she had thought better of it. She didn't want anyone to go in there; she didn't want the group to be split up into search parties. She just sat down and waited; if this Taillefer was in there, he'd come out sooner or later.

And he hadn't been in there; instead he'd come falling out of the sky. Amy had stood up when Raven called for help, but the move had upset her delicate stomach — except her stomach had never been delicate back on Earth.

It was delicate now; she struggled to keep down the supper they had stolen from that poor woman and her children, and as the wizard tumbled into the others and knocked them sprawling, like some horribly unfunny clown act, Amy stood by, off to the side, making no move to help. As she watched the men get to their feet she thought it was a miracle that nobody had broken any bones, and that Stoddard hadn't gotten a concussion from whacking his head on the stones.

At least, she hoped no one had a concussion; in the sickly yellow glow from Valadrakul's hand and Taillefer's staff, none of the faces looked particularly healthy.

"And look what the wind's blown us," Raven called cheerfully, using his good hand to help Taillefer up. "Come you, one and all, and greet him who is come to aid us in our hour of need!"

Amy stayed in her place by the wall; she didn't want to bother greeting the new arrival. With any luck, he'd be creating a portal back to Earth in a few minutes, and she could go home and make an appointment with her doctor and never see Taillefer or any of these other people again.

She couldn't help looking at them, though.

Taillefer was short for a man, no more than her own height, and fat — not really obese, but thick and rounded everywhere, the sort of fat that Amy associated with the word "stout." He was dressed in black, a long fur-trimmed coat over a black tunic and black tights, with gold rings on his fingers, and more gold rings on the carved five-foot staff of dark wood he held in one hand. The rings on his fingers looked ordinary enough, but the gold bands on the staff were glowing dully.

Wizardry at work, Amy supposed. She didn't much care any more; she just wanted it all to be over. At this point she found it more amazing that he hadn't whacked anyone with the staff when he came plunging down out of the sky than that the gold fittings glowed.

And why had he done that plunge, anyway? Why hadn't he just landed by himself? This was the wizard they were trusting to send them home, she thought sourly, a magician who couldn't land on his own two feet?

Singer helped Taillefer brush off the dust, then slapped at the dark smudges on his own uniform; the purple fabric looked dark and ominous in the yellow light.

Amy shuddered. She was starting to get the creeps. Pel had been complaining about how Shadow's country didn't look evil enough; what about this place, then, this ruined castle, with its dark stone walls and black shadows and nasty thorns and vines growing everywhere? In the entire place she hadn't seen a single flower, or an honest blade of ordinary grass. What about right here, where even the silly Imperial uniforms could look threatening?

But that was the peculiar light, and that came from the two wizards, who were supposed to be on the good guys' side.

"The blessings of the Goddess to you all," Taillefer said, in a surprisingly high-pitched tenor and with an accent distinctly different from the peculiar Australian-New York intonation of the other Faerie folk Amy had met. "My brother Valadrakul, I greet you; for the rest, come, let us know one another! Pray, someone among you, make us a light, that my fellow wizard can cool his hand, and I my staff."

"I'll fetch something," Stoddard said; he turned away and began looking for dead brush.

While he and the Imperials set about building a fire, Raven stepped up to Taillefer and announced, "I am called Raven of Stormcrack Keep, and I welcome you to this place, whatever it might be." He held out a hand.

Taillefer clasped the hand and smiled. "Ah, Lord Raven, as you would surely have it," he said, "I've heard much of you. But know you not what this place is, then? Did not my brother in the arcane arts tell you that much?" He turned to look at Valadrakul.

"I saw no need," Valadrakul said, "and we'd more urgent concerns."

"Indeed, I dare say you did, yet 'tis worthy of note where we meet, is't not?" Taillefer grinned in a way Amy did not find comforting.

"Where are we, then?" Raven asked, a trifle annoyed. Stoddard looked up from the armful of brush he and the Imperials had collected.

"Why, this is Castle Regisvert, none other!" Taillefer's grin broadened, then slipped somewhat as most of his audience failed to react.

Stoddard and Raven reacted, however; Stoddard's face went blank, as if he had just decided not to believe what he was being told, and he continued stacking the firewood.

Raven started, then looked about at the ruins with new interest. "Truly, say you?" he asked.

"Aye, truly," Taillefer said.

Prossie and the four Earthpeople still didn't respond, since none of them had ever heard of any Castle Regisvert. Two of the Imperials paused in their efforts.

"So what?" Wilkins asked.

"Why, know you not the tale?" Taillefer asked, astonished.

"We're not from around here," Wilkins answered dryly.

"Then gladly I'll tell it," Taillefer said, his grin returned. "'Twas in the days of old, when Shadow's reach was yet limited, when darkness had not yet fallen upon all the lands, yet strife was widespread, for those who opposed the encroaching evil were not united; aye, in truth, that's the damning disgrace of all our people, and all that was needed for the triumph of Shadow that so oppresses and shames us now . . ."

"Excuse me," Amy called from her place by the wall, "but I don't think this is the time for stories."

Affronted, Taillefer turned to glare at her. "'Tis no mere *story*, wench, but the true history of this place."

"All the same," Pel said, "maybe it can wait. Amy isn't well, and we'd like to get her home. And I want to get home, too, and probably the Imperials do. And we should get Ted there to a doctor."

Ted giggled.

Susan said nothing, Amy noticed; she just stood by and watched.

"Ah, and is this why I was summoned hither?" Taillefer asked. "Has Valadrakul told you that I might bear you to your homes?"

Valadrakul cleared his throat. His still-raised hand was still glowing, but the glow dimmed perceptibly.

"Indeed, I've a fine gift for wind-riding," Taillefer said, "and I might well bring another, though I doubt me I can carry any but one at the time."

"'Tis not wind-riding we ask," Valadrakul said, lowering his hand. Only the faint remaining glimmer of Taillefer's staff and the dim light of the stars overhead remained to illuminate the scene.

"And what then is it?" Taillefer asked. "That sign sent me told me that I was called, and by whom, and to what part of the world, but naught else. What would you have of me, Valadrakul of Warricken?"

A thin tongue of flame flared up in the stack of brush, as Valadrakul worked his magic with a gesture. "Before we talk of that," the wizard said, "let us exchange names, as you said we should. You know me well of old, and Raven has spoken his name; know then that he who stands yonder is Stoddard, of Raven's household, most faithful of all." He pointed to where Stoddard stood, faintly visible in the still-weak firelight. "And of all you see here, good Taillefer, only we three, Raven, Stoddard, and myself, are from this realm."

Taillefer cocked his head slightly. "How mean you, Valadrakul?"

Valadrakul sighed. "I mean that this good man, Pellinore Brown, and likewise Ted Deranian, and these ladies known to me as Amy and Susan, came to us from a land they call Earth; and that these others, Messires Wilkins and Sawyer and Singer and Marks, and Mistress Thorpe, are from the Galactic Empire."

Amy couldn't see just where the wizard pointed as he named all the names, and wished that they had some proper light — even just a flashlight. The fire was growing, and that would help.

The glow of his staff lit Taillefer's face, though, and Amy could see that he was considering them all for a moment, looking about in the darkness.

For a moment, firelight flared, as a particularly dry bit of kindling caught; then it flickered and died down.

"And that would account for their garb, I would suppose," Taillefer said at last, "but that yourself, Valadrakul, and him you name Stoddard, wear the same. And lo, Vala, your hair is much transformed; had you fleas, perhaps, that would not yield without this butchery?"

"We have sojourned in the Galactic Empire," Valadrakul explained, "and there were forced to make do with what attire came to hand." He put a hand to his head. "As for this, 'twas but the result of misfortunes that bear no retelling here and now."

Taillefer nodded thoughtfully. "And Elani? For surely, 'twas she who sent you thither?"

"Dead," Valadrakul replied bitterly. "Slain by Shadow's black beasts."

Amy's stomach lurched, and she called, "Can we get on with it, please?"

Taillefer threw her a glance, then turned back to Valadrakul. "'Tis a grievous loss you speak of," he said, "and when time more freely permits, I'll mourn her as she is due. Erstwhile, howsoever, he that you called the Brown Pellinore spoke of going home. Home to this Earth, is it?"

"Aye," Valadrakul said.

Amy could hear Wilkins and the others trying to help the fire along, could hear the bits of wood scraping on the stone floor and the muttering of their voices, but she could no longer see their faces. Someone was cursing under his breath, but she couldn't tell who it was.

"And you'd have me open the portal, then?" Taillefer asked his compatriot. "'Tis for this that you summoned me and sought my aid?"

"Aye," Valadrakul replied.

"And you'd have it here in Regisvert, I suppose? Do you think me mad, Vala?"

"The place was of your own choosing, Taillefer, that it might be readily found by us all; I'd no mind as to where the portal might be."

"What's wrong with right here?" Amy demanded.

Taillefer turned a disdainful stare her way, his face ghostly in the gloom. "Methought you'd have none of the history, woman," he said.

"I don't need any lectures," Amy snapped. "What's wrong with here?"

Valadrakul sighed and turned to her. The darkness hid his features. "Four hundred years and more agone," he said, "this Castle Regisvert was hearth and stronghold for the Green Magician, sworn foe to Shadow. 'Twas built upon this spot because here the currents of magic are strong, the flow of power rich and full; and as was ever the case, that drew the attention of Shadow, who one dire night came and, after a famous battle of eldritch skill and might that lasted for many days, Shadow struck down the Green Magician, threw down the castle to ruin, and drew the powers of this place into its own web. The magic yet runs strong here — but likewise is it yet linked close to Shadow, and as any touch upon the strands of a spider's web will draw the spider's eye, yet will any spell worked in this place draw Shadow's gaze."

"You tell it briefly, and without interest," Taillefer said, "yet is that the essence of the tale, and of my reasoning."

"Then we'll go somewhere else," Amy said. "We don't care where you open the portal, we just want to go home."

"And I've no doubt you desire it," Taillefer said, "but I'll have none of it. Go where you will, yet I'll not conjure you home."

Wilkins, squatting, looked up from the fire; Stoddard, who had been standing impassively nearby, unfolded his arms from across his chest.

Ted giggled hysterically. "I knew it," he said. "I'm *never* going to wake up from this one. I must be comatose, or maybe dead."

And Amy's stomach betrayed her again; she bent, clutching her belly, and threw up most of her stolen supper.

Chapter Thirteen

Raven frowned and glanced at the black-haired Earthwoman, the one called Susan. She was tending to her sick companion, and her black bag rested on the ground beside her. The madman, ted-Deranian, was leaning against a broken wall, staring at the stars. Pel the Brown and the witch-woman Thorpe were dividing their attention between their fallen comrade and the wizards, while the four soldiers had eyes only for Raven, Valadrakul, and Taillefer.

Stoddard was standing back, beyond the fire, but Raven had no worries where Stoddard was concerned; the man had been true all his life, the most faithful helpmeet any could ask for.

And Valadrakul had returned to his customary silence; he was standing there, looking first to his compatriot in the mystic arts, then to his liege lord, and saying nothing.

None stepped forward to confront this rogue Taillefer, who sought to betray the cause. That was a leader's duty.

That was *his* duty.

And he'd no wish to shirk that duty; he would be only too glad to berate the scoundrel, to demand an explanation, to demolish the fool's every argument against doing as they asked. Yet it would not do to be overhasty. He had expected a tumult of protest when the wizard spoke his defiance, and had bethought himself to enter as the voice of calm reason, quieting the roil; the woman Amy had put an end to that by her illness, puking on the holy stones of Castle Regisvert like an overfed bitch. To speak up whilst her condition was unknown would have been seen as unseemly.

But her attendants were about her, and it would scarcely do to leave Taillefer too long unchallenged.

"Look you, wizard," Raven said, trying to sound calm and reasonable, "wherefore say you this, that you'll not conjure the portal to the realm called Earth?"

"And I'll not," Taillefer answered coldly. "'Tis reason enough."

"Play no games with *me*, Taillefer," Raven snapped. "Say then, why you will not conjure as we ask."

"Because, O Raven, I love my life, and would not see it early ended. Much as I appreciate that all must in time return to the breast of the Goddess, yet am I in no hurry to do so."

"Nor are we, wizard," Raven retorted, fighting down anger. "What does this with the conjuring?"

Taillefer sighed ostentatiously. "See you, Lord Raven," he said, "who has conjured this spell that you ask me to perform? Why, imprimis, there is Shadow, who created it, by what means we know not, for Shadow's ways are unknown to us. An it was human once, we might well doubt that it is yet, and it has lived these many centuries, it draws upon such unlimited powers, it binds together a web of powers and magicks the like of which no mortal has ever known. That Shadow survives the conjuring between worlds means naught for such as myself."

"I know that . . ." Raven began.

Taillefer held up a silencing hand. "Secundus," he said, "there was Quarren, who sought the title Light-Bearer, and who bethought to lead all the wizards remaining in crusade 'gainst Shadow. 'Twas he who first stole the secret of the portals, brought it from Shadow to the light, as it might be said. You well know what befell him."

"He died," Raven said. "I can scarce deny it, he was slain by Shadow. Yet the conjuring of portals was in no way the cause, Taillefer."

"Ah, but know you that in certainty, you who call yourself Raven? And remember, tertius, was Elani of the Scarlet Cloak, who stood among your companions 'gainst the rule of Shadow. And where is she now, O bird of ill omen?"

"Dead likewise, in truth," Raven admitted. "But see you, Taillefer, she died not from the conjuring of a portal, but from merest mischance, that we should be in that forest when Shadow's hellbeasts passed by."

"Say you so, then?" Taillefer shook his head. "An you do, I say you lie. 'Twas no mischance, methinks."

"And I say 'twas just that, wizard," Raven replied, glaring. "I was there by her side; were you?"

"Nay," Taillefer admitted, "yet do I know that which you do not. You and Valadrakul and Elani, you were gone many days, O Raven, vanished from the face of the land — to the Galactic Empire, 'twould seem, from Vala's words. There were reports that hinted at such, from our agents — and yes, I bespoke them, I opened the portals as you would have me do. And every time I did, Shadow's creatures descended upon me, swiftly and with deadly intent, until I dared not do so again. Shadow's reach is long, Raven, and it has ways of knowing that we do not; perhaps it feels tremors in its web, perhaps it sees in ways we do not. Whatever the means, I doubt me not that Shadow *knows,* upon the instant, when any lesser being dares open the gates between worlds. When my compatriot told me that Elani was dead, slain by Shadow's beasts, I knew in an instant that she had conjured one portal too many, and I'll not follow her down that path."

Raven glowered at him. "'Twas not quite the way of it, wizard," he said. "True, that perchance the beasts were drawn by a gate between worlds, but 'twas none of Elani's conjuring. The mages of the Galactic Empire, those they call scientists, opened the portal."

"What matter, then?" Taillefer demanded. "You see my point; 'twas the gate that drew Shadow's attention, whosoever conjured it."

"Yet have you, by your own words, conjured portals and lived to tell of it."

"Indeed, for I fled instanter, when attacked."

"Then do this the same!"

Taillefer shook his head. "Nay, Raven. I have gone too oft to the well, and fear that the bucket must soon give way. These last conjurings were each for but an instant, and each guided to a particular ally in the Empire, yet I scarce won away." He drew back a sleeve and held up his left arm, displaying deep, half-healed wounds, plainly visible even by firelight. "And that was in Old Dunleigh, seven score miles from here, and five score further from Shadow's keep. Here, with no friend upon the other side to guide the spell home, with the need to see half a dozen men and women transported . . I'll not risk it. E'en should I open the gate, it might well deliver these to the wrong spot in yonder realm — I might send them to Stormcrack when I sought Starlinshire, as it were, or leave them in some blasted wasteland, or drop them in the sea, an I take not an hour or more to guide it. And an hour, when every second draws Shadow's ire closer?"

"Yet 'twould be the right world, and surely, the journey home could be made . . ."

"Nay, Lord Raven," Taillefer said, "be you not so sure. Know you, that in the realm these call Earth, there are many worlds? And that in some, the air itself is poison, if there be air at all?"

Raven turned to Pel, who was standing close at hand. "Is't true?" the rightful lord of Stormcrack Keep demanded.

*P*el had not been expecting the question; he had been standing close by, listening intently but silently, hoping that Raven would find some way to talk Taillefer around — certainly, Pel had always found Raven persuasive — but he had had no intention of getting into the argument himself, for fear of messing things up.

But when he was directly questioned, he could hardly stay out. He couldn't answer immediately, though; puzzling out what Taillefer meant took a few seconds. "Do you mean the other planets?" he asked. "Mars and Venus and like that?"

"Aye."

"But I thought you could only open a gate to places where people spoke English . . ." Pel let his sentence trail off, suddenly realizing how stupid it sounded.

"Nay, 'tis the miracle-workers of the Empire, who speak without voice, who can locate only those minds that speak the Good Tongue," Taillefer said. "The spells of Shadow can open gateways unto any realm whose existence is known beyond doubt — that is, any realm of which certain arcane characteristics are known. But where in that realm the portal opens, who wist?"

Valadrakul spoke up. "Friend Pel, though we esteem you greatly now, think you that we had *chosen* your cellars as our point of entry? Had we the fullest choice, we'd have emerged in the audience chamber of a king or prince. And think you that we *chose* that foul desert whither Elani sent us, when Shadow's beasts o'ercame us at Stormcrack?"

Pel was flustered. "But she said . . . she was in a hurry . . ."

"As would I be," Taillefer pointed out.

"Listen, if you could be sure it was on Earth, on land," Pel said, "we'd take it — at least, I would. We'd get home eventually." He glanced at the others for support.

Ted shrugged; Amy nodded; Susan frowned, then shook her head, once, a sharp little negative jerk.

"*I'd* take it," Pel insisted.

"And what of the rest, who would be left behind to face Shadow's anger?" Taillefer asked. "Not to put too fine a point on it, what of myself?"

"You could come with us," Pel suggested, not very hopefully.

"Oh, aye," Taillefer replied sarcastically. "Plunge myself into an unknown corner of a realm where all my spells and powers are for naught, where I know not a thing of the ways and customs; a realm that, alone of the three known, has no way to reach the others, so that never could I return?"

"But why would you *want* to return?" Pel asked desperately. "This world's ruled by Shadow, isn't it? Our world isn't; it's not bad at all, really." He had intended to argue further, but he stopped abruptly when he saw the expressions not just on Taillefer's face, but on Raven's and Valadrakul's, as well.

"Man," Taillefer said, "this world may seem unpleasant to *you*, yet is it my world, my homeland, and I'll not abandon it to Shadow, not leave it in its hour of need."

"Nor will I," Raven said.

Pel looked at Valadrakul, whose expression convinced Pel that he didn't need to hear what the other wizard had to say. The Earthman sighed.

"You won't do it?" he asked.

Taillefer shook his head. "That I won't," he said.

*A*my heard it all, heard first Raven, then Pel argue with Taillefer. Her stomach had calmed, and she was in no danger of vomiting again; she was ravenously hungry, and felt weak and sick, but she was not going to throw up for awhile. She sat against the ruined wall of the castle, surrounded by shadows and gloom, and listened to the men debate the rest of her life.

And she was losing the argument. If someone didn't do something, it sounded as if she would be trapped in this horrible fairy-world forever.

Raven, much as he wanted his guns and soldiers, appeared to have abandoned the argument to Pel. Pel was trying, but he argued like a man, all rationalizations and confrontations, and he was obviously losing. Taillefer felt his life was at stake; he wasn't going to be swayed by that sort of logic.

"But why would you *want* to return?" she heard Pel ask. "This world's ruled by Shadow, isn't it? Our world isn't; it's not bad at all, really."

Amy didn't need to hear; she knew the answers. If anything, Pel had just convinced Raven to switch sides, rather than Taillefer. "Susan?" she said quietly.

"Yes?"

"You have your bag?"

Susan took a moment to consider that.

"I don't think it'll work," she said, "but I'll try it if you want."

"Please," Amy said.

Susan sighed, then pulled her bag up where she could reach into it more easily.

Then she had her little revolver in her hand, the .38 Police Special; she glanced at Amy, who nodded.

"I don't think it'll work," Susan said again, as she rose, pistol ready.

The men had not noticed anything, as yet; Pel was asking the plump wizard, "You won't do it?"

"That I won't," Taillefer replied.

Susan cleared her throat, then raised the pistol, gripped tightly in both hands, and pointed it at Taillefer.

"Wizard," she called, her finger tight on the trigger.

*R*aven turned at the sound of the Earthwoman's voice, expecting nothing more from her than a plea for mercy; it took a second before his eyes adjusted to the dimness, but at the sight of the weapon in her hands his jaw dropped.

Quickly, he caught himself, composed himself.

"Aye, mistress?" Taillefer asked, as he, too, turned. "What would you, and what is this you point at me?"

"This thing I'm pointing at you is a weapon from Earth," Susan explained. "It's commonly called a handgun. If I pull the trigger, it'll blow a hole right through you — ask Raven and Valadrakul, they've seen me use it to kill Shadow's creatures. It's what Raven wants from Earth — we've promised him a supply of guns to use against Shadow."

"Ah," Taillefer said, eyeing the revolver with interest.

"Now, we're going to ask you again whether you'll open the portal to Earth," Susan said, "with the understanding that if you refuse, I'll blow your head off. Will you open the portal?"

Taillefer hesitated, then turned to Valadrakul. "Does this device what she says?"

"Aye," Valadrakul said, blinking at Susan. For a moment, Raven thought the wizard intended to say more, but in the end he left the single word to stand alone.

Thoughtfully, Taillefer turned back to face the Earthwoman. "See you, mistress, the position you put me in," he said. "An you make good your threat, I perish. An I accede to your demands, then too do I perish, but at Shadow's hands rather than yours. Either way, I am dead. If 'tis Shadow that slays me, then mayhap others die with me. Now, consider likewise what you'd accomplish; an I refuse, and you slay me, you do not gain what you seek, for there's none but I who can do it. An I yield, you may yet see Earth, but I die, and there shall be none who can restore the portal for the delivery of the weapons you say this worthy who calls himself Raven seeks; thus, Shadow triumphant, my people forever enslaved. I'd not have that weighing upon my soul in the afterlife."

"I don't need an argument," Susan said harshly. "I need a decision."

"And I say that you shall have one, in a moment — if you see it not yet.

Think you, if you slay me, you shall be forevermore trapped in our world; if you refrain, the chance shall remain, so long as I live, that some way shall be found that I may safely send you home."

"You're refusing, then."

"Aye, mistress; I refuse you."

Slowly, Susan lowered the pistol. Then she shrugged, and said to Amy, "I told you it wouldn't work." She turned away.

And Raven let out his breath.

He had not realized, until that moment, that he had bated it.

Nor had he realized, until the danger was past, that he had thought Susan would shoot. Yet it was with surprise and wonder that he saw her put the weapon away, and saw Taillefer standing unharmed.

Had it been he himself who held the weapon, and who held Susan's position, Raven knew that Taillefer would now be dead.

Which would, as Taillefer had said, be a disaster.

This bore some thought.

"Maybe you should have wounded him," Pel suggested quietly, leaning on one elbow. The stone pavement of Castle Regisvert was cold beneath him. "If you'd put a bullet in his leg, say, maybe he'd have believed you, not called your bluff."

Susan, lying nearby, raised her head and shook it no; Pel could just barely see the movement in the darkness. "Too risky," she said. "What if he bled to death, or the wound got infected? No, it was all bluff, and we lost."

"So what do we do now?"

"We go to sleep, Mr. Brown. It's late, it's been a long day. You heard Raven and Wilkins and Taillefer. We'll talk it all out tomorrow, by daylight."

"But how do we get back to Earth?" Pel heard his own voice rising in pitch; he realized that he must sound almost hysterical.

That was reasonable; he *was* almost hysterical. He *had* to get home. He had to get out of this fairy-tale world, this pulp fantasy story he had found himself in, back to the sane and normal world of lawn mowers and income taxes and marketing consultation, back to the world of Nancy and Rachel. He couldn't stay in Faerie; he simply couldn't take it.

And his only way back was Taillefer, and Taillefer was refusing to cooperate. How could he go to sleep?

"How do we get back?" he repeated, a bit more quietly.

"I don't know, Mr. Brown," Susan said. "I don't know, and no one here knows. You're tired, we're all tired, we're distraught — get some sleep. It'll help."

"But what . . ."

"Maybe Taillefer will be braver by daylight; had you thought of that? People are like that sometimes — *everybody* is, whether they admit it or not. It's easier to take risks by daylight. Go to sleep, Mr. Brown."

Pel hesitated, then rolled over, and tried to sleep.

It was easier than he had expected.

Chapter Fourteen

Amy sat up, stretched, then immediately leaned over and threw up — or tried to; her stomach held nothing she could bring up.

Susan awoke at the sound; Amy saw the attorney's eyes, closed a moment before, open and watching her. Pel, on Susan's other side, stirred.

Taillefer, already up and about, turned and looked at her with interest.

"What ails you, woman?" he asked.

"I dunno," Amy muttered, wiping her mouth with the back of her hand.

"Have you a fever, then?"

Amy shrugged; Susan, who had felt Amy's wrist and forehead the night before, answered, "No fever I could find."

"Is't bad food, perchance? What had you to eat, of late?"

"Garbage," Amy muttered.

"The same as the rest of us," Susan replied.

Taillefer considered that. "Well, betimes a poison may strike one and pass another by, yet . . . how long has this troubled you?"

"A few days," Amy said, wiping her hand on a clump of grass.

"Has it . . . your pardon for my coarseness; has it troubled your bowels?"

Amy shook her head. "Not really. Not yet, anyway."

"Feel you weak and weary, perchance? An so, did that come ere the vomiting?"

"I've felt rotten for weeks," Amy agreed. "But it's just this place — I need to go home!"

Taillefer shook his head. "I think that's not the cause, mistress."

Amy glared up at him. "Oh? Is this something people get here? You recognize it?"

Taillefer smiled crookedly. "An I read the signs aright, mistress," he said, "'tis something that women must surely 'get' in every land, be it here in the True World, or in the Galactic Empire, or on your Earth. Are you wed?"

For a moment, Amy didn't understand what Taillefer meant; the sudden question seemed to come from nowhere, to be completely irrelevant.

Then she saw the connection. The anger drained from her stare, to be replaced with shock.

"Oh, my God," she said.

Pel returned from the bushes still blinking sleepily as he buttoned his pants; he wished the Galactic Empire had developed the zippered fly, but they apparently hadn't. He looked up to see that Amy was crying, and Susan was comforting her — again.

Pel frowned slightly. Whatever was bothering Amy, she didn't seem to be taking it well. It didn't seem to be getting much worse — or any better.

He had heard her asking Susan whether she thought it could be the same thing that killed Grummetty and Alella, that her system was somehow incompatible with this entire universe; he didn't see how that could be it, since no one else was affected, and he certainly hoped it wasn't that.

Well, whatever it was, there wasn't anything he could do about it except help her get back to Earth. The sooner the whole group sat down together and figured out how to do that, the better.

Amy and Susan were sitting against the east wall of the great hall, in the shade; Ted was still asleep nearby. Taillefer and Valadrakul were talking quietly over toward the northeast corner. Raven and Singer and Prossie were doing something together in the sunlit center of the hall, shadows stretching far out to the west — Pel hoped they were getting breakfast. Wilkins and Marks and Sawyer were moving about over at the south end, where thorn bushes had grown up through the broken floor.

Stoddard was nowhere in sight; Pel guessed he was out gathering firewood. The morning air was chilly and damp, fragrant with mosses and weeds, and he still had no shirt; a fire would be welcome.

But there was no need to wait for that; if everyone but Ted was awake, it was time to start discussion.

"So what are we doing?" Pel demanded loudly, of no one in particular.

"Getting breakfast, I hope," Wilkins replied. "We've been trying to catch something here — might be a woodchuck, if you have those here."

The two wizards looked up from their colloquy. "Perchance I might lend a hand," Valadrakul said.

*T*he animal was a badger, not a woodchuck, and managed to claw Singer's arm before being clubbed into unconsciousness by the butts of four blasters and a chunk of wood; it was finished off by Wilkins, who cut its throat with his pocketknife.

Pel watched the operation with morbid interest, but did not help beyond lending moral support; he was not yet accustomed to killing his own food. It seemed like a very messy business — not that he saw much of an alternative here.

He did help build the fire, though.

The meat was edible, at least some of it — Raven cut out the portions he said were fit to eat, and left the rest. Even when properly cooked, however, it wasn't very pleasant eating, and the relatively good parts did not go very far when divided a dozen ways. The smells of blood and dew-wet badger fur lingered, which didn't help Pel's appetite any.

For the rest of the meal Taillefer had a pouch of hard biscuits he shared out, while Sawyer and Marks brought water from a nearby spring.

As they ate, Pel kept looking for Stoddard's return, but there was no sign of the man; when he suggested that a share be set aside for him, Raven simply shook his head.

Amy ate her share quietly, without complaint, and kept it down — she seemed more interested in the biscuits than the meat, however.

The entire party was gathered around the cooking fire in a circle, more or less; the three women were seated together on one side, between Ted Deranian and Albert Singer, while the other men were arranged in no particular order. Pel found himself between Sawyer and Valadrakul; Raven was seated on Sawyer's other side, Taillefer just beyond Valadrakul.

When everyone had eaten, and had brushed crumbs from their hands and clothes, and Valadrakul had collected the offal and gnawed bones in a heap on the dead animal's hide for later burial in sacrifice to the Goddess the Faerie folk worshipped, Pel asked loudly, "Should we get down to business now, or should we wait for Stoddard?"

Raven glared silently at him; Valadrakul looked up from the badger skin to say quietly, "Messire Brown, speak you no more of Raven's man. Stoddard left in the night, whither we know not, without leave nor notice. We can but assume that he has left Raven's service, as did so many others, and that we'll not see him more."

Startled, Pel turned to Raven for confirmation; the nobleman nodded, once.

It had never occurred to Pel, despite Stoddard's complaints, that Stoddard would *really* desert.

"Oh," he said. Then he recovered himself. "Well, then, let's get on with it!"

"On with *what?*" Wilkins demanded.

"On with deciding what to do next, of course," Pel said. "Taillefer says he won't open the space-warp for us, and we don't seem to be able to force him — so how do we get home?"

"Maybe we don't," Wilkins growled.

"And you'll all be made welcome by those of us who yet resist Shadow's foul dominion," Raven said. "Live you among us, and join our fight!"

"I say we go back to the ship," Marks said. "Maybe they've sent a rescue party. Or maybe the lieutenant's got some plans of his own."

"We can check that easily enough," Susan said. She leaned forward to speak past Amy, to Prossie. "Did they send a rescue party?"

*P*rossie had been sitting quietly, not listening, not thinking, but just *being;* it was something she had never really done until very recently. All her life, back in the Empire, no matter where she was sent, no matter where she lived, she had had to either listen, or to actively shut out the constant background noise of other minds; she had never, ever been able to sit and to do absolutely *nothing,* to neither think nor heed the world around her. The Empire did not allow telepaths that sort of isolation; telepaths were watched and guarded, always kept aboard crowded ships or in crowded military installations or in crowded cities. Telepaths, even should one somehow find herself far away from all ordinary minds, were always in contact with the far-flung network of their clan, always open to the common chitchat of their sibs and cousins; even their dreams were shared, built up of the gossip passing back and forth around them and the images that drifted through a shared unconscious.

In Prossie's brief stay on Earth she had been too frightened by the strangeness of mental silence, too lonely, too worried about what would become of her, to really appreciate the virtues of solitude. A jail cell on an alien world, she thought, was hardly the best place for a young woman to look into herself.

And at first, here in Faerie, she had been too busy worrying about survival, too concerned with the politics of Base One, too involved with events — and she had had Carrie, sending to her, listening to her, keeping her in touch.

But since she had cut herself loose, told Carrie to break off, she had begun to drift inward, to look down into the depths of her own mind, depths that she had never really acknowledged to exist until now.

She knew, of course, that minds all exist on multiple levels, sometimes in parallel and contradictory consciousness — she had seen for herself that people could believe things at the same time they saw them for nonsense, and never notice the discrepancy; she had seen that the same person could feel love, hate, and indifference, all at once, toward something. She had known that there were layers of memory and emotion, piled up upon each other ever since infancy, though she had always been forbidden to dig down into all that accumulated experience.

But she had never, before this, thought that there must be such layers in her *own* mind. She had never, before this, tried to explore those layers.

But during the walk across the Starlinshire Downs, the wait for Taillefer at the Castle Regisvert, she had begun to wonder. She found herself thinking of things, almost at random, that she had not thought of in months, or years — and for the first time in her life, she couldn't attribute it to leakage from the thoughts of those around her.

These odd bits of thought, and of memory, must be coming from *her.*

And when she reached that realization, she began to deliberately *look* for them, to search her own memories, her own feelings — as she had been forbidden to, back in the Empire, where the government wanted all their telepaths to be nothing more than communication devices, with no thoughts or desires of their own.

She had never thought of that as something *bad* before. She had been trained to think that the Empire had been merciful and kind in not simply killing all the telepaths, as a danger to the state — or simply allowing hostile mobs to kill them. Everyone she knew had told her that, had *believed* that, and it was almost impossible for her to disagree when she could see that belief in the minds around her. That the Empire had done so because they found telepaths useful she had always known and accepted; that was the price of survival.

But it wasn't *fair.* She had been denied all her own thoughts.

And, she discovered as she slept on the cold stone floor of Regisvert, her own dreams, as well. Her dreams that night were fragmentary and uneasy; her mind was not accustomed to constructing its own, without outside influence.

When she awoke she tried to remember those dreams, and could not; she sat there, groping to recover images, as the soldiers trapped and butchered the badger. She ate silently, letting her own memories drift up from wherever they had been buried, enjoying the sensation of not thinking, not listening, but just being herself.

And then she realized everyone was staring at her, that someone had asked her a question.

Susan repeated, "Did Base One send a rescue party?"

Prossie blinked, and said, "I don't know." Recovering quickly, she added, "I've been out of touch; should I see if I can make contact and ask?"

She saw some of the others glancing uneasily at one another; she saw Wilkins making a familiar, hated gesture to Marks, the clawed finger-wiggling sign used to tease telepaths, the sign that meant "freak" or "monster."

"If you could," Susan said.

"I'll try," Prossie said. She sat up straighter and closed her eyes — which was just for show, not necessary, but it seemed to be called for in this instance.

She didn't say anything to Wilkins, didn't acknowledge his gesture, but inside she hated him with an intensity she had never before allowed herself, a hate that was hot and crawling in her skull, a hate that was the cumulative effect of a thousand memories collected throughout her lifetime, from infancy right up to now, of being loathed just for what she *was*, regardless of what she did, or *who* she was.

Maybe she wouldn't try at all; why should she help Wilkins and his like? How would anyone know?

But it had been Susan who asked, not Wilkins. Prossie wondered why anyone cared, why they thought of it just now — she hadn't been listening to the conversation at all, she realized.

But whether she tried or not made little difference, really; it was up to Carrie, and as she sat, mind open and receptive, she realized that Carrie wasn't listening, wasn't sending, wasn't there at all as far as Prossie could tell. No one else made contact, either.

She opened her eyes and started to speak, then caught herself.

Why were they asking about rescues?

The only possible reason was that they were hoping to go back to the ship and be rescued themselves.

There were monsters back there. Shadow would have taken an interest in the ship by now. To go back there would be insanely dangerous. And even if by some miracle the Empire really *had* sent a rescue party, which they had certainly had no intention of doing when she was last in contact with Carrie, Prossie did not *want* to go back and be rescued.

"No rescue," she said. "They've decided not to risk it. We're on our own."

It was a lie — but who cared? These people would never know unless they returned to the Empire, and Prossie would never go back there, never go back to the hatred and oppression, the rules and limits, the constant barrage of thought.

Right now, though, she thought she had better pay closer attention to what was being said.

"I just want to go home," Amy said.

"Me, too," Pel said.

"I want to wake up," Ted said. "I'm tired of this."

"Same thing," Pel told him.

"I'm not real interested in staying around here, either," Wilkins said. "The question is, what we can do about it?"

"If nobody's rescued the lieutenant," Sawyer asked Prossie, "what *has* happened to those guys?"

"I don't know," Prossie said. "I don't have any way to find out; they're cut off, no communications." She looked Sawyer in the eye.

Sawyer frowned, obviously unhappy with the answer — or with Prossie's behavior.

"I'd send you all home," Raven said, "if 'twas in my power. Alas, 'tis not. Think you, then, on what you'd have in the stead of that — would you join me in the fight 'gainst Shadow? Though in truth I'd rather the weapons of Earth, yet would willing hands be welcome e'en without."

"You won't reconsider?" Pel asked Taillefer.

The wizard shook his head. "Nay," he said. "To open a portal would be to die at Shadow's hand, and I've no wish to die."

Pel looked at him, then back at Raven, then around at the others, at Ted and Amy and Susan, Ted with his bandaged head, Amy leaning weakly against Susan, who stood clutching her big black purse. The wizard Taillefer, the only one here who could get them out of this storybook world and back home to Earth and sanity, but too afraid of Shadow to try; Raven, who wanted guns to fight Shadow; Ted, who thought he was dreaming; poor sick Amy; Susan, with the revolver in her purse . . .

Suddenly, the pieces fell into place for Pel, as he stared first at Susan's purse, then at Taillefer and Valadrakul.

Wizards.

Or rather, he corrected himself, "Wizards," the movie by Ralph Bakshi.

While he had been thinking of all this as something out of a story ever since Grummetty first stepped from the basement wall, ever since he first heard Raven speak, up until now he hadn't settled on just *one* story. He had thought of Tolkien and "Twilight Zone" and a dozen others, but none of those had shown him a way out, back to real life.

"Wizards" was another matter.

Of course, this *wasn't* just a story, this *was* real life, but still . . .

And there was something else. Taillefer was the only one *here* who knew the portal spell, but there was someone else who knew it even better, someone who just might not be quite the villain it was painted.

Of course, convincing anyone else to try that would be difficult. The gun was easier.

"Listen," he said, turning back to Taillefer, "if Shadow were dead, you could send us home, right?"

"Aye, surely," Taillefer said, mystified. "Were Shadow dead 'twould be as a new dawn, and all would be different indeed; I'd have no fear of its creatures, if any even survived. More, methinks the death of Shadow would wreak great change upon the flow of magic through all the world, and all who study the arcane arts would find new strengths to draw on, were Shadow's web sundered. A portal would be but the least of spells, surely, and gladly would I perform it."

"Friend Pel," Raven said, "an Shadow were dead . . welladay, 'twould be glorious beyond measure; 'tis the end I've sought all my life. But how to achieve this miracle? Shadow's life has spanned centuries; it draws unnatural vitality from its nets of power, that it ages not. How then, think you to end this? A blade is as naught; no spell can touch Shadow; no mere mortal can hope to outlive it."

"All right, Shadow can't be killed by anything from this land, but what about a weapon from another world?" He pointed at Susan.

Raven followed Pel's pointing finger, and Pel knew from his expression that he had understood Pel's plan immediately.

So did most of the others.

"Would it work?" Susan asked. "I mean, it's just a bullet, this isn't any sort of big magic."

"It might," Pel said.

"And how would you administer this 'bullet,' Messire Pel?" Taillefer asked. "Need you enter Shadow's fortress? I'd not risk a farthing 'gainst all the gold in Goringham for your chances, then."

"We'd need to get pretty close, yeah," Pel admitted.

"'Tis not to be done, then," Taillefer said, with clear finality.

"No?" Pel demanded, challengingly. "How do you know? You ever *tried* it?"

"I yet live, do I not?" Taillefer retorted. "No, I've not made the trial."

"Then how do you *know?*" Pel repeated. "*I* say it's worth a try — at least, for some of us." He hesitated, then plunged on. "In fact," he said, "I think it might be time for some of us to go see Shadow even *without* the gun. After all, if *you* won't send us home, maybe *it* will!"

Raven stared at Pel, mouth open in dumbfoundment; Taillefer stared for a moment, then burst out laughing.

"Oh, foolish man," he said, when he could speak again, "think you that Shadow will do your bidding, an you walk up to the fortress and ask ever so politely? 'Oh, please, destroyer of kingdoms, ravager of nations, master of all the world, send me home, though I've nothing to pay, and no reason to give that you'll not better to strike me dead this instant.' Is *that* what you'd say, brown one?"

"Something like . . . no," Pel said. He put his hands to his hips and glared at the wizard. "No, *not* like that. Listen, *you* may be a sworn enemy of Shadow, but *we* aren't." He waved an arm to take in both Earthpeople and Imperials. "All we know about it is what we've heard from *you,* and from your friends. How do we know Shadow's any worse than you are? And who says we have nothing to offer it?"

"You speak treason," Raven said quietly, his hand falling to where his sword-hilt should have been.

"You're calling me a traitor?"

"Aye . . ." Raven began.

"Traitor to *what?*" Pel demanded, cutting the aristocrat off short. "I'm a citizen of the United States of America, I'm not one of your underlings, *Lord* Raven! And even if I were — where's Stoddard this morning? For that matter, where's Donald a' Benton, or Elani, or Grummetty, or any of the others? Isn't Shadow the government around here? Seems to me that *you're* the fugitive from the law, and anyone who follows you and doesn't have the sense to give up like Stoddard did is just buying an early death. Where's my *wife,* Lord Raven? Where's my daughter? They're *dead,* from following you . . ."

"They're slain by *Shadow,* Pel Brown," Raven countered. "Would you join your wife's murderer, then?"

"*Who says* it was Shadow?" Pel shouted. "*You* do, and your buddies in the Galactic Empire! *I* don't know who killed her — hell, I don't even know she's really dead, I just have your word on it, yours and the Empire's — *I* never got to see them! *I* didn't see the bodies!" He had stepped forward, as had Raven; the two of them stood with their noses an inch or two apart, shouting in each other's faces.

"Pel," Susan said, putting a hand on his shoulder.

Pel fell silent, but stayed face to face with Raven, glaring down at the shorter man, for a long moment. At last, though, he backed away.

"I don't care what you say, Raven," Pel announced. "Or any of the rest of you, for that matter. Prossie says the Empire's abandoned us, and Taillefer won't send me home; well, the only other person — or *thing* — that can send me home is Shadow, so I'm going to go *see* Shadow, and if I can't make a deal with it, I'll do my damnedest to kill it, and if I do *that,* my price is Taillefer's portal spell. So I'm going looking for Shadow. Now, who's coming with me?"

He looked around at the faces, at expressions of confusion, dismay, and even fear.

"You're mad," Taillefer announced loudly.

"I'll come," Susan said quietly. "At least for now. You may want the pistol, after all."

"Makes no difference to me," Ted said with a shrug. "I'll come."

"Whaddaya think?" Wilkins asked, turning toward Marks and Sawyer.

"I'll go along for now," Singer said.

"I'm in," Marks said.

Sawyer hesitated. "Whatever you guys decide," he said.

"Then we go," Wilkins concluded.

*A*my listened to Pel and Raven argue, listened to the soldiers make their decision. When Susan said she would go with Pel, Amy felt as if something had fallen out from beneath her insides somewhere — how could Susan say that without even a glance at Amy, to see what she thought? Susan was betraying her.

No, she wasn't, Amy corrected herself; Susan was looking after herself. She wasn't really a *friend,* after all — they'd been acting like friends for weeks, but that was because they were the only two American women around; they didn't have anyone *else* to talk to. Susan wasn't really her friend, Susan was her *attorney*; she had to remember that.

And Susan was right, anyway; they had to go to Shadow. If Taillefer was right, if Amy was really carrying Walter's child — she thought she must be, she realized now that she hadn't had her period since early in her captivity on Zeta Leo III, and a baby would have to be Walter's, she hadn't been with another man in almost a year — then she had to get *home*, back to a civilized world, where she could abort it, or put it up for adoption, or do *something*. She didn't want her dead rapist's child. And she didn't want to go through pregnancy and labor and childbirth in this stupid primitive world, this place out of some horrible old fairy tale where for all she knew leeches were the latest thing in medical care.

And she wasn't a young woman, she had no business having a first child at her age — she was used to being childless, she liked it, she didn't *want* a child.

And if she did, she wouldn't want it to be by that sadistic bastard Walter.

She had to go to Shadow with Pel, even if it meant risking death, because just *staying* in this world meant risking death. She could catch a plague, she could die of something in the water, she could bleed to death.

She had to get home, by any means possible.

"I'll come," she said.

*P*rossie had begun to drift away into her own thoughts again, but when she heard all the different voices speaking up, saying whether they would accompany Pel Brown, she listened, she thought back to what she had heard without paying attention.

Going to confront Shadow — that was insane! She had seen and heard memories, back at Base One, from Raven and Valadrakul and Elani and Stoddard; even allowing for added coloration, she knew from those memories that Shadow was cruel and ruthless, willing to commit atrocities to further its ends or remove those who opposed it.

But they were all going along — Susan and Amy and Bill Marks and all of them. If she didn't agree, she would be left behind, with Raven and the wizards, the only foreigner among them.

That would be awful.

And maybe she could convince the others to turn back. Maybe they would come to their senses.

"I'll go," she said.

If she hadn't been trained since childhood not to venture her own opinions, she would have added, But I don't like it.

*R*aven watched with annoyance as voice after voice spoke up, hand after hand raised, agreeing to accompany Pel Brown on his mad errand.

He didn't really have any great *need* for this oddly-assorted group, but he was reluctant to let them go heedlessly and needlessly to their deaths without some further attempt to save them, perhaps to win some benefit from all this disastrous series of events.

And of course, the lot of them might come to their senses when they learned just what they had taken upon themselves. When they saw Shadow's fortress, and realized that none could penetrate it to confront Shadow itself, the survivors might well be valuable additions to the forces of resistance.

They might also, in their madness, learn something useful of Shadow's defenses — surely not enough to allow them to enter Shadow's keep, but something that could be turned to use someday, by those wiser and mightier than themselves.

"All of you are fools," he said, "and I feel I must accompany you as far as I dare, that I might do what I can to save you from your folly.

*T*aillefer watched with mounting astonishment as one after another in the party announced his or her intention of bearding Shadow in its lair, of marching in wide-eyed innocence to certain destruction.

When even Raven and a reluctant Valadrakul agreed to go along, at least for some part of the way, Taillefer flung his hands up.

"May the Goddess preserve me!" he shouted. "You have, every one of you, lost your senses! I'd call on the Goddess to save you all, if I thought it possible even for Her! And as 'tis not, I'll take my leave of you all, lest this madness be catching! Go, then, and die, and I'll pray for your souls!" He spread his arms and spoke the Word of Power he had prepared, and the wind rose, filling his cloak.

He felt the air pressing him upward, felt the currents of power beneath this place, power that led to Shadow, he knew, but power that he could turn to his own ends, at least for now. He drew upon it to conjure the wind that roared about him.

He grew lighter and lighter, until at last the air, and the magical power behind it, lifted him off his feet.

A moment later the others watched as the wizard literally blew away, up into the sky, bound for his distant home.

Chapter Fifteen

*Y*ou're sure there's no magic ring, or mystic gem, or something?" Pel asked Raven as they walked down the western slope, away from the thorn-covered ruins of Castle Regisvert, and down into a broad green valley. Grey clouds hung on the horizon before them, but where they walked the sun shone warmly. A bird sang somewhere in the distance, and the rich scents of late spring filled the air. "Maybe Shadow keeps its heart in a bowl somewhere, or something like that?" he suggested.

Raven shook his head. "I've heard naught, in all my days, of any such device. Shadow draws its power from the magic that flows through earth and sky, and weaves that into its web; it needs no rings nor jewelry, any more than does our own Valadrakul."

"Does Valadrakul weave these same currents, then?" Pel inquired, looking back at the wizard.

"Indeed, he draws 'pon them," Raven agreed, "though not as Shadow does; Valadrakul and the other free wizards, as they tell me, make their magic but from the crumbs that fall from Shadow's table, as it were. They weave no webs outside their own bodies, hold no elaborate traceries at the ready, own no patterns save those in their own minds, but instead pluck away what they can when chance allows, and shape the magicks within themselves." He hesitated, then added, "Ah, in truth, I've most probably made nonsense of it, for 'tis none of mine that we speak of here, friend Pel. If you'd have it right, you'd best speak with Valadrakul, and not myself."

Pel nodded, and dropped back a pace to where the wizard walked.

Valadrakul turned and stared silently at the Earthman as they marched a dozen steps farther down the highway.

Pel realized that this was the first time he had deliberately and directly addressed Valadrakul in normal conversation, and he wasn't sure just how to begin. At last, though, he said, "You're a wizard, right?"

Wilkins, a few feet away, snickered.

"Have you not seen for yourself, Pellinore Brown?" Valadrakul replied.

"I suppose, yeah," Pel admitted. Wilkins snorted, but Pel ignored him. "So tell me about wizards."

Valadrakul blinked, then smiled crookedly. "You'd have me open to you all the secrets of my kind, the mysteries we hold dear, the teachings I struggled for a dozen years to absorb, here as we walk? Think you, perhaps, that what you ask might not be so simple as that?"

"Yeah, well," Pel said, annoyed, "I didn't mean that. I mean, tell me why, if you're a wizard and Shadow's a wizard, why Shadow's so much more powerful than you are."

"And who told you, I pray, that Shadow is a wizard?"

"Didn't you . . ." Pel hesitated. "Or maybe it was Raven — I don't know, but *somebody* told me."

Valadrakul didn't reply, and angrily, Pel demanded, "All right, if Shadow isn't a wizard, what *is* it?"

"'Tis Shadow," Valadrakul said with a shrug. "It needs no other name, for there's no other like it, nor has ever been. What in truth it is, no one knows."

"Didn't one of you tell me that it started out as an ordinary wizard?"

"Perhaps," Valadrakul admitted.

"Then *did* it start out as an ordinary wizard?"

"So 'tis said. And perhaps 'tis true. 'Tis no wizard now, though — not as we use the word."

"So what happened, then?" Pel asked. "How come Shadow's so incredibly powerful, and the rest of you wizards aren't?"

"Good question," Wilkins said. "Took you long enough to get it straight, though."

Pel glared at him for an instant, then turned back to Valadrakul.

The wizard looked thoughtfully at the ground for a moment, and the entire party moved onward a few yards before he spoke again.

"Raven spoke to you of the flow of magic through the world," Valadrakul said at last.

Pel nodded.

"'Tis not exactly a flow, you understand — nor is it precisely in *this* world. The exact nature . . . well, you've not the understanding." The wizard glanced up at Pel.

"All right," Pel said. "Explain it however you can, don't worry about getting all the details right."

Valadrakul nodded. "As you wish." He gazed about at the surrounding greenery. "If you think of the sources of nature's magic as springs, from which flow not water but the invisible energies that we wizards wield, you will have but a poor understanding, for the flow is not as water, nor as light, nor as any other thing in the commonplace world. It permeates all the world, yet varies throughout, from the faintest of traces in one spot to a bursting torrent in another. And when a wizard draws upon it, it is not consumed — the well cannot be emptied. There are flows, but they are not streams — more oft, they're loops, spinning endlessly. And there are points, and lines, and patterns."

"All right," Pel said. "I think I have the idea."

Valadrakul nodded. "Well," he said, "a wizard such as myself, such as all modern wizards, can draw upon whatever energy might be found in the place where that wizard stands, and no more. I can sense these energies, but only dimly; they are not as light to me, but as, perhaps, faint sounds — I can perhaps tell you, that way there is a great power source, but I cannot tell you how far, nor its exact nature, nor can I in any way draw it nearer. At most, if I find a locus I remember, I can perhaps use its peculiar nature to my advantage — as when I used what might be described as a line of magical energy to send a message to Taillefer."

"Okay," Pel acknowledged. "I think I get it."

"Of old, though," Valadrakul continued, "there were wizards who had a greater understanding of these forces, who could perhaps see them, and map them, and distinguish the patterns in them. This higher art, these pattern wizards, these are now thought to be lost — though I'd not swear that none might still lurk in the odd corners, hiding from Shadow. 'Twas pattern wizards who provided much of the art that we lesser wizards use; they were more powerful than we, and for that reason Shadow has made every effort to obliterate them, lest they be a threat to its dominion."

"So Shadow was a pattern wizard?" Pel asked.

Valadrakul shook his head. "Nay," he said, "listen further. 'Tis said that long ago, there was yet a third tier among those who wield magic — those who could not only perceive the patterns, but could *alter* them, could alter the flow of energy, could divert one stream into another, could weave the threads of magic as if they were merest wool, could form matrices of magic that they carried about with them — not the mere patterns of spells trapped within their minds, as we yet do in our small ways, but great intricate webs of the raw stuff of magic itself, that might be formed into whatever spells they needed. They had no need to make do with what powers were at hand, but could draw to themselves whatsoever powers they needed, through these matrices they held. Matrix wizards, these magic-weavers were called."

"And Shadow was a matrix wizard?" Pel asked, remembering what Raven had said about Shadow's webs and networks.

Valadrakul nodded. "Aye," he said. "The greatest of them. And Shadow built about itself a structure that stretches out to embrace all the magic in this world — it gathered in all the lines to itself, drew down the wells, absorbed the matrices of all other matrix wizards, and left nowhere untouched If another somehow learned the lost art of the matrix wizards, and sought to draw into himself even the slightest part of the world's magic, Shadow would sense it, would feel the tug upon its web as a spider feels a fly's struggles. Should that happen, Shadow would reach out and strike down whoever had dared to tamper with its networks." He sighed. "Indeed, 'twould seem that that's why Taillefer would send you nowhere — the portal spell impinges upon Shadow's matrix, tugs at its web, as it were."

"Oh," Pel said. The explanation made sense, he supposed.

Or did it?

"Wait a minute," he said, as they trudged onward. "If Shadow's linked to *all* the magical energy in the world, doesn't it feel something any time *any* wizard works *any* magic?"

"A good question," Valadrakul said. "But alas, we've no good answer. It may be that Shadow senses it as we sense the distant hum of insects, as something always there and not worth the trouble to stop. It may be that our spells are so weak that Shadow sees them not at all, as you and I cannot see the stars in the sun's daylight." He shrugged. "We know not the truth of the matter."

"Oh," Pel said again.

He was hardly satisfied, but how could he demand that Valadrakul tell him something the wizard didn't know himself? Shadow's true nature would have to remain a mystery.

*T*he idea that she might be several weeks pregnant with Walter's child was appalling, but somehow it was a relief, too — it was an explanation, and one that fit all the facts. What's more, it was one that Amy understood, more or less, and one with a definite end in sight. AIDS could take years, other diseases could be sudden or chronic, but pregnancy was nine months, at most, give or take a few weeks.

And it wasn't a death sentence. Childbirth was dangerous, certainly, especially if she couldn't get back to Earth, but she wasn't going to follow Grummetty and Alella and die horribly in a matter of days.

At least for the moment, having an answer, any answer, was better than nothing. And crying all over Susan and Prossie had helped, too.

Perhaps as a result of her lessened worry, perhaps just because her pregnancy was progressing past that point, she was feeling better. She still felt heavy and clumsy in the stronger gravity of Faerie, still tired easily, but her stomach was no longer cramping, and she felt no urge to vomit.

Thank God, she thought, for small blessings.

And being able to think about something other than her own insides and the possibility of imminent death brought her to wondering just what she and the others were doing. Yes, they had to get back to Earth — but were they really just walking right into Shadow's home territory, marching right up to Shadow's lair? Wasn't that, well . . . suicidal?

Did Pel know what he was doing?

She had voted to do this herself, she knew that, but she was having second thoughts now. At the time of the decision she had been panicky, desperate to do anything that would get her home; now she was thinking a bit more clearly.

Would this get her home, or would it get her killed?

And if it would get her killed, what should she be doing instead?

She glanced at Raven, but he appeared to be lost in thought, and besides, he was a liar and a thief, not to be trusted — she thought he meant well, that he was sincere in thinking that everything he did was justified by the need to defeat Shadow, but still, she couldn't trust him.

Valadrakul was better, but he was explaining something to Pel. And those two were the only natives of Faerie left in the party — Elani and Squire Donald were dead, Stoddard and Taillefer had abandoned the group.

Raven kept talking about Shadow as if it were some ultimate evil, and Pel always thought he meant it literally, like some monster from the fairy tales, or a movie villain, but Amy didn't think she believed in stuff like that.

There were real villains, though, lots of them, and if she couldn't quite believe that Shadow was Evil Incarnate, she could believe that it was the local version of Adolf Hitler, or Stalin or Pol Pot or the Ayatollah Khomeini. The woman in the cottage had told Raven some of Shadow's rules, and they'd sounded like something Hitler or Stalin might have come up with.

Well, then, what if she thought of herself as having somehow landed in Nazi Germany? What would she have done?

She'd have tried to get *out*, of course — across the Alps to Switzerland, like the von Trapps, or to England or somewhere.

Except there *was* no Switzerland or England here. Shadow had won its war and conquered the entire world.

So what then?

There was an underground, of course — Raven was proof of that. She had already seen the underground, by traveling with Raven and Valadrakul, and talking with Taillefer, and they'd made promises to get her home, and then they hadn't been able to deliver.

Well, to hell with them, then. She wasn't going to join the underground and become a freedom fighter if they couldn't keep their promises. And it didn't look as if they stood any chance of winning the war, anyway.

Undergrounds never won their wars without outside help, anyway — she was pretty sure she'd read that somewhere.

But to return to her analogy, here she was, in the Faerie equivalent of Nazi Germany, with no way to get out of the country to Switzerland or England. She was going to stay in Germany unless Hitler himself decided to send her home, so she was on her way to Berlin to ask.

Was that going to work?

Well, it might; she wasn't the local equivalent of a Jew, so far as she could tell, or otherwise fodder for the concentration camps. If there *was* an equivalent to the Jews, from what Valadrakul had said she supposed it was wizards. She certainly wasn't a wizard.

She was a foreigner, of course, and Hitler had hated foreigners, but he hadn't just killed them out of hand.

And besides, there was no point in carrying the analogy *too* far.

So they were going to Berlin to ask a favor of Hitler, more or less — and if that failed, Pel wanted to try to assassinate him.

What were the odds of getting away with that?

Probably nil. She just couldn't imagine a bunch of lost American tourists walking in and killing Hitler, which would be the equivalent.

And she couldn't see how they could hope to destroy Shadow, whatever it was, *and* get away with it; despite what Pel seemed to think, this wasn't some silly adventure story. Things like that didn't happen in real life.

But maybe Shadow would send them home.

And what else could she do?

Well, if she were in Germany, she could just settle down somewhere, find work, or someone who would take her in, and just hope nobody reported her to the Gestapo as she got on with her life. She didn't suppose there'd be much call for an interior decorator in a place like Faerie, but she could find something to do, she was sure. And she wouldn't even have to learn the language — the people here spoke English.

When they came to a town, she decided, she'd do that, she'd settle down and make the best of things. Not a farm — she wanted nothing to do with rural life. But sooner or later, surely, they'd find a place with shops and some semblance of civilization, and she could stay there. The others could go on to Shadow's fortress if they wanted, and if Shadow agreed to help they could send for her, but she didn't want to walk in there with them.

She'd have the baby to worry about, of course, if she settled down and stayed.

Well, maybe that wouldn't be so bad; she could claim to be widowed, that she'd left her home because she couldn't manage alone with the baby coming. And just because it was Walter's child didn't mean it would be a monster; she could bring it up properly, and it would probably turn out fine.

And it might die, anyway.

That was a horrible thought, she told herself, but she couldn't help it. Her situation was so awful — trapped in an alien, uncomfortable, hostile world, carrying her rapist's child — that she thought a little morbid speculation was entirely justified.

She looked ahead, at Raven and Pel and Valadrakul, and decided she wouldn't mention anything to them yet. They might not approve. Time enough when they found someplace she could stay, some suitable little town or village.

That woman's cottage had been primitive, but Amy didn't think it was too uncomfortable, really. If she could find a place no worse than that, she thought she could stand it.

She wondered if Prossie or Susan would be interested in staying with her.

*T*he land undulated, Prossie decided. It was a fancy word, but it fit. The countryside was an apparently-endless series of gentle-sloped ridges, and their path led them up and over each one. The westward slopes, the ones they went down, seemed longer and steeper than the eastward sides; that meant they were gradually descending these ripples, coming down from the forest, and that eventually, if they continued, they would reach either the sea or the flat plain of the coast.

It also meant, though, that most of the time they couldn't see where they were going, but each time they topped a ridge the whole world would suddenly be spread out before them, a green expanse of small farms, groves, meadows, orchards that seemed to go on forever, arranged in the rows formed by the ridges — or rather, Prossie corrected herself, the Downs.

From each summit they could see a new valley, and then the tops of the succeeding ridges, fading away in the distance. The horizon was lost in mist from the first few ridgetops, but as the day progressed and the air warmed the mist receded and vanished. From the next two ridges everything was sharp and clear — but then the air began to grow hazy again as the temperature continued to rise. Dark clouds hovered on the western horizon, far ahead of them, but drew no nearer.

There was a pleasant sort of repetition to it all. Prossie supposed that eventually they would arrive somewhere, but she was in no particular hurry; she had been on perhaps a dozen worlds in her lifetime, and despite the high gravity this was one of the most pleasant she had yet encountered. The spaceborne habitats and bases where she had spent most of her time weren't even in the running.

Also, the long walk gave her time to think, to meditate, to remember, and to just *be.*

She thought back to her childhood, remembering when she had first realized that she was a distinct individual. She knew, from reading other minds, that normal babies began to differentiate themselves from their environment when they were just a few weeks old, and had a pretty good grasp on the concept of "I" by the time they were toddlers; telepathic children, though, had a rougher time of it. Distinguishing their own thoughts from those around them, and from the network of other telepaths, was not easy.

Prossie had been slow; she had been almost four when she finally got a firm grip on which thoughts were her own and which came from outside. The key had been when she finally learned to close out other minds.

By then she had learned any number of things that normal children didn't encounter until much later — she knew about sex, from several different viewpoints; she knew about death, and addiction, and lust, and grief; she knew about the dark, sick thoughts that lurked below so many minds.

And she had accepted all that as parts of herself, because she was part of all humanity, a link in the chain of telepaths that bound her species together. She knew that people didn't speak about those darknesses, the raw lusts and searing pain, but it wasn't until years later that she really understood why. She heard people thinking, over and over, that their thoughts were wrong, were different from everyone else, but she had known it wasn't true.

It was so much easier to just accept it all, the foulness and shame and guilt, along with the joy and beauty and peace, and to not think about any of it, to not distinguish any of it as "good" or "bad." It just *was*. It was in everyone, in varying degrees.

Except, of course, in herself, since she was a mere passive receiver, a relay, a servant of the Galactic Empire, not responsible for anything except performing her duty.

But now, thinking back, she knew that she had the darknesses in herself, too. That disgusting Bascombe, the Under-Secretary for Interdimensional Affairs, hadn't had a second thought about sending his own people out to die, just to help his own reputation, and she had, somewhere in the back of her mind, thought she was better than that, that she would never have done such a thing — but hadn't she left Lieutenant Dibbs and the others to die? Paul, who had raped her back on Zeta Leo III, had been awash in fantasies of power and abuse, and she had never done anything like that — but she had never had the chance, and hadn't she deliberately lied to the people here, to manipulate them into doing what she wanted, and hadn't she enjoyed the feeling of power it gave her?

And after all, hadn't she betrayed her own family and her Empire?

But then, her family and Empire had virtually enslaved her from infancy, in their own way just as much as Paul had when he bought her at auction and took her to his home in chains.

Did that make her treason acceptable?

Perhaps it did, but it was still a betrayal. Certainly, her little crimes weren't as bad as Bascombe's or Paul's or the Empire's, but she was no pure little innocent.

And now that she was alone in her head, she could look at that, could take the time to consider her own motives and see just what was lurking down there in the back of her mind.

And she was discovering, as she walked across the Starlinshire Downs, that she had the same drives as anyone else — power and pride and sex and fear and anger, the need for love, the need for acceptance, all tangled together into her own individual mix.

She was thinking about her reasons for serving the Empire so willingly for so long, the fear of punishment, the acceptance by her family, the pride in her work, when she felt Carrie's presence.

She blinked, almost stumbled on the latest upgrade.

"Are you all right, Prossie?" Carrie's thoughts were tinged with worry — nothing serious, just concern for Prossie.

"I'm fine," she thought back, "just fine." To her own surprise as much as Carrie's, her reply carried an edge of annoyance; she had already become accustomed to the mental isolation, the partial sensory deprivation, and she had been enjoying it. The sudden contact came as an intrusion on her own meditations.

"What about the others?"

Prossie looked around as she topped the rise. "Wilkins and Marks and Sawyer and Singer are all fine; the Earthpeople are alive, anyway, and seem to be functioning. Raven and Valadrakul are the only natives we still have with us."

"What about Lieutenant Dibbs and the others?"

"How should I know?" The edge of anger was stronger and more obvious than ever, Carrie could hardly miss it, but Prossie didn't care. "We left them back at the ship; you know that."

"You haven't heard anything more?"

"No."

"What about that wizard who was going to send people home?"

"Didn't work out," Prossie replied. She wasn't really paying very close attention any more; she had just looked out across the valley before them, and realized that this time they weren't just going to pass more scattered, isolated farms.

This time, a town stood in the center of the valley. She couldn't see very much; the afternoon air was hazy and humid, wavering in the heat, but the collection of stone and wood structures half a mile or so away was definitely a town.

"So what's happening, then?" Carrie demanded. "Where are you going? You're walking, I can sense that — where to?"

"We're going to Shadow's fortress," Prossie said, studying the town. The highway widened out to form the main street; another road crossed at the center of town, and a few narrow back-streets filled in the rest.

For several seconds Carrie didn't reply; when she did, she said, "Prossie, that's crazy."

"I know," Prossie said, taking her first step down the slope. "But it should make General Hart happy, shouldn't it?"

Chapter Sixteen

*A*my smiled weakly at the sight of the town. She hadn't smiled much lately;

it felt surprisingly good.

It wasn't much of a town; she doubted the whole thing covered more than about two dozen acres. Still, it was something more than a farm. The buildings lined the main street pretty solidly for a good two hundred yards, with more houses scattered across the surrounding area; she could see signboards hanging above doorways, which meant businesses, and there appeared to be a square at the crossroads, which seemed to imply some sort of local government. A platform was set up in the square, with people on it — Amy couldn't make out any details, but that seemed a pleasantly homey feature.

She thought she caught the scent of wood smoke, but she wasn't sure; and even if she did, she couldn't be sure it came from the town.

It wasn't Goshen, Maryland — but then, Goshen was just a spread-out bedroom community, a sort of annex to Gaithersburg and Rockville, themselves more or less suburbs of Washington. Amy couldn't expect anything like that here. This town was probably the best she could reasonably hope for.

Besides, her feet hurt too much, and she was too tired, to go any farther.

Now she needed to decide just when to tell the others that she wanted to stay here, not to go on and beard Shadow in its lair.

She glanced around, at Raven and Pel and the others. Raven was frowning angrily, though Amy had no idea why; Pel was staring at the town like a baby studying a new toy, trying to see every bit of it at once. Susan had the wary look of a prowling cat; Prossie had on one of her distant expressions, and Amy wondered whether she was talking to someone back in the Galactic Empire, or whether she was just woolgathering.

The other Imperials weren't paying much attention to the town at all, but simply walking on, chatting amongst themselves. Ted, as usual, wasn't paying attention to anything at all, and Amy couldn't see Valadrakul's face from where she walked.

Nobody was saying anything, which suddenly struck Amy as somehow wrong. This was the first town that any of the Earthpeople or the Imperials had ever seen in this stupid world of Raven's; didn't it deserve some sort of comment?

"Raven," she called, "what's the town called? Is that whatsit, Starlinshire, that the Downs are named for?"

Raven turned and glowered at her for a moment before remembering his manners.

"Nay, lady," he said, "'tis but some lesser town, the local market, perchance; Starlinton be greater by far."

"Do you know its name?" Amy persisted.

Raven shook his head. "Nay," he said. "Who's to know every hamlet and village?"

"I just thought you might, where it's on the highway," she said.

"'Tis in Shadow's inner domain, and that's all I wot," Raven answered, turning his gaze forward again.

The road curved as it descended the slope, and trees grew along the verge, so that once the party left the ridgetop Amy could only catch occasional tantalizing glimpses of the town; each time an especially good view presented itself she would pause and stare, then hurry to catch up to the others.

Every time they passed a farmhouse, Amy thought it might be the outskirts of town; every time, she knew she was being foolish to be disappointed when it was not, but she was disappointed all the same.

The sky was beginning to darken, as well, and the already-thick air seemed to be growing heavier; Amy wondered if they might be caught by a storm before they could reach the town and shelter.

At last, however, one house was followed closely by another, and then another, and then by a smithy — the open-sided building with the open-hearth forge at the center was very much like those Amy had seen in historical recreations at Jamestown and Sturbridge Village, and at Renaissance fairs. The fires were banked, however, and the smith nowhere to be seen.

Three large dogs were chained just below the big bellows, however, black dogs of a breed Amy didn't recognize; these beasts watched the party intently as it passed, obviously ready to defend the smithy against any thieves or invaders. Amy was unsure whether she heard one growling, deep in his throat; whether she did or not, none of them barked, nor made any overtly hostile move.

She could smell them, a hot, doggy smell that she did not care for. She could see muscles tense in the nearest dog's forelegs.

These were serious watchdogs, she decided, not pets. She was careful to stay on the highway and not take so much as a single step on the smithy's grounds.

This was hardly a warm welcome to the town she hoped to make her home. This did not appear to be the sort of place where people left their doors unlocked.

But then, most people didn't leave the doors unlocked in Goshen, either.

Beyond the smithy was a row of houses, small and old but reasonably well-kept. Two old men sat on a bench out front of the third one, staring at the group of strangers.

Amy realized that her party must make a curious sight, with only Raven dressed in anything resembling the local garb — and at that, his velvets were the attire of a nobleman, and there was no sign of a castle or palace or manse anywhere in this town, so even he was out of place. Valadrakul wore his embroidered vest, but over an Imperial uniform, and with his hair cut short, where every other native of Faerie Amy had seen wore it long. The five Imperials were all in their gaudy purple uniforms, now somewhat the worse for wear — especially Prossie's, with the ruined sleeves and the slashes in the side. The four Earthpeople were in old, ill-fitting slacks and T-shirts — if that; poor Pel was bare-chested.

Which probably made him the least-alien of the lot, Amy thought. And even bare-chested he was hardly intimidating; Pel Brown was no Arnold Schwartzenegger, by any means. He was taller than any native of Faerie Amy had seen with the single exception of Stoddard, but he was also pale and flabby and narrow-shouldered.

"Should we ask them for directions or anything?" Amy heard Pel ask Raven quietly.

"Nay, why trouble them?" Raven replied. "I'd sooner we sought an inn or public house, that we might eat a decent meal for once, and wash the dust from our throats, and perhaps even from our clothes. When that's done, our hosts will surely tell us if our road's the one we seek."

Pel nodded, and the party marched on past the seated pair in uneasy silence. The four soldiers stopped talking, for once, and no one else spoke, neither visitor nor native.

Past the two on the bench the highway turned a corner, around an immense oak tree. From that point on the road became a street, lined with houses and shops — though the shops had none of the broad display windows Amy would have expected, and were distinguished from the houses mainly by signboards and what was behind the windows, rather than anything about the architecture. Doors and windows were all closed, many shuttered. The houses were relatively crude — rough-hewn heavy wooden corner posts and lintels exposed, the walls between the posts some sort of yellowish, not-very-smooth plaster that reminded Amy of Bavarian postcards, or beer ads, but without the traditional German decoration. Some walls were patched, some stained, some speckled with mildew or just with dirt. Not a single structure in sight stood more than two stories in height, and many were only one.

The signboards did not have writing on them, but only crude pictures — this one of a loom, that of pottery; Amy supposed, with regret, that most of the locals couldn't read. Maybe, she thought, she could make a living teaching reading and writing — but it still didn't bode well for quality of life here.

The highway had become a street, but it had by no means straightened out; it turned and twisted its way through the town, for no reason that Amy could see. There were no sidewalks, no front lawns, very few trees — and those trees there were were just as likely to be in the center of the street as along the side. The buildings were built wall to wall, broken every three or four houses by a narrow alleyway; most of the alleys were closed off with gates, either of wood or black iron. The whole place smelled of cooked meat and cabbage, of dust, and of urine.

The entire place should have been quaint, Amy thought, but mostly managed to be ugly, instead. She wondered whether Shadow had anything to do with that, or whether it was just the prevailing style in this world.

She also wondered whether those recreated villages and medieval towns back on Earth had been prettied up; none ever looked as ugly as this.

There were people on the street, but most of them, upon spotting the strangers, stepped aside, pressing themselves against walls or ducking out of sight completely, into doorways and alleys. No one invited conversation.

This was not, Amy decided, a friendly place — but maybe that was just as well; if people here minded their own business, then they wouldn't bother her, once she settled in, would they?

Besides, if Shadow was the local equivalent of Hitler, *every* town was probably like this.

Then they rounded the next corner, and came in sight of the town square.

For a moment the party became utterly disorganized as most of the group stopped dead in their tracks, while a few — Raven, Valadrakul, Wilkins, and Marks — kept going. Ted and Susan veered to one side, rather than simply stopping; Ted began babbling quietly to himself, while Sawyer said softly, "Oh, my God."

Amy stood and stared.

The platform in the town square was a gallows, a square perhaps a dozen feet on a side, raised seven or eight feet above the street. At either side a post rose well above the platform, supporting one end of a crossbeam.

Three men were hanging from the beam — three corpses, rather. At first, Amy thought that the nooses had been made with extra rope, and that that was what dangled down past the dead bare feet, but at last her mind acknowledged what her eyes were reporting — that the three men had been disembowelled, their bellies sliced open from breastbone to groin, and that those were loops of rotting intestine that dragged on the wooden planks below.

And the black haze around them wasn't in her mind, it wasn't a sign that she was on the verge of fainting. It was a cloud of flies.

The smell, which had been merely an unnoticed unpleasant whiff a moment before, hit at the same moment as the realization of what she was seeing, and she almost vomited. Perhaps because she had been toughened up by her earlier bouts of nausea, or perhaps for some other reason, she managed to fight it down — a small personal victory, but one she appreciated.

When she could think more clearly again, one thought repeated itself over and over in Amy's mind as she forced herself to walk on down the street.

She wasn't staying here. She wouldn't stay here. She couldn't stay here.

*A*t first it appeared that they might have to physically drag Amy to get her into the grubby little tavern, and Pel didn't really blame her — the place faced on the town square, which would have been reasonable enough if it weren't for that bloody gibbet standing there with those hideous rotting things hanging from it. Pel was none too enthusiastic about going anywhere near it himself; quite aside from it being a sickening sight, the stink had made him gag, and he was amazed no one had thrown up.

Raven was far less patient; while the others stared at the corpses, or struggled to say something about them, the velvet-clad aristocrat shrugged and said, "And what would you, then? Shadow deals with its foes thus; 'tis no surprise. 'Twas ever so." He pointed out the tavern, with its sign of a foam-topped beer mug, and urged them all onward.

Susan nodded, and seemed to accept the situation without further comment, but Pel noticed that she carefully avoided looking at the dead men.

Ted, on the other hand, stared at them openly, swallowing occasionally, and then remarked, "I never realized what a sick mind I have. I wonder if that's what they'd *really* look like? And smell like?"

Valadrakul ignored the whole matter, and simply waited for the others to get on with it. Prossie looked ill, but said nothing, and followed Raven's lead into the tavern.

Wilkins started to make a joke about how the hanged men resembled beads on a string, but when he saw the looks on his companions' faces he decided not to finish it. Marks darted quick little glances at the gibbet and said nothing. Sawyer went white, looked quickly at the others, then hurried to the tavern door.

Singer muttered, "Poor bastards," and thereafter kept his head down.

Amy, though, stood frozen in the street, refusing to approach. Raven, standing in the tavern door and waving the others in, saw her and began, "Friend Pel . . ." He pointed, but didn't finish the sentence.

Pel nodded, and hurried back up the street. He took Amy by the hand and said, "Come on. Let's get in off the street."

She shook him off and took a step backward, all the while staring at the hanging viscera.

"Come on," he repeated, catching her arm again. He almost said something about getting a decent meal, but caught himself; given Amy's recent bouts of nausea and what she was now looking at, it was a wonder she wasn't already vomiting, and the mention of food might be the final straw.

She shook her head.

"Look, I want to get out of here as much as you do," Pel told her, "maybe more — but if we're ever going to get *anywhere,* we need to go through this town and out the other side, past that . . past that. And we need to get some f . . . some supplies. And I think maybe we need to talk some more. So come on into the tavern with us, and we'll find someplace away from the windows, where you can't see . . . can't see anything."

Amy hesitated, then said, "I'm not staying here."

"Of course not," Pel agreed. "Come on."

She swallowed, nodded, and came.

Once inside the tavern, Pel found Raven standing by a table near a window and said, "I think we want someplace quieter." He jerked his head toward the open shutters, hoping Raven would take the hint.

Raven did. "Indeed," he said, "so public a place as this is scarce fit for the ladies among us. Your pardon, all, I beg, that I'd not seen this sooner." He turned and led the way to a large table in a back corner of one of the others of the tavern's three rooms.

The entire operation, however, was not particularly large, and even from this rearmost area anyone who wanted to could see out through the archway, the front room, and the windows on the square.

A large man in a grubby apron had stood by, watching, as the party squeezed themselves into the back room, crowding around two tables and occupying all but one of the dozen chairs there; when everyone appeared settled he approached.

"What can I fetch you?" he asked, none too politely.

"Drink," Raven called in reply. "Whatever you have that's fit to be drunk."

The innkeeper, or whatever he was, grunted. "First I'd see the color of your money," he said.

Pel had been anticipating a cool drink, maybe some decent food, and at the innkeeper's words his stomach knotted in frustration. They didn't *have* any money.

Raven frowned, glanced at Valadrakul, and then began to say something, but before he got the first word out Susan had hauled her big black purse onto the table and was rummaging through it.

Raven paused, staring at her.

"Susan," Pel said, "I don't think . . ."

Then he stopped, as she hauled out a wallet and unsnapped the change compartment.

Pel felt suddenly foolish; he had assumed that Susan was going to pull out her pistol and demand a meal at gunpoint, which would hardly have been a good idea — even with a gun, they were eleven against an entire town, without even mentioning Shadow. Furthermore, the locals might not even recognize the little revolver as a weapon.

Susan pulled out two quarters and silently held them up. The innkeeper squinted.

"Silver, is it?" he asked.

Susan tossed the coins on the table, still without a word. The innkeeper reached to pick one up, and Raven's hand shot out, catching him by the wrist.

"Our drinks first," the nobleman said.

"I'm no thief," the innkeeper said, "but I've not seen coins the likes of these before, and I'd study them, to ascertain their worth."

Reluctantly, Raven allowed the man to pick up one of the quarters. He rubbed it between thumb and forefinger, ran a finger around the milled edge, and looked it over.

Pel waited, wondering what the man would make of the copper sandwiched between layers of whatever the silvery metal was — Pel knew perfectly well that there wasn't much actual silver in modern American coins.

"Most peculiar," the innkeeper said, "and whilst 'tis surely worth something, changing it's not to be simple."

Susan fished more coins from her wallet.

In the end, eleven mugs of lukewarm ale cost a dollar and fifteen cents in coin, leaving Susan's change-purse almost empty.

*A*my sipped her ale and stared out the window, ignoring what little conversation was going on around her. The sky had gone grey and the daylight was dim, but it was still far brighter than the tavern's interior, and the gallows stood out vividly.

Those three men had been hanged and disembowelled — hanged by the neck until dead. The evisceration was just an extra; they had died of hanging. Their necks were twisted, their features puffy, their tongues thrust out and swollen; flies were crawling on their faces, on the dark protruding tongues. Their hands were out of sight, presumably tied behind their backs. And Amy couldn't forget the odor that came from them, a thick, heavy odor she never wanted to smell again.

She didn't think this had been the sort of quick, one-snap-and-it's-over, break-the-neck hanging that she had always heard about; she thought this had been slow strangulation. She shuddered, and sipped at her ale, and wished she had something else to drink.

She had never seen a hanged man before. It wasn't like the movies or TV, where the person still looked like a person, just hanging; the features were distorted, and the body and legs seemed somehow thin and stretched.

That might have something to do with how long they'd been hanging, of course, or with having their guts pulled out. The ale suddenly tasted sour at the thought, and she put her mug down.

She wondered why the three had been hanged; were they murderers? Or rapists, perhaps? Was rape even considered a serious crime here?

Or maybe a crime didn't *need* to be serious to merit hanging, here in Shadow's country. Maybe they were up there because they'd stolen a few apples, or a loaf of bread, or talked back to the local magistrate. Maybe they were hanging there just because Shadow didn't *like* them. Had they done anything as serious as Walter and Beth had?

She swallowed, not drinking, but just trying to keep down what she had already drunk.

She had sent Walter and Beth to their deaths at the hands of Imperial troops, and she suddenly found herself imagining the two of them hanging side by side like that, on a gallows, necks twisted, faces discolored, tongues lolling, bodies stretched. She could see just what Walter's face would have looked like, a parody of what she had seen so often when his features flushed and distorted with anger or lust.

But he was a rapist and a murderer, he had killed that other girl, he had beaten Amy repeatedly. He had known what would happen if the Empire ever caught him. He had brought it on himself; nobody had told him to keep slaves, to rape women, to strangle poor Sheila, whom Amy had never met, whom Amy had replaced. He'd thought he wouldn't be caught, that he could get away with it forever, but the Empire had come looking for Amy and the other Earthpeople, and she'd told them what Walter had done, and he'd been hanged for it.

Hanged, with his face congested with blood, his tongue swollen and protruding, body limp and lifeless, no longer a human being but just a *thing.*

Amy shuddered.

That dead thing back on Zeta whatever-it-was had fathered a child on her, too, which only made it worse. What kind of a human being was it who did things like that?

And Beth, who'd been hanged as well, even though she was a slave, the same as Amy had been — the Empire never knew that, had taken Amy's word for it when she said Beth was guilty, too. Plain quiet Beth, who'd helped Walter abuse Amy, and who had mostly stayed out of Walter's way the rest of the time. What kind of woman had she been, to help her master, her captor, against another victim?

But then, Amy knew she had heard of such things before. Patty Hearst had helped the SLA, hadn't she? Amy remembered the name for it, for hostages coming to help their captors — the Stockholm syndrome. It happened all the time.

And it wasn't new. The Sabine women had sided with the Romans against their own brothers and fathers, hadn't they? Why should Beth have been any different? Why side with a loser?

Because it was *right*, Amy answered herself. Because siding with the abuser was *wrong*, it was evil, it just encouraged more abuse.

Would *she* ever have helped Walter with someone new? *She* had resisted — why couldn't Beth?

But of course, Beth had been there for years, not just weeks. Maybe she had fought at first; maybe she had resisted just as much as Amy had, until it finally sank in that resistance did no good. No Imperial troops came to rescue Beth, the way they had saved Amy. Beth had seen Sheila die for fighting back.

What did it matter, anyway, Amy asked herself. Walter and Beth were both dead, and nothing could bring them back. If Beth hadn't deserved hanging, it was a little late to worry about it. Beth had given up, and had died for it, and that was too damn bad, but why was Amy worrying about it? So there were three dead men hanging in the town square — nothing could bring *them* back, either, and what business was it of hers, anyway? She didn't know anything about it.

She did know that she wouldn't be staying in this town, though. She wouldn't stay in a place where those corpses could be left out there. Why hadn't they been cut down and decently buried?

They were meant as a warning, of course, and as far as Amy was concerned, they'd worked — they'd warned her away from this place, once and for all. Anyone who could stay here would be accepting things like that, would be as bad as Beth.

And, Amy reluctantly realized, the same was probably true of anywhere Shadow ruled. She couldn't just settle down, not here, not anywhere.

But walking into Shadow's fortress was suicide, and wasn't that wrong, too?

There was no way out. There was no right thing to do. She was trapped.

She sipped more ale. She wanted to cry, but fought back the urge — not here, not now, not in this town.

Later she intended to cry, but not now.

"What do you suppose they did?" Pel asked, nodding toward the window as he picked at a splinter in the tabletop.

Raven shrugged. "Doubtless they irked Shadow somewise," he said. "As you'd do, by troubling it in its fortress."

"You don't think we should do that, do you?" Pel asked unhappily.

"Nay, I do not," Raven said.

"But what *else* can we do?" Pel asked. "It's our only way home, the only way we can get you your guns, the only chance we have. There are only eleven of us; we can't fight all Shadow's monsters and magic by ourselves."

"Yet that's just what you attempt, is't not?"

"No, it isn't," Pel insisted. "We aren't trying to *fight* them, we're trying to get *past* them, to destroy Shadow itself. Like Frodo and the Ring. Or like assassinating Hitler to end World War II."

Raven shrugged. "These names mean naught to me."

"Frodo's from a famous story about a war against an evil magician — a lot like Shadow, from your description."

"But a mere story?"

Reluctantly, Pel nodded. "But Hitler was real," he said.

"And was this Hitler assassinated, as you propose?"

"No," Pel admitted.

Raven said nothing, but his expression was plain for Pel to read. Raven clearly thought both Pel's examples were silly.

And Pel had to admit that he had a point; this was real life, not Tolkien's Middle Earth — but then, this wasn't Earth at all, and the only experiences Pel had ever had with other worlds had been in books and movies, and in all of those, a few brave and determined people *could* destroy the all-powerful enemy and save the world.

In the real world, nobody had ever assassinated Hitler or Stalin or Napoleon, but how hard had anyone tried? And if he remembered his history right, someone *had* assassinated Caligula, and who knew how many other tyrants had been destroyed before they had reached Hitler's level?

Besides, what *else* was Pel supposed to do?

"Well, what alternative are you offering us?" he demanded. "Just how do *you* propose to defeat Shadow and send us home?"

"In truth," Raven said, "I know not. I would have us find shelter, that we might take what time we need in gathering our forces, that we might await whatever opportunity the Goddess might send — for surely, She will not allow Shadow to rule forever, in despite of Her."

"I don't believe in your Goddess," Pel answered. "We have a saying in my world that God helps those who help themselves; those who simply have faith and wait usually wait forever, if you ask me. And if someone *does* save them, it's other people who *weren't* waiting, not God — or your Goddess, either."

Pel didn't want to wait, sitting around the way he had at Base One, with nothing to do but remember his dead wife and daughter, sinking in morose helplessness. He needed to *do* something. He had set a goal of getting home to Earth, and that was what he intended to do.

Besides, what did he have to lose? Nancy and Rachel were dead; if he got himself killed, as well, so what?

"Then you insist on going on?" Raven asked.

"That's right," Pel said.

Chapter Seventeen

"If this Shadow's so tough with its magic," Wilkins asked, looking around at the scattered bones, "why hasn't it spotted us and sent a bunch of its monsters after us?"

"It probably hasn't noticed us yet," Pel muttered unhappily, as he trudged on down the highway. He looked straight ahead, at the tree-lined highway, trying not to see the bones below or the clouds overhead.

"Well, why the hell *not?*" Wilkins demanded, stopping in his tracks. "It noticed *these* people!" He kicked at a skull fragment.

"We don't know that," Pel insisted, pausing reluctantly. "Maybe it was wild animals or bandits that killed them."

"Bandits?" Wilkins picked up a thigh bone. "Something sucked the marrow out of this, Brown — what kind of bandits would do that?"

"Animals, then," Pel said. "Come on, let's keep moving; I don't like it here. *Whatever* did this, it might come back."

"I never heard of any animal that would do anything like this," Sawyer said, joining the discussion.

"'Twas most likely Shadow's beasts," Raven said, leaning his bandaged left hand against a tree by the roadside. "This looks very much in their fashion."

"Which is what I said in the first place," Wilkins pointed out. "So why hasn't Shadow sent the beasts after *us?*"

"It did, back at the ship," Amy said, not very confidently.

"But not *since* then," Wilkins argued.

Amy shrugged; she was obviously struggling to hold down her lunch. Her bouts of nausea had become far less frequent over the last few days, but she still had trouble when they came across something unpleasant.

Human bones scattered across the highway were definitely unpleasant. Pel had no idea how old these were, or how long they had actually been there, but he didn't think they had been brought there from somewhere else; it looked as if a small group of people had been killed and torn to pieces right there on the spot.

"Maybe they did something to attract attention," Pel suggested. "Used magic, maybe."

"Brown, *we've* been using magic," Wilkins shouted. "Back at the ruin that twit Taillefer was bloody *flying,* and why didn't *that* attract Shadow?"

"I don't know," Pel said. "Maybe we were just lucky that time." He frowned.

"We've been using magic over and over again, Brown," Wilkins insisted. "Our tame wizard here's lit us a fire with his fingers every night."

"We'd no need, had we funds to pay an inn, or had Shadow not done away with all laws of hospitality," Valadrakul pointed out. "But as it is, we've no tinderbox, no other way to make fire. Would you eat your food raw, and sleep unwarmed?"

"It's better than getting ripped apart, like whoever these people were," Marks snapped.

"But we *haven't* been," Wilkins said. "And I want to know why."

Raven said, "Perhaps the Goddess protects us."

"Shit," Wilkins replied.

Pel didn't say anything more; he just turned and marched onward.

For five days now they had been off the Starlinshire Downs and onto flat country that Raven assured them was a coastal plain; they had marched on across Shadow's countryside, passing through towns and villages without stopping, since they had no more coins to spend. No one spoke to them; children, and sometimes adults, ran and hid at the sight of strangers. Even those who spotted them stealing food never called out or protested; they turned away, or simply watched, without intervening.

Most of the towns had had gibbets in the square, and most of those gibbets had been in use, with corpses of varying age. Some had been fresh, as if the travelers had only just missed the execution; others had been little more than bone and blackened skin. Most were men; some were women; and in one village four children had dangled there, naked and eviscerated — three girls and a boy, none older than twelve.

Pel no longer argued that Shadow might just be the victim of hostile propaganda.

The travelers had grown quieter, gloomier, and more nervous with each new atrocity, and the weather had not helped any; the bright sunlight and greenery of Castle Regisvert were only a memory, and they had been walking beneath a heavy overcast since shortly after that first town, where they had wasted Susan's handful of coins at the inn.

Pel almost wished it would rain and get it over with, but it didn't; the clouds hung oppressive and unmoving overhead, growing steadily thicker and darker, but never releasing so much as a drop of rain. Wind rustled ominously in the leaves, but at ground level the air was still and thick and heavy, and smelled of mold.

Pel waited for a moment longer, but Wilkins seemed to have said his piece.

"Come on," Pel said. He started walking. Raven straightened up and joined him; the others followed.

"You know what it is," Wilkins said. "We're walking into a trap, that's what it is. Shadow *wants* us to come to its fortress and save it the trouble of hunting us down. If we turned back, we'd probably have the monsters after us in a minute."

Pel turned to argue, and saw Susan and Prossie staring at Wilkins intently as they walked; they obviously thought the soldier was onto something.

"That's ridiculous," Pel said.

"Why?" Wilkins demanded belligerently. "What's ridiculous about it?"

Pel's mouth opened, then closed.

What *was* ridiculous about it? It made far more sense than Pel wanted to admit.

And what would he do if it were true? To turn back would be to invite attack. True or false, he had to continue.

He turned forward again and kept walking.

*P*rossie glanced up from the half-eaten chicken leg she held and noticed that Wilkins was, for the moment, alone; he was sitting to one side, leaning against the base of a rather unhealthy-looking tree and gnawing on a chunk of poultry, while most of the others were clustered close around the fire.

She rose to a half-crouch and took a quick few steps over to the tree, staying low, as if there were enemies out there watching, ready to shoot — and for all she knew, there were.

She wished she could still read minds; the freedom of mental silence, of being out of the Empire's net, was still new and strange and wonderful, but it was also horribly frustrating to not know what anyone was thinking, to not know if there were people out there she couldn't see. She was unaccustomed to knowing less than the people around her.

It wasn't really frightening any more, but it was frustrating.

And lonely.

"Spaceman Wilkins," she whispered, as she squatted beside him.

He looked up. "Yeah, Thorpe?"

"May I talk to you?" She didn't look him in the eye; non-telepaths never liked it when telepaths looked directly at them — as if the eyes had something to do with mind-reading.

Wilkins put down his chicken and wiped greasy fingers on his already-filthy uniform trousers. "*You* need to talk, Telepath?" he asked belligerently. "About what?"

"Yes, I need to talk," Prossie said, annoyed. "I can't read your mind here."

"That's what you *said,* anyway," Wilkins acknowledged, his tone a little less hostile. "So what do you want?" He glanced at the neckline of her uniform, and she realized that squatting as she had might not have been clever. "If it's what I think," Wilkins said, leering, "I don't know — there's not much privacy, and I never screwed a mutant freak before. You noisy? Mind if the others watch?"

"That's not what I want," Prossie said, refusing to rise to his bait; she guessed that he wanted an angry response. "I just want to talk to you about something you said earlier."

"Maybe I don't want to talk to a mutant," he replied, a challenge clear in his voice.

Prossie stared at him for a moment, wishing she could see whether he was joking, just what mix of fright and anger and hate and resentment and lust he was feeling. His expression was a peculiar one, not quite smiling, a little tense — she had never been good at reading expressions, since she had never had to be. She had always just read the thoughts behind the face.

She couldn't do that now, though, and she finally decided to get directly to the point.

"Do you really think we're walking into a trap?" she asked.

He glanced past her at the others, then back at her, and asked, "Why?"

"Because I don't want to die," she answered bluntly.

"Everybody dies," he said, looking down and picking up his piece of chicken. Whatever emotional game he had been playing with her seemed to be over. "The only questions are when and how."

She smiled bitterly. "True enough, Spaceman, but if I get a choice, I vote for much later, and of natural causes."

"So you don't get a choice," he said, taking a bite of chicken, still not looking at her.

She actually thought for a moment of snatching the food from his mouth, but the remnants of her lifelong conditioning held; she didn't touch him, but she didn't leave, either.

He chewed and swallowed, took another bite, chewed and swallowed, then looked up and found her still there, staring at him. He stared back for a moment, then tossed the rest of the chicken aside.

"What do you want, Thorpe?" he asked. "Who are you spying for now?"

"I'm not spying for anyone," Prossie said. "I'm just trying to stay alive."

"And what if I don't believe that? You've always been a spy; maybe you say you can't read my mind now, but that doesn't mean you've stopped spying. You can still talk to Base One, right? You can still report on whether I've been a good little boy, still loyal to His Imperial Majesty? Well, maybe I don't want to give you anything to tell them. Maybe I don't know who you're working for back there, whether you're a good little soldier or some politician's flunky, and I just don't want to get tangled up in anything."

"I'm not spying for anyone," Prossie insisted. "I can still talk to my cousin, yes, but I haven't heard from her for two days now, and I don't tell her everything, and she's loyal to our family and the Emperor, nobody else. If you think we're working for General Hart or Under-Secretary Bascombe, we're not. And I'm just asking for *me*, nobody else."

"So what do you want from me?" Wilkins asked.

"I just want to know why you think we're walking into a trap, and whether you know of a way out."

"I think it's pretty obvious why I think it's a trap," he said. "If this Shadow is as all-powerful as these people say it is, wouldn't it have to know we're here? I mean, even if it doesn't know anything from its magic, or whatever it is, we've been passing through town after town, in broad daylight, and if it's got *anything* better than messengers on foot, there's been plenty of time for a message to reach it. Valadrakul got a message to that flying nitwit somehow, and I'm pretty sure I've seen smoke used for signalling, so I figure Shadow knows we're here — but it hasn't come after us."

"Maybe it doesn't care," Prossie suggested.

Wilkins shook his head. "You think it's that kind of a thing? Then what were all those people hanged for? What spread those bones around the highway back there? If those were all murderers, the whole region would have been depopulated by now. If they're thieves, you'd think they'd have learned — Raven said this has been Shadow's turf for a couple of centuries now. About the only thing I can think of that people just can't learn to do, even if it gets them killed, is to keep their damn mouths shut — so I think Shadow's the kind of boss who takes loose talk seriously, and doesn't stand for any kind of loose ends. It wouldn't allow a bunch of foreigners to stroll across the countryside any old way they want — not unless it was watching them somehow, and they were doing just what it wanted."

Prossie nodded. She had learned the word "paranoid" from the Earthpeople, and it seemed to fit what Wilkins described; it also matched her own perceptions of Shadow.

"So maybe it's not exactly a trap," Wilkins said. "Maybe it's not going to kill us; maybe if we turn back we'll just find a bunch of cops who'll take us in for questioning, instead of those black animal things. Maybe when we get there it'll offer us all a chance to join its side, maybe go back to the Empire as traitors, saboteurs — I don't know. I do know that either it's tracking us, and knows perfectly well where we are, or else Raven and the wizard have been lying to us and we don't know a damn thing about what's going on here."

"Makes sense," Prossie admitted.

Wilkins studied her, then asked, "So, Thorpe, you can still call Base One, right? You can tell them whether to send reinforcements, or try to pick us up?"

"I can ask Carrie to pass on a message," Prossie agreed, "but that's it. They'll probably ignore it."

"That's about the only way we're going to get out of this, though — if they send in someone else. If you *tell* them that it's a trap, won't they listen to you?"

Prossie hesitated.

"Listen, Wilkins," she said. "There's something I didn't tell anyone — I don't know if you know all the rules we telepaths have, some people do and some don't, but we have rules about what we tell who of what we read, and I'm not supposed to tell you this, but the hell with that."

"What?" He eyed her warily.

"We were set up. I don't know the details, I didn't get it all, but Bascombe deliberately screwed up this whole expedition just to get rid of those people." She waved a hand at the others, sure that Wilkins would understand that she meant the Earthpeople and Faerie folk. "He was listening to Shadow's spies back there at Base One when he picked Carson for command. And when things started going wrong, he and General Hart decided that they want us all dead, so there won't be any evidence that they screwed up. *That's* why I've been so sure we weren't getting rescued."

Wilkins blinked. "Why didn't you tell the lieutenant, back at the ship?"

"You think he'd have believed me? A mutant, telling him he can't trust his own superiors? Lieutenant Dibbs, we're talking about."

"So why are you telling *me*, then?" Wilkins asked. "Why should *I* believe you?"

"Because you figured out that we're being set up again — that Shadow's watching us. So maybe I think you're smarter than the lieutenant. And maybe if you know a bit more, you can figure out how we can get *out* of this."

For a moment the two stared silently at each other; then Wilkins said, "Yeah, I can see what you mean." He glanced over at the others. "Problem is, there are a couple of things we don't know here."

"What?"

"What Shadow wants with us," Wilkins said, "and *which* of us it wants."

"*I* wish the damn clouds would either break up or rain,'" Sawyer said angrily to Pel. "You had to say that."

Pel glared back at him; it wasn't worth trying to talk over the constant patter of the rain, or the splashing as they slogged through the mud. His stolen shirt, taken from a farmer's hut two days before, clung damply to his back and dripped down his wrists; he almost regretted its acquisition.

"Think you he tempted the gods, then?" Raven asked, peering out from under the dripping cloak he held over his head.

"Something like that," Sawyer agreed. He had stolen another farmer's cap that morning, but it was clearly not doing him much good in the steady downpour.

Raven shook his head. "The foolishness of you pagans," he said. "To think our mere words could thus affect the Goddess' scheme."

"You're calling *me* a pagan?" Sawyer exclaimed angrily. He stopped and grabbed Raven by the arm.

Raven turned and struck at Sawyer without thinking; Pel saw him start to wince, and then suppress it, as his mostly-healed but still tender fingers hit Sawyer's wrist.

Sawyer saw it, too, and let go. "Sorry," he said.

"'Tis naught," Raven said. "I spoke ill of your faith; 'twas rude of me."

By now the entire party had stopped; Pel and Raven and Sawyer had been at the front, and the others were now gathered about them, sinking into the mud of the road.

"Oh, come on," Amy said. "If we keep going maybe we can find somewhere to get out of the rain." She turned and trudged onward; she limped slightly, thanks to popped blisters, but seemed to be over her illness. Susan followed her lead, tugging at Ted's wrist to make sure he came, as well.

Prossie, who had been near the center of the line talking to Valadrakul, turned to look over the party, and Pel saw her frown.

Sawyer, too, noticed her expression, and looked over the rest of the group.

"Hey," he said, "where's Ron?"

"Who?" Pel asked.

"Ronnie Wilkins."

Amy and Susan and Ted kept walking, unaware of the consternation as the others all turned and looked around.

"He's gone," Marks said, sounding very surprised. He took off his helmet to look around better, and blinked as the rain drenched him.

"When did you last see him?" Pel asked.

The others glanced at one another.

"At that last village, I guess," Sawyer said. "Just before it started raining."

"He was with us when we left the village," Singer said unsteadily; he was cradling his swollen left wrist in his right hand. The badger scratches he had received back at Castle Regisvert had become infected, and Valadrakul's crude attempts at treatment had done little good; Pel had thought it amusing, or ironic, or at any rate worthy of note, that scratches left by an ordinary badger had turned out to be septic, while the various wounds he and Prossie and Amy had gotten from Shadow's hellbeasts were all healing cleanly.

Maybe ordinary germs couldn't live on Shadow's unnatural creatures.

"I did a count," Singer added. "I *know* he was with us."

"He was here," Marks confirmed.

"How long after that, though?" Pel asked.

Singer shrugged. "That was the last time I saw him," he said. "He was way at the back." He looked at Marks. "I thought he was talking to you."

"He was, for awhile," Marks agreed. "But then he said he wanted to think, so I left him alone and came up to talk to Sawyer."

"I remember that," Sawyer said. "So no one's seen him since then?"

No one had.

"D'you think the monsters got him?" Sawyer asked. "Shadow's things? Or maybe something else, some other magic?"

Singer snorted derisively; Raven smiled.

Valadrakul shook his head. "I doubt 'twas Shadow."

"I think he must've just left," Pel said. "He decided not to come with us, and didn't bother to argue about it."

"He decided not to walk into a trap," Prossie said quietly. "Not when he isn't one of the ones it wants."

The others stared at her for a moment; then Marks said bitterly, "And the son of a bitch didn't ask me to come with him, either!"

"Or any of us," Sawyer pointed out.

"Probably figured he had a better shot by himself," Singer suggested wearily. "Probably right, too."

"Well, he's gone, now," Pel said. He turned, without another word, and began marching onward, following Amy and Susan and Ted.

"We aren't going to try to find him?" Singer asked.

"Why should we?" Pel called back over his shoulder. "He's a big boy; he can take care of himself."

"And where would you seek him?" Raven asked. "'Tis a broad land, and he's had time to conceal himself where'er he would."

Singer blinked at him, then said, "Yeah, you're right." He trudged after Pel.

After a moment's hesitation, the rest came close behind.

"*I*'m going to bunk," Marks whispered.

Prossie turned, startled.

"Like Ronnie," Marks explained. "He was right; why should we *all* get killed? This Shadow thing probably just wants Raven and his wizard pal, or maybe the Earthpeople."

Prossie glanced around. They were in open country now, a low, grassy plain where no trees grew, much of it too sodden to farm; the highway wound its way along the higher, drier portions, past the dreary little farms that mostly seemed to raise various sorts of berries. They hadn't passed anything resembling a village for several miles, and their last meal had been nothing but stolen raspberries — sweet, but not very satisfying.

"Where will you go?" she asked.

"I don't know," he said. "It all looks pretty much the same, so who cares?"

Prossie was considering that when Marks asked anxiously, "So, Thorpe, are you with me?"

"Who else are you asking?" Prossie asked.

"Nobody," Marks replied hastily. "I mean, I figured you and I, we could make like we're married, if anyone asks . . ."

She knew what he meant. Prossie looked at him more closely, considering.

Bill Marks was hardly her idea of the perfect mate; he was of medium height, not particularly well built, with a receding chin and a bad complexion — not really ugly, but not anyone's image of handsome, either. She didn't doubt for a minute that he wanted to carry the fiction of a marriage a little further than answers to questions from nosy natives. The notion did not particularly appeal to her. With the right person, maybe, but not with Bill Marks.

Hell, he didn't even call her by her first name.

"What about Singer and Sawyer?" she asked.

"What *about* them?" Marks asked, flustered.

Prossie looked him in the eye, then turned and looked at the others, a dozen yards ahead.

"Well, you know," Marks said, a little desperately, "Singer's got that bad arm, and besides, the more of us there are, the more likely we'll be noticed, you know, by Shadow or someone . . ."

"Never mind," she said. "I think I'll take my chances with the rest of them, at least for now. You go ahead, and good luck!"

Marks hesitated. "You sure?" he asked.

"Yes," Prossie answered firmly.

She was sure of her decision — but she wished she was sure she was right.

*P*el turned, startled, at a tap on his shoulder, and found Prossie Thorpe just behind him.

"Mr. Brown," she said quietly, without preamble, "I was wondering just what your opinion was on Wilkins."

"My opinion?" Pel glanced around; no one else seemed to be paying any attention. He had half expected to see Nancy glaring at him for talking to another woman this way, but Nancy was dead, she wasn't with them. "My opinion is that he's gone," Pel said. "What do you mean, my opinion?"

"I mean, do you think he got away safely?"

Pel shrugged. "I don't know. He probably did, but I don't know any more than you do. Maybe less, if your telepathy can tell you anything."

"Not about that," Prossie said. "I still hear from Base One sometimes, but they've written us all off as lost."

Pel nodded. "I'm not surprised," he said.

"So do you think Wilkins was right, that he did the right thing by turning back?"

"Or aside," Pel said. "We don't know *where* he went, remember."

"But do you think he was right?" Prossie insisted.

Pel shrugged again. "Who knows?"

"He thought we were all walking into a trap, you know," Prossie said.

"So he said," Pel replied.

Prossie nodded. "He talked to me about it a little; he figured that Shadow might want you, because the warp came out in your house, and Raven because he's the lord of Stormcrack, and Valadrakul because he's a wizard, and so on, but that it wouldn't have any use for a bunch of ordinary Imperial soldiers."

Pel thought that over. "He might've been right," he admitted.

"So what about the others?" Prossie asked. "I mean, I'm a telepath, so maybe I'm one of the special ones, too, but what about Marks and Sawyer and Singer?"

"What *about* them?" Pel asked, trying to figure out what Prossie was leading up to.

"What if they turned back, instead of going on with the rest of us?"

Pel shrugged; he started to say, "It's a free country," then remembered where he was. "They can do what they please," he said. "I'm not their jailer."

"But do you think it would be safe?"

Pel gave her a startled look.

"I mean," Prossie explained, "Wilkins thought that if we turned back, *then* we'd find Shadow's monsters waiting for us, that it was only leaving us alone as long as we stayed headed in the right direction. So if someone it wanted turned back, he would be running right into the monsters. So do you think Marks and Sawyer and Singer would be safe?"

"Why are you asking *me*?" Pel demanded. *"You're* the telepath! And Raven's the expert on Shadow. I'm just . . . I'm just me."

"Raven lies," Prossie said. "You know that; he'd tell me whatever he thought would be best for him. I think I can get an honest answer from you."

Pel looked at her, puzzled. Her eyes were green, he saw — he had never noticed that before. Her hair was a dull brown, her face ordinary.

"You want an honest answer?" he said. "Fine; I honestly don't know. I don't know what's going on; I'm just trying to muddle along. I want to go home. I want my wife and daughter back. Beyond that, I don't care what happens, to me or anyone else. If those guys want to go back to the ship, or go hide somewhere, it's fine with me."

For only an instant, her eyes met his; then she dropped her gaze to the ground, and he was sure he had offended or frightened or embarrassed her somehow. He started to frame an apology, then stopped; he had nothing to apologize for.

Maybe she was just shy. Or maybe she was trying to flirt with him.

He wasn't interested in flirting; he was a married man — or at least, he still thought of himself as one. It was too soon after Nancy's loss to look elsewhere — or maybe he was just too tired, or too scared.

And even if he hadn't been, Prossie Thorpe wasn't exactly what he was looking for in a woman. He looked down at his own muddy boots.

She turned away without saying anything more.

*R*aven was satisfied with their progress — or at any rate, with the speed of it; the direction was not that he would have chosen. Marching to Shadow's fortress still seemed to him the height of folly.

And now they were but a day away, he thought, as he peered out into the blackness of the surrounding night, and that day, if the tales spoke truth, to be spent all upon the causeway across Shadowmarsh, with nowhere to turn or hide. They had seen the marsh spread before them as the sun sank, and that was why Raven had called the night's halt where he did.

Might he not best serve his land and his people and his cause by slipping away, and leaving these foreigners to their own devices? If they were to perish at Shadow's hands, 'twould be a sad loss, but there had been many such losses over the years.

And this was the final moment, the time when he must decide. He had debated the matter with Pellinore Brown over their meager supper, and the Brown remained unyielding — he was bound for Shadow's keep.

Some might accuse a man in Raven's place of cowardice, did he now flee — but what of that? Was he not outcast now? He would know it was not fear, but prudence and hope for the future that guided his steps.

Still, to be marked as coward, even wrongly . . .

He had got that far in his thinking when a cry sounded; instantly, Raven was on his feet, once again cursing the fate that had left him without his sword.

"Help!" a man's voice called, as from a distance. "Oh, my God . . ."

Raven snatched up a brand from the dying fire and waved it, that the air might brighten the sparks; it flared briefly, but the flame did not linger, and he saw naught but startled faces and muddy boots.

"It's Marks," said the man Singer; he, too, raised an impromptu torch in his good hand, and headed for the sound.

The voice cried out again, wordlessly, as Singer and Raven ran up the highway to the east, away from Shadowmarsh. Raven saw that the others, to their shame, stayed behind — even Valadrakul, who, though a wizard, Raven had thought to be a man of honor and some small courage.

The cries stopped well before Raven and Singer reached their source.

When they did reach Marks' body, it was far too late to lend any aid beyond a decent burial; his dead eyes gleamed orange in the feeble torchlight, staring up at the black clouds above, but his face was black with dirt and blood. His throat and chest had been torn open, and Raven knew at a glance that even the finest healer could not have saved him.

"Damn," Singer muttered. "What did it?" He raised his torch, brighter than Raven's own, and waved it about. "Where is it?"

"Shadow," Raven told him, lowering his own brand.

"Are you sure?" a female voice asked.

Startled, Raven whirled, and found the woman called Susan standing a few paces down the road, her black bag open on her shoulder, her hand within — ready, Raven supposed, to bring out in an instant that magical weapon of hers.

He smiled slightly. At least *one* of the foreigners had courage — and the skill to use it, to have followed so silently!

"What else?" he asked her. "'Tis surely another warning — more bones by the roadside for any who would follow us."

"Why just him? Why not all of us?"

Raven turned back for another look at Marks.

"See you," he said, "he sought to flee; we are surely a good quarter-mile from our camp. This man had turned back upon the path."

"And Shadow doesn't want us to do that," Singer said.

"As you say," Raven agreed. "Shadow would not have us turn back."

"You don't think it's a coincidence?" Susan asked. "After all, as far as we know, Wilkins got away safely."

"Insofar as we know," Raven agreed, "but how far is that? And more, the rules may well have changed since Wilkins turned aside; we were not then so near to Shadow's hold."

Susan nodded, the motion just barely visible in the darkness. "So we go on," she said flatly.

"Indeed," Raven agreed. "In the morning, we go on."

In the morning, they would march into the jaws of death, where only the Goddess herself could save them.

And perhaps the Goddess *would* save them; perhaps she had wearied of Shadow's importunities, and would somehow use Raven and his companions as her tools for defeating it.

Or perhaps they would all die, and their souls return to the Goddess' womb. That was death, and Raven did not seek death — but how was he to avoid it, now?

Perhaps, Raven thought later, as he settled to sleep, they should have brought Marks' body back with them, should have buried the poor man's remains and returned his flesh to the Goddess as well as his soul — but no one had suggested it, no one had argued, and the rain had begun anew.

Scores of men had lain unburied in the war against Shadow; one more would matter not.

And Raven knew that on the morrow, he might well be yet another.

Chapter Eighteen

"*T*hat's it, isn't it?" Amy asked, pointing.

Raven nodded wearily. "Indeed, 'twould seem to be. Understand you, I've not been here until now, I've never seen Shadow's keep ere this, but in truth, that we see before us fits every tale I've heard."

Amy had somehow assumed that Raven must have seen Shadow's fortress, but of course, there was no reason he should have. She stared, trying to make out more details.

The rain that had fallen off and on for the past two days seemed to have finally stopped for good, but the air was still thick and damp and hazy. She saw a heavy gray structure built around a central tower that rose in uneven steps, with odd jogs and turrets here and there; it resembled a storybook castle rather more than Stormcrack Keep or Castle Regisvert had, but broader and uglier; no one would ever call this thing "soaring" or "graceful."

She couldn't make out windows or doors with any certainty, nor those things like teeth that ran along the tops of castle walls; that made it very hard to get a clear idea of the size of the fortress.

"How much farther is it, then?" she asked, glancing down at her aching feet.

"Probably farther than it looks," Pel said.

Amy, remembering a few long walks through American cities toward buildings that were visible but distant, nodded as she looked around.

This was no city, though; the gray mass of Shadow's fortress rose from a broad marshy plain that looked almost equally gray. The highway was literally a high way here, a band of yellowish earth built up about two feet above the surrounding reeds and grasses; it was bare, lifeless dirt, no grass or weeds along the verge.

The marshes to either side looked dead, Amy thought; she supposed that was an illusion, that the reeds just weren't as green as the ones she was used to. The dull light that seeped through the thick overcast didn't help at all; it seemed to leach the color out of everything. The place reeked of brine and decay, smothering in the warm, dense air.

To the north she could see wooded hills, and perhaps the clouds were thinner there, because the forests were green enough. Looking back, the higher, drier plain behind them wasn't as drab, either — the trees and the farmers' fields were green, and even the thatched roofs of the scattered houses, and of the last village they had passed through, were brighter than what lay ahead.

The marsh really *was* that sick, flat color, she decided, and she remembered how, back on the Downs, Pel had argued that the countryside didn't look like it was ruled by evil magic.

She didn't remember even the mud flats of New Jersey being as ugly as this, though — though they did smell worse. "Is this more what you had in mind?" she asked Pel.

"What?" Pel started, and looked puzzled.

"I mean this place — is this the sort of place you'd expect an evil wizard to live?"

Pel glanced at the distant shape of Shadow's fortress, at the miles of dun marshland.

"Yeah," he said. "I guess it is."

It certainly seemed to fit the part to Amy. Maybe most of the rest of the bizarre things that had happened since Captain Cahn's spaceship fell in her back yard hadn't fit the stereotypes, but Shadow's fortress looked just fine as an evil wizard's castle, even if it wasn't built in the shape of a skull or anything as silly as that.

"What's that on the road?" Singer asked, pointing with his good hand.

Amy dropped her gaze from the fortress to the highway, and saw what Singer meant — something dark lay on the road ahead, not moving.

"Someone dropped a pack, maybe," she suggested.

"Raven?" Susan asked.

The nobleman turned up his palms. "I know no more than do you," he said.

They trudged onward, but all of them were now moving more cautiously, watching the dark mass on the highway. Amy couldn't decide if it was black or a very dark gray; the poor light didn't make it easy to distinguish.

And its color didn't really matter, anyway.

The thing was about three feet long, she judged, and almost featureless; it looked a little like a huge empty boot, or an irregularly-shaped stovepipe. She had no idea what it was, or what it was doing there — until, when they were perhaps ten feet away, it moved.

It lifted one end and swung it to point at the approaching travelers; the end split open, revealing long rows of sharp white teeth. Amy could still see no eyes, no nostrils, no other features, but the mouth and the teeth were unmistakable. The thing was alive, and hostile.

"A Shadow thing," Pel said.

"Kill it," Sawyer said, drawing his blaster.

Raven's hand dropped to his empty belt; Singer hesitated, hands clutching; Susan shifted her purse but did not reach in.

Valadrakul raised a hand, then paused.

"No magic," Raven warned him. "Not when Shadow's keep looms before us."

Sawyer clicked the trigger of his blaster a couple of times, then turned to stare helplessly at the others.

"Save wizardry, we are unarmed, my lord," Valadrakul pointed out.

That wasn't literally true, Amy thought, remembering the pistol in Susan's purse, but she didn't correct him; it was close enough to the truth.

Instead, she asked, "Do you think that's the one that got poor Marks last night?"

"No," Singer said flatly. He didn't explain, and after a moment's hesitation, Amy decided that she didn't want him to.

For a moment, the nine of them stood in silent confusion; then Ted — Ted Deranian, of all people — marched forward.

"This is stupid," he said. "It looks like I'm not going to wake up until I get through this whole stupid thing, right up to the showdown, so let's get on with it. I'm not going to let some stupid refugee from 'Aliens' stretch it out." He walked up to the monster and kicked at it.

"Go on, get out of here," he said. "You're in the way."

The creature twitched away from Ted's foot, then seemed to hesitate, open jaws wavering.

Then it closed its mouth and slithered away, off the highway and down into the marsh.

"Come on," Ted said. "Let's get this *over* with!" He stamped onward, toward the fortress.

The others, by unspoken common consent, hung back.

"We're unarmed," Pel said. "We're walking into Shadow's fortress unarmed and out in the open."

"'Twas your own proposal," Raven pointed out.

"I know," Pel said, "and you told me at the time it was a stupid idea, and you were right." He hesitated, as if trying to gather the will to turn back.

That was too much for Amy. She wanted to get this all over with. If she was going to die, then she would die, and maybe it would serve her right for sending Beth to the gallows, but she wasn't going to turn back the way Bill Marks had, she wanted to at least face whatever they were up against. "What *else* are we going to do?" she demanded angrily. "Even if it lets us? Do you want to go back and live in some village where they hang *children,* Pel? Where no one talks to us? Or go back to Raven's friends, who don't have the nerve to work a spell to send us home?" Unconsciously, she rested one hand on her faintly-bulging abdomen.

"I wonder if maybe Taillefer could *teach* the portal spell to someone?" Pel asked. "Someone who could use it, and step through with us?"

Amy stared at him, angrier than ever. *"Now* you think of that?" she shouted.

"Don't forget about Ted," Susan said quietly, pointing. Pel's lawyer was a hundred feet away, marching on toward the fortress.

"Valadrakul," Pel said, *"could* Taillefer teach someone to work the spell, without using it himself? Without Shadow noticing?"

The wizard considered the question, but before he could reply, Singer said, "I don't think it matters."

The others turned to him.

"Why not?" Pel demanded.

"Remember Bill Marks," Singer said. He pointed, back along the highway, and the others turned to look.

On the road behind them were half a dozen of the stovepipe-shaped monsters, sprawled across the highway; as they watched, another slithered up from the marsh.

"I don't think *those* are going to let us kick them aside," Singer said.

"Wilkins was right all along," Prossie said. "It's a trap; Shadow *wants* us to come to it, and if we don't we'll all wind up like Marks."

For a moment, they all stared at the creatures; then Pel shrugged and said, "Well, if we don't have a choice, we might as well get going."

He turned and marched ahead, following Ted.

Amy stared at the monsters.

"Come on," Prossie said, touching her arm.

Reluctantly, Amy turned.

"We might as well get it over with," she agreed.

*J*ust as Pel had expected, the fortress was larger and farther away than it had looked; they had first spotted it in the morning, but dusk was falling by the time they finally approached the gates. He was soaked with sweat; so were most of the others. The day was not actually all that hot, but the humidity and the high gravity made it an exhausting march.

Raven had judged their entire journey to be around two hundred miles, once everyone had agreed on what a mile was, and Pel now appreciated just how much that was. Two hundred miles was about the distance from Washington to Philadelphia, about four hours by car, nothing much — but it was a damnably long way to *walk*, through forests and over ridges and across the plain and then through this soggy, unpleasant marshland.

And Pel would much rather have arrived at Philadelphia than at Shadow's fortress; he amused himself for part of this final leg of the journey by trying to remember the exact phrasing of the appropriate W.C. Fields quote, and although he had no way to check it, he finally settled on, "Frankly, I'd rather be in Philadelphia."

They weren't in Philadelphia, though, they were approaching the fortress.

In a way, that didn't seem quite right; they hadn't had enough adventures along the way. They hadn't really had *any* adventures since leaving Castle Regisvert; petty theft wasn't much of an adventure. Wilkins' disappearance hadn't been very dramatic; Marks' death hardly qualified. The whole two-hundred-mile walk had been pretty dull.

In the stories, the journeys were never so boring — or was that just because the authors left out the dull parts?

No, any epic quest was supposed to have real challenges along the way — goblins and monsters, not just rain and irate villagers. And the adventurers were supposed to defeat the menaces through wit and strength and other traditional virtues, not by just trudging onward, day after day.

They hadn't even *seen* the monster that had killed Marks. And while Valadrakul had defeated the giant bat-thing with a spell, that was a long time ago, and far away, and hardly seemed to count.

But this wasn't a story, this was real life, and Pel supposed that if anyone ever wrote it all down, the long dull walk would be relegated to a line or two of scene-shifting.

In any cases, challenges met and menaces defeated or not, they had reached Shadow's fortress.

The marsh came right up to the towering stone walls, but the highway led directly into an open gate. The entire thing was built on a gigantic scale; the outer wall was at least as long as a city block, and Pel judged it to rise ten stories or so — a hundred feet high. The towers were not visible from directly below the walls, but he had seen from the highway that they were clearly at least three or four times as high. Pel hadn't thought simple masonry, with no steel frame, could support so high a tower — but then, it probably didn't; Shadow's magic probably held the thing together.

Just like all those Hollywood movies, he supposed; if by some miracle they *did* play out the traditional heroic adventure and managed to kill Shadow, that whole immense tower would probably fall in and crush them all.

That never happened in the stories — the heroes always got out in time, though the villains might get crushed. Pel didn't care to trust to that sort of thing in real life.

They had no choice, though; a glance back showed him that the highway behind them was sprinkled with those crawling giant-slug-with-teeth monsters. And although Singer had said those weren't what had killed Marks, *something* had killed him — Raven and Singer and Susan all agreed on that. They couldn't turn back; they had to go on in and finish up the story, even if it meant dying.

And maybe dying wouldn't be that bad. If there was an afterlife, maybe he'd see Nancy and Rachel again; if Ted's theory was right, he'd be back on Earth. Maybe Marks was back in the Galactic Empire even now, back with his family, if he had any.

Pel was suddenly bothered that he had no idea whether Marks had had any family. Wilkins would have known, but Wilkins was gone, too — maybe dead, maybe not.

Marks was definitely dead. Elani was dead. Carson was dead. Nancy and Rachel were dead. If Pel died, he would at any rate be in good company.

And whatever death might mean, at least if Pel died he would be out of Shadow's power and out of Raven's world, this whole ghastly thing would be over for him.

And he might or might not die. If they *were* in a story, and one of them was the hero — Raven seemed like the traditional candidate — then that one could expect to win through alive somehow, but the rest of them could die; sidekicks and spear-carriers were always expendable.

And it was always possible that they were just one of the earlier expeditions doomed to fail, so that some later hero might avenge them. Or perhaps the men would be slain and the women imprisoned, for later rescue.

Or maybe it wasn't a story at all, maybe real life didn't work that way. It certainly hadn't worked out well for somebody, he saw; there were more dead bodies, like those in the towns and villages, hanging by their necks from the parapet above the open gate.

Pel had thought he'd gotten used to gibbets and scaffolds and bones and corpses, so at first he didn't really pay much attention when he realized that there were people hanging there; he just tried not to look. The fading light made that easier; so did his sore feet, as they kept his attention elsewhere.

After all, this was Shadow's headquarters; why would it be any different from the rest of Shadow's realm?

Then he heard Sawyer say, "Oh, shit."

He turned, and saw the Imperial soldier staring up at the dangling corpses. Without meaning to, without thinking about it, Pel looked up at them, too.

He swallowed hard.

He had thought he'd gotten used to gibbets and scaffolds and bones and corpses, but this was different.

This time he knew them.

There were six men hanging there, each with his belly sliced open and grayish loops of his intestines torn out and draped across his legs and feet — Shadow apparently wasn't interested in originality in its executions. Six men, and Pel recognized them all. Second from the left was Lieutenant Dibbs; Pel couldn't put definite names to the others, but all wore the remains of the purple uniform of the Galactic Empire, and all their faces, twisted and discolored as they were, were familiar. Of the six, useless blasters still hung on the belts of three. One even wore his helmet.

As Pel watched, they swayed gently in the wind; one swollen hand brushed lightly against the damp gray stone of the castle wall.

If Dibbs had thought this was a story, he'd probably thought he was the hero, and now he was nothing but a warning to anyone who came after him.

Pel realized that he had stopped walking, that the entire party, even Ted, had stopped, that all nine of them were looking up at the dangling corpses.

"Now what?" he asked. He swallowed; his throat was suddenly dry.

"Now we go on," Raven said angrily. "We've yet no choice."

"That's the lieutenant," Sawyer said.

"That changes nothing," Raven answered.

"Where are the others, though?" Singer asked, craning his neck to see the faces. "Where's Dawber? Or Moore? Or Smallwood, or Twidman?"

"Wilkins isn't there, either," Prossie pointed out.

"They're probably hanging around the other side," Sawyer said.

"Why would they be on the other side?" Amy asked bitterly. "We were coming in this way, and Shadow knew it — it hung them up there to tease us."

"Maybe there wasn't enough left of the others to hang up there," Susan said quietly.

"Oh, thanks, lady," Sawyer growled. "You really know how to cheer a fellow up!"

"Or maybe Shadow's just playing with us, trying to make us wonder about the others," Amy said.

"Or maybe they really got away," Pel suggested. "Maybe Shadow's not as omnipotent as it would like." He didn't say anything about it out loud, but he found himself wondering if perhaps Wilkins or one of the others might be the actual hero of the tale. Maybe Spaceman First Class Ronnie Wilkins would appear at the last moment, guns blazing, to save Pel and the others from Shadow's clutches — if he had guns that could blaze here. Blasters couldn't.

Sword flashing, then.

Pel tried to imagine Wilkins with a sword; the image wouldn't come. Instead, he saw him with a switchblade. It seemed more his style.

Ted had stared up at the corpses with everyone else, but had said nothing; now he shrugged and strolled forward, toward the gate, boots crunching on the gravelly road. The sound drew everyone's attention.

Pel didn't mind staring at Ted; he was happy to be distracted from the corpses.

For a moment, no one spoke, as Ted stepped through the open arch onto the stone floor beyond. The crunch of gravel turned to scuffing as he stepped into shadow.

"Our mad friend has the right of it," Raven muttered. "We'll learn nothing more out here; 'tis within that our fate awaits."

"Maybe yours," Sawyer said, stepping back, "but I've had it. I'm not going in there. I'm not the one it wants, any more than Wilkins was."

"How do you know?" Amy asked.

"Because I'm just another soldier," Sawyer said. "I'm nobody special." He pointed to Valadrakul and said, "He's a wizard," then indicated Raven and continued, "and he's some kind of prince or something. Thorpe's a telepath, you're pregnant — you're all special somehow. Your crazy friend has visions, maybe that's important. Mr. Brown — well, I don't know, because I don't know anything about him or the world he came from. That other woman hardly ever says anything, I'm not even sure of her name, she could be *anything*. But Singer and me, we're just a couple of packhumpers and shipjumpers. It let Wilkins get away — why shouldn't it let me go, too?"

"It didn't let Dibbs go," Pel pointed out. "Or Marks."

"It killed Marks so the rest of you wouldn't turn back," Sawyer said. "And maybe the lieutenant put up a fight or something. Look up there, though — there are six of them, out of what, eleven men we left back at the ship? *Where are the others?* Shadow let them go, I tell you, because they weren't important!"

"You're guessing," Pel said.

"We're *all* guessing," Sawyer retorted, "all of us, all the time! We don't any of us have the first idea what the hell is going on here. We don't know what Shadow *is,* or what it wants, or anything, all we can do is guess — and I'm guessing that it doesn't want me, and I'm staying out here."

Pel glanced at the others.

"Let him stay, if he would," Raven said.

"What difference does it make?" Singer asked. "If Shadow wants him inside, it can get him inside." He pointed at the giant-slug things.

Pel looked, back at the monster-speckled highway, then up at the dangling soldiers, then into the gloom beyond the gate. The sun was down, the light dying, but the darkness within the fortress was still far deeper than that without; there were no lights anywhere to be seen.

This was not how Pel had pictured it. Oh, the fortress was suitable enough, the marsh reasonably appropriate if a bit on the drab side, and the dead bodies were a fittingly macabre touch, but the gathering darkness, unbroken by torchlight, didn't seem quite right — it wasn't the shadowy, sinister darkness of dungeons or of midnight, but the soft dimness of twilight, the sort that doesn't scare anyone but just gradually convinces everyone to go home for dinner.

Pel wished he *could* just go home for dinner, and find Nancy and Rachel waiting there for him. He was *trying* to get home — but of course, Nancy and Rachel wouldn't be there.

And the gentle darkness didn't seem right for an assault on the villain's headquarters. The fact that poor mad Ted had gone on ahead, was already almost out of sight in the gloom, didn't seem right. That they were virtually unarmed, no swords, no armor, no secret magic, didn't seem right. That they were walking openly into the front gate, aware that Shadow expected them, didn't seem right — shouldn't they be sneaking in by some secret passage, scaling a back wall, crawling in through the sewers? They had no plan, no organization . . .

And no choice. One of the slug-things was crawling up onto the highway less than a yard behind Sawyer's feet.

"Let's go in, then," Pel said. "And maybe Tom Sawyer'll change his mind when those Shadow things start crowding him." He pointed.

Sawyer whirled and saw the creature behind him. It opened its maw and showed him its teeth, but Sawyer did not retreat.

"I'm not going," he said, still facing the slug. "The rest of you, go on if you're going, and when you're in there, maybe this thing will leave me alone."

"What will you eat?" Susan asked abruptly, startling everyone. "We've had nothing since breakfast, and it's a long way back to the last village."

"Don't remind me!" Amy said.

Pel sympathized; he was hungry, too. He thought he must have lost twenty pounds since he first stepped through his basement wall; he *never* seemed to get enough food, or any *good* food, anywhere in Faerie, nor even in the Galactic Empire before it.

"I'll manage," Sawyer said, still not looking at the others. "It's not *that* far."

The thought occurred to Pel that Sawyer *meant* to die, out here — that he preferred being eaten by those slug things to facing Shadow itself.

Or maybe not. Pel didn't know, and decided he didn't want to ask.

"What the hell," he said, turning back to the gate, "maybe at least Shadow will give us a last meal."

He marched forward, into the darkness of the gate.

Chapter Nineteen

A my had expected something to happen when they were all inside the fortress — the gates to slam shut, or the Shadow-things to surge up and attack poor Sawyer, or lights to spring up, or *something* — but nothing did. She shuffled on into the blackness, hands out before her to fend off stray furniture, feet sliding along the stone flooring.

"Ted?" she called. "Are you there?"

"Shut up!" Ted answered furiously. "I think I'm waking up! I don't see anything any more!"

"That's because it's *dark* in here, you idiot!" Pel snapped.

Amy giggled nervously, and glanced back at the huge gateway. It was still wide open; she could only vaguely make out the gates themselves, grayish shapes to either side. Sawyer was clearly outlined against the dimming sky; he was standing there, facing away from her, in a sort of crouch, as if expecting an attack from the stovepipe things.

She couldn't see anything attacking, though.

"Now what?" she said.

"Damned if I know," Pel said.

"'Tis an excellent question," Raven's voice answered; Amy could see nothing of him in the darkness. She could see Sawyer, and Pel was a shadowy figure to her left, but the others were invisible now.

She could hear footsteps, but couldn't identify them all — were they all here? Was anyone *else* here, lurking in the darkness?

She wondered what sort of room they were in; it seemed to be large, judging by the sounds, and since no one had reported bumping into any walls or other impediments. The air was cooler than outside, and seemed a little drier, a little less of a dead weight pressing down on her.

Then she heard rustling — not clothing, but a different, drier sound. Unbidden and unwanted, the thought of rats immediately leapt to mind.

They had seen a few rats along the long walk, but never very close, and never when they were inside, in the dark, in a strange and forbidding place.

"What's that?" she asked, dropping her voice to a whisper.

Then a light sprang up suddenly, off to her right; Amy started.

"It's me," Susan said, holding up a lit match and a twist of paper. She lit the paper, shook out the match, and held up her impromptu torch. "I thought we could use some light."

"You had *matches?*" Amy said, astonished. "And you never *told* anyone?"

"I only had about three left," Susan replied. "They were in my purse. Valadrakul seemed to do just fine lighting fires, so I figured I'd save them until we really needed them."

Two or three voices spoke up at once; one of them was Amy, asking, "And you think we need them now?"

"My thanks, mistress," Valadrakul said. "I'd no stomach to try my magic here in Shadow's own keep."

Amy didn't bother arguing with Susan about it, though it still didn't seem *fair*, somehow, that she had had matches and not told anyone. Instead Amy peered around in the darkness, trying to see where they were. The paper was burning quickly, and not casting much useful light; Amy tried to take in as much as she could before it burned away.

They were in a huge chamber of bare stone, fifty or sixty feet wide and at least twice as long, the ceiling invisible in the darkness above — and they weren't alone. A ledge or balcony ran along either side of the immense room, about ten feet up, and on those two ledges were crouched dozens of vague black shapes, shapes with heads and legs and claws, with eyes and gleaming teeth.

Monsters.

"Are they statues?" Singer asked. The tone of his voice made it clear that he didn't think so.

"They're moving," Pel answered.

"I'm not sure that proves anything here," Prossie said.

"They aren't attacking," Singer said, a bit more hopefully.

Then the flame reached Susan's fingers, and she dropped her paper torch to the floor; it flared as it fell, then went out on impact.

"'Tis my guess," Valadrakul said in the renewed darkness, "that Shadow retains these creatures ready here, to be sent hither and yon as the whim strikes it. Were we to be slaughtered, surely 'twould have begun."

Amy turned, looking for anything that might reassure her, but the only things she could see were the last few sparks dying by Susan's feet, and the dim gray arch of the entrance. The light outside had died away completely, full night had fallen — and Sawyer seemed to have vanished; she couldn't see anything of him.

"Now what?" Pel asked.

"We wait," Raven said.

"What, until *morning?*" Amy demanded. "No way. I couldn't *stand* it. Susan, light another ma . . . hey!" A thought struck her. "Matches *work* here? Aren't they technology?"

"Of a sort," Pel agreed. "Susan's gun works, too, remember? But my watch didn't. Some things do, some things don't."

"Blasters don't," Singer said bitterly. "If they did, we wouldn't have any problems."

"Anti-gravity doesn't, either," Prossie added. "Nor telepathy." When Singer started to object, she corrected herself. "At least, not properly; I can only communicate with telepaths back in the Empire."

Amy stared at the doorway, wondering what had become of Sawyer. The others all seemed to be here; she had heard Raven and Valadrakul and Pel and Susan and Singer and Prossie . . .

But Ted hadn't said anything since he told her to shut up, and she hadn't seen him when Susan burned her bit of paper.

"Ted?" she called.

No one answered.

"Ted?!" she screamed.

Again, no one answered; the others all fell silent, listening.

Amy could hear rustlings and scratchings from the creatures on the ledges, could hear the breathing of some of her companions, could hear a faint, distant splashing from somewhere out in the marsh — and somewhere, far off toward the interior of the fortress, she heard footsteps, boot leather on stone.

"He's gone on ahead," she said. "Into the darkness."

"Into Shadow," Raven replied.

*P*el wasn't sure why Amy was so certain that Ted had gone on ahead, but it seemed reasonable enough. Ted believed this wasn't real — or at least, he *said* he believed it wasn't real, and acted as if he believed that — which meant that nothing could hurt him. He therefore wasn't afraid of anything, and he wanted to get it all over with. Why *wouldn't* he have gone on ahead?

Pel had been too concerned with his own worries — Nancy and Rachel and his own attempts to get home — to worry much about Ted, but he had decided back at Base One that Ted's disbelief was a defense mechanism, a way to keep from breaking down completely. Convincing himself that it wasn't real was a way to avoid going into a state of perpetual panic; Ted had always wanted to be in control of his surroundings, and didn't deal well with surroundings that didn't cooperate.

Whether the disbelief was genuine, or just a front Ted put up, Pel wasn't sure, and it didn't really matter, because Ted was tough and stubborn enough to act as if he disbelieved no matter what. Pel had proved that to his own satisfaction weeks ago.

Maybe, Pel thought, Ted had decided that whether it was real or not, it was all a story, and he was the hero. Pel could understand that; he'd thought the same way sometimes. If Ted thought of himself as the hero, then he was destined to win out, no matter what.

To Pel, though, Ted looked more like one of those pitiful innocents in a Hollywood movie who gets killed to show the audience just how rotten and nasty the villain is, to show that this is not a game, that there will be blood and death and violence.

"Ted!" he shouted. "Wait!"

"Shut up!" Singer snapped. "Listen, you two, all of you, stop yelling!"

"But . . ." Amy began.

"We're standing in this thing's headquarters, unarmed, in the dark, defenseless, with monsters lined up on either side of us, and you people are *yelling,*" Singer said angrily. "Do you *want* to get killed?"

"Think you that Shadow cares?" Raven asked. "What are shouts to it?"

"Noisy, that's what," Singer retorted. "Why go out of our way to anger our host? Didn't we come here peacefully, to ask it to send us home?"

Pel blinked in surprise — not that blinking made any difference, in the darkness.

They had, hadn't they?

After what had happened to Bill Marks, after seeing Dibbs and the others hanging over the gate, after all the corpses and monsters, Pel had forgotten that it was possible to think of Shadow as anything but the enemy.

"What about Ted?" he asked quietly.

"Let him go," Singer said. "There's nothing we can do anyway, is there?"

"True," Pel reluctantly admitted.

"So what do we do now?" Amy asked.

"We wait," Raven repeated.

"Or maybe we ask Shadow politely for some light," Singer suggested. "Or to send us home."

"You think it can hear us?" Pel asked, peering around into the darkness.

Then, abruptly, before Singer could answer, light blazed; blinded, Pel threw an arm over his eyes. Even through his closed lids, the light that poured around the shielding arm was intensely bright.

Then, gradually, it dimmed, and after a moment Pel risked opening his eyes, arm still raised.

The floor was blue-gray flagstones, joined so well that the seams were almost invisible. His boots, Imperial military issue, were muddy and badly scuffed; the cuffs of his purple uniform pants were frayed and stained. The light was still bright, but bearable.

Cautiously, he raised his eyes and lowered his arm.

Something was glowing overhead — not the ceiling, which was now visible perhaps fifty feet up, but something several feet below the ceiling, something long and straight that ran from the wall above the gate down the length of the room — if it was a room. Pel looked around.

He and most of the others were standing near one end of a chamber that was perhaps fifty feet wide at floor level, but at least sixty by the time it reached the blue-painted ceiling, thanks to the setbacks on either side where the Shadow things stood. However, it was not at all clear whether it was a room or a corridor, because the length was easily a hundred yards, and the far end was not a wall, but a gigantic staircase leading upward.

The walls were pale gray stone, unadorned — granite, Pel guessed. The floor was blue-gray flagstone, unbroken by rugs, carpets, rushes, or any sort of inlay or decoration. The ceiling was hard to make out beyond the glowing rod, or beam, or whatever it was, but it appeared to be plaster, painted the color of the sky in a baroque fresco, that warm, rich blue that made such a fine background for cherubs and chiffon-draped nudes.

Pel couldn't see any cavorting nymphs here, though — just blank blue. The whole place had a rather barren, unfinished look to it. The intense color of the ceiling didn't seem to go very well with the natural gray of the walls.

The light source was an utter mystery; Pel had never seen anything remotely like it. It was as if there were an invisible tube full of glowing gas running the length of the chamber, then vanishing into that immense stairway.

Ted Deranian was more than halfway to the stairs, Pel saw; everyone else was clustered near the door.

Everyone else human, anyway — there were all those creatures on the ledges, too. Some looked almost normal — panthers and apes — while others were tentacular horrors, or just *things* that Pel couldn't describe. They ranged from the size of a cat — assuming there weren't others he couldn't see that were even smaller — up to a gigantic creature near the gate that could only be called a dragon, so large that it appeared to have some difficulty squeezing onto the ledge.

All of them, even in the brilliant white light, were black. Some were flat grayish black, some were glossy black, but all were black, except for eyes, claws, and teeth. Even the dragon was shiny black, from its pointed snout to its snakelike tail, its taloned feet to its batlike wingtips, scales glistening darkly.

And as Pel watched, the dragon moved.

All of the Shadow creatures looked alive, all of them seemed to be breathing, their eyes open and alert, but the others were motionless — or at least staying where they were; a few twitched or shuddered, a few heads turned, claws shifted slightly.

The dragon, though, was stretching its foreclaws and wings, and black horny claws rasped loudly against stone.

Everyone turned at the sound; Pel saw that Raven was rubbing his eyes and waving his head, as if still blind from the flash, while Singer and Amy were blinking. The others seemed to be okay as they turned to look up at the dragon.

It stretched its neck out over the edge of its ledge and peered down at the humans below; Pel could look directly into its greenish-gold eyes, could see the odd frill, or tendrils, or whatever it was that dangled from the monster's chin, and the hard ridges above the eyes.

Then it slithered down from the ledge.

Singer made a dash for the doorway, but the dragon was faster; the soldier stopped dead only a foot or so from its flank as it interposed itself between the humans and their only exit.

"Damn," Singer said, as he backed away. It was the first word any of them had spoken since the flash.

"Now what?" Prossie asked.

The dragon hissed, but made no threatening moves; it simply sat there, between the humans and the door.

"I think," Pel said slowly, "that this is just another version of those slug things — making sure we can't turn back."

"But Sawyer's outside," Singer objected.

"I suppose he was right," Pel said. "Shadow didn't care about him — but it wants the rest of us."

"So what do we do?" Amy asked.

Pel shrugged. "We go on," he said. "At least now we can see where we're going."

Amy's feet hurt — but then, they had hurt for days now. A year ago, she would have said she could never walk two hundred miles, not if she had all the time in the world and her life depended on it, and especially not when she felt so heavy and tired all the time, whether it was from the gravity here or because she was pregnant. She would have said she could never walk so far.

But now she had done it, and as a direct result, her feet ached. It seemed unfair that even after reaching this stupid fortress, she still had to walk farther. Why wasn't Shadow right there at the front door, waiting for them?

It was probably trying to impress or intimidate them, making them walk down this ridiculous huge room lined with monsters; she didn't see what other possible use such a place could have.

Amy had no intention of being impressed or intimidated, though; she thought the room was ugly, was nothing in comparison to, say, the main hall at Union Station in Washington, even if it was a lot longer. And they'd seen plenty of monsters already — the stovepipe things, and the giant bat, and the others they had fought at the spaceship, and the ones that had attacked them back at Stormcrack the *first* time they saw Faerie. She wasn't particularly surprised by more of them.

At least this time they weren't trying to kill her.

That dragon, though, was crowding them.

It didn't actually push anyone, but as they moved forward, it moved along with them, its talons scratching on the stone floor like fingernails on a blackboard, and it wouldn't retreat — if they tried to turn back it stopped and stood there watching them, lashing its tail like an angry cat's, or like a snake squirming, blocking them. If someone tried to go around it it would lunge, and scamper, and cut off whoever it was that had tried to escape.

Singer and Raven had tried to split up and go around both ends, which was when the party had learned that the dragon's tail was prehensile, capable of tripping a man and then picking him up, and also when they had discovered that the dragon's full, extended length was at least fifty feet — it could stretch itself across the entire width of the hall.

It was also amazingly fast.

Amy hadn't tried to turn back; for one thing, that would mean abandoning Ted, who had vanished up the stairs. She trudged on.

At the foot of the steps, however, she stopped and stared upward, dismayed.

The climb had to be a hundred feet — a ten-story building and then some. That bar of light ran right through the center, though she couldn't see any sort of projector. Someone was sitting at the top, with the ragged remains of a bandage on his head — Ted, waiting for them.

It looked as if he *had* to wait; the stairs seemed to end at a wall.

It didn't make any sense; this was a completely stupid way to arrange a building, she thought. Why weren't there any side-passages? Why did everyone have to go up these stairs? How did anyone get into the rest of the fortress?

It was absurd — but it was here, and very solid and real, and she didn't seem to have much of a choice. She sighed, and started climbing.

*T*he dragon was asleep at the foot of the stairs, curled up like a gigantic cat; as Pel mounted the last few steps he looked down past the light-beam at it, bitterly certain that if any of them tried to go back down the creature would awaken instantly.

He wondered what had happened to Sawyer; had the slug-things gotten him, or had he found a way past, or was he still standing out there, waiting, slowly starving to death?

Of course, Pel felt as if he wasn't all that far from starvation himself. Singer's canteen and Raven's waterbag, stolen three days before from a farmhouse on the road, kept thirst under control, but none of them had eaten a bite since their rather meager breakfast of assorted berries that morning.

Less than a day without food, that was nothing, he tried to tell himself, but his stomach disagreed.

You'd think, he told himself, that he'd be used to it by now. He hadn't eaten properly for weeks. Back home he'd always taken food for granted — oh, let's eat Chinese tonight, let's grab a burger, what about a pizza.

He thought that right now he would be ready to strangle a man with his bare hands if it would get him a decent meal.

Maybe Shadow would feed them eventually — or maybe it would starve them all to death here atop the stairs.

Pel had no intention of starving — if that began to look like a real possibility, he'd go back down and let the dragon make a meal of him, or maybe jump into the light-beam — Valadrakul had warned them all, in his archaic phrasing and barbaric accent, that it would fry anyone who touched it, cook them instantly, that it was basically the same sort of magical zap that he had used against the monsters back at the spaceship, but, in the wizard's phrase, writ large.

No one had cared to test the wizard's claim; they had all stayed well clear as they passed it.

Being *above* the light made everything on this upper part of the climb look strange — faces were lit from below, so the nostrils stood out, as if they were all in a low-budget horror film. The stairs were shadowed, making it harder to climb if one looked down. And the space at the top of the stairs was almost dark.

Pel mounted the final step and stopped.

It wasn't *completely* dark here, by any means; they could all see the wall, with its ornate door, just a few feet away, on the other side of the landing at the top.

The door wasn't anything like the gate below, which was easily at least fifteen feet high and ten feet wide, but this door was still big — maybe ten feet high and five feet wide, Pel guessed. It was red decorated with gold, rather like decor in a Chinese restaurant — Pel wished he could stop associating things with food.

Ted was sitting cross-legged on the bare stone floor in front of the door, waiting; the others were standing along the top of the stair, or just now coming up. Poor Amy was the last; she was panting. This was nothing a woman in her condition should be doing, Pel thought angrily.

He was panting, too, he realized.

Tired, hungry, thirsty, virtually unarmed — they were in *great* shape to confront the all-powerful Shadow.

If, of course, they were going to. If they weren't going to just sit here and starve. If they weren't going to wander on through some interminable maze. If they weren't all going to be killed instantly — after all, if Shadow could create that light-beam . . .

How had he ever got into this? Pel reached down to give Amy a hand up the last three steps, and tried to figure that out.

He hadn't gone anywhere or done anything stupid. He'd just been down in his own basement, minding his own business, when this all began happening around him.

And now his wife was dead, his daughter was dead, Elani and Grummetty and Alella were dead, all those Imperials had died for nothing.

When this was over, they'd probably *all* be dead.

Why was he still going on? What good did it do? Why had he bothered to come this far?

Heroes did this sort of thing in the books he read and in the movies he watched, they fought on against impossible odds as their friends died around them, until at last they defeated evil and saved the world — but he was no hero. He wasn't going to save any worlds. He was just going to die.

Well, everybody dies eventually. He might as well get it over with.

He turned to face the door just as it opened.

Chapter Twenty

Amy closed her eyes to catch her breath as she mounted the final step and let go of Pel's hand. She wondered whether that light bar might be radioactive, whether it would do anything to her unborn baby — though even if it did, she really hoped that wouldn't matter, that she'd be able to abort the thing soon.

Although right now it seemed more likely that she would die and take the baby with her.

Suddenly it seemed as if everyone was shouting, and reluctantly, wearily, she opened her eyes.

The doors were opening, and light was spilling out, bright moving multicolored lights that flashed and sparkled every which way — and which seemed to create shadows between them, as if the differing lights canceled each other out in places, creating darkness. The glare blazed in every color she had ever heard of and several she hadn't, painfully bright; she closed her eyes again and raised a guarding hand. If the light bar wasn't dangerous to be near, something here probably was — in all that chaos there had to be some kind of nasty radiation. If it wasn't radioactivity maybe it was ultraviolet or lasers or something, and she'd get skin cancer or cataracts or her hair would fall out.

And there were sounds — rushings and rustlings, like storm winds, or like some sort of machinery warming up. The dead air of the landing stirred to life. She smelled the electric bristle of ozone, and other scents, metallic and harsh, that she couldn't place.

"I'm not going in there," she said, more to herself than anyone else.

"Ted is," Pel told her.

She opened her eyes slightly and squinted, trying to see through the glare, and sure enough, with one arm shading his eyes, Ted was staggering through the big door right into the lights.

"Oh, damn," she said. She hesitated. "All right," she said, after a second or two, "I guess I *am* going in there." She couldn't have explained her decision very coherently to anyone else, but she knew it had something to do with Bill Marks, torn apart on the road; with Tom Sawyer back there with the stovepipe monsters, with Elani who had died protecting her, and with dead Beth on the gallows because Amy had said she deserved it. Amy had reached the point where she thought she was less afraid of her own death than of feeling responsible for any more of the stupid, pointless deaths of others.

She wondered if Pel felt any of the same thing; he was right there beside her as she walked the few steps toward the door. Was he, too, thinking of Marks and Sawyer and Elani? Or was he remembering his poor wife and their little girl, horribly murdered by people who *might* have been sent by Shadow? Was he thinking about revenge, or was he just getting ready to die, to be with his family? Amy had no way of knowing; it was hardly something she could ask him, as even after the weeks of traveling and waiting and traveling together he wasn't much more than a friendly stranger.

And what about Raven, or Valadrakul, or Al Singer? What about Prossie and Susan? Ted still thought it was a dream, he wasn't worried, but what about the others? Was it courage that drove them forward? All of them were moving, all of them were approaching the door, and Amy wondered *why*. Weren't any of them scared?

She had to stop in the doorway; the flickering glare was too intense to continue. The moving air brushed across her face like fingers, like wings, like blowing leaves, sometimes warm, sometimes cool, sometimes gentle, sometimes sharp as wire. Shadow and color shifted too fast for her to see anything clearly.

Ted had gone through the door, and Pel, and Raven, though Amy didn't know how they could stand to do it. Prossie and Susan and Singer were just behind her, still outside; Valadrakul was at her side.

"What *is* all that, anyway?" Amy asked.

"Magic," Valadrakul said. "The raw energies of Shadow made manifest."

"If it's Shadow, shouldn't it all be *dark?*" Amy asked. She inched forward, took her first step into the chamber beyond the door; her arm was across her face, and colors seemed to ripple and flare on all sides. Pink and orange and electric blue swept across her arm, coloring everything she saw. The air felt oddly stuffy now, as it pressed against her, and she couldn't decide if it was warm or cold.

"It could be dark, if Shadow so chose," Valadrakul told her. His voice sounded unsteady.

Startled, Amy glanced at the wizard.

He was trembling.

*T*he air of the room seemed somehow *compressed,* Prossie thought as she lingered in the doorway.

She didn't like the look of the place at all; the shifting, glaring colors made her think of alarms and beacons and a dozen other sorts of warning, all going off at once, or of some sort of huge machinery going berserk. If the warp generator back at Base One had run wild, she thought it might have looked something like this.

No warp generator had ever run wild, though. Prossie knew what various other kinds of machinery would do when they failed — she had scanned through the memories of engineers any number of times, either directly or second-hand, and had seen what happened when anti-gravity drives imploded, when blasters melted down, when everything went wrong. It was a standard part of the follow-up to any disaster in the Galactic Empire to let the telepaths loose on everyone involved so as to find out what went wrong and who was responsible.

And none of those disasters had ever looked anything like this.

A warp generator malfunction probably wouldn't either, she told herself. No warp generator had ever run amok, but Prossie had read the memories of scientists who thought they knew what it would do, and none of them had seen it being this varied and colorful.

Of course, scientists tended to think of such things in terms of numbers and schematics, not light and color.

Whatever was happening here, she didn't like it, and didn't understand it, and she didn't want to face it alone.

"Carrie!" she thought, trying desperately to project, knowing as she tried that in this unnatural continuum, in Faerie, she couldn't.

She could only hope that Carrie was listening.

*L*ight shows, Pel thought, it was all a light show. Like the trip sequence in "2001: A Space Odyssey," or when the ark is opened in "Raiders of the Lost Ark," or any number of scenes in various other special-effects spectaculars.

Except that this one was different because it was all around, not confined to a screen; he wasn't sitting in a dark theater, he was walking *through* the lights and colors, he thought he could actually *feel* them, and whether he could or not, he could certainly feel the air, and smell and taste it, and it had a weird, static-electric, closed-in feeling even though it was moving.

And the lights weren't flashing in some ill-defined soundstage void; as his eyes adjusted he could catch glimpses of a solid room behind the glare, a colonnaded chamber with gilded decoration on white walls — he couldn't see whether the walls were stone or plaster or what, the light was too bright.

No movie was ever so bright, so intense.

The lights moved and shifted, but there were patterns to them, and they seemed to focus on the far end of the room. He couldn't look directly at whatever occupied that space.

Was that Shadow? If so, it seemed horribly misnamed.

It *ought* to be Shadow, though; they had gone through the whole stupid quest, they had fought monsters and thirst and hunger, trudged hundreds of miles, seen half their companions dead, and finally reached and entered the fortress of the enemy. In all the stories, that meant it was time to confront the Evil Power.

Was this it, then?

All that light and color — *was* Shadow misnamed? Was this some other being or force entirely, one that would send them home? One that could bring Nancy and Rachel back to life? One that would make this whole thing just the dream Ted still said it was?

For all Pel knew, this wasn't Shadow, but God. The blinding light seemed more appropriate to God's glory than to a being called Shadow.

Whatever it might be, this was definitely the pay-off, the climax of the whole horrible adventure.

Behind him, he heard Amy and Valadrakul talking, but he didn't pay much attention. His ears were starting to ring, though he didn't know why; the whooshings and rumblings and flappings that had accompanied the colors died away suddenly, so that besides the two voices, neither of them speaking loudly, the only sounds were the tapping of boots on marble, the shuffle of feet and rustle of clothing, and labored breathing from someone nearby — maybe Ted.

"Are you all right?" Amy asked, her voice concerned; startled out of his thoughts about Shadow, Pel turned to see who she was asking.

*V*aladrakul was trembling violently; Amy could see his beard quivering, and his now-ragged embroidered vest was almost slapping the frayed knees of his purple Imperial pants.

"What *is* it?" she demanded, on the verge of panic. She had never seen Valadrakul visibly frightened or upset before.

"'Tis Shadow," the wizard said, almost gasping. "'Tis the matrix. Look you, how 'tis composed — ah, so splendid! Look you, how majestical! What glory is here before us!"

"It's a lot of bright lights," Amy said uneasily. Perhaps the wizard wasn't scared after all, she realized; perhaps it was something else.

"Nay, you look, but you do not *see!* You've not the eyes, you who know nothing of the arcane arts!"

"Tell us, then, what *you* see," Raven said, stepping up close behind Valadrakul. His left arm shielded his eyes; his black clothing seemed to absorb the light, to be the only solid and unchanging thing in the shifting images.

"The matrix," Valadrakul said. "The heart of Shadow — and what name is that, for this is no feeble shadow, but power incarnate! See, each light a strand of the web, woven gloriously together — why, that beam we passed on the stair, I see now how it fits!" Suddenly, the wizard was striding forward into the room, into the light and color; Amy reached out, tried to catch him as he passed, and missed.

"Look you all," he cried as he marched, "whosoever sits at the center, upon that throne, there is the center of it all! I could no more construct a matrix such as this than a sparrow could swim, but oh, I see how it works, I see what every finest fiber must be! You, who sit there, let me try, I beg you — for but a moment, but the merest instant, give me your place!"

"Who sits *where?*" Amy asked, squinting, trying to see through the glare. She could see no one sitting anywhere; Ted was only a vague, dark blur, and Valadrakul, too, was fading into the brilliance.

"Fool," a voice said, a voice none of them had heard before, rich and loud, but not particularly deep. "The matrix does *my* will, not thine, thou pitiful semblance of a wizard. It centers not upon this seat, but upon *me!*"

The words came from somewhere further in the room, deeper in the blaze of light, beyond Ted and Valadrakul, but Amy still couldn't see anything of the speaker.

"Oh, but let me share it," Valadrakul pleaded. "I could learn so *much* . . ."

"*Too* much, perchance," the voice said. "Begone, wizardling; another step, and perish."

"Oh . . ." Valadrakul began. He stepped forward, hands outstretched, reaching for the glory he saw before him.

And then he burned; the initial golden flash was scarcely noticeable amid the lights, but Amy had been watching Valadrakul, staring at him, and the flames were plain enough.

After the flames the blast struck the wizard, and flung him backward, directly toward Amy; she let out a noise, a choking, gasping noise that might have been a scream had she been able to breathe more deeply before it came out.

An instant later a flash of pure white, pale and almost lost in the polychrome glory of Shadow's presence, burst from the flying remains of Valadrakul — Amy remembered the flash when Elani had died, when her magicks had shattered, and knew that Valadrakul, too, was dead.

The body skidded to a halt by her feet, and Amy looked down through flickering colors at the blackened remains of the mage Valadrakul of Warricken.

His vest was reduced to a few scorched threads; the Imperial uniform had held up somewhat better, and was still mostly intact, but every bit of it was charred black, not a trace of purple remaining. A few beard hairs were still sizzling, and the stench of burning hair made Amy gag even before the blackened ruin of the wizard's face registered on her consciousness.

Something white showed through at one spot, and when Amy realized she couldn't tell if it was exposed bone or exposed eyeball she turned away and decided against bothering to keep down whatever wanted to come up. Her life was turning into a horror; vomiting seemed a perfectly appropriate reaction.

Very little did come up, though; a thin spatter of yellowish fluid, nothing more.

*T*hey were all dead, Pel decided as he looked at Valadrakul's smoking remains. The wizard had been blasted just as effectively, and a good deal more quickly, than the Nazis in "Raiders."

Which meant that while this was plainly Shadow, and not a merciful God, this Shadow, to all intents and purposes, was as powerful here as God.

The smell of burned meat reached Pel's nostrils, and he came to the conclusion that this wasn't an adventure story he was trapped in, it was a horror novel, a Stephen King nightmare.

He should be screaming. He should be fleeing in terror — but there wasn't anywhere to go, and after everything that had already happened, after the long walk and the disembowelled corpses hanging in every town and the deaths of Nancy and Rachel, Pel didn't have the emotional reserves to scream or yell or be shocked by Valadrakul's death.

Something in him was already dead, he thought.

And in a few moments, if Shadow's whim ran that way, all of him would be dead, body and soul.

They were *all* dead.

There was nothing more to lose. He turned back to face Shadow, if that was what sat before them in that polychrome glare, and asked, "What did you do that for?"

For a moment, everything was almost silent, save for odd unidentified rustlings, like those that they had heard when the doors first opened, and a faint popping and hissing that Pel realized with a dull, belated shock was the sound of Valadrakul's corpse cooling. The quiet was so total that it seemed as if the surviving humans were holding their breath, and Pel supposed that some of them were.

The shifting labyrinth of light and color seemed to slow and dim slightly.

"Durst thou address me thus, then?" Shadow's voice asked; Pel thought he heard a note of amusement.

"Why not?" Pel replied. He supposed that monsters weren't used to questions like that, but he didn't care. He was too far gone to really be frightened.

"You've got us; we're all dead anyway."

"Think'st so?" The amusement was definite now, and the voice was higher than Pel had realized.

Pel didn't bother to answer, and Shadow continued, "I'truth, some among you might yet live to see daylight more."

"Well, that's up to you, isn't it?" Pel said. "Any whim that strikes you, there isn't anything *we* can do about it, is there?"

"Nay," Raven shouted suddenly, lurching forward, his still-bandaged fingers raised in a defiant gesture. It occurred to Pel, apropos of nothing, that they ought to be healed by now. "'Tis the duty of all free men, of all who love the Goddess, to resist this thing!" Raven called. "Friend Pel, yield not your soul to it!"

For an instant, Pel thought that they had finally arrived at the climax of the story, that it was an adventure with a happy ending after all, that Raven, the storybook hero, had found some secret weakness, some way to resist Shadow's power. He would draw a magic sword and cut through Shadow's spells, or fling some prepared spell of his own.

Then he realized that that wasn't it at all; this was no simple fantasy. This was more horror. Raven had no secret weapon; he had simply cracked under the strain and done something stupid, not something heroic. He had done something stupid, and he would die for it. If there was any hero here, it wasn't Raven after all.

And Pel didn't really think there was any hero. Not after Valadrakul's death. This was real life, and in real life last-minute rescues didn't always come, sometimes innocents died horribly, sometimes the good guys were slaughtered. Just like a horror story. Real life didn't need to be fair, or just, or satisfying; where was the justice in a plane wreck or an earthquake?

Innocents and good guys died meaningless deaths all the time.

He didn't really know anything about Raven's past, didn't know if Raven was an innocent or a good guy, in any sense of the terms, but right now it looked as if Raven was about to die a horrible and meaningless death.

He was. Pel turned as Raven's velvets flared up, in a blaze of fire and spark; black smoke billowed upward around the man's burning black hair into the golden shafts above, spilling into the light like ink into clear sparkling water. The swarthy skin reddened, then blackened, then disappeared.

There was no shock-wave like the one that had flung Valadrakul's corpse at Amy's feet, and although the self-proclaimed rightful lord of Stormcrack Keep had time to give a brief, anguished cry before the flames consumed him, there was no recognizable corpse, but merely a flurry of black ash.

"I'd worry not of souls, little man," Shadow told the smoking, drifting remains and the shocked survivors. "I deal not in souls; the flesh of this world is enough to concern me."

Pel stared for a moment; he heard Singer make a strangled noise somewhere nearby. He knew he should be shocked, horrified, something, but he wasn't. It occurred to him that Raven had been the last of their native companions; everyone who still stood before Shadow came from either Earth or the Galactic Empire.

He doubted that would make any difference if they ran afoul of one of Shadow's whims.

Ｏne by one, Al Singer thought, it's picking us off one by one and there isn't anything we can do about it.

This was not what he'd joined the military for. This wasn't anything he'd ever imagined.

And he couldn't even fight back. Oh, he still had his blaster, but it wouldn't work here except for whacking someone over the head, or maybe cracking nuts.

He glanced at Prossie Thorpe, the expedition's Special — but *she* didn't work here, either, or at least that was what she said. She couldn't call for help, couldn't read the enemy's plans. She could maybe still talk to Base One, but they couldn't send help in time, if at all — and what's more, they *wouldn't* send it.

Colonel Carson, Lieutenant Dibbs — the officers hadn't been much use on this expedition. And Thorpe said that General Hart had written them all off.

What kind of military solidarity was that? The Empire was supposed to stand behind its men, protect its troops just as the troops protected the Empire.

It looked like that was just another lie, like Father Christmas or virgin brides.

He was beginning to wish that he'd never joined up, had never seen little Laura Bailey mooning over the fancy uniforms at the port and had never decided that the best way to get into her pants was to sign away a couple of years of his life.

It wasn't fair, the six of them up against this . . . this *force,* this *thing.*

And they didn't even know what it was.

"Hey," he called, "if you're concerned with flesh, why don't you show yourself, anyway? Do you need all these colors and lights? Are you afraid to let us see you? Are you that ugly? Is that why you killed the wizard, because he could see through this stuff?"

"Wouldst see me unveiled?" Shadow asked, and Singer thought it sounded surprised.

He remembered some of the stories he'd heard as a kid, whispered around a campfire or read aloud by the hearth, about unspeakable monsters — but he didn't care. He was tired of not knowing what was going on. He wanted to see the thing.

"Well, yeah, why not?" he demanded. "You think we'll go mad at the sight, like in the old stories?"

"I'd hope not," Shadow said. "As you will, then."

Abruptly, the colors faded away, the buzzing in Singer's ears was gone, and the blazing lights faded to a soft golden glow from somewhere overhead. His head hurt; whether he had developed a headache in the glare and simply not noticed, or whether the shift had triggered it, he wasn't sure.

He blinked, his eyes trying to adjust to this sudden change, and then took a good look at what the chamber *really* looked like.

The walls were white marble, ornamented with gilded carvings, behind twin colonnades — but some of the gilt was flaking away. The floor was covered in faded carpets, most of them dark red patterned with darker blue. Before them, in the center of the room, was a low stone dais, and on the dais was a dark wooden throne, the straight back and arms carved with strange flowers and impossible beasts.

Slouched in the throne was a woman.

She was fat, but not obese; aging, but not yet old; unattractive, but not really ugly. Her hair was long and dark brown and somewhat disheveled, spilling over her shoulders in tangled curls; her face was soft, with an unhealthy pallor. She looked to Singer as if she should be sitting behind the counter in some inexpensive shop somewhere, shortchanging customers and chasing children away from the candy.

Someone giggled. Singer heard Pel mutter, "Pay no attention to the man behind the curtain," but he had no idea what the Earthman was talking about.

"*You're* Shadow?" Singer asked.

"Indeed, I am," the woman said, and it was the same voice, though not quite as loud.

This was Shadow.

This frumpy, middle-aged woman was the all-powerful Shadow.

"Oh, come on," Singer said.

"Judge not by appearances, child," the woman chided him. "The matrix yet stands, and I am yet at its heart, though thou seest it not; I've but rendered it invisible, not impotent."

"But you're just an old woman!" Singer blurted.

And in his last instant, as he saw the old woman frown, he knew that she really was Shadow, that he had seen Raven and Valadrakul killed for displeasing her, and that now *he* had displeased her. Just because the lights were gone, that didn't mean her power was.

His last thought was to wish that he had never seen Laura Bailey at all, because then he wouldn't be about to die so stupidly, in this horrible alien place. He didn't have the time to think anything more profound.

He didn't even have time to think that at least it was quick.

*P*el watched Singer die, as Raven and Valadrakul had died; the flames seemed more impressive now that the light show was gone.

When only smoldering ash remained, he turned back to Shadow. "Was that necessary?" he asked.

Shadow shrugged. "Necessary or no, 'twas my wish," she said.

"And that's all that matters, isn't it?"

"Aye." Shadow made no attempt to keep the self-satisfaction out of her voice.

"Can we get this over with, so I can wake up?" Ted asked.

Shadow glanced at Ted, at the filthy remnant of bandage on his head, then asked Pel, "Is he deranged?"

Pel hesitated, trying to think which answer would be least likely to reduce Ted, too, to charred fragments.

They were all dead anyway, and maybe he would wake up back on Earth, and he couldn't second-guess Shadow, anyway; he didn't know enough about her. There wasn't any reason to lie. "I'm afraid so," he said.

"Amusingly so?"

"Sometimes."

"Then he lives; I've need of amusement betimes."

"Is that why you brought us here, then?" Pel demanded. "For your amusement?"

"In part," Shadow answered.

"And the three you killed weren't amusing enough?"

Shadow waved a hand dismissively. "What amusement in a hedge wizard who thinks he might wield my power? Many of them have I seen, i' these many years, and all in the end I've slain. And a displaced lordling, in his towering rage? Scores have I seen and slain. The soldier, in truth, was new, but scarce new enough; in these past few days I've seen his like a dozen times over. You saw his companions at the gate, an you troubled to raise your eyes."

"We saw," Pel agreed. "So you'll kill us all, one by one, when we bore you or annoy you?"

"Perhaps," Shadow said, "but perhaps not. I did guide you here, as thou sayest, and 'twas purposeful. Serve me well, and thou shalt live, each of you."

Pel puzzled for a moment over the pronouns in that sentence until he realized that Shadow was using "thou" as singular and "you" as plural; he supposed it made sense. Raven and Valadrakul hadn't used "thou" at all, that he could recall; it was confusing.

Then he forced himself to stop thinking about such trivia. She had just said they might yet live.

It was a story after all, an adventure story. It was real life, but it was following the stories. He recognized it now. This was the part where the villain explained herself, where she revealed her whole evil plan and offered them a chance of some kind, and the hero was supposed to refuse it.

Raven hadn't been the hero — he had died, while the villain still lived, so he hadn't been the hero; heroes could only die while heroically saving others, they couldn't throw their lives away in stupid frontal attacks that left the villain untouched.

Who was the hero, then?

He glanced at the others — at Amy Jewell, clutching her belly and looking nauseated; at Ted Deranian, standing to the side looking bored and impatient; at Susan Nguyen, hanging back warily; at Prossie Thorpe, confused and frightened.

It might be Susan; it might even be Amy. Either of them could be the unexpected hero, the ordinary person who finds unseen strength — Susan with her history of suffering, Amy with her unborn child for inspiration.

Somehow he couldn't see poor mad Ted in the hero role, nor quiet Prossie with her muffled telepathy, her military pose not hiding her general vagueness.

Amy or Susan might fit, but the most likely candidate was himself. He was the one doing the talking, after all. He was the one who had insisted they come here.

He didn't feel very heroic, but then, he'd heard that heroes usually didn't.

Well, if he was the hero — and he still wasn't convinced — he might as well carry on with the role.

"All right," he said. "Let's hear about it."

Chapter Twenty-One

*A*my was impressed with Pel's courage, to stand there and argue with the woman who claimed to be Shadow, or at least to represent Shadow. She wasn't sure it was really very bright, but it was certainly courageous, after three out of eight of them had been murdered.

She couldn't believe how calmly she was taking it, that the three had been . . . had been *fried.* She had been traveling with those people all this time, and now they were *dead,* horribly dead, burned; she wanted to scream and cry and faint, but she didn't dare even do that, because the thing that killed them was still here, all around, and if she did anything it might kill *her.*

And she did not want to die.

Yet Pel was talking back to it — he was brave, but maybe stupid.

She had resisted Walter, but she had known when to shut up, so as not to be killed; she hoped that Pel knew as much.

And for now, she wasn't going to say anything. She didn't want to die.

No one else was saying anything any more, either; were they all as terrified as she was?

Ted was crazy, so he didn't count.

She glanced back at Susan, who was still on the narrow landing beyond the door, not in the throne room at all, and saw her slip a hand into her purse.

Amy remembered that Pel had talked about emulating Bakshi's "Wizards," where the evil wizard was ready for any sort of magical attack, so the good wizard pulled out a pistol and blew him away. She remembered the Arab swordsman in "Raiders of the Lost Ark," too.

Shadow, despite her power, just looked like an ordinary woman; maybe, if Susan shot her, she would just die like an ordinary woman. Maybe she would die, and Amy would live. And if there was ever going to be a time to use that pistol, Amy had to agree that this must be it — but shouldn't Susan get closer? She couldn't be sure she'd hit the woman at all from way back there, let alone kill her with the first shot — and Amy didn't think she'd have time for more than one.

Maybe Susan was waiting for a distraction; well, Pel was providing that, wasn't he?

"Let's hear about it," Pel said.

That was an invitation to a speech if Amy had ever heard one; maybe the

Shadow woman would get talking and forget herself.

Still, Susan was too far away. Amy unobtrusively beckoned her forward, as Shadow said, "I have lived long, little people from realms beyond this world; my magicks have given me years beyond measure, have kept me from aging. I grow, not weary, but bored, and seek distraction."

"What, so you just want to talk?" Pel asked.

That didn't seem very likely; this awful woman would scarcely have driven them here with her monsters just to chat. She probably had something gruesome and disgusting in mind, something worse than anything Walter had done.

Amy hoped that Shadow would die before she could do whatever it was, instead of after, as Walter had.

Shadow laughed, a very unpleasant laugh. Amy turned quickly, ignoring Susan, keeping her attention on the horrible woman on the throne.

"Nay, fool," Shadow said. "I seek to explore new worlds. I've my fill of this one."

She hadn't noticed what Susan was doing — either that, or she didn't care. Amy wondered if Shadow could read minds. Prossie couldn't, here in Faerie, but maybe Shadow could. If so, she was just toying with them all, she knew what Susan had in her purse.

Maybe, Amy thought, I'd better not think about it.

Instead, she tried to concentrate on what Shadow was saying, to involve herself in that — though she hoped it wouldn't matter what Shadow wanted.

Pel frowned. "So where's the problem?" he said. "You're the one who can open those magical portals, right?"

Amy shook her head. Pel was being stupid. He wasn't leading Shadow on well enough.

"She wants native guides," Amy suggested. "People who can show her around, keep her out of trouble." She had moved around to one side a little, hoping to draw Shadow's attention away from Susan. She didn't really think that was what Shadow wanted; she just wanted to keep that nasty old woman talking.

"Near the heart, wench," Shadow answered, "but not to the meat of it."

"So tell us, then," Pel said. "At least, if it's something where we need to help you consciously, and you don't just need a bunch of blood sacrifices or something."

"If it's sacrifices," Amy added, trying not to sound too upset with the idea, "I think we'd just as soon not know." She tried very hard not to look back to where Susan was creeping through the door, nearer to Shadow's throne.

"And what need would I have of *your* blood that would not be served by another's, more easily had?" Shadow asked.

"So tell us about it," Pel repeated.

*T*he villains in the stories never needed so much coaxing, Pel thought; they'd start babbling about their plans at the drop of a hint. How was he supposed to play the hero, and find a way out, if Shadow wouldn't explain what it — or she — was up to? He smiled expectantly at the flabby, blowsy, drab woman that was Shadow.

She hardly looked the part of a world-conquering wizard, but this wasn't Hollywood.

"Know you aught of matrices?" she asked.

"No," Pel said. "At least, not the way you mean it, not if you mean magic ones."

Shadow nodded. "Indeed, magic," she said. "A matrix is a gathering of magical forces, a construction of magicks, a framework."

"Valadrakul said something about webs," Amy said. Pel glanced at her; she seemed to be getting more talkative, all of a sudden.

"Aye," Shadow agreed. "A web, or a net — i'truth, a matrix can be likened to many things, all in some way truthful, yet none a complete description. And there are some — or there *were* — who had the talent for the weaving of them."

Pel nodded encouragingly; she was finally telling her story.

Shadow settled back in her chair. "This was centuries past," she said, "long ere your fathers' fathers were born. There were those of us in the world who learned the making of matrices, and we were friends, and teachers, and students, and rivals, one to another, and sometimes we were bitter enemies. We twined our magicks, erected our structures thereof, each after his own fashion, but each learning from the others.

"Thus it was, for many years, for centuries before my own birth; how it began was lost in the past. Magic was loose and wild in the world, free for the taking, so that any person who could speak the words of a simple charm might use it, but only a few of us, only a very few, had the talent for binding the wild magicks and building matrices that we could take with us, that we could send forth, that we could use for purposes more profound than mere kitchen spells.

"Yet the matrix wizards of that time were mortal, and died, and when each died the matrix he had built crumbled, and the magicks bound therein burst free. See you the way of it?"

"I think so," Pel said. It seemed clear enough.

"See then, in time, certain discoveries were made; a method was found whereby a wizard's matrix might be taken from him intact, and bound to another, should the binder be present when the wizard failed. Further, 'twas learned how one could turn magic upon one's own aging and stave off the ravages of time; a matrix wizard need not grow old, should he attain sufficient mastery."

Pel nodded.

"But see you, then, what this meant," Shadow said, gesturing dramatically. "We had the time to gather to ourselves *all* the magicks, to bind and bind and bind until the wild magicks were no more, until only matrix wizards, or those we permitted to tap our matrices, could work even the simplest spell or cantrip. And further, when that was done, there was no way to gain more, save by the usurpation of another wizard's matrix — and most commonly, by another wizard's murder, for how else to wrest away a well-made matrix? That rivalry that had always been present, that competition amongst us, turned deadly, and we began to entrap one another, to slay one another, to form alliances and partnerships, only to betray one another when better alliances offered." She sighed. "Perhaps were better that had never been, but nonetheless, thus it became."

"I understand," Pel said.

He thought he did, too. Like animals fighting over a prize until only one survived, the matrix wizards had killed each other off — and the survivor wouldn't be the best or brightest, but the most vicious killer of the lot.

And here she was in front of him, presumably.

He wished he could see how to use this against her. Had she built her matrix around a magic ring, or something? There *had* to be some flaw in her power.

"I was called Shadow," she said, "because I kept ever in the background; I'd been a timid child, and change was slow in coming. Yet I was no fool, and I chose my allies and my betrayals carefully, so that in time, I controlled the greatest single matrix ever held." She waved a hand, and brilliant colors rippled through the air for a moment, a reminder of her power. "I took this fortress for my own, slaying the wizard who held it before me, because 'twas in this place that the natural lines of power were strongest. I built my matrix ever larger, in my own time and quietly." She sighed. "But of course, the tallest tree is the one every woodsman wishes to hew down, and my power became too great to conceal. The other matrix wizards banded against me, and spread lies among those who could no longer wield magic, and among those who could tug at the stray ends of it, as it were, but who could not weave their own webs. They made me out a figure of terror and evil; they turned my own name 'gainst me, named me Shadow as 'twere the shadow of death; they spoke of this marsh as a damned, dead place, when i'truth 'tis but an ordinary marsh; they noted my dislike for the sun, and the rains I summon, and made of this something twisted and dark."

Pel could read mounting anger in Shadow's face; these were obviously not happy memories for her. Maybe he could use that somehow. Maybe he could psychoanalyze her into impotence or surrender — except he wasn't a psychiatrist, he was a marketing consultant.

He wondered how much truth there really was in her story, and how much was marketing.

"I'll not deny," she said, calming somewhat, "that I was not, perhaps, the most pleasant of neighbors; 'tis true that I slew those peasants who displeased me, as I do yet, but this was the common practice among the matrix wizards at our height. Why this should be turned against *me*, when all did it . . ."

She caught herself, paused, then continued, "Yet it was. Even that sanctimonious fool who called himself the Green Magician slew half a dozen lovers, yet he turned the peasants against me. Nor was he the worst; the Light, as they called themselves, were all hypocrites and liars — yet their words did their work, and ere I knew it, my reputation was that of the wolf, the scorpion, the vilest beast upon the face of the land. And all, all because I'd dared to build to myself the mightiest matrix of them all." She paused for a moment, then shook her head in remembered disbelief of such injustice.

"So . . ." Pel said, hoping she would give some clue he could use.

"*So,*" Shadow snapped, "in time, I was *forced* by such perfidy to destroy *all* the other matrix wizards, and add their matrices to my own, until at last I controlled all the magic in the world — or at least, I had it at my beck, for in truth the matrix is so vast that I cannot control it all for every moment. Thus, the little wizards of today can pick at it betimes, snatch away a splinter here and there for their petty spells — but what of it? 'Tis naught to *me!*" She waved away the whole matter. "Yet the lies about me persisted, and those poor magicless fools, the peasants and most especially their silly lordlings, still struggled 'gainst me, so that in time I was forced to extend my domain over all the mundane world, as well as the magical. I would suppose that the late claimant to the barony of Stormcrack told you some of that."

"A little," Pel agreed.

"He and his kind existed by my tolerance," Shadow said. "Never were they worth the bother to exterminate."

"I can believe it," Pel said wryly — and honestly. He had not found Raven and his companions very impressive as revolutionaries. He'd seen no signs of a real organization, of intelligence-gathering, of anything but a willingness to oppose Shadow.

And what good was that, if Shadow was as powerful as everyone said?

"At any rate," Shadow continued, "I found myself mistress of all the world — and I grew bored. For centuries, I schemed and fought, always expanding my power — and now I had reached the limits; there were no foes left worthy of my attention, no new lands to conquer. So I drew in to myself, and sought some new entertainment. I experimented with magic, I reached out with senses beyond your poor comprehension — and I succeeded! I found . . ." She turned to Prossie. "I found thy Galactic Empire, with its spaceships, its machines, its telepaths, its many worlds, its myriad wonders and delights, and *there*, I thought, there I saw the solution to my boredom."

"Oh," Prossie said uneasily. Pel glanced at her, then back at Shadow.

He supposed that Shadow meant she intended to conquer the Galactic Empire; that seemed like the sort of thing an all-powerful evil wizard would want to do.

Though to be honest, Pel couldn't really see the point in it when she already ruled an entire world.

Shadow nodded. "First to tour," she said, "and then perhaps to conquer, to play with, to amuse myself with entire worlds — *that* would be an entertainment worthy of me, and one that would last for centuries!"

Pel grimaced.

Boredom as a motive for an inter-universal war of conquest? Not hatred, or anger? Not revenge, or power-hungriness? Just plain old boredom?

Well, why not? When one had centuries in which to become bored, when one already had so much power that there were no other challenges left, why not?

"Carrie," Prossie screamed silently, "do you *hear* this?" She was on the verge of panic, she *knew* she was on the verge of panic, but she couldn't help it. She was trapped and alone here, without her family to support her.

"I hear it," Carrie answered, "but what can I *do* about it? Hart and Bascombe won't listen to me; they don't care."

"She wants to play with whole planets," Prossie said desperately. "How can they not care?"

"Because they won't believe it," Carrie replied. "They can't think on that scale. Besides, why hasn't she already *done* it, they'll ask, and you don't have an answer."

"I might in a few minutes," Prossie replied. She was having trouble accepting Carrie's apparent indifference; this was her *cousin*, her friend, a person she'd shared her thoughts with over and over. It was true Prossie had deliberately left the family, given up her ties to the Empire, but even so, how could Carrie be so uncaring?

It was as if, to Carrie, she was no longer a telepath at all.

She knew that some of her distress must be leaking through, that Carrie knew what she felt, and she waited for Carrie to give her some sort of reassurance.

Carrie replied with the mental equivalent of a shrug.

*N*ow, Pel thought, they were getting to the traditional villain's pitch. They'd gone through the whole self-justification speech; now Shadow could get to the point.

He wondered again how much of her story was true.

"So what does that have to do with *us?*" he asked. "Why didn't you just go invade the Galactic Empire, if that's what you wanted?"

"Because I *can't*, fool!" Shadow shouted. "Think you I'd be here now, could I?"

"Oh," Amy said, "I get it. Magic doesn't work there."

"Ah," Shadow said, pointing at Amy, "*one* among you has some wit!"

"So you can't conquer the Empire directly," Pel said.

"But you sent your creatures," Prossie pointed out. "You could send more, couldn't you?"

"Aye, my creatures," Shadow agreed. "I can send whatever spies and servants I please, and hearken to their reports when they return — and what of it? They tell me of marvels; I would *see* those marvels for myself! Conquest, when I know not what there is to conquer? I can create homunculi, I can raise the dead to fight for me, and i'truth I think I could lay waste all the Empire and claim it for my own, in time — but what sort of ruler would I be, unable to set foot upon my own land? How could I call those lands my own, if I could not see to them?"

Pel blinked.

"Can you really make whole armies of those things?" Prossie asked.

"Certes, I can," Shadow replied. "Do you doubt it?"

"Oh, well, it's been seven years, and all the Empire ever found were scouts and some dead monsters . . ."

"And 'tis all I've sent, thus far, those and my spies, but 'twas no true test of my powers, woman — I have not yet begun. I sought to learn what could live in that unnatural realm of yours; i'truth, the forms that abide well there are sore few!"

"But wait a minute," Pel said. "If you can send whole armies there, why can't you go? Even if your magic doesn't work there, you could go visit, then come back, couldn't you?"

"Ah, now we reach the kernel. No, fool, I cannot. For think you, if I leave this world, and take my matrix not with me, what befalls? And if I open the gate and step forth, but remain not here to hold the gate open, how shall I then return?"

Full understanding of Shadow's dilemma abruptly dawned on Pel.

"Oh," he said.

"Now you see," Shadow said. "And see you this also, I even thought that perhaps I might yield up the matrix, and go forth to dwell forever among the Empire's worlds, with an army to serve me and keep me strong — until I bethought of the passage of time. For what is it that preserves me from senility and death, but the matrix I hold? The Empire's not worth my very life!"

"You mean, like, you'd instantly age a thousand years, or however old you are, without your magic?" Amy asked. Pel immediately thought of movies again — "Lost Horizon" and others, where immortal villains had done just that, fading to dust when their magic was lost.

Shadow snorted in derision. "Nay," she said, "this age of mine is no seeming, but truth. I'd be there as I am here. Howsoever, I'd not *remain* so, but would age as others do, would grow old and in the fullness of time, as the traditional phrase of those with little understanding would have it, I would die. Die! I, face death? I'd not have it, when by staying here I have eternity."

"An eternity of boredom," Pel pointed out.

"Exactly," Shadow agreed. "Wouldst choose death o'er ennui? I'd never."

"I still don't see what you want from us, then." Amy said. "We can't play native guides if you can't go there."

"I think I see," Pel said, with sudden comprehension. He couldn't really believe he had this right, but he couldn't come up with anything else Shadow could want.

And if he was wrong, it wouldn't be the first time.

Startled, Amy turned to him. "What?"

"She wants someone to hold the door for her until she gets back," Pel said.

Shadow nodded. "Precisely," she said. "To hold the door, and to hold the matrix ready, that I may resume it upon my return; if there's none holding it, 'twill crumble, and the wild magicks will be freed again."

Pel couldn't believe it would be this simple. There had to be something wrong with this. Shadow must have safeguards in mind, or some sort of trickery.

"But I . . ." Amy stammered. "You mean you want one of *us* to . . ."

"I would make one of you a matrix wizard in my place, and in my service," Shadow said, with a nod.

Chapter Twenty-Two

Shadow did not give anyone time to protest — not that Pel had any intention of protesting. He supposed some of the others might have said something, if Shadow hadn't gone on speaking.

"See you, none from *this* world can serve; the ability to hold a matrix is lost here. Those who e'er could do so, so they did, and so in their time they all, save me, died," Shadow explained.

"You can't make a whatchacallit, a homunculus, to do it?" Pel asked — not that he really thought Shadow wouldn't have tried that long ago; he was just trying to clear away all doubts, to satisfy his own curiosity and tie up loose ends. It was plain that they were nearing the end of the story, when one of them would be offered Shadow's power.

He wondered who it would be, and whether he or she would accept, and what the consequences would be. Which would be better, to accept or refuse?

This was real life, he reminded himself; he couldn't rely on the most dramatically-satisfying conclusion.

"Nay," Shadow said. "No homunculus nor other creation, nor either a dead man, for while I can instill therein a semblance of life, indistinguishable by any normal means from any mortal born, yet some certain spark is lacking. Perhaps 'tis true that the Goddess lives, and blesses each infant with her gift, and 'tis this gift that lacks; I know not, neither do I care. I know only that 'tis lacking."

Pel trembled slightly; she had said it again, that she could restore the dead to life — and indistinguishably.

"So if none of the locals can do it," Amy asked, "how do you know *we* can?"

"Thinkest I'd not have tried thee?" Shadow answered. "Each of you has been tested and found fit. The Stormcrack lord was not, of course, and the wizardling could have held only the fraction, not the whole. None from the Empire save this one have the gift — yet all the four from Earth do. Perhaps 'tis something in the nature of the worlds whence you come, or perhaps 'tis mere chance, but whatever the reason, so 'tis."

"Maybe it's connected to telepathy, somehow," Pel suggested. "I mean, if Prossie has it but none of the others did."

"You're really sure that no one from your own world can do it?" Amy asked.

"Sure enow," Shadow replied. "Further, an I found one who had somehow escaped destruction, or one born a throwback to times past, how could I trust such a one? For in this land, whoever holds the matrix of Shadow is supreme, and whether it be me or another matters not a whit. You, though — thou and thou and thou — this place is not yours, and what wouldst have here?"

"You don't think any of us would be interested in ruling a world?" Pel asked. Ted giggled; the other Earthpeople ignored him, but Pel was uncomfortably aware how stupid his question sounded.

Still, he felt he had to ask it; he had to know just what the terms were, and why Shadow thought she could make her plans work.

"Not *this* world," Shadow said. "Look you, whosoever I choose shall have of me whatever he will, save that it endanger me not. Wouldst go home, to thy native land? Thou shalt be there instanter, upon my return. Wouldst have power there? Shalt have slaves sent thither to do thy bidding, whole armies, an thou wishest it. Riches untold for the asking, whole worlds at thy feet — for I have riches and power without limit, and shall not stint my faithful servants."

"It sounds good," Pel said slowly. He couldn't resist any longer; he had to ask straight out, "But how do we know we can trust you?"

Shadow glared at him, and flickers of light and darkness obscured her features; bands of color chased one another across the walls, and the air seemed to hum silently.

"Thou durst ask?" Shadow demanded.

"I . . ." Pel's voice caught in his throat.

"Thinkest thou on thy choice, fool!" Shadow shouted. "To trust, and perhaps win wealth and glory, or to refuse, and surely die!"

Pel hesitated.

"And knowest thou," Shadow added warningly, "if thou considerest betrayal on thine own part, that though I shall have not my matrix and the power gained thereby, yet shalt thou have my hand 'gainst thee as long as thou livest, and all my knowledge turned 'pon thy destruction. Thou shalt have the matrix, aye, but shalt have the knowledge to wield it? Shalt have the experience to defy me, and mine own foes in this land, and surely the Galactic Empire as well?"

"So we couldn't use the matrix anyway, you're saying," Pel said, relieved — Shadow's immediate moment of fury seemed to have passed, and besides, he could now see some of her reasoning, which was reassuring.

He much preferred to have the catches out in the open, where he could see them.

"Oh, in this and that, in those appliances requiring neither skill nor finesse, thou might bludgeon a way to thy end," Shadow told him, "but think not that the mere grasp on power without comprehension shall gain thee what I struggled centuries to learn, to compile and constrain to my will."

"But if we go along, you'll send us all safely home, and make us rich?" Amy asked; Pel heard both eagerness and doubt in her voice.

"Nay, 'tis thus not assured," Shadow said. "I'll but grant the whims of the one that serves; the fate of the others shall be for the one to determine."

"Well, I'm sure that'll mean we all get sent home," Amy said, glancing worriedly at Ted.

"If you're telling the truth and don't change your mind," Pel heard himself say.

He didn't know just why he had said it; he didn't *really* want to antagonize Shadow. This was his chance to have Shadow's power at his disposal.

If it was true.

"Look you, then," Shadow said, waving an arm.

The air to one side of the throne rippled oddly, like the air above a hot stove. A dull pressure made Pel's ears ache. He was unsure what he was supposed to look at; the rippling didn't seem to be *doing* anything. He started to say something, then stopped; Shadow was still working at whatever it was, her hands moving in odd, brisk little clutching gestures. Her control of the glare of the matrix was slipping as she was distracted, so that shafts of colored light flitted about, and blobs of shadow rolled suddenly across Pel's field of vision, vanishing before he could focus on them.

For what seemed like an hour, Pel and the others waited for whatever it was Shadow was doing to be complete; a tension grew, and Pel was unsure whether it was entirely emotional, or whether some force was literally charging the air around him.

Shadow's face was lost behind a silvery-pink glitter, and blue sparkles were spattering across the ceiling, when the ripple vanished from the air and she spoke again.

"See you here, then," Shadow said, "a portal to a worldlet in the Empire. Step through, Telepath, and in that place shalt thou be able to hear my thoughts, and to know the truth of what I say, and to so testify to these others."

*P*rossie stared at the spot where the air had wavered as a rabbit might stare at a wolf, her eyes locked on it even though there was nothing there to see.

Here she was being offered what she had never really expected, a chance to return to the Empire.

Could she take it?

After all, she had broken the law; she had betrayed her trust; she had given up her family. If she stepped through, her own family would denounce her and see her condemned to death; she knew that from her last contact with Carrie, from Carrie's indifference to Prossie's danger. If Prossie stepped through and remained in the Empire, she would be hunted down and slain.

But if she refused, Shadow might well kill her here and now.

Reluctantly, she took a step.

"Takest thou a goodly deep breath, Telepath," Shadow said.

Prossie looked up at her, startled.

Shadow smiled cruelly. "Thinkest me a fool?" she said. "Beyond is no world of men, but a bare, bitter rock, with scant air and none that might be breathed by such as thou; thou shalt have but a moment there to look into my soul, and then must thou return or perish."

Prossie blinked. She remembered anew what she was dealing with. This was no ordinary wizard; this was *Shadow*, the cruel overlord of Faerie, the being that had threatened the Empire, had sent monsters and saboteurs to destroy anyone who opposed her. Shadow would think nothing of sending a woman out into the void without a suit, without even a breath-mask — but Prossie could not take it so lightly. She had known a telepath, a great-uncle, who had been present when a ship's hull was breached, and Prossie trembled at the thought, at the stolen memories of men dying in vacuum, of lungs straining for air that wasn't there, of the fierce pressure behind bulging eyes, of sweat and saliva boiling off into the emptiness.

And she remembered something else.

"Wait a minute," she said unsteadily. "No one can read your mind; we tried. My family, I mean — the other telepaths. Reggie died trying."

"Ah, then that was no false tale concocted by the Empire's storytellers?" Shadow asked, and Prossie thought she could see a nasty little smile behind the deep orange glow that hid Shadow's face at that moment.

"No, it's not a tale," Prossie said, gasping, on the verge of panic. "It was true! I read it!"

"Fear not, little thought-thief," Shadow said. "I'd not destroy thee thus. When thou'rt beyond yon gate shall I put aside what I can of the matrix, so that thou might see into my soul without harm."

"You can do that?" Prossie asked, grasping desperately at the hope.

But she still didn't want to read Shadow's mind, and she still doubted she could — to locate a single mind from another universe, in the time she could hold her breath, while exposed to a hostile environment?

And she was just getting comfortable with herself; she didn't want to be plunged into a mind like Shadow's, a mind centuries old and full of foulness and treachery, a mind that was not troubled by the gutted corpses over the fortress entry, not troubled by the fiery destruction, just moments before, of three enemies. Prossie did not want any part of that.

But she didn't want to die, to be the fourth one of the party burned to ash, either.

"An I cannot clear the way enow," Shadow said, "do not force thyself unto madness, nor death, but return straightway; we'll find other means."

Prossie still hesitated — until she saw Shadow begin to frown.

*A*my watched Prossie walk fearfully toward the portal, and she wished there were something she could do, some way to take away Prossie's fear, or to make it unnecessary for her to go — but what could she do? Shadow had told Prossie to go, and disobeying Shadow meant dying.

Maybe if she said she'd believe Shadow without Prossie's word, that she'd take the silly matrix — but she *didn't* believe Shadow, any more than she had believed Stan when he said he wasn't angry, or Walter when he said he wouldn't hurt her, or Beth when she had said she was just as frightened as Amy was herself. She couldn't believe a bully any more; they always lied, always, and Prossie's report wouldn't change anything, because the bullies believed their own lies.

If only someone could do something to make Shadow stop . . .

She glanced back at Susan, who had crept into the room long minutes before, virtually unnoticed. She was moving so *slowly.* Susan's hand was in her purse, closed around something, and she was inching closer to Shadow from the opposite side while Shadow watched Prossie, while Pel watched Prossie, while Ted stared vacantly at no particular part of the whole scene.

Why hadn't Susan shot Shadow while it — or she, whichever — was conjuring up this portal to the Empire? Shadow had been distracted, at least slightly; was Susan expecting a better chance?

Amy blinked, as realization struck.

Susan *was* hoping for a better chance — and she might get it. When Shadow conjured the gateway, it was very much involved in its magical matrix — the colors had been visible, though not the blinding glare they had all seen earlier. And the matrix would almost certainly be able to stop a bullet, even if Shadow was distracted.

But Shadow had said she'd be putting aside the matrix so Prossie could read her mind.

Did that mean she'd be putting aside *everything* that protected her?

Susan apparently thought so.

Susan obviously didn't believe Shadow's lies about sending them home afterward any more than Amy did.

Amy quickly turned away, not looking at Susan, very definitely not looking at Susan, looking anywhere except at Susan, and she watched as Prossie gulped air, stepped forward, and vanished.

*T*he stars blazed brilliantly overhead, the rock was black beneath her feet, the cold tore at her like knives slashing at her bare hands and face as the moisture was torn away. She had to struggle to keep the air in her lungs, the pressure here was very low; she had to be careful to shuffle her feet, not to kick, because the gravity couldn't be more than a few percent of a gee, a good kick could send her right off the surface of this asteroid, or moon, whichever it was, and it might take longer than her oxygen would last before she fell back to the bare stone ground.

And as if the physical pain wasn't enough of a distraction, the thoughts of a galaxy full of people poured in on her, the minds of thirteen billion people all going about their own business, and scattered among them the thoughts of the four hundred other telepaths shone like diamonds in sand; she had forgotten what it was like, it was like a cold wind blowing through her, and like steam boiling in behind, it was hard to remember her own identity at first.

But there was Carrie, calling to her, asking what was going on, calling her by name, and she remembered who she was, and why she was there; she was Proserpine Thorpe, Registered Master Telepath, and she was there to read Shadow's mind. She reached back through the . . through the dimensional barrier, she took the phrase from some unguarded, unrecognized mind somewhere, she reached into Faerie and she could feel her lungs straining, her lips were dry and cracking and her ears were burning with cold and pounding with the roar of her own blood and roaring with the pressure of her breath.

She ignored Carrie, she reached into Faerie and found minds there, she found the familiar first, the patterns she already knew — Wilkins was still alive in a town she didn't recognize, Sawyer was still alive and halfway across the marsh, and then she found Amy and Susan and Pel and Ted, there in the fortress, and Susan was pulling the gun from her purse and Amy knew about it and wasn't saying anything, Ted and Pel didn't see, and the other mind there was Shadow, it had to be, a dark, narrow little mind that seemed to go on forever.

And Shadow wasn't planning treachery, she honestly believed she would keep her promises, but down below that, in the tangle of memories and motivations that Shadow wouldn't allow herself to recall, Prossie saw the dark vicious selfishness that lurked in every human mind. In Shadow it was deep and strong, great and powerful, it had been growing unchecked for centuries, as Shadow's every whim was fulfilled.

She was not lying — but she would betray them and destroy them anyway, in time.

And at that realization Prossie panicked and dove back for the magical space-warp, aware as she did that Susan's finger was closing on the trigger of a .38 revolver that still held two bullets.

*P*el jumped at the sound of the first shot; panicking, he whirled, trying to see what was happening. His first thought was that the building was collapsing, that he had heard a roof-beam crack.

Then he saw the pistol in Susan's hand as she fired again.

"What are you *doing?*" he screamed.

She was only about six feet away, shooting Shadow in the back; she couldn't possibly miss at that range. She was shooting Shadow, and then there wouldn't be anyone who could send them home, there wouldn't be any matrix he could use to bring Nancy and Rachel back from the dead.

Prossie had reappeared by the time the second shot sounded, kneeling on the floor, trembling, gasping, frost forming on her hair and hands and the legs of her uniform, and Amy had stepped back to watch, and Ted was just *standing* there, giggling.

"It's coming apart," Ted cried. "I *must* be waking up!"

And Shadow wasn't falling, wasn't bleeding, she was turning around slowly and deliberately.

Susan dropped the revolver; it clattered loudly on the stone floor as she sank to her knees. She bowed her head and waited, kneeling, as Shadow took a step toward her.

This was all mad, Pel thought. This wasn't how it was supposed to go. This wasn't a proper end to the story. He'd all but forgotten about that stupid gun, about his suggestion that Susan might shoot Shadow. He'd thought Prossie would step back calm and whole and confirm Shadow's story, and the fat old woman would choose someone, probably Prossie — she'd been singled out to test the truth, after all, so wouldn't she be the logical choice?

Any sensible storyteller would have made Prossie the hero of the whole thing. After all, she was a telepath, she'd make a great viewpoint character, she'd always know what was going on. She should have come back upright and proud and confronted Shadow.

Or if Susan was the hero, if it was "Wizards" reenacted, then Shadow should be down and dying, and they'd have had to hunt down Taillefer to get home, they'd be here for weeks or months yet.

But Prossie was on hands and knees gasping for air, Shadow was turning to face her attacker with no sign she'd been harmed, and Susan was bowing her head, preparing to die.

That was what she was doing, Pel realized; Susan Nguyen, who seemed to be able to survive anything, to calmly withstand whatever befell her, was preparing to die.

"Dost think so little of me, then?" Shadow said, in a voice that was strained and terrible. "Thinkest thou I'd have no protections left without the full matrix about me? Did think me such a fool as that?" She took another step, and stood over Susan, who made no answer. "I have endured for centuries, 'gainst wizards, warriors, and time itself; thought thou some simple machine could slay me?" She kicked the revolver aside; it skittered away.

And then Susan slumped forward, fell in a heap at Shadow's feet and lay still.

"Die, then," Shadow said.

Amy sobbed, a deep, bone-shaking sob.

"I don't understand," Pel said hopelessly.

Shadow turned to face him, and glared directly down at him from her throne.

"Dost thou not, then?" she asked. "'Tis plain enough. This wench tried to slay me, with that device from your world, whilst I was distracted and had set aside much of my power; and this other hoped the attempt might succeed. Thus I've stopped the heart of the assassin, and would slay the other — but I think thou'dst have it otherwise, and thus I restrain myself."

Pel blinked.

"Me?" he said.

"Look about you, sir," Shadow replied. "See my choices. A corpse, a madman, and two women, the one who longed for my death, the other a trickster who can hear thoughts — and you, who called out in outrage when that weapon spat its pellets at me. Who, then, shall stand in for me, shall hold the matrix in my stead while I venture forth?"

Pel swallowed hard.

He was no hero. He was just a spear-carrier, someone along to help fill out the party.

But then, this wasn't really a story at all. This was real life. He was being offered his chance. If everything was as Shadow said, it was a chance — his *only* chance — to have everything he really wanted.

He glanced at Prossie, who lay on the stone floor, drawing deep, gasping breaths and shivering with cold.

The telepath looked up at Pel, swallowed, and spoke.

"She isn't lying," Prossie whispered, but the expression on her face was a clear warning.

A warning of what, Pel couldn't guess, and without further thought he ignored it.

"All right," he said.

Chapter Twenty-Three

*P*el had somehow thought that it would all be over in a matter of minutes, that Shadow would transfer the matrix to him then and there, with Susan lying dead on the floor and Amy weeping and Ted giggling and Prossie trying to stop shivering as she brushed the ice from her uniform. He had thought that he could send Shadow through to the Galactic Empire, and then she would come back in a few moments, and he could collect on her promises.

That was nonsense, of course. Shadow, whose appearance was blurring weirdly as she let her suppression of the matrix's appearance continue to slip, explained the situation.

Before Pel could even begin to hold the matrix, he had to become an actual wizard, rather than a potential one; before he could send her through to the Galactic Empire, he would have to learn the portal spell. Shadow would teach him, of course, but it would hardly be instantaneous.

Pel began to wonder if it might have been quicker if Susan had succeeded in killing Shadow after all, and they'd had to track Taillefer down, instead of going through this abbreviated apprenticeship.

"How long will it take?" he asked.

"That depends upon thine own talents," Shadow answered from somewhere inside a halo of shifting colors. "With only a little good luck, three or four days; if thou hast the true talent, as many hours; but if thou'rt such a fool as thou sometimes seemest, then perhaps 'twill be years."

"Are you planning to feed us?" Pel asked.

Shadow flickered, and Pel saw her face glowering through the colors.

*A*my had to admit that the food was good, and the service, provided by odd-smelling black-clad people who never said a word, never opened their mouths at all, was impeccable.

Much of the decor was ghastly, though; she took professional affront at it. She would *never* have allowed one of her customers to decorate a room the way Shadow's dining hall — if that's what it was — was done; she'd have walked off the job first, and to hell with the customer always being right. Punk was all very well, but to line an entire wall with human skulls, several hundred of them . . .

She almost giggled at the absurdity of her aesthetic concerns. Shadow didn't care what the place looked like; she probably had some reason for the skulls. Maybe they were from old enemies, all lined up there as a reminder that she'd killed them all. Maybe they were from servants who'd messed up, to encourage the current crew not to spill anything.

There was no question that they were all genuine human skulls, though; these were not fakes. These were dead people; when Amy thought about it, she had to conclude that to all intents and purposes they were eating in a tomb.

But the heavy, chewy brown bread was rich and filling; the roast beef was tender and had been cooked with onions and some sort of spice that gave it an exotic tang; the wine reminded Amy of the Chianti she and Stan had drunk at that little restaurant they'd gone to when they were dating. She skipped the boiled cabbage — she had never liked cabbage. There were oranges for dessert, and nuts and cheese afterward.

Despite the skulls and the gloomy servants, it was unquestionably the best meal she had had since I.S.S. *Ruthless* almost fell on her in her own back yard. She hoped she'd be able to keep it all down.

Ted and Prossie ate well, too.

She didn't know about Pel, though; he was off with Shadow somewhere, starting his training. She saw servants carrying plates past the table on their way to the workshop, for Pel — and Shadow? Amy didn't know whether Shadow ate, or whether she got all the energy she needed from her magic.

And she wondered about the servants — were they ordinary people, or were they monsters Shadow had made in the shape of humans, homunculi, or whatever they were called?

Or were they something else — zombies, maybe? Shadow had talked about raising the dead at one point, and there was that odd odor.

These people didn't smell *bad*, though, and they weren't black — all of Shadow's monsters, from the stovepipe things to the dragon that had chased them up the stairs, seemed to be black, and none of the servants were any darker-skinned than Raven had been, let alone *black* black. Amy preferred to think that the servants were local people who had found themselves in Shadow's service in perfectly natural ways.

She didn't look at them too closely as she ate, though.

*P*rossie worried about what Pel was really going to do. He had ignored her warning — he *must* have seen it.

Maybe, she thought as she wiped her mouth and winced at the friction on her frostbitten lips, she would be able to warn him once he held the matrix, while Shadow was making her first venture into Imperial space.

She wondered if Pel had thought this through; did he really think that Shadow would ever let him go, alive? She would want to go back to the Empire again and again, she had almost said so — every time she went, every second she was away, she would need someone trustworthy back here in Faerie, holding her matrix together and keeping the space-warp open. She would want Pel here forever, and if he ever refused she would kill him and fetch someone new. After all, once she knew that her idea would work, what would stop her from sending her homunculi to kidnap people from Earth or the Empire?

And there was no question at all about Shadow's callousness or ruthlessness. Susan's cooling corpse had still lain on the floor of the throne room when they were all led away to be fed, and the skin was peeling from Prossie's own ears and mouth and fingers from the cold of that asteroid Shadow had sent her to; no one could expect generosity or kindness from Shadow.

Maybe Pel had some scheme of his own, but Prossie did not entirely trust him to outthink Shadow.

She rose cautiously from the table, cast a final glance at the wall of skulls, and followed a beckoning servant.

*T*he privies were primitive, by Amy's standards, but functional; the beds appeared luxurious, but she found that if she stretched out her feet stuck off the end, and she had never thought of herself as unusually tall.

At least there weren't any skulls in the bedchambers.

She wondered whether Pel was getting any sleep.

She wondered if wizards *needed* any.

*P*el never remembered just how the whole thing was done. Whether this was inherent in the process or the result of some spell on Shadow's part, he had no idea. By morning, as he sat on the rough wooden stool in Shadow's workshop, he simply knew, without being able to put any of it in words, just how one drew upon magical currents, how one manipulated and directed them, how one bound them to one another or to one's own mind. He could sense the currents, could feel and see them; he understood what Valadrakul had seen beneath the haze of color and light, and knew how to ignore that haze himself, if he chose to. He could see the dull lumps of rock on Shadow's crude wooden shelves as glittering foci for magical forces.

He was, in short, become a matrix wizard.

Maybe it was hypnosis, Pel thought when he realized that he didn't know how he had become a matrix wizard. That conjured up unpleasant thoughts of lurking post-hypnotic suggestions.

"Have you . . . I mean . . ." He looked across the dim, dusty workroom at the shimmering darkness that was Shadow's current visible incarnation, and decided against finishing the question.

Shadow guessed more or less what he had been going to say, however. The lone candle flickered as she answered, and the room darkened further; there were no windows, no skylights, no natural light in here at all — only the single candle and whatever magical glow Shadow allowed.

"Aye, I've placed a geas upon thee," she said, "that thou shalt never turn my magicks against me, that thou shalt do me no harm with either thine own hand or through magic the hands of others, and that upon my request thou shalt yield up to me whatsoever I ask of thee."

"That's . . ." That wasn't exactly what he had been going to ask, and it hardly seemed fair to have done that without his permission, but Pel decided against protesting. Shadow wasn't much on fairness, and if she hadn't asked a lot of questions of him while he was in her thrall, so much the better. "That's okay," he said.

He got the impression that Shadow was smiling, though he couldn't see anything resembling a face. "Though 'tis wearisome betimes, Pellinore Brown," she said, "yet I'd never wish to be other than I am, if only because none talk back o'erboldly to me."

Then he realized how he knew she was smiling; he could feel it through the magical matrix.

The candle puffed out, but he could still sense where everything was in the little stone chamber, despite the utter darkness.

A warm golden glow flooded across him, pouring from Shadow's face.

"Come, thou hast the foundation," Shadow said, "and far sooner than I'd hoped; thou hast the true talent, Pellinore. Now, let us build doorways upon that foundation."

There were other spells Pel was far more interested in learning than he was in creating doorways — the spell to raise the dead primarily, and secondarily the spells to create homunculi — but he was in no position to argue. Shadow didn't want him to know all that; she wanted him to serve as her doorman between worlds.

She was looking at him expectantly.

He had the true talent?

He slid off the stool and stood up.

She had said he did, and he had no reason to doubt it, really, but it seemed so odd. He wasn't anyone special; how could he have had some special talent all his life without knowing it? How could an Earthman have a talent for wizardry at all?

Maybe he'd been the hero all along, the young innocent who turns out to be the greatest wizard of all time . . .

But he was no innocent, and not much of a hero, even if he did have the talent. It was more likely that *all* Earthpeople had the talent than that he, Pel Brown, was somehow *fated* to have come here.

But here he was, fated or not, and Shadow was going to leave him holding her matrix, was going to teach him the spell to open portals to other worlds.

And he would have time to experiment with other spells on his own while she was away exploring the Empire.

*T*here were no eggs at breakfast, no coffee, no orange juice, but Amy was satisfied with ham and tea and buttered toast; she passed up the sticky little cakes, and the gooey brown lumps that might have been candied dates. She hadn't thrown up that morning, and she wanted to keep it that way.

Prossie ate a little of everything, though, and Ted ate whatever was put in front of him as if he didn't know or care what it was. None of them paid any attention to the wall of skulls; familiarity had bred contempt.

After the meal, the servants either went away or simply stopped moving and stood where they were; no one gave any sign of where the three were to go or what they were to do. For several minutes they simply sat, looking about the room or at each other, not speaking. Amy looked over the skulls, but they gave no clues — she would not have been very surprised, under the circumstances, if a skull had started talking, but none of them did.

The remaining servants simply stood, and Amy tried for a moment to identify the peculiar scent they produced — a faint chemical smell, vaguely reminiscent of doctor's offices — but she couldn't place it.

And nobody was paying any attention to them; she and Ted and Prossie were being utterly ignored.

She wondered if something had gone wrong somewhere, if Pel had died, or Shadow, and that had shut everything down — but there was no evidence of anything like that.

"Now what?" Amy asked at last.

Ted didn't answer, or even look at her, but Prossie shrugged. "I don't know," she said.

"Do you think we missed a signal or something?" Amy asked.

Prossie shook her head. "No," she said, "I think we're being ignored. Shadow doesn't care about us any more, at least not for the moment. When she needs us, she'll summon us."

"So what should we do?" Amy glanced uneasily at a servant, at the black suede tunic he wore, his motionless hands and expressionless face.

Prossie shrugged. "Whatever we like, I suppose." She hesitated, then added, "But if you were thinking of doing anything Shadow wouldn't like, I wouldn't advise it — she can hear anything, anywhere in Faerie, when she chooses, and she can see through other people's eyes — or for that matter, *anything*'s eyes. She could be looking through mine, or Ted's, or yours, right now — or the eyes of a rat under the table, or one of these servants."

"How do you know that?" Amy asked, startled.

"From when I read her mind yesterday," Prossie explained. "I only had a few seconds, and I was sort of desperate, so I wasn't very selective, I just grabbed at everything I could. I picked up a lot of odd bits, so now I know something about how her magic works." She grimaced. "Not enough to be any real use, I'm afraid; you can't learn skills that way. I just picked up a few random memories of using that matrix thing. She's got centuries of memories of that."

"So she might have been spying on us the entire time, from when the ship crashed until we got here?" Amy asked. "She could have watched us through the eyes of squirrels in the trees, or something?"

Prossie nodded. "I don't know any details, there may be limits, and I didn't hit any memories of anything like that, but yes, she *could* have been spying on us. Not just through squirrels; she could have used your eyes, or mine; we'd never have known it."

Amy shivered. "Did Raven and Valadrakul know she could do that? Or Elani?"

Prossie shrugged.

Amy looked around uneasily, and still found no clues as to what she should do; accordingly, she just sat.

*T*here was a trick to the portal spell, Pel discovered, even for a wizard; it required one to look in a direction that wasn't there, and then draw enough magic into one's perceptions to make the direction real. It was no wonder that no one had discovered it before Shadow, or that it had taken Shadow herself several centuries to come up with it.

It was, in fact, much harder to learn this single spell than to acquire all the basics of matrix wizardry; he had to work at it for most of the day. Shadow let him pull as much energy from her matrix as he needed, so much power that the air in the stuffy little workroom seemed to vibrate with it, the walls glowed pale green, the stones on the shelves buzzed and chimed — but even with all that power, it still took some time before he begin to get the hang of it.

It seemed so strange — as if he had found himself in a funhouse, one where he had to learn to work all the tricks just by wishing. Shadow never explained why the walls glowed green, what the stones were for; she forced him to concentrate on the portal spell.

He tried very hard to concentrate, and at last, in a way he had no words to describe, he began to sense how it would work.

Shadow forbade him to make any attempt to contact Earth, but she guided him in finding the Galactic Empire, in scanning through the worlds therein, in choosing one, and in opening a gateway.

The stone walls fluoresced blue, then vermilion; stones crawled and twisted; but at last he managed to create an opening.

And once the portal was there, holding it open was fairly easy. He simply had to not let the currents of magic slip away.

Colors shifted oddly around him, and he ignored them. He had succeeded in creating his first portal, creating a hole into another world!

Pel marveled at it. He had worked *magic.* He had opened a path between universes! The feeling of power, of accomplishment, and most of all of *strangeness,* was overwhelming; he found himself weeping with no idea why.

Shadow summoned servants from somewhere; the single door of the workroom swung open and admitted one of her silent, black-clad people. She ordered him through the portal, to test it; the man stepped through, vanishing, and a moment later reappeared unhurt. He bowed before Pel.

"Don't they talk?" Pel asked, when the man did not speak, did not say a word about where he had been.

"Not well," Shadow replied.

*T*he remains of breakfast had congealed into an unappetizing mess; no one had ever cleared them away. Amy thought it was time for lunch, past time, though it was hard to be sure when the only light came from a shaft overhead, a square opening in the ceiling that obviously opened to daylight, but which was angled so that she could not see the sky.

No lunch came. Maybe Shadow had forgotten, or perhaps the folk of Faerie only ate two meals a day; Amy could only guess.

She and Ted and Prossie had made no attempt to leave the dining hall beyond visits to a privy that was just up a short corridor; she and Prossie had discussed leaving, had twice almost decided to go back to their bedchambers, but both times they had lost their nerve.

Ted hadn't said anything; most of the time he had just sat there, staring at his thumbs, occasionally glancing around disinterestedly.

All three of them, even Ted once or twice, had walked about the room, stretching their legs; all three had spent some time just sitting, as well. Amy and Prossie had talked a little, and several times Amy had found herself starting to slip into confessions and confidences, only to veer away whenever she remembered Ted's presence. Despite his silence, she thought he might be listening, and she did not care to share her memories, and her concerns about her pregnancy and Stan and Walter and Beth and Susan and all the rest, with a madman sitting a few feet away.

For that matter, while the three servants still in the room gave every appearance of being inanimate, she didn't know whether *they* might not be listening. Amy was now convinced that whatever the servants were, they weren't fully human; ordinary people could not possibly stand so still for so long. These things might be some sort of magical robot, or people under some sort of spell, Amy didn't know; but whatever they were, they might be listening.

And of course, Shadow herself might be listening — any time, any place, Shadow might be listening.

So Amy kept her conversation vague and general, or else trivial.

She was just about to suggest, for the third time, that they return to their bedchambers, when the abandoned servants suddenly jerked to life. Two simply turned and walked out, leaving the door open behind them; the third beckoned for Amy and the others to follow her.

*T*he two of them had moved from the workshop back down to the throne room, where Pel had practiced, opening and closing a portal into the Empire unassisted three or four times, using power drawn from just one strand of Shadow's web; Shadow wanted to be absolutely certain that he would be able to let her back into Faerie.

Pel had discovered some interesting things in the process of this practice.

For one, he had found that Shadow's geas, or post-hypnotic suggestion, or whatever it was, worked; if she told him to open a portal, he had no choice in the matter. He began the spell whether he wanted to or not.

There was no compulsion with other requests or commands, but there certainly was with the portals.

He supposed this was intended to ensure that he wouldn't strand her in another universe. It seemed there was a problem with this in that Shadow would be unable to give him orders from the Galactic Empire, but he supposed she would have thought of anything that obvious and found a way around it.

He had also discovered that it was very difficult to open a *new* portal — each time, after a moment of wild gyration, the spell tried to settle on the exact same spot he had used the time before, like machinery settling into a well-worn groove, or an animal on a familiar path, and had to be forced away. It was downright impossible to open a portal near, but not at, one that had been used before. That explained why Elani's spell gateway to Earth had always come out through Pel's basement wall.

And he couldn't control *exactly* where a portal would come out; he didn't understand why, and Shadow did not explain it, but even when he thought he knew the exact location where his portal would appear, even when he could sense the shape of the other world so clearly he felt as if he ought to be able to step right through without any portal at all, the portal might come out a hundred feet, or a thousand, away from the intended target.

That might explain why Elani's spell had come out in his basement in the first place, instead of somewhere more useful.

Of course, he couldn't really see where it would come out, he could merely sense certain characteristics of the place, characteristics for which he had no words — he could feel them magically, but had no idea how to explain them in words. He guessed that they might relate somehow to magnetic fields, but he didn't really know.

He knew the spell, though, which was the important part. He could open portals.

When Shadow was satisfied that Pel did, indeed, know the spell, she began making her final preparations for departure; Pel leaned against a wall of the throne room and watched.

Every so often he glanced at Susan Nguyen's corpse, lying in a corner where Shadow had left it — she had had her servants remove Valadrakul's scorched remains, and there hadn't been enough left of Raven or Singer to trouble about, but she had perversely left Susan's body. Each time he looked, Pel shuddered slightly.

He had never seen Nancy's body, or Rachel's; he had grieved for them, but he had also been almost numb in some ways, had struggled through moments of disbelief.

He could hardly disbelieve in Susan's death, when the poor little Vietnamese lawyer's corpse was lying right there.

He hadn't known Susan well; he suspected almost nobody had. She had been so quiet, so reserved, so determinedly self-sufficient — and so brave, to attack Shadow like that.

Pel felt a certain shame at that. He had been trying to make deals with Shadow, trying to get himself home, or to get Nancy and Rachel resurrected — but wasn't it Shadow who had been responsible for their deaths, who was responsible, in a way, for his being here in the first place? It was Raven who had brought Pel through the portal into Faerie, but it was Shadow who had driven Raven to it, who had first made contact with other universes and made that contact a hostile one, of spies and saboteurs and plans for war. It was Shadow who was responsible for the disembowelled corpses in every town and village, for the dead soldiers dangling above her castle door.

And Susan, the survivor, the one who simply lived through whatever life through at her, had done a brave thing and tried to kill Shadow, and Pel hadn't helped her, he had protested.

How could he have done that?

At the time it had seemed perfectly reasonable, but now he was ashamed and angry at himself, and angry at Shadow.

Shadow was a monster. She might be his teacher, she might look like a bored housewife, but she was a monster, a ruthless conqueror, even, it might be argued, a genocide, the exterminator of her own kind, the other matrix wizards.

And she held limitless power; he had tasted a little of it himself, and he knew how dangerous she was.

If anyone had ever deserved to die, Shadow did; as long as she lived, no one in Faerie was safe — and now, no one in the Galactic Empire, and Earth would presumably follow.

And quite aside from preventing further deaths, or any abstract interest in justice, Pel wanted revenge. Geas or no, he wanted vengeance — for Susan, for Raven and Singer and Valadrakul, for Nancy and Rachel, and for all the others.

And he intended to have it.

Chapter Twenty-Four

*T*he throne room was full of people, but eerily silent. No one coughed, no one spoke; they all simply stood there as Shadow's patterns of light and color played across them. Amy stopped in the doorway and looked uneasily in, her eyes adjusting to the glare, her ears starting to ring with the odd sensation of pressure that Shadow's presence usually provoked.

The unmoving people were more of Shadow's black-clad servants, dozens of them. Amy was more certain than ever that whatever they were, they weren't really human.

Prossie stopped behind her, but Ted ambled on past them and began pushing his way through the crowd.

"Come you," Shadow called, and the servants shoved back against each other, opening a path. Watching them move, Amy noticed for the first time that they all wore belts bearing sheathed swords.

What was *that* about?

Uneasily, Amy followed Ted, Prossie trailing behind, and the three of them made their way to a wide clear space before Shadow's throne.

Shadow's glory was relatively restrained just now, so they were not blinded, and they could vaguely see a human outline within the glimmering matrix. Pel was standing to one side of Shadow's seat, partially obscured by the shifting colors. In front of the throne was an area of open floor about twenty feet across; all the rest of the vast chamber seemed to be jammed full of servants — homunculi, walking dead, whatever they were, there were hundreds of them, all of them outwardly human.

There were no obvious monsters anywhere to be seen, which struck Amy as a bit odd. Shadow used so many monsters outside her fortress, and in that huge entrance hall; didn't she use them in here?

"Welcome," Shadow said, as Amy stepped into the open area.

Amy stopped.

"You see before you," Shadow announced, "my personal bodyguard. Never in this realm have I had any need of such, but I go now to visit *thy* land, Telepath, where my magicks cannot protect me."

Amy glanced around at the expressionless faces. That explained the swords, anyway — Shadow didn't have any guns to give her guards. And Shadow's monsters couldn't live in Imperial space, which explained their absence, as well.

"In a moment," Shadow continued, "your companion, Pellinore the Brown, will open a portal to a small, pleasant world in the Galactic Empire; my escort will precede me thereunto, and make ready my way. And likewise, you two Earthpeople will step through."

Amy started. "Why?" she asked. "Why aren't you sending us *home?*"

"Because," Shadow explained, "though I have taken what precautions seemed good to me, yet am I wary that our good Messire Brown may not act for love of me. Thou and this madman shall serve me as hostages for his good behavior — an he faults in any way upon my desires, shalt first the madman, and then thyself, be slain."

Amy felt tears stinging her eyes. This just went on and on, world after world, but never Earth. "What about Prossie?" she asked.

"The telepath? Nay, nay, I'm not such a fool as that; an she came, the Empire's soldiers would know my plans and my whereabouts in a trice, and they'd not be troubled by the loss of a handful of you, nor greatly slowed by my swordsmen. I'd flee safely hither, but 'twould be a misfortune best avoided. She's to stay here."

Amy blinked at the indeterminate shape on the throne, and at Pel, there beside it. For a moment she thought an odd expression seemed to appear on Pel's face, as if he were struggling not to smile, but Amy could not be sure through the haze of color.

"Now, Pellinore," Shadow said, "let us begin."

*P*el watched as the black-clad creatures Shadow had called fetches marched, one by one, into the portal he had opened.

Raven had mentioned fetches — weren't they supposed to be the walking dead?

Did that mean that these were dead people brought back to life, or live people condemned to a sort of half-death? Pel didn't know.

He didn't know the name of the planet they were appearing on, either, but he thought it was a green and pretty place, and that the low towers of a city would be visible in the distance from the other side of the portal. He could not really explain how he had found it, or how he knew what it looked like —

one didn't see through a portal, rather, one put a portal through to what one saw, and Shadow had told him through the matrix, in ways words could not describe, where she wanted this one.

He supposed that this troop of black-garbed swordsmen was really a scouting and raiding party, as much as Shadow's bodyguard; he was certain she intended to fight the Galactic Empire eventually, and he supposed she might well conquer it all in time.

And after that, she would probably go after Earth. He really was face to face with a world-conquering menace, just as in all those stories, and one that didn't have any ring to throw in a volcano, nor sword to be broken, nor plug to be pulled — but one he wanted to kill.

He couldn't harm her, though, nor ask another to, and he couldn't refuse her instructions regarding the portal.

He could *think* about harming her, of course; he could imagine her hanged and disembowelled, or torched and burning, or beaten to death, like some of her victims — but he couldn't do anything directly to make his imaginings come true.

The throne room was emptying; he could see Susan's corpse again, no longer hidden by Shadow's slaves.

And he could see Prossie, standing to one side, waiting, as the crowd trickled away through the portal, until finally the last four slaves took Ted and Amy by the arms and led them through.

That left Shadow, himself, Prossie, and Susan alone in the throne room.

"Now, Pellinore," Shadow said, "thou shalt hold this portal open 'gainst my return, and shalt open no others lest they distract thee; understood?"

"I understand," Pel said, annoyed that he could not deny her orders about it. He had been wondering if he might be able to maintain two portals at once, once he was holding Shadow's incredible matrix. It certainly wasn't possible with the little dribble of eldritch power he had access to so far, but Shadow's power was so vast that he doubted the limitation would have held. He had been thinking of opening a portal to somewhere else . . .

But she had forbidden it, and the geas was irresistible.

"'Tis well," she said. "Be ready, now."

And then Pel felt power pouring into him, and felt himself spilling out of his body, as Shadow's magical matrix was transferred to him. The line between himself and the huge network abruptly blurred, and for an instant he was everywhere, all through Faerie, in the currents of magic; he felt the winds and the earth, the seas and the forests, he saw from a thousand eyes at once. An entire world was within him and around him, all at once.

With an effort, he tried to recollect himself.

Maintaining the portal, which mere hours before had seemed a major task, and mere seconds before had taken a conscious effort, was now as thoughtless and automatic as breathing.

Light and color were spilling out around him, he realized once he had managed to relocate himself as being in a specific place, in the throne room of the fortress.

And beside him, a pudgy dark-haired woman rose from her throne and announced, a trifle unsteadily, "'Tis done. Fare thee well until my return, Pellinore Brown."

He was still trying to gather his wits and get a firm grip on reality, and said nothing as she walked, a trifle unsteadily, into the portal.

*P*rossie watched the matrix transfer with interest, as far as she could; at first it didn't seem as if Shadow were giving anything up, but merely as if Pel were developing his own shifting and colorful aura.

Pel's aura grew brighter and brighter, however, far past the level Shadow had been maintaining herself, and Prossie had to look away.

In seconds, Pel blazed with a brilliance fully as unbearable as Shadow's had been when first the party — eight of them, then — had entered the throne room. (Had that really only been the night before?) Prossie closed her eyes against the glare, flung an arm across her face, and turned away, pressing up to the wall.

And still the light grew brighter.

Then, finally, it stopped, though it was so intense that Prossie thought she could see the bones of her own arm silhouetted, black against red, right through the flesh and through her closed eyelids, and that was merely from the light that reached her with her back to the source, light reflected from the gray stone wall.

She heard Shadow's voice, sounding oddly weak, say, "'Tis done. Fare thee well until my return, Pellinore Brown." Although her ears were ringing and blood was roaring through them, she heard footsteps.

And then she heard them stop.

And then Pel's voice roared out, loud as thunder, "Prossie? Are you all right?"

*T*he two men, or whatever they were, pulled Amy forward a few steps, and then released her arms, leaving her standing there in the open air of a meadow; Amy looked around warily.

Shadow's black-clad servants were fanning out across the meadow, stamping down the tall grasses and wildflowers without so much as glancing at them; tiny insects, or at least creatures that resembled insects, whirred and buzzed about as the invaders trampled their habitat, flittering through shadow and oddly-dim sunlight.

There were insects, but there were no birds, and no trees anywhere to be seen; just grasses and flowers and stalky things like oversized weeds. In the distance she could see what appeared to be rooftops, but of an architectural style she'd never seen before.

The sky was a peculiarly purple color, and utterly cloudless above the gently-rolling hills; the sun was far up the heavens but as orange as if it were setting, and its light seemed almost *thick*, somehow — syrupy and rich, but not as bright as sunlight should be.

The air was fresh and cool and spicy, and she felt light on her feet; her back felt straight and strong, and she realized for the first time that it had been aching dully for days, an ache that was now fading rapidly. She took a step, and almost lost her balance.

Clearly, the gravity here was less than in Faerie, and probably less than on Earth — though it had been so long since she had been on Earth she was not absolutely sure of that. The change took some adjustment.

Ted, beside her, tumbled to the ground; quickly, he sat up again and looked about. The four servants who had brought the two of them through the portal were a few steps away, standing as if waiting for something, completely ignoring the two Earthpeople.

"Am I awake?" Ted asked. "It still looks a little funny . . ."

"No," Amy told him, "it's not Earth." She took another tentative step. "I think the gravity's weaker here, for one thing, and look at the color of the sky, and the sun."

Ted looked up at the purple sky, and his face seemed to cave in.

"Oh, *damn!*" he said, and he started crying, heaving deep sobbing breaths.

"I'm fine," Prossie said, "but I can't stand the light."

Until that moment, Pel had not consciously realized that he was emitting light at all; the light had seemed a part of him, and he had somehow not recognized that it existed outside his own perceptions. He struggled for a moment, looking for some way to control the glow, and found it.

He wasn't really much of a matrix wizard yet, he thought wryly, not if it took a struggle just to stop leaking so much light.

He fought down the leakage as best he could, until he thought he was seeing it entirely by magic, then asked, "How's that?"

"Better," Prossie said, warily opening her eyes and turning to face him. She kept a hand up, and blinked often — he supposed that despite his efforts he was still glowing, but more tolerably.

He didn't have time to worry about it; he didn't know what was happening on the other side of the portal, didn't know what Shadow was up to, didn't even know if she could see or hear what was going on, and he wanted to talk to Prossie quickly, before Shadow could do anything about it. This might be his last chance to ever talk freely to someone who understood the situation, someone who could advise him, someone who could tell him he wasn't making a horrible mistake.

"Listen," Pel said hurriedly, "when she sent you through there, and you said she wasn't lying — did you mean that? Was there something else you wanted to tell me?"

Prossie blinked again. "She can't hear us?" She hesitated, then asked, "Are you sure?"

Pel noticed the hesitation, and some little part of him wondered whether Prossie was afraid of him, now that he held Shadow's all-powerful matrix, or whether she was just unaccustomed to not *knowing,* telepathically, how sure someone was.

Or whether it was something else entirely.

It didn't matter, though. "She's through the portal in the Galactic Empire, and I'm holding the matrix," Pel answered. "She can't hear us from there any more than you can read minds from here." He *thought* that was the truth; he hesitated, and then in a fit of partial candor added, "But there might be homunculi listening, and they could tell her what we say — if she comes back and asks them."

The telepath took a second to consider, then replied. "She wasn't lying," Prossie said, "but she could change her mind at any time — instantly. She's selfish and short-tempered and . . . and whimsical. You can't trust her, not about that, not about *anything.*"

Pel sighed, and wind whistled around the fortress tower above him. He was aware of it, aware that the matrix had caused that gust in sympathy to his sigh, as he might have been aware that he had blinked, or that his pulse was beating — he knew of it, but it was unimportant.

"I never really thought she could be trusted," he said, "but what choice did I have?" He tried to keep the sound of pleading out of his voice, and could not tell if he succeeded. "She says she can raise the dead — if it's true, she can bring back Nancy, and Rachel."

Prossie nodded. "She can bring corpses back to life," she agreed. "After a fashion, anyway. That's where a lot of those servants came from, I think — I didn't get the memories very clearly."

"The servants?" Light flickered across the walls in the magical equivalent of a blink.

"The ones in black, like the ones she took through the space-warp with her," Prossie explained.

"Fetches," Pel said. "She calls them fetches. I heard her call them that."

"That's right," Prossie agreed. "Fetched back from the dead — it's not quite what the word means in the Empire, but that's what *she* means by it."

"Then she *can* bring back Nancy and Rachel!" A surge of long-suppressed hope and joy welled up, and for a moment white light flooded the throne room, forcing Prossie to turn away.

The telepath blinked, trying to clear her vision, and for an instant, inadvertently, Pel thought he looked out through her eyes.

"I know you want them back, Mr. Brown," Prossie said, "but I . . ." She stopped.

"But what?" Pel demanded, the hope turning to ash within him.

"But wouldn't she need the bodies?" Prossie asked. "I mean, to bring back your wife and daughter."

Pel sat motionless for a moment, and sickly reds and violets flickered along the ceiling. "I don't know," he said, finding himself involuntarily looking at Susan's body again. "Would she?"

He hadn't thought about that. Maybe he should have asked Shadow about it, tried to make her promise to revive Nancy and Rachel.

But maybe she couldn't, without the bodies. And what if the bodies had to be fresh? Rachel and Nancy had been dead for some time now; he had spent weeks at Base One and on the long journey from I.S.S. *Christopher.*

He didn't want to think about it any more, didn't want to kill his hope completely, and he changed the subject. After all, there were other things that needed to be discussed.

"Listen," he said, "I can't harm her; she put a spell on me, and maybe I could break it if I knew how, now that she's there and I've got this matrix of hers, but I *don't* know how. I can't harm her, and I can't ask anyone else to. But I won't stop anyone else who tries."

Prossie blinked at him, not understanding, her hand shielding her eyes against the glare.

"Are you still in touch with Base One?" he asked.

"I don't know," Prossie admitted. "Not right at the moment. And even if I were, it would take time for them to find her and reach her . . ."

"And she'd see them coming. She'd kill Ted, and maybe Amy, and she'd come back here and probably kill *me*," Pel agreed. "I couldn't defend myself; the spell wouldn't let me. I have to give back the matrix when she wants it, I can't close the portal and trap her there."

"If she were killed, she couldn't bring anyone back from the dead," Prossie pointed out. "She couldn't send anyone home."

"*I* could send people home," Pel said. "That much I learned." He paused, as a thought burst through his mind, a thought that he now saw as so obvious that he could not understand why he hadn't thought of it before.

He had learned how to open a portal; maybe he could learn more.

No one had taught Shadow to raise the dead, had they? She had managed it on her own, by virtue of the incredible accumulation of magical power she had amassed.

It might have taken her awhile, though; she'd had centuries in which to experiment. And he didn't really know anything about the magic he now controlled.

But there were other wizards out there. They could help. And if Shadow were dead . . .

He couldn't harm her, of course.

But he didn't need to stop anyone else from harming her, if someone could figure out how.

And as far as raising the dead went, he certainly had enough corpses around to practice on; even if Raven and Singer were beyond recovery, Susan and Valadrakul remained, and there were the bodies hanging over the fortress gate.

A sudden urgency swept over him as pieces fell into place. He didn't just want to talk to the telepath; he wanted her to *do* something.

He wished she were still able to read his mind; how could he lead her to the conclusion he wanted?

He would have to try.

"Prossie," he said, "I can't leave here, I have to hold this portal open — go down to the gate, will you? I'm going to cut down the men hanging there."

Prossie blinked at him. "What?" she asked.

"Just . . . just go down and look at them. Hurry!"

He wanted to explain further, but he couldn't. The geas stopped him.

It was too much like asking someone to harm Shadow.

*T*he woman called Shadow appeared from the air; Amy saw the arrival from the corner of her eye.

There was no glare of light, no shifting colors, no darknesses or other peculiarities. Shadow was just an overweight middle-aged woman, standing in a meadow and staring about open-mouthed; there was no trace of magic to her — or to anything else here, beyond the everyday magicks of nature, sun and sky and flowers and grass.

"'Tis real!" Shadow said, and her voice seemed weak and thin without her magic amplifying it.

Amy turned, and started to take a step toward Shadow, but then stopped herself.

Here Shadow was, without her magic, and Amy wanted to kill her, she wanted to beat that ugly head against a rock until it broke, to pay her back for Susan and the rest — but she stopped herself.

Because Shadow still had her guards; the four who had brought Amy and Ted through the portal were stepping up beside her, standing at attention, obviously waiting for orders. Their hands were mere inches from the hilts of their swords.

Amy had not lived through so much just to get herself run through by some semi-human creature's sword.

"Yes, it's real," Amy said. "Now what?"

*P*uzzled and wary, Prossie emerged from the throne room onto the landing at the top of the stairs. She didn't understand what was going on, whether Pel was cooperating with Shadow or pursuing some scheme of his own.

It would be so simple, back home, to dip quickly into his mind, maybe not see the details but at least sense which way he was going — but here it was impossible.

Did she *want* to cooperate with him? What was going to happen to her, if Pel was cooperating with Shadow? Where would she go?

Return to the Empire meant death; living here, under Shadow, meant constant fear and probably death as well. And would Shadow allow her to go to Earth with Amy and Ted?

Would Shadow ever allow Amy and Ted to return to Earth at all?

Prossie paused atop the stairs and glanced down.

The black dragon was still down there, looking up at her from below, but then, abruptly, its head burst into flame; for a moment Prossie thought her eyes were playing tricks, or it was an illusion of some sort.

Then the creature bellowed, spitting fire; it crumpled, toppling to one side, and fell, twitching once and then lying still, obviously dead.

"I can't really control them yet," Pel's voice, unnaturally loud, called from behind her. "Run!"

Whatever his plans, Pel was determined, she realized, and while it might have been cowardly, she didn't dare defy him, not when she could be incinerated as easily as the dragon, or as Raven and Singer before it. Prossie dashed down the steps, but slowed as she neared the dead beast.

The beam of light above the corridor was dim and flickering unsteadily; Prossie glanced uneasily up at it as she picked her way carefully past the dead dragon.

Sunlight was pouring in through the open doors, and the eldritch glare of Shadow's matrix shone down from the top of the stairs, so there was plenty of light even should the beam vanish completely; it wasn't darkness Prossie was afraid of, but the uncertainty.

The creatures along the ledges weren't moving; that was some comfort, anyway.

She heard several distant, muffled thumps from somewhere ahead, and she stopped in her tracks.

"Hurry!" Pel called from above, his voice weirdly distorted.

Baffled and frightened and annoyed, Prossie hurried, running down the long, long passage and out into the sunlight, where the six bodies lay.

They stank. Maybe they had before, and the height had kept the odor away, but now the stench was overwhelming, and Prossie shied away involuntarily.

And they didn't look very pleasant, either; they had fallen heavily into loops of their own entrails. Decaying blood and damaged flesh were heaped across the threshold, only partially wrapped in ruined purple uniforms.

Why had Pel wanted her to see this?

Was this some sadistic quirk, forcing her to look at her dead comrades? Was he going mad?

Bloated hands, dead faces, staring eyes; torn cloth, scuffed black boots, black leather belts.

Prossie wished desperately that she could read Pel's thoughts, and find out what she was supposed to see.

Lieutenant Dibbs' mouth gaped open mere inches from another man's bowel, and Prossie had to swallow hard; she looked away, down Dibbs' body, but that was no better, with his slit-open belly, the severed ends of the waistband of his Sam Browne belt dangling into the cavity within, the empty holster at his side . . .

Empty holster.

They weren't all empty.

And Pel was holding the portal open. He couldn't go through it himself, he couldn't harm Shadow — but Prossie could.

Suddenly, she had no doubt at all of Pel's intentions, and she found herself smiling even as she struggled to hold down her breakfast. She scrabbled eagerly at Spaceman Shelby's holster.

"Oh, 'tis wondrous strange!" Shadow exclaimed, oblivious to Amy; the wizard smiled broadly, taking it all in.

Annoyed, the Earthwoman glanced at Ted; he was ignoring her, too, as he stared at the flowers.

And the men in black weren't paying any attention, either. Most of them had formed a hundred-yard ring, while half a dozen hovered warily near Shadow, hands on sword-hilts.

For her part, Shadow was lifting her feet and marveling at the feel of the lighter gravity, staring at the color of the sky, and trying to look every direction at once as she wandered slowly in the general direction of those distant buildings.

"And 'twill be mine," Shadow sang, "all mine!"

Amy snorted.

The ring of men was moving with Shadow, and Amy was, reluctantly, moving as well.

Ted didn't notice, didn't move, until the ring touched him, and two of the swordsmen snatched him up by the arms and dragged him along.

A few feet away, as Amy watched, a swordsman vanished into the portal — presumably by accident, since the opening was invisible. The swordsman had been keeping his station in the moving circle when it reached the portal, and had stepped through.

Amy waited for him to reappear — surely, once on the other side, he would simply turn around and step through again.

He didn't.

Amy blinked; what was happening back there in Shadow's fortress? Why hadn't the swordsman reappeared?

"Hey," she said.

No one paid any attention.

"Hey, *look!*" she shouted.

*P*rossie dashed into the throne room, blaster in hand, just as a fetch stepped from the portal; Pel saw her raise the weapon and point it at the black-garbed slave, but of course it didn't do anything.

Rayguns didn't work here; magic did.

He let one little tendril of arcane force free, just as he had with the dragon, and the fetch burst into flame — as Raven had, as Singer had.

He wanted to shout encouragement to Prossie, but he couldn't, the geas wouldn't let him. He didn't need to stop her, Shadow hadn't worried enough about her safety to appoint Pel as her guardian, but the spell prevented him from doing anything to urge the telepath on.

She didn't need encouragement; she ran through the hot, drifting ash and through the portal without slowing.

*A*my stared as a figure burst from the portal, a figure in a slashed and dirty purple uniform, a figure with a gun in her hand.

The gun fired with an electric crackle and a muffled thud, and a swordsman fell, headless and twitching, as blood sprayed around him; Shadow spun, astonished.

Prossie fired again as Shadow opened her mouth to speak, and Shadow's shoulder exploded into bloody scraps. Whatever Shadow had planned to say was lost as she screamed and tottered, but for another long second the wizard remained upright. Amy glimpsed her face, and saw nothing but surprise; she had obviously not suspected that anything like this could happen.

Shadow had been ready to confront the Galactic Empire with spies and swordsmen, and had not realized how vulnerable that made her. In an instant, Amy understood what that meant. Despite all the reports her agents had brought her, Shadow had never *seen* a blaster, nor any other weapon produced by high technology — or Imperial science — except Susan's pitiful little pistol. She hadn't really comprehended how powerful they were. She hadn't known what she was getting into, hadn't realized how vulnerable she was in this universe where magic didn't work.

She hadn't understood that here, the Empire held a scientific matrix just as powerful as her own magical one.

Prossie fired a third time, and Shadow's chest burst into rags; she toppled forward, and landed face-down in a patch of strange red flowers, her blood staining their leaves and stems almost as bright as their blossoms.

A hundred blades flashed in the alien sun as the black-clad men drew their blades and prepared to defend — or avenge — their mistress.

"Run for the portal!" Prossie cried, as her weapon blasted the belly out of the nearest swordsman.

Amy hesitated at the idea of running *toward* that thing Prossie was firing, but then she obeyed; she stumbled once, forgetting the lower gravity, but she quickly recovered.

She didn't know how it had happened, but she knew an opportunity when she saw it. Pel must have arranged it somehow, despite all Shadow's plans. He had sent Prossie to save them.

And he was waiting for them, back in Faerie.

She hoped that Pel had some way of sending them back to Earth, but even if he didn't, they certainly couldn't stay here.

"Ted!" she called. He looked up. "Through the portal!"

He didn't move, and she was almost there; Prossie was picking off swordsmen one by one, starting with those nearest her, but there were an awful lot of them, and some were coming around behind her.

"Ted, I swear, just get through the portal and you'll wake up!"

Ted hesitated, then stumbled toward the faint waver in the air, but Amy didn't wait for him; she dove past Prossie and through, and landed on freshly-skinned knees on the stone floor of Shadow's throne room.

Or rather, she corrected herself, of *Pel's* throne room.

Chapter Twenty-Five

*P*el wished he could see what was happening beyond the portal, but despite his incredible power he couldn't manage that. A way might exist, for all he knew, but if so, he hadn't discovered it; the portal itself seemed to block whatever he had done to sense where it would go before he had created it, and the trick of seeing through other eyes, even if he had known how to use it, couldn't work in Imperial space, any more than any other magic could.

He saw Amy fall out onto the throne room floor, though; he saw Ted stagger out a moment later, and then Prossie backed from nowhere into the room, still trying to fire her blaster. She was squeezing the firing stud so hard he could hear the clicking over Amy's panting and Ted's shuffling and all the other little noises of their disorganized return.

Then one of Shadow's fetches charged out of the portal, sword raised, and Pel was so startled that the thing was able to take a swipe at Prossie before bursting into flame. The blade cut open one tattered sleeve and drew a line of blood before falling from shriveling, blackening fingers.

Then more fetches came bursting through, mostly one by one, occasionally in pairs or even trios, but each appearing only to flare up instantly and burn away to scattering ash. Amy crawled to the side on hands and knees, out of their path; Ted wandered clear; and Prossie backed away, blaster still in one hand, the other hand shielding her face, and watched as the swordsmen perished.

The stream of burning swordsmen seemed interminable. Since the energy that incinerated them was not his own, and needed no actual guidance but merely a point of release, Pel didn't tire of destroying them, exactly, but the simple repetition was wearying, and the accumulated heat of their fiery extinction did become uncomfortable; by the time the last fetch perished the air of the throne room was sweltering hot, like the inside of a furnace. Amy and Ted retreated up the passage toward the rooms where they had eaten and slept, while Prossie backed out onto the landing at the top of the great staircase.

The whole process quickly took on a surreal aspect — the procession of undead charging forward to immolation, the blackened and melting swords rattling to the floor and lying there in a smoldering heap, all in the flickering, unnatural light of the windowless and underfurnished throne room, had the mindless, irrational repetitiveness of a nightmare.

If any of the fetches ever had the wit to do anything other than charge blindly after the woman who had slain his mistress, he didn't show it — but then, Pel didn't count them, and could not be certain, when they finally stopped appearing, that some weren't still active on the other side of the opening.

Pel would have preferred closing the portal and stranding the fetches on the other side, for the Empire to deal with, but he could not afford the concentration to do that as long as the swordsmen kept appearing; he was unsure just how much the matrix would protect him without conscious direction.

At last, though, the stream of attackers paused, and Pel was able to think about something other than burning.

"Did you get her?" he shouted to Prossie, as he struggled to close the portal. The spell did not yield readily, did not collapse the way his portals had in practice. Something was fighting him — the geas, presumably.

"Yes, sir," Prossie answered, sharply. Pel was startled by the "sir" until he realized that she was simply reverting to military habits.

He was relieved to hear her reply; he had assumed as much, but it was good to hear her say it. And she was quite definite, no "I think so," or "Probably," but a definite "Yes."

And then something yielded and crumbled in his mind, and the portal was gone, leaving only charred sword-fragments and boot-heels and a haze of drifting ash where the fetches had been appearing. The oppressive heat lingered, and Pel could feel himself drenched in sweat, but his mind was clear and sharp — and free.

The geas was gone.

And that, he knew, meant that Shadow was dead.

*T*he grip of the blaster felt good in her hand. The steel cross-graining bit into her palm as she squeezed it, keeping the still-hot weapon steady despite the slick of sweat — and despite its uselessness here in Faerie. It felt good to hold it, and to know that she had killed Shadow with it.

Her hand wanted to tremble, but she wouldn't allow it. Her long-ago training did that much for her, anyway.

She had never shot anyone before. As a rule, the Empire did not arm Specials; they weren't there to fight. They were trained in the use of blasters, just in case, but only on the practice range, with low-power weapons. Prossie hadn't fired a weapon in two or three years — until today. And she had never before used a full-power blast, or shot at a living target.

But now she had — and she had hit what she aimed at. She had killed Shadow.

That she had killed did not bother her, at least not yet; somewhere inside she thought that perhaps it should.

But this was *Shadow*. This was the Enemy. And she, Proserpine Thorpe, outlaw telepath, had killed it.

It felt very good indeed, and she was in no hurry to put the raygun down.

The swordsmen had stopped coming, finally. When she thought about it she realized that they had stopped a moment before Pel had asked her if Shadow was dead. In her excitement she had lost track, for a moment, of the sequence of events.

The portal was probably closed, then. She straightened up, out of her gunner's crouch.

Heat was still pouring out of the throne room, while cooler air drifted up the stairs behind her; she could feel her hair plastered to her scalp with sweat. She turned and looked down the steps.

The beam of light seemed a little brighter than before, though still not up to when Shadow had controlled it; by its glow she could see the dead dragon in the hall below, lying headless on the floor. Purple ichor had puddled around it.

Imperial purple, she thought wryly.

And as if that made some mental connection, she heard her name being called.

"Carrie?" she asked.

*F*or a long moment Pel simply sat there, savoring the calm after the storm. The heat was gradually dissipating, the ashes were settling. The matrix hummed and glowed around him and through him, and he could feel it reaching out through all of Faerie.

Just now, he didn't want to think about it. He knew that he would have decisions to make, important decisions, but just now he wanted to savor his victory.

That was what it was, all right — victory. He hadn't just escaped from Shadow, from Faerie, from the Empire; this time, he had done more than escape. He had played the hero's role after all.

He had won.

*T*he throne room was quiet, and the heat rolling up the passage seemed to be lessening; Amy took Ted's hand and called, "Pel?"

No one answered — but she hadn't called very loudly.

"You said I'd wake up," Ted said accusingly; she jumped, startled, and turned to face him.

"Yes, I did," she admitted.

"I'm not awake yet." Then he laughed, not his usual nervous giggle, but a wild, hysterical laugh. "What am I doing?" he said. "I'm arguing with a *dream?* Because it fooled me?"

"It's not a dream, Ted," Amy replied.

Always before, when she had argued with Ted, or just talked to him, she had felt frustrated and helpless; she had been powerless to help him, to convince him of anything.

Now, though, as she tugged him back toward the throne room, she felt triumphant. "Come on," she said. "We have to get you home."

*T*hat's twice now you've reappeared in Imperial space, and then vanished again," Carrie sent. "We all felt it; a new adult telepath turning up anywhere in the galaxy is hard to miss. And when we tried to locate you exactly this second time, we found some of those Shadow things, but now they're gone, too. Prossie, you said you were abandoning the family and the Empire, but you keep turning up. Who's creating these space-warps for you, and how? Are you working for Shadow now?"

Before Prossie could answer, Carrie added, in a far more emotional tone of thought, "Prossie, what's going on?"

"I killed Shadow," Prossie answered proudly. She looked down at the blaster in her hand, and her mind was flooded with a tangle of emotions. She had sometimes felt something like it in others, in moments of crisis, but this was the first time she had ever experienced such powerful and complex feelings entirely on her own.

And she was really, truly on her own now. "You wouldn't help," she said, "you didn't want to hear from me, but I killed Shadow."

"What?" Prossie could feel Carrie's astonishment clearly. "But . . . did you really? You're serious? How? You'll have to . . . Prossie, can you get back to the Empire, then? They'll want . . ."

Prossie's grip tightened on the blaster, and she cut Carrie off.

"Fuck the Empire," she said. "And fuck *you,* Carrie Hall."

*T*he throne room was ablaze with color and shadow, and stank of smoke; blackened debris was scattered across a wide area.

And Amy noticed that Susan's corpse was still lying against a wall, untouched by recent events.

The shape on the throne was a mass of light, too bright to look at; for a moment Amy could not believe that it was poor Pellinore Brown. It had to be Shadow; the whole thing must have been a trick of some kind.

Then it spoke, and the voice was Pel's.

"I might as well send you all home, I guess," he said. "If I can, anyway."

*"A*re you sure you don't want to go back to your *own* universe?" Pel asked again, for the third time in ten minutes.

Prossie shook her head. "Earth," she said.

It wasn't an easy choice, but it was the right one, she was sure.

If she returned to her own universe she would be a criminal, a hunted fugitive, with no way to hide from her hunters — who would be her own family. They were all slaves to the Empire, all bound up in the web of deception and self-deception, shared delusions and identity. They would track her down, steal from her mind everything she knew about Faerie and Shadow and Pel and Earth and all the rest, and then turn her over to the Empire to be hanged.

And if by some miracle they *didn't* hunt her down, if they sided with her, or even just let her slip away somehow, then they would be as guilty as she — they would *all* be risking their lives. The Empire would not hesitate to wipe the filthy mutants out.

She might have disowned them all, cut herself off, rejected them all — but she couldn't ask that of them.

And besides, she had grown accustomed to the oddly-liberating mental silence of the other realities, and to being her own person; she didn't think she could fit back in the Empire, didn't think she could go back to being a communications device instead of a person.

As for Faerie — even with Shadow gone, even with the entire world's magic in Pel's hands, it wasn't for her. The heavy gravity was wearing, the watery light was unpleasant, the sanitation was abysmal, the whole place was depressingly primitive and harsh.

And although she hated to admit it, she didn't trust Pel any more; she didn't trust *anyone* who held that much power. She was not at all certain whether Pel entirely controlled the matrix, or whether the matrix partially controlled Pel, and she also wondered if some part of Shadow might still linger in that great tapestry of magic. Shadow's original body was dead, yes — but how much of her had been bound up in the matrix?

Not the Empire, not Faerie — that left Earth, which she had only glimpsed, directly and through the Earthpeople's minds back at Base One — Earth, with its amazing alien machines, its complex history, diverse society, and strange, rich culture — television and movies, cars and airplanes, books, music, so *much* to explore! The Galactic Empire had been working toward uniformity for a century, trying with mixed success to impose its single central culture on thousands of worlds; Earth, with its fragmented politics and sophisticated communications, seemed to be going to the other extreme, jamming a million different societies together on a single big planet.

Earth looked like far more fun — frightening and alien, but fun.

"Definitely, Earth," she repeated.

The shifting colors swirled for a moment, and Prossie thought that swirl might have been Pel's magical equivalent of a shrug.

"It's your life," Pel said.

*F*inding Earth was tricky, much more difficult than finding the Empire had been; Pel was not surprised that the Empire's telepaths and science had found it before Shadow's magic.

He would have preferred opening another portal to the Empire first, for Prossie's use — that he could have done in just a few minutes — but she insisted she didn't want to go home, she wanted to go to Earth.

Which meant only creating a single portal, but it also meant that he had to *find* Earth.

And finding the right *part* of Earth was tricky, as well. Nobody had cared *where* on a particular planet Shadow arrived, so long as it was a reasonably pleasant neighborhood and not too far from civilization, but Pel did not think Amy and Ted would appreciate being dumped in the Australian outback — let alone on Mars.

But then, at last, Pel found a place that the portal *wanted* to go, and he realized with a start that he had found his own basement, and the lingering traces of Elani's portal.

His own basement.

He hesitated, momentarily reconsidering his decision to stay.

Then he began the process of prying the portal open.

*T*ed vanished, and Amy took a step toward the portal. Then she paused. "You're sure?" she asked, staring at the throne, trying to see Pel through the glare.

"I'm sure," he said.

"But . . ."

"No, I'm *sure*, Amy," Pel said. "It's a chance to play God. To make everything better for all the people here. I mean, remember what it was like out there, under Shadow's rule! Those gibbets, the dirt, the squalor — I can do a lot of good. Just teaching these people some basic stuff like indoor plumbing, I'll accomplish more than I would in a hundred years as a marketing consultant."

Amy glanced at Prossie, waiting her turn a few feet away, then back at Pel. She knew perfectly well that that wasn't the sort of "playing God" that Pel was really interested in. Oh, he might do it, and it might be a good thing, but it wasn't why he wanted to stay in Faerie.

He wanted to learn to raise the dead, so he could bring back his wife and poor little Rachel. Amy knew that.

But it was his business, not hers.

Poor Susan's body was still lying against the wall; in all the excitement no one had had time yet to do anything for her, or for those dead Imperials out front. Maybe Pel would raise Susan from the dead, too. Maybe he would bring Lieutenant Dibbs and his men back to life, and send them all home.

It seemed vaguely blasphemous and somehow dangerous, but Amy told herself she was being silly. She'd never been devout, and any ideas about it being dangerous came more from horror movies than from logic.

It wasn't her problem.

Her biggest problem was an unwanted baby, and she needed to get back to Earth to get rid of it safely. And just getting back to a normal life — which she could hardly do in Faerie.

She didn't want to play God; she just wanted to go home.

So why was she still here, arguing?

"Besides, Amy," Pel said, "if I leave without turning the matrix over to someone, it'll come apart, and wild magic will run amok — the sort of magic that cooked all those people, Raven and the fetches and the others."

"It will?" she asked, startled. "I thought that it sounded like things were pretty good before the matrix wizards got out of hand." She wondered whether Pel was just making excuses, trying to convince himself.

She wondered, also, if he had any idea what he was talking about. Did he really know any of this stuff? If he'd learned it from Shadow, had she told the

     Worlds of Shadow

truth?

"Well, yeah," Pel said, "but that was before the magic all got collected. It would disperse out to harmlessness eventually, I think, but if I just turn it loose now it'll be like an explosion."

"Are you sure?" Amy asked.

"No," Pel admitted. "Look, Amy, you go on; I can always open the gate up again and go home. But I can't ever come *back* — once I leave, the portal closes and the matrix comes apart. So I want to do whatever I can here first."

Amy glanced at Susan's corpse and shrugged; it wasn't really any of her business if Pel stayed, and maybe he *would* do some good. She stepped through the portal, and as the throne room's eerie colors vanished she saw Prossie coming close on her heels.

She emerged into the dim light of a single bare bulb — if there had been others, as she vaguely remembered there were, they must have burned out. She stepped quickly to one side, so that Prossie would not walk into her.

Pel's basement was hot and musty; the house had probably been closed up all summer, Amy realized. Ted was sitting on the stairs.

"Hello," he said, as Prossie appeared.

Amy glanced at Prossie, and then, reassured that she was safely through the portal, turned and blinked at Ted. Her eyes needed time to adjust to the dimness after the blinding glare of the matrix.

"Are you okay, Ted?" she asked, concerned. "I thought you'd be on your way home by now."

"I don't know," he said. "Am I awake? Why am I in someone's basement, if I'm awake? This is supposed to be Earth, isn't it?"

"It's Earth, Ted, and you're awake," Prossie said gently. "You've been awake all along."

He shook his head. "No, no; that's crazy."

"Well, crazy or not," Amy told him, "you're in Pel's basement, on Earth, and you're safe. Open the door, and let's go home."

Ted shook his head, and Amy saw terror on his face. All through their adventures he had smiled, or simply looked blank, but now that they were safely home he was obviously seriously frightened.

"I don't know what's out there," Ted said slowly. "I don't know who you two really are, if this is real and the dream's over. If I'm here, and not home in bed, it can't have been an ordinary dream — so maybe I'm not awake yet after all. Maybe if I go through that door I'll be back in that castle, or the spaceship, or something. There could be monsters, or slave-drivers, or anything."

"Open the door and see, Ted," Amy said, annoyed with his weakness. She marched across the basement and up the dusty steps, while Prossie trailed uncertainly after her.

For an instant, as her hand closed on the knob and Ted stared fearfully up at her, Amy thought that he might somehow be right, that *anything* could lie beyond that door — or beyond *any* door.

But then she swung it wide and saw only the Browns' hallway, dusty and muggy, and she knew it was over.

*P*el sat on his throne, staring at the portal, for several minutes after Ted and Amy and Prossie had vanished.

None of them reappeared; they were presumably safely back on Earth, but for all he could see they might just as well be dead, or imprisoned. He considered holding the portal open for a moment longer, just in case, but then decided that was silly.

He let his link to Earth collapse into nothingness, glanced back at Susan's body, and got to his feet.

Susan would have to wait; he wanted to practice on someone or something else first. Susan was a friend; he didn't want to bring her back until he could do the job right.

And after he had brought Susan back to life, he would find Nancy and Rachel. Somehow, somewhere, some way, he would find them.

- end part 2 -

Part Three:
The Reign of the
Brown Magician

Chapter One

*H*er car was gone. Amy Jewell had looked out the front door and seen that the curb was empty, and had stepped back inside and closed the door.

Her car was gone.

That had come as a shock at first, but it shouldn't have. After all, she had left it out front months ago.

It was hard to realize that it had really been months, that it hadn't all been a dream, that they hadn't somehow returned to the moment they had left.

But it had been real, and it had been months ago that she had parked her car out front of Pel and Nancy Brown's house in the expectation of being safely back home and in bed by midnight. She and her lawyer had come here to find out why there was a non-functional spaceship in her back yard; she hadn't planned on anything more than an evening of explanations.

She certainly hadn't planned on spending months going through hell in two other universes.

But then, just to see if the stories she had been told were true, she and the others had stepped through a magical portal in the basement wall into a universe she called Faerie, where Shadow ruled — and after that she had been caught up, unable to return, until now.

She had fled from Shadow's monsters into the third universe, dominated by the Galactic Empire, where she had been captured by pirates and sold into slavery; she had spent weeks as a slave before the Empire had rescued from her master, Walter, and his helper Beth.

At least she'd survived — Nancy Brown was killed by the pirates, Nancy's daughter Rachel by her master. Walter had killed a slave once, but he didn't kill Amy.

She was pregnant by that son of a bitch, though. Not that she intended to stay that way. The Empire had hanged Walter and Beth both, and she intended to abort Walter's child, and be rid of it, as well. She'd never managed to have any children when she was married, not even before she had found out what a bastard Stan really was and divorced him, and she wasn't about to start now with *Walter's* kid.

After the rescue she had spent boring weeks at Base One, the home of the Imperial Fleet, and then she had been sent back into Faerie as part of a raiding party that was meant to assassinate Shadow.

She hadn't intended to really attempt anything that stupid; she'd intended to use the Faerie magic to go home the minute the Empire's troops weren't watching her. But then Elani, the wizard who knew the portal spell, had been killed, and she and the others had been stranded again.

So they'd gone on with the plan to assassinate Shadow, knowing it was suicidal.

And it *was* suicidal — most of the party had either died or deserted.

But the most amazing thing in the whole adventure was that they had actually managed it, eventually — Pel Brown and Prossie Thorpe had killed Shadow. Proserpine Thorpe, Registered Master Telepath, who had rebelled against the Galactic Empire and was now a refugee here on Earth with Amy, had shot a powerless Shadow dead.

And Pellinore Brown, a marketing consultant from Germantown, Maryland, had set it up, and now controlled all the power, the magical matrix, that Shadow had held.

And he had sent Amy, and Prossie, and his lawyer Ted Deranian, safely back through the portal in the Browns' basement, and here they were, but Pel hadn't been able to do anything about all the time that had passed while they were going through hell in those other realities.

So of course the car was gone, after so long.

Amy did wonder what had happened to it, though; had it been towed, or stolen, or repossessed, or what?

She realized then that she didn't have her keys, so she couldn't have started it anyway. She didn't have her driver's license, or any money, or anything else — her purse, if it still existed at all, was back on Zeta Leo III, where she'd been Walter's household slave, in that other universe where the Galactic Empire ruled all those hundreds of planets.

Ted's car was gone from out front as well.

Pel's and Nancy's were in the garage; Amy checked, and found them both sitting there, somewhat dusty but apparently intact.

That didn't help much, though; even if she hadn't been bothered by the idea of stealing one of them, she didn't know where any keys were. She supposed one set was still in Nancy's stolen purse — and that was probably on Zeta Leo III, like her own. As for any other set, well, who knew where Pel kept his keys?

She wondered if Ted might know — or if not, whether he might know how to hot-wire an ignition.

Ted, however, was firmly settled in the family room, in front of the TV, watching CNN Headline News, trying to catch up on what he'd missed, and to convince himself . . .

Well, to convince himself of something, but Amy wasn't sure just what. That he'd imagined the whole adventure? That it was all real? That whatever had happened, everything was normal now? For all she knew, he was checking to see whether this was really Earth, and not some twisted alternate version.

Whatever he was doing, he had ignored her ever since he found out that the TV worked, that the power and TV cable hadn't yet been cut off for non-payment.

Prossie seemed to be wavering between the two of them; she was fascinated by the TV, but she also seemed to consider Amy her lifeline, and whenever Amy stayed out of sight of the family room for more than a few minutes Prossie came looking for her, calling her name quietly into the silent depths of the Browns' house.

It was hardly surprising that Prossie felt out of place — certainly no more surprising than the car's absence. After all, this wasn't Prossie's native world.

Amy paused in the hallway as Prossie caught up; for a moment both women hesitated, but neither spoke, and at last Amy led the way.

She wasn't really going anywhere in particular, just looking around; she didn't want to settle down the way Ted had, she wanted to keep moving, to get on home to her own house up in Goshen, but her car was gone and she didn't have any money or identification or credit cards, and she was wearing only the filthy, tattered remains of Imperial military-issue pants and T-shirt. She couldn't catch a bus or call a cab.

She might be able to find something she could wear in Pel and Nancy's closet — she and Nancy hadn't been the same size at all, Nancy had been smaller, but there would surely be something, one of Pel's shirts maybe. She didn't like taking things without permission, but this was an emergency, and she'd only be borrowing it until she could get home.

And besides, it wasn't as if Nancy would ever need her clothes again.

But Amy still didn't have money for a bus or cab.

If the phone still worked she could call a friend for a ride, but she needed to think things through first. Who would she call? What would she say? What had happened all those weeks she was gone? Was the wreck of I.S.S. (for "Imperial Space Ship") *Ruthless* still lying in her back yard?

She wished that thing had never fallen out of the sky onto her land; that had been what got her involved in all this in the first place. The Empire had been trying to establish contact with Washington, and had suddenly discovered, when *Ruthless* popped out of a space-warp over Amy's back yard, that their anti-gravity drive didn't work in Earth's universe.

And no one had believed it was real, so the crew had been thrown in jail down in Rockville, and Ted had bailed them out because Pel had been contacted by people from Faerie who wanted to talk to the Imperials, and then they'd all stepped through the portal in Pel's basement for a quick look, just to see if it was real . . .

Well, they were back now, and Amy wanted to go home, but what about Ted, and Prossie? What would become of them, if Amy left? Prossie had nowhere to go, and Ted seemed so out of touch with reality that Amy wasn't at all sure he could take care of himself.

There were hundreds of questions, and she needed to think, and she thought best when she was moving, when she was looking at things, so she rambled through the Browns' empty house, looking around and trying to think, while Prossie followed along, saying nothing.

Amy thought Prossie probably had at least as many questions of her own, and it was really very thoughtful of her to not ask them yet.

She looked in the master bedroom, but did not explore the closets or dressers — she wasn't ready for that yet. Going through the Browns' clothes would be a little too intimate.

She would get to it, but first she just wanted to look.

Roaming from room to room with another woman tagging after her seemed so very familiar and comfortable that she wasn't sure whether to laugh or cry; it was just like looking over a prospective client's home with the client a step behind. And the Browns could certainly have used an interior decorator — or maybe just a good cleaning crew. The house was a mess.

It wasn't just the dust and general air of abandonment, either. Things were out of place, drawers left open, books stacked in front of empty shelves. Amy couldn't be certain, but she thought the house had been searched. She didn't remember any such disarray when she had been here before; true, that had only been for a few hours, months ago, and she hadn't seen most of the house, but she was fairly certain things were different.

The house hadn't been burgled; the TV and stereo and other valuables were all still there.

Someone, she guessed, must have reported the Browns missing. The police had probably gone through the place, looking for clues — and maybe not just the police, if someone had made the connection to the crashed spaceship. The FAA and the Air Force had been interested in it.

She smiled wryly at the thought as she stood in the door of poor little Rachel's bedroom. Somehow, she doubted the police or the Air Force would ever have figured out that everyone in the house had magically walked through a solid concrete wall in the basement and emerged in another universe, caught up in the conflict between the Galactic Empire and an all-powerful wizard named Shadow.

The smile vanished as she stepped into the bedroom and looked about.

Toys were strewn across the floor; a floppy green-and-red plush alligator lay on the bed, gaping foolishly at her.

Poor little Rachel Brown, six years old, had been sold into slavery and then murdered. There wasn't anything funny about that.

Rachel's mother had been raped and killed by pirates — not storybook pirates with eye patches and peg legs, but serious, workmanlike pirates with guns and a spaceship. Rachel's father had survived, but he was back there in Shadow's place, mourning them both, with some crazy idea he could bring them back from the dead.

Six Earthpeople had walked through that basement wall, and only two had come back — Pel was still in Faerie, and Nancy and Rachel and Susan, Amy's lawyer Susan Nguyen, who she had dragged along, were all dead.

And the Faerie folk who had created the portal were *all* dead — Raven of Stormcrack Keep, and the wizards Valadrakul and Elani, and Squire Donald . . .

No, not quite all, she corrected herself; Stoddard might not be dead — he'd deserted, and might be safe somewhere in Faerie. He was gone, though, and the others were dead. So were at least a dozen of the Imperials who had been involved.

There wasn't anything funny about any of it.

"I want to go home," Amy said suddenly. "Did you see a phone anywhere?"

Prossie blinked at her.

"What's a phone?" she asked.

"*P*roserpine Thorpe is definitely on Earth now," the telepath said, standing at attention and staring straight ahead.

Under-Secretary of Science for Interdimensional Affairs John Bascombe leaned back in his desk chair and looked up at Carrie Hall's face.

Thorpe was the rogue telepath, the one who had gone into Shadow's universe with that barbarian Raven, and the Earthpeople, and that idiot Colonel Carson who'd got himself killed. She was the one who had started refusing orders, or making up her own — crimes that would have gotten her, or any other telepath, hanged or shot within hours, anywhere in the Empire. The Empire couldn't tolerate disobedience in the mind-reading mutants.

She was also Carrie Hall's cousin — all the telepaths, all four hundred and sixteen of them, were a single extended family, scattered across the Empire.

But Thorpe had been in Shadow's universe. Bascombe himself, along with General Hart, had sent her there after she and most of the crew of *Ruthless* had managed to get home to Base One.

Earth wasn't in Shadow's universe.

There were times Bascombe regretted that he had wangled himself this job. It had *looked* like an easy road to advancement, and it definitely had promise, but he kept stumbling across all these complications.

"Earth," he said.

"Yes, sir," Carrie answered, her gaze fixed on the wall behind him.

"You're absolutely sure she's on Earth, Hall? Not on some backwater like her last appearance, or some obscure part of the Shadow reality we haven't seen before, or some other planet in Earth's universe? Or on Terra? I'm told that Earth and Terra are very similar."

"Yes, sir. I'm sure. She's on Earth."

"Do you have any idea what she's doing there?"

Carrie hesitated.

"No, sir," she said.

"You can't read her mind?"

Carrie hesitated even longer this time.

"Sir, it's . . . it's difficult, when she's on Earth," Carrie explained, "especially since she isn't just ignoring me, she's actively trying to shut me out, and even without the use of her own telepathic abilities she knows how to make it difficult for me."

"So you haven't been able to read *anything,* telepath?" The doubt was plain in Bascombe's tone.

"Just . . . just glimpses, sir. It's hard to describe."

"Try."

"I really wouldn't know where to begin, sir. There's a memory of a gunfight in a meadow somewhere, and something about blinding colored lights, and thoughts of death, and the image of a machine showing colored moving pictures, like a miniature movie."

"You can't do any better than that?"

She didn't answer, but he could see the unhappiness on her face.

Bascombe took his time watching that unhappiness before he said, "This renegade, I am told by you telepaths, has popped into real space twice in the past sixty hours. You tell me that these two appearances were over a hundred light-years apart, even though there's no sign of a spaceship involved. At considerable expense we've sent expeditions to both supposed locations, each one with a telepath along. And now you come in here and tell me that she's on Earth. Do you expect us to send another expedition *there*? Do I need to remind you what happened to *Ruthless*?"

"No, sir." Carrie's face was blank again.

"Then what *do* you expect, Telepath?"

"Nothing, sir," Carrie said. "I just thought it was my duty to inform you." Bascombe nodded.

"It was. You did. Now get the hell out of here — and I want you to write up a report on everything you can read from Proserpine Thorpe's mind, and keep on writing it from now until I tell you to stop, and send a copy of the new material to me once a day."

"Yes, sir." Carrie turned and fled.

When she was gone, Bascombe stared at the door.

For decades the Imperial government had relied on those damned mind-reading mutants for much of their intelligence-gathering and long-distance communication. Thorpe wasn't the first one to go bad, and she probably wouldn't be the last, but each time anything like this happened, Bascombe worried; someday they might *all* go bad.

And this time it was all mixed up with the two known alternate universes, with the thing called Shadow that had been sending its spies and monsters into the Empire for the past seven years, and with the party of troublemakers Bascombe and his political rival General Hart had sent to their deaths. And now there was this thing about near-instantaneous travel across deep space.

At least, the telepaths *said* Thorpe had somehow crossed all those light-years in a day or so, without a ship.

If that was true, if hopping between universes could provide near-instantaneous interstellar travel, that could mean that space-warp technology, Bascombe's own little bailiwick in the Department of Science, might be even more important than he had thought.

And if it wasn't true, it could mean that the telepaths had *already* gone bad.

Near the end of the row of gargoyles that drained the rooftop was one with a broken jaw. Its granite chin was gone, and the rusted end of an iron pipe protruded below the stumps of fangs, a jagged hole in the pipe's underside spilling water in uneven splatters onto the stone of the tower's battlement.

The steady rush of water from the others, pouring out over the side, did not bother Pel Brown at all, but the pattering from the broken pipe sounded like a child's running feet, and that sound tormented him. It was as if Rachel's ghost were running endlessly across the parapet.

He wanted to reach out and grab her, pull her back to safety, away from the edge — but she wasn't there.

Rachel would have adored this place, he thought, with its spires and its gargoyles, its spiral staircases and its secret passages. That she had not lived to see it was still unbearable, despite the weeks that had passed since he was told of her death.

He stood under the overhanging eaves, watching the rain, watching the streams of water pouring out into space, watching the one stream that scattered and fell short, watching the repeating pattern of splashes on the stone.

He had, for the moment, suppressed the visible portion of the aura of magic that surrounded him; to outward appearances he was only a man, but he could still feel the matrix he held, the power that flowed around and through him.

He could stop the sound, of course; any time he wanted to, he could stop it. He could blast the gargoyle into powder, if he chose. He thought that with a little more effort he could repair it, gathering dust from the air around it and healing the carved stone.

He did neither; instead, he drew the power to him, reached out into the web, into the power matrix, and found the lines that led up into the clouds overhead. He shifted them, working by feel in a way he had no words to explain.

The rain stopped, as if someone had shut off a faucet. Almost immediately after the last drops plopped onto the tile roof the steady flow from the other gargoyles slowed, and the spattering fall from the broken pipe changed its rhythm, becoming less even.

And that was worse.

It didn't sound like his daughter anymore; it didn't sound like anything. It was as if he had erased the last trace of her. The sky was still grey overhead, the water was still dripping from the eaves, the battlement was still glazed with rain, but no invisible child's footsteps pattered on the stone.

Instead, damp air swirled and whispered across the stone, driven not by wind, but by the magical currents of the matrix.

He pulled the power to him, grabbing at it, hauling it in; magic seethed in his mind and his fingers, and the distinction between himself and the matrix he held became vague and uncertain. A red sheen blurred his vision for a second, and then was swept aside in a shower of crimson sparks that danced wildly across the stonework.

He was glowing again; his control of his appearance had slipped, and a halo of shifting colors flickered around him.

He ignored it, looking upward.

The clouds hung above him, low and dark, and he sent a broad band of scarlet fire snaking upward, lighting them to the color of blood.

The unnatural glow suffused the landscape; the green forests on the distant hills turned black, the gray marshlands that encircled the fortress were tinged with a rusty life, and the castle itself took on a color that had never been seen in nature, not in this world, nor on Pel's native Earth.

It looked like something out of a horror movie, Pel thought, that eerie sky and the thick clouds and the gargoyles, hovering above him.

That seemed perfectly appropriate. He felt as if he'd fallen into a story months ago, and been unable to climb back out. Sometimes it was science fiction, as in the Galactic Empire, with their spaceships and blasters; sometimes it was an epic fantasy, as when Shadow had made him into a wizard and he had turned on her and destroyed her. Why shouldn't it be a horror story now?

He released the knot of power he had gathered — not in a spell, as he had thought he would, but in a simple release, flowing back into its natural patterns — or at any rate, into a form as natural as the patterns could be while still bound together in the world-spanning matrix that Shadow had created for herself and passed on to Pel.

The rain began falling anew, and Pel turned away.

He had no reason to be up here, really. He had been exploring the fortress for lack of anything better to do — or rather, because he was not sure he knew what he wanted to do.

He knew what he wanted to *have* — he wanted his wife and child back. And he knew that he held a power that could allegedly raise the dead.

But he didn't know what he had to do to make it work. He didn't know how to find out.

Hadn't someone said that knowledge was power? Well, Pel thought, the converse didn't seem to be true. He had all the power he could want, but it hadn't gotten him much in the way of knowledge.

He stepped into the tower, closed the door behind him, and started down the stair. The way was dark and narrow, the slit windows covered by dusty shutters, and Pel had no lantern or torch, but he didn't need one — he carried the mobile focus of all this world's magic with him wherever he went, and its glow brilliantly illuminated the surrounding stone walls.

He didn't need to see at all, though; the matrix also let him sense the shape of the world around him in some more direct way he did not understand.

It was amazing how quickly he had become accustomed to carrying this thing about wherever he went, he thought as he tramped down the steps. Shadow had used something like hypnosis on him, he knew — something that used magic, rather than the simple psychological stunts and suggestions of Earthly hypnotists. She had wanted him to learn quickly, not for his own good, but so that he could serve her purposes that much sooner. So he accepted calmly that his senses were altered and enhanced, that he was bound to a network of mystical force as if it were a part of his body, that he could draw on that seemingly-infinite source of energy and therefore no longer grew tired, no matter what he did.

It was mad, really; he was living out an insane power fantasy. Shadow had used this matrix to rule her entire world, and had intended to conquer others, as well; surely, Pel thought, no individual could handle such physical power. It had to be some sort of dream or delusion — a story, not real.

If it was all real, then how could he accept it so calmly?

He paused, and looked about at the shifting glare of colors that shone across rough gray stone.

Was it real?

Of course it was. Poor Ted Deranian had thought he was dreaming, and it had gotten him beaten and abused; Pel wasn't going to make that mistake. This was all real.

But how did he know he hadn't dreamed Ted? And Amy and Prossie, and all the others. None of them were here now to tell him if he was mad or dreaming. He had sent the three of them, Amy and Ted and Prossie, safely back to Earth, and the rest were dead or missing.

He shook his head, and magical currents twisted and writhed around him.

He wasn't dreaming. It was all real. It was as real as anything had ever been; he reached out and touched the nearest wall, felt the cool, hard stone under his fingertips.

It *was* real.

It was real, and he controlled all the magic in this world of magic, and it didn't seem strange at all. It seemed perfectly natural.

He wondered if that was a good thing.

*T*he technician sat up abruptly at the sound of the beep. He blinked at the panel, and his eyes widened as he saw the code number indicating which phone was in use. He reached for his own phone.

"Get me Major Johnston," he said. "We have an outgoing call on the Brown phone."

Chapter Two

*H*e could make the fetches obey him.

It wasn't really much of an accomplishment for a person in Pel's position, but it was a start.

He supposed that making living people obey him would probably be easier; he could just threaten to incinerate them, and they would obey out of fear.

Fetches, however, were already dead. To be exact, they were dead people Shadow had revived as her servants; the fortress held dozens of them.

There were *hundreds* of homunculi in the place, if that was the correct term for all the creatures Shadow had created from scratch, rather than just re-animated — everything from artificial insects to the dead dragon at the foot of the grand staircase, and Pel could sense that there were even bigger beasts outside the castle, such as the burrowing behemoth that had attacked Pel's party at Stormcrack, months earlier, or gigantic bat-things like the one Valadrakul of Warricken had slain in the Low Forest of West Sunderland.

Pel had decided to start with the fetches, though; they were all human in appearance, for one thing, and he was more comfortable with that. For another, he was very concerned with the resurrection of the dead. He didn't want Nancy and Rachel to be mere zombies, like the fetches, but he assumed that any spell that could restore his family would be somehow related to whatever Shadow had done to produce fetches.

He had found three of them simply standing in one of the corridors, lifeless and mute. At first he had stared at them, expecting them to notice him; then he had tried ordering them verbally, telling them to walk.

They had stood there, unmoving, as the shifting colors of the matrix had played across them, rich deep blue and honey-gold predominating just at that moment.

Then he had used the matrix, used his magic, and had found the little tangle of magic in the heart and spine and brain of each fetch, the magic that, he saw, controlled each one's action. He had poked and prodded at one with immaterial fingers — and the fetch had twitched and shivered and blinked.

He had told it, "Speak," and it had opened its mouth, but no sound came out. He had realized, with shocked disgust, that it wasn't breathing.

"Breathe," he had told it, and the chest expanded; air was sucked into its lungs in a hollow gasp, then expelled in a rasping wheeze.

One breath, and it stopped.

Pel shuddered.

"Never mind that," he had said. "Will you obey me, now?"

The fetch had blinked, then nodded, and suddenly seemed alive again — somber and silent, but alive. He had, he saw, had to establish a link between its internal web and the greater web of the matrix, a link that Shadow must have once had, and must have severed at some point — probably when she first transferred the matrix to Pel.

Having established the link he controlled the fetch entirely, just as he controlled the matrix itself.

And that meant he could make the fetches obey him. He would have servants — or rather, slaves — who could run errands for him, do whatever he needed to have done.

That was a good start, he thought. It was a definite step forward on the road to using the matrix properly, and to learning to resurrect the dead.

"Go to the throne room," he ordered. The fetch sketched a bow, then turned and marched away.

It was only a first step, though. There were things he needed to know if he was to bring Nancy and Rachel back from the dead that he couldn't learn just from ordering fetches around, and while the matrix probably contained all the knowledge he needed, somewhere, somehow, he didn't know how to get at it. He needed someone to talk to about his plans, someone who could teach him.

Someone to teach him magic, he thought, as he watched the fetch march down the passage toward the throne room. Pel's lips tightened, and the aura flickered into harsh reds and smoky browns.

He wanted a wizard.

And while Shadow had been the last matrix wizard, the only wizard who regularly raised the dead, while Shadow was dead because Pel had sent Prossie Thorpe to kill her, Shadow had not been the only wizard in the world Pel and his companions had called Faerie.

Even though Shadow had roasted Valadrakul to death, and Shadow's creatures had butchered Elani, Pel thought he knew at least one other wizard who still lived: Taillefer, that fat coward who had refused to open a portal to either Earth or the Empire. After Elani had died, Valadrakul had not known how to open portals to other worlds, so he had summoned Taillefer — and Taillefer had refused to help, for fear of drawing Shadow's attention.

Well, Pel had learned how to open his own portals. And now he could send fetches out to . . . Pel smiled grimly. He could send fetches out to *fetch* Taillefer.

Taillefer might not know how to raise the dead, but he surely could teach Pel *something.*

Pel strode toward the throne room, still smiling.

*A*my hung up the phone. "Donna says she'll be here in about twenty minutes," she said. She smiled with relief.

Prossie didn't smile back. "Then what?" she asked.

"Then she'll drive us out to my place," Amy replied. It was such a pleasure to be able to say that, to be able to take cars and telephones for granted, to know what was going on again! "I guess she can drop Ted off on the way, and then we can settle in. I don't know if there'll be much that's fit to eat after all this time, but we can get into some decent clean clothes." She frowned slightly, thinking and planning. "I don't have my keys, but if I have to, I guess I can break a window to get in. Or maybe I should call a locksmith. I'll have to find one who'll take a check, I don't have any cash. The checkbook's gone, too, but I have extra checks at home."

Prossie nodded, though it wasn't a very enthusiastic gesture. Amy didn't really notice. She was on familiar ground after months of living nightmare; she didn't want to think about Prossie's problems yet. There would be time for that later.

"There's canned soup, that'll still be good," Amy said, talking more to herself now than to Prossie. "And I should have something that'll fit you — you're only an inch or so shorter than I am, right?" She sighed. "I wonder if they stopped delivering my mail? I guess if Pel's phone still works, mine will, too, but there must be about three months' bills waiting. And all my clients will have given up on me — I'll have to just about start the business over again."

She paused and glanced at her companion, but Prossie didn't respond.

Amy continued, "I suppose that spaceship is still in the back yard — did you have anything on board? It might still be there, if nobody's gotten in and stolen it. And I'll need to call the doctor and make an appointment as soon as I can." She shuddered slightly. She didn't like to think about getting an abortion, but it had to be done — she couldn't afford a baby, and anyway, her life was quite disrupted enough without bearing the child of a dead rapist from another universe.

And it wouldn't hurt to have a general check-up, after all she had been through.

"Do you think they might have posted guards around the ship?" Prossie asked suddenly.

Amy blinked at her, startled. "Who?" she asked.

"Your government. The ones who arrested us."

Amy put a hand to her mouth, then admitted, "I hadn't thought of that." Then she lowered the hand and managed an uncertain smile. "But even if they . . . no, they *can't* have guards there; it's private property, and poor Susan had a court order or something. And we haven't done anything wrong."

As she finished her attempt at reassurance Amy realized she could hear sirens; she turned to look out the window. For a moment she stared in disbelief; then she headed for the living room for a better view.

"How did they know?" Prossie asked as she followed Amy. "Do you think they might have telepaths, somehow?"

"No," Amy said. "They don't have any telepaths. They might have the place staked out, though. I didn't think we were that obvious." She paused, then added, "They must have tapped the phone."

Prossie didn't ask what that meant.

A moment later Amy and Prossie were joined by Ted, and the three of them stood at the front window watching as men in suits and uniforms emerged from the two county police cruisers that had pulled up in front of the Browns' home, and from an official-looking car in the driveway, a sedan that had a government seal of some sort on the driver's door.

Amy realized, annoyed, that she hadn't had a chance to go through Nancy's closet; she was still in her Imperial rags. She doubted these people would let her change.

And her hair was a mess — her last bleach and perm had all grown out long ago, and she hadn't even had a chance to brush it in days.

Ted moaned softly.

"We have a report, sir," the lieutenant said, saluting briskly.

Bascombe put down his pen and glowered at the young man.

"A report from *whom?*" he demanded. "From where? About what?"

"From Registered Master Telepath Bernard Dixon, sir!" the lieutenant said, snapping sharply back to attention.

"Ah," Bascombe said. "And exactly which of our mind-reading freaks is this Dixon?"

"Telepath Dixon is currently serving aboard I.S.S. *Meteor,* sir, investigating the reported reappearance of the renegade, Proserpine Thorpe."

"*Which* reported reappearance?"

"Uh . . . the first one, sir. I think." The lieutenant quivered uncertainly. Bascombe sighed.

"Tell me about it," he said.

"Yes, sir. According to Dixon, he has established, working in cooperation with five other telepaths, the approximate location of Thorpe's reappearance — he reports that there is only one system it could have been in, an unnamed system with no habitable planets — the navigator aboard *Meteor* has the catalog number, but it was not included in the report. Dixon is unable to narrow it down any farther; no physical traces have been found, and telepathy, he says, is not sufficiently precise over interstellar distances to be more exact."

"Did he say how he found the system at all?" Bascombe asked.

"Ah . . . that was not included in the report I received, sir," the lieutenant admitted.

"Dismissed," Bascombe said.

"Sir?" The lieutenant blinked.

"I said dismissed. Get out."

The lieutenant almost forgot to salute again as he hurried out.

Bascombe picked up his pen and considered.

He knew how the location was determined; telepaths on a dozen planets had been asked to report which direction Prossie Thorpe had been in, and those were then adjusted by the astronomers to allow for planetary rotation and used as approximate vectors. Where the resulting lines — or rather, cones, since none were narrow enough to be lines — intersected, that was where Thorpe had been.

Meteor had been sent to explore the resulting volume of space; the charts didn't show any inhabited systems there, but the charts could be wrong.

This time, according to Dixon, they weren't. And he'd checked back with five other stinking mutants to see if his distance felt right.

So Thorpe hadn't appeared on an inhabited planet, or even just a habitable one.

That meant a ship.

And that might explain why her stay there had been so brief, only about a minute — she had delivered something to a ship, and then returned to Shadow's world.

But if she were just a courier, why would Shadow, or Raven, or whoever was behind it, use a telepath? A telepath would stand out like a beacon — Thorpe *had* stood out like a beacon.

Someone had wanted the Empire to know something was going on; someone had wanted to get the Empire's attention — but who? And why?

Was it a distraction, a feint? Or was someone trying to tell them something, a message they weren't receiving?

What about Thorpe's other appearance? That one had been narrowed down to two possible systems, one of them, Upsilon Ceti, home to the Imperial colony of Beckett; I.S.S. *Wasp* was scheduled to arrive at Beckett Spaceport in a matter of hours.

If there had been a telepath on Beckett in the first place, maybe life would have been a bit simpler — but four hundred telepaths couldn't cover three thousand Imperial planets, and Thorpe had only appeared in the Beckett area briefly. It wasn't quite as fast as the other, about five minutes instead of one, but it was brief.

Was that a message of some kind? Why Beckett, which was a quiet little backwater?

And now Thorpe was supposed to be on Earth, the only human-inhabited planet in the Third Universe, and this time she was staying there. What did *that* mean?

Did it mean *anything?*

Or were all the telepaths lying? Had Thorpe ever really been in any of those places? Carrie Hall's reports hadn't started arriving yet, but he was fairly certain that when they did, they'd be useless.

Something was definitely going on, but whether the enemy was Shadow, or Raven's band of revolutionaries, or some faction within the Empire, or the telepaths themselves, Bascombe didn't know.

But he intended to find out.

He almost called for a telepath, but then he caught himself; he rose and stepped to the door, and called to his receptionist, "Miss Miller, have a messenger sent to Special Branch; I want orders sent to *Meteor* to stay where they are and search carefully for any signs of activity — ships, gravity fields, lights, whatever."

"Yes, Mr. Bascombe."

He nodded, and retreated back into his office.

The message would be sent by telepath, of course; there was no other way to reach *Meteor* except through Dixon. Sending it downstairs to Special Branch on paper, though, would mean that no telepath would be reading his mind directly.

At least, not legally.

And if telepaths were reading minds illegally, he couldn't stop them in any case — but that way lay madness. Telepaths *could* be listening to any thought, at any moment.

He just hoped they weren't.

"*A*m I under arrest?" Amy demanded, folding her arms across her chest and glaring up at the man in the blue uniform who seemed to be in charge of the whole business.

They hadn't let her change her clothes, and the gesture was as much for the sake of decency as out of annoyance. Her T-shirt was torn on both sides, and she wasn't wearing anything under it.

She tried not to think about that.

Major Johnston sighed. He turned a chair around, sat down, and leaned on the back.

"No, ma'am," he said, "you aren't. However, if that's what it takes to get you to cooperate, it can be arranged."

"On what charge?" Amy protested. "I haven't done anything!"

"I don't know just what charge, ma'am," Johnston said. "I'm not a lawyer; I work for Air Force intelligence, so I know something about the laws, but I'm not a lawyer, and in a complicated case like this . . ." He didn't finish the sentence; instead he shrugged and said, "But there's no question we could find something. You were one of sixteen people who disappeared all at once without any rational explanation, and now three of you — *only* three — have turned up again, one of you apparently gone at least temporarily nuts. I think we could get you booked on suspicion of *something*, kidnapping or assault or something. Withholding evidence, if nothing else."

It was Amy's turn to sigh. At least the officer hadn't included indecent exposure in his list. She wished Susan were there — but Susan was dead. Amy had seen her body lying on the floor of Shadow's throne room, back in Faerie.

Amy supposed that she could have called on the surviving members of Dutton, Powell, and Hough — Bob Hough must be back from his vacation long since — but how could she explain to *them* what had happened, how Susan Nguyen had died? So she had passed up the chance to call her lawyer when this Johnston had offered it.

She had managed to stall her removal until her friend Donna had arrived, so at least someone knew where she was and more or less what was happening, but Donna wasn't going to get her out of jail if these security people, whoever they were, did decide to arrest her.

"Is Ted okay?" she asked. "He was pretty upset."

"Mr. Deranian is, indeed, upset," Johnston admitted. "While I won't tell you any of the details, he seems to be very unsure of his own grasp on reality. He has asked repeatedly to go home, and we may oblige him in that — we're waiting for an opinion from a psychologist on whether it's safe for him to be alone. We've tried to call his sister to look after him, but she doesn't seem to be available."

"But you won't let *me* go home!" Amy protested.

"You, Ms. Jewell, are not screaming and crying and irrational."

Amy glared at him. Johnston glared back.

"What about Prossie?" Amy asked.

Major Johnston sighed again.

"Your other companion," he said, "tells us that her name is Registered Telepath Proserpine Thorpe, formerly of the Special Branch of the Imperial Intelligence Service. Beyond that, I'd prefer not to say at this time." He hesitated. "*Is* that her name?"

"As far as I know, it is," Amy said.

Johnston stared at her for a moment, then said, "All right. You don't want to talk to us. I don't know why not. This whole bizarre case is jammed full of things I don't know. It's been driving me crazy for months, ever since that damned whatever-it-is fell out of nowhere into your back yard and I got assigned to make sense of it. I've been trying to do that without any real information, but I can't. Now, you could give me real information, and you say you won't — but can't you at least say *why* won't you tell me what's going on?"

"Because you won't believe me. Besides, it isn't any of your business."

"How do you *know* I won't believe it?"

Amy closed her eyes. It wasn't really an unreasonable question. Johnston certainly seemed more reasonable than the soldier who had been questioning her before, who had just kept demanding she tell them where she had been for so long, and who had refused to ever accept, "I don't know," as an answer.

"Because," she said, opening her eyes and staring straight at Major Johnston's face, "it's all impossible, so impossible that Ted Deranian doesn't believe it, and he was *there*. That's why he's upset, you know — he thought it was all a dream, and that he'd finally woken up, and then you people came and hauled him away, and that means either it's real, or he's still dreaming." She sighed. "Now, do you expect me to believe that you'll just accept my word for something so incredible that a man who lived through it thinks it was just a nightmare?"

Johnston considered that for a long moment.

"All right," he said, "so maybe I won't believe it. But maybe I will, and what can it hurt to try me?"

"You won't argue?" Amy had visions of trying to tell her story and having every point questioned, every absurdity denied, until nothing made any sense at all.

"I don't know," Johnston admitted, straightening up for a moment. "Try me."

The man's apparent honesty was disarming; Amy shrugged, unfolded her arms, and said, "You ask questions. I'll answer — for now."

*S*hadow had known how to see through other people's eyes, and hear through other people's ears, Pel reminded himself. She had been able to spy on anyone, anywhere in the entire immense world she ruled. It couldn't be that difficult.

He closed his eyes, clenched his fists on the arms of his throne, and concentrated on the webs of magic that reached out in all directions around him.

He could sense things out there, like tiny sparks caught in the meshes of color and darkness, things that he was fairly sure were people, and he tried to focus in on one specific twinkle, tried to see through it — and nothing happened. He didn't connect; he didn't see anything, through his eyes or anyone else's.

Shadow had known how, but Pel didn't. He could sense the shape of the matrix, all the currents and eddies of magic that flowed through Faerie; he could tell when something disturbed those currents, and he was fairly certain he knew when the disturbance was a wizard stealing a little power, and when it was just some harmless peasant stumbling through a place where the magic ran strong. The wizards seemed to have odd little patterns of their own, sort of like fractal designs within the larger design of the matrix. Pel could see that.

But he couldn't see through other eyes.

And he couldn't match up the matrix with the outside world, either; he couldn't make any correlation between magical streams and physical ones, couldn't tell where the web lay on land, where on sea — or where it soared through the air or burrowed underground, or even climbed away from the planet into whatever lay beyond the sky in this strange realm. The network he had inherited from Shadow was centered on the fortress where he sat, but it extended, however tenuously, through this entire universe.

Pel controlled all of it, through his mind and will; he knew its shape, could sense every trickle. He could tell more or less how far out in the network any movement was, and in roughly which direction — but where that was in the ordinary world he had no idea.

He could spot the fetches he had sent out, carrying messages, but though he thought he might be able to transmit a couple of basic commands, such as a signal to return, he couldn't really communicate with them. He could tell which direction they had gone, and could see how far they had progressed in terms of the matrix, but what that translated to in miles he could only estimate, and the farther away they got, the less reliable that estimate was.

Where ordinary people appeared as analogous to white or golden sparks, and wizards seemed to have faint traceries woven inside those sparks, the fetches were something like smoky red embers, and were bound into the matrix itself, rather than being independently-existing structures that sometimes impinged upon the net. It seemed as if Pel ought to be able to at least see through *those* eyes — but he couldn't. He didn't know how. He couldn't see where they were or what they were doing.

He opened his eyes, slumped back in the elaborately-carved throne, and stared through the glimmering colors at the big open doors at the far end of the room.

He didn't look at the spot where Susan Nguyen's body had lain for so long. At least he'd made a little progress on *that* problem — with the help of the fetches he had had the corpse settled on a spare bed, and had put a preserving spell on it as best he could. He had seen how the meats in the fortress kitchen were preserved, and he had painstakingly built up the same magical structure over poor Susan, and it seemed to be working.

But not much else was. He was fairly certain, now, that he'd sent those fetches out on a fool's errand. He hadn't given them any directions; he'd just told them, "Go find wizards and bring them here."

But he hadn't known what directions to give them. He didn't even have a map. He had never *seen* a map of Shadow's world. He wasn't even sure there *were* maps.

He knew the route he had taken to reach the fortress, from the Low Forest of Sunderland across the Starlinshire Downs and the coastal plain to Shadowmarsh; he had looked across the rift valley called Stormcrack and seen Stormcrack Keep, perched on the other side; but where these fit in their world, where Stormcrack lay in relation to Sunderland or Shadowmarsh, he had no idea at all. He thought he remembered Raven mentioning that Stormcrack lay in the Hither Corydians, while the mountains visible from Sunderland were the Further Corydians, but what that meant he didn't know. He had heard other names, as well, but they were just names.

It wasn't fair. In all the stories the hero knew where everything was. There were always maps. Tolkien's books had had maps all over them. Even the movies had maps sometimes.

If Shadow had had any maps, Pel hadn't found them yet.

How could he find anything, or anyone, without maps, without any means of long-distance communication? And while he could sense fetches and wizards in the matrix, he didn't know how to guide the red embers toward the white snowflakes and golden spiderwebs; how could his fetches find anyone?

He had sent them out, a dozen of them, with orders to find wizards and bring them back — Taillefer in particular, but if they found *any* wizard, that would do. But how could they do that? How would they know where to go?

He hadn't thought this through.

He couldn't even send notes; most people in this world seemed to be illiterate, and those who weren't used a different alphabet from the one he knew. He had told the fetches to summon wizards, but he had left it up to them to figure out how to deliver that summons.

They might not be able to; fetches were pretty limited.

He could go out searching on his own, he supposed — but he wasn't sure just how to best use his magic to travel. Conjuring winds that would blow him around, the way Taillefer did, seemed dangerous and haphazard.

And he wouldn't know where to go. It was a very big planet. The matrix seemed to stretch to infinity.

He would have to get organized about this. As Shadow's heir and master of the matrix that controlled all the world's magic, he was, in theory, ruler of all Faerie; he didn't need to run his own errands, or send out all his servants. He could order *other* people to do it all.

And besides, he had told Amy that he intended to be a *benevolent* ruler here, teach these people how to lead more civilized lives; how could he carry out that promise if he stayed holed up here in his castle, with no contact with the outside world?

It was time to start playing his role properly. He would get this place organized — and that would let him fetch wizards who could teach him how to raise the dead.

And if he did some good for the natives in the process, all the better; they could certainly use some help. The towns and villages he had seen on his way to Shadowmarsh hadn't exactly been paradise.

He remembered the gibbets in every village, the disembowelled corpses of the people who had offended Shadow — at the very least he could do away with that sort of thing.

He realized that he could start right on his own doorstep — quite literally on his doorstep, where the corpses of half a dozen Imperial soldiers still lay. He hadn't even done anything about them.

Not that he could do very much, but at least he could have them decently buried.

And after that he could send messengers out to the surrounding villages.

He sat up straight, closed his eyes, and sent out a summons to the fetches still in the fortress, and to the handful of homunculi and other creatures over which he had established his control.

Chapter Three

"I don't care if you believe me or not," Amy said wearily. "It's over, it's done, and I just want to go home and forget about it."

"What about the spaceship in your back yard?" Major Johnston asked.

Amy sighed.

She had to admit that Johnston had done his best to make it easy on her; he hadn't nagged, hadn't argued, hadn't pushed when she said she didn't know something — but on the other hand, he had this annoying habit of finding questions she didn't want to think about.

"I don't know," she said. "What about it?"

"Are you going to just leave it there?"

"Do I have a choice?"

"Assuming you have a choice."

"I haven't decided. Do *you* want it?"

Johnston hesitated, then admitted, "We haven't decided, either. We might; please let us know before you do anything drastic with it."

"Sure," Amy said. "May I go now?"

"Um . . ." The major hesitated. "Not *quite* yet, I'm afraid."

"We've got the report from Beckett, sir," the lieutenant said.

Bascombe leaned back. "Let's have it, then," he said.

"The formal statement is still being written up, sir, but the gist of it is that several unidentified corpses were found in a field outside Blessingbury that could easily have been the place Thorpe appeared. All but one of the corpses were adult males, in some sort of black livery, carrying swords; the one female wore a gray robe and carried no weapon. All had been killed by blaster fire, but no blasters were found; a more careful search is ongoing."

Bascombe blinked and straightened up.

"Swords?" he said.

"Yes, sir. That's what the telepath *said,* anyway."

"The bodies — were they human?"

The lieutenant hesitated. "Well, yes, sir, so far as I know," he said. "The report calls them dark-haired Nordic males, which would certainly seem to *imply* human. I don't think any autopsies have been done yet, though."

"Dark-haired Nordic?"

"Yes, sir, Nordic is the standard term for any pure-blooded white, you know, it's not just the true . . ."

"Shut up."

Bascombe knew Imperial racial classifications as well as anyone; what he didn't know was why any Imperial citizen, except a few holders of ceremonial titles back on Terra, would be carrying a sword.

Shadow's creatures might well use swords, but most of them didn't seem to be genuine human beings. Even the humanoids often had black skin — not the brown of a Negro, but actual black.

On the other hand, the people of Earth were authentic human beings, so far as Bascombe knew. Of the four who had stayed at Base One for several weeks, three had been white, one Azeatic; Bascombe had never seen a Negro Earthman, but that didn't mean much, since that foursome was hardly a fair sample.

Did Earthpeople still use swords? Earlier reports had indicated that they carried projectile weapons, not blades — gunpowder-and-bullet firearms. Perhaps this group had been even *more* primitive, though, or had been uncertain their guns would work in Imperial space. Swords always worked. And they never needed reloading.

Still, swords seemed more appropriate to Shadow's world. Shadow itself relied on its super-scientific "magic," but its slaves didn't seem to, and in fact much of the "magic" didn't seem to operate in normal space.

Or maybe these had been members of Raven's resistance movement. Bascombe didn't think much of Raven of Stormcrack Keep — the man was obsessive and abysmally ignorant, determined to fight Shadow's science with . . .

With swords.

This was all getting very complicated — Shadow, Earth, and Raven were all possibilities.

If the telepaths hadn't made it all up.

"Lieutenant," Bascombe said, "I want one of these corpses brought here to Base One, as fast as possible. Make sure the sword comes with it, and someone who saw everything as it was first found — *not* a telepath."

"Yes, sir." The messenger turned to go.

"And," Bascombe added loudly, "send the telepath Carrie Hall up here."

*M*ajor Reginald Johnston sat at his desk, staring at the fancy silver pen he'd gotten as an award two years before, rolling it between his fingers as he tried to think it all through logically.

Sherlock Holmes always said that when you had eliminated the impossible, whatever remained, however unlikely, had to be the truth — but how did you know what was really impossible?

Which was impossible, and which merely incredibly unlikely?

The three of them were all reasonably consistent in their stories. Details varied, of course, but not to the point of finding any actual contradictions. Deranian insisted that the whole thing was a dream or hallucination, and would only talk about it with a psychologist, and only on those terms; Jewell didn't claim to understand any of it, only to be reporting what she thought she had experienced; but Thorpe, if that was really her name, was the tough one, as she claimed to actually be *from* one of these other universes.

And that should have been easy to disprove, but it wasn't.

So either it was all true, and the United States had blown a chance to make peaceful contact with aliens not just from another planet, but from another universe entirely, or else the whole thing was the most elaborate and inexplicable hoax Johnston had ever heard of.

It didn't make sense as a hoax — but a Galactic Empire in another universe? Wizards and castles in a third?

If it was a hoax, how did the hoaxers get that spaceship there? Why hadn't anything leaked in the months since it crashed? Who was Proserpine Thorpe? Where did she and the others come from? Where did they go?

What did Sherlock Holmes say to do after you had eliminated the impossible, and found there was *nothing* left?

For months, ever since that impossible spaceship had fallen out of nowhere and the case had been dumped in his lap, Johnston had been looking for an explanation. He had thought that when he found some of the missing people he would have that explanation.

He supposed he *did* have an explanation now — but he didn't like it, and he didn't want to believe it.

All the same, he had to cover the bases. If it *is* true, he asked himself, tapping his fancy silver pen on the worn spot on the blotter, if it *is* true, what do I do about it?

A Galactic Empire. An all-powerful wizard.

Hell, it was simple enough, really; the first thing any commander does is collect information, scout out the territory. Even when the territory was in another universe, that rule still held.

And you pass the information up the chain of command, keep headquarters informed — but how in hell could he tell anyone about this one? If *he* didn't really believe it, how could he convince anyone higher up?

And *that* brought him to the first rule, not of military strategy, but of political strategy: CYA.

He would file the appropriate reports, full of qualifiers and ambiguity, and other than that he wouldn't say a damn thing to anyone until he could provide *proof.* He would investigate the hell out of everything, have the Brown house searched right down to the foundations, have Jewell and Deranian and Thorpe watched every minute, send someone to check out whether there was any research being done on . . . on what? Other dimensions?

The Golden Fleece Award people on that senator's staff might know — research like that would be right up their alley.

He put down the pen and reached for the intercom.

*P*el looked over the motley crew he had gathered before his throne. Colored light flickered across black clothing, black leather, glossy black fur — Shadow's color scheme had been pretty limited. Maybe she saw enough colors from the matrix, Pel thought.

He counted nine fetches — kitchen help, mostly, but since Pel could draw all the energy he needed from the matrix, he didn't need to eat, so why should he maintain a kitchen?

There were four hairless, black-skinned homunculi, human in appearance except for their color; three of them, two male and one female, were naked. Pel had no idea what purpose they had served, why Shadow had created them, but he had found them and been able to make them obey him.

There were about a dozen other creatures, but most of them Pel had no name for; Shadow had apparently been fond of experimenting, and had often been generous with claws, teeth, scales, and tentacles. Two could reasonably be called hounds, and one resembled a panther, but the others weren't so easily classified.

Hundreds of other creatures lived in the fortress — if they were really alive — and there were literally thousands more in the surrounding marsh and the forests beyond, but Pel hadn't yet managed to gain control of all those.

He didn't see much use for the sluglike marsh-monsters, in any case. The dragon might have been nice, but he had killed that — which reminded him, he should incinerate the remains before they began to stink.

Most of the rest of Shadow's creatures he just hadn't gotten to yet.

So he had about two dozen obedient servants, of various shapes, none of them particularly appealing.

"All right," he said, "I want all of you to go out of this place, and go out to the villages, and bring back people. Alive. Don't hurt them. I want to talk to them. Understand?"

Roughly a score of heads nodded.

Pel hesitated.

"No children," he added. He didn't want to terrorize any kids. "Adults only. For that matter, make it men only." This was a primitive and sexist world he was in; he didn't want to worry about the sexual politics of the situation. He looked at some of the non-humanoid creatures, and asked, "Can you tell men from women?"

The bobbing movements, hissings, and grunts looked and sounded like agreement.

"Good. Okay, then go." He sat back on the throne as his audience turned away.

He didn't know how to send them after anyone in particular, but he figured that out of any random group of men they might bring in there would be someone he could make use of, as a messenger at the very least, maybe as a deputy or more.

And he had to send several of the things because he didn't know whether he could trust any one of them to do the job, or how people would react. If he only sent one, as a trial, it might get killed by some panicky peasant, or it might fall in a bog somewhere — he wasn't sure how bright most of these creatures were.

Besides, he wouldn't mind having enough of a sample of the population to be at least slightly representative. You didn't test a new product on just one potential buyer; he wanted to have a few people brought in.

They might even find poor Tom Sawyer, if he was still alive out there somewhere.

Pel blinked.

"Wait," he called.

The pack of monsters paused in the doorway of the throne room; two of the homunculi turned back to face him, but the fetches and most of the rest simply stopped where they were.

Spaceman Sawyer was still out there somewhere, either alive or dead, and Pel had completely forgotten about him until just now.

How could he have been so thoughtless?

He had been busy, he had had other problems to worry about, but it was still unforgivable. He had left an Imperial soldier wandering around in Faerie, trapped out there, when he, Pel, could have sent him home to the Galactic Empire in a matter of minutes.

And not just Sawyer, who had turned back at the fortress gate; there was Ron Wilkins, as well, who had deserted the party days before, somewhere in the villages this side of Starlinshire. And there might be other survivors of the Imperial landing party, as well — most had stayed at the ship with Lieutenant Dibbs, and while most of that group had later turned up dead, Pel knew at least a couple were still unaccounted-for.

He could send any of them who were still alive back to their home universe.

And if they hadn't disguised themselves, they'd be easy to spot. They had all been wearing those silly Buck Rogers uniforms the Galactic Empire used.

"Purple," he told his waiting servants. "You find any men wearing purple, you bring them to me. Whatever men you can find, bring them here, but *especially* if they're wearing purple!"

*T*hey had even given her her car back; Amy knew she shouldn't complain. They'd provided some sandwiches — soggy and stale, but genuine Earth food, without any of the strange off tastes of the Empire or Faerie. They'd just been doing their jobs, and that Major Johnston had really been very reasonable, given how incredible the whole thing sounded.

But still, she was furious.

They were going to be watching her house every minute, they admitted it. They were tapping her phone. She wasn't to leave the state overnight.

She ought to have a lawyer; this couldn't be constitutional, watching her like this. But Susan was dead.

Should she call Bob Hough?

She looked right as she came to an intersection, and had to lean forward to see past Prossie; that reminded her of the telepath's presence.

Poor Prossie would need help settling in, and having Bob Hough around wouldn't help any with that. Amy needed to see the doctor, and Bob Hough wouldn't help with *that*, either — in fact, from some remarks he had made during the divorce hearings, Amy didn't think Bob would approve of her getting an abortion, even if he believed her about the father being a rapist and murderer, which he probably wouldn't.

The damn government people would see her going to the doctor, would probably find out all about it — she hadn't mentioned her pregnancy to Major Johnston, since it wasn't anyone's business but her own.

She didn't *want* the government to know about it. What if they decided that the baby was some sort of valuable specimen, living proof that Earthpeople and Imperials could interbreed? Maryland might have legal guarantees of a woman's right to an abortion, but she was pretty sure the feds could find a way around that if they wanted to.

She frowned as she drove on through the intersection. She was making it sound like some trashy late-night movie, thinking about "aliens" breeding with human women — with *her*. This wasn't science fiction, and she wasn't some silly heroine in a tight skirt and heels who was no use for anything but screaming, and Walter wasn't an alien, he was just a bastard — a dead bastard. She didn't want his kid, and she wasn't going to carry it.

If anyone tried to interfere with that, *then* she'd call a lawyer.

*I*t was raining again, and Pel was back on the battlement, looking out over the marsh. Wind whistled around the stone of the tower and sprayed water across the wall, and water pattered unevenly from the broken gargoyle.

He didn't let the sound bother him this time, at least not consciously; after all, he was doing everything he could to bring Rachel back. His messengers had gone out into the world of Faerie, and until they returned, what else should he be doing? The dragon was reduced to ash, Lieutenant Dibbs and the other dead Imperials were buried, and Susan's corpse was as well-preserved as he could manage.

All he could do was wait.

He could feel the matrix surging and flowing around him, all that power at his disposal — but he didn't know what to do with it.

Waiting was always hard, especially waiting alone. If he had someone to talk to, he thought, it might not be so bad.

For a moment he considered opening a portal to Earth and sending a messenger to find Amy Jewell and bring her here. She knew his situation, she had been through it all with him; he could talk to her.

So had Ted Deranian, of course, but he had cracked under the strain. And Prossie Thorpe, but she wasn't from Earth, they didn't have a common background. It would have to be Amy or no one, he thought.

It was foolish, though; Amy was probably getting on with her own life, trying to get her decorating business back on track, catching up on everything she had missed while they were all trapped in the Empire and in Faerie. She wouldn't appreciate being dragged away.

Besides, it would take time to find another fetch or homunculus and break it to obedience, time for it to find its way to Amy once it was on Earth, time to bring her back — by then his messengers would probably be returning.

There were still plenty of non-human creatures around the fortress — hellbeasts, Raven had called most of them — but those wouldn't do; they couldn't live in non-magical universes. The ones Shadow had sent into the Galactic Empire had all died within hours, according to everything Pel had seen and heard. Earth's space was different from Imperial space, but Pel didn't think it was anymore magical.

Fetches and homunculi were sufficiently human to function in the Empire, and presumably on Earth, but he had used up every cooperative surviving fetch and homunculus he could readily find, sending them all out as messengers.

About a hundred fetches had died — or rather, been destroyed; fetches were *already* dead — in the fight with Shadow. That had left the place somewhat understaffed.

He sensed through the matrix that there were still creatures he had not seen deep in the subterranean depths of the fortress, and some of them were probably homunculi — but it just wasn't worth the trouble of going down there and finding them and enchanting them into obedience, and then sending them to Earth, where they wouldn't know how to drive or use the phone and they'd probably just get run over trying to cross a street.

Besides, what good would it really do to talk to Amy? What did she know about Nancy or Rachel, about losing loved ones? It wasn't as if the two of them had been friends before all this started; they hadn't even known each other.

And really, Pel and Amy hadn't hit it off all that well while they were traveling together, either. Pel remembered Amy weeping with exhaustion, Amy vomiting by the side of the road, Amy shouting hysterically . . .

He didn't need company *that* badly.

He would wait.

U nder-Secretary Bascombe looked down at the black-garbed corpse, then over at the sword next to it, and finally up at the soldier accompanying it.

"You were there when they found them?" Bascombe asked.

"Yessir."

"It looked just like this?"

"Ah, well . . . not exactly." The soldier hesitated; Bascombe favored him with an inquisitive glare.

"Well, what I mean is, it was fresher; we didn't have anywhere good to put it on ice on the ship here, sir."

"Oh, of course." He looked down again. "But it was dressed like this? Had the blaster wound in the chest? And the sword?"

"Yessir."

Bascombe nodded. He turned to the doctor beside him. "How long's he been dead?"

"Well, Mr. Secretary, that's hard to say . . ." The doctor fumbled with the buttons of his white lab coat.

"Try," Bascombe said tartly.

The doctor sighed. "Well, sir," he said, "there are conflicting signs. Some of the evidence of overall decay indicates a death within the past three days, while tissue desiccation would seem to indicate a much earlier demise. Seems to me that despite what the sergeant here says, someone's made partially-successful attempts to preserve this fellow's remains. Either that, or he was not at all well for some time before his death."

That figured, Bascombe thought; the entire thing was confusing, so why should even so simple a detail as time of death be any different?

The corpse did prove a few things, though.

First off, it was real — something mysterious *had* happened where the telepaths reported it, it wasn't all a fabrication. Everything the telepaths had reported that could be readily checked on *had* been checked on, and it was all true.

If there *was* some sort of conspiracy or rebellion under way among the telepaths, it was undetectably subtle — and since there was no obvious way the telepaths could have obtained these mysterious corpses, the plotters must also have hitherto unseen, unknown resources.

Second, the corpse was dressed in the manner of some of the people who took part in previous incursions made by Shadow, and armed with a sword; there was nothing to connect it in any way with Earth. No one had ever found any evidence that Earth had inter-dimensional capabilities; the Empire's own crash program had taken five years to produce the space-warp generator once they knew it was theoretically possible to travel between universes, and Earth, which had no anti-gravity, no blasters, and little semblance of the Empire's applied science, had supposedly known of the Empire's existence for no more than a few months.

If Earth was involved, then the Earthpeople had hitherto unseen, unknown resources, and were being undetectably subtle.

In other words, if either the telepaths or the Earthpeople were behind this, the Empire was outmatched — but all the evidence pointed to Shadow.

Shadow was definitely up to something.

The question was, up to *what?*

Chapter Four

One man had died of fright.

Pel hadn't expected anything like that; for a few moments guilt closed his throat, and he blinked away tears.

He *should* have expected it — the poor sucker had been abducted without warning, captured by a pair of zombies and dragged off to the fortress of a world-conquering evil power, a power well known for hanging and disembowelling its enemies.

Nobody out there knew that Shadow was dead, that her replacement was one of the good guys — or at least, *tried* to be one of the good guys.

Not that he was very good at it, he thought as he wiped his eyes and tried to swallow. The storybook heroes never made such stupid mistakes, never accidentally killed innocent bystanders.

Maybe, when he had learned how to resurrect the dead, he could bring this poor fellow back, too.

"Take him to the kitchen," he told two of the fetches when he could speak.

The other involuntary guests all shuddered, glancing at one another and at the corpse as the fetches carried it away.

Pel silently cursed himself, and his eyes teared up again, this time more with frustration than grief. "That's where it's easiest to preserve him until I can revive him," he explained.

It would take some effort to always remember that these people were accustomed to assuming the worst. Under Shadow, assuming the worst was the only way to avoid disaster.

He looked the survivors over.

There were eight, so far, and more on the way — that was really a pretty promising result. None of them were wizards or Imperials; most of them were scruffy and dirty and looked like peasants, but still, this was a good start.

He looked them over, standing or crouching at the eastern end of the throne room, faces averted or eyes shielded against the glare of the matrix and blinking anyway. They obviously had no idea what was going on.

He had debated waiting for the last few, but he had already kept the first arrivals in suspense for over an hour while this group collected, and the others wouldn't reach the fortress for some time yet; it was time to begin.

"I assume you think that I'm Shadow," he said, and without meaning to he let the matrix amplify his voice, so that it boomed and echoed; one man clapped his hands over his ears, and others flinched, but they all turned to listen.

"I'm not," Pel continued. "Shadow is dead. But before she died, she turned her power over to me."

He paused, unsure what to say next; he hadn't gotten that far in preparing a speech. He'd assumed he could just wing it, make it up as he went along — he'd done that often enough in presentations — but he'd been disconcerted by the one who died, thrown off his pace, and now he was struggling to remember what he'd planned to say. He had figured that he would tell these people that the hangings and other executions were to stop, that they were free now — but how did he get to that from the announcement that Shadow was dead?

And if they were free, how could he order them to stop hanging people, or bring him wizards, or do anything else?

And somehow he had pictured himself speaking to a group of well-dressed, dignified village elders, rather than a bunch of terrified farmers who were cowering against the wall in confusion, too scared to speak.

"Shadow is dead," he repeated.

One of the men blinked, and ventured a whispered, "Shadow is dead; long live Shadow."

His neighbors turned to stare at him, then quickly looked back at the blaze of color and light that was all they could see before them.

When Pel, too startled to react immediately, said nothing, about half of the men mumbled, "Shadow is dead, long live Shadow."

Pel slammed a fist onto the arm of his throne, and outside, unheard, magically-driven winds whipped around the fortress walls; Pel could sense them through the matrix. Within the throne room his glow shifted toward reds and blues and shadows, away from the lighter and warmer colors. This was so slow and frustrating! These people didn't understand, and he didn't know how to explain it to them.

"No, no," he said. "Shadow is *dead*; there *is* no more Shadow. I am not Shadow!" He fought down the light and color, so that the men could see him. "I'm just a man, a man who has Shadow's magic."

The peasants peered at him through the lessened glare, then glanced at one another, and after a moment one of them called unsteadily, "Who are you, then?"

"My name is Pel Brown."

Feet shuffled and voices muttered. No one spoke.

Pel realized that his name wasn't much of an answer.

"I came here from another world," he said. "Shadow wanted me to help her with something, but she lied to me, and . . . and I killed her."

It was surprisingly hard to admit that, and for a moment he wondered whether a trace remained of the geas Shadow had placed on him, the magical compulsion not to harm her.

But it was probably, he knew, just guilt. He didn't like to admit to being a murderer, even if it was justified homicide, even if he hadn't pulled the trigger himself. He'd seen Shadow kill his friends for no reason, so even though he couldn't harm her himself, he had set up a situation where Prossie Thorpe would kill her.

He'd conspired to commit murder, and why *shouldn't* he feel guilty about it? Maybe the heroes in books and movies never had any qualms about the villains they killed, but he wasn't any hero, despite what had happened to him, and even if Shadow had been a murderer many times over and a truly evil person, he wasn't happy about her death.

And this man who had died of terror didn't help any; that wasn't justified, it was just carelessness. He hadn't meant it to happen, but it was still his fault.

The peasants muttered among themselves. If he bothered, he could extend his senses through the matrix and hear every word they said, find out if they were blaming him for their companion's death — but why bother? He let them mutter.

He hoped someone would step forward and speak up, ask questions, turn this into a proper conversation — but no one did. He supposed he shouldn't be surprised; this world's culture seemed pretty authoritarian, not much given to discussion.

So it would have to be a speech.

"I have all Shadow's power," he said, "but not her knowledge, and not her . . . her ambition. I'm not going to hurt any of you. I have no desire to rule your world; in fact, I want you to be free, and happy."

One man managed to work up an almost-hopeful expression at that, but that was countered by looks of dread on other faces; Pel supposed that to most of them, *any* talk of change sounded threatening.

He would just have to work past that.

And he knew where to begin; he remembered his horrific walk to the fortress.

"When I came here," he said, "I came down the road from the Low Forest in Sunderland, and I passed through several of your towns and villages, and in most of them there were dead bodies hanging. Who were they all?"

The peasants looked at one another. No one wanted to be the spokesman, obviously. Pel sighed. "You," he said, pointing, "on the end, in the green. Step forward."

The man hesitated, then stepped forward, placing each foot carefully; it looked as if he was having trouble breathing.

"Who were all those people who got hanged?"

"I . . . I know not, my lord . . . your Majesty. In . . . in my own village, the last to be hanged was a man named Norbert . . ."

The colors surged up, flickering orange, as Pel momentarily lost control of his emotions, his guilt and grief turning abruptly to anger as frustration got the better of him.

"Not their *names*, idiot!" he shouted, and the walls echoed back a dull, angry roar. "I mean, what were they *hanged* for?"

The men cowered back against the wall; one moved for the door, but Pel twisted at a strand of his web and the doors slammed shut.

Someone moaned, and Pel forced himself to calm down; he didn't want any more deaths. He didn't even want anyone to faint.

But he *did* want answers.

"Why were they hanged?" Pel demanded. "You, why was this Norbert hanged?"

The man in green glanced back at his companions, found no help there, and after a false start and a throat-clearing, managed to say, "'Twas said he had failed to show the village elders the respect due their station."

Pel glared, though he doubted anyone could see his expression through the magical haze. He had expected something like that, but it was still infuriating. Death for the most trivial wrongs — that had been Shadow's style. No wonder the men were scared. "He didn't kill anybody?"

The man blinked, and made the chopping motion that Pel had learned was the local equivalent of shaking one's head.

"He didn't even *steal* anything?"

Another chop.

All those people, horribly dead for nothing, and it had been deliberate, not accidental like the one the fetches were taking to the kitchen; Pel felt sick. "All right, listen, all of you," he announced. "From now on, you only hang *murderers. Only murderers.* You understand? You can . . . you can beat thieves, or flog them, or throw them in jail, or whatever seems appropriate, but you *can't kill them.* Is that clear?"

Heads bobbed. That gesture was the same here — just another of those annoying situations where things were only *partly* different, just familiar enough to be confusing.

"And you don't disembowel *anyone*, is that clear? Not unless a murderer chops people up with an axe or something, then maybe you can gut him, but *nobody else.*"

"The Elders . . . someone began.

"To hell with the elders!" Pel shouted. "You go tell them to stop hanging people, or they'll answer to me! If they don't believe you, you send 'em here! And look, hey, you can take fetches back with you to prove you were here. I don't want anyone else killed! Shadow's dead, and you don't *do* that stuff anymore!" He was standing in front of the throne now, pointing and yelling; magic swirled and blazed around him, actual flame flaring briefly from the air behind him as his anger sucked energy from the matrix.

The eight men all pressed flat against the wall, hands over their ears, driven back by sheer volume.

Seeing them there, Pel's anger suddenly passed, and he flopped back into his chair.

"And you can clean up your villages, too," he said in his normal tones. "Maybe pave the streets. Put in sewers — some of those places stank. There's no reason you can't live decently, can't have indoor plumbing and all the rest of it."

No one answered, though a few risked uncovering their ears.

"You don't know about all that stuff," he said, with a gesture of dismissal. "It can wait. We'll get to it."

"Ah . . . your Majesty," the man in green said, head down, "if one could be permitted to speak . . ."

Pel slumped back in the throne.

"Oh, go ahead and speak," he said. "Stand up straight and tell me all about it."

"Majesty, we . . . I am but a poor cobbler," the man said. "I know naught of governance or law, and would only go about my business. Wherefore, then, am I brought hither? Why speak to me of roads and hangings and the rest? Would it not be better to call upon the councils of the wise, the elders and those who have a say in such matters? Or perchance, to send forth your own ministers, an you are displeased with our lords?"

"You don't have a say?" Pel asked.

"Nay, surely not," the cobbler said. "I'm neither prince nor councilor."

"You're a person, aren't you?"

The cobbler blinked. "Aye, but . . ."

"Well, then you have a say," Pel proclaimed. *"Everybody* has a say. It's time you people got rid of your lords and ladies and learned some democracy." Blue streaked through the matrix for a moment. "Listen, all of you," Pel said. "From now on, I want things to be run democratically around here. I want you to elect your leaders, not just let them happen. Vote for 'em."

"Majesty, I understand this not a whit."

"I mean I want you to choose your own leaders by getting everyone to vote — each person says who he wants, and whoever gets the most votes wins."

The men stared at him uncomprehendingly.

"It's simple," Pel insisted. "Look, suppose the eight of you were somewhere together and needed a leader. Each of you would say who you wanted to be the leader, and whoever got five or more votes would win."

"But . . . 'tis all very well, but how to know who shall vote?" the cobbler asked.

"*Everybody* votes!" Pel said, waving his hands to include all the world.

"Let *everyone* have a say?" one of the other men protested. "The fools, the children, women? People bearing grudges?"

The others murmured agreement, and Pel stared at them just as uncomprehendingly as they had stared at him a moment before.

It was at that point that Pel realized he didn't *care*. If they didn't want to be democratic, what business was it of his? If they didn't want to build sewers, why should he care? *He* didn't have to live in their stinking villages.

He didn't really care whether they cleaned up their villages, he discovered. He had told them to stop hanging and disembowelling anyone who argued with the village elders, and they had agreed, and that was the really important change. Death mattered. Death was important. The rest of it, elections and building sewers and aqueducts and so on, that could wait, or they could figure it out for themselves.

He had had an idea, when he sent the others back to Earth but chose to stay here, that he might play the great leader, that he might show the people of this world the way to a more modern, more civilized lifestyle, but if they weren't interested, it wasn't *his* problem.

"Suit yourselves," he said, his hands dropping.

His problem was getting his wife and daughter back.

"All right," he said, "forget all that. But no more hangings, no more eviscerations, no torture — none of that stuff. Be good to each other. Shadow's dead. You tell everyone she's dead, and that Pel Brown is running things now." He hoped that that name would reach Wilkins and Sawyer and other Imperials who were still alive, and they could come and find him and he could send them home. "No hangings, and the name's Pel Brown. You understand?"

Heads nodded.

"And there's something else. Something important."

He could see them tense, he could, through the matrix, hear them drawing quick breaths and holding them; he could sense muscles tightening, pupils dilating.

"I want wizards," he said. "I want every wizard you can find, I want every wizard there *is*. Send word out through all the world — every wizard must come to *me*, here in my fortress." He stood up and pointed nowhere in particular, to emphasize his words. "*All* the wizards. Especially Taillefer. They come here, or they're in deep shit. I can find them if I have to, and they know it." This last wasn't as certainly true as he made it sound; he was sure that he could locate anyone who dared to use magic, since all magic was linked into a single network and he controlled that network, and he thought he could tell someone experienced in wizardry by the patterning in their own tiny bit of matrix, but he did not yet really know how to interpret the data, how to convert a sensation in the matrix into a place in the real world.

But that didn't matter.

The important thing was what *they* believed.

He thought for a moment about telling them to find Imperials, too, but then he dismissed the idea. They didn't seem all that bright, and he wanted to keep it as simple as he possibly could. The creatures he had sent out to fetch this bunch hadn't come across anyone wearing purple; probably Sawyer and Wilkins were hundreds of miles away.

"You find wizards. You tell your village elders, you tell *everybody*. Any wizard doesn't come here might as well cut his own throat and be done with it, you understand?"

They were cowering back against the wall, and Pel realized that intangible clouds of dark gray were rolling around the throne room, interspersed with gouts of flame and vivid flashes of crimson — the matrix was picking up his insistence and interpreting it. His guests, or captives, or whatever they were, were probably scared half to death.

He dropped his pointing finger and calmed the roiling currents of magic.

"You get the idea," he said. "No more hangings, and find wizards, and send them here. Now, get out of here, go home, tell everyone." He made the twist in the web of power that would link him to the fetches, and ordered them, "You go with these men, you make sure people believe them about the hangings and the wizards. Take a week, that should do it, then come back here." He waved in dismissal. "Get out of here, all of you."

He slumped back into the throne and watched as the eight men fled, the fetches trudging stolidly after them.

He hoped none of them tripped and fell down the stairs on the way out.

*J*ohnston peered warily down the basement stairs.

Except for being unusually dusty, which came from being shut up and neglected all summer, the place looked perfectly ordinary. It was hard to believe that the doorway to another universe had appeared in this house.

Well, maybe it hadn't — but the house didn't look much like part of an incredibly-elaborate hoax, either.

Carefully, he trudged down the steps. Behind him came a heavily-loaded Air Force lieutenant, struggling to maneuver two cases of equipment safely.

"You'll want to change those lightbulbs," Johnston said, pointing. "The Jewell woman says they're burnt out."

"Yes, sir," the lieutenant agreed, looking up.

"That's the wall, right there, according to the description both the women gave," Johnston said, indicating the bare concrete. "Poke at it if you like, do anything you want that won't damage it — take pictures, measure it, whatever."

"Yes, sir."

"Set the radio up first."

"Yes, sir."

"We don't really expect anything to happen, you understand — but if it *does*, it could be anything, anytime."

"Yes, sir." The lieutenant set the cases on the basement floor.

"Any questions?"

The lieutenant looked around, then shrugged. "No, sir."

Johnston nodded. "Your relief will be here at 1800."

"Yes, sir."

Johnston hesitated, then crossed to the blank wall. He stared at the gray blocks, reached up and tapped one.

Just concrete. His hand didn't vanish into a chilly medieval forest, nor a bare white desert, nor any of the other places Jewell and Thorpe had described and Deranian had babbled about.

"Be careful," he said as he turned to go.

*T*here were advantages, Amy decided, to having vanished in a manner sufficiently mysterious that it attracted the attention of Air Force intelligence. They hadn't paid her bills, but at least they'd collected her mail and kept the post office from returning it all. Their patrols had scared off burglars. And they'd made sure none of the utilities were shut off.

It was too bad they hadn't bothered to answer her phone or explain to any of her clients what had happened. The tape on the answering machine had filled up the first week, mostly with ever-more-angry complaints from the Fosters.

After calling to make her doctor's appointment she had tried to phone all of her clients. Some, including the Fosters, didn't answer; one had moved; one hung up on her. Prema Chatterji was still interested in a consultation, but the others were pretty clearly a total loss. Being called away without warning on "personal matters" for more than three months was not good business.

And after going through the mountain of mail and matching the unpaid bills against her bank balance and the undeposited checks, she knew she was broke, or nearly so — if nothing bounced and she hadn't missed anything and she could transfer from her savings account, she would wind up with a balance of about eighteen dollars.

That wouldn't even pay for groceries to replace what had gone bad. She sighed.

"Is it bad?" Prossie asked.

"Yeah, but it could certainly be worse," Amy said. She looked up, out the living room window at the Air Force car parked out front.

Those people wouldn't let them starve, she was sure. And they were back on Earth, and alive and well.

"It could be a lot worse," she said.

*"I*want agents on Earth and on Shadow's world," Bascombe said. "You tell me how to get them there."

The scientist glanced at the telepath, then shrugged. "We can get them through the warp," he said, "but anti-gravity doesn't work in either of those realities, so getting them down safely is . . . well, it's an engineering problem. And getting them *back* is tougher."

The telepath, a man named Brian Hall, Carrie Hall's brother, whom Bascombe had not dealt with before, said, "You want to use someone who's already there. On Earth, our only possible contacts are Prossie Thorpe and the five we contacted before . . ."

Bascombe interrupted, "I thought there were six."

"Yes, sir; one of them has died."

Bascombe nodded. "Go on," he said.

"Yes, sir. Well, none of those contacts were very satisfactory. Carleton Miletti apparently could only transmit, not receive; though he was aware of our attempts at contact, none of our messages got through. Oram Blaisdell and Ray Aldridge . . . well, frankly, sir, I'm not sure either of them was entirely sane. And the other two, Angela Thompson and Gwenyth — we never got her last name — are both under-age females, which limits their usefulness."

"What about Shadow?"

"We can't read Shadow's mind, sir; we tried, and the telepath who made the attempt died. As for other people in Shadow's universe, we've never managed a solid contact; we don't know why."

"What about our people who went there?"

"I don't know, sir."

Bascombe glared at him.

"I mean, sir," Hall said, "I don't know if any of them are still alive, and no attempt has been made to contact any of them. I doubt any attempt at contact will succeed, but I don't *know* that."

"Try it," Bascombe ordered him. "And get your sister going on contacts on Earth." Then he turned back to the scientist. "And I want your department to figure out how we can get agents safely to Earth and Shadow. Don't worry about getting them back yet; we can take care of that when the time comes."

"Yes, sir." The scientist glanced at the telepath; the telepath carefully avoided the man's gaze.

"Go on," Bascombe said. "Both of you. Get on with it."

"Yes, sir."

Chapter Five

*P*el wondered why he kept coming up to the top of the tower. There wasn't anything new up here; the rain still sounded like a child's footsteps, it hadn't changed any. He'd heard the rain through the broken gargoyle before, seen the landscape spread out on all sides, drawn the currents of power down from the skies and guided them through the clouds. There was nothing new up here.

But there wasn't anything new elsewhere in the castle, either. There wasn't anything he wanted anywhere in the entire place.

A gust of wind blew dripping rainwater toward him; his aura turned it aside with no conscious command. Pel barely noticed; he just stared out over the marsh.

He knew why he was up here; it was because he was bored. He was bored and miserable, and this place, out in the rain, with its vast and depressing view, was nicely suited to being bored and miserable.

Really, it was rather amazing that he was bored and lonely and unhappy. At least in theory, he was the absolute ruler of an entire world; he was an all-powerful magician, with anything he wanted his for the taking.

Except he didn't want any of it.

What he wanted was his family back. Or even, he thought, and hated himself for thinking it, just to know that they were really, permanently dead, and he could never have them back, because at least then it would be *over*, and he could get on to whatever came next — despair, grief, whatever, and maybe someday, if he lived long enough, building a new life for himself.

But this not knowing, this *possibility* of their resurrection, was driving him crazy. He wasn't thinking straight, hadn't been able to keep his mind properly on anything since he had first heard Nancy was dead.

Shadow had *said* she could raise the dead; she had had her fetches, and even though those weren't much better than zombies, there was no reason to think they were the best the magical matrix could do.

After all, Shadow had wanted servants, not companions; she hadn't been doing anyone any favors with her resurrections.

Pel didn't want servants. He wanted Nancy and Rachel back. He wanted to hear *real* running footsteps on the battlements.

He paused, staring out over the marsh.

On the battlements? Did he want to stay *here*, if he once managed to bring his wife and daughter back from the dead?

Probably not. It was lonely here. Controlling the matrix gave him power, it let him move and reshape matter anywhere in this world, and at least in theory it could let him see through the eyes of others, hear through their ears; it made him the unquestioned final authority; but it cut him off from everyone else at the same time. No one had even remembered that his predecessor, Shadow, was human — they'd all called her "it," and treated her as a force of nature.

He didn't think he was at that extreme, but the men he had had dragged in hadn't exactly treated him as another like themselves. He had had the power of life and death over them; when he hadn't made a conscious effort, they hadn't even been able to see him through the seething aura of magical energy that was the visible manifestation of the matrix.

And when they did see him, those peasants in their homespun and leather . . .

He looked down at himself, at the battered purple slacks he still wore. He remembered Raven of Stormcrack Keep, with his black velvet cloak and high boots; Valadrakul of Warricken, with his braids and knee-length vest; Elani, with her red robes.

He didn't belong here. He belonged back on Earth — but with his wife and daughter, and it was only in *this* world that anyone had the power to revive them.

He had the power.

All he had to do was learn how to use it.

And that, of course . . .

He stopped in mid-thought, and stared down at the causeway that connected the fortress to drier land to the east of the marsh. He wasn't sure whether he had seen them first with his eyes or through the matrix, and now he needed a moment to convince himself that they were real, and not some damnable illusion the matrix had created.

They were real — there were people approaching the fortress. Six of them — or really, four people and two fetches.

There was only one explanation, one sort of people who would be coming here.

Wizards!

At last, wizards were coming!

Now maybe he could learn this resurrection business and get *on* with it!

*T*he scientist cleared his throat and glanced nervously at Bascombe. Bascombe glared back.

"Well, sir, it's simple enough to get people to either of the other universes, really; the space-warp generator is completely functional. The problems arise when you require that they arrive safely and be able to get back . . ."

"I don't *care* if they can get back," Bascombe interrupted. "We don't need to worry about that. Cahn and his men got back, most of them, without any help from us."

"Well, in that case, it's just a matter of landing them safely, and as I understand it, no one was seriously injured in the previous warp transitions . . ."

"I don't want them . . . Wait a minute." Bascombe glowered at the man; the poor twit was almost a caricature of a scientist, probably didn't even like to be called that, wanted to be referred to as a physicist, or an electronician, or something — as if all these arcane distinctions made any difference to anyone normal!

But he had a point; Cahn and Carson had both arrived intact. Bascombe considered their arrivals to be unsatisfactory, but he had to stop and think for a moment to put into words, simple words a scientist could understand, exactly what had been wrong with those landings.

"All right," he said, "I want them to arrive quietly, without throwing away any more ships, without attracting a lot of unwanted attention. Can you do that?"

"Well, sir," the scientist said, "I don't see why we couldn't put them in space suits, with a simple anti-gravity unit to get . . ."

"Anti-gravity doesn't work there. What else have we got? Isn't there any way to fly without using anti-gravity?"

The scientist blinked.

"Um," he said.

"Care to be a bit more explicit?" Bascombe let the sarcasm drip from his words.

"Well, we . . . I mean, AG is so cheap and convenient, that we . . . there were experiments, but . . ." His voice trailed off.

Bascombe decided the time was ripe for a suggestion, to get the man thinking positively again. "Why can't we just make the warps come out at ground level?" he asked.

"Oh, because . . . well, we were sending ships before, and the control isn't fine enough, and solid matter . . . the interaction . . . it's not *safe.*"

"So we have to make these holes in mid-air, and let our men just fall through?"

"Well, I —" The scientist stopped dead this time, rather than trailing off.

"You what?"

"Well, there's no reason they couldn't *climb* through. With ropes."

"Ropes?" Startled, Bascombe considered the idea.

It seemed very obvious now, so obvious that he wondered how they had missed seeing it sooner. Maybe because it was *too* simple — getting to another universe involved huge machines, vast quantities of energy, super-science of all sorts; plain old rope didn't fit the image.

They could even have saved most of Carson's group, if they had wanted to.

But then, Bascombe remembered, they hadn't particularly wanted to.

"Ropes," he said.

"At least they didn't cancel my credit cards," Amy said, glancing up as she continued to pull wads of newspaper out of her new purse. "It's a good thing I didn't have all of them with me."

Prossie nodded, then looked down at herself.

Amy had had to guess at the telepath's sizes to some extent, since Imperial standards did not use the same systems as J.C. Penney, but the clothes seemed to fit fairly well.

Prossie didn't look very enthusiastic about the outfit she wore, though.

"Is something wrong?" Amy asked, putting down the purse. She had deliberately gotten something simple and casual for her guest, since Prossie was obviously not ready to go looking for a white-collar job here on Earth, but maybe that had been a mistake.

"It's just so strange," Prossie said. "I've worn a uniform since I was six; except on Zeta Leo III, I've never seen myself in any color but purple."

Amy shuddered at the mention of the slavers' planet. She asked, "Even off-duty? Didn't you ever have, you know, a furlough or something?"

Prossie stared at her as if she were mad, then apparently caught herself and looked apologetic.

"No, of course not," she said. "I'm a telepath; I had to wear full uniform at all times, so that people would know I was a Special."

"So this makes you think of when you were a slave, back there?" Amy asked, with a wave at the blue jeans and black sweatshirt.

Prossie hesitated, then glanced at the tattered, filthy remains of her uniform, lying in a heap on the couch.

"I was *always* a slave," she said.

*T*he first wizard through the door prostrated himself, to Pel's surprise; the man dropped to his knees, then flung his arms up over his head and practically fell forward, until his palms were flat on the floor and his nose was at most an inch above the stone.

The others, with only an instant's hesitation, followed their comrade's lead — even Taillefer, who had met Pel before, when Shadow was still alive. Pel was glad to see that Taillefer was one of the group.

He was not glad that Taillefer's familiar face was plastered to the floor. "Oh, get up," Pel said testily, and inadvertently let the matrix amplify his voice into an angry roar.

The four wizards scrambled hastily to their feet.

Pel stared, looking them over — and doing so while well aware that they probably couldn't see him through the glare of the matrix.

If anyone could see through it, wizards could — but somehow, Pel didn't think these people could.

Physically, they didn't look all that impressive, despite the long robes and fancy embroidery they wore. They were just people, three men and a woman, and not in the best of shape. Taillefer was fat and soft, the woman was bony and unattractive, one of the others had the red scar of an old burn marring one cheek from jaw to eyebrow.

Through the matrix, though, Pel could see that there was a sort of patterning, a power, an inward light and structure to them that the ordinary people he had met since acquiring Shadow's magic did not have.

But it was very weak and faint, like a dim copy of a tiny corner of the great matrix.

He could also see that the wizards were able to sense and touch the matrix in a way no one else had, and he remembered how Valadrakul had been so enthralled by it that he had doomed himself.

None of these four were reacting in quite that way, though they were all certainly fascinated by the flickering tangle of interwoven magic.

"You're wizards?" he asked.

"O great one," the man who had first flung himself down said, "I am Athelstan of Meresham." He bowed deeply and theatrically. "And you, I take it, are Shadow's successor, Pelbrun?"

"Brown," Pel corrected automatically. "Pel Brown."

"Brown Pelbrun, then," Athelstan agreed.

It wasn't worth arguing. "You're a wizard, Athelstan? I know Taillefer, but not you others."

Athelstan cocked his head to the side as if puzzled.

"Aye," he said. "I am a wizard, after a fashion — can you not see as much?"

Pel could see the woman and the unidentified man cringe to hear Athelstan speak so boldly; it certainly was an abrupt change from his first obeisance.

Or had that perhaps been mockery?

"I can see that you can touch magic," Pel said. "But that isn't exactly what I meant."

"Ah." He nodded. "I'truth, O Pelbrun, neither I nor my companions can sense the true patterns, nor shape them; we draw only upon what power we find to hand. Thus, I am neither matrix wizard, nor pattern wizard, but only wizard, plain and simple. Is it this you would have us say?"

"Not exactly," Pel replied. "Look, I *can* use a matrix, obviously — I'm holding the one Shadow built, and I can use it. I have the innate ability that you don't. But I don't know *how* to use it properly, so what I'm asking is not if you have the *talent* of a wizard, but whether you have the *knowledge* of a wizard."

He saw Athelstan glance at the others, who exchanged furtive glances amongst themselves.

"I know enough to fry you all, though," Pel warned. "Don't think I don't."

"O Brown Magician," Athelstan said, bowing again, "ne'er did I doubt it! An what would we, in any event? As you have said, such as we can touch upon a network, but cannot hold it — were you slain, or in other manner the matrix taken from you, the lot of us could hold it not for the merest instant, but instead would most probably be incinerated in its fiery dissolution. You've naught to fear from us."

"Good," Pel said.

"Indeed, meseems 'twould be very much in our interests to serve you honestly and well," Athelstan continued, "for else how shall we flourish, when all the reins of power are held in your own two hands? Look you upon the pitiful estate of all known wizardry, when only we four can be found of the myriad magicians who once flourished in this realm — and this, merely that Shadow was not pleased others should wield the arts arcane. How, then, shall we not rejoice that Shadow has passed, and that a new overlord is come who, by your profession heretofore, seeks not exclusive dominion?"

By the time Pel had interpreted this speech, and debated with himself how to respond, Athelstan had taken his pause for silent consent.

Pel knew that Athelstan was making at least one wrong assumption; he knew that there were a few other wizards besides these four still scattered about the far corners of Faerie — but only a matrix wizard could have seen that, and it didn't matter anyway. He let Athelstan continue.

"What learning we might have we place gladly at your disposal, O Brown Magician," the wizard said. "What would you have of us?"

There it was, the question Pel had been waiting for. He took a deep breath.

"I want to learn to raise the dead," he said.

"*I* want to be useful," Prossie said. "I feel as if I should be doing more, not just sitting here in your house, eating your food and wearing your clothes."

Amy hesitated. "You can't drive a car, though," she said. "You don't have any marketable skills, or any educational record, or anything. I don't know what sort of work you could get. I mean, if I were still in business, I could maybe hire you myself for awhile, but right now . . . I mean, I'm going to be job-hunting myself."

"There must be *something,*" Prossie said desperately; she was on her feet, standing by the living room couch, as if, Amy thought, she couldn't bear to stay seated.

"I'm sure there is," Amy agreed, getting up herself. "Maybe working at McDonald's, if nothing else. We'll want to get you a GED, maybe sign you up at Montgomery College or somewhere — maybe those Air Force people could help . . ." She glanced out the front window at that, at the car that waited out on the gravel shoulder of Goshen Road.

It would be nice to get some use out of all this mess, she thought. "Maybe you could sell souvenirs . . ." she began, as she turned to look out through the kitchen, through the glass panel in the back door, at the spaceship that lay in her back yard.

She stopped in mid-sentence and stared; her mouth fell open.

Prossie asked, "What is it?" She hurried to the kitchen door and looked.

Not realizing at first that Amy was looking out the back, it took her a moment to see what was wrong; she wasted several seconds scanning the kitchen itself, and saw nothing out of the ordinary. At last, though, her gaze reached the window.

"Oh, my . . ." she began.

"Someone better tell the Air Force men," Amy said. She turned and ran for the front door to do just that, leaving Prossie staring wide-eyed out the back, staring at the men in purple space suits climbing down a rope-ladder that seemed to hang from empty sky.

Chapter Six

*S*amuel Best sometimes wondered whether his name had helped him in his career in Imperial Intelligence. Nobody would admit such a thing, of course, but sometimes he wondered whether, on some level, people expected more of him because of his name, and chose him for tough assignments because he was, after all, the Best.

Not that he necessarily believed he actually *was* the best; to think such a thing could lead to overconfidence, and that could easily be fatal.

He did try to be good at his work, though, and in this case that had resulted in delays that had irritated the hell out of that officious twit, John Bascombe,

Under-Secretary for Interdimensional Affairs.

Best didn't much care. Bascombe might be an up-and-coming politician, he might be able to ruin Best's life — but screwing up a field assignment could get a man killed. Better to annoy one's superiors and live than to do as one's told and die.

It had just seemed to be common sense to insist on speaking to anyone in the Empire who had actually *been* in this Shadow place, and it wasn't *his* fault if the surviving crewmen of I.S.S. *Ruthless* had been reassigned and scattered.

It was too bad no one from Colonel Carson's squad had made it back alive, but they hadn't; there were only the six men from *Ruthless.*

Not that they had been able to tell him much, in any case; they had only been there for about twenty minutes, and in an area hundreds of miles from his intended point of arrival.

Still, it was useful to know about the heavier gravity, the lower-than-optimum oxygen content of the atmosphere, the blue-shifted sunlight, the pseudoterrestrial ecology, the appearance of a feudal social structure — and the clothing. Best had no desire to be obvious; he wasn't about to go in in uniform.

The squad sent to the *other* universe, the place called Earth, could make their own decisions; he and *his* boys were going in in the closest approximation of local costume they could manage.

This meant that the Earth squad went first, of course — Bascombe hadn't been willing to wait.

That was fine with Best; he wasn't eager to be the first to try this trick of climbing through a space-warp on a rope ladder. And the fact that the Empire only had one space-warp generator operational at the moment — though he knew that more were under construction, a fact he was not *supposed* to know — meant that he and his three underlings couldn't go anywhere until the Earth squad was through, and the generator shut down, recalibrated, and re-started.

It seemed to be working, though; having finally approved the preparations, he stood behind Bascombe and to the side, hand shading his eyes, and watched through the thick tinted glass as the four space suited figures vanished into the blinding white glare of the space-warp field.

A fifth figure, also suited, emerged from the glare and waved to the control room.

"They're through," one of the engineers said.

"Good," Bascombe said. "Then get this thing shut down and open the warp to Shadow's universe."

"But, sir," someone protested, "If you do that, you'll cut off the men on Earth — the ladder will be sheared off, and we won't be able to retrieve them."

"Roll the damn ladder up," Bascombe said, "and then use it to get Best, here, and his crew, to Shadow's world. Then you can reopen the warp to Earth. We'll do four-hour shifts hanging that ladder in each universe."

"Give them another hour, sir," Best said. "It'll take me that long to get my men ready."

Bascombe turned to glare at him, looked down at the phony peasant garb Best wore, then shrugged.

"Forty minutes," he said. "I want you and your men in the staging area, suited and ready to go, in forty minutes."

"Yes, sir," Best said. He saluted, and stood at attention as Bascombe left the room.

"What an idiot," an engineer muttered when the door had swung shut.

Best didn't bother to reply aloud, but his own opinion was the same.

"I didn't work," Pel said, glaring at the dead dog. It had stopped twitching.

"Well, O Great One," Athelstan said, "did we not say that we knew not the way of it?"

"You said you *thought* you could, if you had enough power," Pel countered.

"Nay, rather, said we that we thought we *might*, had we the power," Athelstan corrected him. "'Twould seem we were mistaken. Ne'er did we *promise.*"

For a moment, Pel just stared at the dog. Then he sighed. "I know you didn't promise," he said. "So you can't do it, you don't know how — but doesn't *anyone* know? *Shadow* knew, right?"

"Yes, it does . . . that is, rather, it *did.*" Athelstan stared at the dog as well.

After a moment's silence, the wizard bestirred himself and said, "Hark, then, Master — we know the theory of old, as we told you, handed down from master to apprentice since the earliest years of Shadow's use of fetches. Our knowledge thereof must, we see, be deficient in some wise. Perchance, though, were we to study an ensample of the *practice* of necromantic art, understanding might be gained thereby."

Pel turned and looked at the wizard.

"What?" he said.

Athelstan blinked, then said, speaking slowly and clearly, "O Great One, had we the chance to *study*, and to test, perhaps to destruction, one that had in fact been resurrected from death, might we then gain the understanding we lack?"

Pel stared at him.

"Your fetches, Lord," Athelstan explained, gesturing at the pair that stood guard by the door.

Pel blinked, then glanced at his unmoving servants, then back at Athelstan.

Something twinged, twitched, tickled at him somehow. He paused.

Something felt odd, and slightly wrong, and he wasn't sure what it was or where it was or even whether it was internal or external. Something was *disturbed,* somehow.

It might have been somewhere out in the matrix, in the web of magical currents that covered this entire world — or it might have been in his head.

Could it have been a twinge of guilt at the idea of destroying a fetch?

After all, he supposed the fetches had been alive once, free people with their own souls and their own interests and their own rights — but they weren't now; he could see that through the matrix, could see how their magical energies differed from those of real live human beings. Shadow hadn't brought them back that far; she had left them mindless zombies. They were already dead, really; why should he feel guilty about dissecting one, or whatever Athelstan had in mind? He had already killed about a hundred of them himself, one way or another, and didn't feel guilty about it. Letting the wizards kill one more was no problem, not really.

If that was what he had felt, then his subconscious was being silly and unreasonable.

If he'd felt something else, something out there in the network somewhere, it could wait. Bringing back his family took priority over anything else.

"Sure," he said. "Go to it."

Major Johnston took a final look around the yard, his gaze lingering on the silly-looking purple spaceship. "You're sure no one could be hiding in that thing?" he called.

"Sure as we can be, sir," a lieutenant replied.

Johnston nodded, glanced up at where the rope ladder had disappeared into thin air, then headed back around the side of the house, toward the waiting cars.

There were four of them, lined up by the roadside; he hesitated for an instant, then marched up to the last one in line, an Air Force-blue sedan.

Amy Jewell looked up at him through the closed window. She showed no sign of rolling it down, so he spoke loudly.

"I'm sorry about this, Ms. Jewell," he said. "I'm going to see if we can get you listed as a civilian consultant, and get you some compensation for your time — you and Ms. Thorpe both. We'll provide alternate accommodations for you, if you'd rather not stay here for now. And I'm afraid we may want to buy your house, if these people are going to keep coming."

Amy shrugged, then nodded. "Thanks," she called, her voice barely audible through the glass.

He patted the side of the car, then straightened up.

More cars were arriving, bringing more men — Air Police, so far; Johnston hoped they'd be enough.

After all, next time the Galactic Empire might send an attack force, rather than scouts or diplomats. If he had had his way, he'd have had a fully-armed squad of Marines here, ready for anything — but he was Air Force, and didn't have the authority to call in the jarheads. A request like that would have to work its way up through channels. He'd started the paperwork, but it would take time.

APs he could do now.

He no longer doubted the existence of the Galactic Empire; he had arrived just in time to see the rope ladder vanish into thin air. He wished he'd been able to reach the place in less than forty minutes; maybe he could have sent someone back up.

But that might not have been safe. The Imperials had arrived in space suits, after all — genuine Buck Rogers space suits, bulky purple things with fishbowl helmets, straight out of "Destination Moon." Maybe they'd needed them at the top of the ladder.

They weren't saying, though.

He glanced at the two civilian cop cars that had been the first things he'd been able to get to the site. Each one had two men in back, space suits and equipment removed, but still in their silly-looking Imperial uniforms.

He marched over to the closer one and peered in the open window. "Care to tell me anything?" he asked.

"Lieutenant James Austin, Imperial Service, H-657-R-233-B-708," the purple-uniformed man said, staring straight ahead without so much as glancing at Johnston.

Johnston sighed. He slapped the car roof.

"Take 'em away," he said.

*P*rossie sat motionless in the back of the groundcar, wishing she could know what the people around her were thinking. Sometimes her mental silence was a blessing, sometimes a curse; right now it was horrible.

The Empire had sent more men — not an envoy this time, no telepaths, but a scouting team, probably, from their actions, Imperial Intelligence.

She wasn't as frightened of the Smarts as most of the people she had known; over the years she had read the minds of several of the dreaded Intelligence agents, and while they generally weren't nice people, they were just people, not the fearsome, emotionless supermen they were reputed to be. She had even worked directly for Intelligence once or twice herself; all the telepaths, the entire Special Branch, were nominally under the joint jurisdiction of Intelligence and the Imperial Messenger Service, always available if the Smarts needed them.

But still, any time Intelligence was involved, matters were serious. The situation was serious *now*.

Especially since she didn't know why they were here.

Especially since one possibility was that they had been sent after *her*.

She knew that the Empire would take a rogue telepath very seriously indeed. If they knew she was here, if they knew she had really, genuinely gone rogue . . .

Otherwise it seemed like quite a coincidence, an Imperial team arriving directly behind the very house she was staying in.

She knew that it wasn't really as much of a coincidence as it first appeared; she had read from the minds of Imperial scientists that something about the shape of space itself made it easier to open a space-warp in the same place every time. If the Empire was going to open a warp to Earth anywhere, this would be the natural place; she was here herself because this was where the warp had come out before.

Still, even if it wasn't a coincidence, why were they here? What did they want? She knew, beyond question, that when she had left Base One with Colonel Carson and Raven and the rest, no one at Base One had had any plans for further contact with Earth, with the possible exception of sending Pel and Amy and the rest home someday. John Bascombe had written Earth off as worthless; General Hart had considered it irrelevant.

Why had they changed their minds?

There was one way she might be able to find out; Carrie had tried to contact her several times. Carrie would know what was going on; she wouldn't be able to help it. Maybe Prossie could coax an explanation out of her.

And maybe not. She and Carrie hadn't exactly parted as friends. Prossie had betrayed her family, betrayed all the telepaths in the Empire, by lying to Imperial officers, disobeying orders, and in general breaking any rule she found inconvenient once she was outside Imperial space and cut off from the mental network she had grown up in.

That she had done so because she could now see that she had been oppressed and abused all her life would not matter much to Carrie or the others; they were still there, under the Empire's thumb, subject to summary execution for the slightest infraction of the telepathy laws. Prossie's rebellion could conceivably endanger them all.

And maybe that was why Carrie hadn't done a thing, hadn't lifted a finger or transmitted a thought when Prossie had been utterly at Shadow's mercy and convinced she was about to die.

Prossie was the one who had broken contact, who had been unspeakably rude, who had been refusing to communicate; maybe Carrie would listen, maybe they could make up. They were cousins, bound together by blood and background — surely a little internecine squabble could be patched up.

But Carrie would have to try again before they could talk. Telepathy was impossible in Earth's universe. Prossie couldn't send unless Carrie was listening, couldn't receive unless Carrie was sending.

Carrie or someone, anyway. There were four hundred and fourteen other telepaths in the Empire, at last count.

And until one of them tried to reach her, Prossie couldn't talk to any of them.

All she could do was to sit in the groundcar, in the thick silence of her own isolated mind, and wonder whether the Empire wanted her, or wanted Earth.

And whether it really made any difference.

*B*est brushed aside leaves and peered down at the ground below.

For the most part the earth was thick with dead leaves and moss — nobody lived here, that was obvious.

In one direction, though, the view was different. There was a clearing ahead, and a very strange clearing indeed. It appeared to have been created or enlarged by breaking limbs off trees, where any normal clearing would simply be a place where no trees grew. Most of the clearing was covered by a black mound of something Best couldn't identify; here and there things showed through the black, some of them bones, some of them unidentifiable. At one side, at the very edge of what he could see, something large and purple protruded from beneath the mound, something that Best thought might be I.S.S. *Christopher.*

Most of it was hidden by trees, so he couldn't be sure; he'd have a better look when he reached the surface.

All around the black mound were signs that people had been there — but not that any were there now.

The area looked entirely deserted, in fact.

That was exactly what Best wanted; smiling but still wary he climbed down the rope ladder into the forest.

Athelstan and the woman, Boudicca, were just finishing their dissection when that odd kink in the matrix suddenly vanished.

It hadn't been guilt. Pel had been forcing himself not to think about it, but when it disappeared so abruptly its absence drew his attention. Nothing internal could have done that; he knew it must have been a twist in the currents of magic, not in his subconscious.

That was reassuring.

So it had been caused by something out there in the world somewhere — presumably a wizard, because what else could affect the magical flow? And from the size of the disturbance, big enough to cause him a real twinge, the wizard must be a fairly powerful one.

Another wizard . . . Athelstan and Taillefer and Mahadharma hadn't thought there were any others left alive. Boudicca, more conservative, had refused to venture an opinion. Pel had known there were other people out there who could touch magic, but had thought they might all be just beginners or dabblers.

Anyone who could make himself — or herself — felt through the matrix like that wasn't just playing around with fire-lighting spells. If this current batch didn't work out at least there might be another chance.

"See you," Athelstan said, pointing to the fetch's heart, "how 'tis with this?"

At first Pel thought Athelstan was addressing Boudicca, but then he realized that both wizards were looking in his direction — not quite at his face, because of the haze of magic around him, but in his direction.

"What?" he asked, leaning forward and trying not to be sickened by the sight of the fetch's opened chest.

At first he saw nothing but gore, but then he adjusted his vision, shielding his gaze with a layer of magic — not because it had occurred to him that that would help, but just to put something between himself and the exposed organs.

And when he did, he saw the fetch not as a human body, but as a magical structure, and he could see what Athelstan meant: the pattern that kept the heart beating, and that was not at all what they had tried to use on that dog.

"Oh," he said. He studied it for a moment, then said, "I could do that."

"So," Boudicca said, sitting back on her heels. "Thus it is."

"I could do that," Pel repeated.

It was simple, really. Not obvious, but simple.

And judging by what he saw in the fetch, it was stable, self-sustaining. It could be done in anything that had the right general structure to it, it didn't have to be a human heart.

Were the homunculi and the rest done the same way?

If so, no wonder Shadow had made so many of them. It would be easy.

Pel tugged at the magic flowing through and around the chamber, and the fetch's chest closed, healing almost instantly.

Athelstan fell back, startled, in a most graceless and unwizardly fashion. Boudicca merely blinked.

That pattern in its heart kept it alive, Pel could see that, and the network that ran through the rest of its body, like a miniature of the matrix itself, let it move and function.

But there was a break in the pattern, a discontinuity, where living creatures continued down into fractal complexity, but the fetch's energies simply flattened out and looped back upon themselves; Pel wondered if Athelstan had seen it.

Excited by this discovery, without thinking what it might do, Pel reached out and repaired the flaw.

The fetch sat up. It opened its eyes and looked about.

Then it started screaming.

Chapter Seven

"I know, I know," Johnston said wearily, "name, rank, and serial number." He waved at the prisoners and sat down. He sighed heavily.

"You know," he said, "we aren't at war with the Empire. Right now we aren't at war with anybody, and we'd like to keep it that way. I think I might know a few things you boys don't, things that your superiors would be interested in — but I'm not going to just hand them over if you people insist on acting like prisoners of war. So far, you're just trespassers and illegal aliens . . ." His mouth twitched a little at that phrase, and he had to stop for a few seconds to keep from laughing.

The four of them sat silently as he recovered. The leader, Lieutenant Austin, was glowering at him; one of the others was looking sheepish, a third was staring at his own knees, and the fourth was studying the ceiling.

"You trespassed on Ms. Jewell's land," Johnston said, "and you're in the country without the proper papers, but you aren't felons, you aren't charged with espionage, you aren't considered hostile or prisoners of war. You're maybe subject to a fine and deportation, and that's about it. Now, I'll offer you a deal — you tell us *why* you're here, and we'll take you back and see if we can send you home. If the opening's still there we can send you through by helicopter, maybe, even if the ladder's gone. You keep quiet, and I'll keep you locked up and incommunicado for as long as I possibly can. It's that simple. If your people want to talk, we can talk — not me, I'm Air Force, but we can get the State Department in on it. If you don't want to talk, you stay the hell out of our space. Simple enough?"

The sheepish-looking one shifted his feet.

"We'll give back the suits before you go, too," Johnston added. "No tricks."

The one who had been watching the ceiling tiles threw his superior a glance, but Austin wasn't buying.

It was obvious who needed convincing here.

"Lieutenant Austin," Johnston said, "I'm not asking for much."

"Too much," Austin said.

Johnston sat back and stared at Austin for a moment; the Imperial looked back unflinchingly.

"So what the hell do you want us to do with you?" Johnston shouted suddenly. "You want to rot here?"

Austin shrugged. "You're holding Imperial personnel against their will," he said.

"You're not in Imperial space, you . . ." Johnston bit his words off short; it wouldn't help any to call Austin an idiot.

He obviously *was* an idiot, but it wouldn't help to tell him that.

"Okay, look," he said. "Maybe you think the Empire's going to come in here, blasters blazing, to rescue you — but did they go after the crew of the *Ruthless?* Did they go after the squad that went with Lord Raven? I *know* about all that. I know your blasters don't work here, your ships can't fly here — this is *our* turf. They couldn't save you even if they wanted to, and I'll bet they don't want to."

Austin was unmoved, but the other three were all visibly nervous now.

"Here's what we're going to do, then," Johnston said. "We're going to send *one* of you . . . let's see . . . Hitchcock. We'll send Spaceman Hitchcock back through the space-warp, and let him talk to whoever's in charge over there, and tell them that we want to talk, we want answers, and that none of you are going anywhere until we get them."

Hitchcock looked up from his folded hands.

"I know we didn't talk when the *Ruthless* came through, because we didn't know it was for real," Johnston said. "Well, now we know. We want to talk. You just tell 'em that, Hitchcock."

"Yessir," Hitchcock said, smiling nervously.

Austin threw him a look that should have been fatal, and Hitchcock wilted into silence, but Johnston leaned back and smiled.

*T*he formerly-dead man — Pel could no longer think of him as a fetch — crouched with his head on Boudicca's chest, shivering silently. He hadn't been eager to answer questions, and Pel hadn't pressed the issue — the man appeared to be unnerved by the memories of spending several years as Shadow's undead servant. Waking up suddenly, with all those memories, had sent him into a screaming fit.

The fit seemed to be past, but Pel still didn't think he wanted to know just what the man was remembering.

The revived dog, on the other hand, seemed perfectly happy with her situation; she sat panting cheerfully as Pel petted her.

"'Twould seem, O Brown Magician," Athelstan said, "that you now have the knowledge that you sought."

"Yeah," Pel said, scratching the dog behind her ears, relishing the familiar doggy feel of the coarse hair and loose skin. She was a pleasant dog, a mutt, mostly hound — she looked something like a coonhound, only smaller.

He felt pretty pleased with himself just now, and he wanted to bask in it for a moment. He'd fixed the fetch, turned it back into a man. He'd brought a dead dog back to life. He thought he had a good understanding of resurrection, and he could use Susan Nguyen as a final trial, bring her back from the dead to sure it would work on Earthpeople. Everything was going well.

He didn't expect it to last, he was sure something would go horribly wrong at any minute now, but he wanted to enjoy the feeling of accomplishment while he could.

"Are we then free to go?" Athelstan asked.

Pel frowned as he considered the question.

"I'm afraid not just yet," he said at last. "Not till Susan . . . not till I know this works every time. And besides, I don't have the . . . the bodies . . ." His throat tightened. The pleasant afterglow vanished as he imagined Nancy and little Rachel lying dead. He forced himself to take a deep breath, and asked, "But I can *make* bodies, can't I? Raven said that Shadow could make duplicates of people — do I need a hair or something from the person, to work with?" He thought of the science fiction stories about cloning people from a single cell, and he thought that it ought to be possible to do something like that with magic.

"Simulacra? Alas, O Great One, I know nothing . . ."

Pel's brows lowered, and thunder rumbled somewhere — not outside the fortress, but in the hallway outside the throne room doors.

Athelstan blanched.

"Perhaps, with some experimentation . . ." he said.

"*I*'m out of this one," General Hart said, shaking his head. "Once you called in Intelligence, I knew enough to get out of the way. It's all yours, Bascombe."

Bascombe, seated comfortably behind his own desk, stared up at the general. "And I suppose you'll deny approving Raven's expedition? We happen to have the paperwork on that one, with your signature all over it."

"Oh, I'll admit to that one, all right," Hart said, leaning back against the gray-painted steel wall. "I did that one through the proper channels, you approved it, everything by the book. I sent Major Southern back to Terra with a full report. And that was just a dozen troopers, two officers, a telepath, and a bunch of foreigners — I didn't send any Intelligence agents, Colonel Carson's no loss, and the telepath was authorized higher up. It's not going to look real pretty on my record, but it's not serious."

"Are you suggesting that my follow-up actions *are* a serious mistake?" Bascombe demanded.

"If they aren't," Hart said, straightening up again, "then why do you want me involved? I can see spreading the blame, but since when would you want to share the credit?"

"I'm just trying to be fair," Bascombe said.

"Oh, of course. You didn't bother to consult me until you heard that the Imperial Marshal and the Secretary of Science were on their way here, but then you suddenly wanted to be absolutely *sure* I didn't mind. *What* a coincidence." He put his hands on Bascombe's desk and leaned forward until his face was a foot or so from Bascombe's. "Not a chance, Bascombe. If there's credit to be had here, you can have it. I've had enough of you. *This* one's all yours, and I hope you choke on it."

*B*est thought he was making good time as he led his little squad through the forest; he just wished he knew where he was going.

Begley, his number two man, had claimed some expertise in woodlore and had reported finding a track that someone had followed away from that huge pile of rotting flesh that covered the wreck of I.S.S. *Christopher.* Best hoped he was right, and that they were following the right people.

The track became obvious after a point, and now Best was leading the way, with Begley, Poole, and Morcambe following close behind. Morcambe was carrying his knife ready in his hand; the others left theirs sheathed.

Best wished he had thought to bring a bow and arrows — but that assumed one could have been found at Base One, which was doubtful.

This silent forest, with its filtered, scattered sunlight and its thick, rich smells, was getting on his nerves. There could be enemies behind any tree. The *Ruthless* survivors had described monsters that came charging out of the woods at them, that burrowed up out of the ground; the thing that had dropped on I.S.S. *Christopher* looked as if it had had wings, before the scavengers and bacteria had started in on, and that implied that it flew. Monsters could come at them from any direction, from above or below, at any time.

And he didn't want to face monsters with just a knife. A bow and arrow would have been only slightly better. He wished blasters worked here, and he wondered just what sort of weird place this was that they didn't.

He wanted to get out of the woods, onto open ground. He wanted to find a native to talk to.

The daylight seemed brighter ahead — was that a clearing? Were the trees thinning?

He beckoned to the others, muttered, "Come on," and picked up the pace.

"I guess we won't need the chopper," Johnston said, staring at the rope ladder that hung from empty air, swaying in the breeze, its bottom rung bumping gently against the side of the spaceship that covered half of Amy Jewell's back yard. He turned to one side for a moment and said, "There you go, Mr.

Hitchcock — your way home. You get up there and tell them that we're ready to talk, and that they don't get their other men back until we do."

Hitchcock nodded, smiling happily as he stepped forward. He already had his space suit on. "Will do, Major," he said. He lifted his bubble helmet into place and began securing the seal.

"Major Johnston," someone called.

Johnston turned to locate the speaker.

"Got a call for you." The voice came from the back door of the house, where a lieutenant was leaning out, the receiver of Ms. Jewell's phone in one hand.

Johnston blinked, then frowned. "This better be important," he said.

"It's Thorpe," the lieutenant replied.

Hitchcock had his helmet in place; he gave Johnston a questioning look, and the major waved him on toward the ladder.

"I still say we should've suited up some of our own men and sent them along," someone muttered.

Johnston shook his head as he started toward the house. "Too dangerous," he said as he walked. "Could be construed as hostile. Trespassing. Invading. We don't know how rough they play." He took the receiver from the lieutenant. "Ms. Thorpe?" he said. "Johnston here." He turned to watch as Hitchcock started up the ladder.

"Sir," Prossie Thorpe's voice said unsteadily, "I tried to talk to Carrie — to Registered Telepath Carolyn Hall. She contacted me."

"Go on," Johnston said. Hitchcock was moving quickly, but it was a long climb, a good hundred feet at least, probably more.

"She . . . she questioned me, but I . . ."

The Imperial telepath's tone penetrated Johnston's focus on Hitchcock's ascent. He looked down at the kitchen floor, at the toes of his shoes, and concentrated on the voice in his ear.

"Take your time, Thorpe," he said.

*P*rossie drew a deep breath and tried to compose herself.

It shouldn't hurt this much, she told herself. She had already *known* she was a rogue, an outlaw; she had already known that Carrie was turned against her.

Still, she hadn't *felt* it until she had taken up direct mental contact with Carrie again.

Then she had felt it, all right — that tense loathing and anger, not just from Carrie, but through her from the entire network of telepaths, the entire extended family.

In fact, *most* of it came from the four hundred, not from Carrie — but then, Prossie knew that Carrie hardly had any real existence apart from the network. All her life she'd lived in the family's web of thought and feeling, just the way Prossie had before *Ruthless* came through the warp.

And much of what the family felt they picked up from the normals around them, the non-telepaths. Carrie was working with John Bascombe and General Hart and people who hated and feared telepaths; it was easy for her to direct that fear and hatred at her traitor cousin.

Still, it was a shock to *feel* it.

And it was a shock to learn why it was so intense.

Bascombe had sent those men to Earth after *her.*

Carrie hadn't meant to let that slip, but she had. She hadn't meant to tell Prossie anything.

And Prossie hadn't meant to tell Carrie as much as she had, either, but any time telepaths communicated directly there would be leakage, there would be things that slipped out. A telepath couldn't completely hide anything without breaking contact.

Hell, even when there was *no* conscious contact, things tended to leak through; telepathy wasn't limited to conscious thought. Anything one telepath knew, they all did, on some level — though they might not all remember it.

Prossie swallowed and gripped the phone, the strange Earthly gadget that was almost like a mechanical telepath, that could transmit voices for hundreds of miles.

"Major Johnston," she said, "I found out what those men were sent after."

"Yes?"

"They think . . . they *suspect* that you and your people have joined forces with Shadow, that you're plotting together against the Empire, and that I came here as Shadow's liaison. They came to capture or kill me, and to see whether such an alliance actually exists. I told Carrie that it doesn't, and that Shadow is dead, and she *should* know I wasn't lying, but I can't be sure."

For a moment Prossie heard nothing, and she wondered whether the phone had broken, or whether some part of its mysterious mechanical workings needed extra time to transmit this particular message, but then Johnston asked, "Can you relay to her for us?"

Prossie shook her head before she remembered that Johnston couldn't see her.

"No," she said. "She and I . . . we can't communicate anymore."

"Damn. You're sure?"

Prossie took a deep breath. "Yes, sir."

"Is there anyone *else* she can communicate with, then? Did they send any telepaths with that bunch we have locked up? And please, don't tell me it's Hitchcock, because he's two-thirds of the way up the ladder out here."

"No, sir. Not Hitchcock or any of the others, so far as I know — none of them are telepaths, and I don't *think* any of them can receive." Prossie blinked. "But there are some possibilities, sir — you know, we sort of made contact with some of your own people before *Ruthless* came through. There were six . . . no, five of them, because one died."

She didn't really listen to what Johnston said to her next, because she knew what it was going to be. She closed her eyes and concentrated, remembering.

"Their names . . . there are three men and a woman, and a little girl. The men are named Oram Blaisdell, and Carleton Miletti, and Ray Aldridge, and the woman is Gwenyth, I don't know her last name, and the little girl's name is Angela Thompson, I talked to her sometimes. I think Carrie's brother Brian was the last one assigned to contact them . . ."

*P*el stared at the object in dismay as he wiped blood and bits of fat and skin from his hands. A thick, soapy smell filled the room.

The thing on the table was made of human flesh, or a reasonable approximation. It had the shape of a woman. He thought he could force it to live, if he wanted to.

But it wasn't Nancy.

He had thought he remembered her every feature, every inch, every detail, but the thing he had created, had grown and gathered and shaped into a semblance of humanity, was not Nancy. The face was wrong. The proportions were wrong.

"I was never a sculptor," he said, flinging down his washrag in disgust.

Behind him stood two fetches and three others; two of the others, the two wizards, stirred at his words.

"Your pardon, O Great One," Athelstan said, looking quickly from Pel to the inanimate body and back, "but I see no flaw in this homunculus. Surely, it . . ."

"It's not *Nancy,*" Pel shouted at him, wheeling to face the wizard. The air crackled with anger, and red light blazed from the walls; Boudicca backed away a step.

"Nay, 'tis not," Athelstan admitted hurriedly, "nor did I say it might be. Yet you've created here a woman — is that not a fair start? To make so fine a semblance as you desire, one needs must have better to work from . . ."

"I don't want a *semblance,*" Pel barked. "I want *Nancy.* And Rachel. My wife and daughter."

"And surely, with patience, you'll have them," Athelstan said. He gestured at the woman who stood stolidly to the side. "Have you not brought this one back from the dead? Can any doubt that you have the power to wreak whatever you will?"

Pel turned and looked at Susan. She gazed calmly back, and he relaxed slightly. He had brought *her* back without any problem.

But he hadn't had to create a body for her.

"Doesn't look much like Nancy, does it?" he asked her.

Susan looked at the lifeless homunculus. "It's a good try," she said slowly, "but it isn't quite right, no."

Pel turned to Athelstan again. "If we had some of Nancy's hair, would that help?"

"Oh, most assuredly! By the Law of Contagion we derive the Law of Parts, and see thereby that the part can be made equal to the whole — from a single hair, in time, we can surely recreate all the pattern of your wife's flesh."

"Do you know how to do it?"

Athelstan hesitated, then glanced at Boudicca.

"I do," the female wizard said.

"Good," Pel said. He looked at Susan, then away.

If he sent Susan back to Earth, why would she return? It was, perhaps, cruel to keep her here, but so far she hadn't *asked* him to send her home, and it was so good to see her alive again, to have the company of a fellow Earthman.

Maybe she wasn't sure the magic that had revived her would hold back on Earth — and for that matter, Pel wasn't entirely certain, either, but Shadow's fetches had lived in the Galactic Empire, and Prossie had said simulacra had lived there; why not a revenant on Earth, then? Susan had left Earth alive, and would return alive, and what difference did it make what had happened in between?

But he wanted her *here.*

He would open a portal to Earth, and send someone to bring him back Nancy's hairbrush, and Rachel's, and the bedroom and bathroom wastebaskets, and anything else that might have hairs or fingernail clippings in it.

But he wouldn't send Susan.

"You," he said, pointing at a fetch. "I have an errand for you."

*T*he lieutenant looked up, startled, at the sound of a footstep. He closed his book.

A man was walking across the basement, a pale man dressed in strange black clothes, paying no attention to the lieutenant or anything else. The man was marching directly toward the stairs.

"Hey," the lieutenant said, dropping Destroyer novel #82 and getting to his feet. *"Hey!* Hold it, you!"

The man in black paid him no attention whatsoever. He began marching up the stairs, his tread heavy on the wooden steps.

The lieutenant hesitated; should he call in, or stop this guy?

If he took the time to call, the man might get away.

He drew his sidearm. "Stop right there!" he shouted.

The man kept on up the stairs.

The lieutenant cursed; he couldn't shoot in cold blood, not just for ignoring him. The man might be deaf. He shoved the pistol back in its holster and ran after the stranger.

He caught him at the top of the stairs, threw an arm around his neck and pulled him back.

The stranger didn't exactly struggle, but he *did* try to keep walking for a moment. When he realized it wasn't working he stopped.

He let the lieutenant carry him back down to the basement, and did not resist as his arm was twisted up behind his back and held with one hand while the lieutenant used the other to work the radio.

The lieutenant had no idea why the silent stranger was being so cooperative, and he hurried to get his message through while the cooperation lasted.

He didn't know that the fetch had been ordered to bring certain items, and no one had told him to hurry.

*"A*ldridge and Blaisdell are easy," Johnston told the FBI man, pointing at the list. "Blaisdell's in Tennessee — you people gave us a report on him, which

is why we decided to turn the job over to you. That, and we hope you can be less conspicuous about picking them up."

"We'll try," the FBI man said dryly.

Johnston ignored the sarcasm. "Aldridge is in Oakland; he's in the papers. Miletti is supposed to be local, but we don't know which jurisdiction, Virginia or Maryland or the District, and we haven't located him yet. Thompson is trickier — we think she might be in Texas, but that might just be something she was pretending. Thorpe can maybe give you more on the little girl . . ."

The intercom buzzed.

"Damn." Johnston pushed a button. "What is it?" he demanded. He was tempted to add, "This better be good," but he didn't. His people all knew that.

"Sir, there's been an incident at the Brown house . . ." his secretary began.

"Damn," Johnston repeated, releasing the button. He got to his feet and grabbed for his jacket.

"If you can keep up," he told the FBI man on his way to the door, "you can come along."

Chapter Eight

"What the hell is taking so long?" Pel wondered aloud.

No one answered. Taillefer and Mahadharma had both slipped away some time ago, and were probably halfway to their respective homes — Pel thought he could probably locate the wizards' auras, or whatever it was the matrix let him see, but he didn't see any reason to bother. Athelstan was off getting himself something to eat — he'd skipped a meal or two while he tutored Pel in the manufacture of homunculi, and was making up for lost time. Boudicca had stepped out to the privy.

The only people in the room, besides Pel himself, were the revivified Susan Nguyen and a fetch. Fetches generally didn't answer questions, didn't talk at all unless directly ordered to do so, and Susan was keeping her own counsel.

Pel wondered whether the fetch had a name. Obviously it had had one when it was a living man, but did it remember that? Had Shadow given it a new name, perhaps?

It probably didn't need a name, though; fetches didn't seem to have any real sense of identity. They were interchangeable zombies, as far as Pel could see.

Pel supposed he should have asked the dead man he'd revived about it — after all, he'd been a fetch for some time before Pel's experimentation had restored him fully to life. He'd been so distraught, though — Pel had thought it kinder to just let him go home.

Of course, Pel thought, he could just restore *this* fetch and ask him. In fact, he probably should restore all the fetches — and he would, when he had a chance, but for now they were useful and he was busy.

"What's it like, being dead?" he asked Susan.

She stared at him, apparently untroubled by the shifting glare of the matrix. "I don't remember," she said.

"Really?"

"Really. I had shot Shadow, and she turned to face me, and then there was a sudden pain, and then I was lying on the floor and you were standing over me, with Shadow's lights all around you."

"That's all?"

"That's all."

Pel considered Susan for a moment. She was something to think about, to distract him from wondering why that stupid fetch needed half an hour to collect a couple of hairbrushes and wastebaskets. He thought back to that insane, terrible confrontation, here in this very room, just a few days ago, really, when Shadow had killed Raven and Valadrakul and Singer one by one.

"Why'd you try to shoot her?" he asked.

Susan blinked.

"I mean," Pel said, "you were always so good at surviving, at putting up with whatever it took to get through. You didn't fight the pirates who captured *Emerald Princess,* or the slavers on Zeta Leo III — you just outlasted them. So why'd you try to shoot Shadow?"

"I don't . . ." Susan stopped, obviously struggling to organize her thoughts. She tried again.

"I don't know," she said.

Pel waited, and after a moment she continued, "All my life, I survived by waiting. When I was a little girl I survived the Viet Cong by waiting until my parents saw their chance. Then I survived the Cambodian pirates who sank our boat by not fighting back while they killed my family and raped me, and I survived the refugee camps by never causing trouble, and I survived the racists and sadists all through school and college and law school by just putting up with their abuse. I always played by whatever the rules were, to survive; I became a lawyer so I could have the rules on my side for once. Whoever knows the rules, whoever makes and interprets the rules, comes out on top. So I didn't fight the spaceship pirates or the slavers — they had the rules, and I didn't."

"So why'd you shoot *Shadow,* then? She made whatever rules she wanted!"

"Because I was *tired* of playing by the rules," Susan said. "I was *tired* of being passive; I wanted to finally do something *more* than survive. If Shadow died, we could change the rules any way we wanted."

"But she killed you," Pel said.

"But she killed me," Susan agreed. "It was stupid. I should have just waited, the same as I always have."

Pel hesitated. She'd tried to be a hero, and she'd wound up dead, and Pel figured that that was what always happened to heroes in real life, but here she was. This was real life, but it was like a story, too — the fact that he was alive and Shadow wasn't proved that. "But it's turned out okay," he said. "I mean, you're alive again, and I guess now *I* make the rules, so you're safe."

She stared silently at him.

*T*he room was cool, but Spaceman Hitchcock was sweating visibly.

Bascombe smiled bitterly at that. As if *Hitchcock* had anything to sweat about! He was probably about to be proclaimed a hero for coming back up the ladder alive, as if that was some great accomplishment. Hitchcock was just scared because he was face to face with Space Marshal Albright and Secretary Markham — the poor little nobody wasn't used to facing the big brass. Hell, he'd be nervous just facing Under-Secretary John Bascombe, and *these* two were probably here to shoot Bascombe's career down in flames.

If he'd had just a little longer Bascombe thought he could have pulled it off, could maybe have moved the Department of Interdimensional Affairs out of the Department of Science and right up to cabinet level.

"Just tell us about it, Spaceman Hitchcock," Secretary Markham said. "Don't worry about the formalities. This Major Johnston offered you a deal?"

"No, sir," Hitchcock said. "He offered the *lieutenant* a deal, and the lieutenant wouldn't take it. Me, they just *told* to come back here and report — I didn't have to do a thing in return."

Markham nodded, and Bascombe frowned.

"And what was it that you were to report, Spaceman?" Marshal Albright asked.

"He said — Major Johnston said to just tell you what happened, and that they want to talk, they aren't hostile. That's all. And that you get the lieutenant and the others back when you agree to talk, and not before."

"And do you think that's the truth?" Albright asked.

Hitchcock blinked. "Do I think what's the truth, sir?"

"That these people aren't hostile."

"*I* don't know, sir. They treated us all right, but . . . well, that doesn't mean much."

"No, it doesn't," Albright agreed. He glanced at the silent figure of his personal telepath, then at the Secretary of Science.

Bascombe wondered how Albright could stand having a telepath with him all the time. It was supposed to be a great honor to have one's own telepath, with one at all hours of the day or night, but that was an honor Bascombe could do without — a damn mutant freak spying on him every second. Bad enough working with them when he was on duty.

Markham had one, as well, of course. Bascombe supposed the telepaths had names and identities of their own, but no one had introduced them; they were just there, part of the background.

That was a drawback to political advancement he had never really considered.

Secretary Markham leaned forward and said, "Spaceman Hitchcock, this Major Johnston is the highest-ranking official we've yet contacted on Earth. Do you think you could go to Terra and tell the Emperor about him?"

Hitchcock went white, and Bascombe winced. In all his years of political jockeying he had never yet had the honor of reporting directly to His Imperial Majesty, and here this poor frightened gee-puller was being offered an audience.

That was an honor Bascombe *did* want — but he wasn't about to get it.

Hitchcock stammered incoherently until Albright finally broke in. "Never mind, Spaceman; I don't think we need to send you to Terra."

Hitchcock relaxed, but at the same time a look of hurt disappointment crossed his face.

"Yet," Albright added. "I'm sure that eventually His Majesty will want to meet you and thank you."

Hitchcock nodded.

Albright and Markham leaned together to confer for a moment, and Albright's telepath leaned in with a word or two as well; then Markham turned and looked straight at Bascombe.

"Mr. Bascombe," he said, "I believe we've heard everything we need from Spaceman Hitchcock for the present, but there are a few things we'd like to ask *you*. If you would be so kind . . .?"

He gestured toward the interrogation chair, where an Imperial guard was guiding Hitchcock to his feet.

Bascombe straightened. Here it was, at last. If he could sell this, he was made. If not, he was ruined.

He rose and rounded the table, watching the telepaths as he went.

"He doesn't look very healthy," Johnston said, eyeing the pale, black-garbed figure. It was a deliberate understatement; the gaunt stranger looked downright corpselike.

"Doesn't seem to be able to talk, sir," the lieutenant said. "I haven't gotten a sound out of him — not so much as a grunt. He just sits there."

"Do you speak English?" Johnston asked loudly.

The stranger didn't stir; he simply sat, staring straight ahead. A layer of grayish dust covered the family room sofa, but this mysterious person didn't seem to notice. Johnston looked at the stranger's hands, and at the largely-undisturbed dust.

He hadn't touched the couch anywhere except where he now sat.

That didn't seem natural.

An airman stood beside the couch, one hand on the stranger's shoulder. Johnston looked at that, and the lieutenant followed his gaze.

"If we don't physically hold him he starts walking away," the lieutenant explained. "Frankly, sir, I think he's mentally disturbed — autistic, or something. We can't communicate with him at all."

"Then how'd he get into the basement here?" Johnston asked.

"I don't know, sir — I didn't see him arrive. Just all of a sudden he was there."

"We might just let him go and see what he does," Johnston said.

No one answered. The black-clad stranger didn't move.

The fellow looked like a corpse, Johnston thought. It was hard to believe he could move at all.

"Let him go," Johnston said.

The airman hesitated, then lifted his hand.

The pale man stood, rising smoothly from the couch without a single wasted motion, and began walking. Johnston, the lieutenant, the FBI man, and one of the three airman followed; at Johnston's command the other two airmen remained in the family room.

Johnston had expected the stranger to aim for the front door, but instead the silent visitor marched up the stairs and into the master bedroom. There he paused for a moment, scanning the room, then headed for one of the dusty, cluttered dressers. He picked up a hairbrush, then another, and another; clutching the three brushes in one hand he turned and scanned the room again.

"Hairbrushes?" the lieutenant asked incredulously.

The stranger spotted his target, and picked up the pink plastic wastebasket from beside a bureau. He dropped the brushes into it and headed for the door.

The FBI man and the airman stepped quickly aside.

"Major, do you know what's going on here?" the FBI man asked.

Johnston shook his head.

The stranger had to step carefully when he searched Rachel Brown's room — the floor was strewn with toys. Johnston saw him hesitate at the sight of the plush alligator on the girl's empty, unmade bed, the first time the man had acted like a human being, instead of a machine.

Or maybe he was just trying to figure out whether the alligator was a hairbrush.

But no, the child's hairbrush was on her bureau, and a wastebasket was at the foot of her bed. The black-clad stranger collected both items and headed back for the stairs, a wastebasket in each hand, hairbrushes in each wastebasket.

"Stop him!" Johnston called to the airmen in the family room.

The pair blocked the foot of the stairs, and the pale stranger stopped and simply stood, as if waiting for them to step aside.

"You aren't going to let him go, sir?" the lieutenant asked.

"I don't think so," Johnston said. "Not yet, anyway. He's got what he came for, I'd say — but why does he want them?"

"Trash, sir?" one of the airmen at the foot of the stairs asked. "He just took the trash?"

"And hairbrushes," the lieutenant said.

"What good would that be to anyone?" the airman who had accompanied the officers asked.

"Maybe he's gonna use voodoo on someone," the airman who hadn't previously spoken suggested. "Get some hair and nail-parings for the voodoo doll, y'know?"

"God knows this guy looks like a zombie!" said the airman beside him.

The others smiled, but Johnston looked at the back of the stranger's head and seriously considered it.

It was true, this guy *did* look like a walking corpse.

Jewell and Thorpe had said that there was a universe on the other side of the basement wall where magic, or something one hell of a lot *like* magic, really worked.

Maybe this fellow *was* a zombie. Maybe his master *had* sent him after hair and fingernail clippings.

He didn't smell like a corpse; there was an odd, meaty, slightly sweet odor clinging to him, all right, but Johnston had smelled corpses, and this odor was definitely not the stink of a dead body.

Maybe, if he was a zombie, the odor had something to do with the magic that had brought him back from the dead.

"Put him back on the couch," Johnston ordered.

The airmen grabbed the stranger by the arms and hauled him into the family room. He didn't resist, didn't protest, just went along as if it didn't matter in the slightest what he did, or what happened to him.

The lieutenant's theory that the man was autistic did seem to fit — but so did the idea that he was a zombie.

"Come on," Johnston said. "I want to see the basement."

"*S*o that dead woman we found on Beckett was Shadow, and an Earthman is running the show in her world now," Albright said.

"If Hall is right about what she picked up from Thorpe, yes," Bascombe replied.

"But Thorpe's a renegade — we can't trust anything she says," Markham pointed out.

"She's a telepath, and she was talking to another telepath," Albright said. "*I* can't lie to a telepath; can she?"

"And this doesn't account for Thorpe's brief appearance in normal space in an unnamed system a hundred light-years from Beckett," Bascombe pointed out.

"That could have been anything," Albright said, waving it away. "It had to be Shadow sending her through, for some reason, and Shadow's dead, so what does it matter?"

"It might," Bascombe said. "Somehow."

"I doubt it," Albright replied.

"Suppose we wait before we leap to conclusions," Markham suggested. "Under-Secretary Bascombe has sent a scouting party into Shadow's universe, after all; why don't we wait and see whether this man Best can confirm Shadow's demise?"

"And if Shadow *is* dead?" Albright asked. "What do we do about this Earthman who replaced her?"

"Why don't we just wait until we hear from Best?" Markham answered.

*J*ohnston crossed the basement, ignoring the card table, radio, folding chairs, and video set-up — which, of course, had run out of tape at the crucial moment.

He stared at the bare concrete wall; it appeared perfectly ordinary in the light of the bare bulbs overhead. Johnston glanced up at the lights, then turned his attention back to the wall.

"There's no opening now," he said. "I wonder how he expected to get back?"

"I don't know," the lieutenant said. "I don't know how the hell he got in here in the first place."

"You didn't see any opening here?" Johnston asked, gesturing at the blank wall.

"No, sir — not a thing."

Johnston frowned. He put out a hand, not knowing what he was looking for, and attempted to tap the wall.

His hand vanished into seemingly-solid concrete; astonished, he staggered, thrown off-balance. Both hands went out, grabbing at concrete that wasn't there, and he stumbled forward, through the wall.

He caught himself just short of going down on one knee and stared at the blaze of shimmering, shifting color before him. The cool, dusty air of the Browns' basement was suddenly thin, sharp, clean, crackling with electricity and redolent of sweat and cold meat; he felt suddenly heavy, the way he sometimes felt the loss of buoyancy upon climbing out of a pool.

He couldn't see anything but colors, as if he were trapped in some incredible light show.

None of them, Jewell and Thorpe and Deranian, had mentioned anything like this inside the portals; they'd said the transition was instantaneous. If he'd gone through a portal, shouldn't he have come out somewhere?

"Hello?" he said.

*A*s he settled back on the dark wood of his throne, Pel had the uneasy feeling that there was something Susan was not telling him.

He didn't know what it could be; he believed her when she said she didn't remember being dead, and he believed her explanation of why she had tried to shoot Shadow, but he was sure there was *something* that she was not saying about her recent experiences.

Did she know something about why the fetch was taking so long? He didn't see how she could; after all, he was the magician, not her. He was the one who could turn a dead body into a fetch, or bring it back to life entirely. He could sense everything that touched magic, through all the world, and she was just an ordinary human being — a lawyer.

What could she know that he didn't?

He was trying to think of some way to ask her when a man stumbled out of the portal.

Startled, Pel let his partial suppression of the matrix' visual manifestations slip. *He* could still see perfectly well, of course, but anyone else would be blinded by the barrage of light, color, and shadow.

He thought for a moment that the fetch had returned, and wondered why he had been startled, but then he got a better look at the new arrival.

It was a man of medium height, middle-aged, a few pounds overweight, and wearing the uniform of an officer in the United States Air Force.

He was unquestionably alive, and not a fetch. He was staring blindly into the matrix glare, eyes watering.

"Hello?" he said.

Pel was in no mood for new complications; for several seconds he considered magically shoving the stranger back through the portal, or even just flash-frying him — burning him to ash would actually be much easier, since it just meant unleashing a little wild energy, where pushing him meant directing controlled energy while maintaining the portal.

But burning him would be murder, and Pel was astonished that it had taken him so long, a good three or four seconds, to realize this.

Besides, this man might know what had become of the fetch, and where the hairbrushes and wastebaskets were.

"Hello," Pel said, letting the matrix amplify and distort his voice into an echoing roar. "Who the hell are you?" he demanded, as he began fighting down the matrix glow.

"Major Reginald Johnston, U.S. Air Force," the stranger said, squinting through glare. "And you, I take it, are Pellinore Brown?"

Chapter Nine

"*I* want my fetch," Pel said. "And those hairbrushes, and stuff."

"No problem," Johnston said. "You keep the portal open, and I'll send him right through." He reached inside his uniform jacket. "Let me leave my card — if you or Ms. Nguyen comes back to Earth, I'd appreciate a call."

Pel blinked at him, at the proffered business card — the little white pasteboard rectangle seemed weirdly out of place here in Faerie, in Shadow's throne room, lit by the light of the great matrix.

He accepted it, not with his hand, but with a tendril of magical energy. From Johnston's point of view the card simply sailed through the air to Pel of its own volition, but Pel could see the strands of magic supporting it, the twisted shape of the air that carried it to him.

"And if there's anyone you'd like me to contact — your firm, perhaps, Ms. Nguyen?"

Susan didn't reply; Pel glanced at her sharply as he picked the card out of the air.

"Sure, tell them she's okay," he said.

Pel remembered that he had two sisters, a mother, and some friends back on Earth who might be worrying about him; he was about to mention that when Johnston spoke again.

"While I understand why you're staying here, Mr. Brown," Johnston said, "why is Ms. Nguyen? You aren't holding her against her will, are you?"

"No!" Pel snapped. He frowned and glanced at Susan again.

She wasn't moving; she was just standing there, watching the two men.

"She's free to go," Pel said. "If she wants to go back to Earth, she can." He hesitated, then added, "I admit I enjoy her company here, though."

"Ms. Nguyen?"

Susan shrugged, and Pel felt a surge of anger. Why was she doing this? She was acting like a zombie; this Major Johnston would think that she was drugged, or hypnotized.

"Answer him," Pel said.

"I'm fine, Major," Susan said. "Thank you for your concern."

Johnston was studying her from a few feet away, but then he shrugged, just as she had a moment before. "Whatever you like," he said. "Mr. Brown, thank you for your cooperation. You don't mind if I leave a man stationed in your house until you return to Earth?"

"Not at all," Pel said, not really concerned. That was on Earth; he wasn't going back to Earth until he could bring Nancy and Rachel with him.

"Um . . . if you don't mind my asking . . ."

"Yes, Major?"

"Have you had any contact recently with the Galactic Empire? I mean, since you reached this place?" He gestured at the throne room.

Johnston had explained about the investigation, about questioning Amy and Prossie and poor Ted, but the inquiry still somehow struck Pel as odd — a major in the U.S. Air Force, in uniform and on duty, talking about a Galactic Empire?

Pel had gotten accustomed to the reality of this strange new world he had found himself in, this not-quite-a-story of wizards and spaceships and monsters where he had inadvertently become master of an entire universe, but it still seemed bizarre and somehow wrong that it could interact so freely with the normal, everyday world of Earth. An Air Force officer didn't *belong* in Shadow's fortress, and shouldn't be worrying about the Galactic Empire.

But here Johnston was, with a serious question.

"No," Pel said. "Why do you ask?"

Johnston hesitated. "I'm not sure whether I should be telling you this, but . . . what the hell. The Empire sent a scouting party through their space warp recently — four men climbed down a ladder in Ms. Jewell's back yard, and were taken into custody."

"What did they want?" Pel asked, puzzled.

"I don't know," Johnston said. "I'd like to find out."

"They won't say?" Before Johnston could answer, Pel remembered his stay at Base One. "No, they won't, will they? Bunch of pompous idiots."

Johnston smiled.

"Okay, well, I don't know anything about it," Pel said. "It isn't really any of my business unless they come poking around here, but if I find out anything I'll send a message through. This isn't America here, but I'm still a U.S. citizen, I guess — I sure don't owe the Empire any favors!"

Johnston nodded. "Thank you, Mr. Brown. That's all we ask."

"Yeah, well," Pel said, *"I* ask for my fetch back."

*B*est sighed and leaned back against the tree.

Two hundred miles to Shadow's fortress — that was going to be a damned long walk.

He would have to walk, though — the locals didn't seem to have any other means of transportation. They knew what horses were, but seemed to take his questions about buying one as nonsense — apparently only the hereditary nobility rode on horseback. And oxen were just for plowing, as far as he could see.

Oxen would be impossibly slow, in any case.

Well, maybe he wouldn't have to travel the entire distance to find out what was going on; surely, news and rumor would spread. So far he hadn't picked up anything useful, but he and his men were still out in the sticks.

At least, he thought as he looked around at the muddy, malodorous little yard where he'd traded an hour's labor in the fields for a meal and directions, he *hoped* they were still out in the sticks.

*P*el watched as Johnston stepped warily into the portal and vanished, back to Pel's own basement back on Earth.

Someday, when he had Nancy and Rachel back, when he got tired of playing with the matrix magic, got tired of this medieval mess of a world with its stone walls, its goddess worship, its open sewers, Pel would want to step back through just such a portal. He wondered if he could do that with one of his own creation.

Probably not. He'd have to get Taillefer back here and have him do it.

This Johnston seemed like a sensible sort, really — not at all like the assholes running the Galactic Empire, Carson and Southern and the others, and not like the ignorant barbarians who made up most of Pel's own empire.

Or maybe it was just a matter of cultural differences, since after all, Johnston was a fellow American, and whatever else the Imperials and the locals might be, they weren't that. Maybe they weren't really stupid; they'd just grown up with a completely different background. Pel knew that foreigners weren't stupid back on Earth, despite what the bigots might say, and he supposed it must be the same with these people.

In any case, it was good to know something of what was happening back on Earth, good to know that Johnston was there, that there was someone to contact in case of emergency. Pel didn't feel anywhere near as isolated as he had just a few moments before.

Of course, that assumed that Johnston had been honest, and Pel would have a possible indication of that in just a few minutes, when his fetch either returned or didn't.

Johnston certainly seemed honest enough, and intelligent — he had figured out who Pel was readily enough, and he had asked about the Empire . . .

Pel frowned. What *was* the Empire up to? Why would they send men to Earth? The crew of *Ruthless* had said they were there to make an alliance against Shadow, but this new batch, from Johnston's description, wasn't doing anything like that.

The Empire seemed to be spying on Earth — but it was *Shadow* that had been the enemy.

Then wouldn't they be spying on Shadow, as well? Or rather, since Shadow was dead, on *him?*

As that thought struck him he felt a sudden twinge, something in the matrix, somewhere . . . he took a moment to analyze the still-unfamiliar sensations the matrix transmitted.

It was somewhere outside the fortress, somewhere far away, but not *too* far — still on the near side of the world. When he tried, he could sense the world's curvature, could feel the matrix reaching around to meet itself, as well as stretching up beyond the atmosphere and down deep into the stone below; compared with all that, this new thing was close by, but he knew it was miles away.

He'd felt it before, he remembered. He had felt the same odd twist in the matrix when Athelstan had first suggested dissecting one of the fetches.

Pel suddenly made a connection.

The Empire probably *was* spying on him — and that's what he felt. He guessed that they'd reopened the space-warp out in the forest where *Christopher* had crashed. They'd opened it when Athelstan made his suggestion. They'd opened it then and sent someone through, and now they'd opened it again — to get a report, maybe?

That was annoying; Pel didn't like the idea of being spied on, and he didn't much want to get involved with the Empire again.

But it didn't matter. If Johnston sent back the fetch Pel could bring back Nancy and Rachel, and then he wouldn't care what the goddamned Galactic Empire did.

"I say we should send a telepath," Albright said. "This dropping a ladder and waiting for messages is stupid. It's a half-assed, asinine idea, relying on this when we could send a telepath and have instant reports whenever we want them."

"Sir," Bascombe said, "may I respectfully remind you that the only telepath to ever leave Imperial space went rogue, and is still loose? Do we really want to risk the loss of another?"

"Bascombe's right, for once," Markham said. "We don't have enough telepaths to send one along with every single expedition. Especially since the freaks can't even read minds once they're there."

"Well, damn it . . ."

"However," Secretary Markham added, cutting off Albright's objection, "I think we might be well advised to see if our mutant friends can pick up a link to Shadow's world. They've read minds there before, haven't they? Have we

tried to follow Best's actions from here?" He turned and looked at his own personal telepath.

"I didn't work on that project, sir," the telepath answered, "and I haven't gone over it all consciously, but it's certainly true that some minds in Shadow's world can be read. Not very many, but more than on Earth. As for reading Captain Best's mind, I couldn't say whether it's possible or not. I would suggest that the Halls would be best suited to make the attempt, as Carolyn Hall maintained contact with her cousin Thorpe for some time while Thorpe was in that universe, and Brian Hall has had considerable experience in interdimensional communication."

"Good enough," Albright said. "Get the Halls in here, then."

*P*el accepted the wastebaskets and said, "Thanks," before he remembered that he was talking to a fetch.

He paused, startled by his own slip.

The fetch had been human once. It wasn't now. Pel could fix that.

He really *ought* to fix that.

After he had Nancy and Rachel back, he promised himself. After that he'd fix *all* the fetches. For now, he had more important things to do.

It was a relief to let the portal to Earth close, finally, and to move on to other things; he collapsed the opening into nothingness, then sent the fetch away with a wave of his hand and stared hungrily into the wastebaskets, at the hairbrushes and the bits of dust and hair.

From that he could grow new bodies — clones, they'd be called in Earth terms; simulacra, they were called here. To the wizards it was a matter of the Law of Parts, of the part containing the whole; Pel tended to think more of the genetic pattern that must be complete in every single cell.

It might be the same thing; he didn't know.

And what's more, he didn't care, so long as it worked.

"*O*kay, we know one of the players," Johnston said. "Brown and his friends look pretty straight and simple, just the way Ms. Jewell and Ms. Thorpe here said, and he's happy now he's got his zombie back; as long as he stays on top there I don't think we have to worry, and he currently holds all the strings."

He paused, and looked around at the others — at his staff, the FBI man, Jewell, Thorpe, and the rest of them.

No one spoke.

"This Galactic Empire's another matter," Johnston continued. "They've got the ability to pop through into our reality, and for all we know they can do it anywhere — though the fact that they came through the same place twice might mean it's not that easy for them. They tried to send an embassy first, and we arrested 'em — maybe that's why the second bunch looks like spies, but it might just be they're twisty, and how we treated the first batch didn't matter. They speak English, but that doesn't mean we know how they think."

Thorpe shifted — deliberately, Johnston realized, to remind him of her presence.

"Thorpe, here, *does* know how they think, better than anyone — she grew up there, and she could read minds — so we've got something to work with, but on the other hand, she doesn't understand how *we* think."

Thorpe almost nodded at that.

"They have one big advantage — they can spy on us, with their telepaths and space-warps, and we can't get at them at all. So we're going to collect everyone we know they can contact and see if we can open some serious negotiations, and we're going to keep an eye on Ms. Jewell's back yard, but mostly, since we *don't* have any space-warps or magical portals or mind-readers, we just wait. Unless anyone has a better idea."

This time it was Jewell who got his attention by clearing her throat.

"Was there something you wanted to say, Ma'am?" Johnston asked.

She looked around nervously, then shook her head, and he made a note to talk to her privately as soon as possible.

G rowing a simulacrum from bits of hair and skin and nail was not the same as creating one from scratch; Pel didn't need to sculpt it, but instead coaxed it along in what seemed a process of unfolding. As he guided the magic through and into it, the little knot of detritus on the workshop table melted together into a little blob, then elongated, expanded, shaped itself.

He had thought that it might grow like a clone, first an embryo, then a fetus, a baby, a child, until Nancy was again a grown woman; he had even idly toyed with the idea of stopping the process a bit early, restoring her to her youthful beauty — not that she wasn't still beautiful, but . . .

But he'd promised himself he wouldn't do that. He wanted *Nancy,* the way she had been when she was killed, not some close approximation.

And it turned out to be a moot point, because the thing didn't develop that way at all; it didn't acquire any recognizable human features until it was two feet long, and by the time it reached three feet in length and became clearly a person stretched out there on the rough wooden table, it was an adult woman in form, not a child. The familiar breasts were fully developed, in proportion to the still-small body; the hips were as broad, in proportion, as the real Nancy's had been.

He cursed himself for thinking "the real Nancy" that way. This *was* the real Nancy, or at any rate it soon would be. And it was enlarging — *she* was enlarging quickly, drawing mass from the magical energy Pel poured into her.

This wasn't cloning, he reminded himself, this was magic — the laws were different here. Here he really could bring back the dead.

Or at least, he could create a simulacrum . . .

He forced that thought away. He *would* bring Nancy herself back from wherever she was, from wherever her soul had gone. He would have an exact duplicate of her body, grown from her own tissue — wouldn't that be enough?

He hadn't gotten the first simulacrum right, but that was different; that time he'd been trying to recreate her from memory.

This time it would work.

It had to.

"M̲r̲. Blaisdell," the man in the gray suit said, "I'm with the government. It appears that we were, ah . . . a bit hasty in sending you home."

Oram Blaisdell stared at the stranger for a moment. He looked over the blue government sedan parked on the gravel by the road, and around at the surrounding hills. Smoke was rising from the Ballard place down the valley, but he couldn't see any of the neighbors watching.

Then he glanced at his son Henry, standing by the door of the house, looking confused and a bit scared.

"What the devil are you talkin' about?" he asked at last.

"I'm talking about your communication with . . . well, you thought they were angels."

"You sayin' they ain't? What the hell do you know about it?" He reached a hand down toward the splitting maul he'd been using, but didn't touch it. He was getting too old to be splitting the damn firewood anyway.

"Mr. Blaisdell, we've learned the truth about those angels," the man in the suit said. "They're quite real, you were right, but they aren't quite what you thought they were."

Oram considered this, threw Henry another glance, then asked, "You humorin' me, so you can get me to some doctor Henry called, or you serious?"

"I swear, Pa," Henry said, "I din't call nobody. He's got a badge 'n' all."

"Rose called, maybe?"

Henry shook his head. "I don't think so, Pa; she din't tell me a thing 'bout it if she did."

Oram studied his boy's face, then looked back at the government man.

"I can understand your doubts, sir," the government man said. "I'm sure you've had some people who thought you were imagining the whole thing, and you think your children might have been worried about you and tried to fool you for your own good, but I promise you, that's not the case. I'm really with the government." He flipped open a brown leather case and displayed a badge and document; Blaisdell didn't care to admit he couldn't read the damned thing without his glasses, and wasn't too sure he'd get it all then.

"We need your help," the man in gray said. "If you agree, we'll be driving you directly to Knoxville and putting you on a plane to Washington — a chartered plane. We'll provide accommodations at the other end, give you an expense account for meals; you'll be free to move about, to use the phone, call anyone you want, but we need to know if the . . . if these 'angels' contact you again."

"You think they will?"

The government man didn't answer that.

"You mind tellin' me what they *are*, if they ain't angels?"

"To be honest, sir, they didn't tell me that."

Blaisdell eyed him carefully. That sounded authentic and true, somehow.

Then he looked around, at the wood he'd been splitting, and at the house it was meant to heat.

"C'n I bring Henry, here? Or Rose?"

"I was told you could bring your family, yes, sir."

"How 'bout a lawyer?"

"If you want, yes — or you can call one locally after you reach Washington."

"C'n I bring a gun?"

"Yes, sir. You aren't under arrest; you can bring whatever you like."

That convinced him. "Gimme an hour to pack," he said.

An hour later he was in the back of the dark blue sedan, on his way to Knoxville, with his old leather suitcase in the trunk and a .357 Magnum in his lap.

*A*t first Ray Aldridge thought he was being sued; it had happened before. Then he thought he was being arrested for fortune-telling; that had happened to a friend of his back in Massachusetts once.

Finally, though, he realized what was happening.

He was being called in as a consultant. A psychic consultant.

He almost babbled with joy as he ran down the steps from his apartment to the waiting car. He was being hired as a psychic consultant to the *FBI!*

This was it. Even if he couldn't help, couldn't come up with a thing, just being called would be enough.

His career was made!

*M*argaret Thompson climbed aboard the plane with her head awhirl in confusion. Angela's invisible playmate was *real?* Her own little girl was getting mental messages from somewhere *real?* That silly made-up name, Basurpathork, was *real?*

Well, not quite — Angie had garbled it. Proserpine Thorpe — what kind of a name was that?

She looked down at her daughter.

Angie was staring wide-eyed at the interior of the plane. "We're really gonna *fly*, Mommy? Up in the air?"

Margaret smiled, despite her confusion. "That's right, Angie, we'll fly right up into the air. All the way to Washington."

*"I*f you guys are I.R.S., I swear I'll sue. It's unconstitutional," Carleton Miletti said, for the hundredth time.

"Yessir. We're not from the I.R.S., sir."

"You better not be." He sank back in the seat and watched the streets of Washington sliding past the car windows on either side.

He didn't understand this. He hadn't received any messages from anyone, didn't know what the hell these people were talking about. He didn't remember anything special this past spring — but then, he'd been busy.

Still, he thought he'd remember any mysterious messages, and he didn't.

It had to be a coincidence, or just his imagination, that that odd feeling of being watched was back.

Chapter Ten

*I*t was Nancy.

At least, Pel thought the woman he had created from hairs and nail clippings was truly Nancy.

She lay there, nude and lifeless, and Pel stared at her, looked over every inch of her, looking for any flaw, any sign that he had failed to perfectly recreate his wife's body in every detail.

Of course, he had only his memory to go on, and he was dismayed by how untrustworthy that was. The curl of the hair was right, the curve of the hip, but was that mole on her thigh in exactly the right spot? Had it maybe been a quarter-inch lower before?

He couldn't be sure.

There were photos back in the house, and he could send a fetch for them, but those wouldn't help — those were portraits and ordinary snapshots, no full-length nudes, nothing that could show him every single feature.

He couldn't be absolutely sure — but as far as he could see, this was Nancy, recreated and intact, just as she had been. Even the smell was right.

But she wasn't alive. Not yet.

He touched her, carefully.

Her skin was cold and dry, her eyes blank; he drew back, shuddering.

This was really creepy, he realized. He had been so intent on it that he hadn't really thought about what he was doing. This was like something out of a Stephen King novel, trying to bring back the dead — or really, maybe it was more like something from "Invasion of the Body-Snatchers," since this wasn't really Nancy's body at all. This was a copy, grown from tiny discarded bits, and the *real* Nancy was still lying dead and mutilated somewhere in the Galactic Empire.

He was back in Storyland, only this time it wasn't some great heroic adventure, it was a horror story. Something terrible was going to happen, he was meddling in things Man was not meant to know . . .

But he had *magic*, damn it. Nothing would go wrong. He could bring her back, safe and sound, in this recreated body. He could do *anything* — he held Shadow's matrix, controlled all the magic, all the creative energy, of this entire *universe.*

He knew he could.

He took a deep breath, clenched his fists, then unclenched them and let out his breath. He gathered in the magic, sucked in energy through the matrix — he didn't want to fail by not putting enough effort into it. He wanted to get it right the first time, he didn't want to go through this again. He had saved out part of the hair and a toenail clipping and some powdery residue he was fairly sure came from hair or skin, but he didn't want to have to use it.

Most especially, he didn't want to have to destroy a botched attempt.

For a moment he thought about calling Boudicca or Athelstan back into the room to advise him, or even just Susan, for moral support, but then he clenched his fists again and quashed the idea. He would do this *himself.* He didn't want anyone else seeing Nancy like this. He didn't want anyone else watching if something went wrong. He didn't want anyone else around, inhibiting him, if everything went right. He didn't want to worry about distractions or explanations or anything else.

He would do it alone.

He drew in the energy, filled the chamber with a thick roiling fog of magic, so dense that the colors seemed like liquid currents in the air, deep orange and blood red and seething molten gold.

He waded through them, feeling the viscous electric force prickling and oozing across his skin, and approached his recreated Nancy. He moved around to the foot of the table and stood there, looking down at her, at toes and legs and the tight curls of hair, and he wrapped the magic around her, felt it soak into her, permeate every part of her.

This wasn't just raising a fetch this time; he wound the pattern of energy in her spine and brain, but at the same time he drew the pattern from the flesh itself, and did something he couldn't describe in words, reaching out in one of those directions that wasn't really there, but which magic gave him access to. He somehow knew that he was reaching through the portals of death itself, to find Nancy's soul and draw it back.

He pulled and wove and pushed and embraced, all at once, all through the matrix — his own hands never touched her — until he felt the power flowing of its own accord, the heart beating strong and steady, the brain waking, the eyes seeing. The flesh warmed, blood surged, muscles tightened and relaxed.

She blinked, and turned her head, first to one side, then the other.

For a moment he held his breath; he let the magic pull away, let her life free itself from the matrix.

"Nancy?" he breathed at last.

She blinked, raised herself up on her elbows, and looked at him.

"Is that my name?" she asked.

"*S*hadow is *dead?*" Best asked, startled. "You're *sure?*"

"Man, where have you been these three days past, since the news first came?" The innkeeper set down the wooden mug of thick, foul-smelling beer. "Aye, Shadow is dead, destroyed at the hand of one Pelbrun, styled the Brown Magician — we've the word of half a dozen travelers on it, one of whom spoke to a man who had been in the very throne room of Shadow's fortress, and had spoken there with Lord Pelbrun."

Best picked up the mug warily, then glanced first at Begley, then at Poole, finally at Morcambe.

Morcambe shrugged.

"It's . . . I mean, 'tis a hard thing to believe," Best said to the innkeeper.

"I'truth, it is!" the innkeeper agreed. "Yet all who come hither from the west attest it true, and it pleases me well to hear it. 'Tis to be a kinder reign, methinks, for Pelbrun's orders have come down to us, that there shall be no more hangings for aught but murther, and that we may serve the Goddess an we choose." He gestured toward the window; Best looked, and saw the gallows in the town square.

He had seen it before, when he and his men had arrived in the village — it seemed a perfectly ordinary gallows. Judging by the stains and general wear it had seen considerable use.

It was empty now, though, and perhaps that was what the innkeeper meant to point out. Presumably, when Shadow was running things, there was usually a criminal or two suspended there.

"What if it's trickery?" Best asked, doing his best to imitate the barbaric local accent, with its flat, harsh vowels and archaic phrasing. "What if Shadow still lives, and is only testing your loyalty?"

The innkeeper shrugged. "What would you have of us? What could *Shadow* have of us, an it yet lives and rules? We're but plain folk; if 'twould destroy us, it may, and what's to be done? Why strive to deceive, when 'twas long said that Shadow had the power to see within every heart, should it trouble itself to do so?"

"What if . . ." Best paused, struggling to phrase his questions. This seemed too good to be true, that the superhuman enemy of the Empire had conveniently died, but he couldn't very well explain that to this brew-soaked barbarian. It seemed more likely that it was all part of some elaborate scheme, perhaps directed at the Empire.

And who was this Brown Magician?

"Enow, good sirs, I've others to tend to," the innkeeper said, after Best had groped unsuccessfully for words for a few seconds. "'Tis a wonder indeed, that we should live to see this day, and I'll give you time to think upon it, and to resolve what you'd say. Drink heartily, and give voice an you'd have more." He turned away and stumped off.

Best looked at Begley. "What d'you think, Bill?" he asked.

"Sounds genuine to me," Begley answered.

"I don't know." He hesitated, then motioned to Morcambe. "Sid," he said, "you finish up, and then head back to the landing site — they're supposed to drop a ladder every four hours, but I wouldn't be surprised if they're off schedule. When they drop it, you climb back and tell them what we just heard."

"What about you?" Morcambe asked.

"I'm going on to Shadow's fortress," Best said. "I intend to see for myself, get a look at this Brown Magician if I can."

Begley shifted uneasily.

"If you and Poole want to back out, we'll talk about it," Best said. "Chances are I'll send you back with reports before I get that far anyway."

"Yes, sir," Begley said, trying unsuccessfully not to look relieved.

*S*hock, Pel told himself. The shock of her death and resurrection had damaged her memory, but it would come back with time, he was sure.

"Yes," he said. "Your name is Nancy Brown. You're my wife."

She sat up, legs still straight out in front of her, and stared at him.

"All right," she said.

"Don't you remember?" he asked.

She frowned slightly. "I'm not sure," she said. "I know things, I remember things, but it's all sort of vague."

"Do you know who *I* am?" he asked hopefully.

She squinted at him. "No," she said. "Except . . . you created me, didn't you? You're the magician who created me?"

Why would she think of magicians? That didn't sound right. Pel was suddenly afraid that something had gone very wrong. "I'm your husband, Pellinore Brown," he said, "and I didn't create you — I've brought you back from the dead."

"Was I dead?"

Pel nodded; his throat suddenly felt thick and clogged with emotion, and he couldn't speak.

"I don't remember that," she said. She cocked her head and looked at him, smiling sweetly, the movement and expression heart-wrenchingly familiar — though it was something Pel hadn't seen since a few days before Grummetty had walked out of the basement wall. His doubts vanished; that gesture was Nancy's.

"You were dead," he said. "You were killed by raiders on *Emerald Princess*, and I came here and killed Shadow so I could get you back, you and Rachel."

"I don't remember that," she said again — not smiling, this time.

"It's probably shock," Pel said. "Traumatic amnesia, or something, like on TV. It'll come back to you eventually, I think."

It struck him how bizarre this scene was — Nancy sitting calmly there on the table, stark naked, while the eerie, shifting patterns of the matrix flickered about her, filling the stone-walled, stone-floored chamber with vivid color.

She wasn't a screaming fury like the revenants in *Pet Sematary*, she wasn't possessed by demons — not visibly, anyway — but she wasn't frightened or upset, either, nor as confused as Pel thought she ought to be. She was just accepting it all — she hadn't asked about the matrix effects, or why he was wearing his present makeshift attire of loose black blouse and homespun trousers, or why she was nude, or most importantly, where she was.

She hadn't asked *anything* except in response to his own words.

It had to be the shock, and the amnesia.

"What should I do now?" she asked, and he was unreasonably relieved to hear her ask it.

"Whatever you want," he said. "I'm so . . . it's just . . . I'm so glad to have you back!"

She turned and dangled her feet off the side of the table. "You missed me?" she asked.

"Of course!"

"How long was I dead?"

"I don't know, exactly — I've lost track of time. Weeks. Months." He watched as she slid off the table to stand on her own two feet.

"Ooh, the floor's cold!" she said. She looked down and danced from one foot to the other.

That was more than Pel could stand. He stepped around the table and swept her up in his arms.

At the feel of her warm, bare flesh, the weight of her in his arms after so long alone, his body responded instantly. He bent his neck and kissed her.

When their mouths parted he remembered himself enough to say, "There's a bedroom down the hall."

He hoped she would say no, or take the initiative wordlessly, or otherwise encourage him to take her here and now, on the rough wood of the table; he feared she would refuse, would draw back, either because she didn't remember him or because, after all, she had just awoken from the dead, she might need time to recover.

For a moment, he wasn't even certain she knew what he meant.

But she smiled and said, "All right."

"M s. Jewell," Johnston said, "I had the impression there was something you wanted to tell me."

Amy Jewell shifted uneasily. "Well," she said, "it's just . . . you said there wasn't any way we could get at the Empire."

"I guess I did, yes," Johnston agreed.

Jewell gestured helplessly.

"I take it you think there *is* a way, then?" Johnston asked. "I assure you, Ms. Jewell, we don't have any secret project that will open a path for us . . ."

"No, not that," she said, dismayed.

"What, then?"

"Well, you can send things through Pel, of course," Jewell explained. "He can open a portal to the Empire anytime you want, and one to Earth, and you can send through whatever you want."

Johnston leaned back in his chair and stared at her.

"That's obvious," he said slowly, "now that you've pointed it out. I'd thought of going through Faerie, of course, but it hadn't occurred to me that Mr. Brown would help us.

"But you know, he might. In fact, why shouldn't he?"

"I don't know," Amy replied.

She still looked uneasy, though — and she knew Brown better than Johnston did. "I think," he said, "that that's something we'll keep in mind, Ms. Jewell."

But he didn't think they'd be in any hurry to ask favors of Pel Brown.

*T*he matrix flickered and dimmed as Pel lay back on the cool bedding. He felt a pool of sweat drying beneath him.

The recreated Nancy lay beside him, saying nothing, smiling blandly.

She had cooperated, had agreed to whatever he suggested — and had suggested nothing herself. She hadn't mentioned the weird pyrotechnics of the matrix, even though she had never seen any of it while she lived. She hadn't said *anything* unless he spoke first. She hadn't resisted when he had proposed things Nancy had always found disgusting; she'd cooperated. She hadn't commented on his endless, matrix-supplied energy.

This wasn't Nancy.

Admitting that to himself caused a hard, sharp, physical pain in his belly, but he had to admit it. This wasn't Nancy.

He sat up again and looked down at the woman beside him in the bed, looked at her as only a matrix wizard could, using the magical network's power to see into her in a way that was more than physical.

This wasn't Nancy. It wasn't really human at all; the soul, if that was what it was, lacked the complexity of a living woman's.

This was an artificial being of his own creation.

He knew that she would do anything he told her to, without argument. She had no visible will or personality of her own. This wasn't Nancy. This wasn't a real woman at all. This was a homunculus, a *thing*, not a real person.

He hadn't raised the dead; instead, he had found the way Shadow had created those duplicates Raven and others had mentioned, her spies, her doppelgängers.

He supposed some men might even think that was enough — but he wanted *Nancy*.

He wept silently, and she smiled up at him uncomprehendingly.

*"T*hey've been collected, all of them, and brought to their capital city," Carrie Hall said. "All but Gwenyth, anyway."

"Why?" Secretary Markham demanded.

"To try to talk to us, I think," she answered uncertainly.

Markham's eyes narrowed. Telepaths weren't supposed to be uncertain. He had an idea, a pretty good one, that a telepath only showed uncertainty when lying — they were never uncertain about what they had read, nor afraid to admit when they didn't know something, but they could be uncertain, briefly, about how their lies were being received.

"It's a very difficult contact," Carrie said, as if answering his thoughts. She was probably doing exactly that — snooping inadvertently, maybe without even realizing she was doing it. Markham knew a lot about telepaths, had worked with them for twenty years, and while everyone knew that snooping without orders was a crime, he knew that sometimes they couldn't help it.

"And the four of them haven't been *told* why they were gathered," Carrie added. "They're guessing, and I'm working from their guesses."

Markham nodded. He turned to Carrie's brother.

"I've located a few possible contacts," Brian said, anticipating Markham's question — as Markham had expected him to. "I've found two of our own people. One is Samuel Best, the head of the intelligence squad Under-Secretary Bascombe sent, and the other is a trooper named Ronald Wilkins, who accompanied Lord Raven for a time and then deserted. He suspects himself to be the only survivor of Colonel Carson's command."

"And what do they know about Shadow?"

"It's hard to read very much, sir — there are currents of energy that interfere. However, both our men have heard that Shadow is dead; Best has sent one of his men back for pick-up, to tell us as much. Apparently Shadow has been replaced by someone or something called the Brown Magician."

"Brown?" Markham glanced at Carrie, and at Bascombe. "Pel Brown, perhaps?"

*P*el debated whether or not he should destroy the false Nancy, and could reach no decision. He sat in Shadow's throne, considering, arguing with himself.

She was a mockery, a thing — but she was alive and she seemed so human, in her complacent and obedient way. She wasn't Nancy — but was she a person, all the same?

He had created her, but did that give him the right to destroy her?

Or the *obligation* to destroy her?

At least he hadn't recreated Rachel, he told himself. Destroying a grown woman would be bad enough, but a false child . . .

But maybe he *should* recreate Rachel. Wasn't a simulacrum better than nothing? He had been so happy to have Nancy back at first, until he had realized it wasn't her. He had so missed the warm companionship of a woman . . .

But he didn't *want* an imitation, damn it! He wanted *Nancy*. And Rachel. Not just this Nancy puppet in his bed.

He looked up and saw Susan standing in the doorway, watching him.

At least *she* was real, and not just a simulacrum, a magical imitation — she remembered her childhood in southeast Asia, remembered how she had died here in Shadow's fortress. A simulacrum wouldn't have known any of that.

That was because he had simply repaired her dead body, forced life back into the corpse; he hadn't had to make a new body for her. He couldn't do that for Nancy or Rachel; he didn't have their bodies.

Red light surged up behind him and lit Susan's face a ghastly color. Pel blinked at her, and forgot all about the imitation of his wife.

He didn't have Nancy's body, or Rachel's.

But maybe he could *get* them.

Chapter Eleven

"The General Secretary has conferred with the Emperor," the telepath said.

"And?" Albright demanded.

"The matter is being left to your discretion; His Imperial Majesty rests his full faith in your decision."

Albright swallowed, glanced at Markham, then nodded.

"All right, then," he said. "That gives us a free hand."

"Or enough rope," Markham replied.

"Or that," Albright agreed.

"I think, in that case, that our course is pretty clear."

Albright nodded. "'The wise warrior does not fight two foes at once,'" he quoted. "Nicholson may be out of style, but it's still damn good advice."

"And, 'Know which enemies to fight, and which to appease,'" Markham replied.

"Right. And, 'Know who the true enemy is.'"

"Excuse me, sir," said Stuart, Albright's personal telepath. "Both of you find this exchange of aphorisms annoying."

Albright glanced up, startled, at the man behind his chair. "Right," he said. "We can both quote Nicholson and Majors, and appreciate their common sense — take that as given. And that probably means that we agree on what we want to do — get back Lieutenant Austin and his men, talk nicely to the Earthpeople, and then shut down the warp and forget Earth. They're not a threat."

"With one exception," Markham said. "If we could develop the space-warp in response to Shadow's inroads, perhaps they can develop something of their own, as well; the telepaths tell me that despite their apparently primitive science in many areas, they have their own areas of expertise in which they're very adept indeed. I'm given to understand that their mechanical communications devices are far better than ours, almost good enough to make up for their lack of telepaths."

Albright frowned. "But they don't have any such thing as a warp substitute *now*, do they?"

"No, but they might someday. Don't worry, Marshal, I'm not arguing with you — I agree, we should close off all direct contact with Earth until we've dealt with Shadow, or the Brown Magician, or whoever is running the opposition at present. I merely suggest that we delegate two telepaths, working in shifts, to maintain a watch on Earth."

Albright nodded. "Of course," he said.

"As for this Brown Magician — I think we want Imperial Intelligence to keep a very close watch there indeed, and for you to keep your men alert to any threat he might pose, but we don't need to assume he's necessarily hostile. After all, we don't know whether he was Shadow's heir, or whether he overthrew it."

"In short, we may have had the interdimensional crisis resolved for us, without our having to fight."

"Exactly." Markham leaned back, smiling.

The Emperor and the General Secretary had left this one to him and Albright, which meant their careers, and quite possibly their lives, were on the line — but he felt sure he was right in his actions. Earth was harmless unless they developed interdimensional travel, and this Brown Magician was a total unknown. No one could blame him for not attacking an unknown force immediately.

Furthermore, cutting off Earth except for a telepathic watch and transferring Shadow's realm to the combined attentions of the military and Imperial Intelligence would leave that nuisance of a political appointee, John Bascombe, with nothing to do. It might keep him out of trouble.

And if not, Bascombe might make a convenient scapegoat, should one be needed.

Albright might still be nervous, but Markham was not.

Markham was quite pleased.

"*H*ello, Angie," Prossie said, kneeling by the little girl's chair.

It was odd to see Angie's face as it really was, and not Angie's rather different self-image.

"Hello," Angie said politely.

Prossie smiled. "Do you know who I am?" she asked.

Angie shook her head.

"I'm Proserpine Thorpe."

Angie stared at her, and frowned. "*You're* not Basurpathork," she said. "That's Mr. Nobody's real name!"

"That's right," Prossie said, nodding. "I was Mr. Nobody. Sometimes. Sometimes it was one of my cousins."

"But Mr. Nobody was just inside my head," Angie objected.

"No, that's just how we talked to you."

"You aren't talking in my head *now.*"

"No, I'm not," Prossie agreed. "I can't do it anymore, I forgot how. But my cousins still can. And we want you to tell us any time they say anything to you, even if they ask you not to tell. All right?"

Angie frowned.

Angie's mother leaned over. "Do what she says, Angie."

"But that's not nice," Angie protested. "That's telling secrets."

"I know," Prossie said. "It *isn't* nice. It's like spying, almost. But you see, that's what my cousins are doing — they're spying on *you*, and your mommy, and lots of other people."

"But Mr. Nobody's nice!"

Prossie nodded. "But there are bad people who are *making* my cousins do bad things. They can't help it." She waited for a moment, watching Angie's face.

"So," Prossie said, "will you tell us if they talk to you?"

Angie scuffed her toe on the blue hotel-room carpet. "I guess," she said.

*A*my lay back in the bed and tried to be calm.

At least, with all the fuss about the Galactic Empire, Major Johnston hadn't interfered with her appointment. Walter's baby was gone, and Amy was rid of the man who had raped her. She wasn't about to forget what he'd done to her, he and Beth, but she didn't need any physical reminders. The bruises were healed, the baby was gone, and she could get on with her life.

She tried to tell herself that.

The abortion had been a nasty, intrusive, humiliating experience. The doctor and the nurses had been nice enough, but the procedure itself . . . well, it couldn't be helped, and it was over. The baby was gone.

She tried not to feel any twinge of regret. She didn't want children, she especially didn't want *Walter's* child, but still, the baby . . .

She shouldn't think of it as a baby, she told herself. The fetus. The tissue. Not the baby.

And it was too late to do anything about it now, anyway.

She could get on with her life.

Of course, she wasn't sure just what sort of a life that was going to be, with her business ruined and her house under martial law and Major Johnston enlisting her as an advisor pretty much whether she wanted it or not. It wasn't as if she'd be going home from here; she'd be going to a fancy hotel in Crystal City, convenient to the Pentagon, at Air Force expense. She and Prossie had adjoining rooms.

That wasn't exactly her idea of a normal life.

One step at a time, she told herself, suppressing a shudder. One step at a time.

I just don't want to talk about it," Ted Deranian insisted, for one final time.

"All right, that's fine," the woman in the blue Air Force captain's uniform said. "When you're ready, though, give us a call. Any time." She shook his hand and started to turn away.

"It wasn't . . ." Ted began. She turned back. He hesitated.

"Was it really . . ." he began again.

"Most of it, anyway," she said, understanding his incomplete question. "I don't know the details; maybe part of it was illusion. Most of it was real, though, yes; you've had an unprecedented experience, one you weren't prepared for, and you've been trying to handle it, trying to cope with things no one should ever have to cope with." She didn't mention that this was a modified version of the standard speech she gave to people who had cracked under the stress of combat or long imprisonment.

She'd never had to counsel anyone who'd fallen into another universe before.

"You go on home," she told him. "Take time off if you need it — we'll certify whatever you need, as far as that goes. You can tell people the truth, or tell them that you've been held hostage by terrorists — that's the easiest cover story, and we'll back you up. Or just tell them it's none of their business. And call anytime — you've got the card." He patted his pocket and nodded. "And we'd like to see you again in a month or so."

"Thank you," Ted said.

He turned and left, closing the door carefully behind him.

"Who did you say this was?" Bob Heyworth leaned back in his chair. Tom Boyle glanced at him from the next desk, and Heyworth waved him away. Boyle went back to typing.

"My name's Ray Aldridge, I'm a professional psychic from California — maybe you've heard . . . no, I guess you haven't."

"I'm not much into psychics, I'm afraid," Heyworth said. "You want me to connect you to someone a bit more in that line?"

"No, this isn't about me," the voice on the phone said. "I mean, I hope you'll mention my name, but that's not why I'm calling."

"What is it, then?"

Heyworth could hear the hesitation before the voice said, "The government's in contact with aliens."

Heyworth grimaced, and asked, "How do you know?"

Tom Boyle glanced at him again, and Heyworth drew rings in the air by his ear to indicate that the caller was a nut.

That wasn't anything unusual; Boyle turned away.

"They told me," Aldridge answered. "They brought me here to see if I could help them."

Heyworth made a wordless noise that meant roughly, "Go on."

"See, they think that some psychic messages I reported back in the spring might have been a genuine contact with these people, who come from a galactic empire in another universe, so they brought me here to see if I'd get any more messages."

"And have you?"

"No, but . . . listen, I know you think psychics are all fakes, and I'm not going to try to convince you of that part, because most of it *is* fake, but look, the FBI brought me here, to talk to people from Air Force intelligence, and they've got people who came from this other universe, and they've been talking about how they have some kind of ship out in Maryland, in a place called Goshen — look, I'm afraid they might be trying to cover it all up, and I don't want that."

Heyworth blinked.

He had seen the phony spaceship in Goshen; the paper had been getting calls about it ever since someone had dumped it there months ago, back in April or May, and like most of the reporters he had eventually gotten curious enough to drive out and take a look at it.

And like all the others, he hadn't found anyone who knew anything about it. The lady who owned the place was never home, the government men who stopped by every so often to check on the place wouldn't talk — no one could make a story out of it. Jessie Wilber from Style had tried to do a sort of human interest piece on the neighborhood reaction to this mysterious object, but it hadn't gone anywhere; most of the neighbors wouldn't talk about it, and the feds had given her a friendly warning that there were privacy considerations, that Ms. Jewell, the home owner, was lawyer-happy.

So at first, when Heyworth made the connection, he thought this might be something interesting after all, that maybe somebody would finally explain that silly contraption and make it something more than a back-page filler.

Then he decided that no, this phony psychic had heard about the ship and had just figured it would be a good way to cash in; really, it was a wonder there weren't half a dozen cults popping up around it already.

But on the other hand — the psychic knew that the government agency watching the ship was Air Force, not one of the civilian outfits, even though the people who checked on it usually weren't in uniform. Heyworth only knew that himself because, in the proper reportorial manner, he had demanded to see ID before allowing himself to be chased away.

But he did know it. So this Aldridge had done his homework, that was all.

"We wouldn't want that either, Mr. Aldridge," Heyworth said. "I don't think we want to talk about it over the phone, though — you never know who could be listening. Is there somewhere I could meet you?"

The relief was plain in Aldridge's voice as he began babbling about a possible rendezvous.

Heyworth didn't know, when he hung up the phone, whether he would bother to show up. Standing a nuisance up was one of the best ways to get rid of him (or her) — but there was always a chance he might get something interesting out of this, and so far it had been a slow day.

He would call a couple of contacts, and see if the Air Force might really have been talking to Aldridge, and if there was anything new on the Goshen spaceship.

"If your reports are accurate, and this isn't all an elaborate fraud," the man in the gray suit said, "then you're right. It's hardly just an intelligence matter anymore, and it certainly isn't just an *Air Force* matter."

"My reports are as accurate as I can make 'em," Johnston replied with a shrug. "And if it's a fraud, they've sure suckered *me.*"

The man in the gray suit made it quite plain, without saying a word, that he didn't consider that to be evidence one way or the other. After a moment of silence, he added, "I'd heard rumors about this spaceship; we all took it for granted that it was a fake."

"So did I," Johnston said, as he pulled the car into Amy Jewell's driveway. He brought the vehicle to a stop inches from a previous arrival's bumper, shifted to PARK, set the brake, and turned off the engine. "If it were just the ship, I'd *still* think it was a fake, and I sure as hell wouldn't have called in the State Department."

"Just what was it that convinced you, then?" the man from the State Department asked as he opened the passenger door.

Johnston waited until they were both standing, then gestured at the rope ladder that dangled unsupported in the air.

"That, among other things," he said, as the State man gawked.

*R*on Wilkins ambled slowly along the causeway across Shadowmarsh, considering the fortress that towered before him and trying to decide if this was really a smart move.

He sure as hell wouldn't have tried it if he thought Shadow was still alive and still in there.

All the reports, though, said that Shadow was dead, and the Brown Magician was in charge, and Wilkins could only figure that the Brown Magician was Pel Brown, which meant that somehow or other he and Raven and the rest had pulled it off, had defeated Shadow.

Which was pretty goddamned incredible.

Wilkins had noticed that nobody ever mentioned Raven, though, nor any of the others. He figured that this probably meant one of two things; either all the others were dead, or some were dead and some had wound up in other universes.

Like back in the Galactic Empire.

Getting back to the Empire sounded like a pretty good idea.

Oh, he might be up for desertion, or something, but nobody over there could know exactly what had happened here, not even the bloody mind-readers; the chain of command had been broken, Lieutenant Dibbs had told Wilkins and the others they could choose for themselves, and it couldn't very well be desertion to walk out on a bunch of crazies committing group suicide, could it? Raven wasn't an officer. Nobody in the whole bunch was except Thorpe, and she was a Special, a mutant, not in the direct chain of command at all, not authorized to give orders.

So Wilkins didn't see that he'd broken any laws, and he didn't think he was important enough to be framed, so going home sounded *real* good.

Someplace with indoor plumbing, and decent food, and clean women who didn't scream if you so much as touched them . . .

Of course, if he was wrong about Brown being in charge, then he was walking right into Shadow's lap and was probably as good as dead — but hey, if he'd wanted to live forever, he would never have signed up to be a soldier.

But he wasn't in any hurry to be wrong. He was perfectly willing to take his time, just in case God decided to give him a sign or something.

So he was walking down the causeway toward the fortress, but walking slowly.

He had the feeling that someone was watching him, as he strolled, and every so often he glimpsed *things* moving in the marsh to either side. The sky was gray and overcast. Combine that with the heavy gravity, the low oxygen content of the air, and the off-color sunlight of this planet — if it really *was* a planet — and the whole place was about as oppressive and unpleasant as he ever cared to see. Leaving it would be a relief.

But he wasn't going to rush into anything.

*S*paceman Second Class Thomas Sawyer, Imperial Military, paused for a moment in his work and leaned on his wooden shovel. Alison and Goody Fitzsimmons were gossiping again, exchanging the latest tales about the Brown Magician across the stableyard fence.

For a moment Sawyer once again considered trying to contact this legendary Pelbrun who had usurped Shadow's role. It almost had to be Mr. Brown.

But that would mean going into that fortress, and Sawyer couldn't bring himself to do that. He'd backed out at the very gate once before — and there was a good chance that Brown remembered and resented that. True, he'd apparently somehow won his battle against Shadow, but how many had died in the process? How many might have lived if there'd been another hand, such as Sawyer's, to help?

Better not to risk it. Life here wasn't all that bad. Rough, perhaps, but not too bad. Alison was a fine young woman, and he thought she was warming to him — that held some promise for the future, maybe more than he'd had in the Empire.

He stood, hefted the shovel, then scooped and lifted more manure into the oxcart.

*P*el sat in his throne, physical eyes closed, and concentrated on the matrix, on bending his magical perceptions in a direction outside the three rational dimensions of normal space.

He had located the reality of the Galactic Empire, and found the place (place?) where the portal had been that allowed Shadow and her hundred fetches to step through.

He didn't want that, though; he wanted to find wherever Nancy and Rachel were.

Where their bodies were, rather.

Nancy had died aboard a spaceship, the *Emerald Princess*; Rachel had reportedly died on the rebel planet, Zeta Leo III. But Pel didn't know what had become of their remains. So far as he could recall, no one at Base One had told him, and he had been too distraught to ask.

He cursed himself for that now.

It seemed possible that both were on Zeta Leo III. Nancy's corpse might have been jettisoned somewhere in space, though.

Or both might have been brought to Base One. That seemed like the sort of thing the Empire would do.

He didn't know where to start; he had a whole galaxy to search. Admittedly, the galaxies of Imperial space appeared to be much smaller than those of Earth's universe, but still, there were thousands of worlds there.

As he groped about, in great sweeping arcs through non-space, he felt odd little tugs and discontinuities, like snags in the fabric of space. At first he thought they were natural; then he thought he was doing something wrong; and then he realized that those were the places where Shadow had opened portals into the Empire.

He paused and considered.

It was interesting to see that portals left a permanent mark in what he could only think of as the shape of space itself. One might even think of it as permanent damage, and he wondered whether he might have hold of something that could destroy entire universes if misused, or even just overused.

He smiled wryly. Stand aside, atom bomb — magic could wreck universes, not just a planet or two!

More importantly, as far as he was concerned, these snags were places Shadow had penetrated into the Empire, and while some of those penetrations had been botched scouting expeditions that ended in a bunch of dead monsters, hadn't she managed to plant spies in the Imperial military?

The Empire had certainly thought so.

A portal that had been used to plant a spy would presumably come out somewhere useful. Someone could step through and ask questions, maybe learn something useful. If he could make contact with the Imperial military, get a message to General Hart at Base One, he could ask them to deliver the remains of his wife and daughter.

He had helped dispose of Shadow, after all, and after they had sent him here, to almost certain death, instead of just sending him home. They owed him one.

Of course, he couldn't go through such a portal himself — that was what had brought Shadow to ruin. He could send someone, though.

Fetches weren't very bright, and couldn't talk, and could hardly blend into a crowd if there was a problem; the locals here would be hopelessly out of place in a relatively civilized space-faring universe of spaceships and aircars.

He could wait for that Imperial spy, or whatever he was, to arrive — but Pel thought it would be better if one of his own people took care of things.

"Susan!" he called.

Chapter Twelve

The State Department man and the deputy from the Imperial Department of Science were chatting quietly on one corner of Amy Jewell's patio, the Imperial's purple space suit an odd contrast with the Earthman's gray jacket. Major Johnston had been carefully not listening to them even before he got into the argument with the newly-arrived FBI agent-in-charge, but he did wonder just what they were saying.

The first official contact between the governments of the United States of America and the Galactic Empire was taking place just a few feet away, and here he was in a stupid jurisdictional dispute.

"The Bureau dumped it on us back in April," Johnston pointed out.

"An error," the agent insisted. "We're correcting that."

"Seems to me that it's not really your concern any more than it's an Air Force matter, at this point. State and the CIA might have a claim, but why you? There's a spacecraft involved, which would mean either Air Force or NASA, but no one's committed any federal crimes. And we do have seniority here."

"Domestic espionage is a matter for the Bureau," the FBI man argued.

Johnston had been keeping half his attention on watching Lieutenant Austin and his two men climb the ladder; now he dropped the argument completely to watch as Spaceman Farmer — a name and rank combination that Earthpeople found funny, but the Imperials apparently didn't — vanished into thin air upon reaching the top. Farmer's bulky purple space suit just disappeared, as if erased.

Barrington followed, and Austin was nearing the top when an AP distracted Johnston.

"Sir, there are reporters out front."

"What reporters?" Johnston asked, turning away.

"Heyworth, from the *Post.*"

"Any video? Photographers?"

"Not that I saw, sir."

Johnston nodded.

He'd known it wouldn't stay quiet forever; *everything* leaked eventually. In this particular case he hadn't even tried for real secrecy; relying on normal discretion and the high unbelievability factor had seemed like a better idea. The nut theories that had been circulating for decades about a government cover-up of alien spaceships had been about the best protection he could have asked for, and classifying anything would only have made people suspect that there was something real this time.

But with the FBI and State involved, and the four psychic contacts, something had to leak, and sooner or later someone would check it out. Johnston did wonder whether it had been the paranoid Miletti or the publicity-hungry Aldridge who called Heyworth — they seemed the most likely candidates.

If it was either of them, it was probably Aldridge; Miletti would more likely have just called more lawyers.

"Should I allow them back here, sir?"

Johnston glanced up in time to see Austin's purple-booted feet disappear. "I don't think we can legally stop them," he said. "You tell Heyworth that this is private property, and he's trespassing at his own risk, but if that doesn't keep him out, then let him past." He wished he'd brought Ms. Jewell along, so she could order the reporters away, but he hadn't thought of it; she was, as far as he knew, in the hotel in Crystal City, a good forty minutes away.

The AP turned and headed back around the side of the house; Johnston watched him go, then glanced at the diplomats.

They were shaking hands; then the State Department man watched as the Imperial representative turned and trotted out toward the rope ladder, lifting his bubble helmet into place as he went.

Johnston blinked.

"If we had our men in place here," the FBI man said, "I think we could find a way to keep these reporters out."

"Oh, I could find a way," Johnston answered. "For awhile. If I told the APs to keep 'em out, they would, legal or not, but why antagonize the press? They'll find out sooner or later, and if we treat them nicely maybe they'll make us look good in their reports."

"We could order them not to interfere in an ongoing investigation."

"And you think that would *work?*"

The Imperial envoy was climbing the ladder, and Johnston was puzzled and uneasy. He had had the distinct impression, when he had ordered Austin and the others released, that this deputy was supposed to serve as the Imperial representative here until an ambassador could be sent — so why was he climbing back up there?

"It's within the Bureau's authority," the FBI man said.

"Okay, fine," Johnston said; he could hear footsteps, and glanced over to see Heyworth coming around the corner, first staring up at the unsupported top of the dangling rope ladder, then at the space suited figure clambering upward. "Fine; you tell Mr. Heyworth that." He turned away and headed for the State Department man, leaving the FBI agent to deal with the reporter.

The man from State was calmly watching as the Imperial ascended.

"What's going on?" Johnston asked.

"Hmm?" The man in the gray suit looked mildly startled.

"What's going on?" Johnston repeated. "Where's he going?"

"Oh, he's just going back to get his staff," the State Department rep replied. "He wasn't sure how many he could bring, what sort of facilities we would have."

"But he'll be back?"

"Oh, yes, of course. He'll be right back. Ten minutes, he said."

Johnston frowned, then turned to watch as the Imperial climbed. He was about fifty feet up now, and climbing fast.

Heyworth was trying to shove past the FBI man to get closer to the ladder, and the FBI man was holding him back; the AP had followed Heyworth and was hanging back, standing by the back door of the house.

"You," Johnston called, "get me a radio."

"Yessir," the AP said, with a salute. He trotted away.

Johnston watched the Imperial climb.

He didn't like this; once that man was back through the warp the Empire would be free of any commitment to Earth. The hostages had been freed — Johnston didn't mind admitting to himself that Austin and the others had been hostages, though he would have vehemently denied any such thing if it had been suggested by anyone else. The crew of *Ruthless* was long gone. Prossie Thorpe was in exile.

Of course, the Empire was perfectly willing to abandon their people anyway; they'd demonstrated that before. Maybe it didn't mean anything that in a few moments they would have none of their people on Earth.

But Johnston didn't like it.

He couldn't *do* anything about it without possibly creating an international — interdimensional! — incident, but he didn't like it.

Ten minutes, the State Department man said.

The AP returned with the radio when the Department of Science deputy was a little over halfway up the long climb.

Johnston got through to the people he wanted at about the three-fourths point.

"Listen, that copter we had on standby," he said, "get it in the air and get it up here. Right now."

He didn't really listen to the acknowledgement.

Heyworth had stopped arguing; he was standing where he was, watching the diplomat climb, just as Johnston and the State rep were. The FBI man was watching Heyworth.

The Imperial reached the top and vanished; the State man clapped his hands together and said, "Well! He should be back in a moment; shall we have a drink while we wait? I'm sure there must be something around here." He seemed to notice Heyworth for the first time, and frowned slightly.

Johnston paid no attention; he was staring at the ladder.

Heyworth turned to answer the man in the gray suit, the FBI man turned to follow the reporter, the AP stationed by the ladder had glanced away, so only Johnston saw the first jerk as the ladder moved.

"Damn it," he exclaimed, as he dashed across the patio. "Grab it!" he shouted at the AP.

The other three men turned and stared in astonishment as Johnston ran across Amy's back lawn and took a wild leap upward, trying to catch the bottom rung of the rapidly-rising ladder. The AP had grabbed hold and was being yanked upward.

Johnston's own grab missed, and barely kept himself from falling when he landed on the grass; by the time he could collect himself for another jump it was obviously far too late. The ladder was being hauled upward at a prodigious rate, and the AP had lost his nerve and dived free, to land rolling on the grass.

"God *damn* it!" Johnston shouted, as the ladder vanished upward into the space warp.

The State Department man stared at the empty air.

"But he said he'd be right back," he said. "Maybe it'll be right back!"

The FBI man didn't say anything; Johnston snorted.

"What the hell is going on?" Heyworth demanded.

Johnston looked around at the others, and a sudden silence fell.

Heyworth was still badgering them, trying to get a response, when the Air Force helicopter arrived a few minutes later, to fly aimlessly back and forth through empty air where the space warp had been.

*S*omeone was entering the fortress, Pel could sense it, but right now he was too busy to care. Susan was ready, wearing a green dress that Pel hoped wouldn't stand out in the Empire — he had seen very few civilians at Base One, and didn't really remember what the women had worn on Psi Cassiopeia II or Zeta Leo III.

Not that he'd seen all that many women there, either.

He did remember the passengers on *Emerald Princess,* though, and he thought this green dress he'd magically created from fabric he'd found in one of Shadow's workshops was a reasonable approximation of the gowns they wore. Simpler, perhaps — he hadn't bothered with any sequins or lace — but along the same general lines, with its high waistline and long skirt.

Susan didn't argue about the dress — but then, Susan didn't seem to argue about anything anymore. After the one burst of uncharacteristic action that had gotten her killed she seemed to have become more passive and tolerant than ever.

She stood there in her seamless new dress, purse slung on her shoulder, a blaster tucked in the purse, and said nothing at all as Pel tried to locate the spot he wanted and open a portal.

He was seated on the throne, the matrix seething about him; Susan stood before him, waiting, eyes closed against the glare. The fetch who had brought the hairbrushes from Earth stood by the back wall, motionless, dead eyes untroubled by the brilliance of the magical display.

Pel could sense the simulacrum of Nancy, still waiting in the bedroom down the stone corridor; he could sense the other fetches scattered about the fortress, and the hundreds of homunculi and other creatures with which Shadow had peopled the place. Boudicca and Athelstan were eating in a kitchen two levels below. Since Pel's takeover a handful of the local peasants had also made themselves at home in the fortress; he could feel their presence, as well. The thousands of monster slugs in the surrounding marsh were also detectable, tiny dark sparks in the magical tracery.

The lone man who had just walked in through the front gate was no one Pel recognized from the pattern of magical energy; that meant it wasn't Taillefer or any other wizard, nor any of the peasants who had spoken to him before. It might, he supposed, be that Imperial spy, though he wouldn't have expected the spy to march in so openly.

Well, if it was the spy, then that was all the more reason to get on with it. The portal would form a few feet to Pel's left, Susan's right, and Susan could just walk right through.

Perhaps he should send the false Nancy, or Athelstan, or Boudicca, or one of the peasants — but he didn't trust any of them, really, and he had thought of Susan first, and here she was.

He twisted the matrix, poured energy through it, and felt reality give way as the portal opened. A cool breeze blew into the throne room from somewhere in the Galactic Empire, cutting through the thick, overheated air.

"It's open," Pel said. "Go ahead."

Susan straightened, adjusted her purse strap, stepped forward — and almost collided with the man stepping *out* of the portal.

*S*amuel Best stared at the fortress.

He hadn't expected it to be quite so ugly.

And he hadn't expected it to be built on a sort of island at the center of a vast open marsh.

There were only two ways to approach the place, so far as he could see — openly, walking along the causeway, or by sneaking through the marsh.

He looked down and contemplated the mud, the sawgrass, the likelihood that there were leeches, ticks, and assorted other vermin, quite aside from whatever defenses Shadow or its successor might have deliberately planted.

He sighed.

"Poole," he said, "it's your turn. Begley and I are going to wait here for orders, because I'm not interested in either wading through a swamp or walking into somebody's gunsights. You go back for pick-up and tell 'em what this place looks like, and that unless something unexpected turns up, we aren't going any farther without a direct order to do so." He glanced at Begley, and added, "If then."

"It's a long way back," Poole objected.

"But it's back home," Best pointed out. "If you'd rather stay, maybe Begley wants to go."

Begley smiled, and Poole shrugged. "I'll go," he said.

"Good," Best said.

*"B*est has hit a dead end," Brian Hall announced. "He's sending his man Poole back for orders."

Markham glanced at Hall in surprise. "What's the problem?" he asked.

"Shadow's fortress — or the Brown Magician's, whichever it is — is surrounded by marsh, sir. The only safe approach is by a completely unsheltered causeway several miles long."

"What about the other man, Wilkins? Has Best contacted him?"

"No, sir," Hall answered. "Wilkins went on into the fortress, by way of the causeway."

"Can you contact either man?"

"Not reliably, sir — neither one is *expecting* telepathic contact, you see, and they're both in the area where the interference is very strong. It's getting hard to read Best, and I can only perceive Wilkins intermittently now."

"It's very suspicious, that interference," Markham said. "Why is it there?"

"I don't know, sir. It may not be deliberate."

"Hmm." Markham frowned. "Well, keep me posted as best you can."

"*D*amn it," Pel said, "strangers aren't supposed to keep stepping out of these things!" He made no attempt to suppress the glare of the matrix as he glowered at the newcomer.

The man was squinting, shielding his face with a forearm, but he didn't look perturbed by the brightness, nor in any way confused or frightened. He wore a black jacket of a cut that seemed peculiar and slightly archaic to Pel, but which was not all that different from some he had seen in the Galactic Empire; beneath the jacket was a purple silk vest, a pale pink cravat, and a white shirt with fancy white-on-white patterning to it — Pel couldn't make out the details of the design past the jacket, vest, tie, and shifting light. The man's pants were slightly flared black slacks with old-fashioned wide cuffs.

The overall effect was of a dandy from some alternate past, where fashion had followed a different route.

And in fact, that was probably just what the fellow was, Pel thought — some foppish Imperial who had wandered through the portal by accident.

But why wasn't he dismayed by his sudden transition into another universe?

"Who the hell are you?" Pel asked. His anger filtered into the matrix, and his voice boomed from the walls as if heavily amplified, while red light flickered overhead and a pale, insubstantial mist swirled coldly around the stranger's ankles.

The well-dressed man turned to face the throne directly, and Pel could see him blinking behind his shielding arm.

"I'm called Peter Gregory," he said. "I take it that you aren't Shadow, though you sit in its stead."

"No, I'm not," Pel said warily. "You knew Shadow?" He had his doubts about that, given Gregory's choice of pronoun.

"Shadow created me," Gregory said.

Pel blinked, and reached out into the magical web that surrounded him. He drew it down onto this Gregory, and really *looked* at him.

He looked human — but Pel could see that he wasn't quite. There were subtle differences, *extremely* subtle, detectable through magic, but probably by no other means. Pel stared intently.

Gregory's inner force, his magical essence, was smoother than a real human being's. It wasn't like the damaged magical core of a fetch, or the simplified one of a homunculus or monster, but it lacked the . . . the *texture* of a human's.

Just the way the artificial Nancy's essence did.

"You're a simulacrum," Pel guessed.

"Yes, sir," Gregory said.

"Was there a real Peter Gregory, then? What happened to him?"

"Shadow killed him, I believe; I'm not entirely sure."

The simulacrum seemed utterly undisturbed by the death of his original, and Pel shuddered; the matrix flickered eerily purple-white for a moment, reflecting his discomfort.

Pel looked away from the simulacrum for a moment and noticed Susan standing beside him, waiting patiently. He also felt the stranger in the fortress, down in the gallery — whoever it was was moving slowly, clearly in no hurry to confront the Brown Magician.

"Go sit down somewhere," Pel told Susan. "It may take awhile to straighten this out."

And he decided he didn't want the new arrival — the Imperial spy, if that's who it was — to come into the throne room just yet; the doors at the top of the stairs swung closed, and a tendril of the matrix sealed them shut.

Susan nodded and headed for one of the side doors.

"Where's Shadow?" Gregory asked as the Earthwoman departed. "Why are you in the matrix now?"

"Shadow's dead," Pel said, preparing to flash-fry the simulacrum if it proved necessary to stop an attack.

Gregory blinked, but did not question that.

"You spied for her, didn't you?" Pel asked.

Gregory nodded.

"Did she tell you what to do if she died?"

"Of course not," Gregory answered. "She didn't think she could die."

That was probably true, Pel thought — but he couldn't be sure; Shadow had been clever.

"Will you obey me now, as you did her?"

"Of course, if you want me to," Gregory replied. "You hold the power that made me, as Shadow did; you sit in her throne, the master of her fortress and her world. You are my God, as she was my Goddess."

Pel smiled, and began to dim down the matrix glare.

"Good," he said. "You spied on the Galactic Empire for her?"

"Yes."

"You know your way around there?"

"Yes."

"Are there other spies, as well? Captain Cahn thought there were."

"Oh, yes, sir; I am simply the one who was waiting by the gateway when it opened. I was due to report some time ago, but the gateway did not open on schedule, so I waited. By the time the opening finally appeared there were three of us taking turns waiting, and there are many more of us, placed throughout the Empire. Some are probably still waiting at other gateways."

"Excellent!" Pel grinned broadly. "Then listen, Peter Gregory — I have a new job for all of you. I suppose Shadow wanted information, and was planning all sorts of elaborate schemes, and wanted to conquer the Empire, but all *I* want are two people . . . two . . . two bodies. There's a woman, medium height, dark hair, named Nancy Brown — she was killed aboard a ship, I.S.S. *Emerald Princess*. And the other's a little girl, Rachel Brown; she died on Zeta Leo III. I want their bodies.

"You go back through that portal and tell the others — do whatever it takes to bring me those two.

"*Whatever* it takes."

Gregory nodded.

"Yes, sir," he said, as he turned back toward the portal.

Chapter Thirteen

"Do firearms work in Imperial space?" Johnston asked, pacing. Amy watched his feet moving across the tile floor of his office.

She was tired, and she wasn't sure how much was the after-effects of the abortion, how much was just weariness of this whole ongoing mess. She was back on Earth, and that was wonderful; Walter's child was gone, which was a relief; but was she *ever* going to get back to a normal life?

Beside her, Prossie frowned. "I'm not sure," she said. "I know that some tribes used projectile weapons before the invention of the blaster, but I don't know if they operated on the same principles as yours."

"Susan's gun worked in Faerie," Amy mentioned without looking up.

"*Magic* works in Faerie," Prossie pointed out. "Did Susan ever fire it in Imperial space?"

"I don't know," Amy said. "I don't think so."

"That copter — if it had got through . . ."

"Pel's digital watch didn't work in Imperial space, *or* in Faerie," Amy said. "I wouldn't want to be on the helicopter if it tried it, especially since the warp's out in the vacuum of space."

"It is?" Johnston was startled. "Is that why they wore the space suits?"

Amy looked up at him, equally startled. "Of course," she said. "Didn't we tell you that?"

"Not that I recall," Johnston said. "It doesn't matter, though. The warp's gone."

"You don't think they'll reopen it?"

"Frankly, Ms. Jewell — no, I don't. And neither do our psychics."

It took Amy a moment to realize who Johnston was referring to; she hadn't thought of that motley collection of people as "psychics." Little Angie Thompson was hardly a "psychic."

"How would they know?" Amy asked. "Did the Empire *tell* them?"

Johnston shook his head. "No, this is something Ms. Thorpe suggested.

There's a good deal of . . . of leakage in telepathic communication, on an unconscious level. Telepaths know things without realizing it, and sometimes convey that information without meaning to. Ms. Thorpe suggested that our four contactees might have picked up such information, and with her help we've developed some techniques for getting at it — questions asked so quickly that the answerer has no time to think, oblique references, and so on."

Amy looked at Prossie, who shrugged. "Back home, we all knew about leakage," Prossie said. "It wasn't safe to mention it, though. It violated the secrecy rules — but the truth was that anything any of us knew, we all knew, on an unconscious level."

Johnston nodded. "Mr. Miletti's been the most useful in that regard. He remains completely unaware of any contact on the conscious level, but he's answered several questions for us by simply replying without thinking about it."

Prossie explained, "We could never establish any conscious contact with Mr. Miletti — but we *knew* he was receptive on some level. I think that when we tried to reach him he must have gotten linked into the unconscious network, just as if he were a part of my family — and since it's unconscious, with no voluntary control, they can't just cut him off or keep anything secret now."

Johnston nodded. "And it's not just Miletti on this particular point, in any case — all four of them agree that the Empire is done with Earth."

Prossie sighed, and Amy wasn't sure if her reaction was relief or disappointment. This meant that the Empire wasn't hunting their rogue telepath anymore — but it also meant that she was cut off from her family, from her entire home universe.

At least, on a conscious level; Amy wondered whether that unconscious link might still be there, just as it was for Carleton Miletti.

Not that it mattered.

"Why are you worrying about guns, then?" she asked. "If the Empire's going to leave us alone, why don't we just forget about them? Besides, you can't get at them anyway, can you?"

"But *they* can get at *us*, Ms. Jewell," Johnston said, "and we have to be ready to deal with them if they ever decide to do that. By your own accounts, this Galactic Empire is a fairly aggressive imperial power, accustomed to doing pretty much whatever it pleases — there's no balance of power keeping it in check, is there?"

"Not that I ever heard of," Amy admitted.

"No, there isn't," Prossie said, very definitely. "The concept of a balance of power doesn't really even exist in the Empire anymore; they see themselves as the rightful rulers of the universe."

"But we aren't *in* their universe!" Amy protested.

"It wouldn't surprise me if they extended their doctrine, though," Johnston said. Prossie nodded.

"But you can't get *at* them," Amy pointed out.

"Well, we weren't planning on a preemptive strike, in any case," Johnston said. "The United States does not operate that way — not as a general thing," he added hastily, as Amy prepared to provide counter-examples. "However, it

seems prudent to consider our options, especially since this cut-off is a display
of bad faith on the Empire's part — they lied to us. We'll definitely want to talk
to Mr. Brown about this when we have a chance — he can provide access to the
Empire, if necessary. You suggested that yourself, Ms. Jewell; we're just taking
your own advice."

That was true enough, and Amy had to admit that she didn't entirely trust
the Empire. Back on Zeta Leo III those Imperial troops had seemed like the
cavalry coming to the rescue, but where were they when the monsters attacked
in Faerie? Where were they during the long march to Shadow's castle? And the
fact that they had sent Amy and the others to Faerie in the first place, instead
of safely home to Earth . . .

Susan Nguyen was dead because of that bit of Imperial arrogance. Not to
mention that about a dozen of the Empire's own men had died, as well.

But still, it seemed as if Johnston was going looking for trouble. The Empire
was gone, Amy and Prossie and Ted were safe at home, Shadow was dead, and
Pel had become a sort of demigod in Faerie — wasn't that a satisfactory solution?

It was good enough for Amy. If she could just get her home back and get
Johnston and all these other people to stop bothering her, she'd be satisfied.

"Furthermore," Johnston was saying, "now that the press has gotten involved, even though they haven't gone public yet, we don't want to get caught
unprepared . . ."

Amy scuffed her feet on the tiles and wished Johnston would shut up and
send her home.

*T*he Gregory simulacrum was gone, and the portal was closed; Susan and
Pel were alone in the throne room, excluding the pair of fetches Pel had
summoned.

And whoever it was outside the throne room door was waiting patiently.
He — or she, Pel couldn't be entirely certain from the perception through the
matrix — seemed to be sitting quietly, not particularly concerned about anything.

That was interesting; all Pel's previous visitors had been very nervous indeed.

Pel opened the door.

A man rose quickly and smoothly to his feet and stood on the landing,
shielding his eyes against the flickering glare of the matrix. "That you in there,
Brown?" he asked.

Pel blinked in astonishment. He stared through the magical light show and
fought down the emanations as quickly as he could.

The man wore peasant homespun and carried a rough sack with a drawstring
— and his boots were black Imperial military issue, dusty and worn, but
recognizable even at this distance. Peasants didn't wear such boots here, and
no nobleman would dress like that.

And the face . . .

"Wilkins!" Pel shouted, and the name rang eerily from the walls, carried by
the matrix.

Wilkins smiled. "Guess it *is* you," he said.

"Come in!" Pel called, delighted to see a familiar face, pleased to know that Wilkins had survived. "Come in!"

Wilkins ambled into the room, his sack over his shoulder, and belatedly noticed Susan. "Good morning, Miss Goyen," he said.

"Nguyen," Pel corrected. Susan didn't respond. Wilkins glanced at her sharply.

Pel was annoyed with Susan; this man was a long-lost friend, and she was just standing there, silent as a fetch. "I'm glad to see you," he said, addressing Wilkins.

"And I'm relieved to see you, Mr. Brown — at least, as best I *can* see you. What's making all those lights?"

"That's the matrix," Pel explained. "Shadow's magic. It's mine now." He completed the suppression, and the last sparkles died away, leaving a slightly run-down colonnaded room of stone, wood, cloth, and gilt. He came forward, hand outstretched, and the two men shook hands.

Wilkins appeared wary of the contact, but Pel kept the matrix forcibly restrained, and only flesh touched the Imperial's hand.

"How'd *that* happen, if you don't mind me asking?" Wilkins said.

"It's a long story," Pel answered.

"I'll listen or not, whichever you like," Wilkins said. "I guessed that something like this had happened when I heard the stories about a Brown Magician, but I wasn't completely *sure* until I heard your voice call my name just now."

"It can wait, then," Pel said. "I mean, you can probably guess the basics. What about you, though?"

"Well, after I got separated from the rest of you . . ."

"After you deserted us, you mean," Pel said, and Wilkins hesitated uncomfortably. "Oh, don't worry — if any of us had had any sense we wouldn't have come here. You kept yourself alive, which is more than Raven or Singer or Valadrakul or even Susan here can say."

Wilkins glanced uneasily at Susan.

"I brought her back," Pel explained. "Shadow hadn't done anything terrible to her — the others were all burned, but Susan had just had her heart stopped. She was dead for a few days, though."

"Is that why she's so quiet?"

Pel frowned. "She was always quiet," he said.

Wilkins swallowed.

"You were saying what happened after you left," Pel reminded him, eager to get the conversation back on track, and onto more comfortable topics.

"Oh," Wilkins said. "Well, there wasn't much to it. I didn't see any point in going on to face Shadow alone, or in going back to the shipwreck, either, because if anyone was going to rescue Lieutenant Dibbs they'd probably done it days ago, so I figured I was pretty much on my own. I just took odd jobs where I could, stole a few things when I couldn't see another way to manage — I was getting settled in, after a fashion, when the word came about Shadow being dead." He looked at Pel. "Is it really dead?"

Pel nodded. "She's dead, all right — Prossie Thorpe blasted her."

"Thorpe?" The expression on Wilkins' face was so odd that Pel wished he could read minds; it looked like a mix of startlement, fear, distaste, and other things as well. "Thorpe? Not you, or that wizard?"

"Well, I set it up, but Thorpe pulled the trigger," Pel explained. "Valadrakul was already dead by then." He mentally upbraided himself for getting back to the subject of death. "So did you see any of the others anywhere? Sawyer, maybe?"

"Wasn't Sawyer with you?" Wilkins asked, surprised.

"He turned back at the gate," Pel said. "And I think there were some of Dibbs' bunch we never accounted for."

"Did you account for *any* of them?"

Pel nodded, reluctantly — here he was again. "Shadow killed most of them; we saw the bodies. I buried them myself, after Shadow was dead." Trying once more to turn the conversation cheerful, he asked, "So, why'd you come here? I mean, I'm glad to see you, but were you just curious to see what had happened, or was there something in particular you were after?"

"I was hoping you could send me home," Wilkins said.

That was so obvious Pel couldn't imagine why he hadn't guessed it without asking.

"I mean," Wilkins added, "I was doing all right here, but it's not exactly a life of luxury, and it's not my *home.* I'd like to get back to the Empire."

The Empire.

Pel had just turned Shadow's entire network of spies loose on the Empire, trying to recover the remains of his wife and daughter.

Wilkins was not just Pel's old companion in adventure; he was an Imperial soldier.

Pel could send him through to the Empire, but the only places he could be sure Wilkins would wind up anywhere sufficiently civilized to be reasonably certain of getting home intact were the points where Shadow's spies reported.

That wouldn't do. Pel didn't know just what was on the other sides of those closed portals, but he had visions of dropping an Imperial soldier into what amounted to an enemy headquarters.

Somebody would get hurt. And the body recovery might be hindered.

"I don't think I can do that," he said.

"W̶e've lost Wilkins," Brian Hall reported.

"What do you mean, lost him?" Markham demanded. "Is he dead?"

"I don't know, sir, but he's in Shadow's fortress — or the Brown Magician's, whichever it is. We can't contact him at all anymore; the interference is much too strong."

Markham put down his pen. "Remind me," he said. "Why was Wilkins going into the fortress to begin with?"

"Because, sir, he believed that this Brown Magician was the same Pellinore Brown who we had sent into Shadow's universe with Colonel Carson and Lord Raven and the others, and he wanted Brown to create a space-warp, or a magical portal, or whatever you want to call it, back to the Empire, so that he, Wilkins, could return here and report in."

"And do you think he's right? That this Pellinore Brown has somehow usurped Shadow's rule?"

"Well, sir, that's what all the evidence indicates, both from Shadow's universe and from Brown's native universe."

Markham nodded. "True enough." He didn't say any more than that aloud, but Hall read the next question from his mind — Markham had authorized such minor intrusions, to increase efficiency.

"I have no idea how Mr. Brown could have accomplished it," Hall said. "But then, I don't understand Shadow's power, either. It really does seem to be a sort of magic."

"Magic is misunderstood science," Markham reminded him.

"In our reality, yes, sir," Hall said, "but in Faerie?"

"The laws of physics may change," Markham replied, "but the laws of logic don't, and science is applied logic. This 'magic' Shadow used, and that our Mr. Brown appears to have mastered, has to have rules and limits and all the rest, all subject to determination by the scientific method. And if he can learn and use them, anyone can."

Hall didn't argue.

"So Wilkins expects to be sent back to us?" Markham asked.

"Yes, sir."

"You think Brown can do it?"

"I don't know, sir. He did apparently send Prossie Thorpe and the others to Earth."

"True." Markham considered for a moment. "It seems to me," he said, "that we should expect Spaceman Wilkins to reappear somewhere in the Empire at any moment now. I want to know when it happens — I want to know where and when, and I want him brought here to Base One as fast as humanly possible. You broadcast that to your whole family, Hall — I want every telepath in the Empire to spread the word. I want Ronald Wilkins."

"Yes, sir," Hall said. He saluted sloppily, and exchanged a glance with his second cousin, Markham's personal telepath.

"I'll tell George," that man said.

Markham wasn't sure who George was — some other telepath, presumably. "And inform Marshal Albright immediately," Markham said. "I don't want any problems with him."

"Yes, sir. I'll tell Stuart." Stuart was Albright's personal telepath. Hall hesitated. "What about Under-Secretary Bascombe?"

"What *about* him? It's not his problem anymore."

"Yes, sir," Hall agreed.

John Bascombe drew a circle on the desktop with his finger. "So we've lost Wilkins," he said.

"We've lost contact," Carrie Hall agreed.

"What about Best?"

"Oh, he's fine; he's reached Shadowmarsh, and is waiting there for further orders."

Bascombe looked up. "And has anyone *given* him further orders?"

Carrie hesitated. "No, sir," she said. "Telepathic communication isn't reliable, so close to the fortress, and his messenger, Spaceman Poole, hasn't reached the rendezvous point yet."

"But we know he's coming?"

"Yes, sir."

Bascombe frowned.

He was out of the matter now, in bureaucratic limbo. He hadn't officially been reprimanded or removed, he was still Under-Secretary for Interdimensional Affairs — but the telepaths and messengers all reported directly to Markham or Albright, and no one invited Bascombe to their conferences or meetings. He had been shunted aside.

And he bitterly resented it.

He had ordered Carrie Hall to bring him up to date. He had had to leave his office and track down an unassigned messenger to find her, and the embarrassment rankled. He had seen her hesitate when he first told her to report what was happening, and he had known that she was trying to decide whether he still had the authority to ask that.

The damnable mutant bitch had probably actually had to check with other telepaths to decide whether or not he, John Bascombe, an Imperial under-secretary, had the right to give orders to a stinking mind-reading freak!

He needed to get himself back into things, and this, he thought, might be the opportunity. No one had given Best his orders yet. It might be a simple oversight, or it might be an attempt by Markham and Albright to cut Imperial Intelligence out of the potential political profits in this operation, or it might be part of an arcane maneuver in a duel *between* Markham and Albright. Albright might be deliberately trying to sabotage Best's mission.

Bascombe thought that in a way, he'd like to see Albright best Markham — it would be a pleasant petty revenge for the way Markham had treated Bascombe — but on the other hand, as a career move, it would be better to back Markham. Albright wasn't in position to help Bascombe as much as Markham was.

And backing Imperial Intelligence against either or both of them was probably a smart move, in any case. Imperial Intelligence was certainly more dangerous to an ambitious career than either the military or the Department of Science, and potentially more valuable. The Smarts could make or break anyone.

And if it was just an oversight — well, he didn't care to be the scapegoat if someone spotted it later.

"Send a messenger," he told Carrie. "Through the warp, I mean. I'll write up Best's orders immediately."

He opened a drawer and looked for paper.

The fact that he hadn't yet decided what orders to write, that he had given no thought to what orders would best serve the Empire's interested, troubled him not at all.

Chapter Fourteen

"It's creepy," Carleton Miletti complained. "I know all this stuff, and I don't know how or why, or what half of it means."

"I don't *care* what any of it means," Margaret Thompson answered. "I just want to take Angie and go home."

"In that case, Ms. Thompson," Major Johnston said from the doorway, "I think we can oblige you."

The five looked up, startled.

"Are you giving up the project?" Aldridge asked.

"No, not at all," Johnston said. "We may want to call you back again, if anything develops. For now, though, events seem to be at a standstill, and there's no reason to inconvenience all of you."

"So you're sending us home?" Miletti asked.

Johnston hesitated; his mouth twisted wryly. "No, Mr. Miletti," he said. "We're saying that Ms. Thompson can take her daughter and go home, if she wants, and Mr. Aldridge and Mr. Blaisdell can go, as well, if they choose — we'll provide transportation right to their doors, and an escort if they want, as well as a lump-sum payment as compensation for the time and inconvenience we've put them to. But they don't *have* to go — we'd be just as pleased if they stayed here."

"They? What about *me?*" Miletti demanded.

"Well, Mr. Miletti," Johnston said, "we do want to keep one contact available at all times, just in case, and you've been so successful that we'd prefer it to be you." Before Miletti could protest, Johnston raised a hand. "We won't insist; you're a free citizen, and if you walk out that door right now I won't stop you. However, I would advise against it."

"Why?"

"Because we would find it necessary to ask other governmental agencies to keep a *very* close eye on you, Mr. Miletti. The I.R.S., for example. And your local police. And of course, the FBI is already involved in this operation."

"You're threatening me with harassment, in front of witnesses!"

Johnston didn't answer that; instead, he went on, "I'm sure that we can come to some comfortable arrangement; we don't insist that you be *here*, only that you be available on a moment's notice, and that you talk regularly with one of our people. I understand you live not far from here; do you have a portable phone? If not, we'll provide one. And a pager. That should be more comfortable than wearing a wire at all times, don't you think?"

Miletti stared at him in horror.

"I still don't see why you won't send me home, Mr. Brown," Wilkins said.

"I told you, it's nothing personal," Brown answered edgily. "It's just that I've sent someone into the Empire to get something I want, and I don't want to risk you interfering."

"Why the hell would I interfere?"

"No reason," Pel admitted. "I'm just being cautious."

Wilkins thought he was being a good bit more than cautious, but decided it wouldn't do any good to say so again. They had been through this argument several times over the last few days, to no avail.

At least this time he'd gotten something vaguely resembling an explanation; up until now, Brown had refused to give any reason at all.

He'd been willing to talk about almost anything else — Wilkins had eventually got the whole story of how Pel Brown had defeated Shadow and become Pelbrun the Brown Magician, told piece by piece and gradually assembled into a fairly coherent whole — but this was the first time he'd said anything about sending someone else into the Empire.

What in all the worlds could the absolute ruler of an entire universe want from the Empire? Why from the *Empire,* and not from Earth? Pel was from Earth; wouldn't that be where he'd want something from?

"I'm afraid I'll have to ask you to leave the room now, Wilkins," Brown said.

Wilkins stared at the polychrome glare for a moment, then shrugged. "Let me know when you can send me home, all right?" he said. Then he turned and walked out, not through the side door that led to the fortress living quarters, but through the big double door that led to the stairs and down to the grand entrance hall.

"I'm taking a walk," he announced. Not that Brown had asked.

Wilkins wanted a breath of fresh air. He'd have to settle for the nasty stuff that covered Shadowmarsh, which was foul even by the standards of this unpleasant world, but at least he'd be out of doors.

"It's honest work," Best said with a shrug. He dropped another handful of berries into his bucket.

"It may be honest, and it's certainly work, but that doesn't mean I have to like it," Begley replied, as he untangled his trousers from the thorns of a berry bush. "How long do we wait? What if Poole didn't make it back, or whoever's bringing our orders gets killed on the way here? What if he can't *find* us, because we're down here in the bogs picking berries?"

"I give it a month," Best replied. "If we haven't heard anything by then, we pack it in and go back to the rendezvous."

Begley looked at him silently for a moment, then announced, "I'm going back up to the highway, to see if I can see anything."

"Please yourself," Best said, plucking another handful.

*F*or a moment, Pel considered opening a portal to Earth and sending a fetch, or maybe Susan, to bring back some clothes and toiletries. Getting a place ready for Nancy and Rachel, complete with familiar clothes and belongings, would keep him occupied, keep his mind off the delays. The simulacra in the Empire seemed to be taking a long time to deliver the bodies.

But then, he was impatient, he knew he was impatient, and after all, they weren't necessarily even on the right *planet.* The Galactic Empire had faster-than-light travel — in their universe there was apparently no reason not to — but it still wasn't anywhere near instantaneous, and each of the thousands of inhabited planets was, if not as big as all of Earth, at least the size of Mars.

It might be weeks, or months, before he had his wife's corpse available to resuscitate. Setting up a room for her now would just add to the frustration. And he'd have to resist the temptation to let the Nancy simulacrum use things — he was constantly fighting the urge to treat her as Nancy, or to try to turn her into a closer substitute for Nancy.

Besides, he reminded himself, he had an appointment. That was why he had sent Wilkins away — it was time to check on Peter Gregory, to see what progress was being made.

He worked quickly; the portal-opening procedure, which Shadow and the other wizards would have called a spell, had become very familiar in the last few days. He twisted his perceptions through the matrix, in a direction that wasn't conceivable to anyone but a matrix wizard, and found the weak spot between realities.

Gregory was waiting; the instant the portal opened, he stepped through.

He looked worried, and Pel felt suddenly nervous. Simulacra weren't prone to worry — generally, they just went along with whatever happened, untroubled by guilt, responsibility, or fear. Pel had noticed that first in the imitation Nancy, who would agree to anything he proposed — he suspected that she would have smiled and nodded and obeyed if he ordered her to cut her own throat. Gregory and Shadow's other spies had all behaved similarly, as if their lives, being artificial creations, had no real value.

Maybe it was because they'd had no childhoods. Maybe it was something inherent in the matrix magic. Pel didn't know, and didn't really care; he'd simply observed that the characteristic was there.

So how could Gregory be worried?

"Master," Gregory said, "Felton's been captured."

Pel blinked, then asked, "Who's Felton?"

"One of our agents," Gregory replied. "Augustus Felton. Shadow replaced him about two years ago. He's a military records clerk. Balding, mid-fifties, overweight . . ."

"That's enough," Pel interrupted. "How'd it happen?"

"As nearly as we can determine," Gregory explained, "Felton was checking through the files, trying to find where your wife's remains were, and when he couldn't find what he wanted in the regular files he tried to get into the records of Imperial Intelligence, and got caught in a restricted area."

"He's in prison, then?"

"We don't know *where* he is — Imperial Intelligence operates very secretively."

"That figures." Pel stared at Gregory for a moment, trying to think. Then he shrugged; despite his two-week stay at Base One, he didn't know what the Empire was like, and Gregory did. "Now what?" he asked.

"I don't know," Gregory said. "Whatever you tell us to do. I'm sorry Felton failed you."

"Not *your* fault," Pel said. He didn't see where this was really a big problem, and he wondered why Gregory had looked so concerned. "You tell everyone to get on with it and get me those bodies, and to be more careful, that's all. And if you can find Felton and get him out, that's fine, but it isn't important. Finding the bodies, *that's* what's important!"

Gregory nodded, his expression again cheerful. "Yes, O Great One," he said with a bow.

He turned, and Pel watched him vanish back through the portal.

It occurred to Pel, a little belatedly, that perhaps he should have ordered Gregory, and through him the others, to keep the search for the bodies quiet — a simulacrum would gladly die rather than disobey orders, or at least so Gregory had assured him, so he wouldn't have had to worry about Felton breaking under interrogation.

But he hadn't given such orders.

Well, Felton would probably figure out for himself that he was supposed to keep quiet.

And if the Empire *did* find out that Pel wanted the bodies, so what?

Celia Howe was not stupid; quite the contrary. She could hardly have risen as far as she had in Imperial Intelligence if she were a fool. All the same, she came very close to making a serious error regarding the proper disposition of the information received from telepathic interrogation of the records clerk, Augustus Felton.

It would have been a natural mistake. After all, if Felton was working for the Brown Magician of Faerie, that made his apprehension an interdimensional affair, and reporting it to the Under-Secretary for Interdimensional Affairs would appear to be the proper, sensible thing to do.

Howe trembled when she thought how close she had come to doing just that.

Fortunately for her career and her political ambitions, she had paused at the last minute — perhaps it was something in the telepath's expression, or perhaps the telepath was illegally projecting a bit, or perhaps Howe's well-developed sense of self-preservation had awakened a bit late — and had reconsidered.

A check of recent reports, and the whereabouts of various appointees, made it clear that Under-Secretary Bascombe was currently out of favor. He was still in office, and would have to be informed if he asked, but if Intelligence, in the form of Howe or her representative, could report directly to someone higher than Bascombe, that would be a better move in the continuing struggle for status and power.

Of course, Howe could have just passed the information to her own superior and let *him* worry about it, but that wouldn't do her any good, not really. She wasn't going to make a friend of Stanley Winter, and Stanley Winter wasn't going to help her advance in the service.

And jumping to the next level up, or straight to the Director at the level above that, would make too many enemies — not just Stan Winter, but others as well. No, she was best served by passing this information out of Intelligence herself, while her written report wound its way through channels to the uppermost echelons.

But telling Bascombe was out.

Though Secretary Markham was the next obvious possibility, Howe hesitated. Marshal Albright was also at Base One, and the military had been active in Faerie. And there was always the possibility of going clear to the top, to the General Secretary or even the Emperor himself — though bothering His Imperial Majesty with something he considered beneath his notice was a good way to end a career completely.

Howe, upon consideration, didn't think this little affair was worthy of the Imperial notice. That left three possibilities.

The General Secretary, of course, had his own ways of obtaining information; he would know soon enough, and he wasn't particularly pleased by attempts at ingratiation.

That left Markham or Albright.

She looked at the notes she had made of the telepath's oral report. Felton's assignment had been to locate and retrieve two corpses — he didn't know why anyone in Faerie wanted these particular bodies, only that he and his cell of Faerie's spy network were under orders to obtain them by any means available.

It was interesting to learn that Faerie's spy network still existed and functioned, despite Shadow's death, and despite Operation Spotlight, which had rooted Shadow's agents out of the ruling circles of half a dozen rebel worlds — and a few Imperial ones as well. Howe had not been aware that other spies continued to operate, and she suspected that her superiors still didn't know it.

And they *were* active, and wanted these bodies, a woman and a child.

Well, who *had* the corpses?

Howe didn't know — but she would find out. If it was the military, she would report to Albright. If it was the Department of Science, she would report to Markham.

If neither organization had the corpses, or if each had one of the two, then she would tell Albright *and* Markham, she decided.

As for learning where the corpses were, she didn't worry about how she might do that. That was exactly the sort of thing Imperial Intelligence had always been best at, she thought with a wry smile — finding where the bodies were buried.

Sometimes Pel considered just sending a messenger to the clearing in the

Sunderland woods, and through that warp the Empire kept opening there, to ask the Empire for the bodies. It surely wouldn't be a big deal for them to deliver Nancy and Rachel.

On the other hand, somehow he suspected that the Empire wouldn't cooperate with even so simple a request. He'd probably get caught up in the bureaucracy somehow, or they'd demand some absurd payment.

Better to get them on his own, if he could. He could always ask the Empire openly if other methods didn't work.

It wasn't, after all, as if the Empire had openly sent their representatives into Faerie. No ambassadors had turned up at the fortress, asking for audience. Instead they were apparently sending spies.

Well, Pel had spies of his own, and Gregory and the others seemed fairly confident that they could, in time, locate Nancy and Rachel.

He sat in his throne, drumming his fingers, while magic and light played in shifting patterns through the air around him.

*B*egley looked eastward, toward the Sunderland forests — though of course he couldn't see that far, even on this oversized planet with its distant horizons. He could see scattered houses, a few trees, thousands upon thousands of berry bushes and acres upon acres of bogland, and the narrow path the locals considered a highway cutting its way through half a mile or so of the countryside before it was lost in the background.

Nothing moved anywhere on the highway, so far as he could see.

He turned to the west, where Shadow's fortress thrust up from the horizon beyond a vast open marsh, at the end of a narrow causeway.

A man was walking on the causeway, a very long way off.

"Someone's coming this way, from the fortress," he called down to Best. "Should we talk to him?"

Best looked up.

"Couldn't hurt," he said. "At least, not if you're careful."

Begley nodded. "I'll be careful," he said.

*W*ilkins ambled along the causeway, bored and aggravated. He should have been back at Base One by now. If it weren't for this mysterious secret project Brown was working on, he *would* have been back.

If he had been stuck here for good, that would have been less than ideal, but he could have lived with it. If he got home, that would be fine. But this dismal *waiting,* caught in between, was annoying.

He scanned the horizon, planning to turn back — after all, he didn't have anywhere else to go, and the hot, swampy air out here wasn't much of an improvement over the dusty dimness of the fortress.

A movement caught his eye.

Someone was standing on the highway, off in the distance — Wilkins couldn't tell whether the figure was man or woman, whether it stood inside or outside the boundary of Shadowmarsh, but someone was standing on the highway.

Wilkins paused, and thought for a moment.

Nothing was happening back at the fortress, so far as he could see. What harm would it do to walk on out and say hello to whoever that was? It would take time, of course — maybe an hour each way — but so what? It would relieve the boredom.

And that might be a woman — maybe one as bored and lonely as he was.

He turned eastward and trotted on.

*T*he messenger crouched quickly and listened.

Yes, those were footsteps, coming toward him through the forest.

He hated this. This was not what he had signed up for. Fighting was one thing; running messages around Base One was another; but neither of those had anything to do with sneaking through a huge alien forest, trying to find a couple of spies on a hostile planet where science was all cockeyed, aircars and blasters didn't work, and he didn't have any roads to follow or addresses to find.

Samuel Best was reportedly waiting at the east end of the causeway across Shadowmarsh — how was he supposed to find that in this wilderness? Was he supposed to ask the natives for directions, and hope they wouldn't put a bunch of arrows in him or tie him to a stake and burn him? It wasn't as if there were any maps — no one had done an orbital survey, or even brought back whatever crude doodles the locals used.

He wished that idiot Bascombe had picked someone else to carry his message. Wasn't this sort of thing what telepaths were for?

He brushed against a bush, then snatched his elbow away as the leaves rustled loudly.

The footsteps stopped.

"Anyone there?" a voice called.

The messenger hesitated. The language was English, but then the locals here supposedly spoke English, as well. The accent didn't seem exotic.

"My name's Poole," the voice said. "That looks like Imperial purple behind that thicket, assuming I'm not imagining things. If it is, I'm on your side."

The voice didn't *sound* hostile. Cautiously, the messenger stood up.

"Good morning," the man who called himself Poole said, smiling. "What brings you here? Are there others? You aren't one of Lieutenant Dibbs' men, are you?"

The man wasn't in uniform; he was wearing a baggy, ugly woolen outfit, brown and dark gray. His hair was blond and short, though, and how would a native know about a Lieutenant Dibbs?

If the truth be known, the messenger had never heard of Lieutenant Dibbs, but somehow that just made it all the more convincing.

"I've got orders for Samuel Best," the messenger said.

"No shit?" Poole grinned. "Well, I'll be damned. He sent me back to get further orders — you've saved me some hiking."

"You said your name was Poole . . ."

"Right — Abner Poole, Imperial Intelligence. I'm with Best. Come on, I'll take you to him."

For a moment the messenger hesitated anew; this was all almost *too* easy.

But then, the man said he'd been on his way back for orders, and where did this miserable trail go other than the clearing where the space-warp came out?

"Right," the messenger said. He stepped out from behind the bushes.

"So what are the orders?" Poole asked curiously, as the two set out westward.

"You'll have to wait," the messenger said. "They're for Best."

Poole shrugged. "Good enough," he said. He strolled on, leading the way toward Shadowmarsh.

*I*t was simple enough to find the little girl; her body had been recovered in a pacification operation on a backwater planet called Zeta Leo III, at the start of the recent campaign to bring Shadow's network of puppet governments into the Empire. The corpse had been brought to Base One, and was in cold storage in the zero-gee lockers near the core of the hollowed-out asteroid.

The military had offered it to the Department of Science, in case someone wanted to dissect it and see if Earthpeople were different from normal humans, but so far no one in Science had shown an interest. After a moment's consideration, Howe removed a few records and made sure that no one ever would.

The other body was much harder to track down. Howe could find no records about it except the interviews with the Earthpeople, where Nancy Brown's death was reported.

Nancy Brown had died during the capture of *Emerald Princess* — but her body wasn't aboard when Zeta Leo III was taken and *Emerald Princess* recovered.

Well, why would the pirates have kept it? They had undoubtedly shoved it out the airlock and left it to drift in space.

Celia Howe frowned. That might be difficult. Finding a floating corpse . . .

They did know the ship's course, and running a heavy gravity generator along the route might turn up something. The Department of Science had done a few fishing expeditions that way in the past.

The military had their own equipment, of course; gravity generators had plenty of uses in combat. There was no need to bring in Science.

It was time, though, to talk to Marshal Albright.

Chapter Fifteen

"We know where one of them is," Gregory explained. "Rachel Brown's body is in cold storage at Base One. We haven't located Nancy Brown yet, though." He hesitated, then asked, "Do you want us to bring you Rachel?"

Pel thought about that, and felt tears welling up; the matrix swirled an uncomfortable shade of blue and splashed up the throne room walls. His throat tightened, and for a moment he couldn't speak.

He missed Rachel so much — but bringing her back here, to a strange place where her father radiated color and light, where zombies walked the halls, and where her mother was dead . . .

And besides, if Gregory and the others were to steal Rachel back, it might alert the Empire and make it that much harder to recover Nancy.

He swallowed, and managed to speak.

"Not yet," he said. "But the minute you find Nancy, get them both."

Wilkins was disappointed; it wasn't a woman, or anyone interesting at all. It was just a couple of berry-pickers working unusually close to the edge of the marsh.

He'd come this far, though, he figured he might as well go on. Especially since one of them, the one who'd been on the highway to begin with, had spotted him; now they were both standing there, talking quietly and watching him approach.

Wilkins didn't really think there'd be any trouble if he turned and headed back to the fortress, but he hated to think they might think they'd scared him off.

"Good morrow, gentlemen!" he called. The locals seemed to consider that a normal greeting.

"And to you, sir!" the taller one called back — not that either of them was particularly tall; the people of Faerie ran a bit short, by Imperial standards, and Wilkins wasn't sure if it was the gravity or the diet that was responsible.

Probably both, he decided.

These two weren't runts, though — just middling.

And they hadn't turned and run, nor called any threats, nor just stood there silently the way most peasants usually did. Maybe they'd be interesting after all.

"My name's Wilkins," Wilkins said — he was close enough now that shouting was unnecessary. A native — a human native, anyway, not the dwarfs or gnomes or whatever they were that he'd met once or twice — would probably have phrased it differently, getting "hight" or "yclept" in there, but Wilkins didn't

feel like dealing with that just now, and these two looked bright enough to
figure out what he meant even if he didn't talk like an old book.

For a moment, the pair of strangers seemed to take that in stride. Then the
taller one's eyes widened.

"Wilkins, did you say?"

Wilkins stopped walking a few feet further away than he had originally
intended. Warily, he said, "Yes, sir — do I know you?" He didn't remember
meeting this fellow anywhere, but he'd offended a few people, mostly women,
and his name might have been spread around.

"Spaceman First Class Ronald Wilkins?"

Now Wilkins' own eyes widened; he stared.

He should have realized. These two were too clean, their blond hair too
short, their beards still only half-grown. "Who're you?" he asked.

The taller one stepped forward and held out a hand. "Samuel Best, Imperial
Intelligence," he said.

Wilkins hesitated for half a second. The man was Intelligence. That could
mean a treason charge, a desertion charge, that could mean *anything* — shaking
that hand might be his own death sentence, and in any case, to Wilkins
touching an Intelligence man would be like touching a rat.

On the other hand, offending an Intelligence man was a very bad idea, very
bad indeed. Wilkins stepped forward and took the proffered hand.

"I hadn't expected to find you alive," Best said, as he released Wilkins' hand.
"Are any of the others with you? Do you know what's happened to them?"

"Which others?" Wilkins asked. "Do you mean the Earthpeople?"

"The Earthpeople, or Lieutenant Dibbs, or anyone . . . look, you have a lot
to tell us. Have a seat, have some of these berries — sorry we don't have anything
to drink." He gestured to the buckets and a hummock of dry grass. "Oh, this
is Begley. He's in Intelligence, too," he added as an afterthought.

Together, the three men settled to the ground.

*H*owe's concern about which cabinet officer to tell had been irrelevant,
she saw; the first thing Marshal Albright had done was to call Secretary
Markham in to hear the news.

"You know, at first glance," Markham remarked, as he twiddled with a pen,
"it would seem perfectly natural for this Pellinore Brown to want to recover
the bodies of his wife and child."

Albright nodded. "I thought of that," he said. "It's the *method* that has me
puzzled — and concerned. Why is he using Shadow's spies? For that matter,
why are Shadow's spies still *here*? Shouldn't they all have been recalled? I suppose
I should have known better than to have believed that Operation Spotlight
had really broken the back of Shadow's whole network of subversion and
espionage, but this Brown Magician was supposed to be on our side — or at
least, not hostile. It seems hostile to be sneaking around this way, though,
instead of just asking for his family. He hasn't communicated openly with us
at all — our only sources of information have been our own spies, both

telepathic and normal. If it weren't for them, we wouldn't even know that Shadow was dead, or who had replaced it."

"And even there, he's deliberately blocked all telepathic contact with his government," Markham pointed out. "No one in his fortress can be read."

"And our telepath on the spot, Proserpine Thorpe, went rogue," Albright agreed. "Probably subverted by this Brown. Hardly a friendly act."

"And Earth's government, the United States — they held our men hostage demanding recognition," Markham added. "Brown's an Earthman originally."

Howe didn't follow this; she wasn't familiar with the Thorpe case, or recent actions on Earth. She saw which way the wind was blowing, though.

"Shall I have Felton shot?" she asked.

Albright and Markham glanced quickly at each other; then Albright shook his head.

"Not yet," he said.

I can just climb up a goddamned *ladder?*" Wilkins demanded. "Why in bloody hell didn't they lower one *sooner,* then, before Dibbs and the rest got butchered?"

Best shrugged. "They don't tell me everything," he said. "Hell, half the time they don't even tell me what I'm supposed to be doing, or half the information I need to do it."

Wilkins snorted. "I can believe it," he said. He looked back at the marsh for a moment, considering.

"Listen," he said, "I don't know what our Mr. Brown is up to out there in his castle, but it's taking too damn long to suit me. Maybe he'd send me home tomorrow — but for all I know, it'd be next year at Donalmas before he saw fit to do it, and if I walk back up to Sunderland I'll have sore feet, but I'll be back at Base One in a fortnight."

Best nodded. "They'll be glad to hear from you, if they have any sense."

"And if they *have* closed the fucking warp, I'll just come back here, and my temper's going to be foul enough after that walk that Brown had damned well *better* send me home!"

Begley laughed nervously.

"Either of you care to join me?" Wilkins asked.

Begley's laughter died; he glanced warily sideways at Best.

Best shook his head.

"'Fraid not," he said. "We have our orders — such as they are — and I said I'd wait here until I got further instructions. So I wait here."

Wilkins shrugged. "Suit yourself," he said.

*W*ilkins has emerged from the fortress," Brian Hall reported.

Markham leaned back in his chair and looked up at the telepath. He didn't need to say anything to convey his question.

"Pelbrun the Brown Magician, ruler of Faerie, is indeed the Earthman Pellinore Brown; Wilkins heard the entire story from Brown's own lips, though he didn't bother to remember most of it, and our link is sufficiently tenuous that we can't recover anything he's not consciously thinking about. Wilkins met our man Best on the road, and the two exchanged information, so we were able to pick up some of the details from that."

Markham nodded, and Hall knew that the details could wait.

"Wilkins is on his way back to our standing space-warp."

"Good," Markham said. Then he frowned. "Wasn't he going to have Brown send him back?"

Hall nodded. "Yes, sir — but Brown refused. He told Wilkins that he had sent someone into the Empire to get something, and could not risk Wilkins interfering with that; he would only send Wilkins when he had obtained whatever it is he's after. Wilkins had no idea what that might be, or how long this might take, and finally left the fortress in disgust. It was sheer good luck that he encountered Best so quickly."

"Sent someone to get something?"

"Yes, sir. It might have been the bodies. It might have been something else."

"Have you been snooping, Hall?"

"Not intentionally, sir."

"But you know about the bodies. I suppose all you telepaths do."

"Not consciously, sir, but the information does tend to leak, and I *am* working on related matters."

Markham knew well that information leaked among telepaths; fortunately, most of them were very good at keeping their mouths shut around most *non*-telepaths. Fear of summary execution could do that.

Of course, they would blab to anyone high enough in the Imperial government the minute someone asked the right question — fear of summary execution did that, too.

"What's Best doing now?" he asked. "Is he coming back with Wilkins?"

"No, sir; he's still awaiting orders. I believe they're on the way."

Markham nodded, leaning back still farther, hands folded across his belly.

Then abruptly he sat up, startled, as the telepath's words registered.

"Orders are on the way?" he demanded.

"Yes, sir."

"I didn't send any orders."

"A messenger went through the warp two or three days ago, I believe," the telepath said.

"At whose direction? Who wrote those orders?"

"It wasn't Marshal Albright," Hall assured him hastily, unable to ignore the suspicion of a political double-cross that suddenly dominated Markham's thoughts. "And it wasn't Intelligence, either; it was Under-Secretary Bascombe."

"Bascombe?" Markham straightened further. "That idiot?"

"Yes, sir."

For a moment Markham stared at the telepath; then he glanced at the door.

"Bascombe sent Best in the first place," he said. "And Best's in Intelligence."

"Yes, sir."

"Does Albright know about this?"

"Not yet, sir — but I'm sure he'll find out. You know how it is."

"Yes, I know — you mutants can't keep a goddamn secret for five minutes." Markham knew that was unfair, that it usually took either Intelligence or someone of cabinet rank to pry secrets out of the telepaths, but he didn't care about being fair right now. "All right," he said, "call Albright's telepath for me, tell him I want to talk. And try not to mention this to Celia Howe — you or any of your family."

"Yes, sir," Hall said. "But . . ."

"I know," Markham said. "Intelligence will find out. But I'd like to talk to Albright first."

*T*he purple uniform was a dead giveaway; Wilkins knew from half a mile away that he had spotted another friendly face. He assumed at first that the other man was a native guide, but there was never any question about the messenger. He *had* to be an Imperial.

Convincing them of his own identity was a bit trickier; the messenger was nervous and knew nothing at all about this world or who'd been there before him, and Poole, unlike Best, hadn't memorized the complete roster of Colonel Carson's ill-fated command.

Once he had convinced them, the conversation was much shorter than his talk with Best — Poole and Simons weren't interested in the details of how he'd survived or who was running things, and had little to add to what Best had already told him.

He gave them directions for finding Best and Begley, got directions to aid his own memory of where the wreck of I.S.S. *Christopher* lay, and then headed on eastward.

*A*lbright and Markham stood side by side, watching as the research ship I.S.S. *Magnet* settled smoothly into her docking cradle. The telepaths had already assured them that the ship had found and collected a dead woman, but even so, Markham had some last-minute doubts. While space was immense, Nancy Brown hadn't been the only one to die aboard *Emerald Princess*; how sure were they that this was the right corpse?

And if it wasn't, was it because the Brown Magician's agents had already somehow recovered the one they wanted?

And what was Brown up to, anyway? Why were these corpses so important to him? Why hadn't he just *asked* for them?

The ship was down, the docking bay doors grinding slowly shut; Markham turned away from the thick glass of the window.

"I want to see this for myself," he said. "You coming?"

"I'll watch from here," Albright said.

Markham shrugged. "Please yourself."

By the time he emerged from the stairwell the gauge by the door showed the docking bay at 30% Terran sea-level air pressure and rising; Markham forced the latch and, with the help of the entry guard, heaved the door open.

Air whooshed past, almost sweeping him out into the bay; his ears popped. He let the wind carry him forward, across twenty feet of steel flooring, until he put up a hand and caught a fin to stop his progress.

The fin was hot steel — one of the guidance vanes for a collection bin on *Magnet*'s side, hot with waste heat from the ship's gravity generators. Markham snatched his fingers away.

He gasped for breath — the air was still thin in here — and glanced up, first at the side of the ship looming over him, then back at the observation area. Albright was shouting something, but Markham couldn't hear anything but roaring wind; he supposed the Imperial Marshal was chastising him for hurrying out here before the pressure was equalized.

Markham didn't care about that; he looked up at the collection bin just above his head. It was tightly closed, the heavy shutter holding in whatever the gravity generators had drawn out of the void.

There were other, identical bins elsewhere, a girdle of five of them encircling *Magnet*'s waist. The corpse could be in any of them, even the one on the underside that was only accessible from the service sump.

The rush of air was slowing, and a loud thump sounded; Markham looked for its source and saw that the ship's main hatch was opening.

"Come on," Markham shouted, "get on with it! I want to see her!"

A helmeted head appeared in the doorway. "She's not pretty, sir," the spaceman said.

"You think I give a tinker's dam what she looks like? Open those shutters!"

"You can get a look at her from in here, if you want."

"Can I?" Markham had never before had any use for *Magnet*, and had little idea how she operated.

"Yes, sir."

"Show me." Markham hurried to the hatchway, where the spaceman reached down and caught his arm, boosting him up the yard or so between the floor of the docking bay and the floor of the airlock.

Together, the two men made their way into the ship's interior, through bare steel passages that gave no indication which of the curving surfaces were meant as walls, which as floors or ceilings. Markham remembered that when the massive gravity generators, capable of drawing in anything that would fit in the bins, were in use, they made it impossible to maintain ordinary shipboard artificial gravity. The crew had to tolerate the spillover, which would draw them toward the generators, so that "up" and "down" would be distorted all over the ship.

When that was happening, Markham judged that this straightforward corridor would become a slanting, treacherous tunnel. The grab bars along one side, he realized, would be rungs of a ladder.

"She's in Number Four," the spaceman said, pointing diagonally upward. He spun the wheel to undog the circular hatch at the end of the passage, swung the heavy portal open, and led the way into a peculiar space, a horizontal cylinder some thirty feet in diameter, webbed with catwalks and struts that were built at nightmarishly contradictory angles. The air here was thick and hot; Markham could sense the heat radiating from the far side.

The gravity generators were just beyond that bulkhead.

The spaceman wasn't giving any guided tours, though; he said, "This way," and pointed to a strangely-angled staircase leading up and to the left.

Markham followed. The spaceman paused long enough at the next hatchway to unclip a hand-held electric light from its bracket, and a moment later the two men were crawling through a narrow steel tube where that lamp's dim glow, largely blocked by the spaceman's body, was the only light. The air was hot and stank of sweat and machine oil.

Then the spaceman stopped and turned — Markham wasn't sure how he managed it in the confined space of what was really little more than a large pipe. He lifted the lamp almost in Markham's face.

"There she is," he said, gesturing.

Markham looked up in the direction indicated, and flinched.

A face was staring down at him through a window — or rather, a ruined red and black thing that had once been a face was pointed in his general direction.

He was a scientist, Markham reminded himself, and he stared calmly back, over his initial shock.

The window was a chunk of glass, or at any rate a clear substance, roughly six inches wide, a foot long, and four or five inches thick, set into the wall of the tube; it gave a view of the interior of one of the collection bins.

The woman's corpse had landed in the bin with the face pressed up against one end of the window; dark hair, grey dust, and a small pinkish something Markham didn't recognize at first covered the rest. More dust was smeared on her face; so was a dark powder that was probably dried blood.

The face had been battered even before she went out that airlock, and weeks drifting in hard vacuum had not been kind; the skin was flaked and torn, the flesh dehydrated and shrunken, bone protruding here and there. Markham looked at the pink thing for a moment, just to get away from that hideous visage, and then wished he hadn't.

The pink thing was the shrivelled remains of a finger, one that was very clearly not attached to a hand.

"She landed a bit hard," the spaceman remarked. "Three fingers snapped right off and bounced around a bit — things get brittle when they've been out there in the cold for awhile."

Markham swallowed bile.

"We got lucky," the spaceman added. "Never had one land with the face on the viewport like that before. Makes it a lot easier to get a look at her. So, that the right one?"

"Good God," Markham said, "you expect me to tell from *that?*"

The spaceman shrugged, and the little light wavered, sending eerie shadows dancing across the dead woman's face. "She's the only woman we found," he said. "We've got dead men in two of the other bins, five of them in all, a couple in *Emerald Princess* crew uniform, so we're pretty sure it's the right bunch, and she was the only woman."

Markham stared up at the corpse. Then he shook his head.

"It's probably her," he said. "I was hoping I'd be able to tell from the descriptions I got, but I hadn't realized . . . well, I didn't account for her condition. We'll need to get Captain Cahn's men to identify her — they knew her when she was alive."

"Should've sent one with us," the spaceman said. "I'd hate to make another trip when we could've done it in one."

"I didn't think of it," Markham said. "I can't think of everything." He shuddered, all enthusiasm gone. "Let's get the hell out of here."

"After you," the spaceman said sardonically, and Markham began working his way back out of the observation tube.

Chapter Sixteen

*B*est settled onto a patch of relatively dry ground and read the inscription on the little packet that the messenger had handed him. The code, still legible despite the smearing, was correct — and really, there could be little doubt that the orders were genuine, under the circumstances.

Not that he was in any hurry to read them; they'd probably mean trouble, and he'd found berry-picking to be fairly pleasant, low-stress work. It would have gotten intolerably dull eventually, but Best thought he could have handled a few more days of boredom.

"We didn't have any trouble," Poole said. "I just told anyone who asked that I was taking a man in purple to see Pelbrun." Best nodded in understanding, but the messenger looked puzzled; Poole explained, "They'd all heard about this proclamation he'd issued, that he wanted all the wizards and all the strangers in purple, and nobody was about to interfere with anyone following the Brown Magician's orders. A couple of centuries of Shadow's rule here gave the locals a healthy respect for authority, and this Pelbrun is the man who *killed* Shadow. You're on his business, you're safe."

"Oh," the messenger said, comprehension dawning. "So *that's* why people fed us, even when we couldn't pay, but wouldn't talk to us? They were scared?"

Poole nodded. "You've got it exactly."

"Someone could run a pretty nice little scam that way," Begley remarked.

"You'd need an Imperial uniform," Best remarked, as he reluctantly tugged at the seal on the envelope. "Not that easy to come by around here. And you'd have to be careful never to be seen heading away from the fortress."

"The direction isn't a big problem," Begley argued. "You could always double back cross-country. And how many of the natives know what a real Imperial uniform looks like?"

"Good point," Best conceded. The wax broke, and he opened the flap.

Before taking the folded paper out he looked up at the others. "Sit down, all of you," he said. "You make me nervous, standing around like that."

"I should be getting back . . ." the messenger muttered uneasily, glancing out across Shadowmarsh. He had obviously picked up a few stories about the place during his nine-day hike down from Sunderland — even if the natives wouldn't talk to him, Best was sure Poole had had a few things to say.

"Without waiting to see if I have a reply, or a report?" Best said mildly. "I don't think they'd like that back at Base One."

The messenger sat down, with an uncomfortable glance to the west.

Best unfolded the paper and read.

From Under-Secretary Bascombe to Samuel Best, with Bascombe's full title, official address, and all the other usual curlicues, while the "to" line read simply, "Samuel Best, in the field." No rank, no unit — everyone in the Empire knew that meant he was in Intelligence. And "in the field" was nicely vague, while being completely accurate — they were sitting on the edge of a blackberry field.

Best smiled to himself at the thought that if he'd been working in the cranberry bog down the highway a bit, the address should say "in the bog." Maybe it should have read "in the rain" — but the rain had stopped.

He was putting it off, he realized. He forced himself to get past the salutations and authorizations and down to the actual orders.

They didn't take long to read; he stared at them in disbelief.

Was this some kind of joke? He glanced down at the bottom.

"John Bascombe, Under-Secretary of Science for Interdimensional Affairs, by appointment, in service to His Imperial Majesty George VIII." And the Great Seal, embossed in light blue.

Nobody would put the Emperor's name and Imperial seal on a joke.

"That's insane," he said. He looked up at the messenger. "This is completely insane."

The messenger, perched uncomfortably on a hillock of wet sand, shrugged.

"Why?" Begley asked. "What do they want us to do?"

Best threw down the letter.

"That *idiot* Bascombe!" he said. "He's ordered us to arrest Pellinore Brown!"

*T*here were two uniformed spacemen waiting in the clearing.

The last time Wilkins had seen the place, the dead body of Shadow's giant bat creature had lain across most of the opening, completely covering the useless hulk of I.S.S. *Christopher*; now much of the monster's substance had been cut away, or been eaten away by the local wildlife, or had simply rotted. What remained was a rather grisly maze of dried black hide and protruding white bone, with a clear path to *Christopher*'s main hatch and various other navigable routes in and out of the mass.

The two Imperials were standing near the center of this macabre tangle; one was leaning against a gigantic rib, while the other was fully upright.

Neither of them had noticed Wilkins yet; he had a habit of moving stealthily any time he walked alone across country, and he was good at it. He had seen men die because they'd made a wrong assumption about how dangerous supposedly-friendly terrain was, and he didn't intend to follow their example.

He didn't make reckless assumptions about supposedly-friendly people, either. In theory, those two men should be his bosom buddies; in practice, he was out of uniform and they probably weren't expecting anyone, and might shoot first and ask questions later.

Not that they could shoot him, really; their blasters wouldn't work here.

They probably weren't used to that yet — he noticed they both had holstered blasters on their belts. And they were in those easy-to-spot bright purple uniforms, while he was in dull, hard-to-see brown. He had other advantages besides simple surprise.

That damned messenger Simons hadn't mentioned any guards, though.

He probably assumed Wilkins already knew about them; he hadn't seemed terribly bright. One didn't get a messenger job by graduating top of the class, after all.

And all this debate wasn't getting him anywhere.

He stepped forward, into a pool of sunlight, and called, "Hey!"

The two turned, startled; the one who had been leaning stood up, and the other's hand fell to his holster flap.

Old habits die hard, Wilkins thought with a smile.

"Hey, yourself," the former leaner called, relaxing somewhat at the sight of him. "Are you Ron Wilkins, by any chance?"

Wilkins blinked, almost as startled by the question as the guards had been by his shout. "How the hell did you know that?" he called back.

"Telepath said you were coming," the guard said. "We were sent to escort you home."

"Telepath?" That made sense. And an escort? As far as he knew, there were two kinds of escorts — honor guards and jailers. Wilkins wondered which kind *his* escort was supposed to be.

Not that it really mattered; he figured he could manage either way. The Empire knew he was alive now, and they had telepaths tracking him; he wouldn't be able to escape if they really wanted him. He didn't have much of a choice about going back.

He stepped forward into the clearing, and let the two soldiers lead him to the ladder.

*T*he crew of I.S.S. *Ruthless* had been dispersed in the course of Operation Spotlight, and then again after Best had tracked them down and consulted them, but Albright had found that two of them, Elmer Soorn and Bill Mervyn, happened to be on Base One. He had the two of them detached from their regular duties and sent to the cold storage lockers, without explanation — and without their sidearms.

Markham met them in the security room.

"You wait here," he ordered Mervyn. Then he crooked a finger at Soorn. "You come with me."

Together, the two men stepped past the guards, and Markham led the way through the vault door into the locker where the corpses lay.

"Recognize them?" he asked, pointing to the two bodies that sprawled stiffly on a dissection table.

"What's this about?" Soorn asked. He glanced at the cadavers — then stopped, and looked more closely.

"Oh," he said.

"You know them?"

Soorn hesitated. "The little girl . . . I know who she was, yeah. That's Mr. Brown's little girl, from Earth. Rebecca, was it? Something like that."

"Rachel," Markham said, his breath puffing out in a cold little cloud. "What about the other?"

"Mister, whoever you are, be serious — look at her! She's been out in space, hasn't she? She's bloody well freeze-dried, barely looks human. And it looks as if her face was smashed in even before she went out the lock."

"You can't venture a guess?"

Soorn looked at the larger corpse again.

"I could guess," he said, "if you promise not to hold me to it."

"Guess, then."

"Well, since you've got her here with the little girl, I'd guess she might be the girl's mother, Mrs. Brown."

"You think she could be?"

Soorn shrugged. "The hair's right, what's left of it. If there were any clothing . . ."

"This is how we found her," Markham said.

"Last I saw," Soorn said, "Mrs. Brown was wearing a borrowed uniform — there were probably half a dozen other women who wore them just aboard *Princess,* though."

"This one wasn't wearing anything when she was recovered," Markham said. "What about the face?"

"The face . . ." Soorn shuddered. "There's nothing that makes it impossible, but who could tell?"

Markham nodded.

"I think that'll do," he said.

Ten minutes later Mervyn rather queasily confirmed Soorn's guess that the body was Nancy Brown's — though he, too, was reluctant to swear to it. He hadn't known Mrs. Brown well, he insisted, and he, too, pointed out the condition the corpse was in.

Secretary Markham had to admit the body was in bad shape, but he was reasonably certain now that it was the right one. He left the vaults feeling rather pleased with himself.

That lasted until he reached his office and found the telepath waiting to report.

"*T*he Empire has recovered your wife's body," Gregory reported, "but they're keeping it, and Rachel's, under heavy guard; we can't get at them."

Pel frowned. "Have you tried bribery?" he said.

Gregory nodded.

This was very annoying; that simulacrum, Felton, must have talked. The Empire knew that he wanted the bodies.

Well, that wasn't really that big a deal. He'd just have to talk to the Empire and get them back openly.

He couldn't go there himself, of course — the matrix would collapse the instant he set foot through a portal, and then he'd never be able to resurrect Nancy and Rachel — but he could send an emissary.

He could send Gregory, of course — but that seemed rather a waste. The Empire might hang him for espionage.

Or they might not believe him in the first place.

No, they had telepaths — they could check.

But could telepaths read the minds of simulacra? And the Empire didn't have all that many telepaths; they might not bother to check before consigning Gregory to the loony bin — or the noose.

This would require some thought.

He could, Pel supposed, send Wilkins as his emissary — that would be a nice little goodwill gesture, and would leave no doubt that the message really came from Faerie.

He cast about with the matrix, and discovered, to his surprise, that Wilkins wasn't in the fortress, nor anywhere nearby.

That was puzzling.

Thinking back, he realized he hadn't seen Wilkins in days — not since he had announced that he was going out for a walk.

Pel hoped nothing had happened to him; he sort of liked Wilkins.

Maybe he'd gone off somewhere; Pel looked further out in the matrix. He couldn't really tell one person from another reliably when they were outside the fortress, and certainly not by the time they were outside Shadowmarsh, but if he saw anyone around who felt out of place . . .

He didn't notice anyone he could recognize as Wilkins.

There were three men coming up the causeway, though — presumably they were coming to see the Brown Magician.

Pel decided he could attend to whatever they wanted, then get back to worrying about the Empire.

"Go back and wait," he told Gregory. "I'll get back to you shortly."

The simulacrum bowed, and stepped through the waiting portal, out of the throne room and back to his little corner of the Galactic Empire.

"*B*ascombe ordered *what?*" Markham stared at the telepath in disbelief.

"He ordered Best to arrest Pellinore Brown on charges of subornation of treason," the telepath repeated. He added, "Specifically, coercing Proserpine Thorpe into going rogue."

"But he's a head of state!" Markham shouted. "He's a bloody dictator, for

God's sake! You can't just walk in and arrest him!"

The telepath just stood there, staring straight ahead, and after a moment Markham calmed down enough to stare back.

"Pel Brown's a head of state, and John Bascombe's an idiot," he said.

The telepath didn't argue.

"All right," Markham said, "Best is in Intelligence, so I assume he's *not* an idiot. What's he doing about his orders?" Markham knew what he hoped Best was doing — sending back a request for confirmation and clarification. That would eat up two or three weeks in transit both directions, and was the only legitimate stalling tactic Markham could think of.

And the clarification would be to tell Best to ignore it, Bascombe's an idiot. Best would see that, surely. Markham's spirits rose.

"He's . . . well, he's more or less planning to attempt to carry them out, sir."

Markham's spirits plummeted again. "He's what?"

"I'm afraid his opinion of Under-Secretary Bascombe matches your own, so he assumes that the orders meant just what they said, and any clarification would confirm that. Furthermore, he and his men — especially his men — are tired of delay, and prefer not to wait around. Therefore, they're planning to enter the fortress and ask the Brown Magician to return to the Empire with them; in fact, they're already on the causeway across the marsh. Given Spaceman Wilkins' experience, they don't expect to be harmed outright. Best has no intention of mentioning anything about an arrest."

Markham stared. He considered.

Then he shrugged. "What the hell," he said. "It can't hurt."

"*Y*ou sound like an Imperial or an Earthman," Pel said, "but there aren't supposed to be any other Earthpeople around, and as far as Imperials go, you're not Ron Wilkins, nor Tom Sawyer, either. What the hell are you doing here? Who are you?"

"No, sir, I'm not Wilkins or Sawyer or an Earthman," the man said, blinking and shading his eyes against the glare of the matrix. "My name's Samuel Best. And I'm here on behalf of the Galactic Empire."

Pel stared, drumming his fingers on his knee and letting the matrix swirl greenly. He glanced quickly at Susan, standing silently to one side, then back at his visitor. There was something familiar about the man — not his physical appearance, but his magical one. Pel placed it finally.

"You're the spy," he said. "One of them, anyway. The ones they sent through the portal in Sunderland's Low Forest. And those two are more of them."

He reached out with the matrix and drew Begley and Poole forward, from the landing into the throne room. Neither of them screamed, which was something of a relief. Peasants always screamed.

"Yes, sir, I am," Best admitted.

"I didn't expect you to just walk in here like this," Pel said. "I figured you'd be sneaking around causing trouble."

"My orders were changed," Best — if that was really his name — explained.

"They told you to come talk to me?"

Best nodded. "Yes, sir. And to respectfully request that you accompany me back to the Empire."

Pel stared. The matrix billowed up in deep blue glow, wrapping around Best. "Why?" Pel asked.

"They want to talk to you about what happened to their men here, and to the telepath, Proserpine Thorpe," Best said — and Pel knew he was lying; the matrix couldn't provide telepathy, but it could, he had discovered, read physiological signs much as a polygraph could.

The matrix darkened.

*B*est could sense that the conversation had suddenly gone bad; the blinding waves of light and color shifted, and what had previously seemed like an outward manifestation of irritated curiosity was now almost openly hostile. He tried desperately to recover.

"I don't really know what they want to talk to you about," he said hastily. "I'm just a spy; they sent me because I was handy, and told me to bring you back to the Empire with me. They didn't say why."

The seething cloud of color surged forward slightly, stopping just short of engulfing him.

Was there really a human being behind that, controlling it? It hardly seemed possible. Best began to suspect that if it truly was Pellinore Brown in there, he was no longer entirely human.

"They think they can just order me around?" that thunderous voice roared.

"I don't know what they think!" Best protested. "I'm just the messenger!"

"Messenger?" The Brown Magician's voice boomed from the walls. "All right, messenger, I've got a message for you to carry!"

*T*he sergeant stared. "Who the hell are you, and why are you dressed like that?" he demanded.

"My name is Samuel Best," the man in the primitive clothes replied. "I was just stranded here, wherever I am, and I need to get back to Base One immediately." He hesitated, then added, "I'm working for Imperial Intelligence."

The sergeant considered that. It wasn't a very likely story; it sounded like something out of the fiction magazines, really.

On the other hand, strangers in crude woolen tunics and baggy tights didn't generally walk in off the street here; the local government here on Delta Scorpius IV was not known for its sense of humor. And ships were coming and going all the time; one of them could have dumped an unwanted passenger here easily enough.

Why anyone would bother to strand someone alive was another matter. If he had been a smuggler or pirate, the sergeant thought, he'd have just dumped the troublemaker out an airlock — but he supposed some outlaws might have scruples about such things.

It wasn't as if sending a man to Base One was a big deal; the regular supply run was headed out there in another two hours anyway. Passing the problem along would be the simplest solution, and if the fellow really *was* in Intelligence, the sergeant didn't want to interfere.

"I'll have to ask you to submit to a search," he said, "and from the look of that outfit, a delousing, too. Do you have any credentials?"

Chapter Seventeen

"He wants the bodies," Best said. "He said I should say that you'd know what he meant, but if you . . . well, in his words, if you try to play dumb, he means he wants the remains of his wife and daughter."

Markham drummed fingers on his desk. "Now he's asking," he said.

"Because we've got them safe and he can't get them any other way," Albright said.

"Or because he knows that we know he wants them," Howe suggested. "He wants us to think he's coming out in the open."

"You don't think he is?" Markham asked her, mildly startled.

Howe shrugged. "I never trust anyone a telepath can't read," she said.

"Sensible attitude," Albright agreed.

"I wonder if we shouldn't tell the General Secretary about this," Markham said. "After all, this Brown is effectively a head of state — a real one, not some penny-ante rebel tyrant — and he's asking us to turn over what might be Imperial property. I don't see this as within the purview of the Department of Science. We were directed to investigate and contain Shadow, and to contact any other interdimensional civilizations we could locate. We've done that — Shadow is dead, and we've got this Brown ready to talk. So we're done."

"As long as the Empire's security is threatened, the military is still involved," Albright said, "but I don't see this as a military matter, either."

Albright and Markham turned to Howe, who shrugged. "I'm not authorized to say anything about Intelligence's opinion," she said.

"Neither am I," Best said. "I'm just a field agent on detached duty to the Department of Interdimensional Affairs."

Best had noticed that John Bascombe, head of that department, was not present; he didn't have to ask why, but he did wonder whether Bascombe was still alive and free. He hadn't heard Bascombe's name spoken since he had arrived at Base One; he'd been sent directly to Markham's office, where the current gathering had formed. It was quite clear that Bascombe was no longer in any position of authority.

Best was fairly sure that initially, Markham would just have removed Bascombe from duty — that was easier to keep quiet. If Bascombe didn't *want* to keep quiet, though, if he protested — well, there were prisons where no word would get out. And if that was too much trouble, a blaster charge was cheaper and more permanent.

In any case, mentioning him did not seem like a good idea, and Best didn't.

This talk about the General Secretary was not comforting, though. Any blame for screwing up that Secretary Sheffield might want to hand out would be directed at higher levels than mere field agents, but Intelligence's internal attitude was another matter. Nothing official would be done, but agents who showed any signs of developing a high profile had a tendency to wind up either in obscure backwaters, or on assignments with excessive casualty rates.

Like 100%.

Best hoped Bascombe, wherever he was, was proud of himself.

Miletti was slumped in the armchair, staring disinterestedly at the TV, when the daily knock came.

"Come in, it's open," he called.

The lieutenant crept in, tape recorder in hand and already running. He'd had practice. The questioning went better if Miletti wasn't paying attention — and both he and Miletti knew that. Miletti wasn't being rude by watching reruns of "$25,000 Pyramid," he was making it easier on everyone.

The lieutenant did wonder sometimes about what shape Miletti was in, physically and emotionally — he obviously didn't enjoy any of this.

That wasn't the lieutenant's department, though; he was just an interviewer. (That sounded much nicer than "interrogator.")

"Any attempts at contact?" he asked.

"They're listening," Miletti said, without looking up.

"Sending?"

"Not sending."

"Any mention of Earth?"

"Nothing new."

"Proserpine Thorpe?"

"Nothing new."

"Amy Jewell?"

"Nothing."

"Pel Brown?"

"Sent a message."

Miletti blinked, startled by his own words.

The lieutenant was almost equally startled — until now there had been no change for a couple of weeks. "What's the message?" he asked.

"He wants the bodies," Miletti answered without thinking. "His wife and daughter."

This was outside anything the lieutenant was prepared to deal with, but he could at least ask the obvious. "Why?"

"Don't know."

"Is the Empire going to deliver them?"

Miletti looked up at the lieutenant. "This is spooky, you know," he said. "I really hate this. And I can't believe it's real. How do you know I'm getting this right, and not just making it up?"

"Not my department," the lieutenant said. "Are they going to give Brown the bodies?"

"That's what's really spooky," Miletti said. *"They* think they don't know yet, but they do, and I know it." The lieutenant needed a second to puzzle that out, and had just got it straight when Miletti concluded, "They aren't going to."

"Hℴow do I report that?" Carrie Hall asked her brother.

He didn't need to ask what she meant.

"You don't," he said. "Bad enough they know we're leaking anything; if they find out we're leaking things that we aren't supposed to know, that *nobody* knows consciously . . . well, hell, maybe he's wrong, anyway. Maybe it's just an opinion he picked up somewhere. Just don't mention it."

Carrie nodded reluctantly.

She didn't like it, though. Telepaths weren't supposed to keep secrets like that — they had orders to report on Miletti, and they weren't supposed to leave out anything important. And there shouldn't be that sort of leakage. There never had been before they started getting involved with these other worlds. Telepaths all knew things they shouldn't, but nobody in the entire Empire had ever tapped into the group unconscious of the telepaths the way this Miletti had.

Earthpeople were apparently slightly different from Imperials, in some very subtle way — or at least, Miletti was. Maybe he was a mutant himself — maybe he would *be* a telepath in Imperial space, if he ever came through a space-warp into the normal universe, and maybe that was why they couldn't shut him out.

They had tried. Miletti was the only psychic they'd found on Earth where they hadn't been able to make any conscious contact at all, even though they knew he ought to be receptive — maybe it was because he'd had enough telepathic talent that he'd learned to shut them out.

But he couldn't shut out their unconscious transmissions — and neither could they. They'd been able to close off the others, but not Miletti.

So for the first time ever a non-telepath, someone who hadn't been brought up from infancy in the Special Branch, who hadn't been trained in keeping secrets, someone who hadn't sworn loyalty to the Emperor and the Empire, was linked into the telepathic network.

Nothing like that had ever happened before they'd begun messing around with other universes.

And Prossie hadn't been an outcast before they contacted Earth. She never would have gone rogue if she'd stayed in the Empire.

And if she had gone rogue anywhere in the Empire she would never have survived if she hadn't had Earth to escape to. Carrie suspected that bad thoughts were leaking through from Prossie on some subconscious level, just as secrets were leaking through to Miletti, and that Prossie's horrible rebelliousness was affecting the entire family — everyone seemed to be thinking strangely lately.

Or maybe it wasn't Prossie, maybe it was just all those minds out there, on Earth and in Faerie, with their alien ways of thinking, subtly different from the ordinary thoughts of the Imperial citizenry.

Could Miletti know a decision that no one in the Empire had consciously reached yet? These Earth psychics were so odd, with their erratic, untrained receptiveness, each one a bit different — could he have really learned that from the telepaths? Did they all really know it? Had they suppressed it?

Could Miletti be precognitive? Imperial science said that was impossible, but reality was different on Earth. Maybe he was seeing the future with his own psychic talent, not reading the telepathic unconscious at all.

And *would* the Empire deliver the two corpses?

Maybe Miletti knew, but Carrie didn't, or at least didn't want to admit it if she did, and she didn't like that.

She didn't like any of this.

"*H*ow long should I give them?" Pel asked, without looking at Susan.

"However long seems reasonable," she replied.

"How long is that?" He glanced at her; as usual, she was standing by the side of the room, not doing much of anything.

That didn't seem right, somehow; shouldn't she be going about her own business, instead of just hanging around him all the time?

But then, what business did she have?

"I don't know," she said.

"Neither do I," Pel muttered. "I don't know how long it takes to get from Gregory's place to Base One, or who'll have to authorize the decision, or how long they'll need to argue about it." He sighed. "Maybe I shouldn't have sent those two away — Begley and Poole, I mean. I just sent them back out to the berry patches, but I could have sent them somewhere in the Empire, and maybe that would have sped things up. Or maybe I should have tried the weak spots until I found a portal that goes directly to Terra — there must be one. Then I could've sent someone straight to the Emperor; he'd have to listen, right? I mean, I'm ruler of an entire universe, right? Even if all I've seen of it is some woods and a marsh and a few villages and this damned depressing fortress." He slumped back in the throne, thinking.

What he had just said wasn't exactly true, Pel realized. That was all he had seen with his own eyes, but he could reach out through the matrix and touch almost any place in Faerie. The matrix distorted distances, and he couldn't sense all of it at once — probably, he thought, just because his brain couldn't handle anything so large — but he had a vague idea of just how huge Shadow's realm was. The space-warp that the Empire maintained in West Sunderland was two hundred miles away — and that was right next door. Even assuming that the scale was constant, which he was fairly sure wasn't true, he could sense things dozens of times as distant as that, which would put them three thousand miles or more away.

And in fact, he believed the scale was logarithmic, which would make that distance tens of thousands of miles.

It still wasn't anything like the Galactic Empire, with its thousands of planets, but surely it deserved some respect, and surely, once his request worked its way far enough up the chain of command, someone over there would see how reasonable it was and would deliver Nancy and Rachel.

No one had come through the Empire's warp out in Sunderland lately, though; there had been that party of three outbound awhile back, but no one coming in.

This would all be much simpler if the Galactic Empire had telephones.

Or maybe not; after all, how could you use telephones between planets? And radio wouldn't work, either; the planets might be closer together than they were in the *real* world, but the interstellar distances were still measured in light-years.

At least he could have run a phone line through that space-warp, though, instead of running messengers back and forth. Not through one of his portals, because then he'd have had to keep it open constantly, and he couldn't do that, but the space-warp . . .

Well, the space-warp came and went, too, but it didn't *have* to, did it?

It all seemed very weird, that there could be a Galactic Empire with space-warps and telepathy and anti-gravity, but no telephones. Movies and telegraphs, but no telephones or TV. The old science fiction stories never had anything like that.

Maybe it had something to do with the different physics involved.

He looked around at the marble walls of the chamber he sat in. More different physics, he thought; if this room were in either the Empire or the real world he wouldn't be able to see a thing, because he'd be sitting in pitch darkness. The only light here came from the matrix he controlled.

Maybe he should do more with that magic. Maybe he should see more of this world he controlled. Maybe, just maybe, he and Nancy and Rachel wouldn't go straight back to Earth once he'd restored them to life.

First, though, he had to get them back. The *real* ones, not cheap imitations like that thing waiting for him in the bedroom.

And she *was* still waiting for him in the bedroom; he had told her to, so she would. She wouldn't leave that room for anything, not even to eat . . .

Was there a chamber pot there? He hoped so. And there wasn't any food.

"Damn," he said. He twitched the matrix, summoning a nearby fetch.

*L*ife aboard ship was usually boring, but Best thought he'd have preferred honest boredom to the endless games of stoking Markham wanted to play. Best could handle boredom, while playing cards with the Secretary of Science was wearing on his nerves. He was never sure whether to play his honest best, or to deliberately lose, and just how badly to lose. And stoking was never one of his favorite games in the first place.

He wished Albright or Howe or someone had come along, instead of staying at Base One; then he or she could play with Markham and give Best a break.

"Burn," he said, dropping the king of cups on the central pile.

"Damp," Markham replied, tossing the king of swords.

Best looked at the table, and drew three.

"I don't know why you need me along, anyway," he said, in an unusual moment of honesty. "I can't tell Secretary Sheffield anything you can't. Hell, I can't tell him anything the telepaths haven't *already* told him; I'm not sure why we're making this trip at all."

"You were there," Markham said, looking at his hand. "The General Secretary always likes to hear things first-hand, likes to talk it out before deciding. Without telepaths." He pulled out a card and threw the eight of diamonds. "Burn."

With a sigh, Best played the knave of sticks. "Damp," he said, and added three points to Markham's score. He glanced up from the scratch pad and happened to catch the Secretary's personal telepath watching.

As if playing stoking wasn't bad enough, he had to worry about the mutant reading his thoughts and telling Markham all the details of his aggravation.

And of his cards, for that matter. Not that Markham would bother to cheat, but he might find out that Best had deliberately overlooked the nine of swords in his own hand. Best didn't think Markham would like knowing that Best was losing intentionally.

But he didn't think Markham would like losing, either.

Well, it was only two more days to Terra.

"Y ou don't know what this mysterious project of his was?" Albright asked.

"No, sir," Wilkins replied. He was already over his nervousness at finding himself questioned by the Imperial Space Marshal, and was now treating Albright as just another officer.

A good one, but just another officer.

And he was getting tired of repeating all this.

"It kept him from sending you home, though?"

"Yes, sir — that's what he said."

"D'you think it had anything to do with these bodies he wants?"

"I don't know, sir; he never mentioned them to me."

"But he could have just sent *you* to ask for them, at any time," Albright said. "Why did he wait until Best showed up?"

"I have no idea, sir."

Albright considered Wilkins silently for a moment, then turned to his telepath.

"I don't like the sound of it," he said. "Tell Secretary Sheffield and Secretary Markham about this."

"Yes, sir," the telepath said.

"I'm going to check," Pel said, already gathering the energies to open a portal.

Susan and the false Nancy didn't argue; Susan stood motionless, and Nancy smiled agreeably. And of course the fetch didn't respond.

Just having someone better to talk to would be a relief, Pel thought. Not that Gregory was much of an improvement.

He reached, and twisted, and the portal opened.

No one was there.

"Damn," Pel said. He picked a fetch.

"You," he said, "go find Peter Gregory."

Chapter Eighteen

By the time Gregory emerged from the portal Pel was furious with impatience, his fingers striking blue sparks from the dark wood as he drummed on the arm of his throne.

"Where the hell were you?" he demanded without preamble, his voice echoing unnaturally. Angry orange currents swirled through the air.

"Down at the port," Gregory replied, unfazed. "I was trying to get word of what's happening at Base One."

"Did you?"

"A little."

"And?"

"The bodies are still under heavy guard. The Secretary of Science is on his way to Terra to confer with the General Secretary."

"Is that it?"

"Yes, O Great One."

Pel glared at Gregory's bland face, infuriated by the simulacrum's calm.

"Get someone to Terra," he said. "Get a message to the General Secretary — or the Emperor, or whoever's in charge. Tell him I want those bodies *now*. Through that space-warp out in Sunderland."

"Yes, O Great One."

"That's all. Go on, get out of here!" He gestured angrily, waving Gregory toward the portal.

Gregory bowed deeply, then stepped backward and vanished.

Pel stared at the slight shimmer in the air where the portal hung. To his eyes, it was virtually invisible — if he strained, he could see the very faintest distortion. To his internal vision through the matrix, though, the portal was a gaping hole in reality, an infinite tunnel of powerful blue-black magic that somehow had no length at all, ending in the utter impenetrable darkness of non-magic space.

He knew it came out on some planet he'd never heard of, Delta something-or-other, roughly half a day's spaceflight from Base One. He'd never found a weak spot that would open directly into Base One; apparently Shadow hadn't had any portals there. He could create new portals, of course, but he couldn't aim them all that well, and trying different places in the Empire at random could take forever. Not to mention that if he ever *did* open a path to Base One, it might come out in the middle of a firing range or something.

So he had no direct route, and the delays were infuriating.

Of course, the Empire's space-warp connected Faerie to Base One, but that was out in Sunderland, ten days' march to the east, and he was stuck here in Shadow's fortress . . .

Wasn't he?

Pel blinked, and the matrix slowed into contemplative green spirals.

Was he stuck here?

Why should he be?

Shadow had claimed this fortress and lived here because it was a natural focal point for the network of magical currents that permeated Faerie, so that it was easier to maintain and control the matrix here — but did that mean this was the *only* place the matrix could be used?

That was silly. Shadow had talked about the early matrix wizards roaming around, taking over each other's strongholds, absorbing each other's matrices; they hadn't all just sat at home like spiders in their webs.

Why *couldn't* Pel go up to Sunderland if he chose?

And that obnoxious coward Taillefer had been able to fly, probably at a pretty good speed — sixty, seventy, maybe as much as a hundred miles an hour, and *he* wasn't any matrix wizard, he was just a little hedge magician, too feeble for Shadow to have bothered hunting him down and killing him.

And *he* could fly. Anything Taillefer could do, the master of the great matrix should be able to do. If Pel could do *that*, if he could fly, he could be in Sunderland in a matter of hours.

Of course, he couldn't take all his fetches and monsters along, or Susan, or the false Nancy — but so what?

But *could* he go anywhere? Could he learn to fly, blown on a magical wind the way Taillefer was?

He could damn well try. At the very least, it would give him something to do while the Empire dawdled.

He stood up and marched for the stairs — not the huge staircase down to that absurd entrance hall, but the narrow steps up to the battlements.

"*A* message from the General Secretary," the telepath said suddenly, startling Best so much he almost dropped his cards.

"What is it?" Markham asked, looking up; at first he seemed annoyed by the interruption, but by the time he finished raising his head and pronouncing those three simple words he was calm again.

"He wants to know if you have anything to add to what's already been relayed telepathically. Regarding the Brown Magician."

"Not that I know of," Markham replied. "Do I?"

The telepath's mouth quirked in a ghost of a smile. "Not that I can see, sir," he said.

"So why is he asking? Can you tell me?"

The telepath nodded. "In light of the interview with Spaceman Wilkins, regarding the Magician's secret project that prevented him from sending Wilkins home, Secretary Sheffield believes that we should cease any further delays or stalling tactics and open direct negotiations with Brown. Therefore, you're to turn around and return to Base One forthwith; he'll be coming out as well, along with several trained envoys."

"Envoys?" Best asked. "What envoys?"

"Well, obviously," the telepath explained, "the Empire hasn't needed actual ambassadors since the Unification, but there's apparently a staff of envoys on Terra, kept on hand in case of need. They've occasionally seen duty in negotiating terms of surrender with rebel worlds, and they're theoretically ready if we ever meet intelligent extraterrestrials."

"I didn't know that," Best marveled. "They think of everything, don't they?"

"They try," Markham said dryly. "Tell the captain of the change in plans."

As the telepath hurried out of the stateroom Markham tossed the four of cups. "Burn," he said.

*T*he wind whipped Pel's hair forward, slashing it back and forth across his face; it occurred to him that he hadn't had it cut in weeks, maybe months, not since he had left Base One. And he hadn't bothered shaving, hadn't had a chance, since then, either; he had a full beard for the first time in his life. He must be a mess.

He wondered if Nancy and Rachel would even recognize him like this. He hoped the beard wouldn't frighten Rachel.

Of course, he could shave it off, once everything was back to normal, once he had Nancy and Rachel back.

But first he had to bring them back.

He stepped up on a merlon — at least, he thought that was what the stone blocks along the edge of the battlement were called. Maybe the right term was crenellations.

It didn't matter.

Below him the wall of the central tower was a sheer drop of a hundred feet or more, down to the roofs and walls of the next layer of the fortress; fifty feet out that, in turn, fell away, for another sixty or seventy feet, and then again and again the stone walls and slate roofs, squat ugly turrets and sinister battlements, until five hundred feet down and two hundred feet ahead lay the stagnant water and thick reeds of the surrounding marsh.

Above him was that single line of gargoyles, and a heavy, leaden overcast.

Around him seethed the light and shadow of the matrix.

He was standing on a stone fifty, maybe sixty stories up, unsheltered by anything but his magic.

Nothing built without steel had any right to be this high, he thought. It must have used magic. Why hadn't it fallen down when Shadow died?

Because the matrix still held, of course. And he held it.

He reached out, down into the fortress; he couldn't sense any specific place where magic held the stone, but surely there were some.

The wind subsided slightly as his attention was distracted, and he shifted a foot to keep his balance.

The merlon was carved, the corners somewhat rounded, in what appeared to be a representation of leaves. It wasn't very well executed, and as he glanced at it through a purple swirl of magical energy Pel thought the result resembled a tooth more than anything else. The lines of the carving provided a bit of traction, but as Pel looked past the stone and past the haze of color at the drop below him he wished the corners were still solid and square.

What was he doing, standing here on top of a tower and deliberately summoning a wind that would blow him off?

This was insane. People couldn't fly.

Not on Earth, anyway, but this wasn't Earth. He'd seen Taillefer do it, and he had Shadow's entire matrix, where Taillefer had had only the leavings of it. Taillefer hadn't lived in a constant shifting mass of magic the way Pel did.

He wasn't going to jump. He wasn't going to step off. If he could conjure up a wind strong enough to *blow* him off, then he'd believe he could make one strong enough to carry him.

He felt the matrix, felt it moving the air, and he drew more power to that movement, summoned strength from earth and sky, and the wind hit him like a wall, sweeping him off the battlements, bearing him up and away into empty space.

"So how do we get a message to him?" Secretary Sheffield asked.

"Send a messenger through the space-warp. It's about a ten-day hike from there to the fortress," Albright replied.

"There isn't anything faster?"

Albright shook his head. "We can't seem to relocate the warp to anywhere within five hundred miles or so of a previously-used location, so we can't get it any closer to the fortress. Brown apparently has some way of contacting his network of spies, so he may well know our decision within a day or two, but we don't have any way of knowing that. We haven't been able to break the ring, or infiltrate, or even identify any members with certainty. We know Felton, and of course we know who Felton's contact was, but that was a woman named Fielding, and she committed suicide before we could capture and interrogate her. We're checking on her friends and associates, but so far we haven't found anything particularly suspicious."

"Felton didn't know any other names?"

"Not for certain. The telepaths are still digging."

"So our only way of contacting Brown is through our own space-warps, and the only one we currently have is ten days march from Brown's fortress — but can't we get some sort of vehicle through there?"

Albright shook his head. "Anti-gravity doesn't work in . . . well, we call it Faerie. The telepaths picked up that name for it somewhere, and it seems to fit. Anyway, anti-gravity won't work — ships and aircars just fall to the ground and sit there."

"What about wheeled vehicles? Or is there a water route?"

Albright hesitated. "We don't *have* any wheeled vehicles," he pointed out. "And I suspect the roads aren't good enough. The warp comes out in a forest, and the pathway out is just that, a path. As for a water route, again, our entry point is in the middle of a forest, with no navigable rivers in the areas we've seen." He glanced at Best, who was seated at one corner of the table, trying hard to be unobtrusive.

"No rivers," Best confirmed. "And there aren't any roads in the forest."

"What about opening a new warp over the sea somewhere?" Sheffield suggested. "It would have to be farther away, but it might be faster all the same. Is this fortress accessible by sea?"

Albright rubbed his noes thoughtfully. "I don't know," he said. "You understand, sir, I haven't seen it myself, and we haven't done any photoreconnaissance. I understand it's in the middle of a marsh, but I don't know any more than that — whether a small boat could get across the marsh is an excellent question." He turned to Best again. "You were there," he said.

"Yes, sir," Best admitted.

"You think a boat could reach this fortress?"

"I don't know much about boats," Best said, "but no, I don't think so. It's a pretty nasty marsh, and I didn't see where it connected to anything better. Besides, how would you power a boat? If you're rowing, that's no better than walking, is it?"

Sheffield acknowledged that with a nod.

"All right, then," he said, "we'll send an envoy to this forest and let him walk from there, and one of the demands will be to find a better way for future communications."

Demands?

This was the first mention Best had heard of demands. He tried to imagine what the Empire might be demanding of the Brown Magician.

And he tried to imagine how Brown would react to any such demands.

He didn't like what he came up with.

R iding the wind was a very strange sensation, something like swimming in a very strong current. And of course, he could steer the current by manipulating the matrix.

And the matrix added to the strangeness, because he could feel that he was simultaneously riding and pulling it. It didn't *want* to have its center dragged away from the fortress.

Pel began to understand why Shadow had sat waiting in her fortress, rather than coming out to collect her visitors; it was uncomfortable being out here. He was stretching his web, forcing the patterns to shift and distort.

He rebelled at any thought of going back, though. He *could* operate out here, and he *would* — he wouldn't be held prisoner by his own power!

Besides, he could sense that the matrix would restructure itself with time; the patterns would slide and shift until they settled into new positions, and the discomfort would pass. It wasn't so much that he was restricted to one spot as that the matrix resisted moving about.

Of course, it would work best and be most comfortable in one of the natural places of power — Shadowmarsh was one, probably the strongest, but Castle Regisvert would work, too, or any number of other places.

He looked down.

He was not at airplane altitudes — he'd started at about five hundred feet, and hadn't risen much above that. He didn't see any need to go higher. From this height he could follow the road without difficulty, from the causeway across the marsh back past the berry fields and plains to the villages, one after another, strung out across the ridges and valleys of the Starlinshire Downs.

The roads branched, the towns held forks and crossroads, but Pel simply remembered that he and his party had traveled almost due west; he kept his bearings and headed eastward.

From this altitude, low as it was, he could see far more of the countryside than he had from the ground. Farms and villages stretched off in all directions; castles were scattered about, but all of them looked abandoned, and most were outright ruins — Shadow had not been kind to the conquered nobility.

Some castles, of course, had belonged to wizards; to the unassisted eye those were built in more or less random locations and were all no more than ruins — some, in fact, more nearly resembled craters than castles. Through the matrix, however, Pel could see that these locations weren't random at all, but carefully sited on the natural magical currents of earth and sky, currents that were now all diverted into the matrix itself, leaving shadowy ghosts of themselves in an odd sort of double image.

Other castles, the more intact ones, tended to be built on commanding hilltops or bends in rivers — defensible positions, in short, and ones that could control a respectable territory. Those, Pel assumed, had belonged to the mundane nobility.

Pel suspected that virtually all of the places of power had been occupied by matrix magicians at one time or another, before Shadow consolidated all the matrices into one — certainly, every one he could see as he blew across the landscape seemed to have a ruin on it.

The matrix griped about leaving Shadow's fortress because that was where it had been centered for so long, but if another matrix magician had won out, it might just as well have been centered in one of the dozen or so other spots he passed — or in the hundreds or thousands of others he knew lay beyond the horizon. He couldn't see those, but he could sense them through the matrix.

If Pel wanted a castle other than the fortress, one where the matrix would be comfortable, he supposed he could rebuild Regisvert or one of the others. If he needed to relocate, closer to the space-warp, that might be a good idea;

the matrix would shift itself to fit the new location, and the present discomfort would pass.

Or he could erect himself a new fortress out in Sunderland, if he chose, but there was little natural magic there; it wouldn't be as suitable as a power spot, and the matrix might never accommodate itself properly.

And it shouldn't be necessary, anyway — he should have the bodies as soon as the Empire could take care of the paperwork, and then he'd be able to take them anywhere, back to the fortress or anywhere he wanted.

The Low Forest was a dark green line on the horizon before him, and the overgrown ruin ahead and to the left, where the power flowed strongly just beneath the ground, was surely the ruins of Castle Regisvert. Pel adjusted his course, and blew onward.

*S*paceman Thomas Sawyer looked up from the pigpen and saw the glowing, seething mass of color and light tear across the sky to the south, moving eastward. The flickering lit the mud and the hogs in quick flashes of color, like a fireworks display.

"What the hell is *that?*" he asked no one in particular.

It had to be magic, of course. They didn't have fireworks here in Faerie, did they?

It had to be magic. So even if Shadow was really dead, there was still magic running loose, and it didn't look like just the stuff people like Taillefer and Valadrakul did.

Sawyer had no intention of getting involved in anything like that. It looked like he'd be staying down on the farm for awhile yet.

*L*ieutenant Sebastian Warner checked the seals on his space suit one final time, then cycled the airlock. He waited patiently while the pressure decreased, and when the signal light came on he undogged the outer door and stepped out into the vacuum of space.

Huge machinery surrounded him, but he closed his eyes and ignored it as he proceeded carefully toward the space-warp, moving hand-over-hand along the rope ladder. Even with his eyes tightly shut the glare was painfully bright, forcing him to work entirely by feel.

This wasn't his first trip through, though; he was an old hand now, and could find his way easily. He had already made almost two dozen quick trips to see how things stood on the other side, and whether anyone interesting was in the area around the base of the ladder.

This time the job description was slightly different — he was supposed to prepare the site for an Imperial envoy, whatever that meant. As far as he was concerned, it was more of the same, and just as dull as ever.

He'd missed the assignment when Spaceman Wilkins was picked up; dull as that was, it had been about the most exciting job anyone had had here since

Warner was given his current duty. James and Butler had got that one, had met Wilkins and brought him up the ladder; Warner had never encountered anyone on the other side.

Warner had hopes of spotting something interesting eventually. Even just one of the primitives finding the ladder while out hunting would do.

If nothing else, it would give Warner a chance to see whether the stories were true, and blasters really didn't work on the other side; he hadn't wanted to test the theory without a valid reason, in case one of those damned spying mutants reported it.

He'd spent the first twenty years of his life without ever being on the same planet as a telepath, but lately it seemed as if he couldn't get away from the bloody freaks.

He was through the warp; he could tell because the gravity had shifted, the ladder now led down instead of forward, and because the intense glare of the warp had faded. Without thinking, he had gotten his feet securely onto a rung.

He opened his eyes on bright, cool sunlight and saw the green roof of the forest spread out below him, and began climbing down toward it.

He was just passing the highest branches when a bright flicker of movement attracted his attention. He turned his head, expecting to see a wild bird or other flying creature of some kind, hoping it wasn't even the most distant cousin of that dead giant bat-thing that lay in the clearing below.

Instead he saw, miles away but approaching rapidly, a thing like a cloud of polychrome light.

He froze, clinging to the ladder, and stared. He'd wished for something interesting, but this was a little more than he'd had in mind.

And it was coming closer *fast*, at least as fast as an aircar at cruising speed.

He shouldn't stay here, exposed, he realized. He should either climb back up and give the alarm, or he should get down to the ground, take shelter, and watch, maybe wait until it had passed and then get the hell back to Base One.

He had no idea what the thing was — some weird natural phenomenon peculiar to this strange world? Some sort of creature? A weapon, sent by the so-called Brown Magician, or maybe Shadow? They said Shadow was dead; he wasn't convinced. Maybe Shadow and the Magician were still fighting this out, and the thing coming toward him was involved in that.

Whatever it was, he had to *move*.

He looked up, at those long yards of ladder exposed in the open air, then down at the shelter of the trees, and he began descending as rapidly and silently as he could.

Chapter Nineteen

Pel frowned as he looked down at the trees beneath. He remembered, a little belatedly, how Taillefer had landed at Regisvert, tumbling out of the sky onto half a dozen waiting helpers.

Pel didn't have any helpers. And tumbling down through the forest canopy looked scratchy.

On the other hand, he had access to more power than Taillefer could ever imagine.

But Taillefer was more experienced and skilled at using his power, and this particular area was one where there were no strong natural currents of magic, so that the matrix was relatively weak.

Relatively weak, but still vastly stronger than anything Taillefer could do. And even here, Valadrakul had been able to blast Shadow's creatures.

The power to do any sort of landing he wanted was unquestionably there, but Pel had to admit that he didn't really know *how* to land, other than to simply let himself fall. And here in the forest, that might mean breaking a leg or putting his eye out on a broken branch.

He supposed he could use the matrix to protect himself from damage; Shadow had certainly taken her personal invulnerability for granted, and with good reason. It might well be that the matrix would protect him even if he did nothing consciously at all.

His instincts rebelled at the idea, though. Letting himself drop into the trees . . .

He couldn't do it. At least, not from this height.

Maybe, if he lowered himself gradually . . .

He looked ahead, trying to judge distances, and spotted something strange, ahead and to the left. Something was sticking up out of the forest.

He had glimpsed it before, from a distance, and had taken it for an odd branch, or a dead trunk, but now he saw he had badly misjudged its size and distance.

He turned and steered for it.

It rose straight up out of the forest, straighter than anything that could naturally be there, taller and thinner than anything natural, and swaying slightly in the wind. Pel couldn't see the top. He could see above where it stopped, but somehow he couldn't see the exact point at which it ended; there was a blind spot.

And the matrix was kinked out of shape there, he realized.

This was the space-warp. This is what he had intended to be aiming for all along, but he'd gotten so involved in the mechanics of flying, and the view of the landscape, that he had lost track of it.

Well, there it was.

He hadn't really expected anything visible, but there it was.

He hadn't bothered to ask Best or his companions how they got through the warp, but now he saw. That thing was a *ladder,* a rope ladder that reached from a space-warp about five hundred feet up to down in the forest somewhere. It was swinging in gentle curves, swaying back and forth in a shallow sine wave.

That would be an uncomfortably long climb and a dizzy, seasick one, but obviously the Imperial spies had managed it.

And Pel could, too. He wasn't about to go up through the warp — he'd lose control of the matrix if he left Faerie for even a second — but he could grab the ladder and climb down to the ground.

That, at least, was the theory; steering himself through the air at perhaps forty miles an hour and boarding a stationary rope ladder turned out to be much more difficult than he had expected. Instead he smacked into it and then slid on past before he could grab hold, sending the ladder into violent, twisting oscillations and drawing a nasty rope-burn across his right cheek.

He made a wide loop, rubbing his injured face and muttering obscenities, then came back for another pass, dropping so much speed that he began losing altitude rapidly.

He hit the ladder hard, and barely managed to clamp his hands onto a rung about three steps lower than he intended. His arms jarred with the impact, and he wondered if he had injured his shoulder, but he kept his grip.

*S*ebastian Warner stared up at the glowing, seething *thing* that hung in the sky above him.

It had struck the ladder and then passed on through, and Warner had seen the ladder still there and thought he was safe, but then it had looped around and hit the ladder again, and this time it *stayed* there.

It looked as if the ladder was being consumed by some sort of eldritch energy cloud. Since no severed end came tumbling to the ground, Warner assumed that it was not actually being consumed, but he was still cut off from the space-warp. He wasn't about to try climbing through *that.*

In fact, he was hurrying to get off the ladder and away, behind a tree, where the thing might not spot him — assuming it could see.

Once there, he turned and watched for a moment. If he hadn't still been suited up, he'd have drawn his blaster and found out once and for all whether the things really didn't work here.

And he'd wished for something interesting to happen. He should have known better. This was something interesting, all right, and it looked like very bad news indeed.

Of course, it could get worse — and as he watched, it *did* get worse.

The thing started moving downward along the ladder.

*P*el's shoulder ached, and his back felt oddly scraped and raw from the now-vanished wind pressure, and the thick, damp, hot air above the forest made his skin itch and his head hurt, but at least he'd finally gotten both hands and both feet onto the ladder.

He began descending, carefully. The ladder swayed more than he would have liked, so he moved slowly.

As he neared the treetops he noticed the light and color of the matrix flitting across the leaves, and decided he didn't like that. It might attract unwanted attention, and besides, it made it harder for him to see whatever there might be to see around here. Shadow had apparently been able to use the matrix to enhance her senses as a regular, permanent thing, but Pel's mastery of it wasn't anywhere near that complete; it took an effort of will to sense anything through the matrix unless whatever he was sensing was somehow *part* of the matrix.

The space-warp was a part of the matrix, in a way; any attempt to use magic was, as well. Fetches and homunculi and the rest of Shadow's servants and creatures qualified, as well, and showed up without any special effort on his part.

Trees, however, didn't.

That was mildly interesting, actually; Pel had always thought of trees as rather magical things. Certainly they were magical in most of the fantasy stories he'd read.

Maybe some *were* magical, but the Low Forest wasn't, or at least the matrix didn't register anything special there, and the energy currents were weak. And Pel's eyes were having some trouble seeing through the magical haze.

He suppressed it, forcing the magical radiation out of the visible spectrum, and then continued climbing.

*T*he instant it had started downward, Warner had taken off his space helmet and begun opening his suit. He had dragged out his blaster, pointed it, and pressed the trigger.

They were right; nothing happened. It didn't so much as buzz.

He shoved it back in the holster, and was debating whether to turn and run when the cloud-thing vanished, revealing a rather battered-looking man climbing slowly downward.

Was that the notorious Brown Magician, perhaps? Or one of his representatives?

He didn't look like much of a threat.

Warner backed off a few paces and found himself a hiding place in the underbrush; then he waited to see what the new arrival was up to.

*P*el was about ten feet up when he spotted the man in the space suit. He smiled, and dropped to the ground, skipping the last few rungs. "Hey, you!" he called, the matrix amplifying his voice.

The man froze.

"Come on out where I can see you!" Pel beckoned.

The man hesitated, then stepped out of the concealing foliage. He had a bubble helmet under one arm, and his free hand was on the butt of a blaster that protruded through an open seam in his vacuum armor.

"The raygun won't work here," Pel told him. "You can try it if you want."

The man's hand dropped away from the useless weapon.

"I'm Pel Brown," Pel said. "I run this place. Who're you?"

"Lieutenant Sebastian Warner, Imperial Fleet," the stranger replied.

"Good!" Pel said, smiling. This was just what he had hoped — and, from the instant he first saw Warner, expected; nobody but the Galactic Empire would have sent someone here in a purple space suit. "You're holding down the fort for your people, I take it?"

Warner blinked. "I'm sorry, I . . ."

"I mean, they left you in charge here? Or is there a whole installation in the next clearing? Maybe you're using the *Christopher* as your headquarters. If you're not in charge, can you take me to whoever is?"

"It's just . . . listen, whoever you are, I don't have to answer any questions!"

Pel abruptly dropped the suppression, and the matrix flared up around them both in red and orange swirls. "No," he said, "you don't have to answer any questions — but you might *want* to. My name's Pel Brown, as I said, but I'm better known here as Pelbrun, the Brown Magician."

Warner made a wordless noise and stared in horror at the surrounding colors.

"Now, I don't see anyone else here, so unless you tell me otherwise I'm going to assume you're it — in which case, Lieutenant Warner, I do have one question to ask you, and if you don't answer it, you're toast." Pel stopped, caught for a moment by the sudden image his own words conjured up of Raven and Valadrakul and Singer incinerated by Shadow's power.

If Pel wanted it, in an instant this Warner really could be nothing but burnt toast — but the idea sickened Pel. Murder him for failing to answer a question?

But he hadn't really meant the threat, Pel told himself. He just wanted his answer.

Then he admitted to himself that maybe he wanted it enough that he *had* meant the threat seriously, when he made it.

He didn't now; he had no intention of harming this poor jerk.

But he didn't want Warner to know that.

"Are they going to give me what I asked for?" Pel demanded.

"I . . . I don't know," Warner stammered. "What did you ask for?"

"*They* know," Pel said. "You don't? Okay, fine, you don't — then I want you to carry a message for me. You go back up that ladder and tell them I want those bodies *now*. They have . . ." He glanced at Faerie's pale sun. "They have until dawn. Maybe fifteen hours. I'm being generous."

Warner glanced up at the setting sun, as well, then swallowed.

"Now, you get back up that ladder and *tell* them!" Pel shouted.

Quickly, Warner started to set his helmet in place, then realized that the sealing buckles and latches along the side-seam weren't closed. He dropped the helmet and began clamping them shut as quickly as he could, as the apparition he had taken for an ordinary man stared at him from a boiling cloud of violet smoke.

A moment later he was suited up and climbing. Pel watched him ascend a few feet; then he sat down on the dirt of the forest floor and sighed.

Warner glanced down, but kept moving.

Pel watched Warner clamber up into the treetops, then out into the sky beyond.

He had given them until dawn, which meant he would be spending the night here, in the woods. He looked about.

The matrix would provide light and heat without any effort at all, but shelter . . . well, he could make it easily enough, but wasn't the wreck of the *Christopher* just over that way?

And seeing what remained of the giant bat-thing would be interesting, too.

Pel got up, dusted off the seat of his pants, and after a final glance at Warner's distant form, he strolled off into the trees.

"*I*t's all clear, I suppose?" Warner's captain said; then he got a look at the lieutenant's face as Warner stepped out of the airlock, his helmet already off and dangling from one hand, and the captain realized that something was wrong.

"He's down there!" Warner said, addressing his superior and ignoring the Imperial envoy who stood, half-in and half-out of a space suit, to one side.

"Who is?" the captain asked, glancing at the array of Imperial brass up in the observation area.

"Pelbrun! The Brown Magician!" Warner answered, ignoring the glance.

"Where?" the envoy asked. "He's supposed to be in his fortress, I . . ."

"He's right there! At the foot of the ladder! He came out of a cloud and found me there!"

The captain looked up again, and caught Albright's signal.

"Wait here," he said.

"*T*he telepaths say it's possible," Markham told the others. "Apparently they don't have a very good grasp of the geography there, especially now that both our contacts have returned to Imperial space, but Brown does appear to have moved out of his fortress somehow."

"So he's waiting for us to deliver the bodies," Sheffield said. "He said he wanted them *there, now,* and he's come to collect them."

"And he's given us a specific deadline this time," Albright commented.

"Which we don't know exactly, since your lieutenant neglected to check his watch," Markham pointed out.

"We wouldn't know it exactly in any case, since none of your people have ever bothered to calibrate the local cycles there," Albright retorted. "Besides, how does this Earthman define dawn? First light? Semicircle at true horizon? Sun clear of the visible horizon?"

"Not much of a horizon in the middle of a forest," Markham answered.

"I don't think we want to wait for his deadline in any case," Sheffield said. "I think we go ahead with our original plan, and send the envoy — the only difference is that he'll be negotiating right now, instead of days from now. Does either of you gentlemen see any reason we shouldn't proceed thus?"

Markham and Albright glanced quickly at one another, but neither spoke.

*P*el had worked his way through the mummified remnants of Shadow's flying monster, studying the bones and skin with interest, puzzling out just why the Imperials had cut away the parts they did while leaving the rest, and was just starting a look through the wreck of I.S.S. *Christopher* when he heard a human voice calling.

He hesitated. It was obvious that the Imperials had used the ship and clearing as a temporary base during their ventures into Faerie, and he was curious about just how they had set it up, and how many of them had been here — and for that matter, whether anyone might still be here.

No, he could tell, magically, that no one was in the ship.

He did want to see the inside — he'd felt a twinge of nostalgia when he first saw the familiar purple paint, now somewhat marred by weather and abuse. He had only been on the ship for perhaps an hour, but it had, after all, been a fairly important hour, the one that brought him to Faerie, where he had a chance to revive his family.

But that voice was probably the Empire's representatives, delivering the bodies, and if he had a choice between thinking about his wife and child as they were, or bringing them back from the dead, he'd be a fool to settle for memories.

Anyone who wanted to find him here could do so readily enough, since the glow of the matrix was probably visible for miles, but still, it wouldn't hurt to let whoever it was know that he was welcome.

"Hello!" Pel called, stepping out of the hatchway. "Over here!"

Perhaps two minutes later he and the Imperial envoy came face to face on the narrow track Imperial traffic had worn between ladder and clearing; Pel stopped dead at the sight of him.

The man was wearing the most outlandish outfit Pel had encountered since leaving Earth, somewhat the worse for having been stuffed inside a space suit for the climb through the warp. The pants were black velvet with broad purple silk stripes down either side, stuffed into shiny black jackboots; the shirt was white silk with elaborate lace ruffles down the front, artfully fluffed up around a diagonal purple silk sash that combined with a purple silk cummerbund to make a bizarre imitation of a Sam Browne belt. Over this, the stranger wore a bright red cutaway jacket with gold braid on the cuffs and shoulders, and the Imperial seal on the breast — a lion and unicorn rampant against a sunburst, a seal that Pel had first seen on the door of an aircar on Psi Cassiopeia II.

Pel couldn't tell whether the gold-and-white ruffled lace collar that flared out from the man's neck was part of the shirt, the jacket, or neither.

The crowning glory of this comic-opera outfit was undoubtedly the hat, a curling, almost brimless, vaguely conical thing of red velvet and white and purple ostrich plumes.

That the sunlight was gone and the only illumination came from the shifting colors of the matrix made this costume all the more bizarre. Pel tried to shift the light toward white, so as to see this thing better, and belatedly thought to make sure that the matrix was transparent, so that this character could see him, as well.

Why on Earth had they sent this person to deliver the bodies, instead of just a soldier or two?

"My Lord Pelbrun?" the man asked, standing straight and snapping his heels together.

"Yeah," Pel managed.

The apparition took off his hat and bowed, with a flourish. After a moment of frozen formal subordination, he rose, reached into an inside pocket, and pulled out a packet roughly the size of a business envelope, which he proffered to Pel. "My credentials, sir."

Too dazed to even laugh, and feeling a twinge of dread, Pel reached out with a tendril of magic and took the packet; it felt like parchment, and was sealed with gold leaf and purple sealing wax. He pulled it open and tugged out a large sheet of paper — or more likely parchment — which he unfolded and glanced at.

It was in elaborate old-fashioned script, and Pel didn't care to bother reading it by matrixlight, but he did notice the signature and elaborate blue seal at the bottom.

Georgius VIII Imperator et Rex.

That sounded pretty official.

"Okay," Pel said, "the Emperor sent you. Who the hell *are* you?"

"My name is Ambrose Curran, my lord, and I am an accredited Imperial envoy. His Imperial Majesty has sent me to negotiate the terms under which he will yield to you the mortal remains of Nancy and Rachel Brown."

"Terms?" Pel needed a second or two to absorb that; he was still bemused by Curran's appearance.

Then it sank in, and the matrix turned angry red as he repeated, *"Terms?"* His voice rang and echoed, and tree-branches creaked warningly.

Chapter Twenty

Ambrose Curran stepped back involuntarily and threw up an arm to shield his eyes as the ragged man vanished behind a blazing, surging cloud of scarlet energy. White and red light flashed across the forest, interspersed with sharp-edged stripes of black shadow where the trees blocked the furious brilliance.

"Yes, my lord," Curran said, "but I assure you, the terms are not onerous in the least. As His Imperial Majesty's representative, I promise you we seek only the friendship natural between two great and puissant lords and their respective realms."

According to accepted protocol that was a proper way to phrase it, but Curran had some doubts as to whether this Brown would like it. From his speech and appearance the man seemed to be rather a rough and ready sort, not a traditional aristocrat at all — and that was hardly surprising, since he was, after all, a usurper.

"I don't want your fucking emperor's *friendship,*" said the roaring voice from the glowing cloud. "I want my wife and child!"

"Of course," Curran said, just managing to keep his voice steady. He wished he knew whether this obscenity was an indication of the Brown Magician's fury, or simply a lower-class usurper's natural style. "And we intend to deliver them, just as soon as we have your assurance that you will cease your interference in Imperial affairs."

"I don't give a shit about Imperial affairs!" the voice screamed, and Curran heard branches crack and fall. The cloud was showing several colors now, changing too fast for Curran to name them all. "I want Nancy and Rachel, I want them lowered down a rope from that fucking hole in the sky you've got up there, and I want it done *now,* or you can kiss your whole fucking Galactic Empire good-bye!"

"My lord . . ."

"Just shut up with that 'lord' crap while you're at it, and get your ass back up that ladder!"

"I have my orders, Mr. Brown . . ."

"Then they've ordered you to die, you stupid son of a bitch! Last chance!"

"And you think they'll deliver if you kill me?" Curran shouted, backing away another step.

The air suddenly stilled, and for a moment an unnatural silence fell. Then the voice spoke again, and to Curran it sounded more like growling machinery than like anything human.

"State your terms, then, errand boy."

Curran did not think this was the time for formality or protocol; he gave his position in the simplest, most direct way he could. "We want your spies withdrawn, that's all. We know we didn't get them all. We want them out of the Empire, and your word that you won't send more. As soon as they're gone, we deliver the bodies."

Again there was a moment of eerie stillness. Then the voice, once again sounding human, said, "That's all?"

"That's all."

"You really want them withdrawn, or would you rather they turned themselves in? You could question them about whatever they did for Shadow before I took over; might be interesting for your cops."

Curran hesitated. That hadn't been covered in his instructions; no one had considered the possibility that Brown could be so ruthless as to turn his own people over to Imperial Intelligence.

It seemed an irresistible opportunity, and after all, if Secretary Sheffield decided it was a mistake, he could just have them all sent through the warp.

Or killed.

"Either one would be satisfactory," he said.

"They'll turn themselves in, then," the voice said. "Easier for me — I don't have any use for them here."

"As you please."

"It may take a few days for word to reach 'em all."

"Of course."

"If you get back up that ladder and get the gears turning on your end, I'll get started on mine. I want those corpses *soon* — you tell your people that. No more stupid delays; as soon as my people start surrendering, you get those bodies here."

"I'll deliver your terms, of course." Curran bowed again.

"Go on, then!"

Curran turned and walked off with as much dignity as he could muster, hoping he wouldn't have any difficulty finding the ladder and donning his space suit in the dark.

He was not looking forward to that long climb.

The welcome at the top should be pleasant enough, though; Brown had, after all, agreed.

*P*el didn't bother to watch as the Imperial geek put his space suit on and started up the ladder; despite his shouting, he knew it would be hours before Curran could get his message through and the bureaucracy could process it. He didn't really expect the bodies to be delivered for a day or so.

Pel shook his head as he trudged back toward I.S.S. *Christopher.*

That outfit Curran wore was really amazing; now that Pel was over his initial surprise and subsequent fury, he could marvel at its absurdity. The Galactic Empire really did have some odd quirks. *Why* would they dress their ambassadors, or whatever they were, like that?

It certainly made them distinctive, anyway.

Which was probably the point.

If that regalia was what ambassadors wore, what did the Emperor wear for formal occasions?

It didn't matter, of course. What mattered was getting Nancy and Rachel back. And that would be easy enough; all he had to do was order Gregory to spread the word — everyone was to pass the message on, then surrender to the Imperial authorities.

That was really reasonable enough; when Pel had first heard that the Empire had terms he had expected something difficult or unpleasant. Once he had his family back, though, what did he need spies for?

He wondered what the Empire would do with them all; Pel didn't know himself how extensive Shadow's network of spies actually was, but he was fairly sure there were at least a couple of dozen. He supposed they'd wind up serving time in prison for espionage.

If they had been real people, Pel might have felt guilty about that, but surely they were all simulacra or fetches or other Shadow-creatures, and from everything he'd seen of those, they had such a flattened emotional response that prison probably wouldn't bother them much.

And maybe he could work some sort of trade later on, buy them free somehow.

Maybe he should have said that he'd withdraw them, rather than suggesting that they turn themselves in — but what would he have done with them all, here in Faerie? They'd have just been in the way.

And it would have taken ages to round them all up.

He stumbled over a broken branch, and, annoyed, vaporized it in a shower of emerald-green sparks.

Then he was in the clearing, the bat-thing's remains rearing up before him in an eerie maze of black flesh and white bone; he marched past without paying much attention, up to the hatchway of *Christopher.*

He'd open his portal to Gregory's place, whatever it was, aboard the ship; he didn't want to do it out here in the open, where stray birds or chipmunks or something might wander through it. He wondered if birds ever flew into the Empire's space-warp up there, to emerge into vacuum and die.

That was a nasty thought.

And for that matter, he wondered why air didn't flow constantly through the opening into the space beyond. Did the warp create some sort of static field, perhaps, that held it back?

He didn't know — and it didn't matter.

The interior of the ship wasn't quite as he remembered it; there were dead leaves here and there, a few seats had been removed, and it appeared that something had chewed at some of the maroon leatherette upholstery.

Squirrels, probably.

The lights didn't work, of course, but the matrix made them superfluous in any case.

He settled in one of the aisle seats that was still clean and intact, and began concentrating on opening a portal.

It was much more difficult than he had expected; the nearness of the space-warp created a fierce counter-pressure that he had to struggle against, and the relative weakness of the matrix so far from any power spot left him with far less energy than he had ever had available before when attempting such a task.

Nonetheless, after about half an hour of effort that left him sweating and trembling, he forced open the portal.

Nothing happened. No one stepped out.

"God *damn* it!" Pel shouted. Fighting to maintain the spell, he reached a magical tendril back into the aft storeroom and swept out everything he could reach.

Steel bottles of oxygen, purple cotton packs and bedrolls, black folding shovels, pieces of space suits, and a great pile of unidentifiable equipment came tumbling through the hatchway into the passenger compartment; Pel let most of it drop as he snatched up an oxygen cylinder and heaved it through the portal.

It vanished, instantly and silently, but Pel was sure it made a suitable clatter on the other side.

He waited.

The portal refused to stabilize completely; keeping it open took a constant effort, and after five more minutes Pel wasn't sure how long he could hold it. The matrix seemed to be fighting him, rather than cooperating.

He found a piece of equipment with glass parts — he had no idea what it was, some sort of scientific apparatus by the look of it — and heaved *that* through the opening.

Then he waited again.

Finally, Gregory's head appeared, and a moment later Pel's chief spy stood aboard the ship, looking around with mild interest.

"Yes, master?" he asked.

Pel cleared his throat, and began explaining.

When he got to the main point, that everyone was to surrender, Gregory's usual bland expression turned uneasy.

"O Great One, are you sure that . . ."

"Sure enough. Do it."

"Yes, master," Gregory said unhappily.

It was the first time Pel had seen such unhappiness on a simulacrum's face, and he felt a twinge of guilt.

"Listen, if you think they'll mistreat you . . ."

"No, O Great One, it's not that," Gregory explained. "It's that we'll no longer be able to serve you. We won't have a master to tell us what to do."

Pel blinked.

Shadow had obviously done a thorough job of indoctrinating her creations — or maybe it was something in the nature of simulacra.

"All right, then," he said, "if you want, and they allow it, you can swear fealty or whatever to the Emperor, and make *him* your new master."

Gregory's relief was evident. "Thank you," he said.

"Now, get back there and get it started!"

C urran was startled to not see any officials in the prep room when he emerged from the airlock. He had expected Markham and Albright and Secretary Sheffield to be waiting impatiently, had thought they would reprimand him for taking the time to remove his space suit.

Instead there was just an ordinary soldier standing there, ready to welcome him back.

"This way, sir," the young man said, gesturing.

Curran followed, puzzled, as he was led out of the warp facility and into the main working area of Base One, down corridors and up lifts until he arrived at the door of a conference room.

Two guards stood at the door. After an exchange of salutes and whispers, one of the guards opened the door and ushered Curran in.

Sheffield stood at the head of a long table, presiding over the meeting; along the sides were Markham, Albright, and Howe, as Curran might have expected — but also John Bascombe, Samuel Best, Sebastian Warner, Ron Wilkins, Brian Hall, Carrie Hall, General Hart, Major Cochran, and at least a dozen others Curran didn't immediately recognize.

Everyone who had attended any of Curran's briefings for this assignment appeared to be present.

All of them glanced up as the door opened.

"Ah, Curran," Secretary Sheffield said. "Come in! We've saved you a seat." He pointed.

Curran took the chair indicated, between Best and Warner, and whispered to Best, "What's happened?"

Best leaned over and whispered back, "One of Brown's agents threatened the Emperor. In person. In the Imperial Palace itself."

"He *what?*" Curran blinked.

"She. We got word telepathically just after you went through the warp — even thought about calling you back, but by the time we could have suited someone else up . . ."

"How'd this person . . . what did she . . ."

"No one knows how she got in, but she was waiting in the Emperor's private apartments when he prepared to retire, and she told him that the Brown Magician wants the bodies *now.*"

"Oh, my God."

"But what's *really* frightening," Best said, "is that she *got away.*"

"How?"

"We don't know."

"I take it, Mr. Curran," Sheffield's voice said, overriding the private exchange, "that Mr. Best has filled you in on the situation."

Curran looked up, startled. "Yes, sir," he said.

"I believe you've just spoken with the Brown Magician — and after this latest stunt, I begin to think he deserves to be called a magician."

"Yes, sir."

"Did he say anything that might shed light on this situation?"

Curran hesitated, swallowed, then stood up, and reported the conversation.

He was still answering questions about the details when the telepaths began delivering the first reports of surrendering agents.

"So what's the general attitude over there?" the lieutenant asked casually.

"Scared shitless," Carleton Miletti replied.

That was different; the lieutenant struggled not to show any interest, since that might break Miletti's semi-trance. "Why's that?" he asked.

"Oh, Brown did something they didn't think was possible, something to do with their emperor," Miletti explained.

"What did he do?"

Miletti shrugged. "No idea," he said. "I didn't catch that."

"Was he trying to scare them into turning over the remains?" the lieutenant asked.

"Probably. They don't know."

"Didn't work, of course."

"Of course not."

*P*el stretched and yawned as he stood in the open hatchway. He'd slept away most of the morning, he was sure. The sunlight spattered across the clearing was not at a particularly low angle.

Leaves rustled overhead, and branches sighed in the breeze, but other than that all was quiet. There was no Imperial deputation waiting to deliver the bodies.

He supposed they might be huddling at the foot of the ladder, but he doubted it. More likely they were signing receipts and filling out forms before releasing anything. Either that, or they were waiting to see how many spies they collected before they paid for them.

After a good night's sleep, Pel was in a far better temper than he had been; he was willing to be magnanimous and patient. The Empire had agreed to deliver the corpses, he had met their terms — it was just a matter of time.

He hopped down from the ship and ambled toward the ladder, smiling.

*T*he first surrenders were on Delta Scorpius IV; from there, they radiated out into the Empire at slightly less than the speed a courier ship could travel.

Word of the initial round reached Base One almost instantly; when Samuel Best had turned up on Delta Scorpius IV, Albright had made sure that the local government there had a telepath on hand at all times. He'd also had men search the area where Best said he had appeared, and had had a guard posted, but had not located any sort of space-warp. Best's description wasn't sufficient to pinpoint the exact spot, but at least they knew which building it was — Best said he had found himself in the office area of an old warehouse.

When the surrenders began, Albright had sent for a report from those guards.

There had been a small disturbance a day or so before the first surrender — objects had appeared loudly from nowhere. A civilian who had been hanging around, one of the people who worked there, had argued with the guards, slipped out of sight for a time, then returned.

They hadn't held him. Albright cursed them all for idiots when he heard that.

They had checked his identity, though — his name was Peter Gregory. Albright ordered an immediate search.

It was two days later that Gregory was found — or rather, that he turned himself in at the local constabulary, announcing that he was the ringleader of the Brown Magician's espionage network.

By then, however, Albright hardly cared. The surrenders had spread as far as Base One, and shock after shock was registering as one trusted person after another announced that he or she was actually one of Shadow's spies, now working for the Brown Magician. The telepaths were constantly busy, interrogating the captured spies — or trying to; many, it turned out, were impervious to telepathy, which explained how they had survived for so long.

No one had expected that.

And no one had expected how *many* spies would turn themselves in. The official count made Peter Gregory #113, and Marshal Albright was morally certain that there were others whose capture had not yet been reported — and that there were many more yet to come.

After all, these were just from a two-day radius around Delta Scorpius IV, and the Empire's full expanse required thirty days to cross.

And while no one in the Emperor's cabinet had surrendered, nor anyone in Intelligence, nor any telepaths — *that* was a terrifying thought! — still, it was a shock when General Hart's aide confessed to deliberately arranging for the inept Colonel Carson to command the expedition to Faerie, instead of the competent Captain Haggerty, to ensure the mission's failure; when an engineer confessed to unsuccessfully attempting to sabotage the entire space-warp program; when Major Harrison acknowledged doing everything he could to ensure hostility between the Empire and Earth . . .

How could there be so many infiltrators?

Why hadn't the telepaths long ago spotted them and reported them?

And the most frightening question of all — if Pel Brown was giving all these agents up, *what was he holding back?*

Chapter Twenty-One

*P*el sat cross-legged on the verandah of his treehouse and glared angrily up the dangling rope ladder.

A little time for paperwork and general dithering was one thing, but this was getting ridiculous. He had been hanging around here for *days,* waiting for the Empire to make good on its promise.

He had kept himself busy. He had constructed the elaborate four-room treehouse, growing some parts and building others, and then furnishing it to suit himself, using pieces of the dead bat-thing and I.S.S. *Christopher* for some of his raw materials; he had sent messages written on tree bark and shaped into gliders, rather like paper airplanes, back to the fortress, to keep Susan and the imitation Nancy appraised of his whereabouts; he had created a few monstrous little servants for himself from bits of tissue he found in the forest — tufts of fur, lost feathers, and the like.

And he'd done all that, made himself this cozy little nest, and all the time, what the hell had the Empire done?

Nothing, so far as he could see!

No one had emerged from the warp since that popinjay Curran had departed.

And nobody responded when he opened the portal to Gregory's place and threw things in — presumably Gregory had, as ordered, turned himself in to the Imperial police.

Well, they'd had quite long enough.

Without looking, he sent an arm of the matrix back to the clearing, a hundred yards away — he'd done this often enough while working on the house that he hardly needed to think about it anymore.

The magic touched *Christopher.* Rivets flashed red and parted, as purple paint blackened and flaked away; a moment later a hull plate, about four feet by eight, popped out of the wrecked ship's hull and floated gently upward.

Black letters etched themselves into the metal surface, spelling out Pel's message: YOU HAVE ONE HOUR TO CONTACT ME AND EXPLAIN THE DELAY.

Then the curved steel sheet sailed up through the treetops, and on through the space-warp at the top of the ladder.

*H*ow many more were there?

Secretary Sheffield's hands trembled as he stared at the latest list. Terra itself appeared to be complete now, as Base One had been for days; the woman who had appeared in the Emperor's own bedroom was secure, under heavy guard. Surrenders had ceased throughout most of the inner Empire, though more of Shadow's agents continued to trickle in elsewhere.

The count was over four hundred in all.

Four hundred, including generals, technicians, records clerks, confidential secretaries, and assorted others in sensitive positions.

And they had thought that after Operation Spotlight, with its haul of almost a hundred, there might still be as many as twenty left.

How had Shadow done it? She must have spent all her free time for seven years infiltrating her agents into the Empire! And some of these agents were people who had well-documented histories going back to childhood, thirty, forty, fifty years ago, but the telepaths were now saying that some of them weren't even truly human. How had Shadow managed that? Had she corrupted records? Had she somehow created false memories in friends and family members? Had she substituted her imitations for the real people?

If so, how had she done it without their closest friends noticing any change?

Had she actually been working her agents into the Empire for decades, not just the seven years everyone had assumed?

And what was Pel Brown holding in reserve? Surely, he wouldn't give up this network for next to nothing. Were these four hundred just the tip of the iceberg?

It was a nightmare.

The list was still clutched in his hand when someone knocked on the door.

"Come in," he called.

The door opened, and a messenger saluted nervously.

"A message has been received, Your Excellency," he said, "from the Brown Magician."

Sheffield looked up, cold dread clutching his heart.

The messenger cleared his throat, and continued, "It was etched into a plate from a spaceship's outer hull. The complete text read, 'You have one hour to contact me and explain the delay.' It came through the warp . . ." He glanced at his watch. " . . . twenty-three minutes ago."

"Good God," Sheffield said, struggling to his feet.

His legs didn't want to support him; he leaned heavily on the table.

They had to keep Brown talking.

"Send a messenger through immediately," he said. "Before the hour is up. The messenger is to say that an explanation will be along within another hour. Use a telepath to get that to the warp crew, if it's fastest — do whatever it takes. Go! Get going!"

The messenger saluted, and turned away.

"Run!" Sheffield shouted after him. "Run, damn you!"

The messenger ran.

*P*el wished he had a watch.

Electronics didn't work in Faerie, though, so his old digital watch would have been useless even if he still had it. Spring-driven watches probably worked well enough, but they didn't appear to have been invented here — at any rate, Pel hadn't seen any.

He hadn't bothered to make a sundial, either.

An hourglass would be in keeping with the local technology, but he didn't have one, and he had no idea how he could calibrate the thing if he created one.

It made it hard to tell how much of the hour had passed. It *felt* as if it had been an hour or more since he had sent that chunk of steel through the warp, but he couldn't really tell for sure.

Just then he felt the kinking of the matrix as something came through the warp. He looked up, blinking against the sun, and tried to focus on the top of the ladder.

Leaves were in the way, but that was easily fixed; a brief flare in the matrix and nothing blocked his view, not even the drifting wisp of smoke that was all that remained of the branches that had obtruded.

The space suited figure was moving slowly and carefully down the ladder, and Pel didn't want to wait; he reached a magical something up and snatched the person off the ladder, swept him spiraling down through the treetops and deposited him with a bump on Pel's own verandah, in the very midst of the glare of the matrix.

"Maybe you should just give him the damn bodies," Markham suggested.
Albright turned, shocked. "Give up our only bargaining chip?"
Markham shrugged.
"Why the hell not?" he asked.
But he knew he was outvoted.

Pel kept the first messenger on the verandah while they waited for the second.

The man was terrified. At first Pel didn't much care; he let the fellow sit there in his space suit with the helmet off, trembling, looking around at the trees, at the twenty-foot drop to the ground, at the shifting polychrome of the matrix.

But it was probably going to be an hour before the next guy appeared, and it wasn't the poor messenger's fault he'd been sent. This wasn't anyone Pel had seen before, not Curran or any of the soldiers.

"You been here before?" Pel asked at last.

"No," the messenger said, shaking his head violently. "I haven't even been in a suit since basic training."

"Why'd they send you, then?"

"I was handy. I'm just a base messenger. Secretary Sheffield was in private, no telepath, so they sent me to give him your message, and he sent me back, and they suited me up and put me through. All the regulars, Lieutenant Warner and Lieutenant James and Lieutenant Butler, were in conference somewhere."

"What about Best, or Wilkins?"

The messenger looked up into the glare, then blinked quickly and turned away. "Who?" he asked.

"Never mind." Pel considered telling the poor bastard to suit up and go home, but just then, as he glanced thoughtfully up the ladder, he saw something glitter in the sun.

The second messenger was arriving.

Again, he reached up and plucked the suited figure off the ladder, and swept it down to the verandah.

As he lowered the newcomer to the wooden beams, Pel smiled.

It was Curran, and his absurd hat was squeezed into the helmet of his space suit, looking rather like an unborn chick inside its egg in one of those grade-school science books. Pel was tempted to shatter or dissolve the helmet to free the poor thing, but he resisted — that would have meant stranding the man here until a replacement could be sent.

Or made; Pel supposed he could make one almost as easily as he could shatter one.

Instead, he waited while Curran undogged the thing and lifted it off.

He then doffed his hat, and while still wearing his space suit he bowed dramatically, surreptitiously shaking the feathers back into shape as he did; Pel watched with amusement.

For one thing, Curran had misjudged Pel's position within the glowing haze of the matrix, and was bowing elegantly to a tree-branch.

"All right, Curran," Pel said, "what's the story? Why aren't the bodies here? I had my people turn themselves in; what's the delay?"

"Your pardon, my lord," Curran said. "We just need some surety, some guarantee, that in fact *all* your agents have surrendered."

"Why? Do you have any evidence that some are missing?"

"No, my lord; we just need proof that you've held nothing back. We were, we confess, rather shaken by how high some of them had penetrated in the Imperial government, and we need to know that there are no more."

"There are no more. I give you my word on it," Pel said. "I ordered *all* of them to surrender." He hesitated. "I suppose it's possible a couple didn't get the word, but if so, they're people I've lost contact with myself, so they're harmless." He waved the possibility aside. "In any case, I've lived up to my side of the bargain — I've turned the lot of them over. Now it's the Empire's turn to deliver."

"The bodies of your wife and child, you mean."

"Right. I want them. Now."

"My lord, if you could give us some *proof* that no spies remain . . ."

"How the hell am I supposed to *prove* it?" Pel shouted. "I gave you my word I ordered them all to surrender; what the hell else can I do?"

"I'm afraid I don't know what would satisfy my superiors, my lord; perhaps they don't know themselves."

"Well, you better go back and bloody well find out!" Pel shouted, lifting Curran into the air. "Or better yet, tell them to go fuck themselves — if those bodies aren't here in . . . in two hours, I'll make the Empire regret it!" He tried to force himself to calm down, and partially managed it. "Look, Curran," he said, "all I'm asking is this one simple thing — two corpses that I know you people already have, stored away in a freezer somewhere on Base One. All you have to do is haul 'em through the space warp and lower them down on a rope — what's the big deal? *You* don't care about them! And *I* don't care about your stupid Galactic Empire — I just want my wife and daughter back. You people have set me conditions, you've put me off, you've lied and procrastinated, and I've done nothing but go along with it, I've acted in good faith, I've had dozens of my servants give themselves up, and God only knows what you're doing with them all. And what have I got to show for it?" His temper snapped again. *"Nothing!"* he shouted. *"That's* what I've got to show for it! Well, to hell with you and your damn empire, Mr. Curran — I want those bodies *now,* within *two hours,* or the Empire's going to be very sorry! You go back and you tell them that!"

Curran might have been trying to say something, but whatever it was, Pel didn't wait to hear it; he sent Curran soaring upward on an arc of raw magical energy, toward and through the space warp.

Curran was still trying to dog down his helmet seals when he vanished.

"It's an empty threat," Albright said. "It has to be. What can he possibly do to us? After all, this psionic super-science of his, his so-called 'magic,' can't operate in normal space, can it?"

"Not that we know of," Markham agreed.

"We've broken his spy ring, haven't we? Four or five hundred of them — he *can't* have any more."

"Then if he hasn't got any more, why don't we just give him the damned corpses?" Markham demanded.

"Because we don't *know.* He's making threats — what's he got to back them up with? We need to know."

"It seems to me that we're antagonizing him for no good reason," Markham insisted. "We're treating him as an enemy, and he isn't one." He paused, then corrected himself, "At least, he *wasn't* one. By now, who knows?"

"Of course he's an enemy," Albright said. "How could he be anything else? He's ruler of a world — of a universe! Naturally, he'll want to expand his power, and that means taking from the Empire."

"Does it?" Markham asked.

"If we give in to his demands," Secretary Sheffield said, "then what's to keep him from making further demands, indefinitely?"

Markham looked at him, startled. "Nothing," he said, "but isn't that just what *we're* doing?"

Pel watched as the sun sank in the west. The two hours were up, obviously; they must have been up long ago.

And there had been nothing. No one had emerged from the warp.

The messenger was asleep on the verandah; Pel walked over and stared down at him for a moment.

He looked young and innocent, asleep there on the wooden platform, with his short blond hair and clean-shaven features, his uniform hidden by the bulky space suit.

Pel kicked him in the back of the head — not particularly hard, but more than a mere prodding. The messenger's eyes snapped open, and a hand flew up to the injured spot.

"Get your helmet on," Pel ordered. "You're going home, and I've got a message for you to take."

The messenger scrambled to his feet, and groped for his helmet.

"It's a very simple message," Pel said. "It's this: It'll stop when I have the bodies."

"What will?"

"You don't need to know that. You just tell them, it'll stop when I have the bodies, and not a moment sooner. Got that?"

"Yessir."

"Good. Here you go."

And the messenger was airborne, heading for the warp.

"Get your helmet on!" Pel shouted after him.

He slowed the ascent, and watched as the kid got his helmet in place; then the matrix flung him upward and out through the warp.

That done, the next step, Pel knew, was to attack the Empire. They'd asked for it, and they were going to get it; no more Mr. Nice Guy.

The only question was how.

Chapter Twenty-Two

He didn't like it, but returning to Shadow's fortress was the fastest way to acquire an army. There weren't any people in the Low Forest; there weren't even a lot of animals to work with. He'd grown himself a few furry little servants, but they were hardly suitable for what he had in mind.

He had an entire world to draw on, of course, but the fortress still seemed like the place to start.

The stone halls were cold and gloomy, and Pel wondered why it had taken him so long to get the hell out of this damn tomb, into the wide green world — the sunlight might be the wrong color, the air strange, and the gravity harsh, but it was better than these dank corridors. He certainly didn't want to stay back here any longer than necessary.

He wished there were some sort of rapid transit possible between the fortress and the vicinity of the space-warp; his wind-riding took between three and four hours by his best estimate. The sort of lifting and tossing he'd been doing with Curran and that poor twit of an Imperial messenger was severely limited in range — he couldn't use the pure magic of the matrix to move things much beyond what he could see, and he had trouble moving himself at all; the winds were faster and safer.

Even a phone line would be helpful, or a telepathic link like the ones in the Empire, but he didn't have one. He was fairly sure that magic could be used to communicate over long distances — he'd seen Valadrakul summon Taillefer from afar, and everyone seemed to think that Shadow had spied on people all over the world — but Pel didn't know how it had been done. Once or twice he had thought he was on the verge of using Shadow's trick of seeing through other people's eyes, but he had never quite managed it, and had no idea what he was doing wrong.

He could, he supposed, round up the wizards again, and ask them — in fact, it might be a good idea. Not that he liked them much, or thought he could trust them.

That could wait, though; first he needed to assemble his attack force.

He swept into the throne room, the matrix flaring up more brightly than it ever had in the wilds of Sunderland, and sent out the magical summons — *every* living thing in the fortress was to come to him.

They came — fetches, homunculi, simulacra, monsters, peasants, dogs, cats, everything. The monsters ranged from little buglike flying things the size of his finger up to a creature resembling a rhinoceros that struggled mightily to mount the steps from the entry, and from the sluglike marsh monsters with their simple tubular bodies to a thing that looked like a hundred-pound cross between a spider and an octopus, with additions — it had stalked eyes, tentacles, jointed legs, rudimentary wings, and mandibles like giant pliers.

The dragon, alas, was long dead, its head blown off by Pel's own magic and the remains incinerated. The gigantic bat-things were far too large to ever enter any building, and the great burrowers were not nearby — but that didn't matter, because Pel didn't think he could create a portal anything that size could fit through.

Within moments the throne room was jammed full, and more were still arriving. The humanoids had clustered closest around the throne, arms or hands flung up to shield eyes from the glare; there was the false Nancy, and the real Susan, and any number of fetches and peasants.

Pel thought for a moment, then began giving orders.

Shelton Grigsby had always had mixed feelings about his post as governor-general of Beckett. Beckett was a pleasant enough place to live — the gravity was light, the air sweet, the sunlight rich, if a trifle unpleasantly reddish, and the locals were friendly and peaceful. The local flora was plentiful and only rarely toxic, the local fauna generally harmless. Of the three thousand worlds in the Empire, this was definitely one of the mildest environments.

The planet was, however, something of a backwater, well out of the political mainstream, and he sometimes regretted giving up the opportunities for advancement he'd have had if he'd held a post back on Terra or one of the other innermost worlds. A governor-general out here could expect to serve until retirement or death; a peerage, or promotion to the Imperial Council or the Emperor's cabinet, was unlikely in the extreme.

He had always consoled himself with the thought that he'd probably live longer without the stress and strain of political intrigue, that he'd given up his ambitions but found peace. He'd certainly never expected any trouble on Beckett, with its placid population of a hundred million or so, spread over four small continents and a score of moderately large cities.

He should have known better, he thought.

But he had certainly never expected any trouble out of Blessingbury. The town was a resort in the foothills of the Darlington Mountains, small but reasonably modern, and well supplied with all the essentials and a good many luxuries — a place for the moderately-well-off to spend their annual vacations hiking, riding, or swimming.

Now, though, Blessingbury seemed to be attracting trouble, rather than tourists.

First there were those mysterious corpses, with their swords, that had been shipped off to Base One and got the Empire to station a squad of soldiers and even a telepath in town.

Now, he had a report of monsters.

He glanced out the window of the limousine; they had bypassed the town itself and headed for the meadows to the northeast, where the corpses had been found and where the monster had been reported.

From up here everything looked ordinary enough.

The car was descending; the chauffeur had his orders, and was following them.

A moment later, Grigsby stepped out and clapped his hat on his head — this was official business, and he had to look the part.

A lieutenant in full uniform stepped up to greet him; Grigsby snapped off a salute, then turned toward the meadow.

It wasn't hard to find the monster; the thing was lying dead, half a dozen soldiers standing in a ring around it.

It was black and hideous, with fangs and tentacles, and Grigsby had no doubt what it was — he'd read all those briefing papers, like a good little official.

It was a Shadow-beast.

But wasn't Shadow supposed to be dead?

"What killed it?" he asked.

"We don't know," the lieutenant replied. "It was still alive and moving when it was first spotted, but it apparently keeled over shortly after, and by the time anyone dared get close it was definitely dead."

"Where'd it come from?"

The lieutenant shrugged. "Who knows? There was a trail in the grass, but it appeared out of nowhere a few feet back."

Grigsby turned to look at the place the soldier indicated — and at that moment, three pale, black-garbed men stepped out of thin air in that exact spot, rayguns ready in their hands.

One of the soldiers reached for his blaster, and an invader blew his head off before the weapon cleared its holster.

Even to the governor's untrained eye, though, the attacker's hand seemed unsteady, his aim poor; only the very short range allowed him to hit his target.

"Down!" the lieutenant shouted, tugging at Grigsby's arm, and Grigsby dropped, stunned by what he had just seen.

That first shot was followed by more; Grigsby heard the electric crackle of blaster discharge and the dull explosions of superheated tissue where the bolts struck, but didn't see any of what was happening as he dropped and huddled in the tall grass, the lieutenant's arm flung protectively across his shoulders.

Then, cautiously, he looked up from behind the carcass of the dead monster.

The grass surrounded them in broken disarray; to one side was the slick black hide of the Shadow-beast. Overhead was the familiar purple sky of Beckett, but the blue-white discharges of blasters discolored it in streaks and flashes.

He couldn't see, from here, who was firing at what.

"What's going on?" he shouted.

The lieutenant lifted up on one elbow.

"There are more of them," he said, "but I don't see . . ."

Another blaster crackled, and the lieutenant dove again. He groped at his belt for his own weapon. "Stay down, Your Excellency," he said. Then he was up on his knees, crouching behind the dead Shadow-beast, using it for shelter as he snapped off three quick shots.

Then blue-white electric fire tore through the air and the lieutenant dropped his blaster and fell, clutching at the bloody ruin of his left ear.

"Drop your weapons!" someone shouted — a woman's voice. "If you don't shoot at us, we won't hurt you!"

Grigsby looked at the wounded lieutenant, at the blaster flashes, and shouted, "Cease fire!" He tugged at the lieutenant's sleeve and told him, "Order them! Cease fire!"

The lieutenant winced, hesitated, then called, "Cease fire!"

The louder discharges stopped almost immediately; the enemy, whoever it was, took two more shots before they, too, stopped firing.

Cautiously, Grigsby pushed himself up on all fours, then rose to a kneeling position and peered over the dead monster's back.

There were eight or nine of the strangers now — eight or nine still standing, at any rate, and others lying on the ground, dead or wounded. Most of them were men wearing odd, primitive clothing — the same sort of clothing, Grigsby realized, as those mysterious corpses that had appeared in this same meadow some weeks back.

Behind the others, though, was a woman — a woman wearing a heavy black jacket but little or nothing else; her legs were completely bare.

What the hell was a half-naked woman doing on a battlefield?

Of the six soldiers who had surrounded the dead monster, three lay unmoving, two of them visibly missing pieces and obviously dead, the third perhaps only wounded; another sat clutching a blackened arm that hung limp; and the other two, who had taken shelter behind the monster, appeared unhurt.

A stray bolt had hit Grigsby's official aircar, and a corner of the roof was now torn, blackened, twisted metal instead of sleek purple lacquer. The chauffeur, Ben Miller, had dived out the other side and now crouched behind the vehicle.

At least, Grigsby thought, Miller hadn't simply flown off and left the others to die.

On the other hand, if he *had* flown off, and hadn't been shot down, he might have summoned aid.

"Who are you? What do you want?" Grigsby shouted.

And where the devil did they come from, he wondered silently. He had seen the first three appear as if out of nowhere, and these others had presumably arrived during the fighting, but there were no tracks, there had been no sound to indicate their arrival.

"If you'll step this way, we'll explain everything," the woman answered, gesturing. Grigsby noticed for the first time that her hands were empty. In fact, he realized, most of the attackers appeared to be unarmed; he only counted three blasters.

Maybe ceasing fire had been a mistake; if those were the same three blasters that the first arrivals had had, they couldn't have very much charge left.

It was too late now, though; he would play along for the moment.

"You, the driver," the woman called, "and you in the fancy suit — you two go first, the wounded go last."

Grigsby had serious misgivings about this, but he reluctantly emerged from what little shelter he had and stepped up to where the woman indicated.

"Here?" he said.

"One more step," she replied.

He obligingly took one more step . . .

And Beckett vanished.

"So what's the total?" Pel asked, looking up from the unconscious lieutenant.

"We now have nine blasters," Susan replied. "However, two of them appear to be low on charge. Eight fetches were destroyed. Nancy and the other fetches are unhurt."

"Fetches are no great loss," Pel said. "Was anyone on their side hurt?"

"Three men dead," the false Nancy reported. "Six captured."

"I can count the captured for myself." Pel, still on his knees, looked around.

There were four soldiers, counting the lieutenant; he had already repaired an injured arm on one before attending to the lieutenant's ruined ear. There was a dignified elderly man in a fancy suit — nothing as elaborate as that man Curran's rig, but this fellow was obviously someone important. And the last man wore a black-and-maroon uniform that Pel had never seen before.

"Someone go get the dead ones," Pel said. He picked two of the fetches and pointed them out by surrounding them in a golden glow. "You and you — bring the three dead men." He glanced at the Nancy simulacrum. "Were they all soldiers?"

"Yes."

"Just the ones in purple uniforms, then — don't bother with the ones in black."

The fetches disappeared into the portal.

Pel stood up, stretched his back, and crossed to his throne. He settled in, got himself comfortable, then largely suppressed the visible manifestations of the matrix, allowing the Imperials to see him.

"All right," he said, "who are you all?" He pointed at the man in the fancy suit. "You first."

"My name is Shelton Grigsby," that gentleman said. "I'm a representative of His Imperial Majesty's government on Beckett."

"What sort of a representative?" Pel asked, curious.

Grigsby didn't answer. Pel shrugged, and pointed to the man in the black uniform. "What about you?"

The man glanced at Grigsby, then said, "I'm Gov . . . I'm Mr. Grigsby's driver."

"What's your name?"

"Ben Miller."

"You're a chauffeur?"

Miller nodded.

"You drive aircars?"

Miller nodded again.

"Good!" Pel said. "That's perfect. You tell me what kind of a representative your Mr. Grigsby is, then, and I'll let you go home."

Miller glanced at his superior, who said nothing, whose expression gave nothing away. The soldiers shifted about uneasily; the lieutenant, no longer under Pel's sleep spell, stirred uneasily.

"Okay, don't tell me," Pel said with a shrug. "I'd think, after seeing me grow that man a new ear and put the other's arm back together, you'd have a bit more appreciation of me than that, but what the hell. Susan, get a blaster."

Susan took a raygun from a nearby fetch.

"Now, unless someone tells me just who this Mr. Grigsby is, what his job is, and what an Imperial representative is doing on your little backwater planet," Pel said, "I'm going to tell this woman to put that blaster to Mr. Miller's ear and pull the trigger." He grinned broadly as he spoke.

It was, he supposed, a pretty cruel joke; these people didn't know that the blaster wouldn't work here. Frankly, though, he didn't much care; he was fed up with Imperial uncooperativeness. He wanted to show he could be ruthless — and he had to do it before they saw him bring their dead companions back to life, or the effect would be ruined.

Of course, he could threaten to fry them all magically, which would be a more *honest* threat, but somehow Pel suspected the blaster would be a more *effective* threat. These people undoubtedly believed in blasters, while they probably didn't believe in magic.

It was Grigsby who spoke up, which obscurely pleased Pel.

"Don't shoot him," he said. "I'm the governor-general of Beckett."

Pel's nasty grin turned into a pleased smile. "Governor-general? Is that what it sounds like?"

"I couldn't say," Grigsby answered. "I've no idea what it sounds like to a barbarian such as yourself. And just who, might I ask, *are* you? You know who we are; who are you? Are you Shadow?"

"No, I'm . . ." Pel hesitated, then gave the name he was known by here — maybe back on Earth he was Pellinore Brown, but not here. "I'm Pelbrun, the Brown Magician. And to me, 'Governor-General' sounds like the highest office on the . . . the planet? Is Beckett the name of the planet? Or is it just an island or a continent or something?"

"Beckett is the planet," Grigsby admitted.

"That's great!" Pel was absolutely delighted; this was a real stroke of luck. This first raid in his planned campaign of terror had just been intended to add to his armory; he hadn't hoped for so valuable a hostage.

He had figured that in any sort of open combat, soldiers from Faerie would get cut to pieces if they didn't have any better weapons than swords and spears, and he didn't have the patience to infiltrate an entire new network of spies and saboteurs. He did have three blasters — the one Prossie had used to kill Shadow, and two others that had belonged to Lieutenant Dibbs' men when Shadow slaughtered them. What he needed was to get more.

So he had sent the monster through, knowing it would die, so that soldiers would come and look at it, maybe post a guard; then the fetches were sent through, three at a time, to kill or capture the soldiers in order to get more blasters.

The first three had gotten killed, but another threesome had been close behind, ready to snatch up the blasters the first set dropped and continue the fight, and then, after a dozen had gone through, he had sent the false Nancy to assess the situation and either sound the retreat or call for the enemy's surrender, whichever seemed appropriate.

And it seemed to have worked. They had more blasters.

The fetches reappeared and lowered a purple-uniformed corpse to the floor.

That was something to practice resurrection on, Pel thought, smiling.

The fetches vanished back through the portal.

"All right, Mr. Miller," he said, "you can go — just step back through that portal, the way those two just did. Then get in your aircar and go — but I want you to take a message back to your bosses for me."

"What message?" Miller said warily.

"Simple enough — you tell those fools at Base One that I'll trade your Governor-General here, and these fine soldiers, for the bodies of my wife and daughter. I get the bodies, I let everyone go. But if I don't get them soon, I start killing hostages. And if I run out of hostages, I'll stage another raid — and probably not on Beckett. My men could pop up anywhere in the whole fuckin' Galactic Empire, Mr. Miller — you tell those bastards that!"

Miller hesitated, unsure what to say; he stared at Pel for a few seconds, glanced at Grigsby, then back at Pel.

"Go on," Pel said, with an impatient gesture.

Miller stepped forward, groping for the opening — and then he was gone.

Pel nodded with satisfaction. It would take time for Miller to get back to wherever he came from and pass the word; it would take time for the message to reach Base One, and for the brass there to decide what to do.

They might well decide the wrong thing; the Empire had demonstrated before just how pigheaded and stupid it could be. Pel told himself that he had to be ready if the idiots said "no" again.

And he only had nine blasters so far.

"Another report," the telepath said. "This one's from my cousin Sharon — I mean, from Gamma Trianguli II. A party of armed men appeared from nowhere, took hostages, broke into the local constabulary's armory, then vanished, taking the hostages with them. They left a note demanding the bodies."

"God," Albright said, resting his head in his hands and staring down at the desk.

"We should have just delivered them in the first place," Markham said. "All the raids have been new arrivals, there haven't been any signs that he left spies or saboteurs in place; we should have believed him and given him the damn bodies."

"That's as may be," Sheffield replied. "We didn't, and we can't now."

"Why not?" Albright asked, lifting his head. "Why the hell not?"

"Because we can't give in to terrorism. We mustn't let ourselves be black-mailed, or he'll have won, we'll have to do whatever he demands. I have His Majesty's backing on this — we will *not* give in."

Albright stared silently at his superior for a long moment, then glanced at Markham.

Markham shrugged.

"For God's sake," Albright said. "He wants something that's his by right, that we *should* have given him long ago, and now you say that we *can't?*"

"Not while he's attacking us. If he returns all our hostages, then maybe we can negotiate. If we choose."

"We *did* negotiate," Markham pointed out. "He agreed to our terms, and did what he said he would, and then we changed the rules."

"We asked for proof, that's all."

"Proof — how the hell was he supposed to prove a negative?"

"Look, it *doesn't matter,*" Sheffield insisted. "The Emperor says we don't give him anything. We don't even talk until he stops the attacks."

"And if he *never* stops the attacks?"

"We're going to *make* him stop the attacks."

"How?" Albright demanded. "We don't have any way of locating or blocking the space-warps he's using; they don't produce the same radiation ours do. They don't produce *any* radiation we can detect. As far as we can tell, they can pop up *anywhere.*"

Sheffield shook his head. "I don't think so," he said. He turned to Celia Howe, who had sat silently throughout the debate. "What's the latest report?"

"We've been interviewing all the captured subjects, of course," Howe replied. "It's been assigned our highest priority. Most of them know very little about Brown, or for that matter Shadow, but they seem willing to tell us what they do know, even those immune to telepathy, though of course we can't be sure those aren't lying. We've resorted to unpleasant methods with some of them . . ."

"Torture," Albright muttered. Howe ignored him.

" . . . and we've been collecting and collating the data as fast as we can. So far, we have not learned of any enemy personnel who have not surrendered to us — each subject has listed all agents known to him, and so far every single one is accounted for. This tends to support Brown's claim that he gave up his entire network, however irrational such an action may appear to us — it may be that we're dealing with a lunatic."

"What about these space-warps?" Sheffield asked. "Have we learned anything more about them?"

Howe shook her head. "There are indications that the portals, as they call them, always manifested themselves in exactly the same place in the Empire, though the location of the opening on the other end might vary somewhat. However, we have been unable to establish whether this was merely a matter of convenience, or whether it's inherent in the system."

Markham and Albright looked at one another. Markham volunteered, "We've been forced to open space-warps in exactly the same spot — we can't get them anywhere within about five hundred miles of where one previously occurred without using exactly the same place. Maybe Shadow's method, whatever it is, has the same limitation."

"If we put all known warp locations under heavy guard," Albright suggested, "perhaps we could stop any further raiding."

"Or perhaps," Markham added reluctantly, "we'd just force Brown to move to someplace five hundred miles away. The Empire's a big place; we can't guard *all* of it."

"At the very least, we should guard every known location on Terra," Albright said. "Are any known here on Base One?"

Howe shook her head. "So far, we know of none on either Terra or on Base One. The Terran cell of Shadow's network received its orders from off-world."

"Then how'd that woman get into the Emperor's bedroom?" Albright asked.

Howe frowned. "I'm afraid I can't answer that; it's a top security matter." She pointed at the telepath. "I *certainly* can't say anything with him in the room. But it doesn't appear to have involved a space-warp portal."

"None of this is important," Sheffield said, cutting off the discussion. "When I said we were going to stop the attacks I wasn't talking about some feeble blockade."

Markham grimaced. "Somehow, I didn't think you meant blockading the portals. So what *did* you mean?"

"I thought it was obvious," Sheffield said.

"So I'm stupid," Markham replied. "Humor me."

"The Galactic Empire is the natural end of political evolution," Sheffield said. "Everyone knows that. It's our destiny to rule the entire human species, and I see no reason that should be limited to our own universe, now that we know others exist. Shadow was an unknown quantity, but Brown — we know about Brown. We don't know *everything*, but enough. He's just a man — and an amateur, at that. It's inevitable that we'll add his kingdom to the Empire, and these raids he's making just mean we need to do it now." He smiled grimly. "We're going to counter-attack, of course. The Imperial Army is going to flatten this upstart once and for all."

Chapter Twenty-Three

The abrupt twist in the matrix startled Pel out of a light doze. He sat up and looked around.

He was in his bed, safe in Shadow's fortress; the light of the matrix blazed gold and crimson from the bare stone walls. The false Nancy lay naked beside him, sound asleep.

What had roused him? There wasn't anything out of place in the bedchamber. Had he heard something?

Not through the foot-thick walls, certainly; he reached out with the matrix and opened the door, while sensing everything that lay in the corridor beyond.

Except there wasn't anything in the corridor.

He reached out farther.

There were fetches and monsters and people going about their business, there were his dozens of hostages all secure in the dungeons and towers; all was as it should be, throughout the fortress.

The weather above was a normal, if unpleasant, drizzle; the marsh was quiet.

Then, finally, he noticed the kink.

The Imperial space-warp had opened again. It had been closed for some time; in fact, he hadn't noticed it open since he had begun his little attempts at convincing the Empire to cooperate. He had flown out to the familiar spot by his treehouse in the Low Forest of West Sunderland a few days before to see if the Empire had come to its collective senses, if the bodies had been delivered before the warp was closed, or at some time while he was asleep or distracted, and he'd found nothing but empty air and woods.

Now it was back — but the place where the space-warp bent a strand of the matrix in an impossible direction had moved; instead of being in Sunderland it was somewhere far off in the other direction.

And it seemed *larger.*

Pel was now fully awake, and angry. What the hell was the Empire up to?

He would just have to go and see.

Captain Hamilton Puckett took a deep breath, tightened his grip on his sword, and jumped, his eyes still firmly closed. His left hand was on the hilt of his blaster — he knew all the experts said it wouldn't work, but he couldn't help it, he still wanted that familiar reassurance, and he'd made sure his holster was slung on the outside of his space suit.

The glare of the warp abruptly vanished, and the red glow it made of the inside of his eyelids disappeared; he opened his eyes, and managed to catch himself just short of falling on his armored face. The drop seemed longer than it should; he hoped that was just an illusion caused by the transition to higher gravity.

He got himself upright, released his blaster, wiped dust from the front of his helmet, and looked around.

People were staring at him — *strange* people, all of them terribly tall and thin, with pale narrow faces and long black hair, wearing flowing green and white clothes. He was standing on bare dirt; in fact, his landing had stirred up a cloud of dust. Around him were crude huts made of some sort of reeds or grasses, and all in all about a dozen faces peered at him from the doorways of the huts or the spaces between them. Their expressions were odd — not fear or anger or anything he could read plainly.

They didn't look happy, though.

Well, why should they? He'd just popped out of thin air in the middle of their village.

"Damn," he said.

The word was oddly muffled by the helmet he wore.

He turned and groped for the warp — the scientists had said they were going to bring it in right at ground level.

They hadn't; it was a good four feet off the ground. He had to back up and take his best running leap in order to get through it, and he imagined he looked like a particularly ridiculous sort of monster as he galloped through the middle of the village in his space suit, waving his sword about.

His jump turned into an exceptionally awkward dive — he'd misjudged either the suit's mass or the local gravity — but he did sail back through into the blinding white light of the space-warp. His landing knocked the wind out of him, and for a moment he lay motionless on the steel walkway.

When he raised his head at last, he saw people signalling wildly to him from the observation area.

He sighed and clambered to his feet; he'd have to go up and report.

They probably weren't going to like this. They'd wanted someplace near human habitation, to avoid impassable wilderness and make foraging easier, but no one had wanted to come out smack in some primitive village. And they'd wanted ground level, where they could just step through, not a four-foot drop.

Well, it wasn't *his* fault; they could shout at the scientists.

But they'd probably want to try again, which would mean someone would have to make another leap into the unknown, and Hamilton Puckett had a pretty good idea who'd be making that leap.

After all, he had experience now. And if he wanted to command the first assault, he needed to scout the terrain — that was the deal the brass had offered.

And it was a deal he intended to keep.

"It's getting bad," Miletti said. "They're escalating, turning it into a war."

Major Johnston considered this for a moment, then turned to Prossie Thorpe. "Ms. Thorpe," he said, "if you don't want to answer I won't press it, but you know more about this than any of the rest of us. In your opinion, is a war between Faerie and the Empire good or bad for us here on Earth?"

"I don't know," Thorpe said.

"How can any war be good?" Amy Jewell asked. She seemed uncomfortable, here in Miletti's living room — and that was, Johnston thought, reasonable enough; after all, Miletti hadn't invited her, and didn't particularly want any of them here. It had been Johnston who had brought them along, in an effort to speed up the process of questioning Miletti and interpreting the data he provided.

If Miletti had been willing to come down to the Pentagon, or Crystal City . . .

But he wasn't. He insisted he could provide more information if he stayed safely in his suburban home, with familiar surroundings and sixty-eight channels of cable TV, and Johnston had decided that there might be enough truth in that to make it a mistake to argue with him, or to order him anywhere.

"If it removes them both as threats," Johnston answered Amy's question. "I'd consider that a good war, for us."

"I don't think Pel was ever a threat to anybody," Thorpe replied.

"He is now," Miletti said, looking up from his television.

"Secure the village," they said. Just what the devil did they think that meant?

Captain Puckett only knew one way to make sure a village was secure, and he didn't like it much. He was fairly certain that Marshal Albright knew what was involved, but Secretary Markham and Secretary Sheffield might not. Someone might get soft-hearted later, and if that happened Puckett supposed he'd take the blame for the massacre and probably spend the rest of his days on a pension somewhere like old man Blackburn, with parents warning their children away from him.

But if he didn't do it, he'd catch hell right now.

He looked over his men once again. In their space suits they all looked alike, faceless gleaming automatons — but the swords they held looked weirdly out of place, throwbacks to some earlier century, as if they were knights in distorted armor rather than Imperial troopers.

He chalked a final warning on the board — REMEMBER! FOUR-FOOT DROP, HIGH GRAVITY! Naturally, the scientists hadn't fixed that — they claimed they couldn't. Puckett had his own opinion on that, but knew better than to say it aloud.

He put down the chalk and signalled the door crew. The big panel slid open, admitting the blinding glare of the space-warp, and Puckett waved his men forward.

He wondered if any of them were yelling as they charged across the open, airless expanse and into the light.

*P*el had never seen this part of his new world before — but that was hardly surprising, since he had never seen most of the place.

He estimated that he had covered at least two hundred miles so far, probably more, and the twist in the matrix was still far ahead of him, somewhere to the southwest. The terrain below was not as lush as the Starlinshire Downs, by any means — there were occasional open areas that looked like little more than bare sand, while trees were few and far between.

Far off to his right, almost on the horizon, he could make out a distant ocean, glittering in the afternoon sun. Behind and to his left were green hills. Ahead, he saw mostly flat scrubland.

There weren't any roads or villages along this stretch; there had been, closer in toward Shadowmarsh, but he had passed them all.

What the hell was the Empire doing, opening a warp out here?

And using it, too; he'd sensed people coming through the warp for some time.

And there were people around the warp before the Empire's people started arriving. Had the Empire found local allies? Maybe some part of the resistance movement that Raven and Valadrakul had belonged to still survived, and wanted to see Shadow's matrix destroyed, rather than passed on.

Well, once he had his family back, Pel wouldn't have any great objection to that. If the matrix exploded and wild magic wrecked what little civilization Faerie possessed, it wasn't *his* problem.

He glimpsed something moving in the air ahead, and almost fell off the wind he was riding before he recognized it as just distant smoke.

It seemed like rather a *lot* of smoke, though.

He reached out through the matrix.

Shadow had had some way to see far-off places magically, through the eyes of the people or animals there, but Pel had never managed it, and he still couldn't contrive to get a look at whatever was happening there — it didn't help any that he was whipping through the air several hundred feet up at about fifty miles an hour.

Sometimes, when he used the matrix, he felt as if he were one of those poor fools with a big fancy computer loaded with expensive software that he only used for balancing his checkbook because he didn't know how to access anything else. Shadow had only taught him to open interdimensional portals; she hadn't intended to turn the matrix over to him permanently. He had picked up a few other things from the other wizards, and there were a few things that simply feeling the matrix made obvious, and then on top of that, every so often he would stumble across something else the matrix could do — such as fly — but he still had the tantalizing feeling that there were a thousand other wonderful things just out of reach.

And some way of seeing what was making that smoke was probably — almost certainly! — one of them.

He could sense the shape of the matrix. He could sense people, usually. But he couldn't *see* anything, or *hear* anything.

The matrix was bent out of shape by the intruding space-warp, and Pel could tell that this warp was bigger than the old one in Sunderland — but why? That one had been big enough to fit a spaceship; what more would they need?

And there were people there. There were a *lot* of people there. Two different kinds . . .

That was strange; he hadn't usually been able to tell people apart through the matrix before, and certainly not at so great a distance. Fetches felt different from natural people; so, much more subtly, did simulacra, and wizards. But other than that, people were people; he hadn't noticed any difference between natives, Earthpeople, or Imperials.

So why did some of the people ahead feel different?

And they seemed *brighter* somehow, as if they held more of that trace of magic that people had, as if they were more nearly linked to the matrix.

The new space-warp had come through at the center of a magical power spot, he noticed; did that have anything to do with it? Had these people absorbed some of the world's magic by living there?

More and more Imperials were arriving, or at least more and more people were coming through the warp, and he assumed they were Imperials. The others, the strange-feeling ones, were scattering in all directions, moving away from the warp.

What the hell was going on? There were *dozens* of Imperials there, a whole *army* of . . .

An army.

There was an entire Imperial army coming through the warp.

An invasion!

The Empire was invading!

They were actually invading Faerie!

How could they be so stupid?

And that explained the smoke . . . or did it? Blasters didn't work here, and the Empire had no conventional firearms, so far as he knew; what weapons would they be using that might start fires?

Angry and worried, he gathered more of the energy of the matrix into the wind that carried him.

*T*hese funny-looking natives were deucedly hard to kill. Puckett's troops were not particularly skilled swordsmen, and their space suits had gotten in the way at first, but all the same, Puckett thought they ought to have been able to handle a bunch of mostly unarmed wogs, regardless of what sort of wogs they were.

Maybe half a dozen of the natives had turned up with ornately carved spears, but the others had had only bare hands. Slaughtering the lot of them should have been easy.

But they *dodged*. And they hid. And they ran, without ever seeming to hurry, and those abnormally long legs of those could really cover territory.

None of them had said a word, none had shouted or screamed, even when Puckett's swordsmen surrounded them and hacked them to pieces. It wasn't natural.

And there must have been a hundred or more in the village originally, but Puckett could only confirm four killed — and he'd lost five of his own men to those spears.

Now, though, the natives had been driven away, their huts burned, and the village was, he could say with some confidence, secured.

And it hadn't been a slaughter at all, really. That was almost a relief. Puckett didn't need to worry about being another Major Blackburn.

Of course, with so many wogs still out there, they'd need to be constantly on guard for counter-attacks, snipers, and the like, since they hadn't killed the villagers; that wasn't in accordance with doctrine. Colonel Scarborough and the rest of the brass might not like it.

Well, Puckett thought as he scanned the situation from his position at one end of the wide steel steps leading up to the warp, the Colonel and the others could just stuff it — it wasn't Puckett's fault that the natives had fled and faded away, or that his men had to arrive in those bulky, awkward suits that were never meant for use on a planetary surface, or that they had to use archaic, unfamiliar weapons.

At least matches worked here. And dropping the steps through at the very first had made transit through the warp easy enough.

The first supply dumps were arriving now, and the men were clearing away the last burning wreckage of the crude native huts; they would have some tents and probably a few more substantial shelters up well before sunset. Swordsmen were patrolling the perimeter, ready to fend off any wog counter-attack. Order and organization were arising out of chaos.

If this campaign was going to last long, though, Puckett hoped the brass would see about getting some different armament. These swords they'd been issued were a bit flimsy — they were just ceremonial swords that had been sharpened, not serious fighting blades, since that was all that was available in quantity on short notice. Some of the men were using their standard-issue knives, instead, and it wasn't just because the knives were more familiar.

And some sort of missile weapons — bows, crossbows, powder firearms, something like that — would help considerably. Even some decent spears or pikes would be useful.

"Captain!" someone shouted.

Puckett turned, and saw men pointing skyward. He shaded his eyes and looked up to the northeast.

"Damn," he muttered.

The brass had assured him that aircars didn't work here, any more than blasters did — and of course, any number of his men had tested blasters; he had, himself. Blasters didn't work, so the assumption had been that aircars didn't either.

But something did, because that wasn't any bird or bat or airfish or pterosaur approaching. For that matter, it wasn't any sort of aircar Puckett had ever seen before, either. Puckett didn't know *what* it was — it blazed almost as brightly as the afternoon sun, but in a thousand changing colors. Tendrils of light and smoke trailed out in all directions, shifting constantly.

Was it a weapon?

The glare dimmed momentarily, and Puckett thought he glimpsed something at the thing's center — something that looked like a man.

Not a man in an aircar or any other sort of machine, just a man, flying unsupported through the air like a leaf in the wind, in the middle of that great insubstantial thing.

And flying *fast*, too.

Puckett wished more than ever for a squad of crossbowmen.

Or rocketeers; would rockets work here? He couldn't see how they wouldn't, but he wasn't a scientist. When he sent his next report he'd suggest bringing rockets. Why hadn't anyone thought of that sooner?

But right now he didn't have rockets, or anything else that could shoot that thing down.

"Maintain your positions," he called. "It may be a diversion — keep alert!"

He hoped it wasn't a serious attack — after all, there was only the one man in there. Maybe someone was coming to parley.

But how would the enemy have known they were there? Had the displaced villagers gotten word back that fast? Base One had said the enemy's central fortress was over three hundred miles up the coast; did the enemy have telepaths, or some equivalent?

Maybe this thing was from a local garrison somewhere.

The flying thing was coming closer; it was crossing the perimeter. Puckett cursed under his breath; he supposed no one at Base One had even *thought* about air cover.

But after all, it was just one man in there.

*T*he ground looked as if it had measles — purple measles. The whole area was speckled with the purple spots of Imperial uniforms. Pel stared down at them in annoyed amazement.

The Empire could organize an entire invasion, but they couldn't turn over two bodies.

The invaders were interestingly arranged, Pel thought; almost in a target. The thickest concentration was right in the center, where he knew the warp was, where dozens of uniformed men were hauling boxes and beams about; then there was a broad ring where they were relatively scarce. Outside that was a ring of men, and then another clear area, only a few advance scouts moving quickly at angles through the scrub.

The warp made a perfect bull's eye.

He passed directly over it, and saw faces turned upward, watching him — but no one was shooting at him.

They probably didn't have anything that *could* shoot at him.

Now, what had this place been before the Imperials arrived? Where were those strange people he had sensed? What had made all the smoke he had seen?

The smoke he could partially explain, at any rate — there were heaps of ash still smoldering. But what had they been originally?

And the people were mostly still alive, but not in the circle the Imperials had established as their beachhead — he could sense them on all sides, a few hundred yards away, as inexplicable as ever.

That was reassuring — at least the Imperials hadn't butchered them all.

He looked at the piles of ash, at how they were arranged, and suddenly Pel realized what they were.

They were houses. This had been a village of those strange people, and the Imperials had come in and burned it all.

They had just marched in and burned people's homes.

What *right* did they have?

Those people weren't Imperial citizens. They weren't rebel slavers, like the ones on Zeta Leo III. They were Faerie folk, going about their own business.

They were Shadow's subjects, not the Empire's — except Shadow was dead.

So they were *Pel's* subjects.

And they'd been attacked because Pel had attacked the Empire. Not because they'd done anything, but because *Pel* had attacked the Empire to try to get his family back.

Damn the Empire!

Magic flowed thick and strong here; the matrix hummed through Pel almost as strongly as back in his fortress, and he could sense half a dozen currents of natural energy intersecting just where that Imperial space-warp had come out.

It couldn't be a coincidence, but how could the Empire have known?

It had to be something in the nature of interdimensional travel, Pel thought. The warp over the Low Forest hadn't been near any power spots, but the Empire had been aiming that one for a particular place; this new one had probably been allowed to come out wherever it was easy.

Maybe that had some connection with why it was impossible to open two portals near one another.

Whatever the reason, the result was that Pel had all the power he could ask for here, enough to dispose of the Imperial intrusion if he wanted to.

He wondered whether the power spot had any connection with the strange people, then upbraided himself. Of *course* it did! They were more attuned to magic, he could sense that — not as much as the wizards were, their auras or whatever they were weren't patterned and formed like regular wizards', but these people definitely had something magical about them. They must have sited their village here deliberately, to take advantage of it.

Were they all some sort of low-level wizards, then? That was something to investigate.

Right now, though, what they all were was refugees, and the Empire was occupying their village, and it was Pel's job, as their ruler and protector, to do something about it.

While he had observed and thought through this much, he had passed completely over the Imperial perimeter; now he wheeled back for another pass.

He had to do something about the invasion — but what?

The simplest thing would be to just unleash some of that magic and flash-fry the Imperials, as Shadow had flash-fried Raven and the others in her fortress, but Pel hesitated. That seemed unnecessarily ruthless.

He could twist the warp into nonexistence, he thought — he wasn't certain, but he thought that it would be possible. That would cut off these soldiers, several hundred of them by the look of it, with nowhere to go, nothing to do but make trouble . . . not a good idea.

He wanted the Empire to hand over the bodies. He wanted them to see that they didn't stand a chance. Cutting off the warp and leaving their men alive wouldn't do that. Simply obliterating the expeditionary force would be more effective — but not quite right, either.

He wanted survivors who would tell the Empire what had happened.

He turned again, this time moving himself toward the rim of the Imperial circle, and began to bend the matrix into the shape he wanted.

"What the devil is it?" Lieutenant Miles asked.

"Haven't the faintest notion," Puckett replied. The glowing thing had passed directly over the camp, swooped back across, then veered off to one side; now it seemed to be circling their perimeter.

But it wasn't *doing* anything, so far as Puckett could see; it flew along at a steady altitude, a few hundred feet up, with all those patterns of light and color and shadow spraying every which way, but doing nothing.

And then something flashed, and someone screamed; Puckett drew his blaster without thinking, swore, and flung it aside, reaching for his sword instead.

Another flash, more screams, and wild shouting, but Puckett still couldn't see what was happening.

Another flash, and another, and another, moving along below the flying thing, in a great sweeping curve just beyond the Imperial perimeter.

And there were men running, falling back from the perimeter, some retreating in good order, others screaming and running, as the flashes blended into a solid ring of fire.

"What's happening?" Puckett snapped.

A sergeant saluted from the foot of the steps. "Sir, explosions all along the perimeter! We're losing men, burned alive — can't see what's causing it, there're no bombs falling, just bang, and some poor fellow goes up in flames."

"Damn," Puckett said. "All right, fall back — everyone fall back. Noncombatants to suit up and get back through the warp immediately; combat troops to stand ready. Miles, sergeant, spread the word!"

Puckett watched as his men gathered inward, contracting toward the warp. The flames had closed the circle now, and were beginning to spiral inward — that flying thing was *fast*.

Another supply team stepped out of the warp just then, their load slung from poles on their shoulders, and stood, staring in astonishment at the surrounding chaos. Puckett grabbed them, turned them around, and shoved them back toward the warp.

"Get back through there!" he shouted. Then he grabbed a man who was about to put on his space helmet, and told him, "Pass the word — no more traffic outbound! Tell them on the other side — we're doing at least a partial withdrawal! Understand?"

"Yes, sir!" the soldier barked, saluting. Puckett noticed that he wore an engineer's insignia — that was good; engineers could follow orders.

"Good! Now get that helmet on and get back there!" He slapped the engineer on the back and turned his attention back to the ring of fire.

This looked very bad. Somehow, he didn't think a partial withdrawal was going to be enough.

*P*el watched as the last survivors vanished through the warp mere inches ahead of the magical flames, still trying to pull on space suits and helmets; he wondered whether they'd make it to safety across the airless expanse between the warp and the rest of Base One.

Plenty of their comrades hadn't even made it that far, of course; the broad burned-over expanse outside the contracting circle of flame was covered with drifting black dust, much of which had been Imperial troops.

And their equipment, of course, as well as some of the native plants and a few structures left from the native village.

Now, everything was gone except the warp itself and the steps leading up to it, there in the heart of the flame.

The steel steps melted and sagged, and Pel reached out for the warp itself, and twisted hard, pouring magical force into it, trying to straighten the shape of space itself.

It resisted for several seconds, then gave, and the warp was gone. He had done it; he had closed it.

He wondered what effect that would have on their machinery, back on Base One.

He hoped it wasn't damaged; then they wouldn't be able to deliver the bodies until it was repaired.

Chapter Twenty-Four

*P*el stood in the center of the blasted clearing and looked around.

This had been a village once, but between the Imperial invasion and his own magical destruction of the invaders, there wasn't much left — just sand and ash.

He wondered what the villagers would do now.

He was tempted to just leave and let them do it — he had his own problems. He would want to retaliate for the invasion, send a message to the Empire.

But on the other hand, it was his fault the Empire had destroyed their village, and he was their ruler and protector; he should do something to help.

With the matrix, he had the power to help.

And he was curious about who these strange people were, why and how they were linked to the matrix.

He considered what he could do.

He considered building them a new village, the way he had built his treehouse in the Low Forest — but this wasn't a forest; there were no raw materials to work with here.

Or were there? He looked down.

There was plenty of sand and ash, and the matrix would provide all the heat he could want. What more did he need to make glass?

Half an hour later he knew what else he needed — knowledge. And maybe practice. The ugly brownish-green stuff he had produced probably qualified as glass, but it wasn't very *good* glass, and his fanciful notion of raising a fairy city of glittering glass spires was obviously not going to work unless he spent a lot longer at it than he had intended.

On the other hand, he had attracted an audience; a ring of people had formed around the edge of the blasted area, all of them watching him solemnly.

These were the strange people, the ones who were linked to the matrix. There were perhaps sixty or seventy of them, men, and women, but no children that Pel could see. They were all thin, with long white faces and straight black hair worn long, wearing peculiar green and white robes.

Pel tossed aside his latest unsatisfactory lump of glass and beckoned. "Come here," he called, using the matrix to amplify his voice. "I want to talk to you."

A man stepped forward, and strode calmly up, to stand a few feet away. He seemed untroubled by the light of the matrix; in fact, the way he stared impassively straight ahead, Pel wondered for a moment if he might be blind.

He was taller than Pel had realized, and paler — and he had pointed ears.

It dawned on Pel that these people weren't exactly *people*, and it struck him what they must be.

They were elves.

Well, why not? This was Faerie, wasn't it? And Pel had met gnomes, and been told that they weren't elves, that elves were something else.

Well, these were elves — weren't they?

"You're an elf," Pel said.

"And you are a human," the man replied, speaking English with an accent Pel couldn't place, but which sounded somehow Asian.

"You're really an elf?"

The other nodded. "And you are called Pelbrun, the Brown Magician."

"Well, I'll be damned."

"As to that, I could not say," the elf replied.

"I never met an elf before," Pel said.

"I never met *you* before."

There was something unsatisfactory about this conversation, Pel thought. The elf's voice was musical and pleasant enough, but shouldn't he be saying things that were deep and meaningful?

Well, Pel's own words hadn't exactly been brilliant.

"Listen," he said, "I'm sorry about the village. I'd hoped I could help rebuild it, but I don't know how. I'm not really a very good magician yet."

"We can rebuild it to our own liking."

Pel looked around. He had no idea what the elf intended to rebuild *with*, but if he said they could . . .

"Don't elves traditionally live in forests?" he asked.

"This is the place Shadow allowed us," the elf replied.

Pel bit his lip and looked around. That explained it.

This place was a reservation. Shadow must have put the elves here to keep them out of the way, just the way whites had put Indians on various badlands back on Earth.

"Listen," he said, "I could move you to the Low Forest of West Sunderland, if you want, above the Starlinshire Downs. Nobody lives there."

"We would starve," the elf replied.

Pel blinked. "You aren't starving here, but you would there?"

The elf nodded.

It seemed to Pel that this fellow was playing the strong silent type a bit more than was entirely wise. *"Why* would you starve there? What do you eat?"

"The earth itself sustains us, magician; we do not eat crude matter as humans do."

For a moment Pel stared blankly at him; then comprehension dawned. *That* was why these people were linked to the matrix! That was what they lived on; they consumed raw magical energy.

No wonder they wouldn't want to live in the Low Forest.

"Oh," Pel said.

And that, he realized, might even explain some of the old folk tales about fairy feasts, about how insubstantial fairy food was.

That also eliminated any possibility of sending elves into the Empire, for any purpose at all — they'd undoubtedly die there, just as the monsters did, or as Alella and Grummetty had.

Not that Pel had seriously been thinking about it, but the idea that they might want to avenge the destruction of their village had occurred to him.

Well, that idea was out.

"Okay, well," Pel said, "I don't know where else I could send you; I haven't learned the local geography yet."

"We are content here," the elf answered.

Pel shrugged. "Suit yourself, then," he said. He looked around at the circle of elves and the sandy wasteland, and decided that he'd tried, and if they weren't going to ask for any help, he wasn't going to give it. Let them rebuild their own damn village. "Stand back," he said.

The elf began retreating.

Pel had never tried taking off from flat ground before — at the fortress he'd launched himself off the tower, and in the Low Forest he had jumped from a treetop, but there wasn't any handy tower or tree to climb, and this desolate circle didn't have anything that would block the wind. Taillefer had taken off from Castle Regisvert; Pelbrun, Pel thought, ought to be able to take off here.

And the elves could take care of themselves.

He took a deep breath and summoned the wind.

"One hundred and eight dead or missing," Albright said, tossing the report onto the table in front of Sheffield.

"For nothing," he added a second later, as he settled into his chair.

"Hardly for nothing," Sheffield said. "We know now that this Pelbrun either has some way of detecting intrusions into his universe, or that he has some form of high-speed communication that allowed the villagers to warn him. We also know that he has extremely effective weaponry using his 'magical' super-science. We've gained some important knowledge — that's hardly nothing."

"What good is it going to do us?" Albright argued.

"You tell me," Sheffield replied. "Now that you know that, what would you do differently?"

"Me? Colonel Scarborough handled this."

"Colonel Scarborough is out of the picture now; what would *you* do?"

Albright stared at Sheffield for a moment, thinking.

"Well, to begin with," he said, "I'd make everything fireproof . . ."

Pel made his counter-raid through the same spot Peter Gregory had used — nine fetches under the false Nancy's direction burst through, shot everyone in sight with their blasters, collected three more blasters from the bodies, then left Pel's prepared message, painted on a non-flammable stone slab, prominently on display.

YOU CAN'T HURT ME, it read, BUT I CAN HURT YOU. DELIVER THE BODIES.

By the time the reports reached Base One, however, Operation Brown-Out was under way. The message was ignored.

"I think they know on both sides that it won't work," Miletti said. "They just aren't ready to admit it."

Prossie looked up at this oracular pronouncement, made not in response to any question, but out of the blue.

She glanced at the lieutenant; he looked back at her and shrugged, then turned away again.

Prossie looked at Miletti, then at the lieutenant, then back down at her book.

Miletti was behaving strangely, she thought — but what did she know of what was normal for these people?

She wished she could read his mind, to see whether the strain and isolation were getting to him, or whether it was something else — but she couldn't.

And it wasn't really any of her business anyway. She was supposed to be studying this planet's history, as part of her assimilation, not worrying about Miletti's mental health. They were keeping her here, letting her sleep in Miletti's guest room, in case one of Miletti's reports needed explanation, but it wasn't really her problem anymore.

For her, the Empire and Faerie were the past; Earth was the future.

*P*el stared at the plateful of corned beef and cabbage.

He wasn't really hungry — but when had he last eaten?

He didn't know. It had occurred to him that he ought to eat, so he had had this dinner prepared and served, but he wasn't hungry.

And he couldn't remember the last time he had eaten anything.

It was obvious what was happening, of course; he was drawing energy directly from the matrix, feeding off pure magic, the way the elves did.

He remembered what was supposed to happen to people who ate of fairy feasts, though — they were trapped in Faerie forever, unable to return to Earth.

That was just an old story, of course, a folk-tale for children . . . but he had been living a storybook existence for months now, ever since poor little Grummetty had stepped out of the basement wall. He had fought monsters, been captured by space pirates, been rescued by a Galactic Empire, defeated an evil wizard, become a wizard himself . . . if all *that* could happen in real life, if he could be sitting here in a magical stone fortress staring at a meal prepared by zombies in a room lit by his own raw magical energy, how could he possibly say that the old fairy tales were nonsense?

He picked up a forkful of meat and chewed.

His stomach protested with a sudden cramp.

He knew why, and he felt a tremor of terror at the realization. He had gone so long without food that his digestive processes were not up to handling anything this rich; he should be starting off with a thin broth, or even just water, as if he had been on the verge of starvation.

But he felt fine and healthy — other than the nausea, anyway.

Maybe he couldn't go back to ordinary food, he thought. Maybe it was too late. Maybe it would just sit, undigested, in his gut.

Maybe he wasn't really human anymore; maybe he was becoming an elf, or something else native to this other cosmos. Maybe all those stories about Shadow being an elemental force, rather than a human being, had been true, in a way. Maybe Susan's bullets wouldn't have killed Shadow even if they had hit her.

Maybe she could *only* be killed when she had become human again by leaving Faerie. And maybe he, too, was changing into something else.

But then, how could he ever go home again? How could he return to Earth once Nancy and Rachel were restored to life?

Shadow had been able to leave, to go to the Galactic Empire — but she had died there. Could she have survived even if Prossie hadn't shot her, or would she have died the way Grummetty and Alella did?

He swallowed.

He would, he thought, just have to wait and see.

He loaded his fork again.

Then he stopped, fork halfway to his mouth.

The matrix had just twisted again. The Empire had opened a new space-warp.

He put the fork down, telling himself that he had to investigate, that doing so was more important than eating this meal.

He wished he really believed it.

Fifteen minutes later the taste of corned beef still lingered in his mouth as he leapt from the fortress tower into the waiting winds.

Captain Puckett eyed the horizon warily as his men hauled equipment through the warp.

This time the damned thing had come out a full eight feet up, and it had taken most of an hour to locate something better than a ladder to compensate for the drop. Some clever fellow had finally located a set of folding bleachers — Puckett had no idea what such a thing was doing anywhere on Base One, but there it was, and it worked fine.

And they hadn't come out in the middle of a village this time; instead the warp hung invisibly above a field of barley. A special squad had captured the farmer and his family — they hadn't resisted, so no one had been killed.

The residents of the neighboring farms had either surrendered or fled.

These weren't any pale, skinny freaks this time, just ordinary people — though they had an odd accent and an old-fashioned way of speaking. They had been terrified at the sight of the Imperial troopers in their bulky purple space suits — after the previous massacre, no one had opposed the suggestion that the troops keep their suits on, despite the inconvenience and discomfort. Helmets could be loosened to save on bottled air, or even removed, but the main suit, which was fireproof, stayed on.

Puckett was happy with that — not that his opinion mattered anymore. No one had openly blamed him for the disaster, but he wasn't even nominally in command this time; he was a "special advisor" to Colonel Bender, along to provide whatever expertise he might have acquired in the course of utter defeat.

He wasn't sure just how much of that expertise applied here. They were some six hundred miles southeast of the site of the previous landing, and the terrain was totally different. Where the other site was barren, this one was lush; instead of whitish sand, the earth was rich black loam producing a variety of crops, while anyplace in sight that wasn't under cultivation was either forest or rapidly returning to forest. Instead of grass huts, the natives had sturdy, well-weathered homes of stone and timber, with intricately carved lintels and shutters and generously stocked with good-quality crockery.

And of course, there was the castle.

Puckett raised his binoculars and took another look at the thing, perched perhaps five miles to the southeast, atop the highest of the surrounding hills.

Stone walls, watchtowers, overhanging parapets — that was a serious fortification there. It wouldn't have stood half a day against blasters and aircars, but against the improvised armaments of this particular Imperial expedition . . .

Well, the Empire's officers still knew how to besiege a fortress, even if they hadn't ever actually done it.

And so far, the castle's occupants had shown no signs of making a sortie against the invaders. The scouts had reported that faces could sometimes be glimpsed on the battlements, watching the Imperial forces as they made camp, but the heavy gates had shut within two hours of the warp's first appearance and had remained closed ever since.

A crow cawed somewhere.

The castle was daunting, in its way, but it wasn't what worried Puckett, not really. Anyone who needed those massive defensive walls . . . well, somehow Puckett didn't think the thing that had slaughtered his men lived in a place like that.

If it had really been the Brown Magician, as Imperial Intelligence believed, then it didn't live anywhere near here; his place, their eventual target, was supposed to be somewhere hundreds of miles to the north, according to the space-warp scientists.

At that thought, Puckett turned his glasses northward and scanned the treetops and the sky above.

And there it was.

At first he thought he'd imagined it, but then he found it again, and focused the binoculars on it, and there wasn't any doubt.

"Colonel!" he shouted. "Colonel Bender!"

The expedition's commander looked up from some papers a clerk was showing him.

"Sir, there it is!" Puckett shouted. "It's coming!"

Bender turned, and by then it was visible even without the binoculars, a seething, constantly changing mass of light and color swooping toward them out of the northern sky.

Bender began shouting, but Puckett didn't wait for his own orders; he clapped his helmet in place and began dogging it down tight.

*P*el didn't bother reconnoitering; it was obvious that the Empire was trying again. This wasn't a power spot, but it was near one, and a strong current of magic flowed through the earth here; Pel reached down and pulled that current upward, then turned it loose.

Fire burst up from the ground, and men screamed — but at first they simply retreated, with their faces scorched but still alive, protected by their space suits.

Pel couldn't allow that. He couldn't just use flame to hem them in or drive them back; since they had worn those protective suits he had to make it plain that there was no defense against the Brown Magician's power.

He reached down to the magical flow again, and brought it up, and this time an Imperial soldier became a walking torch for an instant before collapsing into nothing. He didn't even have time to scream before his suit held nothing but ash.

Then another went, and a third.

The suits made it slower, though; Pel had to manifest the flames inside the men's bodies, and the lack of air made it necessary to use more magic.

Then, as he concentrated on his fourth victim, something whizzed past him, through the matrix.

Then an entire barrage tore through the air toward him, and he recognized them — arrows!

He turned them all aside easily, but it distracted him for a moment.

The Empire was getting more inventive, it seemed; Pel decided that he had best be more cautious. He twisted the light, to ensure that he would be completely invisible behind the cloud of color and shadow, and thickened the air below and before himself, forming a protective barrier.

More arrows flew up at him, and were diverted.

Something made a cracking sound, and something smaller and faster than an arrow tore past — a bullet.

He hadn't known the Empire had guns, and for a moment he was on the verge of panic.

Then he remembered who and what he was.

He thickened his barrier once again and looped back for another pass over the Imperials — he had overshot their entire installation while they were shooting at him.

There were the bowmen, he saw — or rather, the crossbowmen. And there was someone with a muzzle-loading pistol, stuffing a wad down the barrel — was *that* the best the Galactic Empire could do?

That was nothing. Pel carefully targeted the pistoleer as his next incendiary victim, then began on the archers.

By the time he had incinerated a dozen men the Imperials appeared to be in full retreat, most of them running for their precious escape route, and Pel decided that he had made his point; he didn't have to kill anyone else.

"Deliver the bodies!" he shouted, using the matrix to amplify his voice so that everyone could hear it.

Most of them probably didn't have any idea what he was talking about, but word would reach those who did.

"I can close the warp, you know," he called. "I'm letting you go. All I want is the bodies."

One of the Imperials raised a megaphone — it figured that they wouldn't even have a proper bullhorn; their technology was really pretty primitive, outside of the blasters and anti-gravity. Mostly equivalent to the early 19th century, Pel estimated — they weren't very advanced at all, Galactic Empire or not.

"If you continue, we'll destroy the bodies!" the man bellowed.

For a moment, Pel was shocked into silence; he flew on past the Imperials and wheeled about before replying.

"You do that," Pel shouted back, trembling with anger, "and your fucking Empire will never know a minute's peace as long as I live! You think I've given you trouble before, you're fooling yourselves! I haven't *begun!* I can make your lives hell!" He turned again. "You tell your masters that! You go home now, or you die — and you tell your masters that if they damage those bodies they're all dead meat!"

He gestured, and fire burst up in walls around the Imperials, flames roaring twenty feet into the air, driving them back toward the space-warp.

"You tell them that!" he shrieked. *"Tell them!"*

"*H*ow marvelous," Markham muttered, reading the reports. "Now we've made him mad."

"You think he's serious?" Sheffield asked quietly.

Markham looked up in astonishment. "Of *course* he's serious!"

"You think he can make good on his threat?"

"I don't have any idea," Markham said, "but it wouldn't surprise me a bit."

*P*el didn't go back to Shadowmarsh after the warp collapsed into non-existence, leaving ash and debris scattered across some poor farmer's fields. He needed to think.

His fit of temper had subsided, but he was still in no mood to see anyone else just now. The flight back to the fortress would take hours, and night was approaching, but he still didn't want to head back yet.

Instead he sailed over the castle, waving to the tiny figures on the battlements; a few waved back, while most ran to hide. Then he let the wind blow him onward, across unfamiliar terrain; he knew that he could always find his way back, thanks to the matrix that had become a part of him.

And it didn't matter anyway. He had the matrix with him wherever he went, anywhere in Faerie — and he didn't have Nancy and Rachel.

He had to convince the Empire to give him the bodies.

Asking politely hadn't worked. Making token raids hadn't worked. Fighting off their counter-attacks hadn't worked. What could he do that would convince them?

What could he offer them?

Conversely, what could he threaten them with?

He had an entire world he could give them — he didn't care what happened to Faerie, so long as he got his family back and could go safely home to Earth. But how could he ensure that they would deliver the bodies? They didn't trust him, and he didn't trust them; how could they work an exchange safely, when he couldn't go into the Empire, and they couldn't come here without his permission? Why should they believe that he wouldn't just fry them all and take Faerie back once he had what he wanted?

They wouldn't. Bribes wouldn't work. It would have to be threats.

But what could he threaten them with? He had *already* threatened them with raids and sabotage and the like. What could he say that would scare them . . .

"Them."

Just who were they, anyway? Who did he have to scare?

He didn't know; he had talked to a bunch of different officers and civilian officials, but none of them had been very high in the Imperial hierarchy. Somehow, he doubted Major Southern was running things at Base One. There was that General Hart people had talked about — Pel wasn't sure whether he had ever met him.

But they weren't all that important, Pel was sure. They weren't making policy.

Pel didn't know who was making Imperial policy.

He did know who the nominal head of state was, though, and he suddenly thought of what threat he could make, even if he didn't know who he was threatening.

Whether His Imperial Majesty George VIII was a figurehead or an actual monarch Pel didn't know, and somehow he suspected it didn't matter, because in neither case could the Empire's rulers sit by and let him be assassinated.

Pel let the wind lower him gently, and landed in a forest, where magic flowed strongly in intricate patterns through the trees. Cutting wooden slabs was easy, and using his finger as a focal point it was easy to cut letters into them with his magic. The light of the matrix made the gathering gloom of evening irrelevant.

He would not settle for one. He could not risk anything going wrong, and one board might get lost, might be ignored, might land someplace too far from wherever the bodies were kept, someplace that didn't have one of the Empire's four hundred telepaths close at hand.

And he'd send these to places he'd hit before, and places he hadn't — let them know that they couldn't stop him.

He cut slab after slab, and wrote the same message into each of them.

IF THE BODIES ARE NOT DELIVERED WITHIN TWENTY-FOUR HOURS OF THE APPEARANCE OF THIS MESSAGE, YOUR EMPEROR WILL DIE.

Chapter Twenty-Five

"He can't mean it," Sheffield said.

"Why the hell not?" Albright demanded.

"I wish we knew more about him," Markham said. "If we knew why he wanted the corpses . . . maybe we should send someone to Earth, to talk to people who knew him."

Albright snorted. "Not that easy. We cut Earth off; they've no reason to cooperate, and they've got a guard on our warp site. We'd have to open a new one, and then our men would have to find some way to cross hundreds of miles of unfamiliar terrain without being noticed, find the right people to talk to without alerting the local government . . ."

"You don't think they'd cooperate?" Markham asked.

"Why should they?" Albright said with a shrug.

"Given time, we might manage a mission such as you describe," Celia Howe said. "But what good would it do? We couldn't possibly get anything useful done before that twenty-four-hour deadline."

The telepath in the corner cleared his throat, and all four faces turned toward him.

"His Imperial Majesty informs me," the telepath said, "that we are to return this man's family forthwith."

"Well, that's it, then," Markham said, with visible relief.

"But does His Majesty understand that we cannot be sure what Brown intends . . ." Sheffield began.

"His Majesty understands quite enough," the telepath said, cutting him off. "He also desires that we proffer a formal apology, and Secretary Sheffield is hereby recalled to Terra immediately."

The others glanced at one another; they knew what this meant.

George VIII let his governments operate independently up to a point — but when his personal safety was threatened, that point had been passed.

Sheffield was ruined, at least temporarily; the Emperor would undoubtedly convene the Council and the Peerage and ask them to appoint a new government. And until they came up with one he liked he would run the Empire himself.

Whether Albright and Markham retained their posts . . . well, the Emperor hated doing the work of running the Empire himself. He would want a new government installed quickly. That meant as few cabinet changes as possible, and His Imperial Majesty might well instruct the legislature accordingly.

But on the other hand, Albright and Markham were involved in this interdimensional debacle, just as much as Sheffield was.

It was up to the Imperial whim.

Meanwhile, they had little choice but to obey orders as quickly and efficiently as possible. Albright stood up.

"Get me a messenger," he said.

*T*he matrix twisted, and Pel almost fell. A space-warp had opened, one that was fairly close, and big enough to disturb the matrix noticeably.

It was, he quickly realized, in the same place as the second invasion.

He looked down at the forest below with something like regret; he had been enjoying his scenic tour of Faerie. The mountains ahead looked quite spectacular, and he was sure there was plenty more to be seen. He hadn't yet come across more elves, nor any of the little people, the gnomes, as they were called, let alone their homeland of Hrumph.

Of course, Grummetty's comments all those months ago had implied that Shadow had driven the gnomes out of Hrumph — they might have wound up on a reservation somewhere, the way the elves had.

There was so much Pel didn't know.

For some time he had thought of Faerie as a narrow strip stretching from Shadowmarsh to the Low Forest, but now it had finally sunk in that it was an entire *world*.

Perhaps he and Nancy and Rachel could take a vacation here before returning to Earth, take a flying tour of the countryside. They couldn't see all of it, of course — there was far too much, a world larger than the whole Earth — but they could roam about a bit.

For now, though, it was time to see whether the Empire had finally seen reason, or whether he would have to find a way to kill George VIII and hope that George IX, or whoever the next Emperor was, would be more sensible.

He wheeled about and headed back across the wooded hills, accelerating as he went.

Moments later he stumbled to a stop on the charred remains of a barley field, where two steel cylinders lay side by side, a sheet of paper atop one of them.

He picked up the paper and read, "With Our apologies for the delay, and hopes for cordial relations hereafter." A blue seal adorned one corner. The signature was done with something like a rubber stamp and was slightly blurred, but still decipherable — *Georgius VIII Imperator et Rex.* An illegible scribble next to it was presumably the mark of the secretary who had stamped the document in accordance with Imperial instructions.

"Well, that's more like it," Pel said to no one, dropping the paper and turning to the cylinders.

His stomach was suddenly trembling inside him, his knees unsteady.

The cylinders were cold to the touch. Each was held closed by two complex screwed-down latches of some sort; Pel spun the flywheel of each latch on the nearer container and pried open the complicated hooks.

He felt as if he might faint, and his hands were cold, and not just from the cold metal. He was sweating. At last, at long last, he had his wife and daughter back.

Either that, or the Empire was in for unrelieved hell, if this should prove to be some other stupid delay.

He lifted the lid, not breathing, and looked inside.

For a moment he thought that it *was* some sort of trick, that they had substituted some ghastly thing for his wife; then he realized he was wrong.

This thing was Nancy.

She was naked, but so battered and horrific that that hardly mattered. Her skin was pale and discolored, a sickly grayish hue, and large areas were flaking or peeling, as if her skin were badly weathered paint. Her belly was a ruin of blackened, torn meat — the pirates had shot her in the gut with a blaster at point-blank range. She was half-frozen, still stiff, lying in a puddle of condensation.

One of her legs was *cracked,* exposing bone and flesh; Pel supposed it had happened while she was frozen.

And three fingers were gone from her right hand, but a moment later Pel spotted them, little shrivelled pink things lying by her hip.

And her face . . . part of the skin was gone from around her left eye, and her right cheekbone was caved in; a huge purple bruise had apparently formed before death. Her eyes were wide open and staring.

But it was Nancy.

Pel stepped back and sat down abruptly to keep from falling. He felt sick and faint.

He had never thought about what she would look like. He had thought of her looking as if she were asleep.

He should have known better. Especially after some of the things he had seen since — the disembowelled bodies hanging from gibbets in Shadow's empire, the blackened remnants of Shadow's enemies, the corpses he had resurrected himself, the Imperial troops he had killed himself — he should certainly have known better.

He put his head down and took deep, slow breaths, and tried not to think about her appearance.

After a minute or two he felt better — still sick, but fairly sure he wouldn't faint or vomit.

He didn't look at Nancy again; instead he went to the other cylinder and opened the latches.

He hesitated, however, before lifting the lid.

No one had said how Rachel had died. He knew she had died on Zeta Leo III, at the hands of the slave-owners there, but only that. Nancy had been beaten, raped, and murdered by the pirates on *Emerald Princess*; Rachel's death was a mystery.

He had to be prepared for the worst.

He took a deep breath, then opened the cylinder and looked in.

It wasn't as bad.

She was wrapped in dirty white cloth from her shoulders to her knees, and whatever might be hidden by the cloth, Pel wasn't interested in seeing. There were no bloodstains, nothing obviously broken or missing; her eyes were closed. Although she was plainly dead, so pale and lifeless that no one would ever mistake her for a living child, she showed no signs of whatever had killed her. There were a few bruises, though, and her face was smudged with dirt. Bits of dirt clung to her hair, as well, and more dirt was smeared across the cloth . . .

She had been buried, Pel realized. That was why it had taken the Imperial task force so long to find her. They had found her and dug her up and brought her back to Base One after someone, probably her killer, had buried her.

Buried her without a coffin, obviously — just wrapped in an improvised shroud.

Had whoever it was been trying to do the right thing? Or had the killer just been disposing of the evidence?

It didn't matter; all that mattered was that Pel had her back.

He reached down and touched her.

Her skin was cold and dead — *very* cold. Like Nancy, she had apparently been frozen, or at least refrigerated.

Pel shuddered and withdrew his hand, and the motion jarred the corpse; Rachel's head rolled slightly to one side, and Pel saw the purple finger marks on her neck and knew how she had died.

But that was past. She was here now, in a world where magic worked, and her father, who had done nothing to save her when she was alive, would bring her back to life.

He closed the lid and screwed down the latches, then did the same for the other cylinder. A moment later he was airborne, the cylinders following him northward through the sky, toward Shadowmarsh and Shadow's fortress, where Shadow's magic would restore them all.

John Bascombe leaned back and smiled. The news had spread like wildfire, like the shock wave of a supernova — the Empire had yielded to the Brown Magician's demands. The war was over, and the Empire had come out second-best. Sheffield had been recalled to Earth. A new government would be formed.

And John Bascombe, Under-Secretary for Interdimensional Affairs, was pretty sure that Sheffield would take the others down with him — Markham and Albright and Hart and all the rest of them.

But not him. Not John Bascombe. Because he'd been cut out of everything, shunted off to the side; none of what had happened was *his* fault.

Or at least, none of it could be pinned on him, and that was what counted.

And with Markham and the rest surely doomed, that would mean opportunities for advancement. He might not be the new Secretary of Science, but he thought he ought to be able to move up a notch or two. Perhaps General Under-Secretary of Science? Imperial Advisor on Science?

He was musing pleasantly on the various possibilities when the door of his office burst open and two men stepped in, blasters drawn.

They wore the purple and gold of the Imperial Guard. Bascombe sat up suddenly and stared.

"John Bascombe?" one of them asked.

"Uh," Bascombe said.

"John Bascombe, you are under arrest, by order of His Imperial Majesty, George VIII."

"Uh," Bascombe said again, staring.

How could he be under arrest? And it wasn't just Sheffield or the others taking a last-minute revenge — the Imperial Guard didn't take orders from anyone but the Emperor and their own officers.

They didn't ordinarily leave Terra at all — the Emperor must have sent them here especially. It must be a full-scale purge, Bascombe realized.

But he hadn't done anything wrong! Oh, he had intrigued a little, hidden a few little mishaps, but he hadn't done anything *wrong,* he hadn't been one of Sheffield's people . . .

"What . . ." he said, mouth dry. "What charge?"

"Treason," the guardsman said.

And Bascombe knew that whatever happened, whether he lived or died, was acquitted or convicted, that with a treason charge on his record, even if it was dismissed as a mistake, he was never, ever going to be Secretary of Science.

*P*el brought the cylinders through the front gate, up the great staircase to the throne room, where some of the inhabitants of the fortress were awaiting his return.

He didn't pay much attention.

He knew, in a vague, detached sort of way, that he had been awake and active for far too long. He had spent most of the day that was ending in the air, riding the winds hither and yon; he had spent the night before carving wooden message-boards and sending them through portals into the Empire. And that had followed the day in which he located and destroyed the Empire's second attempted invasion.

And he hadn't slept in thirty-six hours or more.

He hadn't eaten anything but a bite or two of corned beef in weeks.

He was letting the matrix support him — and it was doing so, so that he still wasn't physically tired, but he knew he ought to sleep, he knew that he wasn't thinking clearly anymore. It wasn't healthy. It wasn't safe.

But he had the bodies, at last. He had the bodies. He had his family back.

He looked up and saw Susan Nguyen standing in the doorway, and he smiled. There she was, the proof that he could restore the dead.

But of course, he would have to repair the bodies first, Nancy's especially.

And there was the false Nancy now, standing at Susan's side, and she could serve him as a model.

"Come here," he called, "both of you!"

"*D*id you, or did you not, order an officer of the Imperial Intelligence Service to arrest one Pellinore Brown, also known as Pelbrun the Brown Magician?" the presiding officer of the court — Bascombe wasn't sure just what the correct title was, or for that matter what the exact nature of this hearing was — demanded.

No one worried about telling the accused such unnecessary details in an affair like this.

"I don't know," Bascombe said. "Did I? Why does it matter?"

The judge, if that was what he was, sat back in his chair. "Pellinore Brown," he said, "is a reigning head of state. To order his arrest is an act of war. To commit an act of war against a friendly nation in the Empire's name is an act of treason. Now, do you deny issuing that order?"

Bascombe glanced at the silent young woman sitting in the corner of the room. "What difference does it make? You've got a telepath there; you know whether I did it better than I know myself."

"We would prefer to have your own words on the record."

"I don't remember whether I issued such an order," Bascombe said, truthfully. "I may have. I wasn't aware that the Empire had recognized Pellinore Brown as a head of state, or that his nation was a friendly one. I didn't know there *was* such a thing as a friendly nation."

The judge glanced at the woman, who nodded.

Bascombe watched the judge's face, and thought he saw something there, something that might have been a trace of disappointment.

And John Bascombe suppressed a sigh of relief; he was fairly sure that that disappointment meant that at least so far, his answers had not condemned him to death.

At last, when he had been unable to organize the matrix currents properly to repair Nancy's intestines despite three attempts, Pel gave up and found a bed.

He awoke with no idea how long he had slept, and no interest in finding out; he returned immediately to the throne room, to resume work on the bodies.

It took hours; the damage to Nancy's body was extensive, severe, and often subtle. Tissues had been burned, frozen, dehydrated, attacked in dozens of ways, and everything had to be *perfect.*

He took a break every so often; he didn't want to risk screwing anything up through fatigue.

At last, though, he had them both ready, the bodies repaired but lifeless.

They weren't going to *stay* lifeless, though; at long last, he was about to raise them both from the dead.

And Nancy would be first.

"They're in chaos," Miletti said. "The Emperor's royally pissed off by the whole affair. He's convinced the whole thing should have been turned over to the spies right from the start, that the military and the scientists had no business keeping it to themselves and that his Prime Minister or General Secretary or whatever he's called should have known better."

"And how's this affect us?" Johnston asked.

Miletti shrugged.

"They don't care about us," Miletti said.

Then he added as an afterthought, "At least, not yet they don't."

Nancy's eyes opened, and she stared upward for a fraction of a second; then she closed them, tight, and flung an arm across them protectively.

"The matrix," Susan suggested. "She's never seen it before."

Pel had forgotten that; he quickly fought down the glow, reduced it to a dim flickering, no brighter than a few candles. He was relieved that he had allowed Susan to stay when he sent all the others away; he had become so accustomed to the matrix, and to his own immunity to its brilliance, that he might not have identified the problem for a minute or two, and he didn't want to waste even a second.

He remembered how the simulacrum had reacted when she first awoke; if this one did the same thing then he would know he had failed, and it would all be over.

"Nancy?" he said.

The eyes opened again, the arm lifted, and she looked up at his worried face. She looked at the beard, at the unkempt long hair, and then at his eyes.

She blinked, and stared into his eyes for a long moment.

"Pel?" she said at last, and the Brown Magician smiled the most wonderful smile of his life.

Chapter Twenty-Six

*I*t was perfect. It was, Pel thought, really almost perfect. It wasn't at all like that first night with the simulacrum of Nancy. It wasn't like any night ever before, not even their honeymoon.

At first Nancy had asked about Rachel — Pel hadn't told her where Rachel was, or that she was dead; he had merely told her that their daughter was safe, that he would explain everything later.

She had still wondered, in a half-hearted way, but she hadn't argued too strenuously.

And she had asked where they were, and Pel had told her they were in Faerie, but it was all right, Shadow was dead and they were safe, he would explain it all later.

And she had asked about the glow, the strange colors flickering around him, and he had told her that it was magic, but it was under control, he would explain later.

And she had asked about his beard and hair, and he told her he'd been too busy to shave lately, but he'd clean himself up when he had a moment.

And she had asked how she got there, and he said she had been unconscious for a long time, but she was all right now.

And then she had run out of questions and he had taken her in his arms, and it had been damn near perfect.

At first.

But then he woke up beside her, and looked at her sleeping there, and he thought it over.

She shouldn't have been aware of any long separation. She had died just a dozen yards away from him, aboard that ship; they had been together until just hours before. Yet she had acted as if they were reunited after months apart.

They *were*, but how would she know?

Was it just his own altered appearance that had let her know? That shouldn't have been enough, he thought — it wouldn't have had the emotional impact she seemed to have felt. Had she been somehow aware while she was dead? Had he snatched her back from Heaven, perhaps?

Pel had never really believed in Heaven, and he still didn't — but he had never believed in a lot of things he had seen for himself of late.

And she hadn't argued with him about anything, not really. She hadn't insisted on knowing where Rachel was, or who was looking after her.

Well, there must have been something of a shock, going from being raped aboard a spaceship to waking up in a magician's castle.

And she hadn't mentioned being raped, but all the survivors of *Emerald Princess* had said she was raped before the pirates killed her.

There hadn't been any physical evidence that Pel could see, but after all, the body had been in such terrible condition that he wouldn't have noticed anything whether it had been there or not, and why would the others have lied?

So she had been raped — and how could she go so willingly from that to her husband's bed? It didn't seem right, somehow.

That first fetch he had restored had screamed at the memory of what had happened to him; Nancy hadn't. Why not?

Pel frowned, and told himself that he was worrying about nothing, trying to ruin his own happiness with all these niggling little worries. Maybe years spent as Shadow's fetch were far more horrible than what Nancy had lived through. Maybe she didn't remember being raped; he hadn't asked her about it, so he didn't really know. Maybe she had blocked out those last few minutes. Or maybe that was why she *had* been eager enough to not ask more about Rachel, maybe she had wanted something clean and good to wipe away the memory.

This was Nancy. She had known his name when she first woke up. She had asked about Rachel, even if she hadn't insisted. She had responded just about the way Nancy always had, nothing had been wrong or strange — until now, until he sat here thinking too much.

Had she been a little slow to react to things, a little detached?

Well, she had been *dead*.

He got up and had the matrix drape a robe about him, leaving Nancy undisturbed.

There wasn't anything wrong with her.

There wasn't, he told himself as he walked down the stone corridor, finding his way in his own light, anything wrong with her.

But somewhere in the back of his head he remembered something Shadow had said before she died.

The exact words were hard to recall, given her archaic phrasing, but he thought he had it. "I can instill therein a semblance of life, indistinguishable by any normal means from any mortal born," she had said, "yet some certain spark is lacking."

She had been referring to the ability of a resurrected person to use magic, to hold a matrix, Pel reminded himself. Nancy could never be a magician — but who cared?

That was all Shadow had meant, Pel told himself.

It was still Nancy. She was alive again.

And in an hour or so, Rachel would be, too.

*H*is Imperial Majesty George VIII drummed his fingers on a six-hundred-year-old table and considered his disgraced General Secretary, delivered directly from the spaceport to the palace and rushed hastily through security.

"Bucky, whatever were you thinking of?" he asked.

"I don't know what you mean, your Majesty," Sheffield replied uneasily.

"We mean why did you persist in antagonizing this Brown person? You know better than that."

"I'm not sure I do, your Majesty," Sheffield said. "I did what seemed best to me."

"We're disappointed, then. Why in the world didn't you just give him his dead wife back? What possible harm could that have done?"

"I am not quite sure, your Majesty, and I preferred to err on the side of caution. Secretary Markham seemed to believe that the so-called 'magic' at Mr. Brown's disposal might be able to make some use of the woman's remains."

"And what possible use could be worse for us than getting Brown furiously angry?" the Emperor asked. "And not only that, Bucky, but you *lied* to the man — you promised delivery, then balked. He did everything you asked — do you realize he ordered his entire network of spies to swear loyalty to us? To us, personally? That was more than anyone asked, and entirely his own idea, and he didn't even bother to mention it. The man was being as friendly as he could be, and how did we respond?"

"Um," Sheffield said. "But your Majesty, he . . . the Empire cannot afford to appear weak."

"Oh, nonsense. The Empire *isn't* weak, so it doesn't really matter how we appear. Except that it's much easier to stab someone from behind, and an enemy will never turn his back, while a friend won't give it a second thought, so we *should* have done all we could to appear friendly. We should have turned over the bodies immediately."

Sheffield swallowed. "So Secretary Markham came to believe," he said.

After all, just because his own career was ruined, that didn't mean that he had to drag innocents down with him.

"And what did Albright, your other partner in crime, think?"

"I'm not sure he voiced an opinion, your Majesty. Marshal Albright quite properly thinks in terms of means, rather than ends, as a military man should."

"A good soldier knows when to offer suggestions, Bucky, even if he doesn't try to force them on anyone," the Emperor said gently. "It may be time for Marshal Albright to retire honorably."

That wasn't so bad, really, Sheffield thought.

"General Hart will be court-martialled," the Emperor said. "John Bascombe's already up on a charge of treason, and he's guilty, but I don't think we'll hang him, as he's not so much dangerous as he is stupid. The telepaths identify those two as responsible for a great deal of the bumbling prior to Mr. Brown's ascension, and some of the mishaps afterward." He smiled. "The rest, we're afraid, was largely your own doing — well-intentioned, but wrong."

"The telepaths, your Majesty?"

"Oh, yes, Bucky — there's nothing in the world more useful in untangling a mess like this than the network of telepaths. We wish we had a million of them, not just a few hundred."

Sheffield shifted uneasily. He wanted to say something about the untrustworthiness of the mutants for anything beyond interrogation and long-distance communication, but he couldn't think how to phrase it properly.

"You don't like them, do you?" the Emperor asked. "The greater fool you, then. Don't you know they're just people? They want to be liked and appreciated, and most people hate their guts — they must be miserable. All you have to do is like them a little, and they'll love you in return. And we *do* like them." He grinned. "They could tell if we were faking, after all." The smile faded.

"And right now," he said, "we can't think of anyone better to run things until they're straightened out than the telepaths."

He paused, then added, "Under our own direction, of course."

Rachel sat up and blinked.

This time Pel had suppressed the visible portion of the matrix in advance; he sat there looking as ordinary as he could contrive to look. He'd combed out his hair and trimmed both his hair and his beard somewhat, but he hadn't managed to shave.

He hadn't shaved for several days before he and Rachel were separated, so that shouldn't be *too* strange, and otherwise he thought he looked pretty much as Rachel would remember him.

Except for the robe, anyway; he hadn't bothered to find any Earth-style clothing. And they were in a bare, candle-lit stone chamber that wasn't terribly friendly looking.

"Where am I, Daddy?" Rachel said.

"You're in a place called Faerie, honey," Pel replied.

"You're dressed funny," she said. Then she looked down and squealed, "And I'm not dressed *at all!*"

"You've been sick, Rachel, very sick," Pel said. He hesitated, then asked, "What's the last thing you remember?"

Rachel looked up at him, thought for moment, then said solemnly, "The bad man squeezing my neck." She added, "It hurt a lot."

Pel swallowed. "The bad man is gone," he said. "The soldiers in the purple uniforms came and took him away, and he's gone forever. But he'd hurt you so bad it took magic to fix it, so I came here and learned to do magic, and here you are, all better."

"Do I have to stay here?"

"No," Pel said, smiling as he tried to keep his eyes from tearing, "no, you can go home if you want."

"What about you and Mommy? Will you go home? Is Mommy all right?"

"We're both fine, honey," Pel said.

"She isn't dead?"

"No, she isn't dead," Pel said. He managed to keep himself from adding, "Not anymore." Rachel wouldn't have understood.

"Can I see her?"

"Sure," Pel said. "Come on."

"So he's got the bodies back," Johnston remarked as he led Amy and Prossie down the front walk of Miletti's suburban home. "Think he can really resurrect them?"

"Shadow said she could raise the dead," Amy replied.

"But Pel isn't Shadow," Prossie pointed out. "He's got the power, but does he know how to use it?"

"You sound like someone in a bad movie, saying that," Johnston said. He hastily added, "No offense meant."

"Pel obviously *thinks* he can do it," Amy said.

"Or at least hopes he can," Prossie corrected her. "And for all we know, Shadow was lying in the first place."

Johnston opened the car door for the women.

"I don't think she was lying," Amy said, as Prossie climbed in. "But I think she said something about the resurrected people not being quite the same."

"Like in *Pet Sematary?*" Johnston asked. "They come back evil, or something?"

Amy shook her head, then seated herself. "I don't think it was anything like that; just they're a bit less lively, or something."

Johnston shrugged. "Well, it still sounds like a happy ending to me, then," he said.

He slammed the car door and circled around to the driver's side.

*P*el watched as Nancy and Rachel embraced. He had wiped away his tears, but was still grinning so broadly that his jaws hurt.

They didn't cry, he noticed. Neither of them did. They smiled, but that was all.

But then, he reminded himself, they didn't know they'd been dead. Nancy had seen Rachel alive and well just minutes before the pirates hauled Nancy out of the storage locker and raped her; Rachel had been safe with her father the whole time, for all Nancy knew.

And Rachel didn't really understand what had happened to her, or to her mother.

Still, he had somehow expected weeping.

Nancy looked up, and asked, "Pel? Are you ready to explain what's going on?"

Pel hesitated.

"I'd rather not, just yet," he said.

"If Rachel weren't here?"

Reluctantly, Pel nodded.

"I'll get Susan to keep an eye on her," he said.

"Susan? Susan Nguyen?"

Pel nodded again.

"She's here?"

"Yes."

"What about the others? Ted and Raven and Amy and the rest?"

"Ted and Amy are back home on Earth," Pel said. "Raven is dead. Most of them are dead, and the rest have gone home; it's just Susan and I who are still here."

"Why?" Nancy asked.

"Why what?"

"Why are the two of you still here?"

"I had to get you two fixed up," Pel said. "And Susan stayed to help, I guess. I offered to send her home, but she didn't want to go."

"That's odd," Nancy said. "*You* offered to send her home? What about Elani?"

"Elani's dead," Pel said. "I'm a wizard now."

Nancy stared at him. "Go get Susan," she said. "You have a *lot* of explaining to do, Pel Brown."

Pel stepped to the doorway, but that was just for appearance's sake; he used the matrix to summon Susan with a gentle tug.

She had been waiting down the hall, as he had told her to do; she was there within seconds.

"Go with Susan, Rachel," Pel said, giving his daughter a gentle shove. "She'll try to find you some proper clothes."

Rachel looked up and said nothing. She was still wrapped in the crude shroud she had been buried in.

Together, silently, Susan and Rachel left the room, and Pel turned to his wife, who sat up in bed, wrapped in a sheet.

"I was dead, wasn't I?" Nancy said. "I remember that man pointing that raygun at me and pulling the trigger, and I remember this incredible pain. I wasn't just unconscious, was I?"

"You were dead," Pel admitted. "For months."

"And Rachel?"

Pel nodded. "She was killed a few weeks later. Strangled."

"And Susan?"

"Susan, too. Shadow stopped her heart."

"The others?"

Pel shook his head. "Nobody else who's still alive."

"So if we died . . . well, what about you? Are you dead, too? Is this some sort of afterlife?"

"No, I didn't die," he said. "There were a couple of times I wanted to die, or was certain I was about to, but I never did."

"So what happened? How can you be a wizard? Did you make a deal with the devil, or something? Or with Shadow?"

"I'll explain," Pel said. He took a deep breath, and began.

He told her how *Emerald Princess* had been captured by pirates under the direction of one of Shadow's agents, how the passengers and crew had been sold as slaves on Zeta Leo III, how he had worked in the mines until the Imperial task force came and liberated them all — and found Rachel dead.

He explained how the Empire had sent the survivors back into Shadow's world on a suicide mission to get rid of them, how some of them had made their way cross-country to Shadow's fortress, gradually realizing that that was what Shadow had wanted them to do, because she wanted someone to serve as a placeholder, keeping her magic for her, while she explored the Galactic Empire.

He told Nancy how Shadow had casually killed anyone who displeased her, reducing Raven and Singer and Valadrakul to ash, and had settled on Pel as, as he bitterly put it, "her human bookmark."

And he described how Prossie had taken a blaster from one of the dead soldiers and had followed Shadow into the Empire and shot her dead.

He didn't mention that it had been his idea.

"Shadow was just an old woman?" Nancy asked.

"As human as I am," Pel replied.

He went on to explain that he had sent Amy, Ted, and Prossie to Earth, because Prossie had broken some law and couldn't go back to the Empire. He had stayed in Faerie to see if he could restore Nancy and Rachel to life, and after various difficulties, he had managed it.

He didn't mention his abortive attempts to introduce democracy and social justice to Shadow's world; he only told her he had wanted to resurrect her — and, of course, Rachel.

Susan, he explained, had been for practice.

"And here we are," he said.

"What about Raven?" she asked. "Are you going to bring him back next?"

"I wasn't planning to," Pel said. "I don't think there's enough left."

"What about any of the others?"

Pel shook his head. "I'm not God," he said.

"But you brought *me* back, and Rachel, and Susan . . ."

"Susan was right there, and I needed to try, to see if I could do it," Pel said. "And you and Rachel — I *love* you. I had to bring you back."

"Oh," she said.

Just that, flatly, and Pel felt slightly sick at the sound of it. "What do you want me to do?" he asked. "Bring back everyone who dies? I'd never have time for anything else, and I'd never keep up, anyway. It's not my responsibility."

"I guess not," she said. "So, what happens now?"

"Whatever you want," Pel said. "We can go home to Earth, if you like, and just forget any of this ever happened — but if we do, we can't ever come back here. When I leave Faerie, the matrix will come apart, and I'd never be able to restore it, and there won't be anyone here to open portals for us."

"Is that what you want to do?"

"I don't know," Pel said. "Maybe not right away. I mean, there's a lot we could do here first — we could see the world. It's a big world, as big as our own, and I don't know much about it."

She nodded.

"Listen, do you want to get some clothes?" Pel asked. "I can open a portal back to Earth, and you could go get stuff for Rachel and yourself while I wait here."

Nancy glanced down at herself. "That might be a good idea," she said.

"Oh," Pel said, remembering, "but you'd want to wear something — there's this Air Force intelligence officer camped out in our basement."

"Would he let me go upstairs?" Nancy asked.

"He ought to," Pel said.

Nancy considered, then said, "I guess I won't bother, yet."

"All right."

The conversation was becoming uncomfortable, and Pel wasn't sure why. It didn't feel right.

But why not? They were just talking, calmly discussing the situation . . .

And that was it. How could they be so calm? He had just brought Nancy back from the *dead*, turned a mutilated, months-old corpse back into his living, breathing wife — shouldn't they both be laughing and crying and screaming?

And Nancy's last memories . . .

"You said you remember dying? Being shot?"

Nancy nodded.

"Do you remember what happened . . . just before that?" Pel asked nervously.

"You mean being raped?"

Pel nodded silently.

"I remember," she said quietly.

"Do you . . . do you want to talk about it?"

She shook her head. "It's over."

"They're dead," Pel said suddenly, the words rushing from his mouth unwanted. "The Empire tracked them down and hanged them, hanged everyone involved, all the pirates, they've been dead for months."

"It doesn't matter," Nancy said.

And that, Pel knew, just wasn't right.

He didn't say anything then. He still tried to tell himself he was imagining it.

But half an hour later the real Nancy encountered her simulacrum in the passage.

She didn't scream, or even start; she simply turned to Pel and asked, "Who's this?"

"I tried several ways to bring you back before I got it right," Pel said.

"Oh. Is that really what I look like?" She eyed the duplicate with mild interest.

The duplicate looked back, complacent and smiling.

Pel looked back and forth between the two of them.

The real Nancy hadn't screamed, hadn't shouted at him, hadn't shuddered. She didn't even ask if he had bedded the simulacrum, either directly or merely hinting.

Something was very, very wrong.

Chapter Twenty-Seven

"Why don't you run and play?" Pel asked.

"Don't want to," Rachel said.

"Do you want to go home? Back to Earth?"

"Don't care."

"Don't you miss Harvey, and all your friends?"

Rachel shrugged.

He turned to Susan. "Damn it, what's *wrong* with her?"

"She was dead," Susan said.

"She was dead too long, that's what it is," Pel said, turning back to stare at Rachel.

She was sitting cross-legged on the floor of the throne room, watching the changing colors of the matrix, and seemed quite content to do so indefinitely.

"They were *both* dead too long," Pel said angrily. "It's all because the goddamned Empire had to play their stupid games, and wouldn't just hand them over! I mean, what the hell is wrong with them? *You* aren't any different!"

"You didn't know me back on Earth," Susan said, but Pel didn't notice; he was working himself into a rage. Rachel watched quietly as the matrix became saturated with angry reds and began to seethe in tight little claw-shaped curls.

"The Empire had to play their fucking little power games," Pel said through gritted teeth. He turned to Susan. "I want fetches," he said. "With blasters."

"Fifteen dead," the telepath said. "That's not counting the attackers."

The Emperor drummed his fingers on the arm of his chair. "Three of them, we believe?"

"Yes, your Majesty," the telepath replied.

The Emperor shot a quick glance at Sheffield, who said nothing; the telepath said, "Yes, your Majesty, he is thinking that he told you so, that he warned you this would happen. He is also remembering that we haven't gotten back the hostages the Brown Magician claimed to have — roughly a hundred and fifty in all, he believes there were — but at least we've presumably recovered three blasters, and the others must be running low on charge, which will make it impossible for these raids to continue indefinitely."

Sheffield's expression was resigned, with no trace of self-righteousness that the Emperor could see. "He can always get more blasters," the Emperor said. "He started out with just three or four, didn't he, Bucky?"

"Yes, your Majesty," Sheffield admitted.

"We wish we knew what he wants," the Emperor said, drumming his fingers again. "We gave him the bodies, and he hasn't *made* any other demands." He gazed thoughtfully at Sheffield, then at the telepath, and at last he shrugged.

"The simplest way is probably the best," he said. "Send that envoy, Curran, through the warp, and have him *ask* Brown what he wants."

"Yes, your Majesty," the telepath said, bowing.

*T*he matrix kinked suddenly, startling Pel so that he almost dropped Rachel.

He was lifting her over his head, bouncing her up and down, trying to make her laugh — and failing. He was trying to keep a smile and a good attitude, to have fun, but Rachel's solemn little face wasn't helping at all.

And now the Empire had opened another warp.

"Screw 'em," Pel said to Rachel. "Let 'em burn villages if they want to. I don't care anymore."

He didn't mean to pay any attention, but as he lowered Rachel to the floor he couldn't help noticing that the warp was in the Low Forest, in Sunderland.

They probably wanted to talk, then.

Screw 'em.

*C*urran explored the treehouse thoroughly, evicting a squirrel and several birds in the process; the strange little servants, creatures like furry, misshapen dwarves, stood aside and let him search. None of them could speak — or at least, none of them *did* speak, so they could not tell him anything.

It was quite clear, even without confirmation from the servants, that the Brown Magician was not here, and had not been here in some time. He did not appear to have been near the shipwreck, either.

That left Curran in something of a quandary. How could he negotiate with someone who wasn't there?

The only solution seemed to be to go where Brown was, and while he didn't know for certain, the best guess was that fortress, in the place called Shadowmarsh — two hundred miles to the west.

And the only way to get there was by walking.

Curran sighed. He really didn't have any choice; his orders had come directly from the Emperor himself.

He started walking.

"*W*here do you want to live?" Pel bellowed.

"I don't care," Nancy repeated.

"You *have* to care!" Pel shouted at her. "*Think* about it, for God's sake! You can live here, where I have all the magic in the world and we can probably use it to live forever, or you can go back to Earth, where we can go back to a normal life, see your folks, all your friends, where I can talk to my mother and my sisters on the phone — where you'd *have* phones, and indoor plumbing, and books and TV and radio and we have a goddamn *VCR,* instead of magic! How can you not care?"

She shrugged. "It just doesn't matter to me."

Pel stared at her, frustrated beyond all control.

She had been alive again for a week, and all the initial euphoria was gone.

She didn't argue. She didn't complain. She didn't laugh. She never seemed to do anything on the spur of the moment, or show any real enthusiasm for anything.

She wasn't as obedient and agreeable as the simulacra; this was a different thing altogether. Instead, Nancy and Rachel seemed as closed and impervious as Susan.

But it had seemed *natural* in Susan, because she had always been quiet and reserved and calm, all the time Pel had known her.

Nancy hadn't. Nancy had had spirit.

But she didn't now.

And worse, neither did Rachel.

Pel couldn't stand it.

He raised both arms over his head and blasted a hole in the ceiling.

It didn't matter; he could repair it later. But the boom and the shower of dust and debris were oddly satisfying.

For a moment.

C urran staggered along the causeway, hoping that he could make it to the fortress before he collapsed.

His fancy coat was long gone, stolen in the first village he had passed through; the cummerbund had been traded for a meal, the silk sash for a night's lodging. The hat had fallen off in a storm, and never been recovered.

The soles of his shiny black boots were worn paper-thin, but still intact, though one of the nails holding the right heel had worked its way up through the sole and was now poking into his foot, so that he limped slightly.

The ruffles on his white shirt were stained, torn, and flattened; the shirt itself was more brown than white now.

His velvet pants had shredded, and been replaced with a stolen pair of soft leather breeches.

He hadn't shaved in almost a fortnight, his hair was shaggy and uncombed, and he had developed a nasty cough that he hoped wasn't anything serious.

Mostly, though, he was simply exhausted. A two-hundred-mile walk through a hostile country was no joke, and this country had definitely turned out to be hostile.

In fact, it had appeared to be on the verge of anarchy. His clothing had marked him as a figure of fun, not someone to be taken seriously as a threat, which had probably saved his life, as several groups he had encountered had seemed prone to strike first and ask questions later.

The Brown Magician did not appear to be a strong ruler. There were apparently several factions claiming to act in his name, and he had done nothing to settle the disputes.

As several people mentioned, Shadow had never allowed this sort of thing.

All the same, the Brown Magician was the ruler, as everyone agreed, and he was undoubtedly the one behind the raids into Imperial space, so he, and no one else, was who Curran had to speak to.

The causeway really seemed unreasonably long; why had Shadow, or whoever it was, built that fortress so far out in the marsh?

Curran staggered again, and decided he really needed to just sit down for a moment and rest, he wouldn't go to sleep or anything, he would just sit down, maybe close his eyes for a second . . .

*A*t first, Pel didn't recognize the bedraggled figure the fetches held upright before him.

Then the ruffled shirt caught his attention, and something clicked.

"Ambrose Curran?" he asked. "The Imperial envoy?"

Curran, still not entirely conscious, nodded weakly.

"Good heavens," Pel said. "What happened to *you?*"

Curran managed to mutter, "It's a long walk."

"So it is," Pel agreed, amused. "You came through the warp in the Low Forest? That was almost two weeks ago!"

Curran nodded again.

"Here, take him somewhere and feed him and get him rested up," Pel ordered the fetches. "Mr. Curran, you take your time, and come back when you feel up to talking. And don't worry, I haven't been launching any more raids lately."

He watched as the fetches dragged the semi-conscious envoy away, and shook his head in amazement.

Were all those *other* warps delivering envoys and ambassadors? The Empire had been opening space-warps every day or two, in various places, and then shutting them down again after one or two people had come through; Pel had assumed that they were all spies.

But maybe not.

He hadn't worried about it in any case; he hadn't *cared.* If the Empire wanted to subvert and conquer Faerie, it wasn't any skin off *his* nose — he still controlled all the magic, so they couldn't touch him or his, and he could leave and go home to Earth anytime he wanted.

At least, he could if he could get Rachel and Nancy to agree.

And Susan, too, he supposed.

So far, though, the three revenants had not expressed any interest in returning to Earth.

They hadn't voiced any objections, either; they were frankly disinterested.

It was really very depressing. Pel no longer blamed the Empire; Susan assured him that she was just as changed as the others, so the delay couldn't have been all that important.

The change was just that extra spark Shadow had referred to. Whatever it was, it was gone, irretrievably.

Pel had talked to the revenants, argued with them, studied them with all the magical resources at his disposal, and still hadn't found anything broken that he could fix, anything missing that he could replace. All of them readily acknowledged that they were changed; they could remember thinking that things were important, they could remember laughing and crying and caring, but all that was gone. When they had first come back there'd been something, all three agreed on that, but it had faded and vanished, like a pleasant dream upon waking. It might have just been a lingering habit of caring, rather than the emotions themselves, but whatever it had been, even that was gone now.

And it didn't matter to them. That was the worst part, Pel thought — that they didn't *care* that they'd lost something. That they didn't care about *anything*.

Including him.

He had asked Nancy, one night, if she still loved him. He had expected her to either say, "Yes, of course," or to say something about how he had let her be killed, how he had let her down.

But she hadn't said anything like that.

She had shrugged.

"Not really," she had said.

"Not really."

What was he supposed to do now?

How could he make her love him again?

He didn't know; it had been eating at him for days.

So Curran's arrival was a welcome distraction. He hoped the little diplomat would recover quickly.

"Miletti still says there's nothing new," Major Johnston said, and Amy guessed what was coming.

She'd been anticipating it for the last few days, really; things had been so quiet since that one final raid, and the Empire sending an envoy.

"There's absolutely no sign that the Empire's taking any interest in Earth anymore," Johnston continued. "They're still involved with Faerie, more or less, but the situation has lost its criticality; Mr. Brown is no longer counterattacking, or resisting minor Imperial incursions. Miletti says they even sent another telepath into Faerie the day before yesterday, the first one since Ms. Thorpe — they'd never have risked that when Brown was taking active countermeasures. And apparently Brown isn't really running Faerie, anyway; he's holed up in that fortress of his, ignoring everything."

Amy nodded.

"My point, Ms. Jewell, Ms. Thorpe, is that there's no longer any perceptible threat to the national security here — and it's damned hard to convince most people that there ever was one; nobody wants to believe in invaders from another dimension, even if they've seen the evidence. I can't justify my requests for funding any more consultations. I've managed to get Miletti into the budget as an ongoing special surveillance, which means I've got at least six months before they review what he's costing us and eliminate it, but you two were outside consultants, and orders are to end the project, which means paying you your expenses and per diem to date and saying good-bye."

"I understand, Major," Amy said.

"We'd hoped that Miletti might want to keep Ms. Thorpe on as his guest," Johnston added, "but he says he prefers to have her leave."

"I'd rather stay with Amy, anyway," Prossie said.

"If it's any comfort, the cuts also mean pulling out our observation post at your house," Johnston said. "We'll be paying you a lump-sum compensation for that. It won't be very much, but maybe it'll tide you over for awhile."

"Thank you," Amy said.

For a moment, she and Johnston looked at each other, not saying anything; it had really all been said, but neither was in a hurry to cut the conversation short.

At last, Amy stood up.

"I guess that's it, then," she said. "Thank you for your consideration, Major."

"You're very welcome, Ms. Jewell, and I'm very sorry for all the inconvenience. Feel free to call me if there's anything you need to discuss — you have the number." He hesitated, then added, "And if we've misjudged, and the Galactic Empire starts dropping paratroopers in your back yard, you call me right away, any time, day or night, and then you get out of there — you've done more than your share."

"Thank you," Amy said again.

"So what brings you here?" Pel asked, looking Curran over as he stood in his ragged shirt and leather pants, squinting against the glare of the matrix.

The last time Pel had seen the Imperial diplomat had been out in the Low Forest, in his treehouse, and it occurred to Pel that Nancy and Rachel might like that treehouse. Especially Rachel.

Or at least, they would have before they died; now they probably wouldn't care.

"I was sent in response to your raid on the guildhall on Iota Cephus IV," Curran said. "His Imperial Majesty wishes me — or *wished* me, at any rate — to extend his fondest greetings, and to inquire what prompted this unwarranted attack on his people. He believes — believed — that this must be the result of a misunderstanding, and asked what could be done to rectify the situation." He cleared his throat. "I feel constrained to use the past tense, because of the long delay in my arrival. We regret that we have no faster way of reaching your capital."

"My capital?" Pel looked around at the white stone columns and walls. "It's not a capital, it's a goddamn fortress. As for that raid, if it's the one I think it was, it wasn't a misunderstanding, I was just royally pissed off — *imperially* pissed off, in fact." He smiled bitterly at his feeble joke.

Curran hesitated. "I'm afraid I don't recognize the idiom, but I take it to mean you were angry about something. Was it something that the Empire was responsible for?"

"No, no." Pel waved a hand in dismissal. "Nothing like that. A personal matter. At the time I thought it was the Empire's fault, but it wasn't."

"Then all is well between yourself and His Imperial Majesty, and His Majesty's servants?"

"As far as I'm concerned, sure. I'm still pissed . . . still annoyed that you people took *so* damn long to deliver what you'd promised, but that's all."

"Then may I convey to His Imperial Majesty your assurances that there will be no further attacks on his dominions?"

"No," Pel said, "because I haven't decided about that. I may just attack again, if I feel like it. But I'm not currently planning anything."

Curran hesitated. "His Imperial Majesty may not find that entirely reassuring."

"Fuck His Imperial Majesty, then," Pel said. "It's the best answer he's going to get."

Curran swallowed uneasily. "There are two other matters," he said.

"What?" Pel asked. He was getting tired of this. Curran wasn't anywhere near as funny without his fancy costume.

Of course, not much was really funny anymore, with Nancy and Rachel the way they were.

"The lesser is to ask, on my own behalf as much as my government's, if it would be possible for you to transport me back to the Empire magically, to save me the journey back to the forests of Sunderland."

"Sure," Pel agreed. "I can't guarantee where in the Empire you'll come out, though; I never learned all the place names."

"Thank you, sir." Curran bowed.

"What's the other?"

"Please remember, sir, that I have been out of touch for almost a fortnight, so this may no longer be relevant, but part of my original charge was to request the return of the hostages you took in the course of the prolonged misunderstanding between yourself and certain former ministers of His Imperial Majesty's government. It was His Imperial Majesty's understanding, perhaps faulty, that they were to be returned when the bodies of your wife and daughter had been delivered. That was done some time ago."

"The hostages," Pel said. His last trace of good humor vanished. Curran was no longer funny at all.

Pel had completely forgotten about the hostages. They were undoubtedly still somewhere in the dungeons beneath the fortress — Shadow had burrowed out miles of dreary passages, lined with cells and chambers, and Pel had ordered the prisoners taken there and looked after . . .

And then he'd forgotten all about them.

"Yes, sir," Curran said. "I was told that there were over a hundred, including His Excellency Shelton Grigsby, Governor-General of Beckett."

"No," Pel said, "you can't have them. I'm keeping them."

"But, sir . . ."

"You tell His Imperial Flatulence that I'm keeping them until he gives back all my spies, *and* gets all his spies out of Faerie, and *proves* it. He expected me to prove it when my people turned themselves in, let's see how *he* does it!"

"Sir, His Imperial Majesty had no part in that unfortunate . . ."

"It's his fucking empire, isn't it?" Pel demanded.

Curran struggled for words.

"Then it's his goddamn responsibility." He shifted in his throne. "I've had enough of this. Just shut up for a few minutes, Curran, and I'll open a portal for you — but I'll send the hostages back when I'm good and ready, and not a moment before."

Curran hesitated, opened his mouth, closed it — then bowed, and stepped back.

Pel reached out into the matrix and began preparing a portal into the Empire.

As he did, he tried not to think about those neglected and forgotten hostages.

He wondered where they all were, and whether they were still alive.

I hate to pull it," Johnston said, looking over the latest budget statement. "We don't have anyone who can watch Faerie for us the way Miletti watches the Empire. And Brown might turn up at any time."

"Well, sir, what if he does?" the lieutenant asked. "Won't that mean it's all over?"

"Except for the lawsuits," Johnston agreed. "His sisters are trying to have him declared legally dead, and they're fighting his mortgage company, which wants to foreclose, and he's got some problems with unfinished business from his consulting firm."

"None of that's really any of our concern, though, is it, sir?"

"The mortgage might be, but no, not really," Johnston admitted, putting down the clipboard. "All right, we pull out, and his sisters can have the house."

*P*el sat in his throne and stared for a long, long moment at the empty air where Curran had stepped through the portal to the Empire — to somewhere in the Empire, Pel didn't know where. He hadn't worried about which portal he had opened.

All those hostages . . . He still had all those people down in the dungeons, and he'd completely forgotten about them.

But what did it really matter? What did anything matter, if his wife and daughter didn't love him anymore?

He looked up at the hole in the throne room ceiling, raised a hand — then lowered it again.

What did *any* of it matter?

Chapter Twenty-Eight

"He didn't say what he wanted from us?" the Emperor asked, baffled.

The telepath replied, "Mr. Curran says it was his impression that Mr. Brown didn't really want anything. It was his impression that Mr. Brown was depressed about something, and simply didn't want to deal with us."

"We don't understand," the Emperor said. "Ask Mr. Curran if he thinks further approaches might be more productive."

The telepath did not reply for several seconds, as the question and answer were relayed. Then he said, "It's Mr. Curran's belief that further approaches by representatives of the Empire might be productive, but might equally well be disastrous — Mr. Brown is, Mr. Curran judges, in a state of extreme whimsicality, liable to do anything at all, for no reason whatsoever."

"And he might launch another raid at any time?"

"So he said, your Majesty."

"And he's not returning the hostages?"

"He is not, your Majesty."

"That's intolerable. Really."

"Yes, your Majesty."

His Imperial Majesty George VIII marched back and forth along the antique carpet, thinking hard. "We don't understand this man," he muttered. "And we can't send one of you to read his mind, because you can't. And those spies of his that we spoke to knew nothing about him. He's an enigma, an alien . . ."

He stopped pacing and looked up.

"What about his family?" he asked.

"His wife and daughter . . ." the telepath began.

"No, no, we know about them," the Emperor said, dismissing Nancy and Rachel with a wave of his hand. "Does he have no brothers or sisters, no close friends we might interview?"

"I don't know, your Majesty. There were the other Earthpeople who traveled with him . . ."

"Yes, there were!" the Emperor said, raising a finger triumphantly. "Yes, exactly! There were those women, what were the names . . ."

"Amy Jewell, your Majesty, and Susan Nguyen, and there was the madman, Ted Deranian."

"Yes, well, a madman won't do us any good, but what about the others?"

"Susan Nguyen appears to be living in the fortress in Faerie, your Majesty, and Amy Jewell has returned to her home on Earth."

"Has she?"

"Yes, your Majesty."

"And is she, by any chance, the one whose home lies almost directly below our arrival point on Earth?"

"Yes, your Majesty, she is."

"Oh, that's excellent, then! Fetch her immediately!"

The telepath blinked. "Your Majesty?"

"Oh, read our bloody mind, will you? It's so much quicker."

"Yes, your Majesty," the telepath agreed.

"They want the Jewell woman to talk to Brown," Miletti said, between gulps of bourbon.

"What for?" the lieutenant asked, startled.

"How the bloody hell should I know?" Miletti shouted at him. He threw the glass of bourbon on the rocks at the lieutenant's head, but missed. He glared angrily, then realized his drink was gone and snatched up the half-empty bottle, cuddling it close.

"How should I know?" he repeated. "How do I know any of this?"

He swigged bourbon.

The lieutenant watched him warily for a moment, then went to call the major.

Amy marveled at her kitchen.

When the Air Force men had pulled out they had cleaned up, and had done, she had to admit, a better job on the kitchen than Amy had ever done herself. The place was spotless.

The rest of the house wasn't quite so good — there was a cigarette burn on her couch, and some sort of brown stain on the carpet in the upstairs hall, though mostly it was all right.

The kitchen was wonderful, though; it shone, from the chrome faucets to the brass-plated doorknobs. They had even scrubbed the windows.

She looked out through the sparkling-clean glass at the remains of I.S.S. *Ruthless*, still lying out there in her yard.

She remembered someone saying that some of the machinery aboard was partly made of platinum; maybe she could salvage that and sell it to a jeweler?

Or maybe she could sell the whole thing to an amusement park somewhere — she ought to be able to get at least the cost of hauling it away.

"It's still there," Prossie said, as she leaned over Amy's shoulder.

"A little bit of home, huh?" Amy asked.

Prossie shook her head. "Maybe," she said, "but it's not anything I'm nostalgic about."

"No?"

"No. I miss my family, and I miss my talent, but I don't miss being in the military. And actually, even though I miss being able to read minds, it's nice to be alone sometimes, too, to know that my thoughts are my own." She stepped back, away from Amy. "I don't suppose that's anything you'd understand — your thoughts have *always* been your own."

"Well, the way you mean, yes," Amy agreed, "but there were certainly times when I paid too much attention to what other people thought." She hesitated, and asked, "Have you settled on what you want to do yet?"

"I want to study psychology," Prossie said, "and probably become a therapist — that's the right word?"

Amy nodded.

Prossie smiled wryly. "After all, I'm the only person on this planet who's ever *really* known what other people are thinking." She sighed. "But it's going to be expensive, isn't it? I'm still not used to worrying about money like this; back home . . . I mean, back in the Empire, I was government property, and everything I wanted was either provided for me or forbidden."

"Maybe we can find you a scholarship somewhere."

"I wouldn't know how to begin," Prossie said. "And after all, I don't even have a . . . a diploma?"

"That's the word," Amy agreed. "But we can get you a GED easily enough, I'm sure."

"I hope . . ."

Prossie stopped in mid-sentence, her mouth falling open.

Amy whirled, guessing even before she looked out the window what had so surprised Prossie.

The ladder that had unrolled out of thin air was still dancing and swinging, not yet settled into place.

*P*el stared moodily at the two Nancys as they sat talking over their dinner.

He hadn't bothered to eat lately; somehow, it didn't seem to matter. All the others had to eat, though.

Usually he didn't watch, but he had happened along the corridor as the Nancys and Rachel and Susan were dining, and had looked in, and there they were.

He wondered what they talked about. Neither of them showed any interest in talking to *him*. The simulacrum was always ready and eager to do what he told her, but she wasn't much of a conversationalist, in his experience.

And the revenant — he no longer thought of her as "the real Nancy" — was always polite, but disinterested.

Rachel was listening solemnly to both women. Pel had noticed that she seemed unable to tell them apart, and called them both "Mommy."

Pel had no trouble distinguishing between them, so long as they were awake — their manner was sufficiently different that he could tell which was which the moment a word was said or an expression displayed.

But he wasn't sure he cared anymore.

He wasn't sure he cared about anything.

He had planned to go down to the dungeons and find the hostages, something he'd been meaning to do for a couple of days now, but now he reconsidered.

What did he care where they were, or what shape they were in?

What did it matter?

He was the Brown Magician; he could do anything he wanted, could have anything he wanted.

But he didn't know what he wanted.

No one answered at the number Major Johnston had given her; Amy slammed the phone down angrily, then picked it up and dialled again.

It rang and rang, without response.

So much for all his fine assurances!

She turned back to the window, bent down, and looked up.

A space-suited figure was climbing slowly down the ladder, with a white flag clutched in one gauntlet and an immense pack on his back.

That flag was promising; they weren't coming in with drawn weapons. Amy still wasn't inclined to trust them.

Major Johnston had told her to flee if any Imperials showed up, but he had also told her to call first, and she hadn't gotten through. Didn't the man have phone mail, or an answering machine, or something? It was incredibly inconsiderate of him to have stranded her like this.

She heard a car on the road out front, which was nothing unusual, and she would not ordinarily have even noticed it consciously — except this one stopped. She heard tires on gravel, and then the engine died.

She looked, but couldn't see anything from her post in the kitchen.

"Here, you watch out back," she told Prossie, handing her the phone. "If anyone answers the damn phone, tell them what's happening."

Prossie silently accepted the phone as if she expected it to explode at any second, and Amy marched through the archway to the living room, where she looked out the front window.

The car out front was dark blue, with "U.S. Air Force" stencilled on the door, and a familiar figure was climbing out.

No wonder she hadn't been able to reach him at his office! He must have been on his way even before the ladder appeared. Miletti must have delivered a warning.

Why the hell hadn't Johnston called ahead, to tell her he was coming?

She strode to the front door and flung it open, but before she could say a word, Johnston called, "Ms. Jewell! Are you all right?"

"I'm fine," she called back.

She started to gesture and say more, but Johnston called, "We saw the ladder as we drove up — is someone coming down?"

"Yes," she called.

Johnston turned and nodded to the uniformed man who had just climbed out the other side of the car. "Come on," he said.

Side by side, the two men trotted around the house.

Annoyed, Amy stepped in and closed the door, then marched back through to the kitchen.

"He's just reaching the ground," Prossie announced.

She was still holding the phone; Amy took it from her and hung it up. Then she looked out the window over the sink.

Sure enough, the Imperial was on the ground and undogging his helmet, the white flag still in his hand. Johnston and the other man — a lieutenant, was he? — were coming into sight around the corner of the house.

The man lifted his helmet off and said something, but Amy couldn't hear it.

Johnston answered, and she couldn't make that out, either.

Damn it, she thought, this was *her yard,* and if people were going to talk here she wanted to hear what was said. The man looked harmless, and there weren't any more coming down the ladder, she could see that for herself.

She opened the back door and stepped out before Prossie could say a single word in protest.

The man in the space suit turned to her the moment she emerged and said, "Miss Jewell?"

"*Ms.* Jewell," she corrected him.

"You don't have to talk to him, Ms. Jewell," Johnston called.

"But *I* must talk to *Mrs. Jewell,*" the Imperial said. "That's my assignment."

Amy blinked in surprise. "What?" she said.

"You don't have to be involved, Amy," Johnston said.

"That's all right, Major," she said. "I want to hear this."

The Imperial smiled, glanced at Major Johnston, then took a step toward Amy and began his explanation.

"We could just leave him alone and hope for the best," Sheffield suggested.

The Emperor nodded. "We could, Bucky," he said, "but hoping for the best generally isn't the best way to get it."

"You think *I* can talk sense into him?" Amy said, a hand to her chest.

"We think you have a better chance than anyone else," the Imperial envoy said. "If you're willing, I have a space suit in my pack that we think will fit you."

"What about his . . ."

Amy stopped.

She had never met Pel's mother or sisters, but she had heard him talk about them. His mother was not a well woman, and Amy couldn't imagine how she would cope with finding out that not only were other universes real, but her son was now the absolute ruler of one.

And besides, that would take so long — locating them, and explaining everything, and talking them into it.

And she was curious — what had happened, all these weeks since she had returned to Earth? Miletti's reports had given her a vague idea, but she didn't really *know,* and she was curious. Why was Pel behaving so unpleasantly? What horrible things had the Empire done to him? What had really happened to Nancy and Rachel — had Pel been able to resurrect them?

And there was another point.

"Will you pay me?" she asked. "In gold?"

Johnston shifted his weight uneasily. The Imperial blinked in surprise.

"I'm sure that could be arranged," he said.

"Good," Amy replied. She started to say, "Let's go," and then remembered something.

Prossie was watching from the house.

"Can you get an Imperial pardon for Proserpine Thorpe?" Amy asked.

The Imperial frowned. "That's the rogue telepath?"

Amy nodded, waiting.

"I don't know," the Imperial said. "I wasn't authorized to say anything about that." He looked unhappy. "Will you wait while I report in and ask?"

Amy looked at him, then at Prossie's face in the kitchen window, then at Johnston and the lieutenant.

"No," she said. "Let's go. Major, would you please see that Prossie's all right till I get back?"

Then she stepped forward, reaching for the Imperial's pack.

*P*el was sprawled across his throne, staring up at the still-unrepaired hole in the ceiling, when he felt the space-warp in the Low Forest reopen.

Another spy, he supposed. He wondered idly what the spies were finding out that was worth reporting back.

Maybe he should go see for himself. Back before he had resurrected Rachel and the second Nancy, he had been thinking about touring Faerie; maybe he should do that. Nancy and Rachel weren't interested, but who cared what they thought?

Maybe he should just kill everybody. Reduce the Nancys and Susan and Rachel to ash, and then go flying about frying anyone he came across.

There was the spy, coming through the warp. He could feel it.

He thought about going back to Earth, but if he didn't bring Nancy and Rachel he would have to explain what had happened to them, and he might well wind up either in the loony bin or on trial for murder.

And if he did bring them, he would have to explain why they were so . . . so . . . so *dead*.

And he would have to live with them, and that house in Germantown was a lot smaller than Shadow's fortress.

And his business must have collapsed into utter ruin long ago. If any of his clients still remembered him, it was probably as someone who had skipped out on a breach-of-contract suit.

Poor Silly Cat must surely be dead.

What was there to go back to? Here he was immortal and all-powerful . . .

A second person had come through the warp; that was a trifle out of the ordinary. The Empire had mostly sent singles, not pairs.

If he went back, and took Nancy and Rachel, and no one noticed how their personalities had changed, there were other differences that someone would notice eventually. It had taken Pel some time to realize, himself.

As far as he could see, their hair and fingernails no longer grew. Nancy hadn't had her period since she died — Pel suspected that neither had Susan, but he hadn't yet asked her outright.

He suspected that Rachel wasn't growing, that she would remain six, physiologically, for the rest of her life.

Or maybe all of that had something to do with the magic here in Faerie, and would reverse itself back on Earth — but if it didn't, how could he explain it?

A *third* person through the warp — how odd!

And if it did reverse . . . did that mean that they were immortal here in Faerie, but mortal on Earth? Could he ask them to give up eternal life?

He didn't know what he could ask. They owed him their lives, after all.

And he didn't *know* what would happen back on Earth.

And they wouldn't give any opinion on the subject, they both insisted they didn't care.

A fourth?

Pel blinked and sat up.

Maybe this wasn't just another spy mission. He waited.

A fifth. Then a sixth. Then a seventh.

Then nothing; he waited, but no more emerged.

Still, seven people — that was really a bit much.

He decided to go see what they wanted.

*T*he Empire had obviously learned a few tricks, Amy thought as she looked at her escort.

Five of them still wore their gaudy purple uniforms and blond crew cuts, but there wasn't a blaster in sight; instead, they carried swords. Very practical-looking swords. And they wore daggers on their belts. Two of them had crossbows slung on their backs, with bandoliers of quarrels.

The sixth man had the appearance of a native guide; he wore a gray woolen tunic with a purple armband on each sleeve. He had a dagger, as well, but no sword; he had been introduced back at Base One as Samuel Best, and although no one had mentioned a rank, and there was no sign that he was an officer, he was clearly in charge of the expedition.

One of the uniformed troopers was Ronnie Wilkins; it was a relief to know he had somehow survived and made it back to the Empire.

The other four she didn't recognize; she had been given their names, but hadn't remembered them.

Amy herself was wearing a sort of modified hiking outfit that the Empire had provided — purple T-shirt, leather walking shorts, black army boots. They'd offered her weapons, but she had declined.

Best and three of the others were sorting supplies in the clearing beside the mummified remains of Shadow's bat monster, while Wilkins and the last stood guard, blades drawn, at either side. The space suits were all safely stowed in the wreck of I.S.S. *Christopher,* and stocks of food and clothing were being distributed and bundled for carrying.

"Too bad we couldn't get horses," one of the men muttered as he hoisted an immense pack.

"They're working on it," Best replied. "They've got a carrier now, they just don't have anywhere to stable them at Base One. You need a lot of fodder."

"Well, if they'd just brought them straight through, they wouldn't need to feed them," the other argued.

"Oh, yes, they would," Best said. "You see any grass around here? We're in the middle of a forest."

"You could get out to the Downs before the horses'd starve."

"Well, they didn't do it," Best said. "So we'll just have to walk — assuming that Brown doesn't come to us." He turned and motioned to Amy. "Come on, Mrs. Jewell," he said. "I've got the lead, then Howard, then you."

"Which pack is mine?" she asked.

"None of them," Best replied. "Orders — you travel light, in case you have to run for it. We take care of you."

"That doesn't seem fair."

Best shrugged. "It's our job," he said. He trudged toward the trail to the west; a trooper fell in behind him.

The others waited, and Amy reluctantly followed.

The others fell in behind her, and the party of seven marched into the woods.

*S*even of them, and then the warp had closed again; Pel was baffled. What could a group of seven be doing? It was too many for spies, too few for an invasion.

Well, he would know soon; he could sense them in the forest below. He let the wind slacken, and descended slowly toward them.

The trees were in the way; he couldn't see anything. Annoyed, he blasted a clearing ahead of the Imperial party, and dropped down into it.

*T*he light ahead seemed odd, Amy thought; there was a sort of sparkliness to it, something strange about the colors that filtered through the trees.

She didn't *think* it was just the unfamiliar sunlight of Faerie.

She had forgotten how uncomfortable Faerie was, with its pale light and heavy gravity and thick, moist air. Going to talk to Pel had seemed exciting and noble back on Earth, or at Base One, but now it was beginning to seem stupid. She had made this two-hundred-mile walk once, and it had been hellish; so why had she volunteered to do it again?

At least she didn't have morning sickness this time.

She was about to remark on the colors when flame erupted ahead of her, like a bomb-burst; she flung an arm up to shield her face as heat and light blasted at her. The ground shook, and a deafening roar rolled through the forest; the compression of the air washed over her like a great ocean wave, forcing her back. Her hair whipped out behind her, dragging her head back painfully.

"Oh, hell," Best said, barely audible over the ringing in her ears.

Amy lowered her arm, expecting to see a blazing forest fire ahead.

Instead she saw a flickering, shifting mass of color, cloud, light, and shadow, like a Hollywood special-effects light show run amok. She felt a tightening in her chest.

"Shadow," she said.

But Shadow was dead, she remembered.

"Pel," she said.

And a voice spoke from the matrix.

"Amy?" it said, in a sound of thunder. "Amy Jewell?"

Chapter Twenty-Nine

*A*my didn't care very much for flying even with a plane, and after the initial thrill wore off this magical wind-riding of Pel's was far worse. The wind was a constant, unpleasant pressure; she couldn't speak over it. There was a constant sensation of falling, which she found slightly nauseating.

And it was cold, too.

And frightening.

And it went on and on; they had been airborne for hours. The sun had long since passed its zenith and was moving down the sky ahead of them.

Amy had also looked down at some of the villages they passed over, and been depressed to see that they looked dirtier and less pleasant than she had remembered.

At least all those dead bodies hanging on gallows were gone; she didn't see a gallows or gibbet anywhere. That was certainly an improvement.

She glanced sideways, first at Wilkins, to her right, then at Best, to her left. Pel had decided to bring them along, but none of the others, and hadn't bothered listening to any argument, he had just snatched the three of them up.

She wondered how Pel knew Best.

They were above the marsh now, and there was the fortress ahead of them, drawing quickly nearer; they were flying lower, and slowing down . . .

A moment later they landed, hard, on the causeway outside the gate. Pel stayed on his feet, but the others tumbled to the ground.

Best landed rolling, and got quickly to his feet, dusty but unhurt. Wilkins hadn't done quite so well; he'd scraped one palm trying to catch himself, and seemed to have hurt his shoulder.

And Amy herself stretched full-length in the dirt, painfully bruising herself several places, scraping skin from her chin and hands and forearms.

She got slowly to her hands and knees, wincing as she put weight on her palms, and cursing herself for not remembering how roughly Taillefer had landed at Castle Regisvert.

The gate was standing open, and Pel was standing in the opening, his glow suppressed enough that he was visible as a vaguely human outline. "Come on in," he said.

Amy got stiffly to her feet, and followed Pel and Best. Wilkins brought up the rear.

The matrix lit the entry hall, and Amy looked about in mild surprise.

The hall was empty. The monsters were gone from the ledges on either side. Odd bits of debris were scattered about, mostly what appeared to be ash, and the entire place had a dusty, unkempt air, exaggerated, perhaps, by the weird, unsteady, colorful light.

The little party made their way the length of the hall, past a blackened, scorched-looking area and a few smudges that Amy hoped weren't bloodstains, onto the great staircase.

The great tube of light was gone completely. Pel noticed Amy looking at the hole where it had emerged, and said, "That was one of the magical currents turned visible — I don't know why Shadow bothered. I don't."

He marched on ahead, seemingly unwearied by the long flight, up the stairs and across the landing into the throne room. The matrix glow lingered sufficiently for the others, rather more worn, to make their way up the steps at their own pace.

Amy's legs ached by the time she stepped into the throne room, arm raised to fend off the glare.

"Pel?" she called, as she advanced cautiously into the light. "Could you turn it down?"

"Sure."

And the glow was gone — or rather, reduced to insignificance, to just enough to light the throne room pleasantly. Amy could see Pel's face.

His hair was fairly long and hung in greying tangles around his head; his beard was shaggy and uneven as well. Both appeared to have been cut at least once since she had last seen him — but it hadn't been very recently. He had obviously not concerned himself with his appearance lately.

Well, the telepaths had said he appeared to be depressed, and that would fit. She moved cautiously nearer.

Best and Wilkins stepped to the doorway, but waited there as Amy walked warily into the room to talk to Pel.

They'd done their job; they'd gotten her to Pel safely. The rest was up to her. This was what the Empire was paying her a small fortune in gold for; this was what she had agreed to when she had coaxed from the Imperials a promise to commute Prossie's treason sentence from death to exile.

Amy looked around the room, trying to collect her thoughts.

She didn't remember that hole in the ceiling. She didn't remember the litter along the sides of the room, or the thin layer of ash that she scuffed through as she approached Pel's throne. She didn't remember the damp, faintly musty odor.

It reminded her of a pre-teenager's bedroom — the sort of kid who never cleaned up, and screamed if his parents dared move a single candy wrapper.

"So, how's it going?" she asked.

Pel shrugged. "Hard to say; how've you been doing? I guess the Empire sent you to talk to me about something?"

"I'm fine, thanks — the Air Force people have been very nice about everything. And yes, they tell me that the Emperor himself suggested I come talk to you."

"Really? Wow." Pel sprawled comfortably in his throne; Amy looked around for somewhere she might sit, but found nothing.

After all, this was a ruler's throne room, she realized; she wasn't supposed to sit in the presence of royalty, or wizardry, or whatever Pel was.

"So here you are," Pel said, "and it's good to see a familiar face, and I hope we can talk awhile before I send you home again, but what was it the Emperor wanted you to say?"

Amy hesitated; she hardly knew where to begin. This wasn't going the way she had pictured it.

"Come on, let's get the business out of the way," Pel urged.

"He thinks you're upset about something," Amy said. "Or his advisors do, or the telepaths, or someone; I never talked to the Emperor, of course, just a bunch of officers and bureaucrats, but they seemed nicer than the ones we dealt with before."

"Maybe you're just more used to them now."

"Maybe," Amy agreed. "Or maybe I'm not so scared. They weren't trying to send me off to fight Shadow, after all, they just wanted me to talk to you."

"I'm as powerful as Shadow was," Pel remarked. "Or pretty nearly, anyway. I can't do a lot of the stuff she did, but I can do plenty."

"So I've heard." She hesitated, then asked, *"Are* you upset about something?"

Pel looked away, at a door in a side wall that had stood slightly ajar; now it slammed shut, though no one had touched it.

He looked back at Amy.

"Yeah, I guess I am," he said.

Amy glanced back at Best and Wilkins, who stepped back discreetly.

"What is it?" she asked.

Pel swallowed, and looked entirely human for a moment.

"It's Nancy," he said.

"Nancy's dead?" Amy asked.

She wasn't sure just what had happened to Nancy. She knew that the Empire had delivered her corpse to Pel, she knew that Shadow had claimed to be able to raise the dead, and Pel claimed to have all Shadow's power, but had Pel really brought Nancy back to life?

"Yeah," Pel said, and Amy could hear the pain in his voice, "she's dead. She's up and walking, but she's still dead, as far as I'm concerned."

"You're sure?"

Pel slammed a fist into the back of his chair, and plumes of golden flame flared momentarily into existence on all sides, then vanished.

"Of *course* I'm sure, damn it!"

Amy took a step back, but then Pel burst into tears.

"Oh, God, Amy," he said, "of course I'm sure!"

*I*t didn't really matter what she said, Pel thought; it was just good to have someone he could talk to, someone he could explain it all to, someone from Earth, someone *real*, someone who would understand.

He hadn't known Amy back on Earth, he had only met her at that first gathering in his house, when Raven of Stormcrack Keep and his little band of resistance fighters had led Captain Cahn and his crew, and Amy and her lawyer, and Pel and his wife and daughter and *their* lawyer, into Faerie.

For five minutes, Raven had said. Just to see. Just so they would know it was real.

How long had it been? Pel had lost track of time; here in the windowless depths of Shadow's fortress, where he didn't need to eat or sleep, he had let days slip by uncounted. The seasons were different here, the year longer than Earth's — it was autumn here, wasn't it? Back in Maryland winter had probably come and gone.

Five minutes, Raven had said.

And he and Amy and the others had been trapped into this adventure, this long storybook adventure that should have ended with Shadow's destruction and Pel's ascension, when everyone was supposed to live happily ever after.

Or with Nancy and Rachel's resurrection, when Pel had regained what he had lost, and once again, should have lived happily ever after.

Happily?

He wept openly, he sat on the floor with Amy's arms around him and cried miserably.

Best and Wilkins retreated to the stairs, embarrassed, and Pel had started to shut the doors, until Amy had reminded him that if he did that, the two Imperials would be in the dark.

So he had left the doors open, and he didn't care if they heard him crying. He was the goddamned Brown Magician, he could reduce them to ash with a thought, and he would cry if he wanted.

His wife and daughter were dead to him, and there was nothing he could do about it.

*A*my held Pel and let him cry; she had to keep her eyes closed, and even so they stung with the glare of the matrix, because Pel's control of its brilliance had slipped with his loss of control of his emotions, but she didn't turn away or let him go. She held him and let him cry.

At last he stopped, and fought the matrix down, and she opened her eyes to find him looking up at her, his own eyes red and weary.

"Thanks," he said. "You look awful."

"So do you," she said, repressing a sudden urge to giggle. It was all so ridiculous, him lying there in her arms as if he were her lover, but with his hair and beard going every which way and his silly black robe like some comic-book wizard's cloak making him look like an ancient lunatic.

"Sorry."

"It's okay."

Pel sat up, and Amy released him.

"So what are you going to do?" Amy asked.

"About what?"

"Well, I meant about Nancy, but as long as you're asking, what about the Empire? I mean, they sent me here to ask if you'd send home their hostages, and promise not to attack them again, and all that. Normalize relations, I guess you'd say."

Pel shook his head. "I don't want to normalize relations. I want to be left alone. As long as they do that, I won't bother anyone. And they can have the hostages back; I don't even remember where I put them. They're somewhere in the fortress dungeons, I guess; I'll let them go, and they can go back to the space-warp with Best and Wilkins."

"You won't open a portal for them?"

"No." Pel shifted around to face Amy properly. "No, I'm not going to do that. I wouldn't know where to send them; I don't know where any of the openings into the Empire come out." Amy doubted that that was true, but she didn't want to argue it. "And besides," Pel continued, "it's too much contact with the Empire; every time I've dealt with them it's been trouble. Let them take care of their own."

Amy shrugged. "I guess that'll have to do, then."

"It ought to."

"I think it will."

For a moment the two of them sat silently; then Amy looked around, before the silence became awkward, and remarked, "It's gotten a bit dusty in here; you've been letting the housekeeping go, I guess."

Pel looked up at the hole in the ceiling. "I always was a bit of a slob," he said.

Amy hesitated, then asked, "So what are you going to do about Nancy?"

Pel shrugged. "What *can* I do? She's my wife — my responsibility. I was the one who brought her here and brought her back to life. I have to stay with her and try to go on loving her." He sighed heavily. "I suggested that she go back to Earth without me, but she didn't want to. She didn't really *mind,* but . . . and besides, after what happened to Grummetty and Alella, I wasn't sure it was a good idea."

"So why don't *you* go back to Earth?"

"Leave her?" Pel looked at Amy, startled.

"You said she was dead, Pel; if she's dead, let her go."

"But she's alive, really, she's just different."

"If she's not the woman you married, let her go; if Rachel's not your daughter anymore, let Nancy have her."

Pel turned away. "That's easy for you to say."

"Pel," Amy said, "have I ever talked to you about my ex-husband, Stan?"

Pel didn't answer, and Amy continued, "One day I saw that he wasn't the man I'd thought I'd married, that I didn't know him and didn't love him, and I divorced him — and it was the smartest thing I could have done. Staying in a bad relationship isn't a good thing to do."

"This is different," Pel said.

"Yeah, I suppose it is — but is it *that* different?"

Pel got up and began brushing dust and ash from his black magician's robe.

"I can't go back to Earth," he said, not looking at Amy. "I'm the Brown Magician, the ruler here. I control all the magic. If I leave, the matrix will come apart and all the magic will run wild."

"If you're happy here," Amy said, "then stay."

"It's not . . . I mean, I'm *needed*. Without me there'd be chaos."

"So you're running everything, the way Shadow did?"

"Not the way Shadow did," Pel replied. "No hangings — I've outlawed the death penalty for anything short of murder. And no eviscerations even for that. And I don't keep a close watch on everything the way she tried to do; I never learned how she did all that stuff."

"So what *do* you do?"

"I . . . well, I stopped the Empire from invading."

"They said *you* raided *them* first, and your men killed innocent people."

"Well, they'd lied to me! They cheated me!" The matrix flared up redly for a moment, and Amy decided not to argue with that.

Instead, she said, "So you attacked them?"

"Just some little raids."

"And they counter-attacked, but you stopped them?"

He nodded. "That was easy. I just let some of the magic turn to flame, and burned them up, drove them back into the space-warps."

"Same as Shadow would have done."

Pel nodded again, not looking at her.

He had closed himself off again, Amy thought; that moment of emotional release, when he had wept in her arms, was past.

The matrix was flickering in and out of visibility around him, like spreading multicolored flames; a swirl of fine black ash rose up for a second in a gust of magical wind.

Amy wondered where that ash had come from. What had Pel burned here? Had he burned people?

He had admitted burning those Imperial soldiers. He had committed murder, had taken human lives — and he didn't seem to think it was important.

She took a step back, suddenly frightened.

"Pel, I think I'd like to go home now," she said.

He turned to face her.

"I've said what the Empire wanted me to say," she said, "and I've given you my opinion about what you should do about Nancy and Rachel, and that's all I came to do. So could you send me home?"

For a moment he didn't answer.

"All right," he said finally. "Give me a minute."

*J*ust before she stepped into the portal, Amy turned to face him for a final word.

"Be careful, Pel," she said. "The way you killed those soldiers, and everything, the way you've let yourself go — be careful you don't turn out like Shadow."

And then she was gone, back to Earth, to the basement of his own house, in Germantown, Maryland.

Angrily, he dropped the portal, let it collapse into nothingness as the matrix resumed its proper shape.

He wasn't like Shadow. He was a caring, considerate person. He wouldn't hurt anyone.

He'd killed those soldiers, but they weren't *real*, they were just Imperials . . .

And why weren't they real?

And he'd killed Shadow herself, of course, or at least set her up, and he'd destroyed all those fetches, but they weren't really *alive*, were they?

He'd killed a lot of Shadow's monsters, by sending them into the Empire to die, but they weren't people.

He had an excuse for everything — but he had an awful lot to excuse, didn't he?

Why hadn't he just gone back to Earth in the first place? Everyone would have been better off.

He tried to tell himself that no, the people of Faerie wouldn't have been better off, they wouldn't have had him there to protect them — but how much protection had he actually provided? Would the Empire have attacked the elves, or those farms, if Pel hadn't goaded them into it?

And most of the time he had just shut himself up here in this fortress, brooding over his own concerns, driving himself to distraction with his problems and ignoring everyone else.

He didn't know a thing about Faerie, really. Had he ever talked to the people here? Did he know what they wanted?

He shook his head.

He really didn't. He'd made a half-hearted attempt, back at the beginning, to be the good ruler, but instead of listening to what his people wanted he had told them what *he* wanted, an end to executions and an attempt at democracy.

That was hardly anything to be proud of.

He wasn't doing anyone any good here — least of all himself, trapping himself here, surrounded by his own failures and by a world that he couldn't help seeing as somehow unreal, no matter how solid the stone walls might be.

The door at the side of the throne room opened, and Susan Nguyen — or at least, the thing that used her body and shared her memories — looked in.

"Go get Nancy and Rachel," Pel barked. "Both Nancys."

If he was going to do something irrevocable, if he was going to leave her, he had to let her know.

If she asked him to stay, or asked him to take her with him, he would do it, he knew that.

But if she didn't, if she said she didn't care, what would he do?

Amy was right, he had to be free of Nancy, Nancy was dead and holding onto her wouldn't help. And the longer he stayed here in this fortress, in this world, the more like Shadow he became.

Maybe it was something in the matrix; maybe it was something in human nature. He didn't know, and it didn't matter. Having that power always there, straining to be free, waiting to be used, was changing him for the worse.

He had to leave Faerie. He didn't know how to release the matrix completely any other way.

And he couldn't pass it on; there was no one in Faerie who had the talent. Shadow had said so; that was why she had chosen him in the first place. The talent for matrix wizardry had been bred out of the inhabitants of Faerie, and among the Imperials she had only found it in the telepaths; only among Earthpeople was it reasonably common. And the only Earthpeople still here in Faerie were revenants or simulacra, who could never hold magic.

So he would release it, and the matrix would come apart, and wild magic would be loose in the world — and would that really be so bad?

Shadow had said it would, but Shadow could have been wrong, could have lied.

Pel couldn't see how it could be so bad. It would be wild and free, and Shadow would have seen that as bad, but was it really?

And no new matrix wizards would arise, to gather the power together again — the talent had been bred out. The magic would *stay* free.

Pel almost wished he could be here to see it.

But he couldn't; he had to go.

Back home to Earth, to Maryland . . .

To Maryland?

Well, to Earth, certainly; he had no desire to live in the Galactic Empire, under the absolute rule of His Imperial Majesty George VIII.

But Maryland?

Back there where his business was ruined, and there were probably a hundred lawsuits and legal complications to deal with because of his sudden disappearance?

Back to that house full of memories of Nancy and Rachel?

Why?

"You wanted us?" Nancy's voice called from the door.

"No," Pel said. "I mean, yes. Come here, all of you." He sat up in his throne and watched as the three women and the girl approached.

"If I were to leave," he asked, watching the passive faces, "permanently, would you prefer to come with me, or stay here?"

"It doesn't matter," Susan said.

"Whichever you like," the simulacrum said.

"I don't really care," the Nancy revenant said.

"I don't care a whole lot either," Rachel said.

And that, Pel thought, settled it.

"You're all free," he said, already feeling for the shape of the matrix and the links to Earth. "All of you, do whatever you want from now on. And everyone else in the fortress is free. My last command to you four — or request — is to make sure that the Imperials in the dungeons are all free to go, and that Best and Wilkins can find them."

The four just stared at him.

"They're on the stairs," Pel said, with a wave of his hand. "Best and Wilkins, I mean. Go tell them the hostages are free."

Susan glanced at the others, then turned and headed for the big double doors.

The others just stood there, watching him.

Pel stared back for a moment, then decided that he'd had enough of them. He would make his departure from atop the tower, where any discharge from the disintegrating matrix would dissipate harmlessly into the open air.

And he wouldn't want to go empty-handed, he realized; there was no telling where he might wind up.

He didn't have to rush off this very minute . . .

But soon.

Chapter Thirty

*I*t was raining, and the water was spilling from the hole where the broken gargoyle had been, spattering across the battlements. Pel remembered the sound of Rachel's running footsteps, and smiled a wistful smile.

The tiny revenant downstairs didn't run and play. Rachel was gone.

He took a final look out at the gloomy countryside, at the grey marsh and the distant hills, at the long line of freed hostages marching away down the causeway, then reached out and twisted the matrix in an impossible direction, reaching for the opening to Earth, but turning aside from it, veering away to somewhere else on the planet.

Then the portal was there. He hefted the bag of gold coins in one hand, the pack of clothing and toiletries in the other, and stepped through.

And with a horrible wrenching the matrix came free, tore itself from his mind and shattered, and he staggered forward into total darkness, dazed, wondering if he had gone blind; he staggered, and fell, and landed on sand.

For a moment he lay there, face down, gathering his wits.

It was strange to be in darkness; he hadn't seen true darkness in months, not since he first accepted the matrix from Shadow.

The possibility that he might be dead occurred to him, but the sand beneath him was cool and solid, and he heard a soft whispering that didn't sound like anything he would expect in the afterlife.

It sounded like the sea.

He rolled over, the gold coins clinking as he shifted them, and looked up at stars, millions of stars, twinkling white above him.

He wasn't blind; he'd arrived at night.

He sat up, and saw pale bands moving; he blinked, and saw that it was surf, phosphorescent surf rolling in to the beach on which he had arrived.

"And just wot didjer think you were doin' there?" a voice demanded from behind him. "This beach is closed to the public!"

The accent was Australian.

Pel smiled.

He'd always wanted to visit Australia.

"Sorry," he called, getting to his feet. "Which way out?"

*B*est looked up at the warning rumble, shielding his eyes with his hand to keep the rain out.

The matrix was a shimmering mass that completely surrounded the top twenty feet or more of the central tower; now, as he and the others looked up at it, it expanded, like impossibly fast-rising dough, seething rapidly outward . . .

And then it exploded, not with a bang, but with a scream, and colors and patterns scattered wildly across the overcast sky; for a moment a cloudbank flickered red, another was crisscrossed with green tracery like the veins of a leaf, purple fire dripped sizzling down the tower, carrying molten stone with it. Creatures flapped and scrambled in the clouds.

Then it was gone, and the broken stump of the tower ended in a jagged line of blackened stone.

But the raindrops were faintly glowing and slightly iridescent, and somehow Best knew that magic was raining onto Shadowmarsh and all of Faerie.

He shuddered. He didn't like magic.

"Come on," he said. "Two hundred miles to Sunderland and Base One — let's go!"

*B*rown's really gone?" the Emperor asked.

The telepath answered, "Yes, your Majesty."

"Who's in charge, then?"

"The local governments appear to be reasserting themselves," the telepath replied. "The surviving remnants of the old nobility, Shadow's councils of elders, and the like. There's no central government; apparently, there never really was much of one. Either that, or it disintegrated upon Shadow's death."

The Emperor nodded, considering.

"We think," he said, staring at the rug, "that we will find it entertaining and profitable to pick up territories piecemeal in Faerie. An attempt to conquer it all at once would be impractical, and to risk a new Brown Magician arising would be foolish. Better to involve ourselves in it little by little, and stop any potential threat before it looms too large."

"Your Majesty's plan is, of course, wise," the telepath said.

George VIII looked up, pleased. "You really think so?" he said. "All of you?"

*B*rown's gone," Miletti repeated. "Faerie's doing a planetary imitation of Yugoslavia."

"You're sure of that?"

"I'm not fucking sure of *anything,*" Miletti said, "but it's my honest report."

The lieutenant nodded. He turned off the tape recorder and put it away.

"In that case, Mr. Miletti," he said, "I have good news. Our budget's been cut, and if there's no longer any plausible threat from either the Empire or Faerie, we don't need to monitor the telepaths anymore. That means we don't need you; the major says you're free to do as you please, and we'll be removing our equipment and ending the regular visits. We'll be mailing your check out on Monday."

Miletti stared at him for a long moment, then looked down at the bourbon bottle in his own right hand.

He dropped it to the carpet.

"About time," he said. "Thank you!"

*H*e's gone somewhere," Johnston's voice said, "but we don't know where; he never appeared at his house."

Amy looked out her back window at the spaceship in her yard.

"I don't blame him," she said. "Thank you, Major."

She hung up the phone, and realized that she was smiling. And why shouldn't she? The Empire's payment had plummeted out of the sky half an hour ago, enough gold to get her decorating business off the ground again. Prossie was in the other room, studying American history for her GED, and no longer had to worry about the Empire. Everything wasn't what it had been before *Ruthless* appeared, but it was good enough; all the complicated and nasty adventures in other worlds were over, and it was time to get on with her life.

She was happy with the situation.

She hoped Pel Brown was as happy, wherever he was.

She thought he might be.

*A*nd in a small town on the Australian coast, a barefoot, strangely-dressed man with an American accent wandered down the village high street with a bag of gold coins in his pack — Faerie gold, to be sure, but he was reasonably certain that it wasn't going to disappear or turn to offal.

Of course, he wouldn't be able to sell any until the town's only jeweler opened his shop in the morning, so he had decided to walk the night away.

The air was warm, and rich with the smell of the sea; the stars of the southern hemisphere were bright and strange overhead. It was a beautiful night for a stroll, and the world was rich with possibilities.

He walked on, whistling.

- end -

About the Author

Lawrence Watt-Evans is the author of more than two dozen novels, more than a hundred short stories, and assorted other works. Further information can be found on his webpage at http://www.watt-evans.com/.

www.ingramcontent.com/pod-product-compliance
Lightning Source LLC
Chambersburg PA
CBHW020737020826
48980CB00018B/625/J